The Prairie Trilogy

Includes:

Prairie Rose

Prairie Fire

Prairie Storm

PRAIRIE ROSE
A Town Called Hope

NUMBER 1

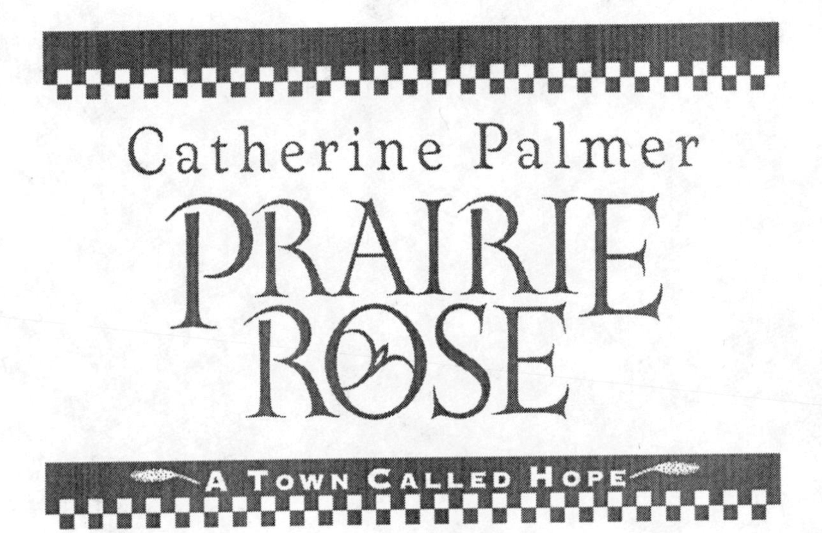

Tyndale House Publishers, Inc.
WHEATON, ILLINOIS

Visit Tyndale's exciting Web site at www.tyndale.com

Unless otherwise indicated, Scripture quotations are taken from the *Holy Bible,* King James Version.

3 IN 1 ISBN 0-7394-0311-7

Printed in the United States of America

For my husband

Timothy Charles Palmer

Twenty years of promises kept.

I love you.

His name is the Lord—rejoice in his presence! Father to the fatherless . . . God places the lonely in families. Psalm 68:4-6, NLT

So you should not be like cowering, fearful slaves. You should behave instead like God's very own children, adopted into his family— calling him "Father, dear Father." For his Holy Spirit speaks to us deep in our hearts and tells us that we are God's children. Romans 8:15-16, NLT

CHAPTER 1

Kansas City, Missouri
May, 1865

TALKING to God from the outstretched limb of a towering white oak tree had its advantages. For one thing, it meant that Rosie Mills could see beyond the confining walls of the Christian Home for Orphans and Foundlings, where she had lived all nineteen years of her life. For another, she had always felt as if she were closer to God up in the old tree. That was kind of silly, Rosie knew. God had lived in her heart ever since she gave it to him one night at a tent preaching service, just before the War Between the States. But the best thing about praying in the oak tree was the constantly changing scene that unfolded below.

Take these two men coming her way. The first—a dark-haired fellow in a chambray shirt and black suspenders—minded his own business as he drove his wagon down the dusty street. He had a little boy beside him on the seat and a load of seed in the wagon bed. The other man followed on a black horse. All the time Rosie had been praying, she had been watching the second fellow edge closer and closer, until finally he was right behind the wagon.

"Seth Hunter!" the horseman shouted, pulling a double-barreled shotgun from the scabbard on his saddle. "Stop your mules and put your hands in the air."

The command was so loud and the gun so unexpected that Rosie nearly lost her precarious perch on the old limb. The milkman across the street straightened up and stared. Down the way, the vegetable seller and his son halted in their tracks.

"I said stop your team!" the horseman bellowed.

The man on the wagon swung around and eyed his challenger. "Jack Cornwall," he spat. "I might have known."

He gave the reins a sharp snap to set his mules racing lickety-split down the road. Jack Cornwall cocked his shotgun, lifted it to his shoulder, aimed it at the fleeing wagon, and fired. At the blast, Rosie gave a strangled scream. A puff of pungent gray smoke blossomed in the air. A hundred tiny lead pellets smashed into the seed barrels on the back of the wagon. Wood splintered. Seeds spilled across the road. The mules brayed and faltered, jerking the wagon from side to side.

"Whoa, whoa!" the driver of the wagon shouted. "Cornwall, what in thunder do you think you're doing?"

"Give me the boy, or I'll shoot again!" Cornwall hollered back.

"He's my son."

"You stole him!"

"He's mine by rights." The wagon rolled to a halt directly beneath the oak tree where Rosie perched. "I aim to take him to my homestead, and neither you nor anybody else is going to stop me, hear?"

"What do you want him for—slave labor?"

"You forgetting I'm a Union man, Cornwall? We don't trade in human flesh like you Rebs."

"And we don't go stealing children out from under the noses of the grandparents who took care of them since the day they were born."

"My *wife* took care of Chipper—"

"Wife?" the man exploded. He edged his horse forward, once again leveling his shotgun at Hunter. "You claiming my sister would marry some good-for-nothing farmhand?"

Rosie gripped the oak branch. The two men were barely three

feet beneath her, and she could almost feel the heat of their hatred. This was terrible. The little boy the men were arguing about was hunkered down in the wagon, terrified. He couldn't have been more than five or six years old, and as he peered over the wooden seat his big blue eyes filled with tears.

Rosie didn't know which of the men was in the right, but she wasn't about to let this Jack Cornwall fellow shoot someone. She spotted a stout stick caught in a fork of the tree. Maybe she could use it to distract the men, she thought as she shinnied toward the slender end of her branch.

"Your sister married me, whether you believe it or not," Seth Hunter snarled. "I'm this boy's father, and I mean to take him with me."

"I didn't track your worthless hide all the way to Kansas City to let you just ride off to the prairie with my nephew. No sir, Chipper's going south with me. My pappy's not about to let you work his grandson to the bone on your sorry excuse for a farm."

"I told you I don't plan on working him. In fact, I'm headed for this orphanage right now to hire me a hand."

"Hire you a hand," Jack scoffed. He spat a long stream of brown tobacco juice onto the dirt road. "What're you aiming to pay him with—grasshoppers? That's all you're going to be growing on your homestead, Hunter. Grasshoppers, potato bugs, and boll weevils."

"I've got a house and a barn, Jack. That's more than a lot of folks can say, including you. And any young'un would gladly trade that orphanage for a home."

I would, Rosie thought. She was beginning to side with Seth Hunter, even if he had stolen the little boy. The other man was big, rawboned, and mean-tempered. For all she knew he planned to shoot Seth dead with his shotgun. And right in front of the child!

The branch she was straddling bobbed a little from her weight as she inched along it toward the stick. Truth to tell, it was the boy who stirred her heart the most. Neither man had even bothered to ask the child what he wanted to do. And where on earth was the poor little fellow's mother?

"A house and a barn," Jack said, his voice dripping with disdain. "What you've got is dust, wind, and prairie fires. That's no place to bring up a boy. Now let me have him peaceful-like, and I won't be obliged to blow your Yankee head off."

"You're not taking my son." Seth stood up on the wagon. His shoulders were square and solid inside his homespun chambray shirt, and his arms were roped with hard muscle and thick veins. Badly in want of cutting, his hair hung heavy and black. His thick neck was as brown as a nut. With such a formidable stature, Rosie thought, he should have the face of the bare-knuckle fighters she had seen on posters.

He didn't. His blue eyes set off a straight nose, a pair of flat, masculine lips, and a notched chin. It was a striking face. A handsome face. Unarmed, Hunter faced Jack. "I already lost Mary, and I'm not—"

"You never had Mary!"

"She was my wife."

"Mary denied you till the day she died."

"Liar!" Seth stepped over the wagon seat and started across the bed. "If your pappy hadn't tried to kill me—"

"You ran off to join the army! We never saw hide nor hair of you for more than five years till you came sneaking back and stole Chipper."

"I wrote Mary—"

"She burned every letter."

"Mary loved me, and none of your lies will make me doubt it. We'd have been happy together if your pappy would have left us alone. He ran me off with a shotgun. I was too young and scared back then to stand up to him, but I'll be switched if I let him do it again. Or you, either."

"I'll do more than that, Hunter." Jack steadied the gun. "Now give me the boy."

"Over my dead body."

"You asked for it."

He pulled back on the hammer to set the gun at half cock. Rosie held her breath. No. He wouldn't really do it. Would he? She reached out and grabbed onto the stick.

"Give me the boy," Jack repeated.

"If you shoot me, they'll hang you for murder."

"Hang me? Ha! You ever hear of Charlie Quantrell, Jesse James, Bob Ford? They're heroes to me. I've joined up with a bunch down south to avenge wrongs done in the name of Yankee justice. Nobody messes with us, Hunter. And nobody hangs us for murder. Besides, I'm just protecting my kin." He pulled the hammer all the way back.

Seth stood his ground. "People are watching every move you make, Jack," he said. "They know who you are. Don't do this."

"Chipper, come here, boy."

"Stay down, Chipper."

"Hunter, you Yankee dog. I'll get you if it's the last thing I do."

Jack lifted the shotgun's stock to his shoulder. As his finger tensed on the trigger, Rosie gritted her teeth and swung her club like a pendulum. It smashed into the side of Jack Cornwall's head and knocked him sideways. The shotgun went off with a deafening roar. Like a hundred angry hornets, pellets sprayed into the street.

At the end of the limb, Rosie swayed down, lurched up, and swung down again. Acrid, sulfurous-smelling smoke seared her nostrils. As screams filled the air, she heard the branch she was clinging to crack. She lost her balance, tumbled through the smoke, and landed smack-dab on Seth Hunter. The impact knocked them both to the wagon bed, and her head cracked against the wooden bench seat. A pair of startled blue eyes was the last thing she saw.

"Glory be to God, she's awake at last! Jimmy, come here quick and have a look at her."

"Aye, she's awake, that she is."

The two pairs of eyes that stared down at Rosie could not have been more alike—nor the faces that went with them more different. The woman had bright green eyes, brilliant orange-red hair, and the ruddiest cheeks Rosie had ever seen. The man's green eyes glowed like twin emeralds from a gaunt face with suntanned skin stretched over sharp, pointy bones. He sucked on a corncob pipe and nodded solemnly.

"Seth Hunter, the lass has come round," he said. "Better see to her. She's a *frainey*, all right. She's so puny she'll keel over if she tries to stand up."

Her head pounding in pain, Rosie was attempting to decipher the lilting words her two observers had spoken when Seth Hunter's blue eyes—now solemn—appeared above her for a second time that day. He stroked a hand across her forehead. His hand was big and warm, his fingers gently probing.

"I don't feel right about us leaving her here, Jimmy," he said. "She's still bleeding pretty bad from that gash on the back of her head. But if we don't take off soon, I reckon Jack Cornwall will be back on my tail. I've got to get Chipper out of town. I want him home and settled as quick as possible."

"Sure, the wagon's loaded down with our tools and seed we came for," Jimmy said. "The *brablins* have their peppermints, and they'll be eager to start licking on them. If we set out now, we'll be home not a day later than planned."

"I know, but I just . . ." Seth touched Rosie's forehead again with his fingertips. "Ma'am, can you hear me? I want to thank you for what you did. I never expected such a thing. I owe you, that's for sure. If I had any money, I'd give you a reward, but—"

"Home," Rosie said. She didn't know where the word had

come from. She'd never had a home, not from the very moment she was born.

"We'll see you get home, ma'am," Seth said. "The delivery boy for the mercantile here said he recognized you. He's gone to fetch your mother."

Mother? Rosie studied the rows of canned goods, bolts of fabric, and sacks of produce that lined the floor-to-ceiling shelves in the mercantile. She knew the place well. She had been here many times, shopping for the orphanage's kitchen. She gradually recalled how she must have come to be lying on the sawdust-covered floor with her head throbbing like a marching band. She even knew the name of the man bending over her. But how could the delivery boy be fetching her mother?

"I don't have a mother," she said.

"No mother!" The ruddy-cheeked woman leaned into view and clucked in sympathy. She placed a clean folded cloth over Rosie's gash. "Can such a thing be true? Aye, lass, you're cruel wounded in the head, so you are. Perhaps you've lost your wits a bit. Sure, we wouldn't want you turnin' into a *googeen* now. Can you recall your name at all?"

"Rosenbloom Cotton Mills."

"She's disremembered the sound of her own name, so she has!"

"No really, that's who I am. Rosie Mills." She struggled to sit up, and the woman slipped a supporting arm around her shoulders. "My mother . . . you see . . . she put my name on a piece of paper."

"But you just told us you didn't have a mother."

"I don't. Not one I ever met, anyway. The piece of paper with my name on it was inside the stocking with me when I was discovered."

"You were discovered in a stocking?"

"I was a baby at the time. Newborn."

"A baby! *Ullilu*, Jimmy, did you hear the wee thing? She was left in a stocking."

"A foundling."

Jimmy pronounced the word Rosie had despised from the moment she learned its connotations. For nineteen years she had worn that label, and it had barred her from adoption, from marriage, from all hope of a family and a home. Taking no notice of the expressions on their faces, she pulled her pouch from the bodice of her dress.

"I keep the paper in here in this little bag I made from the toe of my stocking," she said. "As you can see, my name is written out very clearly: Rosenbloom Cotton Mills."

She unfolded the tiny scrap that was her only treasure. Everyone gathered around. As it turned out, there were many red-haired, green-eyed visitors at the mercantile that day, and most of them weren't more than three feet tall. Clutching red-and-white-striped peppermint sticks, they elbowed each other for a better look.

"Appears to be a stocking tag from that mill over on the river in Illinois," Jimmy said. "You remember, Sheena? We passed it on our way west, so we did."

"*Whisht*, Jimmy. If the lass says it's her name, who are you to start a clamper over it?" Sheena gave Rosie a broad smile that showed pretty white teeth. "Now then, we're to set out on our way home to Kansas in the wagon—Jimmy O'Toole and me, our five children, and our good neighbor, Seth Hunter. We're most grateful to you for the whack you gave that *sherral* Jack Cornwall. We never met a man as fine as our Seth, God save him, and we won't see him come to harm. So, if you think you'll be all right now, we'll—"

"Rosie? Rosie Mills?" A woman who had just entered the mercantile spotted the injured girl and clapped her hands to her cheeks. She glanced at Sheena O'Toole. "I'm Iva Jameson, the director of the Christian Home for Orphans and Foundlings. What on earth has happened to Rosie?"

"I . . . I was up in the oak tree," Rosie said meekly, dabbing at her wound with the cloth, "and then along came Mr. Hunter's wagon . . . and I—"

"You should have outgrown tree climbing long ago."

"But it's where I pray, ma'am."

"Rosie, shame on you for such tomfoolery—and at your age!"

"Maybe I should explain, ma'am." Seth stepped forward. "What happened was mainly my fault. I'm Seth Hunter, and I was on my way to your orphanage with my son this morning when things took a wrong turn."

"I see, Mr. Hunter." Mrs. Jameson eyed the little boy standing forlornly beside him. "Would this young man be your son?"

"Yes. This is Christopher. They call him Chipper."

"Chipper. Now, that's a fine name for such a strong, handsome lad." The director knelt to the floor. "And how old are you, young Chipper?"

"He's five," Seth said. "Listen, ma'am, we don't have much time here. The O'Toole family and I—we've got homesteads waiting for us over in Kansas, and we need to get on the trail."

"Are you a widower, sir?"

There was a moment of silence. "Well, yes," Seth said finally. "I reckon I am a widower."

"You're uncertain?"

"I just hadn't thought of it that way. My wife . . . Chipper's mother . . . I went to fetch her and I learned she had died."

"I'm very sorry about your loss, sir," Mrs. Jameson said. "These are difficult times indeed. I'm assuming you were planning to ask the Christian Home for Orphans and Foundlings to look after your son while you find another wife."

"A wife?" Seth's voice deepened. "No. Absolutely not. No, I'm taking the child with me."

"Oh, I see."

"I was on my way to the orphanage because I'm in need of a strong boy," Seth told Mrs. Jameson. "Maybe you can still help me.

See, I want somebody who can work with me on the homestead. There's plowing and planting and such, but I wouldn't push him too hard. In fact, if you've got a boy who's good with young'uns, I mostly want him to keep an eye on Chipper. I can't offer pay, but I'll give him room and board. I'll give him a home."

Rosie stiffened and took Sheena O'Toole's hand. Holding the cloth to her hammering head, she pulled herself to her feet. What had Seth just offered? A *home. I'll give him a home.*

"I'm sorry, Mr. Hunter," Mrs. Jameson said, "but we're not an employment agency. Why don't you place an advertisement in the newspaper?"

"I don't have time for that. I've been away from my claim more than two weeks already, and my fields need plowing. Don't you have somebody who could help me out?"

"I understand your predicament, truly I do," Mrs. Jameson said. "But all our oldest boys went off to the war. We don't have anyone at the Home much over twelve, and I don't believe—"

"Twelve would do. If he's strong, it won't matter how old he is. Look here, ma'am," Seth said, "I'm an honest man, I'm a hard worker, and I won't do wrong by anybody. I'm offering the boy a chance to get a good start on life. A home of his own."

Rosie sucked in a breath. A *home*. A chance to make her unspoken dream come true! She was strong enough to do most any job. She could learn to plow. She could plant and dig and hoe. And she knew she could look after that boy.

"I'm so sorry, Mr. Hunter," Mrs. Jameson said, "but I simply couldn't send a twelve-year-old off with a stranger. We find our children jobs in the city. With the shortage of men these days, even our younger ones are working at the liveries and helping with refuse collection—"

"Shoveling stables and picking up garbage? I can offer a boy a better life than that."

"But I can't just give you a child. It would be worse than slavery."

"Slavery? I'm holding out a chance at a new life. I'm offering this boy a future. I'll turn him into a strong, useful man."

"I'll be your man!" Rosie called out. She took a step and began to sway. Sheena leapt to her side, placing an arm around her waist to keep her from falling. "I'll go with you, Mr. Hunter. I'll help you with the plowing, and I'll take care of your son. I know I can do it."

Seth Hunter stared at her. The little boy beside him gaped at the unexpected declaration. Even Sheena O'Toole eyed her in wonderment. Rosie didn't care that she had astonished them all. This was her chance—and she intended to take it.

Mrs. Jameson turned on her. "Don't be ridiculous," she snapped. "The cook will be searching the whole house for you. At this hour of the morning, you're to be in the kitchen ladling out porridge."

"Yes, ma'am . . . but . . . but I believe I'll go to Kansas with Mr. Hunter instead. I'll be his worker. I'm good with children, and I can learn anything." She swallowed and forced herself to meet those bright blue eyes. "Sir, won't you take me with you? I'm nineteen—almost twenty—and I can do a good day's work. I promise you won't regret it."

So far Seth Hunter had said nothing. Rosie knew she was losing ground. Mrs. Jameson would never hear of her going away with a stranger. And what man would want a skinny foundling to help him on his homestead? But he had offered a future. A home.

"I'm a very good cook," she continued. "Just ask anyone. I bake the best apple pies. I can clean and scrub, and I know how to take a stove apart and black it top to bottom good as new. I'm wonderful at hoeing, and nobody makes pickles better than mine. It sounds like I'm boasting, but it's true, Mr. Hunter. You'll see how thankful you are to have me."

Seth looked her up and down, his blue eyes bringing out a flush in her cheeks and making the back of her neck prickle. She glanced at his son. Chipper was grinning. A broad space where he'd lost his two front teeth gave his face the look of a small, round jack-o'-lantern.

Mrs. Jameson harrumphed. "Rosenbloom Cotton Mills, I shall not tolerate such nonsense. And as for praying in a tree—"

"Mrs. Jameson's right," Seth said to Rosie. "I was mainly needing a farmhand. I don't reckon you'd be strong enough."

"I'm strong enough, Mr. Hunter," she countered, squaring her shoulders and setting the bloodied rag on a countertop. "Besides, you *owe* me. You said so yourself."

"Indeed you did, Seth." Sheena wasn't quite as tall as the younger woman, but her stocky stature gave her the look of a determined bulldog. When she spoke again, her voice held a tone of foreboding. "Speak the truth and shame the devil."

"I admit I'm obliged to the girl," Seth said. "She saved my life, and I intend to pay my debt by sending her a reward from Kansas. A dollar here, another there, as my crops come in."

"She wants to go with you to Kansas. That's the reward she claims," Sheena said.

Rosie's heart warmed to the woman at her side. Somehow, Sheena understood the depths of Rosie's need. Somehow, she *knew*.

"She's a *donny* thing, Sheena," Jimmy put in, "but she'll not last two weeks on the prairie before—"

"You're no great help to her, are you now, Jimmy O'Toole?" Sheena interjected. "She's a poor slip of a thing with no mother and never a home to call her own. She knew not a *stim* about our Seth, yet she saved his life, so she did." She fastened a glare on Seth. "Now then, Mr. Hunter, what do you have to say for yourself?"

Seth took off his hat and scratched the back of his head. He assessed Rosie and appeared clearly unhappy with what he saw. He crossed his arms over his chest and stared out the mercantile window for a full minute, his eyes narrowed and his jaw clenched. Finally, he gave a grunt of surrender.

"I reckon I'm going to take the girl." He turned to Mrs. Jameson. "I'll only need her for the growing season—six months at the most."

"Sir, Miss Mills is an unmarried woman." Her words were clipped. "You can't just take her into your home like that. It wouldn't be Christian."

"She can live in the barn."

"But Rosie isn't married!"

"A family down the river brought in a girl from Sweden, so they did," Sheena put in. "She takes care of their children and cooks their meals. Two or three families in Lawrence hired young women who used to be slaves to work for them. I even heard of a family—"

"But Mr. Hunter is not a family. He's a widower. He's a single man!" objected Mrs. Jameson.

"And that's how I'm going to stay, too," Seth said, turning on Rosie. "So if you have any crazy ideas about—"

"No," she said quickly. She had to reassure him—had to make this work. "All I want is somewhere to live."

"Don't be foolish, Rosie," Mrs. Jameson cut in. "You know nothing about this man. You have a place with us."

"A place, yes. But not a home." In spite of Mrs. Jameson's scowl, Rosie lifted her chin. "I'm going to Kansas, ma'am, with Mr. Hunter."

Seth hooked a thumb into the pocket of his denim trousers and cocked his head in the direction of the orphanage. "Go fetch your things. I'd just as soon be gone when Jack Cornwall talks the sheriff into letting him go."

"I don't have anything of my own to fetch, sir. I'm ready to leave this very minute."

"You don't have anything?" He frowned and glanced at Mrs. Jameson.

"We're an orphanage, Mr. Hunter," the director explained. "We do well to put food in the children's stomachs. Rosie's fortunate to have a pair of shoes."

Seth studied Rosie up and down for a moment, his blue eyes absorbing her faded dress, worn shawl, and patched boots. Finally he shook his head. "All right," he said. "Let's go."

Rosie pressed her cheek against that of the woman who had taken her in so many years before. "Pray for me, Mrs. Jameson. And give my love to the children."

She turned quickly so she wouldn't change her mind and hurried out of the mercantile. Seth Hunter lifted Chipper onto the spring seat, helped Rosie into the back of the wagon, and climbed aboard himself. Jimmy O'Toole settled his wife and their five red-haired children among the sacks, barrels, and tools. Then he joined Seth on the seat.

Rosie tucked her skirts around her ankles before allowing herself one last look at the Christian Home for Orphans and Foundlings just down the road. What had she done? Oh, Lord!

After releasing the brake, Seth flicked the reins to set his team plodding down the street.

"Don't give her bed away, Mrs. Jameson," he called as the wagon passed the Home's director, who was already marching purposefully back toward the orphanage. "I'll have her back in six months."

"It's a long way from Kansas City to my homestead," Seth said as the wagon rolled out of town. "Ever been to the prairie, Miss Mills?"

She was sitting bolt upright, her head held high as though she intended to drink in the sights and smells and sounds of everything along the way. A ragged bonnet covered the lump on her head, and only a few wisps of brown hair drifted around her chin. Skinny as a rail, she had a straight nose, high cheekbones, and a long neck.

If it weren't for her eyes, she'd be about as pretty as a fledgling prairie hen. But her eyes glowed, huge and brown, like big warm chocolates, and when she blinked, her thick lashes fluttered down to her cheeks in a way that made Seth feel fidgety.

"I've never been anywhere," she said, turning those big eyes on him. "Except to the mercantile and church."

"My place is a long way from any market or church."

"I don't mind, Mr. Hunter. The Lord promises, 'My presence shall go with thee, and I will give thee rest.' I'm not afraid."

"You're a brave lass, so you are," Sheena O'Toole put in. The children were nestled around her, busily sucking on their peppermint sticks. "In truth, at times the prairie can be a lonely place."

"Oh, I've been lonely all my life."

Rosie said it so matter-of-factly that Seth almost didn't catch the significance of her words. When he did, he knew he had to set things straight right away. He didn't want her getting any ideas.

"Look, Miss Mills," he said. "I agreed to let you come along because I owe you. I'm giving you room and board in exchange for hard, honest work. I don't promise any luxuries, and I won't require your company evenings or Sundays. I've been alone a lot of years, and I like it that way."

He knew she didn't fully understand his situation, but he had no intention of going into the details. He had shelved the memories of a brief young love, a secret wedding, and the tumult that had followed. He had lived as a husband for less than a month before his wife's parents banished him from their property. When he had learned he had a son, he was in the Union army and camped on a battleground three hundred miles away. He had not seen his wife again.

"The boy stayed with his mother," Sheena O'Toole whispered in explanation. "Seth was fighting in the war."

"My mama lives in heaven now," Chipper whispered, turning

his big sapphire eyes on Rosie. "She's not coming back to take care of me anymore."

Seth hadn't heard the boy speak more than a word or two in the days he'd had him. Chipper had a high, sweet voice, a baby's voice with a slight lisp from his missing teeth. But not much about him reminded Seth of Mary. Sturdy, black-haired, and blue-eyed, the child was a spitting image of himself.

"I bet you miss your mama," Rosie Mills said from the wagon bed.

The dark head nodded. "I do miss her. And I don't like *him*." He jabbed a tiny thumb in the direction of his father. "He's a Yankee."

"Oh, but he's much more than that. He's your papa, too. That means he loves you, and he's going to watch out for you."

"I don't care. I want to live with Gram and Gramps. I like them better than any Yankee."

Seth glared at the little gap-toothed face. He didn't know how to talk to a five-year-old. Mary's parents despised their son-in-law, and they had poisoned his own child against him. When he returned for a wife he hadn't known was dead, he had learned they'd lost their farm and were moving to southern Missouri. It was then he had decided to claim the son he had fathered. Now he was beginning to wonder if he'd made a mistake.

"Did you know your mama's love lives in your heart, Chipper?" Rosie asked, leaning forward and taking the child's chubby hand. "Why, sure it does. Whenever you're lonely, you can think about her."

"Where does *your* mama live?"

"She doesn't know, Chipper," Sheena said. "Poor Miss Mills never met her mama."

"But I know my father very well," Rosie said. "God is my father. He's always looking out for me, always wanting the best for me, always with me. If I need help, I can talk to him any time."

"Sounds like a better father than *him*." The thumb jabbed Seth's way again.

"I imagine he could be a pretty good papa in time. You'll just have to teach him, Chipper. Now, what do you think a good papa would do with his son while they were traveling to the prairie in a wagon?"

Seth frowned at the road. He didn't like this turn of conversation. Not at all. He wanted to concentrate on his land, to plot out every one of his one hundred sixty acres, to imagine how his crops would grow. He wanted to talk over new ideas with Jimmy O'Toole. He didn't know what to do about the little boy beside him. Or the woman with the big brown eyes.

"He'd sing," Chipper said. "A good papa would sing."

"Oh, that's easy." Rosie laughed at the boy's suggestion. "Come on, then, Mr. Hunter. What shall we sing on our way to the prairie?"

"I don't sing."

"I told you," Chipper said. "He don't even sing."

"Everyone sings," Rosie said. "It's the easiest thing in the world."

"That it is," Sheena agreed. "As easy as dreaming dreams."

"Here's a song about heaven, where your mama lives, Chipper. Let's all sing it together:

"Precious memories, unseen angels,
Sent from somewhere to my soul;
How they linger, ever near me,
And the sacred past unfold."

Rosie's voice was high and lovely. It wrapped around Seth's heart like a pair of gentle arms, warming and comforting him. He did his best to ignore her, but the pleading in the woman's sweet voice softened him.

"Precious memories, how they linger," he joined in roughly, keeping his attention trained on the road ahead.

"How they ever flood my soul;
In the stillness of the midnight,
Precious, sacred scenes unfold."

CHAPTER 2

THE TRAIL that followed the Kansas River toward the open prairie bustled with traffic as Seth Hunter's wagon rolled west. That first day of the journey, Rosie counted three stagecoaches filled with excited travelers heading for the frontier. Two more coaches returning east passed the wagon, their passengers worn and weary from the long journey. A pair of bearded prospectors led a plodding mule bearing their pickaxes and shovels, and dreamed of quick, easy riches. A group of dusty cowboys drove a large herd of cattle east toward the Kansas City stockyards. They had traveled all the way from Texas, the men called out as they passed. The ever-changing pageantry was enough to keep the five O'Toole children chattering, arguing, and speculating for hours.

Just before they stopped in Osawkie for the night, a swaying black buggy raced toward the travelers. "Mrs. Dudenhoffer near Muddy Creek is indisposed," the driver, a physician, called out as his horse rounded Seth's wagon. "We're afraid it may be twins this time."

"God save you, kindly doctor!" Sheena O'Toole shouted back. Then she shook her head at Rosie. "Twins. May the good Lord have mercy on the poor woman's soul."

Rosie knew the birth of twins could kill, and there was little anyone could do about it. A widower with small children would have a hard lot on the prairie. Any man in such a dire situation would be desperate to find himself a hardy new wife. And he couldn't be choosy.

Rosie mulled this thought as they crossed Rock Creek the following morning. At Muddy Creek a circuit preacher approached on his horse. He gave the travelers a friendly wave. "On your way home?" he called. "God bless!"

"Good morrow to you," Sheena replied. "Shall we have the privilege of a visit, sir? We homestead on Bluestem Creek. There are two families of us, and we've been without preaching all winter."

"Bluestem Creek? I'm afraid I always circle around you folks. Your creek runs too high to cross most of the year."

"Humph," Jimmy O'Toole grunted. "I understood you crawthumpers could walk on water."

Seth chuckled as Sheena gave her husband's shoulder a swat. "As you can see, Reverend, we're in grave need of prayer and preaching. Do keep us in mind."

"I will," the preacher said. "And I'll see if I can manage a visit."

Lifting his hat, he gave the group a broad smile and spurred his horse past the wagon. Rosie took note that with his bright yellow hair and well-cut suit, the preacher could almost be called handsome. Not in the same way Seth Hunter was handsome, of course, but the preacher was tolerable looking all the same.

As the wagon neared Indianola, Rosie pondered the unfolding panorama of the prairie and the hope it inspired. Toward evening, she came to a momentous conclusion regarding the six months she would spend on the Hunter homestead. She might actually find someone who would be amenable to the notion of marriage with a woman lacking pedigree, money, or a fancy education! In fact, she already had taken note of several prospects. A lonely widower. A traveling preacher. Even a Texas cowboy. The land was filling quickly with men in need of good, strong wives. The possibilities were endless.

Rosie glanced at Seth Hunter on the wagon seat beside Jimmy. Her new employer was in want of a wife, though he wouldn't admit it. He had made it clear that he would never allow another woman into his life. She suspected his first marriage had been one of true love—at least on Seth's part. He had devoted himself to a young woman whose family despised his northern heritage and abolitionist sympathies. In defiance of her parents and brother, he had married Mary Cornwall, written countless letters to her while he was away in the war, and laid claim to their young son so he could keep a part of her with him always.

Though she was dead to the world, it appeared that his wife was very much alive in Seth Hunter's mind. Rosie sensed it would take a special woman to win his heart—a woman who had much more to offer than the ability to bake apple pies and black a stove from top to bottom.

Though the travelers were just across the river from Topeka, Rosie spent her second night of independence sleeping under the open sky, an ebony umbrella sprinkled with stars. Seth had expressed concern that Jack Cornwall—assuming he had been released from custody and was recovered from the knock on his head—might be able to track the party down if they stopped in Topeka. Besides, Sheena wouldn't hear of allowing her *brablins* to spend a night in such a wild city.

The next day they began the long journey toward Manhattan. As the wagon rolled west, the land began to flatten, the trees gave way to tall golden grass, the streams slowed down and straightened into long silver ribbons. The sun beat on the travelers like a merciless golden hammer.

Throughout the day, the mules plodded wearily down the baked, dusty trail. Every twelve miles, they passed a station on the Butterfield stagecoach route—a refreshing, timely stopping place to trade and water the mule teams. Seth, in a hurry to elude his possible pursuer, paused as briefly as possible.

The sunburned O'Toole children grew restless during the long journey, the young ones whimpering and the older ones fussing at each other. Not even passing through the Potawatomi Indian reservation could perk them up. Seated between his father and Jimmy O'Toole, Chipper slumped over on the front bench, shoulders hunched. Sheena fanned herself as she mourned the lack of a canvas wagon cover, and Jimmy mopped his forehead.

"Why then, Seth, do you think that *sherral* Jack Cornwall is coming after us even now?" Sheena asked as the sun rose to its apex. Like a mother hen, she had settled her five children around her. The two youngest drowsed on her lap. "Sure, I won't have harm done to any of my wee ones."

"I doubt he'll be able to track me down right away," Seth said over his shoulder. "The sheriff had him in custody, and a couple of townspeople gave the story of what happened between us in the street. I hope Cornwall will stay locked up for a while, anyway."

"Aye, but then what? Does he know where you homestead?"

"All he'd have to do is ask around."

"Will he come for you?"

"It's the boy he wants."

"Chipper, you're a good lad, aren't you?" Sheena asked softly. "You don't want your papa to come to harm. Why then, let's have the preacher in Manhattan write a letter to your grandparents and tell them how happy you are."

The little boy turned and scowled at her. "I don't wanna live with no Yankee papa," he said, speaking aloud for the first time that day. "I want to go home to Gram an' Gramps. I want my mama."

"Enough about her," Seth snapped. "You have a papa, and I don't want to hear any more talk about your mama."

Rosie bristled at the man's harsh tone. Surely he could understand the boy missing his mother. Seth Hunter wanted a son, but he clearly had no idea how to be a father. If he intended to weld the two of them into a family, he would have to do better than chastise the little boy and forbid him to mention the mother he was so obviously mourning.

Rosie couldn't deny she knew little about the business of being a family. But after nineteen years at the Christian Home for Orphans and Foundlings, she did know a great deal about children. Above their basic needs of food, clothes, and shelter, they wanted kindness. Discipline. A good Christian example to follow. And fun. All children deserved fun.

"Let's play Cupid's Coming," she said, elbowing Erinn, the oldest of the O'Toole children. At eight, Erinn was well versed in the responsibilities of child care. "You and I will start, and we'll go around the wagon, ending with your mother. How's that?"

"Cupid's Coming?" Erinn asked, her green eyes bright. "But we don't know that game."

"It's easy. I'll start. We'll use the letter *T* for the first round." Rosie frowned for a moment, pretending to study the situation. "Cupid's coming," she told Erinn. "Now you ask, how?"

"How?"

"Tiptoeing."

"Cupid's coming," Erinn told her brother, six-year-old Will.

"How?"

"Talking," Erinn said.

Will turned to Colleen. "Cupid's coming."

"How?" she asked.

"Terrifying!" Will shouted, forming his hands into claws. Everyone laughed. Even Chipper managed a half grin.

Colleen nudged her father on the wagon seat. "Cupid's coming."

"How?" he asked.

"Ticktocking."

"Cupid's coming," Jimmy told Chipper.

"How?"

"Tapping."

Chipper looked at his father. Then he glanced back at Rosie. She gave him an encouraging wink.

"Cupid's coming," the boy said.

Seth gave the reins a bored flick. "How?"

"Tripping."

"Cupid's tripping?" Seth exclaimed. "Well, I guess that's the end of the game then."

"No!" the children shouted. "Come on, Seth! Play with us."

"Excuse me," Rosie cut in. "I'm afraid Mr. Hunter didn't take his turn quickly enough. He'll have to pay a forfeit."

Seth turned slowly, his blue eyes locking on Rosie's face. "A forfeit?"

She lifted her chin and stuck out her hand. "That's right. Pay up, sir."

Seth frowned and patted his empty shirt pocket. "I'm afraid I'm fresh out of—" He stopped, leaned out of the wagon, reached into the tall grass growing by the trail, and snapped the prickly head off a dry stem. He tossed Rosie the small black ball. "Purple coneflower."

She held the gift in the palm of her hands. "This is a flower?"

"Seeds. You'll have to plant them if you want flowers." Seth turned to Sheena. "I choose the letter A. Cupid's coming."

"A? Why, Seth, that's impossible!" Sheena squawked.

"Cupid's coming," he repeated.

"How?"

"Annoying," Seth said, giving Rosie a look.

The game faltered after that. The letter A only managed to make its way to Will, who came up with "apples" and was disqualified. He paid his forfeit with a peppermint-sticky kiss on Rosie's cheek.

She was tucking her purple coneflower seedpod into the pouch she wore around her neck when Seth pulled the wagon up to a small frame building, unpainted and sagging. "Holloway's Stagecoach Station," he called. "I've had enough of Miss Mills's songs and games for one morning. We'll stop here for lunch."

"Hurrah! Come on, Chipper!" Will grabbed the younger boy by the hand. "This station has a creek out back—with tadpoles!"

"Don't get muddy!" Sheena called. She woke the littlest ones and began handing them down to Seth and Jimmy one by one. "I pray Mrs. Holloway has some of those delicious pickles. I want to buy a few. I'd love the recipe, but Mrs. Holloway won't give it out. Selfish, if you ask me."

"Come on then, my treasure," Jimmy said. "You know you'll copy the taste of Mrs. Holloway's pickles in your own kitchen, as fine a cook as you are."

"Blather, blather, blather," Sheena said with a chuckle.

She and Jimmy walked toward the station as Seth lifted a hand to help Rosie down. She slipped her fingers onto his palm, aware of the hard calluses that bore testament to his labors. Lifting the hem of her skirt, she stepped onto the wagon wheel. Before she could jump down, Seth wrapped both hands around her waist and swung her to the ground.

"Cupid's coming," he said in a low voice. "Afflicting."

"Appalling," she shot back, meeting his steady blue gaze.

"Agitating."

"Alarming."

She pulled away from him and hurried toward the station door, aware that her cheeks must be as hot and red as a pair of sun-ripened tomatoes. Why was he tormenting her this way? Did he despise her?

"Agonizing," he said, following her with long strides.

She sucked in a breath and stopped. "Abusing."

He smiled. "Amusing."

"A . . . a . . . admitting."

"Admiring."

She stepped through the door into the cool shadows. "I can't . . . can't think . . . oh, alligator."

"Ha! Too slow. You lose." He stood over her, seeming twice as tall as he had in the Kansas City mercantile. "I'm afraid Miss Mills wasn't able to give an answer quickly enough. She'll have to pay a forfeit."

Rosie swallowed. "What do you want? You know I don't have anything."

"Agreeing."

"To what?"

"No more games. No more songs. No more silliness. Leave my son to me. Take care of him—feed him, see that his clothes are patched, make him go to bed at night—but that's all. Come fall, Miss Mills, I'm taking you back to Kansas City. I don't want Chipper sad to see you leave. He's *my* son. Got that?" He turned into the station.

"Cupid's coming," Rosie said softly behind him.

Seth swung around, a frown drawing down the corners of his mouth.

"Accepting," she finished. Spotting Sheena admiring a bolt of calico, she set off toward the counter.

As Seth chewed on a slab of salt pork as tough as old leather, he studied Rosie Mills from under the brim of his hat. He didn't like her. Didn't trust her. She was too cheerful, too perky. Worse, she was defiant. In opposition to his direct orders, she had continued her charming, winsome ways with the children. With her songs and games, she had easily won them over. Look at them.

Under the shade of a big black willow tree, Rosie had arranged everybody in a circle and was marching around tapping them one by one as she chanted:

"Heater, beater, Peter mine,
Hey Betty Martin, tiptoe fine.
Higgledy-piggledy, up the spout,
Tip him, turn him 'round about.
One, two, three,
Out goes he!"

In a moment, the whole pack of children was racing around like a bunch of prairie dogs with rabies. Rosie ran among them, her bonnet ribbons flying and her skirts dancing at her ankles. How could anyone who had nothing—no home, no family, not even a blanket or a spare petticoat—be as happy as that?

No, Seth thought, it just didn't make sense. In fact, it was downright suspicious. What was she after, this Rosie Mills? What was she planning to get out of this little adventure of hers? What scheme did she have up her sleeve?

Even worse than her unsettling cheeriness was the way Chipper responded to Rosie. Ever since Seth had reclaimed the boy, Chipper had spoken barely six words to him—and not one of them was charitable. Seth could hardly blame him. After all, until three days ago, they were complete strangers, and with little explanation he had scooped up the boy, toted him to his wagon, and driven off with him.

Sure, Chipper understood that Seth was his father. Thanks to his grandparents, the boy had been well versed in the story of the Yankee "scalawag" who had sired him. Chipper didn't like his father, didn't trust him, wanted nothing to do with him. But the child clearly adored Rosie Mills.

"Oh, Chipper!" she exclaimed as he tackled her, and she tumbled to the ground in a heap. "You caught me, you little rascal!"

"You're it, you're it!" Barefooted, he danced around her. "Rosie's it!"

"I can't!" She threw back her head, stretched out her long legs, and gave a breathless laugh. "You've worn me out, all of you."

"Let's go down to the stream again before Papa calls us to the wagon," Will suggested. "We'll catch a frog and take it to Bluestem Creek. Come on, Rosie! Come with us!"

"You go ahead. I need to catch my breath."

"Please come," Chipper begged, pulling on her hand in an attempt to make her stand.

"Really, sweetheart, I can't. Go with Will. He'll show you how to catch a frog."

Seth watched as the children traipsed over the hill and down the slope toward the creek. The moment they were gone, Rosie pulled off her bonnet and crumpled it in her lap. A pained expression darkening her eyes, she gingerly touched the back of her head. Then she began to take out her hairpins one by one. She loosed the thick ropes of her brown tresses. Her hair slid to her shoulders, then tumbled down her back to the ground in a puddle of shiny silk.

Seth stared. He'd never seen such hair. Long hair—masses of it—draped around the woman like a brown cape. Even more amazing was the great pile of it that sat in the grass around her hips. Rosie Mills had enough hair for three women. Maybe four. Unaware of Seth's staring, she bent over her knees and probed her head.

"Sheena," she called softly. "Sheena?"

Seth frowned. Sheena was inside the station buying pickles. Jimmy was with her, trading one of his famous knives for a cast-iron skillet. Rosie touched her head again and looked at her fingers.

"Sheena!"

"She's inside," Seth called. He set his plate of salt pork in the wagon bed and started toward her. "Something wrong?"

"My head. It hurts where I hit it the other day. I'm afraid . . . am I bleeding again?"

Seth didn't like the notion of getting too near the woman. His new employee had an unsettling way of looking into his eyes as though she could read his thoughts. And she smelled good. He had noticed that when he helped her down from the wagon. She smelled clean and fresh—like starch mingled with lavender. Most of all, he didn't want to touch that silky sheet of her hair.

"I shouldn't have been running," she was saying, "but I thought if the children played hard, they might sleep in the wagon this afternoon. It would shorten the trip for them. Would you mind taking a look at my bump, Mr. Hunter? If I'm bleeding, I think I should put some ice on it. Maybe the stationmaster would spare . . . Mr. Hunter? Would you mind?"

She turned those big chocolate eyes on him, and Seth walked over to her like a puppet on a string. Before he could stop himself, he was kneeling beside her and drinking in that sweet lavender scent. She sifted through her hair with long fingers.

"It's just there," she whispered. "Can you see anything?"

He touched the warm brown strands. "You've got a swollen lump—"

"Ouch!"

"Sorry. I don't think it's bleeding again. I could buy you a chunk of ice."

"No, I'll be all right." She threaded her fingers through her hair. "I would hate to spend good money on something that's going to melt. I just don't want to stain my bonnet, you understand. This is the only one I have, and it's very precious to me. Priscilla gave it to me two years ago, before she left the Home."

"Priscilla?"

"My best friend. When she married the vegetable seller's oldest son, he bought her three new bonnets—not to mention a green twill skirt, a pair of new stockings, and a wool shawl. Wool. Pure, white wool. So, seeing as she didn't need it, she gave this bonnet to me for Christmas."

Seth blinked. He'd never heard anyone rattle on the way Rosie Mills could. Despite the bump on her head, she jumped from one subject to the next like a rabbit in a spring garden. As much as he wanted to ignore her, Seth couldn't quite suppress his intrigue.

"Cilla lived at the Home three years," Rosie went on, oblivious to her employer's bemusement. "She came to stay with us after her parents died in a terrible fire. All her relatives lived in England, and they couldn't afford boat passage for her even though she ached to go to them."

"I'm sure she did," Seth managed, searching for an adequate response to the woeful tale. "Poor Cilla."

"It was very sad. But I wouldn't feel too sorry for her, if I were you. Cilla wasn't a foundling, you know. She came from a respected family, and she was very pretty. Blonde. Curls everywhere. Anyway, the vegetable seller's son decided she would make a good wife. So they married, and now she has a baby girl and another on the way."

"Not to mention three new bonnets, a skirt, and a pair of stockings."

The corners of Rosie's mouth turned up. "Don't forget the wool shawl."

"Lucky girl to win the heart of the vegetable seller's oldest son. Must have been true love."

"I don't know about that." She shrugged and began to twine her hair into a long rope. "What matters is Cilla's settled, and I miss her. I won't have this bonnet ruined."

Seth studied the wad of thin calico. The bonnet was a pathetic scrap, patched and frayed. Cheap cotton, it might once have been navy, but it had faded in the sun to a pale shade of cornflower blue sprinkled with small white rosebuds.

"Is that what *you're* after, Miss Mills?" Seth asked. "Bonnets and stockings and wool shawls?"

"Good heavens, no! Those are earthly treasures. The Bible tells us not to store them up. They won't last. I'm after something much more important."

"I figured as much."

She lifted her focus to the tips of the arching willow branches. "Faith," she murmured. "I want to grow in faith. Hope. The hope of heaven. And love. To share the love of my Father with people who've never known it."

"Lofty dreams." He gave a grunt of impatience. "Look, Miss Mills, you left everything familiar to risk traveling to the prairie with a stranger. You must be thinking you'll get something practical out of it."

Her brown eyes searched his face. "Yes," she said softly. She leaned toward him. "This is a secret, so please don't tell anyone. I've made up my mind. I want to get married, Mr. Hunter."

"What?" His heart jumped into his throat and froze solid. "Married?"

"Not to you! Don't draw back like a snake just bit you." She laughed for a moment as though the idea of anyone wanting to marry him was a great joke. "Of course not you. Someone else. Almost anyone will do. While I'm living on your homestead the next few months, I'm going to search for a husband. If I can find someone fair-minded and strong, a kind man and a hard worker, I'll ask him to marry me."

"You'll ask *him?"*

"Why not? I don't have a thing to offer but a pair of good hands and a strong back. Who would ask me?" She leaned back and giggled again as though this were the funniest notion she'd heard in weeks. "Oh, laughing makes my bump hurt."

Seth watched as she twirled the rope of her hair onto her head in a big glossy mound of loops and swirls. Still chuckling, she deftly slipped hairpins here and there. She gave her creation a quick pat to assure herself it was secure, then she swept her bonnet over it and tied the ribbons into a loose bow under her chin.

"Keep your eyes peeled for me, Mr. Hunter," she confided. "I don't much care what the man looks like or how old he is. It makes no difference how many children he's got. As long as he's good and kind."

"And hardworking."

"Yes." She studied him. "Why are you smirking at me, Mr. Hunter?"

"It just seems a little strange that you've made up your mind to go out husband hunting like a trapper after a prized beaver."

"And why not? The Bible tells us it's good for a man and woman to marry. I don't know why I should be obliged to spend the rest of my life working at the Christian Home for Orphans and Foundlings when there might be a lonely man somewhere who could use a good wife."

"I guess you never considered that it might be nice if the fellow loved you. And you him."

"Love? Please, Mr. Hunter. Have you been reading novels?"

Seth studied the woman's brown eyes. He didn't know what had made him kneel under the willow tree and talk to this creature in the first place. She jabbered like a blue jay. She giggled like a schoolgirl. He didn't trust her around his son. No telling what ideas she might put into the boy's head. Any woman who would walk away from a secure position to go to work for a stranger . . . any woman who would set out on her own in search of a husband . . . any woman who would ask a man to marry her . . . any woman like that was too downright bold. Too forward. Too impetuous. It just wasn't proper.

Rosie Mills didn't seem to have the least idea what love was all about. She would marry a man the way a store owner would take on a hired hand. No feeling. No emotion. No passion behind it.

That wasn't how he and Mary Cornwall had felt about each other. He had been half crazy over that girl. The way she swayed when she walked had set his heart beating like a brass band. The way she batted her eyelashes at him turned his stomach into a hundred butterflies. And when she had stood on tiptoe to kiss him on the cheek that afternoon in the barn . . . well . . .

Seth hadn't known Mary very long when he asked her to marry him. But the way she made him feel was love. True love. No doubt about it.

"I don't know a thing about love except what the Bible says," Rosie announced, cutting into his pleasant memories. "Love is patient, kind, forgiving. Never jealous or proud. Love is never demanding or critical. I imagine I could love just about anybody, Mr. Hunter. Couldn't you?"

"Nope." He stood and swatted the dust from his knees with his hat. "I hate Jack Cornwall's guts, and if he tries to take my son again, I'll kill him."

"Kill him?"

"Besides that, I'd never marry some bold, insolent woman who thought she could do the asking. If I ever marry again, I'll have more in it than patience, kindness, and forgiveness. You don't know the half of what it takes to make a marriage."

Rosie got to her feet. "Maybe I do know the half. I may never have had a family to grow up with or a man turning somersaults over me, but I watched the family who lived across the street from the Christian Home. I climbed up in the white oak tree every morning to say my prayers, and I studied that family. I saw how they lived, working together day and night. I watched the children grow. I saw funerals and weddings and birthday parties."

"Working together day and night is not all there is to marriage," Seth said, growing hot around the collar.

"Maybe it's not all, but it's half!" Rosie Mills tilted her chin at him, her brown eyes sparking like coals. "Half is what *you* know—the kind of love that forces a man to marry a girl against her parents' wishes, love that makes him write her from the battlefield and steal away her son and keep her alive in his heart even when she's dead."

"Stop talking about my wife!" Seth exploded.

"I won't deny I've never known that kind of passion," Rosie went on. "But *I* know the other half of what makes a family. It's commitment. It's holding on through thick and thin. It's surviving through freezing winters and burning summers and sick children and not enough food in the pantry. That's what it is. Commitment like that is plenty to make a marriage, and I'm going to find myself a husband no matter what you think, Mr. Seth Hunter!"

"Good luck to the man who hooks up with the likes of you!" he roared, his mouth just inches from hers.

She swallowed and blinked. To his utter dismay, her brown eyes filled with tears. She gulped. "I'll . . . I'll just go and see if Sheena found her pickles. Excuse me."

Rosie swung away, her palm cupping the bump beneath her bonnet. Seth watched her go, a slender twig of a woman with hair like a river, dark coffee eyes that glowed when she laughed, and enough spunk to survive the worst life had to offer. It occurred to him as he went back to his plate of salt pork that Rosie Mills would probably make some man a pretty good wife.

CHAPTER 3

As ROSIE stood inside the stagecoach station watching Sheena and Jimmy count their purchases, she fought the lump in her throat. Once again, she had to confess she had stepped out on her own instead of turning to her heavenly Father for direction. In setting off for Kansas with Seth Hunter, she had been willful, selfish, and headstrong. To the best of her knowledge, she hadn't offered up a single prayer for guidance before climbing onto that mule wagon bound for the prairie. And now she would have to suffer the consequences.

Seth Hunter was a hard man. An angry man. A bitter man. He didn't want tenderness or compassion. And he certainly didn't seem to like anyone standing up to him. Unfortunately, his new hired hand was everything he found intolerable.

Rosie had always assumed a girl who had spent her life in a place like the Christian Home for Orphans and Foundlings ought to be meek, contrite, humble. Instead, she fought a constant battle with her willful nature.

Precisely because she had grown up in the Home, she had learned to rely on her wits and to trust her instinct. On an impulse, she could devise a game that would transform toddlers' wails into giggles. She could create meals when there was nothing in the kitchen pantry but a bag of bug-infested beans and a few withered carrots. She contrived ways to keep the orphans warm during blizzards. She improvised a pull-rope swinging fan to keep the kitchen cool in summer. If a townsman gave the Home a sack of old, half-rotten potatoes, Rosie had the children cut out the eyes, plant them in the kitchen garden, and grow a bumper crop. If a church donated an extra quilt, she cut apart the patches and used them to mend the holes in every child's clothing.

If Rosie had an idea, she acted on it. More often than not, her ideas were good ones. But sometimes . . . sometimes the consequences were disastrous.

"It's me, Father," she prayed as she leaned against the rough plank wall of the stagecoach station. "It's always me first, isn't it? You must be so tired of my willful stubbornness. Every day I do nothing but rely on myself. *I'll* climb the oak tree. *I'll* whack Jack Cornwall on the head. *I'll* go to Kansas with Seth Hunter. *I'll* find a man to marry me."

She shook her head in dismay. Why couldn't she remember to pray before she acted—instead of after?

"Father, forgive me," she murmured. "I do so want to have a home and a family. Help me to leave it up to you—"

"Rosie?" Sheena's green eyes studied her. "Are you muttering to yourself, then?"

"No, no—"

"Seth's just told us the knock on your head has been troubling you. He's fretting about you, he is."

"About me?"

"Aye, and now I hear you muttering to yourself. Perhaps we'd better try to find a doctor so he can have a look at your head."

"No, really, Sheena. I'm fine."

"You're certain? I'm sure I saw you—"

"I was praying."

The woman's green eyes widened. "First you pray in an oak tree. Now in the stagecoach station?"

"Our Father is with us everywhere."

"That he is, and a good thing, too. All the same, I wouldn't go talking to him just anywhere. People might wonder at it, you know." Sheena handed Rosie a wrapped bundle. "Now then, here's a gift for you from Jimmy and me. We want to see you started off right in your new life."

Rosie stared at the package in her hands. No one had ever given her anything new. Ever. Not in her whole life.

"Well, don't just stand there throwing sheep's eyes at the thing," Sheena said. "Open it."

Swallowing hard, Rosie unfolded the rough white cheesecloth. "A skillet! Cast iron. Oh, Sheena, it's beautiful."

"Jimmy traded one of his knives for it. He makes the best knives in all Kansas, he does."

"Mr. O'Toole!" Clutching the heavy skillet to her chest, Rosie danced across the room and flung an arm around the tall, gaunt man. "Thank you. Thank you so much!"

"Now then—" he began, but he stopped when she planted a big kiss on his cheek.

"A skillet! I wish I could show this to Mrs. Jameson. She wouldn't believe how beautiful it is! And so big. I'll bet a person could fry fifteen eggs in this skillet. If the kitchen at the Christian Home had a skillet like this one . . . You know, the skillet we have now is so thin at the bottom . . . everything burns . . . and the other has a hole in it . . . Why don't I send this one to Mrs. Jameson and the children? Would you mind if I gave it away?" She glanced at Jimmy. A look of confusion in his green eyes, he shook his head.

"Oh, thank you! Mr. Holloway, will there be a stagecoach or a wagon passing through here on its way to Kansas City?"

"Only ten or fifteen a day," the stationmaster said. He was eyeing the O'Toole children, who had filtered into the building and were peering into his cases—sticky fingers, lips, and noses pressed against the glass. "What is it you want with a stagecoach back to Kansas City, Missy? Ain't that where you folks just come from?"

Rosie set the iron pan on the countertop. "Mr. Holloway, will you please send this skillet by stagecoach to the Christian Home for Orphans and Foundlings? I've never been able to give anyone a gift. Tell them it's from me: Rosenbloom Cotton Mills."

The stationmaster scowled at her. "What kind of a dumb-fool name is that?"

"It's a beautiful name. It's the name my mother gave me."

"That ain't no name. It's a place. In Illinois, to be exact. I order my stockings from Rosenbloom Cotton Mills. Look here."

He reached into his glass case and brought out a pair of cotton stockings the exact shade of gray as the one Rosie had been put into as a baby. He tunneled his hand down to the toe and pulled out a scrap of white paper.

"See there, it's right on the label: *Rosenbloom Cotton Mills*. They make stockings, underwear, and gloves. I've been ordering from Rosenbloom Mills for fifteen years." He shooed the children away from his cases, and they scampered outside. "Now what's your real name, Missy? I don't know nobody in their right mind who would give a skillet as good as this one to a passel of worthless urchins. Half of them is of indecent birth."

"But Mr. Holloway—"

"It ain't right even to look at them devils—born to loose women and not worth the food that's fed 'em. Even God don't want nothing to do with the likes of foundlings. Ain't you read what the Good Book says? The book of Deuteronomy: 'A bastard shall not enter into the congregation of the Lord; even to his tenth generation shall he not enter into the congregation of the Lord.'"

Rosie caught her breath. "No . . . the children . . . we—"

"Who are you, anyhow?" Holloway went on. "The way I see it, anyone who goes by an alias is hiding something."

Her heart hammering, Rosie touched the small pouch she wore

on a string around her neck. The toe of the stocking . . . and inside it, the square of neatly printed paper. *Rosenbloom Cotton Mills*. For years, she had convinced herself her mother had written out that beautiful name for her newborn baby. Hadn't she tucked the tiny child into the stocking so her daughter would be safe and warm? Hadn't she cherished the child she had been forced to leave behind? Didn't the silent, long-lost mother mourn for her daughter every day—wondering where she was, praying for her safety, aching to hold her again, just as her child ached to be held?

The image Rosie had denied all her life burst into her thoughts with the force of an exploding bullet. She had been conceived by accident. Born unwanted. Stuffed into a sock. Abandoned on a stack of moldy hay in a livery stable. Expected to die.

The name was not a precious gift. It was a stocking label.

"You gone deaf, girl?" the stationmaster spoke up. "If you want me to send this skillet to Kansas City, you'd better give me your true name."

"Rose Mills," Seth said, stepping up to the counter and jabbing a finger into the man's chest. "That's who she is, and it's as good a name as yours or mine. Now send that skillet to the Christian Home like she said, or I'll see that nobody the other side of Bluestem Creek ever stops at your station again."

"You look here, Mister—"

"Now then, Seth." Jimmy O'Toole put an arm around his friend's shoulder. "Sheena's got her pickles, and the *brablins* are already climbing onto the wagon. Let's be on our way, shall we?"

"The sooner the better." Seth gave the stationmaster a final poke. Dropping his hat on his head, he grabbed Rosie's arm. "Let's go."

She barely had time to lift the hem of her skirt as Seth propelled her out the door onto the rickety front porch. She half ran to keep up with his long stride, and Jimmy hurried his wife along behind them.

"By herrings, that Holloway is a wicked fellow," Sheena puffed. "I hope it gets there. The skillet, I mean."

"It will."

When they reached the wagon, Jimmy helped Sheena climb aboard. As he pushed his wife from behind, the three oldest O'Toole children pulled on their mother's arms. Sheena couldn't hold back a giggle at her family's arduous effort, but Seth was in no mood to join the fun. He swept Rosie off her feet and tossed her over the side of the wagon like a sack of seed. Climbing onto the front, he flicked the leather reins. As the wagon began to roll, Jimmy gave his wife a final shove. Then he scampered around to the other side and climbed aboard.

"Whoa, Seth!" Sheena called, thumping him on the back. "You've nearly gone off hot-foot without my Jimmy! What's got you so scalded?"

"Holloway. The man doesn't deserve the privilege of running a station. Someone ought to take away his post office commission."

"Aye, he charges double what the merchants get in Kansas City," Sheena said. "Two dollars for a gallon of molasses. Seventy-five cents a pound for butter. Did you see his eggs? Sixty cents a dozen. Sure the man ought to be strung up for highway robbery."

"He'll charge what the market can bear," Jimmy said. "Holloway's got a good location, so he does. Hardly a soul can make it from Fort Riley to Kansas City without stopping at his station."

"Of course, if *we* had a better crossing at Bluestem Creek," Sheena suggested, "we could cut off Holloway and his high prices. We could—"

"Now you've done it." Jimmy shook his head at Seth. "Her blather won't let up for hours. 'If you would only put in a ferry, Jimmy. If you'd just build a bridge, Jimmy.' Seth, why don't you give my wife an answer, and see if you can put a stop to her ballyragging."

As the adults talked on, Rosie leaned her head against a keg of seed and shut her eyes. She couldn't make herself care whether some Kansas creek had a ferry or a bridge. She didn't even mind that Mr. Holloway overcharged for molasses and butter. Her head throbbed where she'd hit it, but the pain was nothing compared to that in her heart.

Rosenbloom Cotton Mills, that beautiful name. It wasn't hers. It belonged to a factory that made underwear. No mother had loved her newborn baby and tenderly laid her in a warm, safe place until she could be discovered by someone who had the means to care for her. Rosie had been abandoned. Cast away. Unwanted.

She fought the tears that welled in her closed eyes. The station-master's rebuff rang in her ears. *Even God don't want nothing to do with the likes of foundlings. Ain't you read what the Good Book says? The book of Deuteronomy. A bastard shall not enter into the congregation of the Lord—* Rosie forced the memory to stop. She couldn't believe such a thing was really in the Bible. No matter what Mr. Holloway said, she had to believe God loved her. Thanks to his mercy, she had been found. Taken in by the Christian Home. Fed. Clothed. Taught to read and do arithmetic and sew. Given honest work to keep her hands busy.

But nobody had ever wanted her. Her mother hadn't wanted her. She hadn't been chosen by any of the families who looked over the children for adoption. She hadn't been picked by any of the young men who came courting the older girls at the Home.

Even now. Seth Hunter didn't want her. Though he had come to her defense against Mr. Holloway, he had made it clear that Rosie was a bother to him. Annoying. Afflicting. Agitating. He hadn't wanted to take her to his homestead in Kansas. And he didn't like her spending time with his son.

Stay out of my life, was the message his blue eyes conveyed. *Keep away from me and those I love. I don't want you.*

"Sheena's right," Seth was saying as Rosie struggled to keep her tears from spilling down her cheeks. "If we had a better crossing at Bluestem Creek, we could cut Holloway right off the trail. The only reason people stop at his station on Walnut Creek is because they can't cross the Bluestem until they get almost up to the springs."

"So why don't you build a bridge, Seth?" Sheena asked. "It would bring you closer to our place, as well—just across the creek instead of half a day's travel upstream and back down again. Sure the stagecoaches would love it. And the military, too. Can you imagine? A straight stretch from Laski's Station to LeBlanc's Mill. It would cut off almost a full day's travel. Maybe you could charge a toll, Seth. Make enough money to pay for the bridge—and a little extra to save besides."

"You want fifteen stagecoaches a day passing across our property, Sheena?" Jimmy asked. "You want settlers stopping and begging you for eggs and milk? You want them slipping into our fields and picking our corn? You want soldiers poking around in your kitchen garden to see if they can find a spare spud for their stew? You want to be cooking for thirty at dinnertime instead of seven? I say let Holloway have the lot of them, and bad luck to them every one."

"And what if a fire burns our fields like it did poor Rustemeyer to the north, Mr. Contrary O'Toole?" Sheena hurled back. "What if a cyclone comes along and blows away our house? Did you ever think about that? Sure we could use the money then, couldn't we? What if we have a drought? What if—"

"What if St. Patrick drives all the snakes back into Ireland? What if all our spuds turn into gold nuggets? By all the goats in Kerry, woman, I'll not have fifty *spalpeens* a day traipsing across my homestead. I don't care how much you want a bridge, I'll not build it!"

"Then I will," Seth said. "I'll build it just downstream from my house, over near the barn. Jimmy, with your permission, I'll clear a path from the main trail across the corner of your land to that spot on the Bluestem where folks cross in a dry month. Nobody would come near your house, but I'll let them stop at mine for water and feed. You know it would do the both of us good to have a bridge."

"That Jack Cornwall would get to you quicker if he had a nice, straight road to ride down," Jimmy said.

"And you and I would be closer to each other in case we need help. It would even tie in Rolf Rustemeyer—"

"That *German?*"

"Yes, and you're Irish, LeBlanc's French, and Laski's Polish. Why not build a bridge to connect us? At harvesttime it would shorten your trip to Topeka, and I could get to the mill twice as fast." He paused. "*And* we'd cut off Holloway."

Sheena laughed. "There you have it! Cut off the scoundrel and his pickle-hoarding little wife."

"You'd cut off Salvatore Rippeto, too," Jimmy said. "Or did you forget about our Italian neighbor?"

"Sure, he and Carlotta would thank us kindly for such a thing. That poor woman's got so many wee ones she can barely keep her eye on them—not to mention tending all the travelers."

"Aye, build your bridge then," Jimmy said. "I knew it would come to this one day. Civilization. Before you can count to ten, the preacher will be dropping by to tie up our Sundays with his crawthumping. And then somebody will get the elegant notion to put in a mercantile. And a saloon. And a schoolhouse. In no time, there'll be lawyers and doctors and all manner of scalawags swarming us."

"And St. Patrick will drive all the snakes back into Ireland," Sheena said. "To tell God's truth, Jimmy O'Toole, you are the sourest man that ever lived. There's not a chance in all the world that Seth Hunter's little dugout will become the next Topeka."

"Dugout?" Rosie said, coming suddenly alert.

"Sure and what else did you expect?" Sheena asked. "A white clapboard with roses and morning glories twining the front porch? You're on your way to the prairie, my girl."

Rosie sank back against the seed keg and shut her eyes. The prairie. No bridge. No mercantile. No church. No school. Not even a house.

Unwanted, unneeded, unloved, the girl with no name was on her way to live in a hole in the dirt of the barren, windswept prairie.

"It makes me think of ironing," Rosie said to Sheena.

Seth frowned. What was she on about now? Ever since they'd left Holloway's Station on Walnut Creek, Rosie had been uncharacteristically quiet. No songs. No whistling competitions. No riddles. No long, drawn-out fairy tales about princesses and ogres. At first, it had been a blessed relief. Seth thought he'd had enough silliness to last a lifetime.

But then the O'Toole children began to whine and fidget. Sheena complained about the heat. Jimmy complained about Sheena. The whole cacophony was regularly punctuated by Chipper announcing he wanted his Gram and Gramps, and he didn't want to go live with "no Yankee."

Seth had almost rejoiced when he heard Rosie's voice from the back of the wagon. "I don't know what I expected," she said, and everyone grew quiet. "But this certainly isn't like anything I ever imagined."

"What are you talking about, lass?" Sheena had asked.

"The prairie," Rosie had said. And then she made her comment about ironing. No doubt this was going to turn into a riddle game or something, Seth mused. At least the sound of her voice had calmed the children. Even Chipper seemed to be listening to what Rosie would say.

"Ironing," she repeated. "You know how it is when you do the laundry? You start with a shirt fresh off the clothesline, and it's as rumpled and wrinkled as Missouri is full of hollows, hills, creekbeds, and bluffs. Then you begin to iron. The wrinkles smooth out, and the rumples flatten down. The hills vanish. The streambeds stretch out straight and smooth. And it's the prairie."

Sheena laughed. "What do you think of it then? Do you like this pressed down, flat land, Rosie?"

The young woman sat silently for a moment. "I think the prairie is the ugliest thing I've ever seen."

Seth swung around. "Ugly?"

She turned her big chocolate eyes on him. "Ugly. Boring, too. It's flat and dry and all but bare of trees. There's nothing to stop the wind. The water is so sleepy it makes hardly a sound. And the grass—it seems to go on forever like an endless pale-green-and-yellow sea. I know God created the prairie, but I can honestly say I've never seen anything so ugly in all my life."

Seth stiffened. "You call soil as thick and rich as chocolate cake ugly? You call a sky that stretches from one horizon to the other like a big blue bowl ugly? Miss Mills, you don't know a thing about ugly."

He glared at her. The prairie was his home, his certainty, his hope. The prairie was the source of his faith. In his lifetime, Seth had known enough pain to turn him away from God—a father who walked out on him, a war that tore his country apart, a best friend blown to bits by a cannonball, a wife whose parents despised him, a love who died in the bloom of her life. But the prairie refused to let Seth's bitterness and doubt claim his soul. The prairie was proof of a future, proof of heaven, proof of God himself.

"You call this ugly?" he asked, bending over the side of the wagon and snapping off a bunch of long-stemmed red blossoms. "This is Indian paintbrush. See these pink-and-yellow flowers? Goat's rue. Those little white flowers? Pussy's-toes. The purple ones? Bird's-foot violets." He reached down and plucked another handful of tiny blue flowers. "Blue-eyed grass. And here's yellow-star grass."

He tossed the wildflower bouquet into Rosie's arms. She caught it and clutched it with both hands. Her brown eyes were wide, as though she feared he might put her out of the wagon any moment and abandon her on the ugly, boring prairie.

Seth had half a mind to do just that. On the other hand, for some reason he couldn't explain, he wanted Rose Mills to see what this land meant to him. He wanted her to understand that it was his life.

"It's not just an endless sea of yellow and green. Right from this wagon seat I can count seven different kinds of grass. There's prairie dropseed over there and two kinds of broomsedge along the trail. See that patch of light green? That's Elliott's broomsedge. It'll be a brown orange come fall. This other kind looks almost the same, but it's not. The leaves on the seed stalks are broader, and they'll turn bright orange."

"There's little bluestem," Jimmy chimed in. "It's a sort of blue-green, so it is. And you see that stand of purple-stemmed grass over there, Miss Mills? That's big bluestem. By mid-August, the seed heads will divide into three parts."

"They look just like turkey tracks, so they do," Will O'Toole said. "I see silverbeard bluestem, Papa. Look down, Rosie, just by the wagon wheel. Silverbeard is very short. Do you see it?"

Holding tight to her bouquet, she nodded. "I never imagined—"

"I see Indian grass!" eight-year-old Erinn piped up. "Look just over there! It's so tall. Taller than me."

"And there's switchgrass!" Will said.

"I see sideoats grama," little Colleen pointed out.

As the children began exclaiming over the grass and flowers, Sheena patted her bonnet. "Sure, you've not said a word to Rosie about the animals, Seth Hunter. The prairie is teeming with animals, so it is. Deer, antelope, jackrabbits, prairie chickens, wolves—"

"Don't forget buffalo," Will cut in. "Sometimes we see them crossing the prairie by the thousands, so we do."

"And grizzly bears," Colleen added, touching Rosie's arm. "Sure, they like to follow the buffalo herds and eat up the weak shaggies. You'll want to beware of grizzly bears."

"She should beware of snakes, too," Erinn said. "You'll want to look out for copperheads, Rosie. If a copperhead bites you, well . . . you're done for."

Will squared his shoulders. "But there's lots and lots of other good snakes. We've ribbon snakes and garter snakes and bull snakes, not to mention prairie ringnecks and prairie king snakes—"

"All right, all right!" Rosie exclaimed, holding up her hands in surrender. "There does seem to be more to it than I thought. Just . . . just give me time."

"You've got six months," Seth said. "When I take you back to Kansas City after the harvest, you can tell me then if you still think our prairie is ugly and boring."

Rosie was smelling the bundle of wildflowers, but he could read the pain written in her eyes. She didn't want to go back to Kansas City. As unappealing as she found the prairie, she considered her old life a far worse prospect.

Chances were good she would find herself some farmer and marry him. Then her husband could put up with her songs and whistling and chatter. It sure would be quiet when autumn rolled around. Nice and quiet.

"There's Rippeto's Station!" Will shouted. "I see it! I see it!"

Sheena patted Rosie's arm. "Here's where we part ways. After a good night's sleep—"

"Good night's sleep?" Jimmy snorted. "With Carlotta's *brablins* hollering their lungs out?"

"Tomorrow morning," Sheena continued, "our Jimmy will put all the O'Tooles on the wagon we left at Rippeto's. Then we'll set off down the western bank of the Bluestem. You and Seth and the boy will travel down the eastern bank. Sure we'll see each other's wagons almost the whole twelve miles, but there's no way to cross."

"Until Seth builds his elegant bridge," Jimmy said, "and paves the way for Jack Cornwall and every other scoundrel from New York to California."

"*Whisht*, Jimmy," Sheena said softly. "Aye, Rosie, you're almost there. By tomorrow you'll have what you've always dreamed of. Home. A beautiful home."

Seth gave the reins a flick. "Six months," he said. "And the only home she'll have is the barn."

CHAPTER 4

BEFORE heading east to Kansas City with Seth Hunter, the O'Toole family had stored their wagon in Salvatore Rippeto's barn. Now loaded down with the seeds and farming equipment they had purchased, the wagon rattled across Bluestem Creek. Sheena and her children waved good-bye, and Rosie was never so sorry to see anyone go. As Seth turned his own wagon south, she felt more alone than she had in all her life. Not only was she lonely, she was concerned at what the day might bring. And she was tired.

The night at the Rippetos' had seemed as endless as Jimmy had predicted. Carlotta regularly shouted at one or the other of her ten children—evidently the only means she knew to control them. Salvatore hammered in his loft until well after dark. Four stagecoach passengers stretched out on the floor and snored loudly enough to raise the roof. Two military men talked for hours on the porch. And in the darkness, little Chipper sobbed.

It had been all Rosie could do to keep from creeping over to the grieving child and taking him in her arms. But she remembered his father's stern command to keep away. She was to provide for the boy's needs and nothing more. But wasn't compassion a need? Didn't a child have a right to comfort and love?

"We'll be at my place a little after noon," Seth said as he guided his mules downstream. It was clear to Rosie that the man kept his focus on himself and his own interests—and not on those around him. "Most of this land's unclaimed, though it was surveyed before the war. We'll pass Rolf Rustemeyer's place in a few hours. He's the fellow just north of me. German. Can't understand a word he says."

Rosie studied the man on the bench beside her. The nearer they drew to his homestead, the more civil Seth became. His blue eyes shone in the early morning sunlight. His dark hair lifted and feathered beneath his hatband. Rosie thought she even detected the hint of a smile at one corner of his mouth.

But the change in Seth's demeanor hardly made a difference to her. All she could see was how coldly he behaved toward his son. He gave no heed to the little boy's tears. He never laid a hand on the child or whispered even the slightest word of comfort. His indifference toward his son infuriated Rosie, and she began to wish she had whacked Seth on the head instead of Jack Cornwall.

"Rustemeyer's been working on his claim a lot longer than I have," Seth said, oblivious to the fact that she was attempting to bore holes through him with her glare. "He's been looking after my place while I've been away. I think I'll see if he has a notion to help me build the bridge."

"You just told me you couldn't understand him," Rosie said.

Seth glanced at her, one eyebrow arching a little at her retort. "Not much. It's all *ja* and *ach* and *nein*. But we manage."

"Does he have any children Chipper could play with?"

"Rolf's not married."

"Well then, Chipper, you'll just have to help your father build that bridge so you can walk over to the O'Tooles' house to play." Rosie bent down and kissed the little boy's hot, damp forehead. "Who do you like best of all the O'Tooles? I thought Erinn was very pretty with her long red braids. Do you like her?"

"Will," Chipper said softly. "I like Will best."

"I like him, too. Did you hear him going on about the snakes? I'll bet you and Will could have a fine time out by the creek. He can teach you all about the prairie, and you can teach him some games. What's your favorite game? Hopscotch?"

"Tag."

As the hours passed, Rosie did her best to draw out the little boy—and to ignore his father. She had come to the conclusion that Seth Hunter had kidnapped his son in the vain hope of recapturing a part of his dead wife. But he had no inclination to love Chipper for the special person he was. To Seth, the boy was a prize. A trophy. He would kill Jack Cornwall for the right to keep that trophy. But he had no idea how to truly cherish such a treasure.

Chipper had stopped crying and was beginning to catalog all his favorite foods when the wagon rolled to a stop. Rosie looked up to find Seth setting the brake and climbing down from the bench. In the distance, a blond giant of a man waved from his plow.

"Rustemeyer!" Seth called. "Good morning."

"*Guten Morgen*, Hunter! How you are?"

"Pretty good, and you? We've just come from Rippeto's."

"*Ja*, Rippeto. *Sehr gut*."

Curious, Rosie slipped down to the ground and started after Seth across the newly tilled field. Rolf Rustemeyer was no taller than Seth, but he had been built like a granite bluff. His thighs looked like two tree trunks. His hands, great slabs of ham, gripped the wooden plow handles. His hair hung to his shoulders in thick golden waves. When he smiled, his grin spread from ear to ear.

"Ah, Hunter, You have *Frau!* Vife, *ja?*"

Seth swung around. Seeing Rosie behind him, his eyes darkened. "Wife? No. She's going to work for me. Work."

"*Sehr schön!* Beautiful, *ja?* Pretty."

Rosie stopped. She stared up at the hulk of a man, her heart pounding. Unmarried. Hardworking. Friendly. *And* he thought she was beautiful. Had she just met her future husband?

"Name?" he asked. When Rosie said nothing, he placed a hand on the rock slab of his chest. "*Ich bin* Rolf Rustemeyer. "

"I'm Rosie," she said. "Rosenbloom Cot . . . uh . . ."

"Rose Mills," Seth finished when she faltered. "She's come to look after my boy. Clean a little. Cook."

"Ah, *die Köchin!*" Rolf rattled off a long string of unintelligible words as he gestured toward his land and the ramshackle dugout in the distance. Then he finished with a grand smile. "*Ja?*"

"I don't know what you said!" Seth shouted, as though talking louder might somehow make Rolf understand. "I . . . want . . . to . . . build . . . a . . . bridge! Will . . . you . . . help . . . me?"

Rolf frowned. "*Helfen?*"

"What?"

"*Ach!*" He turned to Rosie. "*Sprechen Sie Deutsch,* Fräulein Mills?"

"A bridge," she said. "Over water. Bridge."

"Britsch? *Über dem Wasser?*"

Rosie looked at Seth. He looked at her. "This puts me in mind of the time Tommy Warburton came to live at the Home," she said. "He was as deaf as a fence post, poor little fellow. We had to draw pictures and point to things just to try to make him understand." She paused. "Look here, Mr. Rustemeyer. A bridge."

Hiking up her skirt a little, Rosie knelt to the ground. She drew her fingers through the soft, rich dirt. "This is the creek. The water."

"*Das Wasser?*" Rolf asked.

"*Das Wasser.*" She set a pebble by the stream. "This is you, Mr. Rustemeyer. And this pebble is Mr. Hunter. Over here across the *Wasser* is O'Toole. *Ja?*"

"*Ja!* Bluestem!" He was grinning like a coyote that had just gotten into the chicken coop. "*Ja, ja, ja!*"

Rosie picked up a stick and broke it in half. Then she laid it across the line she had drawn. "Bridge. To go across, see? Across the *Wasser.*"

"*Eine Brücke!*"

"*Ja!*" Rosie said. "*Eine Brücke!*"

"*Sehr gut!*" Then Rustemeyer rattled off another string of German that seemed to indicate he understood the idea very well. And he liked it.

Rosie glanced at Seth. "What's he saying?"

"Your guess is as good as mine."

She studied the big German. "Come to Mr. Hunter's house. Tomorrow. Build the *Brücke*."

"*Am Morgen früh? Ich kann nicht. Ich habe eine Kuh die krank ist.*"

"I don't know if he'll come," Rosie said.

"I'd say it's doubtful."

She shrugged her shoulders and turned back toward the wagon. Suddenly from behind, Rolf Rustemeyer grabbed her arm and swung her around. Rosie clapped a hand over her mouth, her breath in her throat.

"Fräulein, very pretty!" he said, falling to the ground on one knee and sweeping his frayed straw hat from his head. "Beautiful."

Before Rosie could suck air into her lungs, Rolf Rustemeyer planted a firm kiss on the back of her hand. She jumped back, bumping into Seth.

"Oh, my!" she gasped as Seth caught her shoulders. "Gracious, what are you doing, Mr. Rustemeyer? What's he doing?"

"Looks to me like he's courting." Seth stepped up to the kneeling German and lifted him by one suspender. "Listen, Rustemeyer, she's mine. Understand? The fräulein belongs to me."

"*Für* vork, *ja?*"

Seth paused. "That's right. She works for me. I brought her all the way from Kansas City. You leave her be."

"*Ja, ja.*" Rustemeyer nodded as Seth took Rosie's arm and started back across the field. "Goot-bye, fräulein! Beautiful!"

Seth helped Rosie onto the wagon beside Chipper. As she arranged her skirts, she took a peek at Rustemeyer from under the brim of her bonnet. The German wasn't bad to look at, though he did need a haircut and a wash. He was a hard worker. He seemed kind enough. And he thought she was beautiful.

As Seth started the mules, Rosie brushed a hand across her cheek. Her skin felt hot. Her mouth was dry. She thought she might be sick.

Beautiful? Nobody had ever said a word about how Rosie Mills looked—one way or the other. When she happened to catch her reflection in a window, she saw nothing but two big brown eyes, a tall gawky body, and the same blue dress she had worn for three years. Beautiful?

"Rustemeyer ought to learn some English," Seth said in a clipped voice. "And if you ask me, he needs to take a bath more than once a year."

Rosie felt a grin tug at her lips. For some odd reason, the big German's attentions to her had irked Seth. Of course, if she found someone to marry right away, she wouldn't be able to look after Chipper. Maybe that was what bothered him.

"Mr. Hunter," she said. When he turned his head, his eyes shone as bright blue as the sky. Her heart stumbled over a beat, but she lifted her chin. "I'll have you remember the war is over, and Mr. Lincoln freed the slaves."

"What's that supposed to mean?"

"It means I don't belong to you, Mr. Hunter. Not my arms for the working. Not my words for the speaking." She paused. "And not my heart for the courting."

Seth searched the trail for the first sign of his house. He had always liked that view—the roof coming into sight, and then the wall, his cows, the chickens, the fence, and finally his barn. For some reason, his pulse was pounding like a marching band. He couldn't wait to show off his place. And it wasn't just his son whose eyes would shine.

He glanced at the woman on the bench beside him. Ever since their encounter with Rustemeyer, Rosie had ridden in silence, her head held high and her eyes scanning the horizon. *Pretty*, the German had called her. *Beautiful*.

Seth gave a snort and studied the woman a little harder. Truth to tell, Rosie Mills wasn't half bad to look at. For one thing, she had those big brown eyes. In her eyes, a man could read everything she felt. Happiness, anger, fear, sorrow—her emotions were as obvious as the sun in the sky.

When Rosie was happy, her joy was about as hard to keep from catching as a case of hiccups. Anger flashed like lightning from those eyes of hers. And sorrow—Seth didn't know when he'd ever seen such pain as that written on her face when Holloway badmouthed her background. No matter that Rosie Mills was stubborn and willful and a lot more jabbery than Seth liked, nobody deserved the kind of abuse she'd taken from the stationmaster.

But pretty? Her nose was straight enough. Her cheekbones stood out high and sharp. Of course, a month or two of good food might fix that. And her mouth . . . her mouth . . . Rosie's lips—

"There it is!" she cried, turning those big chocolate eyes on him. "I see a roof! Is it your house?"

Seth cleared his throat, glad she had diverted his attention. "That's it. I built it myself."

As the mules pulled the wagon the last hundred yards, he couldn't deny the pride of ownership he felt. He had dug every inch of soil out of the ground with his own two hands. He had cut the blocks of prairie sod and laid them one atop the other to build the half-wall that fronted his dugout. He had chopped two of the scarce trees on his land and split them into boards. He had laid out his slanted wooden roof and covered it with more sod. And there it was. Perfect.

As he sat gazing on his dream, his future, Rosie stared in silence. Finally, she turned to him. Her brown eyes were luminous.

"Oh my," she whispered. "You live in a cave."

"I don't wanna live in no hole in the ground with no stinkin' Yankee," Chipper announced. "I wanna go back and live with Gram and Gramps."

Seth stared at the two of them, his face rigid. He couldn't believe what he was hearing. His farm—the labor of his hands, the legacy he would leave behind him—

"This is it, like it or not," he snapped. "This is where we stay."

Rosie stared at the dugout, her face as pale as winter prairie grass. "Home," she whispered.

Never in her life had Rosie seen anything quite so forlorn, so unwelcoming, so dispiriting as the cave in the ground Seth Hunter called home. Truth to tell, it was more like a three-sided cutaway into a low hillock than a house. As she walked up to the door, she noted that he had sided the front of the soddy with long planks. He had installed four long windows—though they had only oiled paper for panes—and a semblance of a front porch with an overhanging roof. The house itself was tucked into the hill, its roofline even with the ground. In fact, should anyone want to, he could drive a wagon right up the hill and over the sodded roof of the house without a pause.

Rosie let out a breath. This was no Kansas City cottage. There was nothing even to lend an air of beauty. No white paint. No pink-flowered curtains. No brick walkways. No picket fences. No roses or daffodils or tulips. It was . . . a burrow.

"I bought a stove from a fellow upstream who couldn't prove up his claim," Seth said, lifting the wooden bar across the front door. "He sold it cheap. You'd better light it if we're to have any supper tonight."

Rosie swallowed and stepped around a chicken on her way toward the door. Chipper sidled up against her, one thumb stuck securely in his mouth. Taking his free hand, she gave the little boy the bravest smile she could muster. "Your father built this," she whispered. "This is a prairie house."

"Looks more like a mole's house to me."

"You—!" Seth swung on the child, his finger outstretched. "I'll have you know my place is twice as big as Rustemeyer's, and I've got a better stove and a bigger bed than O'Toole—" He caught himself. "Just get your hide in here and start peeling spuds."

Rosie stood just outside the doorway. She easily read the hurt that ran beneath Seth's anger. And she understood it. He had built this house. It was his pride. His only possession.

Dear Father, she prayed silently, bowing her head under the open sky. *Please help me to see the beauty in this place. I know you can make good of all my willful mistakes. I'm almost sure you wanted me to stay back at the Home, but here I am with Seth Hunter—and I don't know why, nor what I'm to do for you. Oh, Father, please make a godly plan of my terrible mistake. Please bring joy and peace—*

"Are you coming inside?" Seth called, leaning one shoulder against the frame of his door.

Rosie breathed a quick "Amen" and hurried toward the house. As she brushed past Seth, she looked up into his eyes. They were as hard and blue as ice, and she suddenly knew she must do all in her power to soften them.

Not just his eyes, a voice spoke inside her. *Soften his heart.*

"I'm going to check on my cows," he said. "I'll bring in some meat from the smokehouse."

He started out, but she caught his arm. "Wait, Mr. Hunter. Please . . . will you show me around?"

"I thought you knew how to light a stove."

"I do. But . . . this is your home. You built it. Please, I'd like you to show it to me."

He looked down at her, his jaw tight. She saw a flicker of some emotion cross his face. And then he stroked a hand down the door.

"Walnut," he said. "You won't find a harder wood in these parts. Took me three days to build."

"And the hinges?" Rosie said. "They're leather. They look strong."

"Deer hide."

"I can't imagine anything that could break down such a sturdy door."

She gave him a bright smile as she walked inside. But there, her heart sank further. Darkness shadowed the cavernous room. A filmy cobweb stretched across one corner. A dank, musty smell mingled with wood smoke permeated the air, and the few pieces of furniture stood around on the uneven dirt floor like lonely soldiers.

"Here's the stove," Seth said, striding across the room. His head nearly touched the low ceiling. "I've only had it a couple of weeks. I reckon it could use a good cleaning."

Rosie swallowed at the sight of the large sooty stove with its rusted pipe and blackened burner lids. Half afraid of what she might find, she gingerly opened the oven door. A brown mouse lifted its head, gave a loud squeak, and jumped out at her feet. Rosie gasped and leapt backward as the mouse fled across the floor with Chipper racing after it.

"Mr. Hunter," she said, setting her hands on her hips. "Have you ever used this stove?"

He took off his hat and scratched the back of his neck. "Well, uh, not exactly. I figured I'd get Sheena over here one of these days to teach me how to work it."

Rosie brushed off her hands. If there was anything she knew, it was cooking and cleaning. Maybe God could use her to set up this household—if only for little Chipper's sake. In fact, the more she looked around the place, the easier it was to imagine what she could do with it. Scrub the table. Air out the mattress. Polish the stove.

"I built this table out of pine," Seth was saying. He stroked his hand down the three smooth boards of the long trestle table. "And the chairs. If you know anything about caning . . ."

"I do," Rosie said, studying the four seatless chairs. Obviously, Seth had been using a set of stumps assembled around the table for his perch. Those would have to go.

"And here's the bed." He cupped the ball on top of the foot post. "It's got a straw mattress. No bugs."

Rosie inspected the frame. To her surprise, the bed revealed skilled craftsmanship—its joints solid, its pegs tight, and its posts carefully carved, sanded, and polished. Curious, she returned to the table. It, too, displayed even planing and careful joinery. The chairs—though they lacked seats—stood level and rigid. And in the center of each chair's back a design of flowers and scrolls had been carved.

"You did this work?" she asked, straightening. "You built these things?"

Seth shrugged. "My uncle taught me carpentry. I always liked working with my hands." Before she could marvel aloud at the handiwork, he turned away. "See what you can do about that stove, Miss Mills. I'll be back in a few minutes with some meat."

"Eggs, too, please!" she called after him. "If you have any."

As he disappeared through the door, Rosie let out a breath. "Well, Chipper," she said softly. "Here we are at home. How do you like it?"

"I hate it." He picked up a potato from the basket at his feet and hurled it across the room. "Hate it, hate it, hate it!"

Rosie gathered the little boy in her arms and held him tightly as he began to sob. Never mind what Seth Hunter wanted, she thought. This child needed love—and she intended to see that he got it. If not from his father, then from her.

Seth decided Rosenbloom Cotton Mills's real name should have been Twister. The skinny little gal was a regular cyclone around the house. Declaring the stove too filthy to use, its chimney blocked with creosote and its ash pit jammed, she fixed a lunch of cold smoked venison. She boiled greens on an open fire, along with a few potatoes and some coffee. After lunch she broke down the stove, dragged it out the front door piece by piece, and began to scrub and polish.

While Chipper wandered the creek bank picking up kindling, Rosie scoured every pot and pan in the house. She hauled the mattress outside and threw it on top of a spice bush to air. Then she toted the sheets and bedding down to the creek and washed them in the cold water—declaring that she would do it again with hot water after she had the stove put back together.

By the time evening rolled around, she had reassembled most of the stove and all of the bed. Along the way, she had managed enough chitchat to wear out any man's eardrums. "Don't you have a broom, Mr. Hunter? Never mind, I'll make one tomorrow. I'm so glad you have a well. I thought sure I'd be obliged to make that trip to the creek five times a day. You need some new paper in your windows, Mr. Hunter. These oiled panes are all fly speckled. We had real glass panes at the Home, but I don't see how a person could ever bring glass out here to the prairie. It would shatter the first time the wagon hit a bump, wouldn't it? Don't throw those ashes away! I'll want to make lye for the soap. Have you seen any beehives around here, Mr. Hunter?"

As he went back and forth from the house to the barn, Seth couldn't help but marvel at his new employee. While he cleaned the cow stalls and checked on his chickens, the little brown-eyed twister sashayed around like there was no tomorrow. By the time she banged two pots together to call him to supper, he had to admit bringing Rosie Mills from Kansas City might not have been such a bad idea. The delicious aroma drifting through the front door of his house made his stomach groan in anticipation.

Seth washed his hands and face in the pot of warm water Rosie had set on the front porch. Still dripping, he walked inside to find the long table spread with wilted poke salad boiled with chunks of salt pork, fried sweet potatoes, and a mountain of steaming scrambled eggs. Seated on a stump at the table, his hair combed and his cheeks scrubbed, Chipper regarded the feast with wide blue eyes. Slowly, half unbelieving, Seth walked across the room and stared. He hadn't eaten a meal like this in . . . in years.

"Did you wash up, Mr. Hunter?" Rosie asked, breezing into the house carrying a plate piled high with turnovers. "I put a bowl of hot water—" She stopped and looked Seth up and down, breathless, as though the sight of a wet man had cast a spell over her. "I see you found it."

He raked a hand back through his damp hair. "Where did this come from? All this food?"

"Here and there." Coming out of her trance, she set the turnovers on the table. "You have a wealth of greens right outside the door. Poke, dock, plantain. I found some dried apples in the cellar. I hope you don't mind—"

"No, no. It's fine. Use anything you want. I'll make sure we always have fresh meat. Rabbits and quail, if nothing better. Anything in the smokehouse is yours. I dug a cellar when I moved out here late last summer. It still has a few things I managed to winter over."

"There'll be twice as much next spring," she said, sitting on a stump across from Chipper. "You'll hardly believe how good I am at pickling and canning. My cheeses and sausages are wonderful—though at the Home we never seemed to have enough to go around. Everyone says my—" She stopped and clapped a hand over her mouth. "I'm boasting. You'd better pray quickly, Mr. Hunter."

She stretched out her hands to him and Chipper and bowed her head. Thrown off-kilter by her action, Seth cleared his throat. Across the table, the boy slipped one hand into Rosie's, but he firmly tucked his free hand into his lap. Deciding the whole business of holding hands was for children, Seth propped his elbows on the table and closed his eyes.

How long had it been since he had prayed? During the war, maybe. A battle. Cannonballs bursting all around. A prayer for preservation. A cry for safety. Nothing more. He couldn't remember the last time he had spoken with God. Or listened. After all, God had allowed the Cornwalls to banish him from their property, allowed his best friend to be killed, allowed Mary to die.

"Are you going to pray before the supper gets cold, Mr. Hunter?" Rosie asked, slipping her hand into his. "At this rate, the turnovers won't be worth feeding to the chickens."

Seth glanced at her. Then he looked down at their clasped hands—his large and hard, hers much softer. An ache started up inside his chest. He couldn't speak. Could hardly move.

"Dear Father," Rosie said softly, "I thank you so much for our safe journey across the prairie. Thank you for this beautiful home Mr. Hunter has built. Thank you for providing us with this fine supper—surely more than we can even eat. In the name of Jesus Christ I pray. Amen."

Rosie gave Seth's hand a gentle squeeze. Then she picked up her spoon and began to dish out the scrambled eggs. "I have never, never in my whole entire life felt so happy," she said. When she looked up at him, Seth saw that a streak of stove blacking smudged her cheek and a puff of white flour dusted the end of her nose. Unaware, she gave him a warm smile.

"Have you ever been this happy, Mr. Hunter?" she asked.

Scooping up a spoonful of greens, Seth couldn't bring himself to answer. He felt a strange tickle at the back of his throat. And he had the terrible feeling he was going to cry.

CHAPTER 5

ROSIE had been happy at supper. But when she saw where she was to spend her summer nights, her spirits flagged. The barn smelled to high heaven. What little hay was left over from winter had grown stiff and moldy. Three milk cows and the mules used the barn for shelter. The chickens roosted in its rafters. And as she climbed the rickety ladder into the loft, Rosie gasped and stiffened in shock. On the moonlit barn floor below her, a five-foot-long blacksnake slithered out from under a tuft of loose hay and disappeared behind a wagon wheel.

"Don't worry about that fellow," Seth called up. "He's not poisonous. He keeps the barn cleaned up for me—eats mice."

Wonderful, Rosie thought. *How comforting.*

"Are you all right up there?" Seth asked.

Rosie looked over the edge of the shaky platform. "What about grizzly bears?"

"We don't see them around much. They follow the buffalo."

"Wolves?"

"Same." He shoved his hands into his pockets. "Would you like to keep my rifle on hand?"

Rosie shook her head. She could cook and clean and can and pickle—but she didn't have a clue how to shoot a gun. Seth glanced around the barn before looking up at her again.

"Well, then," he said, "good night, Miss Mills."

"Wait, Mr. Hunter!" she called out. "Please send my bonnet back to the Home. It's to go to Lizzy Jackson—after I die, I mean."

"Die?"

"Just see that it goes to Lizzy. She's wanted it ever so long, though Cilla gave it to me instead. I'd like Lizzy to have it."

Seth shook his head. "You're not going to die in the barn tonight, Miss Mills."

"Tomorrow you might put a bolt on the door."

"I can do that."

"Thank you, Mr. Hunter." Rosie drew back from the edge of the loft, but through the chinks in the floor she could see Seth staring up at where she'd been standing. She thought he had half a mind to allow her to sleep in the house—though she wouldn't do it. Such a thing would be improper. No, she would just make do in the barn, with the mice and the snakes. . . .

Seth finally left, and the absence of the lantern plunged the barn into darkness. Fortunately, through the open planks in the roof, Rosie could see the stars. They reminded her of how big God was, how powerful, and how very loving. The knowledge that a God who had created such beauty loved Rosie Mills—loved her enough to die for her—sent a wash of warm peace drifting through her. In spite of her fears, she curled up on the hay and pulled a threadbare quilt over her knees.

Seth woke with the sudden sense that something had gone wrong. He grabbed his rifle and sat up in bed. On the floor, the pallet beside the big bed was empty. The door hung ajar, admitting a draft from the night breeze.

Chipper? Confound it, the boy had run off. Or maybe Jack Cornwall had come in the cover of darkness and stolen the child away! Seth stepped into his boots, pulled on his shirt, and hitched his suspenders over his shoulders. Which would be worse? If Cornwall had taken Chipper, Seth would have no choice but to follow his enemy until he had tracked him down. This time, their confrontation would be bloody. Maybe even fatal.

But if Chipper was wandering around alone on the prairie, no telling what kind of critters he'd run into. True, wolves and bears followed the buffalo, but they kept a close watch on their whole territories. A straying child would be easy prey—weak, frightened, defenseless. . . .

His heart tight in his chest, Seth hurried outside. The moon was high overhead, a brilliant white coin. Chipper could see well enough in this light to travel a long way. And he'd been exploring the creek all afternoon. Bluestem Creek was tricky, even when it ran low.

A cold sweat dampening his shirt, Seth dashed toward the barn. He would have to wake Rosie. Two searching would be better than one. If Cornwall had kidnapped Chipper . . . if anything happened to the boy . . . his son—

"He's a very good man." Rosie's soft voice drifted down from the loft as Seth stepped into the barn. "He drove his wagon all the way to Missouri to get you because he loves you so much."

"He don't love me," a gruff little voice countered. "He don't even know me."

Chipper! Seth sagged against the barn door frame and let out a deep breath. The boy was in the loft with Rosie.

"He hasn't had time to get to know you, sweetie," she said. "And after all, you do keep calling him an old Yankee. I'm sure he doesn't think that's very polite."

"I don't care what he thinks. He's a rotten, mean, good-for-nothin' Yankee."

"I see." Rosie was silent for a moment. "By the way, Chipper, exactly what is a Yankee?"

"A bad man. Evil. Gramps used to tell me if I was naughty,

he'd turn me over to the Yankees, an' they'd string me up by my thumbnails."

"Oh, my!"

"They're ugly monsters with big yellow teeth an' hair all over."

"I don't think your father has yellow teeth . . . although he does seem to have a lot of hair."

"An' they come up behind you and *grab* you!"

"Oooh. Yankees do all that?"

"He grabbed me, didn't he? Probably tomorrow he's gonna string me up by my thumbnails." His voice went quavery. "I'm sorry I stole that piece of strawberry pie off the windowsill, Rosie. Gram switched me good for it, an' I figured that was enough. But then that Yankee came an' took me away—"

Chipper broke into sobs. From the barn floor, Seth could hear Rosie's soothing words of comfort and reassurance. He sat on the crossbar of a sawhorse, unwilling to interrupt—even though he sensed it was wrong to eavesdrop. All the same, the boy's words had stunned him. Chipper thought of his father as a monster? He believed he'd been taken away from his grandparents as a punishment for stealing a piece of pie?

"Let me tell you about Yankees," Rosie said to the little boy. "They're not such bad folks, really—once you get to know them. In fact, they believe in some very good things. Yankees believe that all people ought to be free."

"Even slaves?"

"Slaves are people, too, aren't they? They're just like us, only a different color."

"They're black."

"Yes, they are. Apples can be red or yellow or green—but they're all still apples. Each color is just as good as the other. Slaves are people even though they're black. Indians are people even though they're brown. And you and I are people even though we're white. Yankees believe no person should be able to own any other person. Your papa fought in a war to see that everybody—no matter what color their skin—could be free to walk around, do as they please, and live exactly as they like."

"That ain't true! If my papa wanted me to be free, why did he take me away from Gram and Gramps?"

Seth clenched his jaw, waiting for the reply. It was a good question—and it revealed more wisdom than he expected from a child as young as his son.

"Your papa loves you more than you can ever imagine, Chipper," Rosie whispered, and Seth felt a shiver run down his spine at the caress in her words. "God loves us so much we can't understand it. And your papa loves you in the very same way. He wants only the best for you. He knew your mama had gone to heaven—the woman he treasured most in all the world—and he figured you needed someone big and strong to look after you. Who better to look after a little boy than the papa who loves him most?"

"That Yankee loved my mama?"

"Sure he did. Just as much as you loved her." She paused a moment. "Tell me about your mama, Chipper. Tell me everything you remember."

"Mmm. She was pretty. She had yellow hair. Big long curls of it."

Seth smiled, remembering Mary and her curls. That hair had been her pride and joy. It was all her mother could do to make her wear her bonnet. As often as she could, Mary would whip it off and flounce her curls around. To the young farmhand she had set her cap on, she had looked like a porcelain doll—gorgeous, expensive, and untouchable. Until that day in the barn when she had stood on tiptoe and kissed him.

"Mama liked to cuddle me in the rockin' chair," Chipper said. "She used to sing, too, but . . . but I don't want to sing those songs now."

"Did she read stories?"

"Naw. Mama didn't like to read. She said readin' was borin';

school was borin'; hard work was borin'. Dancin' was fun. She liked to dance."

Seth had never known the motherly side of Mary. The thought of her holding a baby and rocking . . . singing . . . But he had watched her dance. *Oh, Mary.* How the young men would stare when Mary Cornwall whirled across the floor.

"Mama liked to go to town to buy things," Chipper said. "An' she would take me along. We would walk down the board-walk together sayin' hello to all the men an' ladies. I used to like to watch her get dressed. She had pretty clothes—lots an' lots of dresses an' petticoats. She would stand in front of the mirror an' turn around an' around. I would help her get her hems straight."

"I'll bet that was fun," Rosie whispered.

"Uh huh. But when she got sick, she wouldn't rock me or sing. She just lay in bed gettin' skinny an' yellow an' . . . an' Gram would cry in the parlor . . . an' Gramps would run me out of the room. Until one day they called me in where she was lying still an' cold—"

"Chipper!" Seth called, cutting into words he couldn't bear to hear. "Chipper, are you in here?"

Silence fell over the barn. A small voice whispered. "He's gonna whip me."

"Chipper is up here with me," Rosie called down. "We were just having a little visit."

"That's enough jabbering, boy," Seth said. "Get on back to the house. If you keep us up all night, nobody will be fit to work in the morning."

"Yes, sir," Chipper said softly.

In the moonlight, his white shirt moved down the ladder. The child jumped barefoot onto the dirt floor and started past his father. Just as Chipper scampered out the door, Seth reached out and nabbed him.

"No more midnight journeys, young man," he said, lifting him high. He could feel the child trembling in his arms. "You hear me?"

Blue eyes that matched his own stared back at him. "Yes, sir. Please don't whip me, sir."

"I don't hold to whippings. My papa gave me enough of those to last two boys a lifetime. But if you pull this again, I won't like it, hear? Now get on back to bed."

He set the child on his feet, and Chipper hurtled out the barn door like a wolf was after him. Seth shoved his hands down into his pockets and looked up into the loft. He could just make out a pale face and a pair of dark, luminous eyes.

"I thought I told you not to baby him, Miss Mills," he said. "I don't want him getting attached to you."

"But he *is* a baby, Mr. Hunter."

"He's five years old."

"A mere child. He needs comfort. Who's going to give it to him?"

"Not you."

"Then who?" She crept to the edge of the loft and set her bare feet on the first rung of the ladder. "Why won't you comfort him, Mr. Hunter? Why must you always brush him aside?"

"I came and got him, didn't I? That ought to show him I care what happens to him."

"But every time he mentions his mother, you shout at him."

"I do not shout!"

"Yes, you do!" she insisted. "Chipper will live with the pain of his mother's loss until someone lets him cry it out. Do you want that for your son? Do you want him to live with the same open wound that tears at your own heart? Both of you loved Mary—"

"You be quiet about my wife!" Seth started toward the ladder. He had half a mind to climb up there and clamp a hand over Rosie Mills's blabbering mouth. What right did she have to talk about Mary? What did she know of the love . . . the pain . . . the loss . . . ?

"I won't be quiet," she said defiantly. "'Like as a father pitieth his children, so the Lord pitieth them that fear Him.' Where is your compassion, Mr. Hunter? Where is your pity? Why can't you treat your child as a son ought to be treated—with love?"

"I'll treat him the way I think he ought to be treated. Who are you to tell me how to look after my son? What do you know about it, anyway? What makes you an expert?"

The figure on the loft ladder sagged. "You're right," she whispered. "I'm sorry, Mr. Hunter. Please forgive me. I don't know a thing about families."

Uncomfortable at her sudden silence, Seth shifted from one foot to the other. "I didn't mean it that way."

"I never had a mother." The words were barely audible. "Never knew parents of my own. You and Mr. Holloway are right—"

"Don't lump me together with him."

"I won't interfere again. You must be whatever sort of father to Chipper you want to be. You must be the sort of father you had—"

"No," Seth cut in. He would never be like that man. He stopped himself from blurting out the truth about his own childhood. "Leave Chipper to me. I'll look after him."

"Yes," she said softly. "You do that."

Seth turned to the barn door. "And if he comes here again, send him straight back to the house."

As he stepped out into the moonlight, he could hear Rosie's voice. "Yes, sir," she said in the same resigned tone his son had used. "Whatever you say, Mr. Hunter."

Rolf Rustemeyer did not show up to build the bridge the following morning. Rosie kept one eye on the trail as she fried eggs and salt pork over a fire she built outside. She could see nothing but pale green grass stretching endlessly to the horizon. A jackrabbit bounded across the road, but that was all. No Rolf.

Sometime in the night Rosie had concocted a drama in which the big blond German rode up on his mule and carried her off to his homestead—like King Arthur and Guinevere, or Prince Charming and Cinderella. Rosie had read those stories over and over to the children at the Christian Home. Fortunately, Mrs. Jameson had permitted the fairy tale book a place with the copies of the Bible, *The Pilgrim's Progress*, Dante's *Divine Comedy*, and Milton's *Paradise Lost*. What Rosie wouldn't have given for a Sir Lancelot. Or even a Frog Prince.

Instead, she spent the morning putting the rest of the stove back together and searching for kindling along the creek bank. When she discovered an old willow tree about a mile downstream, she asked Seth to cut some branches for her so she could weave seats for the chairs. Chipper followed her everywhere, but Rosie made a point to give kind yet brief responses to his thousand questions.

After lunch, Seth sent Chipper off with a burlap bag to gather dried buffalo and cow chips for the fire. Rosie didn't like the idea of the little boy wandering alone across the burning prairie, but she kept her mouth shut. What did she know about being a parent, she reminded herself. Seth continued his plowing, even through the worst of the heat. And Rosie made up her mind to work just as hard as father and son.

She took down the tattered window paper and tacked up the gauzy cheesecloth in which her skillet had been wrapped. This screen let in scant light, but it kept the flies and mosquitoes outside where they belonged. Then she fashioned a broom by shaving a sapling into fine splints and binding it with a rawhide thong. She swept the pounded dirt floor of wood chips, food scraps, and other evidences of bachelor habitation. Small piles of rodent droppings made her wish that the household included a cat.

By dinnertime, Rosie had cleaned the chimneys on all the lamps and nailed up shelves for the pots and pans. Then she had cooked a big supper of corn bread and stew. Chunks of squirrel meat swam with potatoes, wild onions, and beans in a rich broth that made even little, sunburned Chipper perk up.

When Seth walked into the soddy and spotted the table with its steaming cauldron, golden brown corn bread, and bouquet of wildflowers, his blue eyes lit up like a summer afternoon. "Miss Mills," he said as he sat down. "I'm beginning to believe I made a wise choice in bringing you out here. You're as fine a cook as any I've known."

Rosie flushed as though he had called her Helen of Troy. Her hands shook as she poured fresh milk into his mug. No one had ever said Rosie was fine at anything. She knew she was a good cook by the way everybody at the Home ate and ate—and then asked for seconds. She knew her cherry pies were delicious because she had tasted them herself. But "as fine a cook as any I've known" was the biggest compliment she'd ever received. It was even better than Rolf Rustemeyer calling her beautiful. After all, any number of women could be called beautiful. But to be the finest cook a man had ever known . . .

"There's a gooseberry bush upstream aways," Seth said. "We'll have pawpaws and chokeberries, too."

"I do make good pies," Rosie said, and quickly realized how vain her words sounded. "What I mean to say is—"

"I'm sure you do. I'll look forward to tasting them." He glanced at his son. "And Chipper, at this house you can eat all the pie you want."

The little boy's blue eyes darted up in surprise. "Really? Really, truly?"

Rosie could hardly believe her ears as she sat down across from the little boy who had been too astounded to glower and label his father a Yankee. Seth nodded, and one corner of his mouth turned up in the hint of an actual smile.

"And now," he said, "shall we bless the food?"

The shout that echoed from the barn many days later sent Seth's heart straight into his throat. He dropped his seed planter in the furrow and took off running. Chipper jumped up and spilled a bowl of potato peelings on the ground as he raced after his father. Seth had just hurtled the low fence that ran around the barn when he heard the cry again.

"Oh, my! Oh, my!"

"Rosie?" Forgetting her formal name, he burst through the door. "Rosie, what's wrong?"

"Grain sacks!" she exclaimed. "Piles and piles of them!"

Seth stopped, breathing hard. "Grain sacks?"

Chipper skidded to a halt beside him. "What happened, Rosie?"

"Just look what I've found!" Rosie grabbed a bundle of empty flour sacks and hugged them tightly. "It's a treasure. Better than gold! Better than diamonds! There must be fifty of them. Maybe a hundred! I was searching for eggs because the hens seem to be roosting anywhere—and I think you'd better build a coop, Mr. Hunter—but anyway I came across this mound covered by canvas here at the back of the barn. Straw was scattered everywhere and the cobwebs were thick, so I almost went right past it. Then something whispered to me to lift up the corner of the canvas. So I did, of course. Believe me, I've learned to obey those messages I get from the good Lord above. At first I couldn't believe my eyes, but then I took my skirt and began to dust—"

"Miss Mills, what are you jabbering about?" Seth exploded.

"Grain sacks! Look at them all. When I dusted them off, I realized what I'd found. These bales are all white and stamped 'Hunter,' but these others are printed with flowers and stripes and . . . and here's a check and a plaid . . . blue and yellow and green . . . oh my, is this an actual paisley print—"

"Miss Mills!" Half fearing she'd lost her mind, Seth grabbed Rosie's shoulders. "They're grain sacks."

"I know! Aren't they beautiful? Oh, Mr. Hunter, what do you mean to do with them?"

"The ones with my name will go to the mill in the fall. The

others are extras. I got them off that fellow who went bust. He sold the whole batch to me for fifty cents, and I figured if I had a bumper crop some year—"

"Might I use a few of them, Mr. Hunter?" she broke in, her lips moist and her brown eyes glowing.

What could he say? "Use as many as you want."

"Oh, Mr. Hunter!" She threw her arms around his chest. "Thank you!"

For an instant, shock rippled through Seth. The woman smelled so sweet . . . of fresh air . . . lemongrass . . . wild pinks. Her cheek was warm and downy against his neck and her eyelashes soft, so soft, on his skin. In his arms she felt small, slender, fragile. And real. Soft and feminine and very real. She pressed against him in the briefest of hugs, and then she whirled away.

"Catch, Chipper!" she sang out and tossed the little boy a bundle of grain sacks. "We'll have curtains! A rug! Pillows!"

He giggled and flung the bundle back at Rosie. "Your turn!"

"Mr. Hunter!" She swung around and tossed it to Seth. "You'll have a new shirt by Sunday! Checks or stripes? Blue or brown?"

"Well, blue is nice enough, I reckon," he said, watching in amazement as she pulled open the bale and began tossing sacks into the air. "But I think you should—"

"Pink roses for a tablecloth. Morning glories in the windows. Cherries for a kitchen towel." And then she began to sing as she took Chipper by his chubby little hands and danced him around and around the barn.

> "Shout! Shout! We're gaining ground!
> Oh Halley, Hallelujah!
> The love of God is coming down!
> Oh Halley, Hallelujah!"

Seth stared at the woman and the little boy spinning in giddy circles over the joy of finding a few empty grain sacks. Laughing,

Rosie picked up a sack and tied it around Chipper's shoulders like a cape. She tucked another into her skirt to form an apron. Then she draped a third across Seth's arm, linked his elbow, and swung him into a jig.

"The devil's dead and I am glad.
Oh Halley, Hallelujah!
The devil's dead and I am glad.
Oh Halley, Hallelujah!"

Seth was surprised at how easily his feet slipped into the once-familiar steps of the dance. How many years had it been since he had danced? But there was no time to reminisce. His little twister was circling him around the barn, kicking up her heels, and waving grain sacks like patriotic flags as she belted out the song.

"The devil's dead and gone to hell.
Oh Halley, Hallelujah!
I hope he's there for quite a spell.
Oh Halley, Hallelujah!"

Seth joined in, unable to hold back his favorite verse.

"My uncle had an old red hound.
Oh Halley, Hallelujah!
He chased the rabbits round and round.
Oh Halley, Hallelujah!"

Rosie sashayed him across the barn while Chipper skipped and hopped around them like a squirrel. When the song faltered into la-da-das, Rosie grabbed a handful of hay and threw it up into the air. Dancing away from Seth, she twirled amid the falling stems as they settled on her bonnet and skirt. He stepped back to watch her, but she took his hand again and pulled him into the dance.

"You'll settle down no more to roam.
Oh Halley, Hallelujah!
Grain sacks will make your house a home.
Oh Halley, Hallelujah!"

"Red and yellow, green and blue. Oh Halley, Hallelujah!" Chipper shouted from the third rung of the loft ladder. "I like Rosie 'cause she is nice. Oh Halley, Hallelujah!"

"Oh, Chipper, that's a good one!" Rosie sank onto the floor laughing. "I can't dance another step!"

A shadow blocked the door. "Fräulein Mills? Hunter?"

Seth swung around. "Rustemeyer."

"*Guten Morgen.*" The man stared at the hay-covered woman who sat gasping on the barn floor. "How you are?"

"Uh, we were just . . . Miss Mills found some grain sacks." Seth jerked the flowered bag from his arm. "We were dancing."

"*Der Tanz.*"

"I'm going to sew curtains," Rosie sang out, rising and attempting to brush off her skirt. "I'll braid a rug."

"*Ja?*"

Rosie glanced at Seth. He watched in wonder as the young woman's cheeks colored. Then she shrugged her shoulders and, if his eyes weren't deceiving him in the dim light, she winked at him. "Excuse me, please. I was searching for eggs."

Slipping between the two men, Rosie practically ran out of the barn. Chipper studied the situation for a moment, then he took off after her. Seth crossed his arms over his chest.

"What do you want, Rustemeyer?"

"*Die Brücke?*" the German said. He pulled a stem of hay from Seth's collar. "Britsch?"

"The bridge," Seth said. "You came to build?"

"*Ja, ja.*" He glanced out the window at the young woman carrying a basket of eggs toward the soddy. "Fräulein Mills. Beautiful."

Seth gave a grunt and started toward his tool chest. As a matter of fact, Fräulein Mills was beautiful. Especially when she was dancing in the hay. Or laughing like a bell. Or throwing her arms around a man's chest. *Oh Halley, Hallelujah!*

CHAPTER 6

ROSIE felt so excited about the grain sacks that she forgot to daydream about becoming Rolf Rustemeyer's wife. While the two men walked down to the creek to survey for the new bridge, she and Chipper quickly hoed the little garden Seth had planted just outside the house. It was a good spot, and she hoped late summer would bring an abundance of healthy vegetables.

Rosie dug grass sprouts and weeds from among the emerging onions, turnips, potatoes, beans, and corn. Chipper picked cutworms, potato beetles, and harlequin bugs until he had filled the bib pocket of his overalls. While Rosie hauled water from the well to the garden, he smashed the pests under a big stone.

Gardening done, Rosie sent Chipper off to collect buffalo and cow chips while she settled down in the soddy with the grain sacks. By lunchtime she had hemmed four curtains of pale green fabric printed with blue morning glories, dark green vines, and curling tendrils. She made rods from peeled branches and hung the curtains so they stirred in the breeze at each window.

After lunch with the men, she fashioned a tablecloth of pale periwinkle blue stripes and a matching straw-stuffed cushion for each of the cane seats she had woven earlier that week. Her fingers were sore from stitching, but she had promised Seth a shirt by Sunday. The man certainly did need one. Though he washed his face and hands at every meal, he never took off the only shirt he had, and it was in dire need of a wash. Chipper needed new clothes, too. Of course, Rosie herself had only the one dress, but she managed to wash it now and again, hang it up in the night air, and wear it again by morning.

Determined to fulfill her promise to her employer, she selected a pair of grain sacks that had been dyed a beautiful sky blue—the exact color of Seth's eyes. As she slit the sides of the sacks, Rosie thought about those blue eyes. When Seth had laughed that morning in the barn, his eyes had lit up and begun to sparkle. They fairly glowed against the deep tan of his face—as though they were lit from inside with a hot blue fire. Rosie felt her stomach do an odd little flip-flop at the mere memory of the way Seth Hunter had looked at her as they danced.

She wished she could say it had been a look of fascination, intrigue, or maybe even admiration. But Seth probably thought his hired hand was a little touched in the head, the way she had been so silly about finding the grain sacks. Rosie didn't care. After all, the first chance she had, she was going to ask Rolf Rustemeyer to marry her, and she felt pretty sure he would say yes. He thought she was beautiful.

She draped the grain sacks over one shoulder and set out from the house toward the creek to find Seth and take his measurements. As she tramped down to the water's edge, an odd thought occurred to her. She had met Rolf Rustemeyer three times now: the other day on his land, earlier that morning in the barn, and at lunchtime. What color were his eyes?

A pontoon bridge. Perfect. The bridge would drop when the creek ran low—as it did right now. It would rise when the creek ran high. Seth's infantry unit had built and crossed a hundred pontoon bridges during the war. He knew the bridge across the Bluestem would need to support the weight of heavy wagons and be stable enough to keep travelers from toppling into the water. The construction would require strong cables, two or three flat-bottom skiffs, wood planks for the walkway, and secure piers on each bank. But how to explain the structure to Rolf Rustemeyer?

Seth rubbed a hand around the back of his neck as he studied the big German. Maybe the thing to do was call on Rosie. At lunch, she had managed to teach the fellow the English words for meat, potatoes, and bread. She could get a few facts across to him by pointing things out with her hands or drawing pictures in the dirt.

On the other hand, Seth wasn't crazy about the way Rustemeyer ogled Rosie. The man had no manners. He followed her around like a big, shaggy dog. When she set out the lunch, he would have wagged his tail if he'd had one. And he ate like he hadn't had a decent meal in two years. He probably hadn't. Most bachelor farmers had a hard time tending to both crops and housekeeping. Like every unmarried male homesteader other than Seth, the German would be eager to find himself a wife. Though isolation and language barriers had kept him from the few social gatherings on the prairie, Rustemeyer wouldn't overlook an unmarried female living so close at hand.

No, Seth thought he'd better try to explain the pontoon bridge to the German without Rosie's help. After all, she belonged to *him*. No, that wasn't quite right. She worked for him. And the more she worked around the house, the better he liked having her here. No doubt about it, Rosie could cook. Clean, too. The garden looked good. Chipper stayed busy. Even the floor—

"Fräulein Mills!" Rolf hollered, waving one of his big beefy paws. "How you are?"

Seth glanced up to see Rosie coming down the creek bank, her skirt dancing around her ankles and a smile lighting up her face. She was toting some blue grain sacks over one shoulder. As she approached, Rolf nudged Seth.

"Pretty, *ja?*"

"What is it with you?" Seth said, his voice more irritated than he liked. "Look, Rustemeyer, the fräulein works here. Understand? She works for me."

"*Ja*. Not vife."

"No, she's not my wife."

"*Gut*. *Sehr gut*." The German grinned broadly. "*Ich bin glücklich*."

Seth gave a grunt. "Whatever that means."

"Hello, Mr. Rustemeyer," Rosie said as she stepped up to the two men. When she looked at Seth, he could see a pair of pink spots on her cheeks. "Mr. Hunter, I've come to borrow your shirt for a moment. I need to make a pattern."

Seth glanced at Rustemeyer, who was scanning Rosie up and down. He wished she would get on back to the house. "Maybe tonight, Miss Mills. We're busy right now."

"But I promised you a shirt by Sunday. If I wait to measure until tonight, I'll never get it done. Tomorrow I'll be baking bread, and the next day I'll be making soap, and the day after that I mean to hunt for strawberries. With the gardening and cleaning and gathering chips and such, I barely have time to sit down for a moment. You need a new shirt so badly, Mr. Hunter, and this blue color I've found will make your eyes . . . your eyes . . ."

The pink spots on her cheeks blossomed into red roses. Seth couldn't hide the grin that tickled the corners of his mouth. So, Miss Mills wasn't all housekeeping and chores. Her eyelashes fluttered down, and she cleared her throat.

"This fabric is a very nice shade of blue," she said, lifting her chin. "It will hide the dirt well, and that shirt you're wearing is so dirty it could walk around on its own. Now take it off and let me measure it. As soon as you're wearing the new one, I'll give the other a wash and you can have it back—if it doesn't fall to shreds at the first touch of soap and water."

"All right, you can have it. While I get out of it, see if you can explain a pontoon bridge to Rustemeyer."

"You'll have to explain it to me first."

Briefly, Seth outlined his proposal for the bridge. He had two skiffs himself—one he'd bought off the farmer who went bust—and he suspected Rustemeyer had a third. They could braid regular rope into heavy cable, build piers out of stone and mortar, and add the plank walkway last. With hard work, the construction shouldn't take too long.

"Think you can get that through his head?" he concluded, jabbing a thumb in the direction of the curious German.

"All you have to do is draw him a picture, Mr. Hunter." Rosie turned away and knelt to the ground. She began to sketch. "Here's the bridge. *Brücke*. Here's the water. *Wasser. Ja?*"

"Sie sprechen Deutsch!"

Rustemeyer squatted down next to Rosie and gazed at her with those big puppy-dog eyes of his. Seth had the urge to topple him straight into the creek.

"You must learn better English," Rosie said. "Now you and Mr. Hunter are going to build a pontoon bridge. Floating on the water, see? The small boats will float. The water can go up and down, but the wagons can still cross over the bridge."

With some gratification, Seth watched Rustemeyer shaking his shaggy blond head. Not even Rosie could make the big hound dog understand. Seth dropped his suspenders and pulled his shirt over his head. When his eyes emerged, he saw that Rosie was walking down to the creek. In one hand she held a stone. In the other, she carried a leaf.

"The stone sinks," she told the German. "You see? It goes under the water. But the leaf floats on top of the water. The bridge must float. Like the leaf. *Float*."

"Float? *Nein. Ich verstehe nicht*."

"Oh, he doesn't understand, Mr. Hunt—" Rosie caught her breath as Seth tossed her his shirt. Her focus dropped to his bare chest, then darted quickly back to his eyes. The flush on her cheeks spread down her neck, and she hugged his shirt as though it were some kind of shield.

"Excuse me," she muttered. Turning away quickly, she hurried to the spot where she had laid the blue fabric. "I'll just measure this now."

"You do that," Seth said.

He rubbed a hand across his bare chest and gave Rustemeyer a victorious smirk. *See if you can make her blush*, he wanted to crow. *Go ahead and kneel at her feet. Kiss her on the hand. Tell her she's pretty. Trail her around the house. I don't notice her turning pink when you look at her, you ol' shaggy dog.*

"The bridge is going to float, Rustemeyer," he shouted. He had the feeling if he could just talk loud and slow enough, the German would understand. "A . . . pontoon . . . bridge. Like . . . like boats."

"Boat? *Das Boot! Ah, die Schiffbrücke! Ja, ja!*" Rustemeyer splashed out into the creek, spread his long arms wide, and indicated with his hands how the pontoons would float.

"*Ja*," Seth said. "That's right. You got the idea."

Excited now, Rustemeyer began a long discourse in German. He pointed at his farm, gestured toward the creek, and formed his hands into circles and parallel lines. As he talked, he strode back and forth in the water. He drew marks on the bank and set stones in little piles. After a while, Seth gave up trying to make sense of it and wandered over to where Rosie was working on the new shirt.

"I think Rustemeyer understands about the bridge," he said, hunkering down beside her. "It could be tricky getting the cables across the stream. It would be nice to have O'Toole's help. Even so, I don't reckon it'll take us long to build it, once we gather enough lumber."

"I haven't seen many trees around here." Rosie was laying out his shirt as a pattern on the blue cloth. She kept her attention squarely on the fabric. "You may have quite a time getting boards."

"I bought a big load of lumber off that fellow who went bust. It's stacked out behind the barn. There's enough for the bridge and a good start on the house I plan to build after I've proved up my claim. I built my barn from that wood. Most folks around here don't have frame barns, you know."

"It's a very nice barn."

"You been sleeping OK out there?" He wished he could entice her to look at him. He liked the way it flustered her to see him without his shirt. "That blacksnake hasn't bothered you, has he?"

"Not a bit."

"You reckon I ought to invite the O'Tooles over after we get the bridge built?"

"That would be nice. Chipper's been lonely."

"Maybe we could have a dance in the barn." He paused and leaned toward her. "Like this morning."

Rosie bit her lip but kept her attention on her work. "I've never been to a real dance," she said softly as she began to cut the fabric. "I wouldn't know how to fix things up right."

Seth sat, stretched out his legs, and plucked a stem of grass. He hadn't enjoyed talking with a woman this much since . . . well, he didn't know when. Mary had always been the one causing him to stumble over his words. The way she had batted her eyes and flounced around him had left him all but dumbfounded. Truth to tell, he had felt like a puppet around her—always ready at her beck and call, always subject to her whims. And Mary Cornwall had had a lot of whims.

But with skinny little Rosie—this brown-eyed twister—he was the boss. He could make her laugh. Make her blush. Make her mad. Look at her now, furiously cutting away on that shirt. All day long he had been thinking about the way Rosie had flung her arms around him. He had liked that. Liked it a lot.

"I reckon a barn dance might be fun, Miss Mills," he said, chewing on the grass stem. "Come late spring everybody's working so hard that a break would be good. Maybe you and Sheena could plan the party. What do you think about that?"

Rosie nodded and kept cutting. "Who would come? Everybody's so spread out."

"The O'Tooles, of course. Casimir Laski's a nice fellow. His family could visit. They'd have to stay the night. And then there's LeBlanc. He's the French fellow who owns the mill. He's got a passel of pretty daughters. I'm sure they'd love to dance."

Rosie stopped her cutting. She was silent for a moment. Then she flipped Seth's shirt into his arms and stood. "I certainly hope you won't forget to invite Mr. Rustemeyer," she said, looking straight into his eyes. "I'm sure he would be more than welcome by the women at the dance. And by the way, he appears to be miles ahead of you in building the bridge."

Before Seth could stand, Rosie was striding away with the scraps of fabric fluttering in her hands.

"*Auf Wiedersehen*, Fräulein Mills!" Rustemeyer called to her from the heap of stones he was gathering to build a piling.

She swung around and waved. "*Auf Wiedersehen!*" Before she turned again, she gave Seth a curt nod. "Good day, Mr. Hunter."

Rosie knelt by the window at the back of the barn loft and laid her forehead on her folded hands. Though several days had passed since her encounter with Seth by the creek, she still felt terrible inside. Her sewing had been far from perfect. Yesterday she had spilled a pot of peeled potatoes across the floor and had to haul water from the well to wash them all. And this morning she had scorched her skirt on the coals of the outside fire. It was her only skirt, and she had been vainly musing about whether Seth had noticed how it showed off her small waist. Now all he would see was the ruffle of charred holes peppered across the hem.

Consequences. Oh my, but she deserved consequences. She had

been so silly with Seth. Dancing in the barn. Ordering him to strip off his shirt. Flaunting Mr. Rustemeyer at him as though the German were a serious beau.

"Father," she prayed softly, squeezing her eyes tight to keep from crying. "I've been willful again. You've allowed me to come out to this wilderness for a much higher purpose than grain sacks and barn dancing, and I think I'm beginning to see what it is. It's Chipper, isn't it?"

She stopped, opened her eyes, and looked up at the sky as if she could read the answer in it. Clouds like scraps of white lace floated across the blue. From the window, Rosie could see the two men working below. The bridge would cross the stream some distance beyond the barn, and they were gathering stones from the fields nearby. Seth was hammering, while Rolf Rustemeyer set stones in place, his huge arms bulging with the effort.

"I think you've put me here for Chipper," Rosie said, squeezing her eyes shut again so she could concentrate. "Father, what do you want me to do for that precious child? He doesn't love Seth. His mother is gone, but I'm not allowed to take her place. I wouldn't even know how to be a mother, and Seth won't act as a father should. He won't so much as touch Chipper. I don't see how they're ever going to become a family, Father. By rights, there should be a mama and a papa and their little boy, all together and all happy. But things don't always go right, do they?"

Rosie thought about her own birth as she clasped the little stocking-toe pouch she still wore around her neck. No, things didn't always go right. Why had God sent her to help Chipper and his father learn to love each other? She didn't know anything about families—as Seth had rightly reminded her. If she angered him too much, he might tell Rolf Rustemeyer about her past. Then the German would probably never agree to marry her.

"Oh, Father!" she whispered. "I don't want to go back to the

Home. I want to build a family out here on the prairie. I want a husband. I want a house of my own. I want children—"

She cut off her words. Willful. She was so willful!

"I surrender," she said out loud. "Whatever you want, Father, I'll do. Wherever you send me, I'll go. Even if it's back to the Home. Please show me how to help Chipper. And please . . . please . . . keep my thoughts from Seth Hunter's blue eyes . . . his black hair . . . broad chest—"

"Rosie! Rosie, where are you? Where's Chipper?"

At Seth's shout, Rosie jerked upright and leaned out of the window. She could see the tall man racing up the slope toward the soddy, his shirttail hanging out and his hat tumbling from his head. Rustemeyer pounded paces behind, long blond hair flying.

"Fräulein!" he bellowed. "*Achtung!*"

"Rosie! Rosie!" Jimmy O'Toole, pant legs sopping wet, came huffing after the German.

"I'm here!" Rosie shouted down from the barn window. "Has something happened to Chipper?"

She tore across the loft and skidded down the rickety ladder. Just as she landed on the floor, Seth burst into the barn. "Rosie, where's Chipper? Have you seen him? He's not in the house!"

"I sent him for buffalo chips."

"When?"

"Hours ago. After lunch. What's wrong, Seth? Is Chipper hurt? Jimmy, what are you doing here?"

"We've had a message from Casimir Laski," Jimmy said. "He wrote us that he's had a letter from his brother in Topeka. The brother said a man's been asking in all the businesses around Topeka if anyone knows of a Jimmy O'Toole or a Seth Hunter. It must be that *sherral* who tried to shoot our Seth in Kansas City. He's still after the boy."

"Jack Cornwall," Seth spat.

"Are you sure?" Rosie asked, her spine prickling at the sound of the name.

"Who else could it be?" Seth took Rosie's shoulders. "Can you remember which direction Chipper went? Did he follow the creek? Or did he head out onto the prairie?"

"He went upstream toward Mr. Rustemeyer's farm."

"Come on, Jimmy. Rustemeyer, you stay here and look after Rosie. If Cornwall comes around, shoot him."

"I can't go, Seth!" Jimmy broke in as Seth began trying to explain the situation to the German. "What about Sheena and the *brablins?* I must wade back over the creek and see that they're all right."

"I'm going with you," Rosie said to Seth. "I won't sit about waiting for word of Chipper when I have two strong legs to search for him myself."

She tied her bonnet ribbons as she ran from the barn. Seth quickly caught up with her. They hurried down to the creek and began to follow it north toward Rolf Rustemeyer's farm. The German had vanished, Rosie realized.

"Did the message say Jack Cornwall has already come out to the prairie?" Rosie asked. "Does he know where you live?"

"I'm not sure. But he'll find out soon enough." Seth paused and looked at her. "If he's taken Chipper, I'll kill him."

Rosie shook her head. *No,* her heart cried out. *No!*

"Footprints!" he said, grabbing her arm. "He went this way. Chipper! Chipper!"

Doing her best to match Seth's long-legged stride, Rosie crossed a fallen log and skirted a cottonwood tree that had sent long roots into the water. She felt sick inside. Seth would shoot Jack Cornwall. Or Jack Cornwall would shoot Seth. Either way Chipper would be the loser. The child would suffer the most.

And which of the two selfish men cared about the boy himself? Neither. He was the trophy. The prize.

"Chipper!" Rosie cried out. "Chipper, where are you, sweetheart?"

"Confound it, I've lost the prints."

"There they are. Just ahead." Rosie brushed a tear from her cheek. "Jack Cornwall won't hurt him. You must remember that. Chipper may be frightened, but at least with his uncle he'll be safe."

"Safe?" Seth barked. "What are you talking about? Chipper belongs to me!"

"*Belongs* to you?"

"He's mine. Cornwall has no right to him."

"Why do you want him? Why do you even care?"

"He's my son!" Seth stopped running and swung around to face Rosie, his blue eyes crackling. "He's all I have."

"You can't *have* people, Mr. Hunter. Chipper doesn't belong to you. He's God's child. If you truly love your son, you'll care first about his safety."

"Stop preaching at me, woman! You don't know anything about true love. You don't know anything about families."

"And you do?"

"Better than you!"

"And how is that? You treat the child like a hired hand. Fetch the water. Pick up buffalo chips. Eat your supper. Go to bed. A father should be . . . he should—"

"What? What should a father do, Miss Know-it-all?"

Rosie drew back at the venom in his voice. "You had a father. What was he like?"

"It's not your business what my father was like. And it's not your business how I see fit to bring up my son. You don't know anything about me or my son. You don't have a father, so don't—"

"God is our father, and what better example could there be? He's loving and kind, tenderhearted and patient. You must learn to know your son, Mr. Hunter. He needs your love so desperately!"

Rosie realized she had grabbed Seth's shirtsleeves in her fists. She unclenched them and stepped back. Then she stumbled up the creek bank and climbed onto the flat prairie. Pushing through the tall grass, she searched for the trail.

Dear God, she must never shout at Seth again! The look on his face! How dare she be so brash? He would turn her out of his household and send her back to the Home in Kansas City. And she would deserve his rejection. She had no right to tell him how to raise his son. She must learn to stop caring so deeply about people. God had given Chipper to Seth—not to her! She must let go. *Let go.*

"Hi, Rosie. What are you doin' out here?"

At the familiar voice, she whirled around. Not twenty feet behind her, Chipper trundled along dragging the burlap sack filled with dried buffalo droppings. He stopped and gave her a grin.

"Are you huntin' wild strawberries, Rosie?" he called.

"Chipper!" Rosie raced toward him. "Oh, Chipper, honey. There you are! We've been searching all over for you."

He laughed as she swept him up in her arms. "Rosie, you're so funny! You're not a thing like my mama was. You're silly!"

"I *am* silly, Chipper. You're right about that. But I do know that your papa—"

"Miss Mills, listen, I—" Seth emerged over the rise and stopped. "Chipper!"

"Rosie's dancin' again," the boy said. "See, she's swingin' me around an' around."

Seth's face darkened. "Miss Mills, I want you to take my son back to the house immediately. I'm going to scout around my land for any signs of Cornwall. Chipper, from now on, don't go anywhere without me or Miss Mills around. You hear?"

"Yes, sir." The child's blue eyes lost their joy. "I was just pickin' chips. Rosie told me to."

"That's fine. You're . . . you're a good boy to do as you're told. Now go on home."

"Yes, sir."

Chipper stepped into the shelter of Rosie's skirts. She glanced down at the child; then she looked at his father. In the child she recognized the fear and distrust of a hunted animal—a baby rabbit or a kitten when confronted by a ferocious dog.

In the father she saw something entirely different. Seth was a man bound by ropes. Constrained by iron bands. Held by a leash too strong to snap. If he could break free, what would he do? Rush to the child and beat him? Hurl Rosie to the ground to break her impudent spirit? Chastise them both for their failure to conform to his will?

No, that wasn't what Rosie saw in Seth at all. To her amazement, what she sensed was the man's intense desire to run to his son and gather him in his arms. A need to laugh with relief. A need to weep away the fear of losing something priceless.

Stunned, Rosie stood for a moment, staring at Seth and trying to pray away the chains that shackled him. But he didn't escape. Instead, he turned stiffly and began walking down the trail toward Rustemeyer's farm. Going to check his land. Going to find Jack Cornwall. Going to do all the things he thought a father ought to do and none of the things his soul cried out for.

"Come, Chipper," Rosie whispered, taking up the burlap sack. "Let's go back to the house. And along the way, I will think of a plan."

"What sort of a plan, Rosie?"

"A plan to unlock your papa's heart."

CHAPTER 7

THE MINUTE Rosie and Chipper disappeared around a bend in the trail, Seth sank onto a rock and buried his face in his hands. Chipper was safe! When that little dark head had come into view, it had been all Seth could do to keep from shouting hallelujah. Like a child at Christmas, he had longed to grab the little boy—his precious gift—and squeeze him tight.

Like a child—that's how he had felt. He had wanted to act like a little boy himself, and he knew he could never display such behavior. Not in front of his son. Not in front of Rosie.

Despite what she said about him, Seth *did* know how to be a father. Or at least how *not* to be a father. He would never whip his son with a leather belt or a stripped tree limb until the child's tender flesh tore. He would never hurl abuses: "Stupid boy," "Idiot," "Can't you do anything right?"

No, Seth would treat his own son with respect. Decency. He would expect hard work, and in return he would provide shelter, food, clothing. He would see that his son learned how to read and write. Most important, he would never abandon the boy. Never.

Seth raked a hand through his hair and looked up at the setting sun. From the time he was ten years old, he had grown up without a father. The man who had given him life simply walked away one day and left his wife and children to fend for themselves. A penniless woman. Four little boys. Fatherless.

"No," Seth said, standing. He had lost his own wife. Chipper had lost a mother. But as long as Seth lived, the boy would have a father. A good father.

What did Miss Rosenbloom Cotton Mills know about it anyway? Named after a stocking label. Abandoned in a livery stable. Raised in an orphanage. What right did she have telling him how a father ought to act?

Seth stuffed his hat down on his head. Now that he'd calmed down a little, he needed to get back to his house. He didn't like the idea of leaving Chipper. If Jack Cornwall got his hands on the boy, he'd whisk him back to Missouri before Seth could stop him.

And Rosie. He didn't want to leave her alone either. Not with Rustemeyer lurking around the place. That country bumpkin German might just figure out a way to tell Rosie he wanted to marry her. In spite of the way she shouted at Seth—in spite of her stubbornness, her bossiness, her irritating, audacious, and downright silly ways—he wasn't about to let Rustemeyer cart her off.

No sir.

As Rosie and Chipper came in sight of the soddy, Rolf Rustemeyer and the entire O'Toole clan rushed out to meet them. Sheena had convinced Jimmy to ferry her and every one of their redheaded children over Bluestem Creek in his flat-bottomed boat. Now they all swarmed the returning wanderers.

"Rosie, you've found Chipper!" Sheena exclaimed. "Glory be to God! The child is safe!"

"*Und* Hunter?" Rolf asked. "*Wo ist* Hunter?"

"Mr. Hunter is searching his land." Rosie handed Chipper over to little Will and his sister Erinn. "Stay near the house now, sweetheart. Don't let him run free, Erinn."

As the children scampered to play in the barren front yard, Sheena slipped her arm around Rosie. "I've a big pot of Irish stew on my stove at home," she said gently. "Sure you must all come for supper. Even the German. Jimmy, don't say a word about him not talking straight. Rustemeyer does the best he can, so he does. Rosie, do say you'll come. We must plan what to do if that *sherral* Cornwall turns up. And Jimmy's been doing some thinking about Seth's pontoon bridge. We have that flat-bottomed boat that'll be all but useless to us. Sure I do believe he'll be joining in the building of the bridge, won't you now, Jimmy?"

By the time Seth returned to the house, Sheena and Rosie had rounded up the children. Jimmy tried to invite Rolf to dinner, but the German couldn't understand his rapid speech and wild hand gestures. Finally it was left to Rosie, who pointed toward the O'Toole place across the creek and then to her stomach. At that, Rustemeyer nodded and started walking toward the creek.

Seth insisted that he didn't want to leave his house unguarded, but Jimmy convinced him of the need to discuss a plan. It took two trips in Jimmy's boat to ferry everyone across the water, but as the sun dipped into the prairie grass, the settlers were trekking the half mile to the O'Tooles' snug soddy.

"So what do you think of our Seth, now?" Sheena whispered while she and Rosie were setting the long table. "He's a hardworking man, is he not? And handsome. Have you ever seen a pair of eyes like that on a man?"

"Seth's eyes? Hmm. I think they're blue, aren't they?" Rosie gave a shrug and walked to the cupboard to fetch some spoons.

"You think! Sure, my Jimmy's green eyes put me in mind of the fair Emerald Isle. But I won't lie to you. That Seth Hunter can turn a woman's heart with one glance, so he can. Don't you think so, Rosie? Haven't you noticed?"

"I've noticed that eyes are not the only thing to a man. It's his heart that counts with me."

"And what man has a better heart than Seth Hunter? Will you tell me that, now?"

Rosie glanced out the window where the three farmers stood talking and smoking pipes. Moonlight brightened the swirls of white smoke that drifted around their heads. Seth was laughing about something, his head thrown back and his chuckle deep.

Rosie turned away. "I believe Rolf Rustemeyer has a good heart."

"The German!" Sheena squawked. "And what do you know of his heart?"

"I know he's a hard worker. He seems kind enough. He's very smart. Strong, too—you should see how hard he works on the pontoon bridge. And he doesn't shout at me."

"Shout? Does our Seth shout then? Surely not! It would take a mighty great lot of ballyragging to induce that sweet man to shout."

Rosie flushed. "I can't believe *any* amount of trouble would compel Mr. Rustemeyer to shout. He's very nice."

"Nice is he? And what does Mr. Rustemeyer say about all the hard work you've done stitching curtains and tablecloths? Has he paid you compliments? Does he approve of your labors?"

"I don't know—"

"What's his favorite food then? Does he like rabbit? Or does he prefer squirrel?"

"Well, I really don't—"

"How many children does he want? Does he believe in God? What plans has he made for his homestead?"

"I don't know!" Rosie said so loudly that the men turned from their conversation and looked at her. She grabbed the ladle and began to dish out the stew. "I don't know very much about him," she said to Sheena in a low voice. "He speaks German."

"That he does."

"But it makes no difference to me. If God allows it, and if Mr. Rustemeyer will have me, I'm going to marry him."

Sheena thunked a bowl down on the long table. "Now *that* I should like to see."

"I'm sure we'll be very happy together."

"As my dear mother always said, 'Marriages are all happy. It's having breakfast together that causes all the trouble.'"

Rosie cocked her hands on her hips. "You're just like Seth. You think I don't know how to make a good marriage. You think just because I was brought up at the Home, I'm ignorant of what it takes to be a good wife. That's not true, Sheena! I can sew and cook and wash as well as any woman. I know how to tend children. I would never let the pantry run bare or allow my little ones to run around with holes in their socks. And I can be kind to a husband, too. Even though I sometimes shout—"

"*You* shout? I thought it was Seth doing all the shouting."

Rosie flushed. "Sometimes . . . sometimes we shout at each other."

"Do you now? Well, that's a good beginning." Sheena slipped her arm around Rosie's stiff shoulder. "Aye, lass, shouting shows you have feelings—and you're not afraid to show them to each other. Sharing what's in your heart gives life its purpose. It's what makes marriage a godly gift. Marriage is much more than darning socks and keeping the pantry stocked, so it is. It's the two of you together, through thick and thin."

"I can go through thick and thin with Mr. Rustemeyer. With any man, for that matter—as long as he's kind and hardworking."

"And what will you say to Rustemeyer when one of your wee ones comes down with the diphtheria? Or cholera? Will you cry on the German's shoulder then? Will you pour out your heart to his listening ear? And in the long cold days of winter when the snow is piled against the door so nobody can go outside for a week at a time—what will you talk about to Rustemeyer then?"

Rosie gave the stew a stir. "I could teach him how to speak English."

"Perhaps. And then you might learn that he loves none of the things you love, he believes in nothing you've given your heart to, he shares none of your dreams." Sheena let out a deep sigh. "God

Almighty tells us that when two marry, they become one flesh. I cannot explain how that is, Rosie. But you must believe me when I tell you 'tis true. Why not set your heart on a man who needs you as Seth needs you? He's a man you could love with a fire that would carry you through every cold, dark night. Why not love him?"

Rosie studied the men as they stood talking outside under the stars. Thin as a fence post, Jimmy was speaking animatedly about the pontoon bridge. Rolf Rustemeyer took a deep draw on his pipe and stared up at the moon. Seth—tall, straight-backed, and handsome—glanced into the house for a moment and looked at Rosie. Then he turned away.

"Sheena," Rosie said softly, taking her friend's hand. "A long time ago, Seth became one flesh with his first wife. I don't believe that bond has ever broken, and I know I don't have the power to sever it. Look at me, Sheena. I'm skinny, I'm a foundling, and I'm afraid that sometimes I'm very . . . very silly. Seth's blue eyes don't look on me with honor or passion or love. I'm nothing to him. I'm as bad as one of those cutworms—a pest that has invaded his well-ordered life. Sheena, please try to understand. If I'm to have a marriage at all, it will have to be with a man who has no more notion of love than I do. A man like Rustemeyer."

Sheena's green eyes sparkled in her round face. "Aye," she said. "You have no notion of love. And that is why, when your brown eyes meet with Seth Hunter's blue ones, the two of you turn into a pair of *googeens*. Sure the feeling between you is thick enough to cut with a knife."

"It is not!"

"I'll hold you, it is. But never mind. Marry the German, Rosie. Gaze all winter long into his eyes." She paused. "What color are Rustemeyer's eyes, by the way?"

Rosie swallowed. "Brown."

"Are they, now? Well, that's very nice, I'm sure." Sheena walked to the door. "Come inside, all of you, and leave your planning until tomorrow. Sure you'll never plow a field by turning it over in your mind. Jimmy, please send Erinn after the rest of the *brablins*. Put out your pipe, Seth. There's a good man. And Mr. Rustemeyer, take a chair. That's right. Well, glory be to God. Rosie, have you noticed what a fine pair of eyes Mr. Rustemeyer has? They're gray, so they are. As gray as iron."

Seth straightened in his chair and listened to the sound in the distance. A dull rumble. He glanced across the room. Rosie and Sheena were in one corner putting the littlest ones to bed. Chipper was telling riddles with the other children. Jimmy had gone out to check his stock, and Rustemeyer had fallen asleep by the stove.

Seth stood and walked to the door. He stepped outside and sniffed the heavy air.

"Miss Mills," he called. Rosie lifted her head, and their eyes met. "Storm's coming. We'd better get home."

Without a moment's hesitation, she rose and took Chipper's hand. "Come on, sweetheart. Bedtime."

Sheena woke Rustemeyer while Rosie tugged on her bonnet and pulled Chipper's hat over his brow. Seth checked the sky again. The storm was a long way off but moving fast. Like a hundred snakes' tongues, lightning flickered across the black sky. A strong breeze skittered over the tops of the grass, infusing the air with the sweet scent of cool rain. Wings outstretched, an owl drifted over the face of the moon.

By the time Seth and the others had said their good-byes and hurried down the half-mile trail to Bluestem Creek, the lightning had crept closer. Wind pulled at Seth's hat and whipped Rosie's skirt against her legs. Thunder rolled like a drum across the prairie. Chipper began to cry.

"Water's rough," Seth said. "We'll have to be careful with the boat. Rustemeyer, help Miss Mills."

For some reason, the big German had no trouble understanding the request. As Seth lifted Chipper in his arms, Rustemeyer swept Rosie off her feet and set her in the bottom of Jimmy O'Toole's boat. She let out a shriek of surprise and clapped her hands over her bonnet. Too late. The scrap of threadbare fabric whipped off her head and sailed across the creek.

"My bonnet!" she cried. "I've lost my bonnet!"

Rustemeyer began to speak in German, but Rosie was insistent.

"I don't know what you're saying! My bonnet blew away!"

Seth set Chipper in the boat and pushed off toward the other bank. Within moments, they were across. "Go fetch the lady's bonnet," he said to Rolf. "Her hat. Go . . . and . . . get . . . it!"

"*Aber der Sturm!*"

"Forget the storm. Get the bonnet. It's her only one."

As they climbed out onto the bank, rain began to patter across the parched ground. "Let's run for the house!" Seth said against Rosie's ear.

Throwing one arm around Chipper, he lifted the boy to his hip. He circled Rosie with his free arm, and they began to run into the mounting wind. Grass whipped at their legs. Blowing dust stung their skin. Rosie's hair pulled loose from its pins and billowed to her waist, a whirling, tossing sheet of silk.

"What about Rolf? I wish he hadn't gone after my bonnet!"

"He'll be fine." Seth said the words with more confidence than he felt. Lightning cracked across the sky in hissing white bolts. Thunder shook the ground beneath their feet. Chipper's little arms squeezed tightly around Seth's neck, and he could feel that his own cheek was wet from the child's tears.

Holding Rosie close to protect her from the stinging rain, he raced down the muddy trail toward the vague outline of his soddy roof. They passed the barn. Ran through an open gate. Dashed across the yard. Releasing Rosie for a moment, Seth lifted the bolt across his door and shouldered it open.

"Dry the boy off by the stove," he told her. "I'm going to check on my cows."

As Seth splashed back across the yard, he could see Rustemeyer in the flashes of lightning. Empty-handed, the man was sprinting toward the soddy. So Rosie's bonnet had been lost. The only gift she'd ever had.

If Rustemeyer hadn't been so bound and determined to scoop Rosie up in his arms, her bonnet would never have blown away. Crazy German. No doubt he'd want to spend the night. And stay for one of Rosie's breakfasts. And build the bridge all day just so he could be near her.

Seth gave the barn door a kick. It swung open. Inside, his three cows turned their heads to give him sorrowful stares. Poor gals might as well have been standing outside for all the good that plank roof did them. Rain streamed down in miniature waterfalls. Two hens had huddled up in a pile of dry hay. A narrow cascade dribbled down the loft ladder.

Though it sometimes seeped in a heavy rain, there was a lot to be said for a sod roof, Seth thought as he made his way back to the house. It kept the interior cool in summer and warm in winter. A twister could blow right over it without disturbing the people huddled underneath. And a fire was hard put to burn the thing down.

He was feeling pretty good about his situation until he stepped into the soddy. Rosie was bent over the big bed tucking Chipper beneath the covers. Behind her, Rustemeyer stood gaping at the mass of shiny hair that fell from the top of Rosie's head to below her waist.

"Shut your trap, Rustemeyer," Seth growled as he brushed past the German on the way to the stove. "If you hadn't lost her bonnet, she wouldn't be in such a fix."

For some reason, Seth didn't like the idea that Rustemeyer knew about Rosie's hair. It had been a secret vision, something that Seth realized he had thought about more than once while lying alone in his bed at night. Rosie's long brown hair mesmerized him, ribbons and streamers of it draping around her shoulders and down her back. He had touched her hair—just that once—and he'd be switched if he would let Rustemeyer get his big paws into it.

"Better put up your hair," he said to her, and the words came out more harsh than he intended. "It's dripping on the floor."

She cast him a wounded look as she moved toward a chair at the table. "I'm sorry it bothers you. I don't have a bonnet now. I lost most of my pins."

Seth looked at Chipper. He hadn't intended his comment to sound as though he disapproved of her hair. Rosie's hair fascinated him, lured him. The little boy was staring out over the hem of the sheet, his blue eyes fastened on his father.

"I like Rosie's hair down," Chipper whispered. "It's pretty. Don't you think so?"

Seth turned to the stove and cleared his throat. "A woman ought to have a bonnet. It's not right to go bareheaded in front of strangers."

"We're not strangers. Rosie's our friend."

Seth nodded. "Yes, but a bonnet keeps the sun off."

"It's nighttime now." Chipper edged up on his elbows. "Rosie, I think your hair looks like maple syrup."

Across the room, the young woman laughed. "Wet and sticky?"

"Long and brown and flowing everywhere. I never saw such long hair. How many years did it take you to grow it?"

"All my life. I've never had reason to cut my hair before. But now that I've lost my bonnet and my pins—and since it bothers your father so much—"

"No," Seth cut in. He felt hot around the collar at the very idea that she might shear off those long, billowing tresses. Her hair was her glory, the essence of her beauty, the expression of her very soul. How could he tell her so without sounding like a sentimental fool?

"Leave your hair," he said, absently fiddling with the stove's warming oven, as though he might discover a bedtime snack or something hidden inside. "You can tie it up under one of those grain sacks."

"If it troubles you—"

"No, it's . . . it's fine." He faced her. She was holding the pile of her hair in her hands, looking down at it as though it was somehow separate from her. In the lamplight it shimmered—strands of gold, threads of copper, tendrils of bronze—as her fingers slipped into it. "The boy's right. You shouldn't cut it. It suits you."

At the admission of approval, Seth glanced at Rustemeyer. Though he couldn't comprehend the conversation, the German was studying the scene with great interest. Seth didn't like the way those puppy-dog eyes had fastened onto Rosie. Not at all.

Rustemeyer didn't deserve the gift of a look at Rosie's beautiful hair. He didn't know her the way Seth did. There were things about Rosie that made her different from other women. Special. The way she had danced with the grain sacks in the barn. The way she tilted her chin when she laughed. The way her arms felt when they slipped around Seth's chest. No, Rustemeyer didn't know Rosie, and Seth felt an unbidden urge to set his stamp on her. To somehow set her apart . . . to make her his.

But how? And why? Just to keep her away from Rustemeyer? A flash of possessiveness was no reason to toss his whole life into chaos. And admitting he wanted to keep Rosie Mills to himself would certainly create havoc. After all, he didn't really need her. Or want her. Did he?

"Are you warming up, Chipper?" Rosie was asking as she ruffled the boy's damp hair. "I don't want you to catch cold."

"I'm warm . . . and I'm so sleepy," Chipper whispered.

"That's good. I'm going out to the barn now, sweetie."

"Good night, Rosie."

"Wait a minute. You can't sleep in the barn," Seth said as she started for the door. "Rain's pouring through the roof. You'll get wet."

"I'm already wet."

"You won't sleep."

"I'll make my bed under the wagon where it's dry."

"But the snake—"

"I will not sleep in your house," she said firmly. "It's bad enough you find my hair shameful to look at. I won't have people saying evil things about me for staying in a house with two unmarried men."

Lifting the latch, she slipped out the door. Seth glanced at Chipper. The boy was staring at him, blue eyes accusing. Rolf Rustemeyer wore a grin of pity mixed with triumph. Seeing that, Seth made up his mind to follow Rosie. He threw open the door and stepped into the rain. She was hurrying ahead of him through the sheets of water, her feet splashing from puddle to puddle as she raced toward the barn. A bolt of lightning cracked like a whip across the prairie, and she paused, startled.

His heart hammering against his ribs, Seth used the moment to catch up with her. "Miss Mills."

She swung around. "Mr. Hunter? You should go back inside. You need to watch over Chipper. What if Jack Cornwall shows up?"

"Rustemeyer's with the boy." Breathing hard, Seth studied her damp face. Her features were lit by pale moonlight shining through the rain clouds. "We made a plan tonight, Jimmy and I. We're going to send word to all the coach stations along the trail. If anyone spots Cornwall, we'll have advance warning."

She nodded and looked at the barn. "Then I'd better go on. It's late."

"Wait. About . . . about your hair." He shifted from one foot to the other. It was bad enough to stand outside in such a downpour. Bad enough to force his presence on a woman who was clearly anxious to get away from him. And now that he had Rosie alone—all to himself—he didn't even know what to say.

"My hair?" she repeated.

"I . . . I just don't think a man like Rustemeyer ought to take on airs like he does."

"Airs?"

"The way he looks at you. As though he thinks he has a right to see your hair."

Seth rubbed a hand around the back of his neck. This wasn't coming off well at all. Rosie stared up at him, water running down her cheeks and dripping off the end of her nose.

"What I'm trying to say is that it's Rustemeyer that bothers me," Seth tried again. "Not your hair. Not that it's hanging down. Loose."

"I lost my bonnet."

"It wasn't your fault."

"He picked me up."

"He shouldn't have done that. It wasn't his place."

"Well, he didn't want me to get . . . wet." As she said the word, the humor of the situation lit up her brown eyes. Her mouth twitched. "I guess I'm wet anyway."

"Are you sure you won't sleep in the house?"

"No. I'll be fine." She gave him a smile. "Good night, Mr. Hunter."

"Good night, Miss Mills." As she turned to walk away, he caught her hand. "About your hair—"

"Yes?"

"Don't cut it. You could make a bonnet out of grain sacks. For the sun, I mean. Just to keep the heat off your face. Not because I don't like to see your hair down. I don't think it's shameful. That wasn't what I meant."

Rosie tilted her head to one side. "Mr. Hunter, are you trying to tell me that you like my hair?"

"I reckon it's not too bad." He cleared his throat. Though he was wet and shivering, he felt exactly like a chicken roasting on a skewer. With Mary Cornwall, conversation had been so different. She had giggled and teased and flirted around him until he could hardly think. Truth to tell, Mary hadn't thought much either. She was all air and light. A serious thought never crossed her brain. But Rosie demanded honesty. Those brown eyes confronted him with an expectation of truth. He squared his shoulders.

"Miss Mills, the fact is you have the prettiest hair I ever laid eyes on," he burst out. "The shame would be if you cut it off just because Rolf Rustemeyer was careless enough to lose your bonnet. If you like, you can sew yourself a new bonnet to keep off the sun and wind. But as far as I'm concerned, you can leave your hair loose from now until kingdom come. If the truth be known, you've prettied up my homestead a lot since you came. And I'm not just talking about the new curtains."

As he finished speaking, Seth realized he was still holding Rosie's hand. She was staring up at him, her eyes shining beneath the droplets beaded on the ends of her lashes. Before he could further embarrass himself, Seth loosed her hand and turned back toward the house. He knew his boots were slogging through mud, but for some reason he had the strangest sense that he was walking on air.

CHAPTER 8

ROSIE woke under the wagon to find three chickens, a rooster, seven baby chicks, and a very wet puppy cuddled up beside her. A puppy? Where had it come from? She reached out to touch the ball of yellow fur, and the rooster let out a squawk. Feathers flew. The puppy yipped. The barn snake slithered from a clump of hay near Rosie's shoulder. At the unexpected sight of the black, shiny undulation, she sat up and banged her head against the axle—in the exact spot she had hit it the day she fell from the tree into Seth Hunter's arms.

"Ouch!" Clutching the bump and ruefully recalling the tumult of her life since that first moment with Seth, she straggled out from under the wagon. The puppy regarded her with sleepy eyes. Then it began to wag a short, stumpy tail. "Well, good morning to you, too. Where's your mama, little fella?"

The puppy waddled forward and pushed its wet black nose against Rosie's palm. She rubbed the soft fur, aware that the movement of sharp ribs beneath meant the creature hadn't been eating regularly. A bowl of fresh milk would help that.

"Come on, then," she said, hoisting the wiggly bundle into the crook of her arm. "You might as well join the rest of us misfits here on this forlorn prairie. You and I have no parents. Chipper has lost his mama. Seth doesn't have the first notion how to be a good father. And who knows what became of his folks? Not one of us understands how to make a family, so you might as well join in the muddle."

Rosie stepped out of the barn into a bright, hot morning. Steam rose from the plowed fields around the dugout. My, but the neat furrows were a beautiful sight! The promise of a bountiful harvest and a future of hope filled her heart with an unspeakable joy. She started for the soddy, but at the sound of regular pounding coming from the direction of the creek, she stopped. The bridge. Seth and Rolf were building the bridge. On a Sunday!

Picking up her skirts, Rosie marched down the bank toward the water's edge. "Mr. Hunter! Mr. Rustemeyer! Have you forgotten what day this is? It's Sunday!"

The two men stopped their hammering and gaped at her. For the first time that morning, Rosie realized how she must look. Her dress was damp, hemmed in mud, and stuck with bits of straw. Her hair hung in a long tangle past her waist. In between licking her cheek with a soft pink tongue, the little yellow puppy nipped at her chin with his tiny milk teeth.

"It's Sunday," she repeated, attempting to hold the puppy back.

"I told you there's no church around here." Seth set down his hammer. "Until we get this bridge built and cut a trail to the main road, the circuit preacher won't even come by."

"All the same—I think it's only right to honor the Sabbath. Sing. Read the Scriptures. Pray. Don't you agree?"

As Seth gazed at her, Rosie felt the heat rise in her cheeks. What was he staring at? Did she look so appalling in her muddy dress? Or was her long hair distracting him again? Maybe it was the puppy.

"He was sleeping with me this morning," she said, holding up the little ball of fluff. "Under the wagon."

Seth gave the dog a quick glance, then he focused on Rosie again. "Did you sleep all right? You look cold."

"I'm all right. But it's Sunday, Mr. Hunter. You really shouldn't be hammering, should you?"

"I can't see how it matters."

"Of course it matters. You're working. We are to honor the Sabbath and keep it holy."

"I'm building a bridge."

Rosie stroked her hand over the puppy's head as she studied the pile of lumber near the water's edge. Bridges linked people together. Bridges brought circuit preachers. Missionaries. Church builders. Building a bridge on the Sabbath might not be too great a sin in the eyes of the Lord. Still, it couldn't please him to ignore a holy day.

"I think we should turn our hearts to God," she insisted. "I think we should read the Bible."

In Seth's blue eyes, she recognized the flicker of anger. She knew what he was thinking. His skinny, mule-headed farmhand was contradicting him again. Being stubborn. Willful. He clenched his jaw, and she steeled herself against his wrath.

"All right," he said, slapping his hands on his thighs. "I reckon our angel of mercy has spoken. Rustemeyer, it's time for church."

"*Was ist los?*"

"Church." Seth pronounced the word loudly to the German as they followed Rosie toward the soddy. He didn't much like the idea of stopping their work on the bridge just to sit around reading and singing hymns all morning. The creek was running full after the rain the night before; the high water had prevented Jimmy O'Toole from crossing to help with construction. If they hoped to have the bridge built before the crushing heat of summer set in, they would need to work on it every day.

On the other hand, Seth was beginning to sense that Miss Rosenbloom Cotton Mills had a good head on her shoulders when it came to how things ought to be done around a homestead. Maybe she *was* a fatherless foundling who had grown up in an orphanage. But since she'd come out to the prairie, Seth had eaten three square meals a day, slept on clean sheets at night, and lived in a house with curtains at the windows, a cloth on the table, and flowers in a jug. More important, in Rosie's presence, Chipper's sullen attitude had begun to fade. If she thought it was right to pray before meals and sing on Sundays, who was Seth to argue?

"It's Sunday," he said to Rustemeyer. Then he pointed at heaven and folded his hands. "Time to pray. To God."

"*Gott. Ja, ja.*"

"We'll sit in the sunshine," Rosie said. "That way we can dry off."

As they approached the soddy, Chipper came dancing through the front door. He was wearing the nightshirt Rosie had sewn, and at the early hour his hair was still rumpled from sleep. "A puppy! Rosie, you have a puppy! Can I pet him? Can I hold him?"

Chuckling at the utter delight in the child's eyes, she handed over the pup. "He's hungry now. We must feed him some milk right away."

"What's his name? Where did you find him? Where did he come from?"

"God sent him to us. He's our gift from heaven. He has no mama, no papa, and no name. But he's a very special treasure all the same."

"Like you, Rosie!" Chipper said. Then he turned to his father. "He's just like her, isn't he?"

At the implications behind the question, Seth stiffened for a moment. Then he gave his son a deliberate grin. "Muddy and damp, you mean? With lots of tangled hair?"

"Not that!" Chipper said, breaking into a giggle. "I meant that the puppy has no mama or papa, and neither does Rosie."

"I reckon you're right." Seth rubbed a hand roughly between the puppy's two perky ears. "Miss Mills is wet, homeless . . . and a very special treasure. Our gift from heaven."

Rosie's mouth dropped open, and Seth couldn't resist giving her a wink as he sauntered toward the soddy. But inside the darkened room, he could hear his heart hammering in his chest. Now why had he gone and done that? Why did the opportunity to tease and disconcert her give him such amusement? Why couldn't he keep his focus on practical matters—instead of on Rosie's long brown hair and warm smile? What was happening to him?

Last night Seth had followed her into the pouring rain like some lovesick fool. He had held her hand. He had told her he liked her hair. It was pretty, he had said. She was pretty. Now he had all but admitted she had become special to him. How could such foolishness have come about? He felt half dizzy inside. Light-headed. Off balance.

He had to put a stop to this, or she would get ideas. Wrong ideas. Carrying the heavy, black, leather-bound Bible his mother had given him, Seth strode back outside. He arranged himself on a big stump near the woodpile and spread the book open across one knee. Rosie crouched on a log, draping her skirts out to dry in the sunshine. Rustemeyer sat down near her. Chipper stroked the puppy as it lapped at a saucer of milk.

"All right," Seth began, determined to take control—of himself and the entire situation. "We'll start at the beginning. Genesis."

"Deuteronomy," Rosie said. "Please."

Seth frowned. "That's a bunch of laws and rules, isn't it? I think we should start at the beginning—the way a book ought to be read."

"But Mr. Holloway said there's a verse about . . . about foundlings." Her voice was small, wounded. "He told me I'm not supposed to go to church. It's forbidden . . . for people like me."

"What's wrong with you, Rosie?" Chipper asked. "Why shouldn't you go to church?"

"Whoever my mama and papa were, I don't expect they were married to each other. God likes for people to marry each other before they have babies, Chipper. He wants . . . families." She swallowed, and Seth thought his heart was going to tear open at the pain written so visibly in her brown eyes. "You know, I've been to church all my life, but now I wonder if I've done wrong. Maybe . . . maybe God hates the sight of people like me in his house. Mr. Hunter, would you find that verse? It's in Deuteronomy. I want to know what it says. I want to try to understand."

Seth scratched his head. It couldn't be right to talk about touchy subjects like illegitimacy with children around. Could it? And Rustemeyer was getting restless. The German didn't understand a word of the conversation. He kept glancing in the direction of the unfinished bridge. Worst of all, Seth couldn't even remember where Deuteronomy was situated in the Bible.

"Maybe we should just read a psalm and be done with it," he said. "My mama used to read them to us kids all the time after Papa went off and . . . when she was feeling lonely. Or sad."

"Deuteronomy," Rosie repeated. "Please, Mr. Hunter."

What could he say to those brown eyes? Seth flipped around through the pages until he found the book. It was near the beginning of the Bible—almost like starting in Genesis.

The first batch of chapters had to do with the Israelites wandering in the desert. He bypassed that part as too boring. Then came the Ten Commandments. Those had been hanging on the wall in the house where Seth grew up. The neat sampler sewn by his mother had stated God's laws in bold black cross-stitch. And Seth had watched his father methodically break every one of them. He elected to skip over that part of Deuteronomy, too.

"All right, chapter six," he said. "Maybe Holloway's verse is in here. 'And thou shalt love the Lord thy God with all thine heart, and with all thy soul, and with all thy might. And these words, which I command thee this day, shall be in thine heart: And thou shalt teach them diligently unto thy children, and shalt talk of them when thou sittest in thine house, and when thou walkest by the way, and when thou liest down, and when thou risest up.' That sounds good enough to me. OK, who wants to pray?"

Rosie blinked. "But that's not the part about the foundlings."

"It's about children. It says to love God and teach your children about the Bible."

"It's not what Mr. Holloway was talking about."

"All right, all right." Seth lifted his hat and raked a hand through his hair. To tell the truth, he didn't really want to find the part about the foundlings. It might upset Rosie. Seth couldn't stand the thought of her eyes filling with tears the way they had in Holloway's station. Fact is, if the Bible made Rosie cry, Seth would be tempted to chuck the book in the creek. Though he believed in God—Jesus' death on the cross, the resurrection, and all that—he'd never seen much good come of religion in his own life.

After his papa had run off, Seth used to pray every day for God to bring the man back. But he never did come back. Seth had longed for a father—a good, strong father—more than anything in the world. But all his praying hadn't done a lick of good.

"You know there are an awful lot of verses in here," he told Rosie as he flipped through the pages. "Chances of finding that particular one are mighty slim."

"I'm praying for you to find it," Rosie said. "The Lord will lead you there."

Seth shrugged in resignation. "Here's something about the church. Chapter 12. 'But unto the place which the Lord your God shall choose . . . thither thou shalt come. . . . And there ye shall eat before the Lord your God, and ye shall rejoice in all that ye put your hand unto, ye and your households, wherein the Lord thy God hath blessed thee.' Sounds to me like God wants everybody to go to church—and even have a good time eating and rejoicing. OK, *now* who wants to pray?"

"Keep reading," Rosie said. "You haven't found it yet."

Seth turned through passage after passage about which animals to eat, what to do about murder, and who ought to marry whom. Just when he was ready to shut the book and get back to the bridge, his eye fell on Deuteronomy 23:2. He read it silently. Read it again. Finally, he looked up at Rosie.

"Go on," she whispered.

"'A bastard shall not enter into the congregation of the Lord; even to his tenth generation shall he not enter into the congregation of the Lord.' I don't believe that," he exploded. "What's a child got to do with how his parents behave? It's not right to blame a child for what his father did. You can't hold innocent children accountable for their ancestors' sins and failures. That's a bunch of bunk."

He dropped the Bible to the ground. "Enough," he went on. "We've got to get to work on the bridge. Pray, Rustemeyer. Do it in German. I don't care to understand it anyhow."

Rustemeyer stared at Seth. "*Was ist los?*" he asked, gesturing angrily at the fallen book.

"You're not supposed to throw the Bible in the mud," Chipper said. "Only a nasty ol' Yankee would do that."

"What do you know?" Seth snapped, his own father's harsh voice echoing in his head. "What do you know about anything?"

Chipper shrank into himself and buried his face in the puppy's fur. Rosie sat forlornly on the log, her shoulders sagging, her focus on her lap. Rustemeyer glowered.

"So much for Deuteronomy," Seth barked, standing. "So much for the whole worthless Bible. So much for religion and church and a God who doesn't love people for who they are and not what they came from."

Hot, frustrated, confused, he stomped off toward the bridge. At least building was something he knew how to do.

On the first day of June, Rosie, Chipper, the new puppy, and the entire O'Toole clan gathered to watch Seth drive the last nail into the pontoon bridge that spanned Bluestem Creek. He, Rolf Rustemeyer, and Jimmy had worked on the project every minute that they weren't plowing, planting, or hoeing. Rosie had used her own spare minutes to sew a flowered scarf that would hold back her hair. But they didn't have another Bible study, even though two Sundays passed during the building of the bridge.

Rosie could hardly see the point in forming a group to worship God. The preacher at the church in Kansas City had said that wherever two or three believers were gathered in Christ's name, he was there among them. But now Rosie knew that God didn't want her—an illegitimate child—to worship in a gathering of his believers. As far as she could understand the verse in Deuteronomy, it would be just plain wrong for her to bring them all together again like a small church. Her very presence would defile the gathering.

Since that Sunday morning after the rain, nothing had gone particularly well around the homestead. The harmony had been spoiled. To Rosie, it felt like Satan had used the moment of discord to jump right in and throw everything out of kilter. Seth was so angry about the verse in Deuteronomy he had stopped praying at mealtimes. Chipper crept around like a lost lamb. He seemed half fearful that Jack Cornwall would jump out from behind a bush and grab him—and half hoping he would. It was hard to tell what Rolf Rustemeyer was thinking.

If Rosie and Seth had begun to build a bridge toward accepting and understanding each other, it too had been destroyed the morning of Deuteronomy. Rosie felt that her stubborn insistence on observing the Sabbath had led Seth to reject God—and Seth in turn had rejected her. He worked day and night, and he hardly gave her a second glance. There were no more long midnight conversations, no more teasing compliments, no more dances in the barn. For some reason, Seth's disinterest in her hurt almost as much as the discovery that God didn't want her to set foot inside his church.

"Casimir Laski sent us a message this afternoon," Sheena O'Toole whispered to Rosie as the two women led everyone who had observed the ceremonial pounding of the last nail across the new bridge for a celebratory evening meal at Seth's soddy. "Jack Cornwall has been spotted around the Red Vermillion River, so he has. Word is he's been asking the whereabouts of the Hunter and O'Toole homesteads. He's working his way closer to us, Rosie. Sure, you and Seth must keep a sharp eye on the wee one. First thing you know, that *sherral* will kidnap the boy and ride hotfoot back to Missouri."

Stopping in the front yard, Rosie dipped a spoon into the large black cauldron that hung on a tripod over the outdoor fire. The stew she had made that morning looked delicious, and it smelled even better. With fresh greens from the prairie, wild onions and carrots, and the very last of the stored potatoes, the concoction would fill hungry stomachs well. Best of all, Sheena had whipped up a batch of Irish dumplings, which floated in the broth like puffy white pillows.

Rustemeyer, who had ridden over for the celebration, leaned across Rosie's shoulder. "Fery goot," he said. "Schmells fery goot."

"Thank you, Mr. Rustemeyer. I'm glad you think so," Rosie replied. She had grown accustomed to Rolf's awkward attempts at speaking English. He reminded her of the toddlers at the Home—the way they stumbled over words and put sentences together in funny combinations.

"You are velcome." He executed a neat bow, which sent Sheena into a fit of giggles. Ignoring her, the German picked up a stack of bowls. "I helpen you, fräulein. *Mit der Suppe*."

"With . . . the . . . soup," she pronounced carefully.

"Vit . . . dee . . . zoop."

"All right." Rosie looked up into the German's gray eyes as she ladled the bowl full of stew. Rolf had spent a great deal of time at Seth's homestead in the past weeks, and Rosie was accustomed to his presence. In fact, she hardly noticed him. He worked hard. He was cheerful. He treated Chipper kindly. And he ate like a hungry horse.

But other than creating a need to calculate extra portions into her meals, Rolf had been invisible to Rosie. She had been so busy setting up the household, weeding the kitchen garden, baking, washing, ironing, and sewing that she hadn't given a second thought to her plan to marry the big blond German. Now she realized she had only five months to make it happen. She ought to start paying him some heed.

"You did a good job on the bridge," she said, handing Rolf a bowl. "Good work."

"*Ja, ja.*" He smiled. "You are velcome."

She didn't think he had understood. Oh well, he certainly fit every item on her list for an ideal marriage partner: strong, honest, hardworking, kind. Rolf was a good man. He didn't disturb her the way Seth did. He never teased or argued. He never complimented or criticized. He never said anything at all. He just happily went about his work, pausing only to devour grizzly bear-sized portions of whatever she put on the table. Rolf was the perfect mate.

Seth, on the other hand, was complicated, intelligent, edgy, and a demanding perfectionist. When he looked at Rosie, the blood in her temples began to pound, and her heart jumped into her throat. If he inadvertently brushed her hand, strange fiery tingles raced straight up her arm. She found herself listening for his whistle at dawn when he came across the yard to milk the cows. And at night, when he walked her to the barn to light her path with the lantern, she searched for things to say just so she could hear his deep voice.

Truth to tell, Seth Hunter had become a constant presence in her thoughts. He made her feel nervous. Challenged. Alive. Very much alive. She couldn't understand what it meant. Her feelings about him reminded her of the stories she had read to the children at the Home—stories about princes and princesses falling in love.

"Love?" she said out loud. The very thought of that word in connection with Seth Hunter threw her for a loop.

Rolf handed her another empty bowl to fill. "Lof," he repeated. "*Was ist* lof?"

"Love? Oh, it's nothing." She swallowed hard and waved away the word. "Some people think it has to do with marriage. Husbands and wives. People have a wedding, you see. They marry. They live together and have children. Getting married is—"

"What are you talking to Rustemeyer about?" Seth demanded.

He had approached the fire so quietly Rosie hadn't heard him. When she turned toward Seth's voice, she saw that his blue eyes were blazing, and the muscles in his jaw flickered with tension. Behind him, a group of travelers—six mounted horsemen—were talking with Jimmy O'Toole some distance from the soddy.

"Who are those men?" Rosie asked. "Where did they come from? Is Jack Cornwall among them?"

"No. They're all right. Casimir Laski sent them from his station. They were hoping we had finished building the bridge so they could cut a few miles off their trip. They're cattlemen on their way to Salina to pick up five hundred head and drive them to Kansas City." Seth eyed the stew. "Do you have enough to feed them?"

"Of course."

"Good. Rustemeyer, see to their horses." At the man's blank look, Seth leaned closer and said loudly. "*Horses.*"

"You won't make him understand by shouting," Rosie said. She pointed at the lead rider's horse. "Help, please."

"*Ja, ja.*" Rustemeyer gave Rosie a warm smile and headed off in the direction of the visitors. She watched him go, and she felt happy that with each new word he learned he was fitting in better with prairie society.

"Mr. Rustemeyer is doing very well with his English, don't you—"

"I don't want you to marry that man," Seth cut in, his voice hard. "You hear me, Miss Mills? Rosie?"

At his use of her first name, she glanced at him in surprise. "And why not? I can marry whoever I want to."

"No, you can't. Not him."

"Rolf is a good person. He's kind. He's hardworking." She stirred the stew for a moment. "Do you think he wouldn't have me? If he knew . . . about Deuteronomy, I mean?"

"It doesn't have anything to do with Deuteronomy."

"Then what? Why wouldn't he—"

"It's not you. It's . . . well, it *is* you. You're . . . you're . . . you're mine. My worker, I mean. I brought you from Kansas City, didn't I? You're sleeping in my barn. Eating my food. I need you. Need you around the house. You do good work. Chipper likes you. I won't have you going off to marry Rustemeyer."

Rosie stared at Seth. The tips of his ears had gone bright red, and she could see a little vein jumping in his forehead. What on earth had upset him so? The thought of her marrying Rolf Rustemeyer had him fairly steaming. But why? Did he dislike the German so much? Or did he consider Rosie his own personal servant over whom he had absolute power? Or did his concern have something to do with Chipper? Or was there something . . . something else . . . behind it?

Slowly she turned back to the stew and set the lid on the cauldron. The feel of Seth's eyes on the back of her neck set her skin prickling. She took three deep breaths, and then she straightened.

"You don't understand," she said evenly. "You don't understand me at all."

"I do understand. You think you have to hook onto some man in order for your life to have any meaning. You think your mama rejected you, and you think God rejected you. So the only way you're going to have a future is if you latch onto a husband. Anybody will do. You don't think enough of yourself to believe that you could matter to another person."

"I don't matter to anyone."

"You matter." He shifted from one foot to the other. "You matter to Chipper."

"You told me not to matter to him. You don't want me to mean anything in his life. And now you expect me to give up the hope of marriage and a family for a five-year-old child? A child whose father plainly told me to keep my distance from the boy?"

"Arguing again, are you?" Sheena said, taking the ladle from Rosie's hand. "Well now, that's a good sign, so it is. But if the pair of you stand around ballyragging all evening, we'll none of us have any supper. So come along, and put this nonsense behind you for the time being. You can go at it again later. In private."

Sheena gave Seth an exaggerated wink, and Rosie wished she could crawl into a hole. When she glanced around she saw that Jimmy O'Toole, the five O'Toole children, Chipper, Rolf Rustemeyer, and the new visitors were all arranged in a circle, holding their bowls of stew and staring at her and Seth. Even the puppy had squatted near the fire to see what would happen.

Seth cleared his throat and grabbed his bowl. "Welcome to our guests," he said. "Thanks to Mrs. O'Toole and Miss Mills for the supper. Thanks to Jimmy and Rolf for their help building the bridge. Let's eat."

"Let's pray first," Rosie cut in, brushing past Seth. "It's only right. I'll do it."

Before she could cower in the presence of so many guests, she stepped into the middle of the circle and bowed her head. She hadn't prayed in a very long time. Not since the Deuteronomy Sunday. But all that time, she had felt such an aching emptiness inside her heart. Now, though the words seemed difficult to form, she knew it was right to honor this special event with a prayer.

"Dear Father," she began. Her next breath caught in the back of her throat. Father. *Father!* God was her father. Of course. She had believed it for years. She had stated it so boldly: *But as many as received him, to them gave he power to become the sons of God.*

Rosenbloom Cotton Mills was not illegitimate. God himself had made her his own child. *And because ye are sons, God hath sent forth the Spirit of his Son into your hearts, crying, Abba, Father.*

"Dear Father," she repeated. But the sudden knowledge of his redeeming love, his unconditional acceptance, his constant grace filled her heart. Overwhelmed her. As a joint heir with Christ, she could walk into any church with her heart full of the assurance of her heavenly Father's eternal, unchangeable welcome.

As tears spilled down her cheeks, Rosie turned away and ran sobbing into the twilight.

CHAPTER 9

ROSIE? Rosie, where are you?" Sheena's lilting voice called out.

Rosie blotted her cheeks with the hem of her skirt. "I'm over here, Sheena. On the big stone near the willow tree."

"I see you now!" Puffing a little from her run, the Irishwoman lifted her skirts and clambered down the bank. "You gave us quite a scare, running off the way you did in the middle of your prayer. Sure, Seth wanted to come after you, and Rolf, too. It was all I could do to hold Chipper back. Even my Jimmy was set to hotfoot it across the prairie in search of you. You've earned yourself quite a gaggle of lovesick men, so you have."

"Oh, Sheena." Rosie scooted over on the flat stone to make room for her friend. "Don't be silly. For all Seth has tried to accept me, he finds me as frustrating and irritating as a goat-head burr."

"Aye, you've gotten under his skin, so you have. I'll warrant the man's in love."

"Sheena! Please don't tease me." Rosie swallowed. "Anyway, I've seen the error of my thoughts in that direction. I've been looking at Seth in a human way—instead of as God sees him. Tonight—just now—my Father spoke to me, Sheena."

"Spoke to you? Glory be, but you're a strange wee thing, Rosie Mills. God in heaven spoke directly to you? I can't credit it."

"Then you've never experienced it." Rosie briefly explained

about the Deuteronomy Sunday and its outcome. Then she told Sheena how the moment she had called her heavenly Father by name, the meaning of the cryptic verse had become crystal clear. "When you pray, Sheena, you mustn't do all the talking. You've got to listen, too. Listen to what he's telling you."

"But how can you be sure it's God speaking—and not some little imp of the devil inside your head?"

"That's easy enough. Everything God says is true. He can't lie. Satan is the father of lies, and he finds great joy in distorting the truth. He confuses us and fills our heads with doubt and despair. But if I take what I believe God has said to me and hold it up to the Bible, it should reflect his Word. In fact, when I hear my Father's voice, it most often comes in words straight out of the Scriptures."

Sheena sat for a moment, pondering. "I don't know that I've ever listened to God, Rosie. But I'll try. Truly I will. And I'm thankful you've seen that scrap of Deuteronomy clear to its rightful meaning."

"My greatest flaw is taking the reins of my own life and trying to guide myself. When I do, everything gets twisted, and I go off on the wrong path."

"Do you believe God's path led you out here to the prairie?"

"I don't know. But I'm certain he can bring a blessing from it if I continually give myself to him."

"Do you plan to ask God which man he wants you to marry, Rosie?"

"I can't think about marriage, Sheena. When I do, I get so confused. I can't see God at all. I just see myself and . . . and someone else."

"Seth Hunter?"

Rosie twisted her hands together in her lap. "It should be Rolf."

"Well now, you've certainly set every man's heart aflutter with your shenanigans tonight. What do you mean to do about it,

Rosie? Which one will you have? Will it be Rolf Rustemeyer? Or Seth Hunter? Or will you wait for some other man to come along?"

For a long time, Rosie sat in silence, turning the questions over and over in her mind. Finally she laid her hand across Sheena's. "I only know one thing. I'm going to try to stop listening to my own heart and start listening to God. He knows the plans he has for me. If I care enough to follow him, I'll find the right path."

"You're a good girl. Seth would do well to put his past behind him and look to his future."

"He is thinking of his future. He cares so deeply about Chipper. He told me he didn't want me to marry Rolf because he knows Chipper needs me right now."

Sheena let out a squawk. "By all the goats in Kerry, girl, it's not Chipper that needs you! It's Seth himself, so it is."

"I don't see why. I've hardly done a thing but sew him a blue shirt and put three meals a day on his table." Rosie searched her mind, trying to make sense of the messages she had read again and again in Seth's blue eyes. Yes, he did seem to need her. Every time he caught her eye he seemed to be saying, *Don't go. Don't leave me.*

"It's the prairie," she said finally. "If Seth needs me at all, it's because he understands that I can make a difference in his life out here. If I can keep the kitchen garden growing, keep Chipper healthy, keep the clothes and the bedding washed and mended, then his days will be easier. He spoke once about all the dangers he faces. Wind. Hail. Prairie fires. Plagues of insects. Cyclones. I should find a way to help . . . help Seth through all that. Whether he knows it or not, he does need me, Sheena. God can use me in his life."

Sheena gave a little chuckle and shook her head. "I'll warrant the good Lord can use you in Seth's life—one way or another." Standing, she gave a stretch. "Now, my sweet lass, we'd better get back to the soddy, or they'll send a search party after the both of us, so they will."

Filled with a new sense of mission, Rosie lifted her eyes to the heavens. God had given her five months—five months to do his will on the prairie. If her Father wanted her to have a husband, he would provide one. Until then, she must set about to do his will as a single woman in possession of a strong back, willing hands, and the determination to provide for the well-being of her employer.

Seth was pacing by the campfire when Rosie and Sheena emerged arm in arm into the circle of light. His relief at seeing the younger woman was so great, he had to fight himself to keep from letting out a whoop of joy and swinging her up into his arms. Instead, he stopped his pacing and set his hands loosely on his hips as Chipper and the other children swarmed around her. Even the puppy, whom she and Chipper had named Stubby, danced in delight, tugging on the hem of Rosie's skirt and yipping in the excitement of the moment.

"Rosie's been talking to God again, so she has," Sheena declared to the gathered company. She accepted the rough willow chair offered by one of the visiting cattlemen. "Our Rosie talks to God—*and* she listens when he talks back to her."

The cowboy laughed. "Maybe we should build her a shrine or somethin'."

"Make light of it if you will," Sheena went on, "but to Rosie every place on earth is a shrine. God talks to her anywhere."

"Quite a little saint, is she?" The man took off his tall-crowned Stetson and surveyed the slender woman. Then he looked at Seth. "Your wife?"

"She works for me. Takes care of my son."

The man let out a slow whistle. "I'd keep a sharp lookout if I was you, my friend. A man gets lonely on the trail, and she's a mighty purty little thing. Can she cook?"

"Fery goot cook," Rolf Rustemeyer said. "Fräulein Mills *ist* fery goot cook. Maken fresch bread, potato, egg, chicken. *Ist* goot *für* eaten—breakfascht, lunsch, zupper."

"What's he talkin' about?" the cowboy asked Seth. "Is he French or somethin'?"

"German." Seth struggled with the urge to tell the men to keep their eyes off Rosie and their thoughts to themselves—she wasn't free for the looking. But she *was* free. She had kept her heart pure. No man had claimed her. He shoved his hands into his pockets and started toward her.

At that moment, the cowboy stepped in front of him. "Ma'am, that was a real fine supper you fixed," he said to Rosie. "As fine a supper as I've ate in many a month."

Rosie had been carrying Chipper on one hip. Now she let him slide to the ground. "Thank you, sir," she said, her face lighting up. "They were Sheena's dumplings."

"I'd be much obliged if you'd allow me and my men to pay you for the meal. What would you say to fifty cents?"

"Fifty cents!" Rosie gasped.

"*Per,*" the man added proudly. "Pay up, fellers."

"Now just a minute." Seth held up a hand. "We don't take money for food. This is my homestead, not a boarding house. If we have extra, we share it."

"Well, sir, that's mighty generous of you. Mighty generous. If you feel thataway, why we'll just bed down over in your barn for the night. Awful late to be hitting the trail again."

Seth's spine prickled. "The barn's off limits. Head over the bridge to LeBlanc's mill. He's got a bunkhouse all set up, and his wife serves breakfast. If you start out now, you'll be there by midnight."

"Midnight! C'mon, now. If you don't want us in your barn, we'll put our bedrolls down by the crick."

Seth crossed his arms over his chest. He wasn't about to allow six lonely cowboys to sleep within half a mile of Rosie Mills—let alone as nearby as the creek. "Now listen here—"

"Sure, you gentlemen can stay in my barn," Jimmy O'Toole said, laying a hand on Seth's shoulder. "It's dry enough if you can stand the smell."

The cowboys eyed each other. Finally their leader turned back to Seth. "Say, farmer, by any chance do you know a feller by the name of Hunter?"

"What's it to you?"

"Just curious. We been hearing about this Hunter rascal all the way from Topeka. Seems he once took a woman against her will and used her most cruel. Then he run off and left her alone and in a delicate condition. More'n five years later, he showed up and kidnapped the child the poor woman had borned before she died a terrible death. There's been talk of puttin' a bounty on the scalawag's head."

"Is that so?" Seth stared hard at the man, his blood boiling in his veins. "Where'd you come by such a farfetched story as that?"

"Folks talkin' about it everywhere. There's a feller by the name of Cornwall huntin' for the missin' boy. It's him as is thinkin' of a bounty. They say if he puts one on Hunter's head, it'll be for a hundred dollars."

Seth wanted to laugh out loud. Jack Cornwall didn't have a hundred dollars to save his yellow-bellied soul. The war had stripped him of house and farm—his only means of livelihood. He'd be hard-pressed to come up with ten dollars, let alone a hundred.

"A hundred dollars could make a lot of folks sit up and listen," the cowboy went on. "You ever heard of this Hunter feller around these parts?"

"I mind my own business," Seth said. "But I can tell you one thing. Before I'd set off chasing any man for a bounty, I'd take a close look at Jack Cornwall's hundred-dollar reward."

"*Jack* Cornwall, is it?" The cowboy gave his cronies a grin. "Well now, I reckon you know more about this matter than we do."

"Bad news travels fast."

The man laughed. "Shore enough! I guess we'll be crossin' that bridge of yours then. Keep us in mind if you hear of Hunter. We'd be the first in line to ride out in search of a hundred-dollar bounty. If we don't get to Salina purty quick, we're gonna be flat broke."

"You'll need at least two dollars apiece tonight," Rosie said. Seth watched in amazement as she approached the cowboys. Head held high and shoulders squared, she confronted them. "If you want to cross the Bluestem Creek, you have to pay the bridge toll."

"Bridge toll!"

"You don't think that bridge built itself, do you? Lumber doesn't come cheap and easy out here on the prairie. Unless you men intend to ride all the way up the Bluestem to the shallow crossing at Salvatore Rippeto's station, you'll have to pay the toll."

"But that's twelve dollars!"

"Twelve dollars exactly," Rosie agreed. "We crossed plenty of bridges ourselves on the way here, and it's a fair price." She stuck out her hand, and the six cowboys dug around in their pockets for the silver coins. Grumbling, the men handed over their money and then shuffled off toward their horses.

As the cowboys rode away, Rosie took off her scarf, shook out her long hair, and tied the coins into the scrap of cloth. "I will take it upon myself to keep the money safe," she said.

Rolf Rustemeyer—who evidently had comprehended the nature of the transaction—burst out into a deep, hearty chuckle. Sheena gave her a hug as the children cheered. Even Jimmy clapped her on the back.

From a distance, Seth listened as the cowboys' horses clattered across the new pontoon bridge. He was glad he had put a heavy bolt on the barn door. Glad he had begun to shingle the roof. Glad the puppy always slept beside Rosie. But he had a bad feeling that his efforts might not be enough to keep her safe.

Swallowing hard, he fought the strong urge that welled up

inside him. He wanted to protect Rosie. Shelter her. Care for her. It was different from the way he had felt about Mary Cornwall, who had lived so near her ever-vigilant papa. This feeling toward Rosie was stronger, and it filled his chest with an ache so powerful he could hardly suppress it.

But he didn't want to care so deeply about Rosie Mills! Didn't want to care about *any* woman. He had vowed never to fall into that trap again. Throughout his youth, all he'd ever wanted was a family. When he was grown, he hoped for a wife, children, a home. He wanted to be father and husband. He was sure he could do a better job of it than his own father had.

With Mary Cornwall he had tried. He had gone into that marriage with all the hopes and dreams a man could carry. And look what it had brought him. Anger, banishment, loss. He had a son who didn't love him. His brother-in-law had become an enemy who planned to kill him. Chances were that before the summer was out Seth would have a bounty on his head. And his wife—the wife with whom he had planned to spend his years—was dead.

Seth studied Rosie as she cleaned up from the supper, her hair flowing around her like a long silk cape. Beautiful. Rosie Mills was beautiful. But if he allowed himself to care about her—to commit his future to her—he might lose her. Just the way he'd lost Mary.

No. He wouldn't do that. Hardening his heart, Seth made up his mind. He would train his focus on his work. He would try as hard as he could to be the kind of father he thought Chipper needed. And . . . yes, he would encourage Rolf Rustemeyer to make Rosie his wife.

June brought such excitement, such joy, that Rosie knew she had done well in turning her heart toward her Father. Overriding everything hung the anticipation of the dance celebrating the new bridge. Rosie and Sheena took on the project with all the enthusiasm their blossoming friendship brought. It was hardly more than a twenty-minute walk from one soddy to the other, and they were constantly back and forth—talking, planning, even doing chores together.

Seth had decided to shingle the barn completely, and with each passing day Rosie's home became more snug and secure. She hung a curtain in the loft window and set a stool beside her mattress. She even made herself a pillow. Stubby slept at her feet, and at the slightest disturbance, he barked with all the ferocity of a wolf—albeit a very young, slightly yappy wolf.

The barn had been chosen as the site of the dance. Rosie scrubbed the rough plank walls top to bottom, and she and Chipper kept the stalls cleaned and filled with freshly mown hay. Even if it rained on the momentous afternoon, the barn could hold almost everyone invited to the party.

Sheena's list seemed to grow by the day. The Polish family, Casimir Laski and his wife, would come. Salvatore Rippeto had sent word that he and his wife and all their children were planning to attend. LeBlanc and his reputedly beautiful daughters were coming. They were said to be sewing new dresses expressly for the event.

Even Holloway and his wife—as community neighbors—had been invited. They hadn't responded to the invitation. Rumor had it they were angry about the bridge that had effectively cut their station off from the flow of traffic down the main road from Topeka to Salina. But Rolf Rustemeyer would be at the dance and so would all the O'Tooles, as well as a collection of homesteaders from around the area. With music and dancing and wonderful food, the celebration promised to be the highlight of the prairie summer.

As if all this weren't enough to keep her busy, Rosie had discovered a new source of activity: toll-taking.

"Here comes a party bound for the west," she told Sheena one afternoon as they stood in Seth's yard stirring soil-based pigment into the vat of milk paint they had made. They had decided to paint the barn a deep red. "Is it three wagons? Or four?"

"Three. That's nine dollars."

Rosie laughed and set down her paddle. "I never thought tending a bridge could be so rewarding. Did you know I've started taking goods in trade, too? Several travelers didn't have cash to pay the toll. Rather than make them travel all the way to Holloway or Rippeto, I accepted other things. Tea. Flour. Buffalo skins. Blankets. I've put everything in a big chest that I found in the barn."

Sheena studied the wagons as they rolled slowly toward the bridge. "Does Seth know?" she asked. "About the trade goods, I mean?"

Rosie chewed on her lower lip for a moment. She didn't like to do anything without Seth's approval. He hadn't seemed too happy about the toll-taking in the first place. He never asked where she put the money or what she planned to do with it. In fact, he more or less ignored the bridge and the growing stream of travelers who crossed it each day. There could be no question he would object to taking away the hard-earned goods the settlers brought with them in order to establish their new homes.

All the same, Rosie knew if she let one wagon or stagecoach cross without paying, word would spread, and nobody would want to pay. There were plenty who could afford it—cowboys with their pockets stuffed full of earnings from their latest trail ride, miners heading back east from the gold fields of California, peddlers and politicians, fur traders. All travelers knew they would have to pay ferry and bridge tolls. It was an accepted part of the journey. But Rosie had no doubt Seth would despise the notion of taking goods from settlers. On the other hand, how could it be right to turn poor travelers away just because they couldn't produce a silver dollar or two?

"I haven't told him," she admitted to Sheena. "I don't think he'd like it much."

"You might ask his opinion on the matter, Rosie. What's the harm in it?"

"Seth doesn't . . . he doesn't exactly talk to me anymore, Sheena. Ever since that night when I ran away to the creek to talk to God, Seth has been angry with me. Not exactly angry. He just doesn't seem to know I'm here. He never looks at me. He barely speaks."

"By herrings, I don't believe it. Seth doesn't speak to you? Why not?"

"I don't know. I suppose he's upset that I left the company that night. Maybe he's upset that I charged those cowboys a toll. Maybe it has something to do with Rolf Rustemeyer. I don't know. Seth and I can't seem to talk to each other without a squabble. We had been arguing just before I ran off that night. Remember? Seth was ordering me not to marry Rolf Rustemeyer, and I was telling him I could marry whoever I pleased. I didn't think it would make him so furious. But it did."

"He's jealous."

"No, Sheena. You're wrong there. Seth doesn't care for me. If he did, he would behave differently. You should see how he is with Chipper these days. He takes the boy with him everywhere he goes. They plow together, hoe together, even cut shingles together."

"Seth's afraid if he doesn't keep a close watch on his son, Jack Cornwall will kidnap the boy."

"That's part of it. But there's more, Sheena. Seth is trying hard to be a good father. It's a beautiful sight to watch the two of them together in the fields—though I must admit I can't see that it has bound them any tighter. Chipper holds back his heart."

"He must have learned that trick from his papa."

Rosie smiled. "Don't be so hard on Seth. He's a good man."

"Then why don't you tell him the truth about the trading you've been doing?"

"What difference can it make? I'm simply doing what I believe God has told me to do. I'm laying up provisions for Seth and Chipper. I'm taking care of them. Seeing to their welfare. If it comes in the form of silver dollars or extra blankets, what's the difference?"

Unwilling to hear Sheena's response, Rosie lifted a hand in greeting to the wagon team leader. He set the brake and climbed down. "Mornin', ma'am," he said.

"Welcome to Hunter's Station."

"Hunter's Station, is it?" Sheena murmured behind her. "Now isn't that a lovely how-do-ye-do?"

Rosie cast her a disapproving look. Then she turned back to the team leader. "Are you headed for Salina?"

"That's right, ma'am. Any news on the condition of the road that direction?"

"We had word this morning that it's dry and clear all the way to Salina. You'll have a delay at the Pawnee City ferry crossing. The town is right there at Fort Riley, you know, and I think a lot of the soldiers are leaving for home now that the war's over. They tell me it's a rope ferry, and it's been horribly backed up with traffic. The wait is several hours. Sometimes even a whole day. You'd do best to get there first thing in the morning. The ferry starts up at dawn."

"Much obliged to you, ma'am." The man smiled warmly beneath the walrus mustache that covered his upper lip. "Suppose we'll be able to find a place to spend the night in Junction City? My wife is coming near to her time—for the baby, you know. It's our first—and she sleeps better in a bed."

"There are two hotels. Good ones, I hear. The store is not too well stocked, but you can get flour and sugar. They're always low on coffee and soap, but they have plenty of cornmeal."

"Turns out we won't be needing all the coffee we brought. Didn't realize we could make the stuff just as easy out of chicory root."

"Oh, yes, and soap is simple enough, too."

"Soap? Is that right?" He scratched the top of his head. "Come to think of it, I don't recollect that we even brung any soap with us. We been traveling so long, we haven't given much thought to washing."

Rosie had sensed that fact right off. "You must take some of my potash with you." She started toward the barn with the man following. "Most of the time, I use lye to make my soap; you leech it from wood ashes. But these potash crystals are much more convenient. I just boiled down some lye to make them yesterday. Give the crystals to your wife, and see that they're kept well away from children. Any woman who has lived on the prairie can teach her how to use the potash to make soap. Sheena taught me. It's really not hard at all."

In the barn, she handed the man a crock containing half of her hard-earned supply of potash crystals. Truth to tell, it was a little painful to part with. The process of turning lye into potash was slow and smelly. But Rosie couldn't stand to think of that poor woman not even having a bar of soap to wash her new baby's clothes. The man cradled the crock like it was a treasure of gold.

"I don't have much to pay you with, ma'am," he said in a low voice. "We're trying to save what we've got for hotels and food. Would you take something in trade?"

"The potash is free. My gift for the new baby."

Again, the warm smile formed under the man's huge mustache. "I don't suppose you'd take some of my coffee in exchange for the bridge toll, would you?"

"Coffee . . ." Rosie pondered the offer for a moment. "A pound will do. One for each of the three wagons."

The grin grew wider. "You don't have any blankets for trade, do you, ma'am? We been colder at night than we expected."

"As a matter of fact, I do have blankets." Rosie could hardly believe her good fortune. She had more blankets than she knew what to do with in the big chest. But coffee—now that was a treasure hard to come by. Real coffee had a flavor that chicory couldn't match, and everyone at the barn dance would appreciate the unexpected pleasure.

She hauled two long planks from Seth's remaining lumber pile and laid them side by side across a pair of sawhorses. Then she opened the storage chest at the back of the barn and began to take out her trade goods. "I have five blankets," she said, laying them across the makeshift counter. "This one is really nice. Pure wool. I'd need more than coffee for it, though. I took this blanket in trade for the toll on seven wagons."

The man's eyes widened as Rosie took out a handmade quilt, a crock of pickles, and a small keg of nails. In a flash he left to fetch his wife from the wagon. Pretty soon, she and the travelers from the other wagons had gathered in the barn to look over the items. Even Sheena craned her neck to admire a little round mirror someone had traded in.

"Would you be willing to take a packet of needles for that ball of yarn?" the man's very pregnant wife asked. "I'd like to knit booties for the baby."

"Silver needles?" Rosie asked. You could never be too careful about this sort of thing. The woman nodded. Rosie smiled. "And let me tell you that coreopsis will make the most beautiful yellow dye. Be sure to gather the flower heads when they're in full bloom."

"What about blue? I was thinking of blue booties."

"Indigo—but it's not water soluble, so it's very hard to work with. I'd stick with yellow, if I were you. Do you like that knife, sir? I'd be willing to take an extra ax head you might have. Or a razor."

"Look, she has dried apples, Mama!" a child cried out.

"They're all the way from Pennsylvania," Rosie said. "Do you like apples? Here, take this one. Your mother can have a few more apples in trade for that half-pound of lard she seems so eager to be rid of."

"Oh, thank you kindly, ma'am. We haven't had apples for weeks. Can I take five?"

"Take seven. That way you can bake a pie. Or a big juicy cobbler. I've found children love cobbler, especially if you add just a pinch of—"

"Miss Mills." The icy voice gripped Rosie's stomach like a vise. She looked up to find Seth Hunter—hat in hand, sweat dampening his brow, hands planted on his hips—staring at her from the door of the barn. "Would you mind telling me what you're doing?"

CHAPTER 10

SETH could hardly believe his eyes. Right there in his barn stood Miss Rosenbloom Cotton Mills and fifteen complete strangers haggling over coffee, blankets, mirrors, and sewing needles. Where had she gotten all these things? Who were these people? What were they doing in *his* barn?

"Oh, hello, Mr. Hunter," Rosie called, giving him a wave. She smiled, but he could see that her face had paled at the sight of him. "We're just working out an exchange for the bridge toll." She dropped her voice. "And a few other things."

Seth crossed his arms and stared at the unexpected scene. Chipper skipped over to Rosie's side and gave Stubby a pat. The dog wagged his tail. "Where'd you get this stuff, Rosie?" the boy asked as she handed a man a knife and took a big iron soup ladle in trade. "This looks almost like a regular mercantile."

"That's a funny thought, Chipper," Rosie said, giving Seth a wary glance. "You know good and well this is just the barn. I keep a few things stored away in case somebody would rather trade than pay the toll."

"A few things! You gots *lots* of things. You even gots beads and shoes and a pair of scissors. What's in these cans?"

Seth stepped forward and lifted a tin. *Oysters!* Oysters were a luxury item only the rich could afford. How had she managed to get her hands on five tin cans of them? Beside the cans sat a ream of writing paper. And bullets. Rosie had a stack of ammunition that could keep Fort Riley in business for at least half a day. Where on earth had it all come from?

"If you had a post office here," the man with the huge mustache told Rosie, "you could set up your own store. Your prices are fair. You deal honest with folk. And you got good quality merchandise. All you need is a post office commission, and you'd pick up twice the trade."

"Oh, I wouldn't want to do that," Rosie said. "I have so much work to do around the house."

"Put your son to work doing chores."

"Chipper isn't my son. He belongs to—" Again she gave Seth a nervous glance. "He belongs to my employer."

"You mean you're a hired hand? Well, your boss would be smart to put you to running the mercantile and hire someone else to do the cleaning."

"That would never do," Rosie mumbled. "Really, we're very satisfied with things the way they are. This is all just for . . . just for the toll bridge."

As he passed, the man gave Seth a long look. "I'd think about that post office commission if I was you. She's got a good eye for business, that one. She could turn you a handsome profit."

Seth kept his focus trained on Rosie as the line of travelers wound out of his barn and back to their wagons. When she began to pack all her goods back into the chest, he decided it was high time to take up the differences between them. If she was going to work for him, she would have to do things his way. And the sooner he got her out of his homestead and married off to Rustemeyer the better.

Rosie Mills was trouble. Every time he looked at her, something twisted up inside him. A knot of pain formed in his stomach and began to torment him in a gently luring voice he found impossible to resist. *She's beautiful, isn't she? She's a good woman. Chipper adores her. She sure knows how to run a house.* No matter how hard Seth would try to silence the voice, it only grew louder. *Take the risk, Hunter. Reach out to her. Open your heart and let her heal you.*

"No," he said out loud.

"What?" Rosie swung around, her arms full of brightly colored wool blankets.

"I said no. You do not have my permission to do this."

"Do what? Take a few items in trade for the bridge toll? I can't see what harm it does, Mr. Hunter. You heard the man yourself. I'm fair and honest."

"No." He placed his hands palm-down on the makeshift counter. "I don't want you to do it."

"But trading helps everybody. The poor man had brought enough coffee to drown two armies, and he needed blankets for his wife." Rosie leaned across the counter and whispered conspiratorially. "She's going to have a baby. Their first."

Seth stared into her big brown eyes. Big warm chocolate eyes. A pang ran straight through his heart. That awful knot began in his stomach, and the voice began. *Kiss her, Hunter. Shut up and kiss that pretty woman.* He couldn't breathe.

"If you're worried I'm not taking in enough cash," she said, "I can assure you there's plenty. And it's well hidden, too. Is that the problem?"

"No," he managed. *No, the problem is you, Rosie Mills. You scare me. You make me want to hope again. You make me want to dream of things I was sure I had put away forever.*

"Don't think I'm hoarding all these goods for myself," she said. "No sir. I can promise you everything will be divided equally among the three men: you, Jimmy O'Toole, and Rolf Rustemeyer. Just say the word, and I'll split up the goods, and that'll be the end of it. But let me tell you, Mr. Hunter, that bridge you men built is as good as a gold mine. We've got floods of travelers coming across it every day—going both ways. Don't we, Sheena?"

"Aye, that we do," the Irishwoman called. She and Chipper were playing with the puppy.

"Settlers, cowboys, fur trappers, even some rich landowners from back east. They all stop by here—every one of them—and we make a trade. Well, how do you think I got those oysters? It was a Mr. Hercules Popadopolous. He's a Greek fellow who said he owns half of New York state. He gave me the oysters in trade for a large buffalo skin I had accepted from a trapper who had bartered it from an Indian. I told the Greek man it wasn't a fair trade, but he insisted mine was the first real buffalo hide he'd ever seen, and he was bound and determined to have it. And what do you think he did when I handed over the hide? He knelt down on the ground and kissed my hand just like I was a lady from the Middle Ages, and he was a knight in shining armor. I told you about that, didn't I, Sheena?"

"That you did," she called.

"Did you see the mirror?" Rosie went on. "It was given to me by a gentleman from Virginia—a Confederate general. He said he had lost everything in the war, and he was going to California to make his fortune in land speculation. But I don't think he really had lost everything, because you should have seen his carriage. And all the things in his trunk! The mirror was the least of it, let me tell you. He had gold chains and candlesticks and pieces of cut lead crystal. I warned him he might get robbed if he didn't watch out. He paid his toll in cash, but then he turned around right before he crossed the bridge and handed me that mirror. And do you know what he told me, Mr. Hunter?"

Seth swallowed. If he didn't say something soon, Rosie Mills would talk herself blue in the face. Worse, the more she talked and the harder he looked into her brown eyes, the crazier he felt. Crazy enough to kiss her. Crazy enough to just haul right off and ask her to marry him.

"No," he said. "No . . . I . . . I don't know what he told you, but

I do know that you'd better not be taking oysters and gold mirrors off single men, Miss Mills. It's not safe. You don't know the first thing about these fellows. They could be robbers, or confidence men, or worse."

Her face paled. "They seemed nice enough to me. They just stopped by to pay the bridge toll—like they would at any other town or station that had a creek."

"But this is not a town, Miss Mills. It's not even a station. This is a homestead. Do all these travelers know who lives here? Have you told them my name is Hunter?"

Rosie glanced at Sheena, and her pale face went even whiter. "You'd better tell him," Sheena said.

Rosie knotted her fingers together and swallowed hard. "I did mention . . . that is, I have said on occasion . . . I more or less did say—"

"She calls it Hunter's Station," Sheena said, coming to her feet. "And what of it, Seth? This is your place, isn't it? What harm is she doing? Why are you acting the *sherral* about her trading? She's a good woman, and people like to do business with her. All she's done is—"

"Is spread the word from New York to California the exact location of my homestead!" Seth exploded, his fear overriding every need he felt to hold Rosie and bury his pain in her embrace. "Don't you see? Now everyone knows. *He* knows."

"Jack Cornwall?" Sheena said.

"Shh!" Seth cast a quick look at his son. Chipper was studying the three adults as Stubby attempted to nip off a mouthful of his hair. "Don't mention that man's name aloud."

"And why not? Chipper knows his uncle is searching for him. Don't you, boy?" Sheena held out a hand and pulled Chipper to his feet beside her. "But you live here now with your own good papa. Even if that Jack Cornwall came to fetch you, would you go with him? Would you go away and leave your own soft bed? Little

Stubby? My fine Will and all the other wee friends you've made? And Rosie? Would you leave her?"

Chipper stuck his hands in his pockets and eyed Sheena. Then he looked at his father. His blue eyes narrowed. "I might," he said.

"Would you then?" Sheena asked, her voice high. "To tell God's truth, I never would have thought it. And you such a fine boy. Such a good boy. Your papa needs you here, so he does. I can't think why you'd ever want to go away with that Jack Cornwall."

Chipper stuck out his chin. "Uncle Jack and me always make popcorn strings at Christmastime. He lifts me up high, and I hang the strings on the tree. And Uncle Jack gots a mouth harp that he plays when I'm sitting in his lap. When my mama died, Uncle Jack held me tight and we cried and cried. He loves me."

"Oh, but Chipper, your papa loves you too!"

Seth could hear the Irishwoman's voice, but he could stand the pain in his chest no longer. He felt as though his heart had been ripped away. Turning on his heel, he walked out of the barn. A razor-sharp lump formed in his throat. His eyes burned. If he could just make it back to his plow. Just bury everything in the rich prairie soil.

"Seth!" Rosie's hand slipped into his and pulled him up short.

He couldn't make himself look at her.

"Don't take what Chipper said as a rejection of you," she said softly. "Learn from it. Didn't you hear what he loves about his uncle? It's the touching! His uncle lifts him up to hang popcorn strings on the Christmas tree. His uncle lets him sit in his lap. And they cry together. Seth, please hear what your son is trying to tell you. If you want his love—and I know you do—you must touch him! Wrap your arms around him! Let him come into your heart!"

Seth clenched his fists. His own father had never behaved in such a way. Never held or touched him. How could it be right? Wouldn't the boy turn out weak? A sissy? Wouldn't he disrespect a father who showed tenderness of heart?

He could feel Rosie moving closer to him. Her hand slipped up his arm, and she leaned against him. "Please, Seth," she whispered. "You've built such a wall around yourself that no one can come inside. You won't let anyone care for you. You won't let anyone love you. Please, please don't shut us . . . shut him—Chipper—out of your life."

"I don't . . ." He struggled to express himself. "I don't understand . . . how . . . how to touch him."

"But it's so easy."

"No!" he exploded again, turning on her and taking her shoulders in his hands. "No, it's not easy. I can't . . . I've never . . . my father didn't . . . I can't do it."

"You can learn," she said, her brown eyes melting the edges of his frozen heart. "Ask God to teach you how to touch Chipper. Pray, Seth. Pray for the wisdom to win your son's love."

"Pray? You heard the verse from Deuteronomy. If God can shut his heart to a foundling child, what makes you think he'd listen to me? Why would I want to ask him anything?"

"No," Rosie said, laying her hands on his chest. "We read the Scripture all wrong that morning. I understand it now. Anyone who surrenders his heart to Christ becomes a child of the heavenly Father. I'm an heir to the kingdom of God, Seth! I can walk boldly before his throne—and I can call him my father . . . my daddy . . . my papa. He welcomes me, and he welcomes you, too. He'll teach you how to be a good father to Chipper. Ask him. Ask him!"

She laid her cheek on his shoulder for a moment; then she turned and pulled out of his arms. He watched her as she walked back to the barn, her long hair blowing in the early summer wind. *I love her.* His soul spoke the words, and he realized they were a prayer. *I love her, and I don't know what to do about it. Teach me. Teach me . . . my heavenly Father. Break down the wall and show me how to love my son. Guide my hands to touch him, hold him, draw him into my heart.*

Seth felt the tension slide out of his arms. His fists unknotted. The lump in his throat melted. Tears spilled down his cheeks. *And about Rosie, God. Tell me what to do about Rosie.*

The barn wore a coat of bright red paint. Chipper sported a new white shirt, a pair of sturdy canvas overalls, and a handsome haircut. Seth almost matched his son in his own starched white shirt, blue denim trousers, and carefully combed hair. Rosie could not have been more proud of her handiwork as the two stood side by side to greet the stream of guests driving over the new bridge for the party.

Seth had insisted Rosie make herself a dress from a bolt of blue gingham he had noticed in her storage chest. She had protested. After all, she had given a wagon's toll and an iron stew pot in exchange for that fabric. Surely it would bring a nice trade-in someday.

But Seth had told Rosie he was tired of that old skirt with the burned hem, and it was high time she had something new. As for the chest and Rosie's trading business, he reluctantly told her she could continue trading for bridge tolls as long as she kept a close eye out for trouble, especially trouble in the form of one Jack Cornwall. And she was no longer to refer to the barn as Hunter's Station. If it needed a name, she would have to come up with something else.

Pleased to have his permission, Rosie set to work sewing herself a new blue gingham dress. By the afternoon of the dance, she finished the hem and slipped on her creation. It was pretty. She couldn't deny it. The bodice had puffed sleeves, and the skirt billowed out from her waist to her ankles in a cloud of airy fabric.

If only she had a bonnet, she would feel like a queen. But as hard as she tried, she could not fashion a bonnet brim that would stand stiffly in place. Everything she attempted flopped down in her face, until she was forced to abandon the project and put her hair up in a high bun. Fortunately, she did have pins and a ribbon—having traded the gold mirror for them.

"Glory be but you're the vision of a lady!" Sheena exclaimed as she and Rosie carried trays of doughnuts from the cooking fire to the barn. "Has Seth laid eyes on you yet?"

Rosie shook her head. "No. He was in such a hurry to be out and about as the guests arrived. Before I dressed, he and Chipper went out to the bridge to welcome everyone. He's been looking forward to showing off the bridge. To tell you the truth, I think Seth is very proud of the work the men did and all the bridge has meant to our community."

"Community!" Sheena laughed. "Sure, you always think bigger than the rest of us, don't you, Rosie? We build a little pontoon bridge, and you turn it into a grand gold mine. Seth puts up a rickety barn, and you have it shingled, painted red, and transformed into a social hall before half the summer's passed. Two families live across a stretch of creek, and suddenly we're a community."

The sight that greeted the two women as they entered the crowded barn seemed to confirm Sheena's description. Ladies in their brightest dresses set out bowls of blackberries and fresh cream, strawberry pies, gooseberry pies, and raspberry cobblers. Salt pork boiled with greens and cabbage sent a delicious aroma around the barn, a fragrance that mingled with the scents of warm gingerbread and freshly baked biscuits. Rosie had never seen such a vast quantity of food. And to think it had all come from what she once considered a barren prairie.

"Fräulein Mills!" Rolf Rustemeyer swept off his hat and gave Rosie a low bow. "Ist fery goot party you maken."

"Thank you, Rolf. But you must remember Sheena fried all the doughnuts, and it took the two of us and all the children to paint the barn red."

"Ist fery goot barn," he agreed.

Rosie favored him with a radiant smile and went back to arranging the trays. Rolf tapped her shoulder. "Fräulein Mills, *bitte*. Vill you vit Rolf Rustemeyer *tanzen?*" He did a few polka steps across the floor. "*Der Tanz*. Fräulein vill vit me *tanzen?*"

"Dance?"

"*Ja*. Danz!" He waggled a finger back and forth between them. "You *und* me?"

Rosie looked up into his eager gray eyes. Rolf was such a good man. Such a kind man. Such a hard worker. He wanted to dance with her. Maybe he would ask her to marry him. Maybe even tonight, and then everything would be settled.

"I can't," she said quickly. "I don't know how to dance. I'm sorry, truly I am. But I grew up in an orphanage, you see, and we didn't have socials there. I can't dance."

Rolf frowned. "*Ja*, you danz. I zee you in barn vit Hunter. You danzen fery goot."

"Oh, that was just silliness. I had found the grain sacks, remember? I don't really know how to dance. Not properly."

Rolf snapped his suspender. "You not *freundlich* vit me? You not liken me?"

"Of course I'm your friend, Rolf. I like you very much."

"Danzen vit me. First danz."

Rosie let out an exasperated breath. "All right, I'll dance the first dance with you. But I'm warning you, my dancing is likely to turn your toes black and blue by morning." She paused, waiting for him to chuckle at the image she had created. Instead, he bowed with a flourish and strode away, his mission accomplished.

Oh Lord, how can I marry Rolf? Rosie prayed as she gazed down at the raspberry cobblers. *I can't talk to him. He doesn't understand me. We won't be able to laugh together. We won't even be able to pray together! Father, please don't make me marry Rolf.*

But even as she prayed the words, Rosie knew Rolf was her best option. Though her heart was filled with Seth, he kept her shut away. He lived behind a barricade of his own creation. If she were ever to build a family, she must find a willing man. Why not Rolf?

"Rosie, you look beautiful!" Chipper cried, spotting her from the door of the barn and making a mad dash to her side. "Your dress is all checkerdy! It gots puffs and buttons and everything. You look like a princess. Don't she look like a princess?"

He turned to his father, who had just stepped into the barn. At the sight of Rosie, Seth drew in a deep breath. He jammed his hands into his pockets. His blue eyes blinked, as if unsure of what they were seeing.

Rosie's heart began to hammer like a woodpecker on a fence post. Seth took a step toward her, and she swallowed hard. Was her hair still up? Had the bow drooped? Was her hem hanging straight? Had she remembered to button every button? Would he notice the little snag in her sleeve?

"Evening, Miss Mills," he said as he approached. "Chipper's right. You do look like a princess."

Rosie tried to smile, but she felt like her lips were stuck to her teeth. "Thank you."

"Is that the blue gingham I found in the storage chest?"

"Yes." She clamped a hand over the snag on her sleeve. "It might have been better used as curtains."

"It's perfect as a dress. It suits you."

He stopped and stared at her. Rosie felt a flush crawl up the back of her neck and settle in her cheeks. Never . . . never in all her life had she seen a man who looked as handsome as Seth Hunter did tonight—and he was staring at her!

"There's . . . lots of . . . of food." She tried to smile again.

"Your hair sure is pretty. I've never seen it like that. So high up on your head."

"Is my bow crooked?" She nervously fingered the scrap of blue ribbon. "I wasn't sure how it looked. I traded . . . traded the mirror. For the hairpins. And the ribbon."

Seth took another step forward. "Miss Mills . . . would you do me the honor of dancing the first dance tonight?"

"Yes!" She let out a rush of air. "Oh, yes, I'd love to."

"Until then," Seth said, tipping his hat.

"Until then," she replied, favoring him with a slight curtsy. "Excuse me." Feeling faint, Rosie walked out of the barn for some fresh air. She was being so silly! He had only asked her to dance. Just a simple request. *Will you dance the first dance with me tonight?*

The first dance? The significance of his words tumbled through her. She couldn't dance with Seth. She already had agreed to dance the first dance with Rolf Rustemeyer! This was terrible. She would have to tell Rolf she hadn't understood him. No, that would be a lie. She *had* understood. But she had forgotten Rolf as soon as Seth walked into the room. It was Seth who took her breath away. Seth who made her heart beat twice as fast. Seth Hunter.

Oh, what was the matter with her? Why did she feel this way? So mixed up. So anxious. All she wanted was to be near Seth and look into his blue eyes. Was this what he meant when he once told her how it felt to be in love?

Had Seth felt this way about Mary Cornwall? No wonder he couldn't abandon his wife's memory. Seth had been right that this . . . this incredible feeling must somehow be important in making a marriage work. There were two parts to it, weren't there? The lifetime commitment *and* this wonderful . . . frightening . . . amazing . . . feeling!

"Fräulein Mills?" Rolf touched her arm. "You are zick?"

"Sick . . . no . . . I'm all right. I just . . . oh Rolf, you're such a good man, such a very kind man, and I really do think I ought to marry you. But the trouble is with Seth, you see. I can't stop thinking about him and feeling so very odd inside when he looks at me. It wouldn't be at all right if I were your wife and yet I felt this way whenever I thought of Seth. Even though I know . . . I know very well . . . that he loves his wife, and he won't ever forget her . . . I can't make myself feel good about . . . What are you staring at?"

"*Die Musik!*" He grabbed her arm. "*Komm*, fräulein. Ve danzen, you *und* me!"

"But Rolf!" Rosie grabbed her skirts to keep from stepping on them as the big German whisked her back into the barn.

At the far end near the loft, a platform had been set up. A fiddle, a harmonica, an accordion, and a banjo had been assembled along with musicians who claimed to play them passably well—though this was a matter of opinion. As the music swelled through the barn, couples formed into squares and began to dance in time to the caller's directions.

"All to your places
And straighten up your faces.
All join hands and circle eight.
Ladies face out and gents face in
And hold your holts and gone again."

The caller let out a loud whoop, and Rolf twirled Rosie around and around among the other dancers. Still dismayed at what she had done—agreeing to dance with two men—she could barely keep her feet untangled. She had never square danced in her life, and she didn't know which way to turn or where to go. Rolf didn't seem to care in the least. Laughing, he caught her around the waist and spun her once, twice, three times around the square in an awkward imitation of the other dancers.

Assembled around the barn, the elderly men clapped and stomped their feet in time with the rhythm. Young girls—LeBlanc's daughters, Rosie assumed—giggled in clumps of two and three as the young single farmers paused to chat with them. Wives cut cakes and poured lemonade or joined with their husbands in the dance. Wishing the song would end, Rosie searched the barn for Seth.

"Goot danzen," Rolf said as he galloped past her. "Ist fery fun, *ja?*"

Rosie grinned bravely and sashayed with him beneath a long arch of upstretched arms. If Seth saw what she had done, he could turn away from her forever. He would believe she had chosen Rolf over him. He might even think she wanted to marry Rolf, as she had so firmly told him.

But she didn't. She knew it—knew beyond the shadow of a doubt—that she could never marry Rolf Rustemeyer.

"You fery pretty!" Rolf half-shouted as he jigged around her. "I lof you!"

What? Rosie flushed in mortification. Had Rolf just announced that he loved her—in front of everyone? As she examined the faces of the other dancers, she realized no one had understood his meaning. But she knew. She knew!

Oh, where was Seth? Why didn't he step in and claim her? She had no more formed the thought in her mind when a man's firm arm slipped through hers. Linked at her elbow, he twirled her out of the square and away from the crowd.

"Seth," she began, breathing hard. "I must explain—"

But when she looked up, it wasn't Seth's blue eyes that met hers. A slow smile spread across the man's face as recognition dawned in hers. "Howdy, ma'am," he said. "Any idea where I might find Chipper tonight?"

Rosie caught her breath and jerked her arm away from his. The man was Jack Cornwall.

CHAPTER 11

"AREN'T you the little gal who whacked me on the head back in Kansas City?" Jack Cornwall asked.

Rosie couldn't speak. Fear had caught in her throat and blocked her urge to scream. She clutched the edge of the table behind her.

"Yeah, I'm sure you're the one. You were up in a dang tree. So, you and Hunter hooked up together, I hear. I hope he didn't play you for the fool the way he did my sister."

Rosie shook her head. She wanted to explain, wanted to shout for help, wanted to run away. But nothing happened. She merely stood staring at the man with her mouth hanging open and her knees locked beneath her.

"Where's my nephew?" Jack asked. A tall, raw-boned, rangy man, he studied her with a pair of eyes the color of hard, cold slate. Thick brown hair hung to the collar of his battered leather coat, and a sweat stain ran around the band of his hat. "I didn't see him playing out front with the other children. What have you done with him?"

Not with the other children? Rosie quickly searched the throng of dancers. Where was Chipper? And where was Seth? Why couldn't he see what was going on? Why didn't he come? Had Jack Cornwall done something to him?

"Listen, ma'am," the man said, "I really don't want to make a scene here. Truth is, I've spent the last four years fighting Yankees like Seth Hunter, and I'm a little tired. But I never have liked winding up on the losing end of things. So if you don't tell me where the boy is, I may have to get rough." At that, he reached out and took Rosie's arm in a firm grip.

"Wait . . . what are you—?"

"I'd hate to have to hold you as a hostage," he cut in. "After all, I don't know what you mean to Hunter. But you whacked me on the head and landed me in jail. He violated my sister and kidnapped my nephew. And the fact is—I don't really much care what becomes of either of you. I want the boy. Now tell me where he is."

"I-I-I don't—"

"Fräulein?" Rolf Rustemeyer stepped up beside her. "I danzen, *und* I not zee you no more. *Was ist* hoppened?"

Rosie let out a breath of relief. Rolf was a good three inches taller than Jack Cornwall and at least fifty pounds heavier. "Rolf, get Seth. You've got to find him. This man . . . this man—"

But her captor had released her and melted into the crowd of dancers before she could even make the German understand the problem. Frantic, she searched the room until she spotted Cornwall's dark hat as he left the barn. He was gone. Into the cover of night. Chipper was somewhere out there unprotected. And Seth. Where was Seth?

Grabbing her skirts, she brushed past Rolf. As she stepped into the throng, the big German caught her arm. "Fräulein, you danzen vit him? *Der* man vit *braunen* hat? I liken you. You maken goot zupper *und* breakfascht. You fery goot fräulein. Fery pretty. But you danzen vit him? Not goot. *Nein, nein, nein*—"

"Rolf, stop talking!" Rosie cried. "We have to find Chipper. That man with the brown hat wants to take him away. Where's Seth?"

"Hunter? You danzen vit Hunter now? But I vill danzen vit you."

"Oh, just move!" Rosie let out a cry of frustration and pushed him aside. Unwilling to cause panic in the crowd but terrified for Chipper, she elbowed her way among the dancers. "Excuse me, Miss Rippeto. Pardon me, Mr. Laski."

By the door, Jimmy O'Toole stood picking his teeth with the end of a hay stem. He spotted Rosie and straightened as she grabbed his arm. "Sure, you look as if you've seen the ghost of St. Peter himself," he said. "What's the matter now, Rosie?"

"Jack Cornwall is here!"

"Here?" He looked around. "In the barn?"

"He just left. He's after Chipper. Where's Seth?"

"I saw him walk out of the barn at the start of the first dance. He looked angry enough to chew nails, so he did."

"Where did he go?" She shook her head. "No, never mind about Seth. We have to find Chipper. Tell Sheena. Get some of the men together. Cornwall has threatened trouble."

Leaving Jimmy to round up help, Rosie dashed out of the barn. The children were playing prisoner's base in the light of lamps hung from the circle of wagons in the yard. Rosie grasped Will O'Toole by the shoulders and stopped him in his tracks.

"Will, where's Chipper?" she demanded.

"He's around here somewhere. He was playing with us a few minutes ago. What's wrong, Rosie?"

"I want you to help me find him. Now."

"But the game—"

"Never mind about the game. Find Chipper. Take him to your papa right away."

Her heart tight in her chest, Rosie raced toward the soddy. Three women stood tending the outdoor fire and trading gossip. They insisted they hadn't seen the little boy, but Rosie threw open the door and hurried into the house.

"Chipper? Are you in here, Chipper?" The soddy was empty. Fear clutching her stomach, Rosie fell to her knees. "Oh, Father, please help me find Chipper! Please don't let Jack Cornwall take him away. Chipper belongs to Seth. Seth needs him so much. Father, please show me how to find Chipper. And where is Seth?"

Seth sat on the flat rock by the willow tree and flipped a pebble into the creek. Things were about as good as they ever had been in his twenty-four years. He owned one hundred and sixty acres of fertile land. He had a house, a barn, two mules, three cows, a couple dozen chickens, even a dog. His crops had come up healthy and strong, their straight green rows promising him a stable future. Spring wheat, oats, sod corn, and barley should turn a decent profit come fall. The kitchen garden would provide lettuce, beans, cucumbers, tomatoes, and roasting ears for the table. The bridge had been a good idea, bringing toll money and opening the path to easier travel. All in all, things looked mighty fine.

And they looked terrible. Seth shook his head and tossed another stone into the gurgling water. Chipper didn't love his father. Didn't even call him "papa." In fact, the boy clearly preferred the puppy to his own flesh and blood. The dog could make Chipper's blue eyes light up with joy. Rosie could make the child laugh that bubbly chuckle that tore up Seth's insides. But in spite of all the time Seth had spent with his son, Chipper remained wary, his little heart carefully guarded against the man he had been warned never to trust. No matter what he tried, Seth couldn't seem to break down that sturdy wall.

And then there was the matter of Rosie herself. A few weeks ago, Rosie Mills had fallen into Seth's arms and knocked him flat. He'd never recovered. But Rosie seemed bound and determined to marry Rolf Rustemeyer. What did she see in that big German hound dog? Must be something pretty special. Though she had promised Seth the first dance, she had forgotten her pledge as easily as she had slipped into Rolf's embrace.

Seth hurled another pebble into the water. Why did he care? If Rosie married Rolf, she'd have a good life. With all those hearty meals under his belt, Rolf would sure be happy. And Chipper could visit them often. They'd probably have children of their own pretty soon, and Rosie would have everything she'd ever wanted: a home, a husband, a family. She had told him that was all there was to marriage, and it was more than enough for her.

Rosie didn't understand the kind of mixed-up, heart-stopping, breathtaking whirlwind that could tear through a person's soul. She didn't think that kind of love mattered. And she was right. It didn't. So why did Seth feel it every time he looked into her big brown eyes?

"Seth!" Rosie's voice startled him out of his reverie. "Seth Hunter, where are you?"

"Here," he called. "By the creek."

Rosie raced down the bank and nearly crashed into him. Stopping short, she took his hand and squeezed so tightly the blood stopped flowing through his fingers. "I've been looking all over for you!" she said. "He's here. He's right here. And Chipper's missing. I can't find him. I don't know where he—"

"Who's here?"

"Jack Cornwall."

"No!" Seth jumped to his feet. "Where is he? Did you bring the rifle?"

"Seth, you can't fix this with violence. That's not the way. You have to find Chipper. You have to get to him before Cornwall does."

"Wasn't he with the other children?" Seth was running through the darkness now, careless of snagging branches and roots that caught at his feet. As Rosie lagged behind, he grabbed her hand and hauled her along so he could keep pumping her with questions. "Is Jimmy searching for Chipper? What about Casimir and

Salvatore? They brought their horses, didn't they? Have you checked the soddy?"

He could hear Rosie sobbing as she tried to answer. By her despairing response he knew her message must be true. Jack Cornwall had found his enemy. He would take Chipper. Possibly he already had. Unless Cornwall was stopped, Seth would lose his only son.

As the thought tore through him like a knife, he dropped Rosie's hand and raced ahead. At the barn, the dance was breaking up. Women called frantically for their children to round them up and hold them close. Men were standing in clusters, forming search parties. When Seth got to the barn, Jimmy stepped out into the circle of light.

"No one can find the boy around here, Seth," he said. "We haven't seen any sign of Cornwall either."

"What do the children say?" Seth asked.

"They thought your son was playing with them, so they did. Erinn told her mother that when the music started up, she saw Chipper wander away from the others. But she lost track of him in the midst of their game." Jimmy held up a lantern. "We're going out in groups of three and four, Seth. Some of us will take the road to LeBlanc's Mill, and the rest will head for Laski's Station. Sure Cornwall can't have gotten far."

Seth agreed to the plan, and he watched as the men rode off into the darkness. The women bustled their children into the wagons. Seth went from child to child, asking what each one remembered about the evening. Chipper had wandered away. But where?

"Why would he have left the others in the middle of a game?" Seth asked Rosie when she appeared at his elbow. "The music and dancing had just started up. Where would he have gone?"

"You went down to the creek at the same time," Rosie said. "Maybe he followed you. Why did you leave?"

Seth rubbed a hand around the back of his neck. He could see that the question in her brown eyes was an honest one. "I wanted to think," he said finally.

"In the middle of a barn dance? Seth, you're the host. You should have stayed among the company. If you had been there, Jack Cornwall wouldn't have been nearly so bold. The first thing I knew, he had me by the arm and was asking all about Chipper."

"The first thing *I* knew, you were dancing with Rolf Rustemeyer. Why didn't you ask your beau for help with Cornwall?"

Rosie's cheeks flushed a brighter pink. "Rolf didn't have any idea who that man was. He doesn't speak English well enough to understand."

"He must have spoken well enough to ask you to dance." Seth spat the words and turned away from her. Rosie didn't deserve his wrath, even though she was chastising him for not being in the barn when Cornwall appeared. She blamed him for Chipper's disappearance.

And he blamed himself. He had known good and well that Cornwall was lurking. Searching for him. Intending to steal the boy. Why had Seth relaxed his guard for a minute?

Self-loathing tore at his gut. He could almost hear his father's words provoking him. *How could you be so stupid? You're no good. . . .*

"No!" Seth shouted as he ran down the path toward the creek. *I'm better than that. I'm better than you were. I'd never walk out on my family. I'd never abandon my son. I love my son. I love Chipper!*

"God!" He stumbled over a tree root and fell to his knees. Clutching handfuls of the moist, reedy river grass, he shook his head. "God, please help me find him. Show me where he is!"

He climbed to his feet again and continued down the creek bank, peering into the darkness, calling his son's name. In all the confusion, he hadn't remembered his rifle. If he ran into Jack Cornwall, he would need to be armed. Let the man so much as touch Chipper, and Seth would blow his head off.

No. Rosie had said that wasn't the way. No violence.

Then how was he supposed to win his son? Cornwall would never stop pursuing Chipper. Seth would have to kill the man to stop him.

Kill Mary's brother? Murder her beloved Jack? No, he couldn't do that.

God, help me! Seth's heart cried out again and again as he wandered the creek bank calling his son's name. In response he heard nothing but the quiet murmurs of the prairie. An owl hooted. A raccoon scurried from the water's edge. Crickets stopped their chirping the moment they sensed his footfall. The moon rose in the black velvet sky, but even its bright light revealed nothing but clumps of bluestem grass and the trunks of cottonwood trees. It was no good. The boy was gone, and Seth knew he would have to ride after his son and the man who had stolen him away.

He turned back toward the soddy. By the time he reached the barn again, most of the families had packed up and driven away. Jimmy and some of the others were still searching the roads, Sheena told him as she herded her children over the bridge. The rest of the men had given up the hunt. The yard was empty of wagons. The fire had been reduced to ashes.

Rosie moved out of the shadows into the moonlight. Her bun had come down, and the hem of her blue gingham dress was muddy. He could tell she had been crying.

"Any sign of him?" she asked.

He shook his head. "I'll ride out at dawn. Cornwall will be heading for the Missouri border. After the war, the family was planning to move to the southeast part of the state. Jack's father owns a little plot of ground near Cape Girardeau. At least I'll know where to start looking."

"You'll be going after him then?"

"He's my son."

She covered her mouth to stop the sob that welled up. "I'll stay here. I'll tend the homestead until you come back."

"I may be gone for months. You go on over to Rustemeyer's place where he can look after you. He'll find a preacher somewhere. You'd be better off getting married to him early in the summer when you can do him some good in the fields."

"Marry Rolf . . . but . . ." She knotted her fingers. "But . . . but you'll want me to hoe your fields, won't you? What about your crops?"

"If need be, I'll start over again next year."

"You won't have seed money." She followed him into the barn. "If you don't bring in a harvest this fall, you won't have the money to outfit yourself for next spring. And you'll need cash to travel. Take the bridge tolls, Seth. Rolf and Jimmy won't mind."

"All right. I'll take my share. Divide the rest between the other two, but keep back some for yourself. You earned it." Seth studied the interior of his barn and shook his head. Too bad Cornwall had spoiled the party. "Where did you move my saddle?" he said as he walked toward the back of the barn. "I'll need to take both mules so I can travel faster. Did you get a look at what Cornwall was riding? Did he have a horse?"

"I didn't see him come into the barn. I just turned around and there he was." Still searching Seth's face, she stopped beside the large chest in which she stored the supplies she traded for bridge tolls. He could tell she was struggling hard to hold back her tears. "You must take some blankets, and there's a little molasses. . . . Seth, before you go, I want you to know . . . I didn't intend to dance the first dance with Rolf. I wanted to dance with you. But . . . but he pulled me into the barn—"

"Never mind about what happened." He looked into her brown eyes, wondering if this was the last time he would see her, trying to memorize those beautiful eyes and sweet lips. "You did right to organize the search and come after me."

"But I want you to understand. It's not Rolf. It's you. It's you that I . . . that I care about. I never meant to—"

"Don't talk about it, Rosie. Rustemeyer's a good man. You'll be happy with him. He'll take care of you."

"I know he would, but—"

"That's how it has to be. There can't be anything else. I need to go, Rosie. Do you have any ammunition left?" Seth looked down into the open storage chest.

There lay Chipper. Huddled into a ball. His cheek nestled against a wool blanket. Sound asleep.

"Chipper! Chipper, you little rascal!" With a groan of disbelief, Seth scooped the drowsy boy up in his arms and hugged him tightly. "Thank God! Thank God, you're here!"

"Oh, sweetheart!" Rosie threw her arms around both of them. "We were so worried about you. We couldn't find you."

"Really?" Chipper blinked sleepily and rubbed a little fist in his eye. "Were you lookin' for me again?" He yawned, then he drew back and stared solemnly at his father. "Are you mad at me? Are you gonna yell an' scold me?"

Seth nestled his cheek against his son's warm skin. "No, no," he murmured, trying to dam the emotion that welled like a fountain in his heart. "Chipper, you had me so worried, son. I walked up the creek all the way to Rustemeyer's place looking for you."

"You did?" A smile crossed the boy's mouth. "An' I was right here in the blankets all along. I guess I fooled you, huh?"

"I reckon you did."

Seth sensed that Rosie had moved away, and he missed her presence. Yet at this moment he wanted nothing more than to hold his son. Hold him on and on. He lowered the lid on the storage chest and sat down, cradling the boy against his chest. "I don't want to lose you, Chipper," he murmured. "You're my only son."

"I wasn't lost. I was just sleepy."

"I bet you were." Seth brushed a strand of hair from his son's forehead. The baby-softness of the skin startled him. He ran a finger from the boy's brow to his cheek. Soft. So soft. How was it possible this child was his own flesh and blood?

Blue eyes that matched his own gazed up at him. "You sure you ain't mad?"

"Nope. Truth is, I'm mainly feeling real happy right now. I don't ever want to lose somebody I care about as much as I care about you. See, when I was a little boy—not too much bigger than you—my papa decided to go away on a trip. And he never came back."

"Not ever?" Chipper pondered this for a moment. His long black lashes fanned his cheeks. "Like mama did. She went away, an' she ain't never coming back."

"A little bit like that, I guess." As he ran his hand over the boy's dark silky hair, Seth turned over the comparison in his mind. Finally he decided it was accurate enough. His own father had left—run off and abandoned the family. Chipper's mother had died. But the loss was the same. The emptiness was the same. The need for a parent's love was exactly the same.

"That's why I left the other kids playing prisoner's base," Chipper said. "I heard that music, an' I got to thinkin' about my mama. She just loved to dance."

"I remember. I used to dance with her a lot."

Chipper glanced up, startled. "I forgot about that. You knew her too, didn't you?"

"I sure did. I loved her."

"Me too. I looked an' looked for her in the barn, but then I remembered all over again that she wasn't comin' back. That's when I got sad an' grumpy an' tired. So I thought about Rosie's wool blankets that she traded for bridge tolls, and I climbed into the old storage chest to listen to the violin music and think about mama. I wanted to cry where nobody would see me." Again, the blue eyes searched Seth's face. "Do you ever do that?"

Seth nodded. "Yes. I do that sometimes."

At the admission, Chipper smiled and snuggled closer into his father's arms. Seth could hardly believe the sensation. The boy's little legs curled up tight, fitting perfectly into the curve of his father's lap. A pair of matching bare feet—tiny toes peeping out from the hems of his overalls—rested on Seth's denim jeans. Tentatively, the father reached out and touched one of those little toes. How small. Amazingly small. And as perfect as a pearl.

Then his wondering gaze moved upward to the child's thin arm. Lightly scattered with pale, downy hair, the arm was propped in perfect position to admit the boy's thumb into his mouth. Was it all right for children to suck their thumbs? Seth had no idea. But something told him that a little boy whose mama had died deserved whatever comfort he could find.

Poor Chipper. Again Seth stroked his fingers through his son's soft warm hair. The scent the boy carried on his skin drew the father like the aroma of baking bread. It was the smell of little boy—of sunshine, winds, dust, green grass, and puppy dog. Two months Seth had lived near this child, and he had never come close enough to smell that smell. That wonderful smell. Seth laid his cheek on his son's head and gathered him tightly in his arms.

"I'm sorry, Chipper," he began, and then he realized he couldn't go on. "I'm sorry I—"

"It's OK." The boy laid a small hand on his father's arm and caressed the coarse dark hair in the same tender way his own arm had been stroked. "You know something?" he said. "You gots a lot of hair, Papa."

Seth gulped back the lump that threatened. *Papa.* Chipper had called him Papa. Amazing.

"You'll have a lot of hair, too, when you get bigger," he managed.

"Will I look like you when I grow up?"

"You already look like me."

"Do I?" Chipper examined Seth's face. "I don't think so. You gots little black whiskers all over your chin."

"You'll have whiskers, too."

"You reckon?"

"You're my son, aren't you?"

"That's what everybody tells me." Chipper snuggled back into the fold of his father's arms. "You know something else? I don't think you're too bad of a Yankee. I bet Gram an' Gramps just didn't know you very good."

"They didn't know me very well at all. They were scared I wouldn't make a good home for your mama and you. If things had turned out differently, I would have brought both of you out here to live."

"I don't think mama would have liked it out here too much. No mirrors."

Seth laughed at the image of Mary Cornwall attempting to dress herself without a gold-framed pier mirror. "That might have been a problem."

"There's not even a town with sidewalks where she could say hello to everybody an' show off her new dresses an' bonnets."

"Well, that's true, too."

"Now, Rosie is really different from mama. Rosie don't care about mirrors an' showin' off. She fits just right out here on the prairie."

"She sure does."

"Rosie gots lots of good ideas about things. Like bridge tolls. An' barn painting. An' cooking squirrels. An' making clothes out of grain sacks. I love Rosie a lot. Do you?"

Seth looked around, saw that Rosie had left the barn, and nodded. "I reckon she's a pretty special lady."

Chipper leaned around and looked into his father's eyes. "Maybe you ought to marry Rosie and get you an' me another good mama."

"I might just do that, Chipper," Seth said softly. But as he spoke the words, he read the pain of loss in his son's eyes. Taking a wife would bring Chipper the comforts of a mother's love. It would bring Seth the joy of marriage. But it would also bring the risk of loss. For a woman, life on the prairie meant hardship, disease, and the dangers of childbirth. Could he and Chipper bear to lose another love? Was the hope worth the risk?

And what about Chipper himself? Seth had no guarantee that he could keep his son nearby. Cornwall threatened that hope for happiness. If the man stole Chipper, life would seem empty—all but unbearable.

"How come you're always thinkin' you lost me?" Chipper piped up. "How come you always go runnin' up an' down the creek like a chicken with its head cut off? You don't let me go nowhere by myself. Not even to sleep in the old storage chest. How come?"

Seth lifted his son's chin. "You know your uncle is looking for you, Chipper. He wants to take you away with him. But I don't want you to go." He gently kissed the child's forehead. "I love you, Chipper. I love you very much."

Chipper wriggled around in his father's lap until he could slip his arms around Seth's neck. "I love you, too, Papa."

When Seth lifted his focus, he saw Rosie had returned to the barn. She was standing in the doorway, a lantern in one hand and a pitcher of milk in the other. Her brown eyes were misty as she studied the father and son.

"I thought we might as well make use of some of this food that was left behind," she said softly. "Chipper, would you like a big slice of strawberry pie before bed?"

"Strawberry pie!" The child slid off his father's lap and raced across the floor. "I was sleepy before, but now I'm hungry."

Seth stood. As he watched Rosie cutting pie and pouring milk and as he studied his son's dark head and bright, happy eyes, he knew the answer in his heart. Yes. He wanted to marry Rosie. He wanted to take the risk.

But as he approached, she leaned toward him. "Seth, Jack Cornwall was inside the soddy while we were all out searching," she whispered in his ear. "He's stolen your rifle."

CHAPTER 12

ROSIE?" Sheena's high-pitched voice rose at the end of the word. "Rooo-SIE?"

Rosie watched through the soddy's open front door as her friend came scurrying over the pontoon bridge like a mama duck with her five little ducklings in tow. Bonnet ribbons flying, Sheena waved a sheet of white paper over her head. "I've had a letter from Ireland! All the way from God's country. Rosie, where are you?"

Rosie wedged the final loaf of bread into the hot oven and pushed the door shut. The little soddy felt warm enough inside to bake bread without the oven, she thought as she mopped the back of her neck with a cool, damp handkerchief. It would be a welcome break to talk with Sheena for a few minutes—even though it was less than an hour to lunchtime and Seth would be looking forward to a meal.

"I'm here, Sheena." Wiping her hands on her apron, she stepped out of the soddy. It was almost July and not a breath of breeze stirred the still summer air. Across the prairie, the tall grass stretched out like a vast, golden-threaded blanket shimmering in the heat. The limitless surface was marred only by the small green patches that made up Seth's fields. Rosie mused that even though the cultivated acres broke the God-created symmetry of the prairie, they offered the promise of food and sustenance for his people.

As she walked toward Sheena, Rosie turned over in her mind the amazing fact that she had come to love the prairie. Every spare moment she could carve out of the day, she wandered out across the majestic plains—picking wildflowers for the dinner table, watching the antelope graze, marveling at the glorious sky that rolled overhead in waves of depthless blue. The thought of ever returning to the confines of a brick orphanage, high limestone walls, and air darkened by smoke made her shudder. Yet she had made up her mind to obey God's direction, no matter where he led.

"It's just as I'd hoped," Sheena called, puffing up the last few yards to the soddy's front yard. "Better than I'd dreamed! I've had a letter from Caitrin. You know my little sister? My beauty? My sweet, precious Caitie?"

"Yes, you've told me about Caitrin," Rosie said, dragging a bench into the scant shade of the little soddy's overhanging roof. "Sit down and give me all the news."

"Better yet, I'll read it to you!" Sheena shooed the children off to find Chipper in the fields. Then she set a pair of spectacles on her nose, unfolded the letter, and spread it across her lap. "Sure it's taken me all morning to make sense of the writing, but I believe I have it. Listen to this." She began to read in a slow, halting voice. "'My dearest Sheena, All is well with the family and me. How are you? How is Jimmy? How are all the wee ones?'"

Here Sheena paused and took off her spectacles. "Caitie's never met any of them, you know. Not even Erinn, and she's already eight years old. Can you imagine? I've not clapped eyes on my dear Caitrin for more than eight years."

"I know you've missed her terribly."

"Haven't I?" Sheena shook her head and went back to the letter. "'I have made up my mind . . . not to wed Seamus Sweeney—'" Again Sheena stopped reading. "Seamus Sweeney is a fisherman's son and a rotter, if I do say so myself," she confided. Her green eyes flashed. "I never knew what Caitie saw in him. Of course, it was our papa who set the whole thing up, so he did. Papa is the fishmonger in our town, and he thought it would make a good partnership to join with the Sweeney family in business and in marriage. You know, Caitie's always been such a good girl, Rosie. She's always done everything she was told, so she has. I feared she would marry that *sherral*, even if she didn't want to. But now she hasn't after all!"

"Good for Caitrin."

"So you say, but can you imagine what my papa thinks about this? Sure, he'll be in great kinks. At any rate, I'll read again. Now where was I? Oh, yes. 'Dearest Sheena, I am . . . com-coming . . . to see you.' There you have it! She's coming to see me, Rosie! Coming here—to America. Can you credit it? I'm sure I can't. Listen to this. 'I shall see you in . . . August.' Now isn't that what it says, Rosie? August?"

Rosie leaned over Sheena's shoulder and studied the letter. For the difficulty her friend was having in reading it, Rosie had expected a poorly written document. Instead, the handwriting was neat, the words crisp, the message carefully spelled out.

"Yes, it's August," Rosie said, reading quickly through the message. "Caitrin's coming to Kansas at the start of the month, and she wonders if there might be a teaching position anywhere near you."

"Is that what she's written? Teaching. Well, I couldn't make out that word at all. *Teaching*. Why would you put an *a* in a word like that, Rosie? Sure it ought to have a double *e* by all rights. You know I never went to school but a year or two. But Caitie—well, she's been all the way through, so she has. She's very smart. Yes, indeed. Our Caitrin is a well-rounded young lady. I suppose she believes she could earn wages as a teacher in America."

Rosie considered the situation for a moment. "You have five children, Sheena. As you said, Erinn's already eight years old, and

Will is six. Chipper's five. Then there are the youngest of the Rippeto children. Mr. and Mrs. LeBlanc have all those daughters, too. Casimir Laski might even want to send his son."

"Sure, the boy is seventeen!"

"But he can't read a word. At the start of the barn dance, I handed him a list of the guests and asked him to mark off who had come. He couldn't even read his own name, Sheena. How will he make anything of himself without an education?"

"A man doesn't need to know how to read and write to plow a field. My Jimmy couldn't spell his name if he tried. But it's all the same to me. I love him anyway." She studied the letter for a moment. "Still, it would be wonderful if our Caitie could teach the children in the winter months, wouldn't it, Rosie?"

"Yes, it would. It sounds like she needs some kind of work to do now that she's not going to marry."

"Oh, she'll marry. Caitie's a fine, beautiful girl, so she is. She was only fourteen when I left Ireland, but she's twenty-two now and well into the age where she ought to find a husband. Besides that, she's a stunning lass. Red hair in grand big curls falling all over the place. And such eyes. Sure, you never saw such pretty green eyes in all your days. I have no doubt the young farmers will scramble to court Caitie the moment she gets here. She won't have any trouble finding a husband. But no . . . no, I think teaching would be a nice diversion for her. I believe I'll send a message to the Rippeto and LeBlanc families. Do you suppose Seth would let us use his barn for the school?"

Rosie shifted on the rough-hewn bench. The idea of a red-haired, green-eyed beauty charming Seth Hunter into marriage had caused her an uncomfortable pang. Even though Seth had not given many hints as to his feelings about her, Rosie had sensed that things between them had begun to change—soften—ever since the night of the barn dance.

Now Sheena wanted her beautiful red-haired sister to use Seth's barn as a schoolhouse? To see him every day? The barn was Rosie's home, her only place of solitude, her haven of rest. . . .

"Sure you won't be needing the barn by winter, will you?" Sheena asked. "You've told me you might well be wedded to Rolf Rustemeyer by that time. And if you don't marry the German, Seth means to cart you back to Kansas City—not that I'd want you to go, of course. But the barn would be free, wouldn't it?"

"Well, the cows—"

"Caitie could teach the children in the loft! There's lots of room up in the loft, so there is. Oh, Rosie, I cannot wait for you to meet my little Caitie. She's the prettiest thing! A fair flower! I shall have to plan a party to welcome her. Glory be, that reminds me of the second bit of news. There's to be a picnic on the Fourth of July. An Independence Day celebration—and it's hardly a week away. LeBlanc is hosting it, so he is. His wife is planning to hold a box-lunch auction for all the unmarried girls. You know the LeBlancs have all those pretty daughters. I'm sure the missus is hoping to hook a husband or two at the picnic. But the box-lunch auction will include you, too! And won't you be in demand with all the young farmers? Sure you will! Now if Caitie were here, there'd be a fair brawl over her, so there would. I'm half glad she isn't, aren't you?"

Rosie nodded, her mental image of the young green-eyed Caitrin transforming moment by moment into the most glorious creature who ever walked the earth.

"The money is going to a very good cause," Sheena explained. "LeBlanc wants to put up a church, so he does. If we can raise enough to buy the lumber, perhaps the men will build it in the fall."

"A church!" Rosie cried. "But where? Will it be beside the mill?"

"No, no. LeBlanc owns only the land his mill is sitting on and the water rights. It's not a proper homestead. No, he's asking someone else to donate an acre or two for the church. Sure, I'm going to press my Jimmy for it. Wouldn't that be wonderful? A church on our own homestead. Perhaps we'd even have a minister for it one day."

Rosie couldn't imagine the reticent Jimmy O'Toole wanting a church full of people on his property. But if Sheena made her case forcefully enough, it could happen. A church . . . with hymns and preaching and evening socials. The thought of it fairly transported Rosie.

"You're in a dream world," Sheena said, elbowing her friend as they sat together. "What do you think of LeBlanc's proposal? Our very own church, right out here on the prairie."

"It would be wonderful, Sheena. And with all the people passing through, the minister could touch so many lives."

"Aye, the traffic across our bridge has nearly doubled by my count."

"*More* than doubled in the last two weeks." Rosie glanced across the fields to see if Seth was coming. Then she leaned closer to her friend. "The storage chest in the barn is already full again, and I've traded for two more big trunks. Every time someone wants to trade instead of pay the toll, I have to haul everything out and set it all up. I'd love to leave the merchandise out for view—put up pretty displays and even build counters. But I don't want to worry Seth. He's so concerned about Jack Cornwall showing up again, and I don't want him to think my trading post would draw trouble."

"Your trading post, is it?"

Rosie shrugged. "Sheena, I could put a stop to it all. And I would—if I thought this might harm Seth or Chipper in any way. But I-I'm afraid I will have to go away one day, and I want to leave them with something. I know Seth doesn't really like my trading. But it's what I have to give. If I could get a post office commission, I'd have so much traffic I would have to put up a hotel."

"Great ghosts, that reminds me!" Sheena tugged a second letter from her pocket. "LeBlanc brought this along with my letter from

Caitie the last time he picked up the mail in Topeka. Look, it's for you, isn't it?"

Rosie stared at the travel-stained white envelope. "It's from the Christian Home. It's from Mrs. Jameson."

"Well, stop casting sheep's eyes at the thing and read it."

The letter was Rosie's first contact with the place where she had lived so many years. They had been years of struggle, loneliness, and an aching hunger for love. Half of her heart commanded her to pitch the letter into the stove and burn it up. Destroy that part of her life forever and look forward. Only forward.

But those years had been good ones, too. She had learned about her heavenly Father. She had gone to school and read the fairy tale book. She had made her way in a world where only the toughest survived.

Taking a deep breath, she slit open the envelope. "'Dear Miss Mills,'" she read aloud. It was Mrs. Jameson's handwriting. "'Thank you for the iron skillet. By this generous gift, I see you are making something of yourself in the world. I trust that in your efforts to improve yourself you have not strayed from the straight and narrow path—'"

"What does she mean by that?" Sheena cut in. "Does she think you earned the money for the skillet in some low manner?"

"Mrs. Jameson is very strict. She wants the best for me." Rosie read again. "'I trust that in your efforts to improve yourself you have not strayed from the straight and narrow path that was paved for you at the Christian Home for Orphans and Foundlings. I must tell you that your presence is sorely missed.'" Rosie lifted her head. "They miss me, Sheena!"

"Of course they do. You're a wonder, you are."

Rosie began to read again. "'Your presence is sorely missed. The main cook quit her position, and you are needed to fill in, along with Jenny and Pearl. I am counting on your return in the fall, as Mr. Hunter assured me. I do not like to think that we at the Home have given you all these years of care and sustenance only to have you walk away from us in a time of need.'"

"Of all the—!"

"'If you manage to earn any money while you are away,'" Rosie read on, "'I expect you to bring it when you come. We need a new washtub. Sincerely, Mrs. Jameson.'"

"Ooo, I should like to get my hands around her neck!" Sheena exclaimed, demonstrating just what she would do to the orphanage director. "She wants your money for a new washtub, does she? She expects you to race back to that dreadful place just because she gave you a bed and a little food all those years? Well, I've news for her. You deserve a life better than that, so you do. You're a good girl, a hardworking girl, a fine Christian girl. You're going to marry Rolf Rustemeyer and live in his soddy and have yourself a home and a family. And that's that." She clapped her hands over her knees. "You won't give that letter another thought, will you, Rosie? Rosie?"

Rosie stared down at the sheet of white paper. "Sheena, Mrs. Jameson is right. They do need me at the Home. I did run off and leave them in a difficult position. From the moment we drove away from Kansas City in Seth's wagon, I sensed I had been willful and selfish. I certainly didn't pray about coming out to the prairie before I took the first step, and I'm not sure I've done a bit of real good for the Lord since I've been here."

"Of course you have! You're the best cook, the most caring—"

"And I don't think I want to marry Rolf Rustemeyer after all."

"Really, now? I can't say I'm surprised, though I thought you had your mind made up on it. What about Seth then? You know I've wanted you to marry him all along."

"Sheena, I care about Seth. Truly I do."

"You love him."

"Maybe I do. But he loves his wife."

"She's dead!"

"I know that, but it doesn't make any difference to Seth. No woman can take his wife's place. I think he's afraid."

"Afraid of what?"

"Afraid to let someone into his life in that way again. He was hurt so badly by what happened. Now all he can think about is keeping Chipper safe from Jack Cornwall and trying to get his crops in. Sheena, I have to accept the truth that Seth is never going to love me. He's never going to marry me. And my heart . . . my heart doesn't want to marry Rolf Rustemeyer."

"Your heart? I thought you said the heart had nothing to do with marriage. Didn't you tell me that all a woman needed to do was find a good, hardworking, honest man?"

Rosie shrugged. "I think . . . I think I might have been wrong. There may be more to it than that. I've come to believe there's a certain feeling people sometimes have. It's like in Mrs. Jameson's fairy tale book when the story says, 'The prince took Cinderella in his arms and began to dance with her. The rest of the evening, he had eyes only for the beautiful, mysterious woman.' And in Beauty and the Beast: 'though she knew he was outwardly a beast, she saw the good in his heart, and her own heart beat the faster for it.' You know, Sheena, I always thought eyes gazing at each other and hearts beating too fast were just pretend. Make-believe stories for children. But now I'm not so sure."

"Who taught you differently, Rosie?" Sheena took her hand. "Was it Seth?"

"It wasn't Rolf, I can tell you that." She let out a deep sigh. "It's all beyond me. God knows I'd best be back at the Home, where I'm certain of what I'm supposed to be doing and I can't get myself into any greater trouble than climbing trees."

"Does God know that? How can you be so sure?"

"He's been watching what a poor job I'm doing out here. Oh Sheena, I'm such a wreck." Rosie bent over on the bench and buried her face in her hands. "I do love Seth," she whispered. "I love him so much I can hardly stand it. I love Chipper, and I want to try to be a mother to him. I want to marry Seth and feel his strong arms holding me close. I want to know what it's like to kiss . . . to kiss him. Oh, Sheena, this is just awful."

"Fräulein!" Rolf's booming voice brought Rosie upright in an instant. At the edge of the yard, the big blond German was climbing down from his mule. "Happy lunschtime to you!"

"Hello, Rolf." She blotted her cheeks with the corner of her apron. "How are you today?"

"I *komme* eaten vit you!"

"The bread!" Rosie gasped. She hadn't given a thought to the midday meal since Sheena came traipsing over the bridge. A glance out to the fields confirmed that Seth, Chipper, and all five O'Tooles were trudging toward the soddy. "The bread is probably burned to a cinder. All they'll have for lunch is ashes. Oh Sheena!"

"Go on then, Cinderella. I'll take my wee *brablins* home with me whilst you feed your two Prince Charmings." Sheena gave her friend a squeeze. "You must talk to God about this matter of your love for Seth. He'll find you a way through it."

"Thank you, Sheena," Rosie said as she left the bench and made for the soddy door.

Rolf caught her hand just as she stepped inside. "Fräulein, I vill *mein* money haf. Dollars."

"Rolf, my bread is burning. I don't have time to figure out what you're trying to say." She resorted to Seth's habit of shouting at the German. "The . . . bread . . . is . . . burning!"

"Dollars," he repeated. "Britsch money of Hunter, O'Toole, *und* Rustemeyer. You gif me? *Ja*, you gif to me *mein* money?"

"You'll have to wait, Rolf. I must get my bread." Rosie pulled away from him and hurried into the soddy to find black smoke billowing from the oven door. Her bread was ruined. Ruined! There would be nothing for lunch but a few slices of cold salt pork. Everything was a mess. Rolf wanted his money. Sheena's entrancing sister was coming to Kansas. Jack Cornwall was trying to steal Chipper. And Seth . . . oh, she had confessed out loud that she loved Seth. Now it was in the open, and she felt as confused and upset as though a hive of bees had taken up residence in her stomach.

"Rosie?"

She whirled around, the smoking lump of bread clamped in a hot pad. Seth stood in the doorway, a tall silhouette framed by golden noon sunlight. "Rosie, are you all right?"

"No! No, I'm not all right." She thunked the loaf pan on the table and marched toward him through the smoky haze. "You want me to marry Rolf. Rolf wants his money. Sheena's beautiful sister is coming. Cornwall is trying to take Chipper away. Mrs. Jameson needs a new washtub! And worst of all . . . I-I've burned my bread!"

At that, she burst past him and ran right out the front door. She ran by Sheena and Rolf and Chipper and all the gaping little O'Tooles. She ran all the way down to the creek, halfway to Rustemeyer's homestead, and straight to the biggest, tallest tree she could find.

Then she yanked off her apron, kicked off her shoes, and began to climb. Straight up. Up to the very highest branches of the cottonwood tree. And there she sat—thinking, praying, even crying a little—until the sun sank below the prairie. She didn't go down for lunch. Not even for supper. Seth had cooked meals before she came, she reasoned. He could do it again. She needed time to put her world back in order.

When everything seemed quiet at the homestead, she finally returned to the barn. She climbed the ladder into the loft to get ready for bed. And Seth walked in to check on her.

"Are you there?" he asked, holding up the lantern.

"Yes," she said.

"Did you talk to God up in the tree?"

"Yes." She could see him through the chinks in the floorboards, though she knew he couldn't see her. It hardly mattered. Just the sight of him brought everything back in a rush. And she knew that all her hours in the cottonwood tree had been for nothing.

"Did you and God get everything worked out?" Seth asked.

"No."

"Do you want to talk to me about anything?"

"No."

He fell silent for several minutes, and she used the time to study him. It was all as true as she had feared. He was handsome and wonderful and kind. Her heart beat helter-skelter every time she looked into his blue eyes. Her thoughts, dreams, hopes were filled with him. She loved Seth. Loved him in the strongest possible way she could ever imagine. And she could do nothing about it. Nothing.

"Good night, then, Miss Mills," he called up.

"Good night, Mr. Hunter."

Rosie was acting mighty strange, Seth mused as he loaded a stack of blankets into his wagon on a bright Independence Day morning. She wouldn't look at him. Would hardly talk to him. He had asked her if there was a problem. But she always got a look on her face like a big grizzly bear was after her. She sort of shrank inside herself and told him she just couldn't talk about it.

After a while, Seth had decided it must be one of two things. Either she was upset that Rolf had taken his part of the bridge money, or she had gotten worried about going back to the orphanage.

He had spotted the letter lying on the ground that day after she burned the bread and ran off to climb the tree. He had read the letter, even though it wasn't his business, so he knew that the Jameson woman wanted Rosie back. Or maybe she just wanted a new washtub.

On the other hand, Rosie's consternation could have something to do with Sheena's little sister coming out to the prairie to teach school. Maybe Rosie was worried about having to give up the loft. Seth knew she was pretty attached to her little room. She'd decorated it with flowers and bows and little things she found out on the prairie. He wasn't about to make her give up her bedroom, but every time he tried to reassure her, she told him she had something to do. He was beginning to think lassoing a dust devil would be easier than talking to Rosie Cotton Mills.

"Are they going to have races at the picnic, Papa?" Chipper asked, tugging on his father's pant leg. "Three-legged races and sack races?"

"I'm not sure, son. We'll find out when we get to the mill."

"Can we bring Stubby with us? He wants to come. Please, Papa?"

Seth glanced down at the dog. Long-legged, lanky, and growing about an inch a day, the mutt certainly belied his name. His feet were the size of saucers, and his wagging tail had become a downright hazard. Seth had the feeling Stubby might end up the approximate height and weight of a small bear.

"Sure, we'll take Stubby," he replied, lifting the boy into the wagon. "Where's Rosie?"

"In the barn. She's fixing up her box lunch."

"She already packed the lunch." Seth glanced down at the large basket with its cheerful red and white checkered cloth. Rosie must be confused. Lately, she had been doing absentminded things like that a lot. Put salt in the rhubarb pie instead of sugar. Dropped a sack of beans all over the floor. Pulled up a whole row of radish sprouts and left the weeds to grow in their place.

"Naw, *this* ain't Rosie's box lunch," Chipper said, peeking into the basket. "This lunch is for us. You an' me. Rosie gots her own."

"What for?"

"Don'tcha know? Whoever pays the most for Rosie's lunch gets to eat with her."

"Well now, what kind of a crazy idea is that? She doesn't need to make money that way. She's already got all those bridge tolls. And the barn is beginning to look like a bona fide mercantile. Why would she need to sell her picnic lunch?"

"It's for the church, Papa. The money goes to the new church. Ain't you heard about it? Sheena's been telling everybody." His blue eyes brightened suddenly. "There's Rosie! Tell Papa about the auction, Rosie. He don't know a thing about it."

Seth turned, and for the second time that summer, his breath dammed up and his heart flopped over in his chest. Pink. Rosie was pink! She came strolling out of the barn, her dress a billowing, bouncing butterfly of pink calico. Tucks and ruffles and bits of lace and ribbons dangled everywhere. A frill of white eyelet petticoat peeked out from the hem. A fringed cotton shawl draped over her shoulders. She had piled her hair up on her head and pinned white ox-eye daisies into the loops and curls. And in her arms she carried a small woven basket covered with a matching pink calico cloth.

"It's a box-lunch auction," she said, setting the basket into the wagon. "Mr. LeBlanc is hoping to raise enough money to build a church."

Tongue-tied as a gigged frog, Seth helped Rosie onto the wagon bench, then climbed up beside her. Where had she gotten the dress? Had she done her hair up by herself? And how come she smelled so good? Half stupefied, he flicked the reins and set his mules on the trail for the five-mile drive to the mill. His hands felt clammy. He wasn't even sure he could remember the way.

"I bet all the men are gonna put down money for Rosie's lunch," Chipper said. "She's the best cook around."

"Why thank you, Chipper," Rosie said. "I just hope we can bring in something to help with the new church."

"You're gonna put down money, aren't you, Papa? You're gonna try to eat lunch with Rosie, aren't you?"

"Your papa eats lunch with me every day," she reminded him.

"Breakfast and supper, too. I'm afraid he wouldn't find it very exciting."

Exciting? Seth was feeling something closer to panic as he glanced at the beautiful woman beside him. He had looked forward to this day ever since he'd heard about the picnic. Maybe he would finally have the chance to talk to Rosie a little. Possibly even collect that dance she owed him.

And now? Now he would have to be the highest bidder just to eat lunch with her. A cold sweat broke out down his back as he thought of the leather wallet he kept in his pocket. He had brought a little money in the expectation there might be lemonade for sale, or ice cream. What did he have on him—twenty-five cents? Fifty?

"You want to eat lunch with Rosie, don't you, Papa?" Chipper asked. "Look how pretty she is. All in pink. You won't let somebody else get her, will you? Somebody like Mr. Rustemeyer?"

"Chipper!" Rosie said with a laugh. "Leave your papa alone. I've packed you both a big lunch of fried chicken and hard-boiled eggs. It doesn't matter to your papa who eats with me today."

Seth clenched his jaw. It did matter. It mattered a lot. How much was Rustemeyer likely to bid? Seth stiffened. The big German had emptied his third of the savings. And now Seth understood why.

CHAPTER 13

FOR the first time in her life, Rosie felt pretty. Her hair looked just right for an Independence Day picnic. She had spent hours raveling and knotting threads on a white flour-sack shawl to make a fringe. And the dress Sheena had let her borrow could not have been more perfect. Oh, she'd had to take in the side seams a few inches, and the hem was so short that her petticoat kept peeking out, but truly she felt just like Cinderella at the ball.

In fact, it appeared many of the young homesteaders at the picnic had decided to vie for the role of Prince Charming. If Rosie chanced to sit on the swing that Mr. LeBlanc had hung from an oak branch, five men appeared in a cluster to ask for the privilege of pushing her. If Rosie walked toward the front steps of the LeBlanc house, three men were at her side to escort her up to the porch. If she commented on the sunny day, four umbrellas shot up to shade her. If she mentioned a slight thirst, six glasses of lemonade were thrust in her direction. She felt silly and flattered and, most of all, amazed. Could a pink dress do all that? Were these men desperate to find eligible single women? Or did she actually look as pretty as she felt?

"Sure, you're the belle of the ball," Sheena whispered as Rosie placed her box lunch on the long table set up for the auction. "I wager you'll earn the most money for the new church, so you will."

"I hope I can help. But as for earning the most money—haven't you noticed Yvonne LeBlanc? She's lovely. And don't forget Maria Rippeto."

"Aye, they'll win a few bids, I'm sure. All for the good of the church. But who have you cast your eye on, Rosie? Is there a man you'd especially favor to win the privilege of your company? I hear Gabriel Chavez has been speaking favorably about you. He's a good-looking man, though I understand his farm is very rocky."

Rosie studied the dark-haired immigrant from Mexico. Mr. Chavez was indeed a dashing fellow. So were several of the other young homesteaders. But all morning Rosie had been conscious of one man in particular. Seth Hunter.

Seth remained oblivious to Rosie's attentions. Concerned that Jack Cornwall might use this public gathering for another kidnapping attempt, he kept his concentration on Chipper. He had borrowed a pistol from Jimmy O'Toole. He had mentioned to a few other men to keep an eye out for trouble. And he had spent every moment of the morning with his son.

Father and son ran together in the sack race and the three-legged race. They even tried the wheelbarrow race—though Chipper collapsed so many times that Seth finally scooped up his son and dashed the rest of the way to the finish line. They were disqualified, of course, but everyone cheered as Chipper gave his papa a noisy kiss on the cheek. Only once or twice did Rosie catch Seth looking at her. And then he averted his eyes so quickly she wondered if she'd been mistaken.

"It's auction time, messieurs, mesdemoiselles!" Mr. LeBlanc called out when it was nearly noon. "Everybody gather around."

Instantly the whole crowd moved toward the long table where seven pretty baskets sat in a row. The four eligible LeBlanc daughters and Rosie stood in a line to wait their turns. Mrs. Violet Hudson made the sixth contestant. A widow with three children and a baby on the way, she was struggling to hold onto her homestead after her husband's death. The seventh basket belonged to Maria Rippeto, a black-haired beauty with flashing eyes who was reputed to be a terrible cook.

The bidding began with the LeBlanc girls, and as Rosie waited her turn, she searched the crowd for Seth. *Please. Oh, please. Where are you, Seth?* She considered praying over the matter and decided such a small thing wasn't worth God's attention. Then she remembered her Father was interested in every part of her life, and she began to lift up such fervent prayers that Sheena had to caution her to stop muttering out loud or everyone would think she had gone around the bend.

Before long, the proposed community church could boast twelve dollars and sixty-five cents in its building fund, and all the eligible LeBlanc daughters had earned themselves company for lunch. Rosie was next in line. She stepped up behind her basket and looked out over the crowd. Seth and Chipper were sitting at the back of the gathering, their matching blue eyes pinned on her. She took a deep breath. *Please, dear God. Please give him courage. Please let him make an offer for me. Just the smallest offer. That's all I need.*

"What am I bid for the pleasure of taking lunch with Miss Rosie Mills?" Mr. LeBlanc called out. "I understand she is a fine cook. And very pretty, too. Who will start with ten cents? There. Mr. Williams bids ten cents. Do I hear fifteen? All right then. Mr. Hill has fifteen cents. How about twenty? Twenty?"

"Twenty-five cents," Seth called out.

Rosie's heart leaped into her throat. A whole quarter! *Thank you, Father!*

"I hear twenty-five cents from Mr. Hunter. Do I hear thirty?"

"Thirty," Mr. Hill called.

"Forty," Seth answered back.

"Fifty," two other men said simultaneously.

"Seventy-five cents," Seth called out.

For a moment, all was silent. "Eighty cents!" Mr. Hill shouted.

"One dollar!" Mr. Chavez hollered back.

Rosie stood numbly as the price of her lunch box went up and up. One fifty. Two dollars. Two seventy-five. Seth and Chipper picked up their basket and walked away with Stubby. In the deep shade of a pine tree, they spread out the red checkered cloth and began to sort through the pieces of fried chicken Rosie had cooked early that morning. Her eyes filled with tears. Three dollars. Three twenty-five. Four dollars. Five dollars.

"Five seventy-five!" Mr. LeBlanc called out. "Mr. Hill has offered five dollars and seventy-five cents for Miss Mills's lunch box. Do I hear six dollars?"

"Ten dollars," Rolf Rustemeyer boomed, coming to his feet. "I gif ten dollars for lunsch of Fräulein Mills. Fery goot lunsch. Tank you."

The crowd sat in stunned silence as Rolf walked up to the table, hooked one beefy arm through the handle of Rosie's picnic basket and gave her a curt bow. "*Ja*, Fräulein Mills? You eaten lunsch vit me?"

Rosie cast a last look at Seth and Chipper and nodded. "Thank you, Mr. Rustemeyer. The church will be very grateful for your donation."

Her heart aching, Rosie shook out a blanket and spread the lunch under a shady tree. Rolf tucked a napkin into the collar of his blue work shirt and beamed at her. She did her best to smile in return. *Is this what you want from me, Father? Do you want me to learn to love Rolf? Is this your plan?*

"Was you maken?" Rolf asked, peering into the basket. "Chicken? Fery goot. *Ist* goot, *ja?* You eaten togedder vit me?"

"It's very nice."

After she murmured a brief prayer of thanks, Rosie filled the two plates with fried chicken, boiled eggs, and fresh strawberries. Rolf took off his boots and crossed his legs. One big toe poked through his worn sock, and Rosie felt her heart soften toward him. Poor

Rolf. He needed looking after. And who better for it than a woman who longed for a home and a husband?

"Fery goot chicken," he said around a mouthful. "I zo hoppy to eaten vit you."

"It's a pleasure." Rosie realized she didn't have much else to say to Rolf. After all, how many times could he tell her that he liked her cooking? She glanced at Seth. He and Chipper were getting up from their blanket, their attention trained on the auction table.

"Mrs. Hudson has made a fine lunch of ham sandwiches and potato salad," Mr. LeBlanc was saying. "Now who'll start the bidding? Can we start with ten cents? . . . Do I hear ten? . . . Well, how about five?"

"Ten!" Seth called out.

"I hear ten cents from Seth Hunter. Do I hear fifteen? . . . Come on boys, this is for the church."

Violet Hudson, a small woman with light brown hair and big olive eyes, stared bravely out at the crowd. The swell of her stomach lifted the front hem of her dress so that her worn-out boots and darned stockings showed. Seth and Chipper paused at the back of the gathering. "Fifteen cents," Seth said.

"You can't bid against yourself, Mr. Hunter," LeBlanc said. "All right, we've got fifteen. Do I hear twenty?"

"Twenty," Seth said.

"Twenty cents. Do I hear twenty-five?"

"I bid fifty cents," Seth said.

Everyone laughed, even Violet Hudson, whose pale cheeks had flushed to a bright scarlet. LeBlanc declared the bid a winner, and Seth marched forward to take his prize. Rosie watched as the delighted woman picked up her basket and handed it to Chipper. The little boy grinned.

"I vill *ein Haus* builden," Rolf said, tapping Rosie on the arm. "Vit britsch money."

"A house? You're going to build a house?" Her heart sank as

Violet, her three children, Chipper, and Seth gathered in a circle to eat lunch. "You already have a house, Rolf. Don't you?"

"*Ja, ja, ja.* But I vill *ein* voot *Haus* builden."

"Voot?" Rosie shook her head. "What do you mean? What's a voot house?"

"Voot. From trees."

"Wood!"

"*Ja, ja, ja.*" He laughed. "You liken voot *Haus*, fräulein?"

"Yes, I suppose so. I don't mind our soddy, though." She looked over her shoulder. Seth and Violet were chuckling about something. Violet rubbed Stubby's ears. "We've been very happy."

"*Ja?* You vill be hoppy togedder vit me?"

"You and me?" Rosie focused on Rolf again. "I'm having a lovely time now. Thank you for buying my lunch."

"You vill lif in *meinem* voot *Haus?* Cooken, vaschen clothes, maken *Garten* grow?"

"Live in your house?" At the sudden change of tone in Rolf's questioning, Rosie felt nervousness prickle up her spine. She fanned herself. "Well . . . I-I don't know exactly what you mean."

"*Ja? Ist* goot?"

"I don't know, Rolf. I mean, when would your wood house be built?"

"Vinter."

"There's the problem then. I have to go back to Kansas City by wintertime. I'm very sorry."

"*Nein, nein.* You *kommst* vit me. You helpen me."

Rosie felt so hot she was sure the daisies in her hair would start dropping petals any moment. Was this a marriage proposal? Did Rolf actually want her to become his wife and move into his house? *No, dear Lord. Please not this. Not now.*

"You want me to work for you?" she asked. "For room and board? Like I work for Seth?"

"*Ja, ja.*" He nodded. Then, seeming to realize the significance of her question, he shook his head. "*Nein!* Not vorken only. You marry vit Rolf Rustemeyer. Haf baby. *Ja?*"

"Wife."

"*Ja.*" He smiled, his warm gray eyes filled with hope. "*Ist* goot? Voot *Haus*. Vife. Childrens. *Ja? Ist* fery goot."

"I don't know, Rolf. I thought I knew. A month ago I would have said yes just like that." The words gushed out of her—all her pent-up emotions. "I should probably say yes right this very moment. But so many things have happened. I suddenly feel so strange inside. I'm sure you can't understand, because I don't think you've felt this feeling before, Rolf. If you had, you wouldn't be asking me to marry you. It's clear you don't feel it. You're talking about cooking and washing, and all the things I thought marriage was about. But it's more than that. At least I think it ought to be more than that. There ought to be some sort of passion between a husband and wife. Do you know what I mean? Rolf?"

"*Ja, ja, ja.*" He nodded absently. "Danz? *Ist* danz now? You danzen togedder vit me, *ja?*"

He grabbed Rosie's hand and pulled her to her feet. A space had been cleared in the mill yard, and many of the young couples were hurrying to form squares. The makeshift band struck up a tune. People began to clap. Rolf whirled Rosie onto the floor.

She danced. In fact, she danced all afternoon with hardly a moment to sip at her glass of lemonade. She danced with Rolf and Mr. Hill and Mr. Chavez and all the young men who had bid on her box lunch. Then she danced with all of them again. Every time she danced with Rolf, he talked about his voot *Haus*. But she managed to avoid giving him an answer to his marriage proposal.

In fact, she realized that the more she talked, the less Rolf understood. This provided a perfect solution to her dilemma because every time Rosie became nervous, she talked too much. Their attempts at conversation shut down, and the focus returned to dancing.

Rosie knew she needed to pray. Desperately. But she couldn't very well run off and climb a tree. And she couldn't concentrate on anything with all these young farmers bidding for her attention. Finally she resorted to quick whispered pleas—accompanied by furtive glances at Seth. He had taken a seat at the edge of the dance floor. Violet sat beside him, and they talked. They laughed. They pointed at things and laughed some more.

Rosie had never considered that playing the part of Cinderella at the ball could be a miserable experience. As the sun set, Mr. LeBlanc lit lanterns around the dance floor. By that time, Rosie's feet felt like lead weights. Her shoulders wanted to sag. A length of eyelet lace trailed from her petticoat where Rolf had accidentally stepped on it.

Worst of all, she couldn't find Seth. He and Violet had disappeared long ago. How could she blame them for enjoying each other's company? They had so much in common. Both had lost spouses. Both had small children. Both were trying to manage farms on the prairie. They made a perfect match.

As Gabriel Chavez bowed to Rosie after a particularly spirited dance, she spotted Rolf eagerly elbowing his way toward her. *No*. She couldn't take it anymore. Not another dance. She swung around and stepped out of the circle of light.

A warm hand cupped her elbow. "Miss Mills? Would you care to dance with me?"

"No, please. Thank you, but I'm . . . I'm—"

"Are you too tired, Rosie?"

She looked up into Seth's blue eyes. Her heart spun around, and the pain in her blistered toes evaporated. "Tired? Me? Of course not. Never."

"Are you sure?"

"I'm fit as a fiddle."

"Well, come on then. I reckon it's my turn with the fairest flower of the prairie."

Rosie gave a silly, dizzy giggle as he escorted her onto the floor. Just then, the band struck up a waltz. A collective gasp came up from the crowd. Waltzing was considered by many a sinful and wicked thing. Some of the elderly glowered at the change in the music to three-quarter time. Some stomped off in disgust as the tempo slowed down, the squares dissolved, and couples began to move in time to the dance. Rosie herself had heard that waltzing was the devil's tool. But she and some of the girls at the orphanage had practiced the steps and turns in the attic, and none of them had felt the least bit sinful afterward.

"I reckon it's OK to waltz at a church benefit," Seth said, taking Rosie into his arms. "Don't you?"

"It's for a very good cause." Wild horses could not have dragged her away.

Rosie felt exactly like she was floating. Seth's blue eyes gazed down at her. His dark hair gleamed. One hand slipped around her back and the other clasped her fingers. Her feet positively had wings.

"I don't think God has a specific command against waltzing," Seth said. "Although if we looked hard enough we might find it someplace in Deuteronomy."

She laughed. "If it's a sin in the Bible, Mrs. Jameson could probably find it for us."

"Mrs. Jameson is in Kansas City. You're here."

"Yes, I am."

"I'm glad of that." He leaned close to her ear. "You're beautiful, Rosie Mills."

She thought her knees were going to buckle. "It's . . . it's Sheena's dress."

"It suits you."

"My petticoat shows."

Oh, that wasn't polite. She shook her head, embarrassed. She was talking about her underthings! In front of him!

"The dress is a little short, is what I meant to say," she mumbled, and she could hear her own voice begin to speed up in her nervousness. "I really don't mind. About the petticoat, I mean. I'm not ungrateful. In fact, I'm very grateful. I had the blue gingham, but then Sheena said she had brought this pink one all the way from Ireland. She couldn't fit into it anymore after all the children, so the dress was wasting away in her trunk. She suspects her sister Caitrin might be able to wear it when she arrives. Caitrin is coming from Ireland next month for a long visit, and I'm . . . I'm talking too much, aren't I?"

He was smiling at her, the corner of his mouth tipped up just a little and his gaze lazily studying her face. "I like the sound of your voice."

She couldn't think of anything to say after that, so she just drifted along in the soft, sweet music and enjoyed the sensation of Seth Hunter standing so close and holding her in his arms. He smelled very good. Like lemons. She felt the greatest urge to lay her cheek on his shoulder. God had given Seth such strong shoulders—shoulders that could hold up the world. Her daisies began to drop out of her hair one by one, but she didn't care. Seth whirled her around and around until her feet lifted off the ground, her dress billowed, and her heart soared.

When the music stopped, she was so surprised she let out a little gasp. Like coming out of a dream. But it wasn't a dream, and the reality of persistent Rolf Rustemeyer was bearing down on her again. "His wood house," she said, taking a step toward Seth. "He'll want to talk about his wood house."

"Rustemeyer's building a house?"

"He took all his money out of the savings, you know."

"I know."

"Please. Can we go home now?"

Seth tucked Rosie's arm under his. "We're . . . going," he shouted at Rustemeyer. "Chipper . . . is . . . tired."

Rosie could feel Rolf staring at her as she and Seth left the dance floor and walked toward the old pine tree. Good manners dictated that she thank Rolf for his company and for the bid that won her lunch box. She should give him some response to his proposal of marriage.

But she squeezed her eyes shut against her conscience and let Seth guide her away from the gathering. *Forgive me, Lord. If you want me to marry Rolf, I'll try. But not now. Not yet. Please, not yet.*

Chipper was curled up asleep on the blanket, his head on Violet's lap and Stubby at his side. Seth knelt beside the young widow and picked up his son. "Thank you, Mrs. Hudson," he said in a low voice. "I enjoyed the afternoon."

Her eyes deepened. "You're so kind, Mr. Hunter."

"Good night, then."

"Good night." As he turned away, her fragile voice stopped him. "Mr. Hunter, you'd be . . . you'd be welcome to stop by our place anytime. If you're passing thataway. Or if you'd just like to come . . . to come calling on me. Me and the children, I mean. You could bring Chipper to play."

"Thank you, Mrs. Hudson. I'm much obliged."

As Rosie and Seth walked toward the wagon, she reflected on the plight of the lonely widow with her three children and a baby on the way. Guilt began to eat at her again. Maybe it wasn't right to ache so deeply in the hope of winning Seth's love for herself. Violet Hudson needed him more than she did. And Rolf was a good man—an honorable man—who wanted Rosie for his wife.

Back in Kansas City this would all have seemed so simple to her. The widower marries the widow who needs a father for her children. The German bachelor marries the homeless woman who has always wanted a house and a family. How much more logical could the arrangement be?

But then Seth slipped his hands around her waist and lifted her up onto the wagon seat, and Rosie laid a hand on his broad shoulder—and Seth, only Seth, was right for her! He tucked a blanket under his sleeping son's head, loaded the dog, and walked around the wagon to join her.

As the mules pulled them onto the road home, Seth reached over and draped Rosie's fringed shawl over her shoulders. "Cold?" he said.

"Mm."

It was the hottest night of the year. But he left his arm around her, and she snuggled against him. Never in her entire life had she known a feeling so wonderful. So secure. So absolutely perfect.

"Did you enjoy the picnic?" Seth asked.

"Mm." Rosie felt like she was drifting on a soft white cloud. She didn't care about the picnic. She didn't care about anything.

"That fried chicken you made sure was good."

"Mm."

"I guess Rustemeyer liked it."

"He likes everything I cook," she murmured.

Seth fell silent for a moment. "I reckon Rustemeyer took his money so he could outbid everybody."

Rosie's cloud began to fade just a little. "He wants to build a wood house. That's why he took his money."

"A wood house. What's he want to do that for? Doesn't he think a soddy is good enough for him?"

"He's just thinking of the future, Seth."

"The future? What else does he have in mind for the future?"

An alarm bell went off in Rosie's head, and her fluffy cloud vanished completely. "A wood house," she said. "He's been thinking about a wood house."

"I think he took the money in order to win you at the auction. And I think he wants to build a wood house so he can put you into it."

"Rolf didn't win me at the auction. He won my box lunch."

"And the right to your company."

"Are you angry because he outbid you?"

"Angry? I'm not angry." He removed his arm from her shoulder and flicked the reins. "If that hound dog wants to spend his hard-earned money on a box lunch, that's fine with me. I just don't see the point of spending ten dollars on a few pieces of cold fried chicken."

"The money goes to the new church. And what's wrong with my fried chicken?"

"Nothing. There's nothing wrong with the chicken you made. It was good chicken. Better than Violet Hudson's ham sandwiches, that's for sure. But ten dollars? Ten hard-earned dollars."

"Those were bridge-toll dollars. The hard work Rolf put into the bridge was paid off a long time before those ten dollars came along. If he wants to put ten dollars into the new church, why shouldn't he?"

"If you hadn't kept on with those bridge tolls of yours, he wouldn't have ten dollars to pay for a box lunch."

"You don't like it that I take the bridge tolls, do you? You never have liked that. But I've been doing it for you. You and Chipper. I want to give you what I can. I want to leave you something."

"We have all we need." He let out a hot breath. "We have you."

Rosie grabbed the edges of the plank wagon bench. *Please, Father, help him to open his heart. Let him see how much I care.*

"Rolf Rustemeyer's ten dollars mean nothing to me," she said carefully. "Though I'm glad they'll help build the new church. And as for his wood house—"

"I'll build a wood house one of these days." Elbows on his knees, Seth stared out into the darkness ahead. "I have big dreams for my place. I want fences and cattle. I want a better plow and a new seed planter. I plan to chink the barn, and put a floor in the well house, and buy a horse. And I'll build a frame house, too—double storied with real glass windows and a big front porch. I'd like a new wagon. Maybe I'll even get myself a carriage with a black-cloth top and a pair of big, shiny—"

"Seth." Rosie laid her hand on his arm. "Wood houses don't matter. Not to me."

He turned and studied her for a long time. She could feel his eyes searching her face in the moonlight. He dropped the reins and lifted a hand to her hair. Slowly, very slowly, he sifted his fingers through the loose strands. He picked a daisy out of a curl and rolled the stem between his thumb and finger. Then he leaned forward and touched his lips to hers. The kiss was gentle, firm, and over in a breath.

"Rosie," he said. "I meant what I said. Chipper and I . . . we're glad you came. Both of us. Me, especially."

"Especially you?"

"Especially me." Then he bent over and his hands cupped the back of her head. When his lips met hers in a long, satisfying kiss, her breath hung in the back of her throat. She slipped her fingers up his arms to the solid round muscle of his shoulders. He pulled her closer, and his mouth found hers again.

"Rosie," he whispered.

She started to answer, but something popped against the side of her head—a tiny lead pellet. And then another hit her in the cheek. On the neck. In the ear. She drew back in pain.

"Shotgun!" Rosie cried. "It's Jack Cornwall!"

Waving her hands over her head, she fought the hundreds of tiny missiles that suddenly came at her from every angle. Was Chipper all right? She could hear him wailing in the back of the wagon. Stubby began to howl. Oh, Lord! They would all be killed. "Seth, he's shooting at us!"

Seth kept one arm around Rosie as he struggled to capture the reins of the bolting mules. "It's not Cornwall," he shouted. "Take cover, Rosie. We've got grasshoppers!"

CHAPTER 14

IT TOOK all the strength Seth could muster to keep the frightened mules on the track. Chipper screamed in terror as Rosie hauled the boy into the front of the wagon and wrapped him in a blanket. Stubby raced around in circles, yapping and howling. All around them, invisible except for the teeming shadow they cast over the moon, the grasshoppers flew. They settled on Seth's hatband. Climbed up the legs of his jeans. Nestled in Rosie's hair. Rode the leather driving lines like a long string of hideous ornaments on a monster's necklace.

While Chipper whimpered and Rosie cringed against the bench, all Seth could think about were his crops. Would the grasshoppers eat his corn? He had heard the stories, of course. Terrible tales of devastation from the few homesteaders who had been in Kansas long enough to remember the insect plagues. If he lost his crops, he'd be all but ruined.

"Giddap!" he shouted, flicking the reins and sending the hoppers off in every direction. "Come on, Nellie. Don't quit on me now, Pete."

But the mules wouldn't take another step. All around their long ears the grasshoppers flew, their wings buzzing, crackling like the rush of a prairie fire.

"We'll have to walk home," Seth said to the bundle of blanket that was Rosie and Chipper. "You go on ahead, and I'll catch up. Can you manage the boy?"

The bundle nodded. As swarms of grasshoppers flew into his face and hit him on the head, hands, and chest, Seth climbed down from the wagon. Crunching his way over the insects that had landed on the trail, he grabbed the mules' bridles and spoke whatever soothing words he could think of.

Stubby snapped at the insects as Rosie helped Chipper out of the wagon. They walked past Seth, a moving shroud. He put one arm around them and peeked under the drape covering Rosie's face. "You know the way to the soddy?" he said.

"I can find it."

"Here, take the gun." He pressed the pistol Jimmy O'Toole had given him into her hand. "If you see Cornwall, don't stop to think. Protect yourself and the boy."

He knew Rosie would rather do anything than carry a gun. But she took the weapon in silence. "Seth," she whispered, "what will we do?"

He said the only thing that came to mind. "Pray."

Then he kissed her cheek and lowered the blanket to cover her face. She moved away into the swarm, and he returned to his team. Frightened and confused, the mules were straining to escape the harness. Old Nellie had made up her mind to stay put, and she was doing her best to sit down between the leather trace lines. Pete wanted nothing more than to run. He pulled against the neck yoke, thrashing his head around in torment as the hoppers assaulted him.

Seth muttered a prayer for Rosie and Chipper and then concentrated on the mules. He had invested most of his army savings in the mule team and wagon. If they ran off, hurt themselves, or overturned the wagon, he'd be in deep trouble. Crushing grasshoppers with every step, he worked to calm the terrified animals. Pete's mouth grew bloody from straining against the bridle bit, and Seth's heart sank. Even if the grasshoppers didn't eat up his crops, Pete wouldn't be much use until he healed. Nellie kept trying to sit.

As the moon climbed through the night, the swarm in the sky gradually began to taper off. But Seth realized he couldn't afford to relax. The grasshoppers hadn't flown away. Instead, they had settled. Everything Seth touched—the driving lines, the wagon, the road—was covered in tiny, restless insects.

"God!" he groaned as his team finally began to pull the wagon forward. "Why, God? Why this? Why now?"

Seth walked along, his boots crackling like a trek across an icy field. *Pray*, he had told Rosie. Pray? What for? What good had God ever done him?

Seth thought about the Deuteronomy verse and how deeply it had hurt Rosie. She had made peace with it somehow. She felt an absolute assurance that God was her Father—and that knowledge made her whole life worthwhile. Maybe God was Seth's father, too. But truth to tell, God didn't seem that different from the earthly father he'd known.

Just when Seth had needed him most, his father had run off and left the family—abandoned them. Left them to their own devices. Sure, the family had survived. Barely. Seth had begged God to send his papa home. The man never returned.

Then a second crisis in his life had led Seth to cry out to God. When Mary's father had run him off the farm, Seth had been sure his life was over. What had God done to answer a desperate prayer for reconciliation? He had tossed Seth into the Union army to fight one battle after another, march thousands of miles—so far away from Mary that he hadn't known she was expecting a baby. Hadn't known when she died. Hadn't even known she was sick.

On his own, Seth had fought his way back from the edge of despair. He had signed up for a homestead, bought a team, built a soddy and a barn. Then he had traveled back to Missouri and had taken what was rightfully his. His only son. Along the way, Rosie had dropped into his life. Rosie—an unexpected, unearned gift from God if ever there was one.

And now—now he could lose her, lose his land, lose his son. Lose everything.

"God!" he shouted again into the black sky. At the cry, old Nellie stopped in her tracks. Seth pulled on the collar. She balked, shaking her head from side to side. Frustration boiled up inside him. He slapped the mule on her rump. She sat down.

Heat pouring through his veins, Seth dropped to his knees. "God, take these confounded grasshoppers away!" he said through clenched teeth. "Keep them off my crops. Keep them out of Rosie's garden."

He angrily backhanded a tear off his cheek. "I want Rosie, you hear me, God?" he said. "I want Chipper, too. He's my son. I have a right to him! If you let Cornwall have him, I'll kill . . . that . . . that . . ."

He couldn't go on. He brushed a handful of grasshoppers off his thigh and set his hand in their place. Rosie wouldn't like it that he was shouting at God. He doubted she would call that praying. But it was the best he could do.

If he was honest with himself, Seth had to admit he hated God. Hated him just the way he hated his own father. Maybe God had created the world, but he'd sure bungled up the rest of the job. He was never around when a man needed him. It was a lot easier for God to let people struggle against impossible odds than to step in and protect them. Take these vexatious grasshoppers for a perfect example.

"God!" Seth shouted upward again. "If you let these bugs eat my crops, I'll never talk to you again. You hear me? I'll know you're no better than my good-for-nothing papa. I'll know you don't care what becomes of me. You hear?"

Seth grabbed a grasshopper that was wandering down the back

of his collar and hurled it to the ground. Then he got up and brushed the squashed grasshoppers off the knees of his jeans. Old Nellie had decided to stand up again. Seth took her and Pete by the harness and led them toward the bridge. Ahead, the sun was just beginning to rise.

"They're eating up your scarf, Rosie," Chipper said. He stood beside her outside the door of the soddy and held up the tattered scrap of cotton. Six grasshoppers clung to it, their tiny mouths working furiously at the thinly woven fabric.

"They're eating everything."

"What are we gonna do, Rosie?"

"Pray. That's what your papa said we should do. I've been praying ever since the first grasshopper hit me in the head last night. I'm not going to stop now."

"I reckon you might as well stop. God ain't listening."

"A good father always listens to his children. And God always answers our prayers."

"I don't think God's gonna answer this prayer, Rosie. It's too late. The hoppers are eating up most of Papa's corn—an' your potatoes, an' the beans, an' everything we gots."

Rosie knelt down amid the grasshoppers clustered around the soddy. "The thing you must always remember is this, Chipper: God *always* answers our prayers. Sometimes he says, 'Yes, my child, I will do that for you because it fits in with my plan for the way I want the world to go.' And sometimes he says, 'You'll have to wait awhile. I'm not ready to do that yet.' And sometimes . . . sometimes, Chipper, our Father says, 'No, that is not what I'm going to do, my beloved. I have a better plan for you, so please try to trust me through this difficult time.'"

Chipper studied the fields beyond Rosie's shoulder. His blue eyes were troubled, and the corners of his little mouth turned down. "Which way you think God's going to answer us this time, Rosie?" he asked. " 'Cause it sure looks to me like them grasshoppers have ate up everything Papa planted."

She turned and looked out over the stretch of land Seth had so carefully plowed and planted. Bare stalks covered with living, moving insects pointed upward like knobby fingers accusing God of betrayal. The willow tree by the creek was stripped bare. Nothing remained in the garden beside the kitchen but a few pale yellow stems. The grasshoppers had even eaten the pith out of the pumpkin vines.

The pests had attacked the soddy, too. Rosie's broom lay on the ground, chewed from handle to bristles. Holes riddled her storage baskets. Her cleaning rags were nothing but tatters. If not for the stream, she, Seth, and Chipper would have nothing to drink. Even the top of the well was filled with grasshoppers.

The animals had suffered beyond belief. The cows refused to eat, and Rosie was concerned that their milk might dwindle to nothing. The mules stood forlornly in the barn, their brown eyes speaking of their misery. Stubby squeezed himself under the bed and wouldn't come out.

"Chipper, we are going to have to wait on the Lord," she said softly. "Though I'll admit I can't imagine what he can do about this."

"He better think of something quick. 'Cause here comes Papa."

Rosie stood as Seth strode through the grasshoppers toward the soddy. His eyes red-rimmed, he grabbed Rosie's hand and set a knobby, half-chewed potato into her palm. "They got into the root cellar," he said. "That's all I could find."

"I'll make dinner," she said. She put on the best smile she could come up with, but Seth shouldered past her into the soddy.

Rosie and Chipper hauled water from the creek and built a fire using their cache of stored buffalo chips. She decided to make a big pot of potato soup—something that might warm their stomachs and clear their heads. But the moment she lifted the lid on the stew pot, fifteen grasshoppers jumped into the steaming water.

Finally, she pushed the potato in among the buffalo chips and left it to bake. At least the grasshoppers wouldn't be able to get through the coals to eat it.

The grasshoppers stayed for nine days. They ate the cornstalks. They ate the wagon ropes. They ate the wooden milk bucket. They ate every leaf, bush, blade of grass, and weed in Seth's one hundred sixty acres of homestead. They even ate up the old dress Rosie had worn from the orphanage to Kansas.

And then one morning a wind blew in from the west. All the grasshoppers took wing. Within an hour they had gone—a great black cloud of buzzing, swarming pests that nearly blotted out the sun.

Startled at the sudden silence, Rosie stepped out of the soddy to see what had happened. Stubby slinked out from under the bed and stood beside her. Chipper and Seth were walking up from the stream carrying a bucket of water between them. Rosie crossed her arms over her stomach and stared at the two of them, fighting tears. For nine days, they had lived from one moment to the next—fighting for survival with little time even to think.

Now . . . now what?

"Didja see that, Rosie?" Chipper asked. "The grasshoppers went away! They flew right straight over me an' Papa. It was like black smoke—only real loud. I got scared, thinkin' the hoppers couldn't find anything left to eat and was gonna come after us next. But Papa said to hold on tight to his hand. So I did. Sure enough, they left us alone."

Chipper and his father set the water pail down in the yard beside Rosie. She picked a few grasshoppers out of the water and tossed them onto the ground. Then she looked up at Seth. Neither of them had slept much since the invasion. Instead, they had sat together on the bench just outside the soddy. Saying nothing, they had joined hands and waited. Waited through the long, swarming nights until the hot, swarming days began again.

"Now whatcha gonna do, Papa?" Chipper asked. "What's next?"

Seth looked down at his son. Then he lifted his head and met Rosie's eyes. "I'm ruined," he said.

"No." She shook her head. "Please, Seth, don't say that."

"Pack up."

"Seth, why? What are you saying?"

"I'll take you back to Kansas City."

"Kansas City! But I don't want to go."

"It doesn't matter what you want. It doesn't matter what I want. I don't have anything to offer. When you came out here, I promised you room and board in exchange for looking after Chipper and keeping house. Your bed's half eaten up. And God knows I don't have anything but what I can shoot to feed you. You'd best go."

Rosie sank onto the stool beside the front door. In the distance she could see the O'Toole family filing over the bridge. Rolf Rustemeyer was coming from the other direction. No doubt they would all want to compare and assess the damage now that the hoppers had finally gone.

"Lord, what does this mean?" she murmured, bending over and squeezing her eyes shut as Seth and Chipper went out to meet their neighbors. "Were the grasshoppers your sign of wrath against us, Father? Are you punishing me for coming out to the prairie without asking your permission? Is it my willfulness in not letting you choose my husband for me—for loving Seth so much? Was it something Seth did? Or Rolf? Or Jimmy? Why Lord? Why did you allow the grasshoppers? And why are you sending me away now?"

"Great ghosts, has she lost her mind?" Sheena asked Seth. "Did the pestilence send her over the brink?"

Rosie looked up. "I'm praying, Sheena."

"She does it all the time," Chipper piped in. "Out loud, too. She says God answers all our prayers. Sometimes yes, sometimes wait awhile, and sometimes no. But he always makes everything turn out good for the people who love him."

Sheena, Seth, and Jimmy all stared down at Rosie as though she had indeed lost her mind. She picked a grasshopper out of her pocket and gave a little shrug. "I do believe it," she said. "The Bible says it."

"What good can God make of our troubles now?" Jimmy asked. "Sure, the lot of us are finished. Finished clean. It's as bad as the potato famine in Ireland, so it is. Only this time I've my wee *brablins* and hardly a thing to feed any of them."

"No foot *für* eaten?" Rolf Rustemeyer asked.

"No food," Sheena said. "We've eaten the last of our salt pork. Do you have any food, Mr. Rustemeyer?"

"*Nein.*" The German shook his head. "No foot."

"We gots oysters," Chipper said. "Rosie gots 'em in the barn in her big tradin' box."

Rosie glanced at Seth, and the look in his eyes made her heart begin to hammer. "Yes, we *do* have oysters. Now why didn't I think of that before?"

"What else is in there?" Seth asked.

"Coffee. And canned brandied peaches."

"I've got pickles at our place," Sheena added. "Shortening, too. They didn't get at that."

"I have a jug of maple syrup," Rosie went on. "And mackerels—big fat ones in cans. And a keg of lard."

"I haf tea," Rolf said.

"What with oysters and mackerel and canned brandied peaches, we will be a fancy lot, won't we?" Sheena said. A grin tugged at the corners of her mouth. "At least we've something to get by on."

"Until what?" Seth asked. "We won't be able to make it through a Kansas winter on a few oysters and some lard, Sheena. The crops are ruined. There won't be a harvest. That means no winter stores.

No produce to sell in Topeka. No grain to haul to LeBlanc's mill. And no money to buy seed."

"We have a little money," Rosie said. "The bridge tolls. Rolf took his already, but there's forty-three dollars and seventy-five cents each for the Hunters and the O'Tooles."

Jimmy O'Toole's face went from white to pink to bright red in the space of three seconds. Seth's mouth dropped open. Sheena fanned herself with both hands.

"Forty-three dollars, did you say?" she puffed.

"I'm pretty sure of it. I counted it out for Mr. Rustemeyer right before the picnic."

"By all the goats in Kerry, my sweet lass, you've saved us!" Jimmy O'Toole cried. He grabbed Rosie's hands and pulled her up from the bench. "You and that wobbly pontoon bridge have saved us!"

"Forty-three dollars *each?*" Seth asked.

"And seventy-five cents." Rosie hugged herself tight, hoping against hope that the light in Seth's eyes meant what she thought. She had done the right thing. She had helped him.

"Rosie!" He threw his arms around her and swung her up into the air. "You crazy girl! Taking bridge tolls left and right. Trading for oysters and mackerel. Going on with it even when you knew I didn't like it. You did it! You saved us!"

He planted a big kiss right on her cheek. Rolf laughed and gave her a kiss on the other cheek. Then Jimmy O'Toole kissed her hand. Chipper kissed her elbow. Stubby started barking. Pretty soon the whole group was dancing around the yard, stepping on squashed grasshoppers and singing and shouting at the top of their lungs.

"We'll go to Topeka," Seth said. "Rolf and I. There isn't time to go all the way to Kansas City. We'll bring back whatever we can lay our hands on to plant. If we're lucky, we can all put out winter squash, bush beans, cabbages, and even tomatoes."

"Will you buy carrots?" Sheena asked. "We can still plant those. It's only mid-July."

"Carrots. Collards, too. They can take cold as low as fifteen degrees. We can put out mustard greens. It's too late for onions and potatoes, but we might get turnips."

"I'll stay here with the women and *brablins*," Jimmy said. "Every day I'll plow under the ruined crops and get the fields ready. I'll plow two or three acres for me one day. Three for Seth the day after that. And then three for Rustemeyer."

"Chipper, you'll be coming with me." Seth took his son's hand. "We'll leave right away. The sooner we get going, the sooner we can come back and start planting again. Rustemeyer, go get your things. Rosie, it's time to clean out the savings."

The gathering dispersed with far more enthusiasm than when they had assembled. But Rosie couldn't prevent the wave of despair that swept over her as she watched Seth and Chipper head into the soddy. Yes, her bridge tolls had saved them. Yes, she had done her part to help.

But what would it all mean? Just moments ago, Seth had been ready to send her straight back to Kansas City. Were his feelings for her so shallow? Did his affection depend on healthy crops and lots of money? Did he still see her as merely someone to look after Chipper and keep the house?

Brushing aside fragments of dead grasshoppers, Rosie dug her fingers into the corner of the barn floor where she kept the bridge tolls hidden. In moments she had unearthed the heavy crock in which she stored the precious cache. Silver dollars gleamed in the bar of sunlight that filtered between the barn siding.

"Father," she whispered as she touched the cold metal. "I may have saved Seth's homestead with these dollars. But I haven't made him love me. We haven't become a family. We're still just three misfits. Four, if you count Stubby. I don't have a home to call my own. Chipper doesn't have a mother to care for him. Seth doesn't have a wife to share his love. Nothing seems settled between us. I promised Chipper you would turn all our troubles into good. But, Father, oh Father—"

"Still praying, Rosie?" Seth was standing at the far end of the barn, a chewed-up leather bridle in his hands. "I thought you might have given up on that by this time."

She stood beside the heavy crock. "No, Seth. I still believe."

"Believe what?" He walked toward her. "I asked God to get rid of those grasshoppers—"

"And he did."

"Nine days too late."

"Our Father never promised to do his work by our timetable."

"*Your* Father sure has a funny way of showing his love. You'd think if he cared the least bit about you, he wouldn't have let those grasshoppers head in this direction."

"Our Father never promised a life free of trouble."

"Then what's the use of praying?"

Rosie bent down and picked up a silver dollar. "Praying is talking to God. Praying is how you let him know you love him. It's how you know you can trust him."

"Trust him for what?"

"Trust him to be with you—through grasshoppers and whatever else life on this earth brings us."

"You really think God is out here on the prairie with you? How can you go on believing that?"

"Because praying is also listening. And when I stop to listen, I can hear God's voice speaking to my heart. I feel his comforting presence. He's my rock. My redeemer. He has saved me from a fate much worse than grasshoppers, Seth. It's the least I can do to trust him with my earthly troubles."

She tossed the coin to him. "I wanted to help you," she went on. "I thought this would do it. But now I understand it takes much more than forty-three dollars and seventy-five cents to save a man. It takes faith. It takes hope."

"It takes love," he said. He was silent a moment, regarding her with intense blue eyes. When he spoke again, his voice was low. "Do you love me, Rosie Mills?"

She looked away quickly, wishing for a bonnet to hide beneath. Her cheeks flushed at his bold question. But he wanted an answer. She would give it to him.

"Yes, I do," she said, squaring her shoulders and meeting his gaze. "I love you, Seth."

"How?"

"What do you mean?"

"How do you love me? The way you said you'd find love when we talked back at Holloway's Station? Look at me. I'm a good, honest, hardworking man—just like Rolf Rustemeyer. Just like Gabriel Chavez, David Hill, Matthew Smithers, and most of the rest of the homesteaders. You danced with me. You danced with them. You let me kiss you. You let Rustemeyer kiss you. Is that how you love me, Rosie? The same as all the rest of them?"

She gulped down a bubble of air. *What do I say? How do I tell him?* "I love you as my Father loves you," she managed.

His eyes hardened. "Your Father doesn't love me a lick."

He slung the bridle over one shoulder and turned to leave the barn. Rosie caught his sleeve. "Do you want to take me with you as far as Topeka?" she asked. "Do you want me to go back to Kansas City, Seth?"

He swung around and grabbed her shoulders. "I want what no one can give me—a guarantee they won't leave . . . or die."

"Oh, Seth, I—"

He was breathing hard. "Go back to Kansas City, Rosie. Or stay here. The choice is yours."

"Seth," she said softly, "true love involves trust. It's all about faith—trusting the one you love and trusting God to protect your union. The shield of faith in our Father helps us endure."

"Do you still think that's all there is to it? Endurance? Just signing the pledge on the marriage license and then working together day in and day out?"

Rosie shook her head. "No," she whispered. "I think it's more."

"Are you willing to give your heart to a man?"

"Do you have the courage—the faith—to make a pledge?"

He dropped his hands from her shoulders and looked away, struggling against emotion she could barely comprehend. "I'm trying," he said.

She blinked back the tears that threatened. "Then I'll stay."

CHAPTER 15

THE TRIP to Topeka should have taken a day and a half. But Rustemeyer had insisted on hitching his horse alongside Seth's mule to pull the wagon—and the two creatures could not have been more unsuited. Pete was a plodder. Seth had always been able to rely on the mule, whether it was to pull a plow across three acres of tough sod in a day or to haul a loaded wagon over the uneven prairie trails. Rustemeyer's feisty mare, on the other hand, thought she had the world by the tail. She pranced, she flirted, she complained about the heat, she shied and balked and generally made poor ol' Pete miserable.

Seth couldn't help but compare the mismatched team to his marriage to Mary Cornwall. She had enchanted him, but he couldn't deny that in time her lightness would have worn thin. As much as he had adored her, Seth understood now that Mary would have made a poor partner in the life he had always dreamed of for himself.

Rosie Mills, on the other hand, was perfect. She actually enjoyed the prairie. Not only had she accustomed herself to the daily chores, she had taken on the extra labor of managing the bridge. Though the stream of strangers crossing his land bothered Seth—especially where Chipper and Jack Cornwall were concerned—he knew Rosie's ingenuity had saved his farm.

Leaving her there with nothing but Stubby to protect her had been hard. Now all Seth could think about was loading his wagon with supplies and heading back to the homestead. Though he wasn't quite sure he was ready to marry Rosie, he couldn't imagine life without her.

Three days after they'd left the homestead, Seth, Rolf, and Chipper finally arrived in Topeka. During the following seven days, they traveled from mercantile to feed store to farm, and they bought whatever seed and healthy plant stock they could lay their hands on. It was a tough assignment. Every grasshopper-eaten farmer in Kansas who had put a little money back seemed to have the same idea. The town teemed with men, prices rose, tempers flared. But finally Seth and Rolf managed to fill their wagon and set off on the return trip.

"Are we really goin' home now?" Chipper asked as they crossed Soldier Creek one evening and headed toward the Red Vermillion River. "Or are we goin' out to another farm to buy plants? I wanna go home, Papa."

Seth smiled. *Home, Papa.* He had never thought two words could sound so beautiful. *Home . . . Papa.* Even if the crops completely failed this year, Seth knew he had accomplished something far more significant. To Chipper, the Kansas soddy was home. And Seth was Papa.

"We're on our way home," he said, ruffling his son's thick dark hair. "If we can get Pete and Gertrude to cooperate, we'll be there late tomorrow night. How does that sound?"

"Sounds good. I can't wait to see Rosie. How 'bout you, Papa? Have you missed Rosie?"

Seth didn't have to ponder that one. "I sure have. I've missed Rosie a lot."

"Fräulein Mills *ist* goot cook, *ja?*" Rolf said.

Seth shook his head. *Food* again. It seemed like they'd spent half their time in Topeka searching out boarding houses and hotels where the German could buy himself a hearty meal.

"Rosie's more than a good cook, Rustemeyer," Seth told him. "She's a good woman."

"*Ja*, vasch clothes. Grow potatoes *und* carrots in *Garten*. Sew pretty dress. Pink, *ja?* Maken britsch money. Goot fräulein."

"Rosie's a good fräulein, all right. But there's more to her than cooking and gardening and sewing."

"She's pretty," Chipper said. "She gots all that hair!"

"Dances good, too," Seth added. "And she's smart."

"Schmart? *Was ist* schmart?" Rolf asked. "*Schmatz?* A big kiss?" He demonstrated the German word by making loud smacking noises with his lips. This sent Chipper into fits of laughter.

"No, no!" the boy said. "Not kissin'. Rosie's *smart!*"

"*Schmerz?* Fery sad?" Rolf gave a big frown and pretended to cry.

"Not *Schmerz!*" Chipper giggled. "Smart. Smart!"

As Seth watched the sun sinking into the sea of rippling bluestem grass, he wondered how to explain Rosie's complicated intelligence. For one thing, she had good old horse sense. The woman could take a pile of grain sacks and decorate a whole house. She could make a meal out of a single potato. She could turn wood ashes into lye for soap or pigment for paint. And she wasn't afraid to try where others might have failed.

But there was more to Rosie. The woman thought about things. Deep thoughts. She was interesting to talk to. She'd read some books, and she liked to discuss ideas she had. Seth had never met a woman like that, and Rosie's intelligence was something he treasured.

"She thinks," he said, tapping his head to illustrate his point to Rolf. "She's smart."

Rolf frowned. "Schmart? I can not . . . not unterstanden." Then he shrugged. "Rosie *ist* goot fräulein. Vill be *meine* vife."

"Your *wife?*" Seth and Chipper said at the same time.

"Vife, *ja*. In vintertime Rosie vill *komm* to *mein Haus und* marry vit me. *Ist* goot, *ja?*" He gave them a broad smile. "I build voot

Haus, und Rosie vill babies haf. Rosie *und* Rolf: *die* family Rustemeyer."

Seth stared out at the long flat trail ahead. Had Rosie actually agreed to marry the German in the winter? Had she accepted a proposal of marriage from Rolf and never bothered to tell Seth?

Maybe she hadn't thought it important to tell him. After all, more than once that summer Seth had made it clear he was going to take her back to the orphanage in Kansas City in the fall. Sure he had kissed her once, but the grasshopper infestation had kept him from courting her properly. Maybe that kiss hadn't meant to Rosie what it had meant to Seth. Maybe the whole time she was kissing Seth, she had already agreed to marry Rolf Rustemeyer.

"Rosie's gonna marry *you?*" Chipper asked the brawny German. "Are you sure about that?"

"*Ja, ja, ja*. She marry vit me. I build *Haus für* Rosie. Haf childrens togedder. Big family. *Ja?*"

Chipper looked up at his father. Seth could feel the blue eyes boring into him. "I thought *you* liked Rosie, Papa."

"I do like her."

"I thought you loved her."

Seth clenched his jaw. "I do love her."

And she loves me, he wanted to add. But what had Rosie told him in those hurried moments before he left her to go to Topeka? *I love you as my Father loves you*.

What kind of love was that? Surely not the marrying kind. Maybe she was saving that kind of love for Rolf Rustemeyer.

"Why don't you marry Rosie, Papa?" Chipper asked, tugging on his sleeve. "We need a mama."

"Rosie's not *my* mama, Chipper—"

"She's not mine either, but it don't matter. We need her. We like her. We want her."

"Stop your team, Seth Hunter!" The unexpected voice behind the wagon startled Seth. He swung around. Jack Cornwall had ridden his horse to within ten yards of the wagon, and his shotgun was leveled straight at Seth's head.

"I said stop your team, Hunter," Cornwall repeated. "Stop or I'll blow you straight to kingdom come."

"Don't do that, Uncle Jack!" Chipper shouted, standing as Seth pulled on the reins. "Don't shoot him!"

"Get down, Chipper," Seth barked. White heat poured through his veins. He grabbed his son's arm and pushed the boy to the floor of the wagon. "Put down your weapon, Cornwall. You can see we're unarmed. You're scaring my son."

"*Your* son? Chipper no more belongs to you than my sister did. Turn him over to me, and maybe I'll think about letting you live."

"Not a chance." Seth stood slowly, his heart hammering. He knew Cornwall had been lurking. Now the predator had cornered his prey. In moments, Seth could be lying in a pool of blood. Unless . . . *dear God, help me* . . . unless he could calm the man, reason with him, persuade him to let them go.

"Give up this craziness, Jack," Seth said, squaring his shoulders. "You know I don't want any trouble with you. I'm a peaceable man, and I'm taking good care of the boy. Why don't you go on back to Missouri? Your daddy and mama need you a whole lot more than Chipper does."

"A lot you know! They raised that boy from the time he was born. I won't leave this trail tonight without him. Now turn him over."

"I won't do it."

"I'll kill you."

"Don't kill him!" Chipper cried, jumping to his feet again. Tears ran down his cheeks. "Uncle Jack, don't shoot. Please don't shoot!"

"Get down, Chipper. Rustemeyer, hold him!" Seth glanced at the German. In Rolf's lap lay a gleaming coat pistol. Seth's focus flicked to Rolf's gray eyes. Understanding passed between them.

"I want you to keep Chipper covered," Seth said, leaning over and pressing the boy under the seat. As he did, he palmed the pistol. "Stay down now, Chipper, you hear me?"

"Don't make me kill you, Hunter!" Cornwall shouted. "Though I reckon your Yankee hide wouldn't be too sorely missed."

"You're not going to kill me, Cornwall. You're going to turn your horse around and head back east. You're going to tell your daddy you tried your best to get Chipper, but I wouldn't turn him loose. And then you're going to make a life for yourself in Missouri where you belong."

"I don't belong in Missouri," Cornwall said, cocking the shotgun. "My home was lost, Hunter. The likes of you stole my land. The likes of you burned our family house and ruined our crop fields and robbed us blind."

"Is that what this is all about? Are you still fighting the war, Jack? Well, I got news for you. It's over. You killing me and taking Chipper to Missouri isn't going to change that one bit. The war is over. Now it's time to get on with life."

"I'm aiming to get on with life. My life includes that little boy you kidnapped. He's my sister's son, in case you forgot. Mary's son. He's all we've got of her. And we mean to have him."

"You won't get him," Seth said. He cocked the pistol he had kept hidden behind his thigh. "Now turn around and head east. Chipper stays with me."

"You good-for-nothing Yankee!" Cornwall lifted the shotgun to his shoulder. "I'll take him if it's the last thing I do!"

"Don't do it, Jack!" Seth raised the pistol.

The shotgun roared in a flash of fire and black smoke. Seth squeezed the pistol trigger as he flung himself over the seat into the wagon bed. A cry rang out. The animals bolted. Chipper screamed. Rustemeyer jerked at the reins and struggled to keep the wildly racing team on the road.

Among the seed barrels, Seth elbowed himself to his knees.

He'd been hit. He could feel the pain in his left thigh and calf. But he was alive. Chipper was alive. Rolf was alive.

In the dim light, Seth could see Jack Cornwall's horse cantering behind the wagon in crazy circles as its rider fought to stay in the saddle. A bright red stain blossomed on Cornwall's right shoulder.

"Go home, Jack!" Seth shouted at his assailant. "Don't make me kill you! Get on home where you belong."

As the wagon swayed down the trail into the twilight, Seth clambered back over the seat. "You OK, Chipper?" he asked, hauling the little boy up into his lap. "You all right, little feller?"

"I thought he was gonna kill you, Papa," Chipper sobbed.

Seth's heart warmed. "I won't let him do that. I've got to stick around to take care of you, remember?"

"But I don't want you to kill Uncle Jack either, Papa. Please don't hurt him. Promise?"

Seth let out a breath. His leg was beginning to throb, and he had noted a red stain on Rolf's sleeve. The German had taken some buckshot, too. They would need to find a farmhouse and get some warm water and bandages. He rested his cheek on Chipper's head. "I'll do my best not to hurt him, son," he said gently. "I reckon you care about your Uncle Jack. And your Gram and Gramps, too. Maybe there'll come a day when all of us can make our peace. But until then, I aim to keep you with me. See . . . I love you, Chipper. I love you."

"I love you, too, Papa." The soft lips touched Seth's cheek.

"*Mein* arm *ist* bad," Rustemeyer said. "Bloot *kommt*. You haf blood *kommt*, too, Hunter."

"We'll head for the stagecoach station on the Red Vermillion. They'll doctor us." Seth studied the German. The big hound dog. His rival. "Hey, Rustemeyer," he said. "You saved my life by pulling out that coat pistol. Thank you."

"Tank *you*." Rustemeyer smiled. "*Ist* goot haf *einen Freund, ja?*"

"*Ja*," Seth said. "It's good to have a friend."

While Seth was away, Rosie poured herself into her work. When she wasn't milking the cows, gathering eggs, cooking, washing, or mending, she plowed. Seth had taken Pete to Topeka, but old Nellie seemed to understand the gravity of the situation.

The mule patiently bore Rosie's attempts at putting on the harness and hitching the plow. She even accepted Rosie's first counterclockwise rows—and she didn't grumble too much when Jimmy pointed out that all the ground would have to be plowed again in a clockwise direction. In fact, old Nellie seemed to appreciate Rosie's gentle touch. She only sat down once or twice a day. And when she ate up the last scrap of Rosie's scarf, she acted as if she had done her new mistress a favor.

So Jimmy loaned Rosie a straw hat and taught her how to turn under the grasshopper-eaten corn stubble. Every afternoon, when the rest of the chores had been done, she and Stubby trudged out into the field. With each row Rosie plowed, she said a prayer. She felt as though she were knitting her prayers into the very soil of Seth's homestead.

Bring him peace, *Father.*

Open his heart, *Father.*

Strengthen his faith, *Father.*

As the fields were transformed from desiccated ruin into fertile black soil again, Rosie felt her own heart grow ripe. It wasn't just hope that strengthened her. It was love.

She missed Seth. Missed him desperately. Even though he was gone, she realized he had become a part of her every waking hour. She could hear his voice in the rush of Bluestem Creek. In the shimmering haze of the summer heat, she could almost see him working—his shirt cast aside and his muscles straining as he hammered the planks that would link his homestead to the world or guided the plow that would ensure his future. She could smell his essence in the strong, fresh breeze that drifted over the prairie grasses. And every time she thought of his sweet kisses, the ache inside her heart grew stronger.

When Stubby began barking at two men driving a wagon into the yard one afternoon, Rosie's heart leapt. Abandoning the plow and old Nellie, she picked up her skirts and hop-skipped over the loamy rows, the dog scampering behind her. But as she ran toward the wagon, she realized the two men weren't Seth and Rolf at all.

A gentleman with a thick brown beard and no mustache lifted a hand in greeting. "Miss Rose Mills?" he called.

Rosie slowed to a walk, a lump the size of a sourdough biscuit forming in her throat. It wasn't Seth. Almost two weeks had gone by, and July was drawing to a close. Where was Seth? How could she keep on going when the hunger in her heart was so great?

"Mills—is that your name, ma'am?" the man asked.

Rosie approached the wagon. "I'm Rose Mills. What can I do for you, sir?"

"We hear you got a mercantile out here. Is that right?"

She studied the two men from a safe distance. Though they looked peaceable enough, she began to wish she had brought Jimmy O'Toole's pistol with her. What if they were friends of Jack Cornwall?

"I take bridge tolls," she said. "Sometimes travelers want to trade goods with me instead of paying cash. It might seem like a mercantile to some. But it's not."

The man climbed down from his wagon, took off his hat, and extended a hand. "My name's Bridger, and I'm from Topeka."

"Topeka!" Rosie's heart contracted in fear. "What's happened to Seth?"

"I don't know nothin' about anybody but you, ma'am. Word is, you got a mercantile out here on the Bluestem. Folks tell me you trade fair, and you do honest business."

"Are you from the government? Have I done something wrong?"

"Matter of fact, I *am* from the government. I'm with the United States Post Office, and I got a proposal to make you. Since late spring, about ten, fifteen folks come into my building in Topeka—seems like three or four of 'em a week here lately—and they been askin' me to give you a post office commission. And now that half my people under contract went bust after the grasshoppers came through, I'm aiming to do just that. How's it sound to you?"

"A post office? Here? But I don't know if . . . Seth might not . . . what about Mr. Holloway's station?"

"Gone belly up. Your place put him out of business, and the grasshoppers finished him."

"Oh, my." Rosie couldn't help but pity the man, even though he had been unpleasant to her. "Mr. LeBlanc might want a post office."

"Already asked him. Says he's got enough to keep him busy runnin' the mill."

"But I don't really have a mercantile."

"I don't much care if all you got is a cowshed. If you'll let me send the mail out here so folks around can come and get their letters, I'll give you a commission."

Rosie lifted her chin. A United States post office. That sounded mighty respectable. What could Seth find wrong with it? In fact, it would be an honor.

"Yes, sir," she said, feeling almost as though she should salute the bearded gentleman. "I shall be much obliged to serve my country in that fashion."

The man's mouth twitched a little. "Very good. Now, I'll need a little information from you." He pulled a piece of paper from his back pocket and took a pencil from behind his ear. "What's your full name?"

"Rosenbloom Cotton Mills."

He scowled. "Like the place over in Illinois where they make stockings and such?"

"Yes," she said, trying not to let shame overcome the pride of the moment. "But everyone calls me Rosie."

"Age?"

"Let's see. I reckon I must be twenty by now." She hoped he wouldn't ask what day she was born.

"Birthplace?"

"Kansas City."

"You got any warrants out against you? Ever been in trouble with the law?"

"No, sir."

"All right, then. Miss Rosenbloom Cotton Mills, you're now hereby an official commissioner of the United States Postal Service." He handed her a sheet of paper. "You got a name you want to call this place?"

"A name? What for?"

"So's folks can put an address on their letters."

Rosie pondered. Seth had not liked it when she'd called the barn Hunter's Station. But she wouldn't feel right about naming the post office after herself.

"Well, you think about it," the man said. "Meantime, I want to hand over the first mail delivery to you." He hauled a sack out of the back of his wagon and set it in her arms. "There you go. This covers the territory in a good part of this county."

"But how will people know to come here for their mail?"

"We'll put out the message from headquarters in Topeka, and you can let folks know as they pass across your bridge. Word'll spread quicker'n you think. Now, ma'am, this post office is gonna increase your traffic by a goodly bit, so I reckon you ought to be prepared. You might want to keep an eye on them fine-lookin' chickens of yours. Folks has been knowed to take just about anything that's not nailed down. And if I was you, ma'am, I'd set me up a real mercantile double-quick. This commission is your key to some good business."

He tipped his hat and climbed back onto his wagon. Rosie hugged the bag of mail. She could only hope Seth would understand. The mail could bring customers and their money—money that could help during hard times on the prairie. Mail also meant contact, a chance to touch the lives of hundreds of other people. Maybe she could even share her faith—the hope of a future of joy through Jesus Christ. Hope for a bountiful future. Hope for Seth. Hope in God.

"Wait!" she called. She waved at the men on the retreating wagon. "Wait, please! I have the name. I want to call it Hope."

"Hope?" The post office man considered for a moment, then he gave an approving nod. "All righty. I'll be back in a week—bringin' the mail for a town called Hope."

CHAPTER 16

"A *TOWN!*" Sheena hooted as she plunked a crock of fresh honey on the makeshift counter in Rosie's barn. "Here it is barely two weeks Seth has been gone, and already you've taken a post office commission, set up a mercantile, and founded a town! He'll be fit to be tied, so he will."

"I'm afraid you're right." Rosie set a basket of eggs beside the honey and propped up a hand-lettered sign: *Eggs: 50 cents a dozen.* "But Seth will have to accept the facts. He can't deny prairie farming is uncertain business. Without the bridge toll money, Seth, Rolf, and Jimmy might have gone under just the way Mr. Holloway did. If God gives us the opportunity to secure the future by granting us a post office, why should we throw the gift back in his face?"

"But a *town?*"

"This is not a town, Sheena. It's one soddy and a barn. The gentleman needed an address, so I invented a name."

"Aye, and the first time Seth sees a letter addressed to Hope, Kansas, arriving at his barn on the postal coach—"

"Halloo!" The high female voice cut off Sheena's warning of doom. "Is anybody home?"

"It's a traveler," Rosie whispered to Sheena. "So, are you with me in this, or not? Together we can run this mercantile and divide the profits. It's hope, Sheena. Hope."

"I'm with you. Although when Jimmy gets wind of it, there'll be the devil to pay."

"Come on then. Let's greet the first customer to the Hope Mercantile." Rosie smoothed down her apron. She wished she had a bonnet. For all the trading she'd done, she had not been able to part any woman from her headgear. It seemed every female traveler had been forewarned about the prairie sun and its propensity for baking skin to a leathery brown.

Patting her bun, Rosie stepped out of the barn, Sheena at her side. A woman in a bright green dress threw her arms open wide and ran toward them.

"Glory be to God, Sheena!" the woman cried. "The *brablins* said I'd find you here! Don't you know me? I'm Caitrin!"

"Caitrin?" Sheena's eyes went wide. "Caitie? 'Tis really you?"

"Aye, Sheena! I'm here. I've come at last!"

Laughing, the two women flung their arms around each other. Each kissed the other on both cheeks, and they began to weep. "*Cead mila fáilte!*" Sheena cried. "A hundred thousand welcomes, Cait! Oh, Rosie, she's here. My sister is here!"

"Sheena, Sheena, let me look at you!" the woman said, turning Sheena around and around. "You're so lovely!"

"Me? Aye, 'tis you Caitie! You're all grown up, so you are, and as pretty as a shamrock in your green dress. Look at your hair! What have you done with it? Oh my, aren't you the stylish young thing in all your ringlets and silvered combs? Have you ever seen such *shingerleens* as these, Rosie?"

Rosie shook her head, but Sheena paid no attention to her friend's response. She was completely enraptured at the arrival of her sister. And no wonder. Rosie herself could hardly believe such a beautiful creature existed—let alone that she had deigned to set her delicate feet on the prairie.

Caitrin's curling hair glowed like a red-hot fire. Her emerald green eyes sparkled with life. Her cheeks flushed with the most delicate shade of damask rose, and her lips shone in a perfect porcelain pink.

Anyone could see that Sheena and Caitrin were sisters by the turn of their noses and the tilt of their eyes. But where Sheena was short in stature and had been pleasingly rounded by years of childbearing, Caitrin stood tall and elegant, as fine-figured as a queen.

And her dress! Rosie gaped at the wondrous creation in emerald green lawn. The full-hooped skirt had been trimmed in ribbon and braid. Fabric-covered buttons ran up the fitted bodice in a neat row. A loose coat with a small ribbon at the neck had been crafted of matching green fabric. And perched on that glorious mass of long red curls sat the most elegant pillbox hat.

Abashed at her own faded blue cotton dress, Rosie backhanded a smudge of dirt from her forehead and shoved her work-worn hands behind her apron. Lucky to have a petticoat, she had never even considered the luxury of hoops. As for buttons, Rosie had managed to put together a collection of odd-sized fastenings—not one of which matched the other.

As she sized up Sheena's sister, Rosie sensed something unpleasant—and all too familiar—rising inside her heart. It was envy. She had learned the voice of envy well in her years at the Home. Now it was whispering again, and she could hardly deny the truth of its message. She felt like a skinny, bedraggled little prairie dog next to this astonishing creature.

"Isn't she lovely?" Sheena cried, turning Caitrin in Rosie's direction. "Isn't my sister the most elegant lass in all the world?"

"I believe she is," Rosie agreed.

"Nonsense, Sheena. You're as full of blarney as you always were!" Caitrin laughed, and it was the merriest sound Rosie had ever heard. "In all your chatter you've failed to introduce me to your friend, so you have. I'm Caitrin Murphy and pleased to make your acquaintance."

The young woman extended one of her gloved hands. Rosie

shook it in wonderment at the woman's friendliness. Could it be possible that Caitrin was not only beautiful but kind? This was worse than Rosie could have imagined.

"And you are—?" Caitrin asked when Rosie remained tongue-tied.

"She's Rosie, so she is," Sheena explained. "Rosie Mills. She's my dearest friend in all the world. Not only that, but she's a bold young thing with a good *killeen* of God's common sense between her ears. I'll have you know she's built a town, so she has—and all by herself."

"A town?" Caitrin glanced around at the flat prairie. "But where is it?"

"Sure, you're standing directly on the main street of Hope, Kansas."

The young woman looked down at her feet. "I don't see a street, Sheena. I only see . . . dirt."

"It's a post office," Rosie said. "We have a post office here. And that makes it a town. Sort of."

"And where do you live in town?"

Rosie's envy couldn't quite suppress the warm feeling that filled her at Caitrin's valiant attempt to accept the absurd situation. "I live in there. In the barn."

"That's not a barn," Sheena said. "It's the town mercantile."

"Sheena?" Caitrin reached out and took her sister's hand. "Are you feeling well?"

At this comment Sheena burst out laughing and gave her sister another bear hug. "I'm well enough to be sure, Caitie. Has Jimmy clapped eyes on you yet?"

"Not yet. The children told me he was away in the fields."

"I'm not surprised. He's been working day and night. I never have a spare moment with the man. Sure, he's taken on the farming for two other fellows while they've gone off to fetch supplies—Rolf Rustemeyer and Rosie's Seth."

"You're married?" Caitrin asked, turning back to Rosie. Her green eyes were wide with interest. "Have you any children?"

"No, I'm—"

A shriek from Sheena cut off her explanation. "Glory be to God—it's them! It's my Jimmy, so it is! And look who he's leading. Seth and Rolf!" She picked up her skirts and started running in the direction of the approaching wagon, Stubby running behind her as fast as his lanky legs would take him. "They've come home! Jimmy! Jimmy, look who's here! It's our Caitrin. Our beautiful Caitie! She's come all the way from Ireland. Everyone's here together at last. What a day, what a glorious, wonderful day!"

Rosie grabbed her apron and quickly dabbed the perspiration from her neck and cheeks. Seth was home! She could see him sitting tall and straight on the wagon, his black hair gleaming in the sunshine. The very sight of him told her that her heart had not lied. He was everything she had been dreaming of. Beside Seth sat Rolf Rustemeyer. And little Chipper between them.

"The men have been to Topeka," she explained to Caitrin. "They've come back with seed and plant stock. We had a grasshopper invasion, you see, and we thought we were all ruined, but then—"

"You must run to your husband and son, Mrs. Mills. They'll be anxious to see you. Don't mind me in the least."

"Oh, Seth is not . . . he's not my husband."

"No? But I thought Sheena said—"

"I'm only Mr. Hunter's employee." Rosie bit her lower lip as she studied the fair creature who was even now assessing Seth as the wagon pulled up to the barn. Every fiber of Rosie's heart warned her to build a barrier of protection around Seth and Chipper. They were hers. They belonged to her by right.

"Seth and I . . ." she began. But she knew what she wanted to say wouldn't be true. Seth had never given her the hint of a promised future with him. Though her heart claimed him, he was free. And for all Rosie knew, God might have brought Caitrin Murphy to the prairie to become Seth's wife. It would be wrong to step out against that plan. She must submit to his will, not her own.

"Seth and I don't . . . he hasn't courted me. I work for him, that's all."

"But he's looking at you as though you were a honey rose and him starving for sweetness." Caitrin elbowed Rosie. "Go to him, now. Sure, I know a moonstruck man when I see one."

"Miss Murphy, you don't understand—"

"I'm Caitie to you. Here, let me pin up your hair." The young Irishwoman reached up and poked on Rosie's bun for a few moments. Then she whipped a small silver comb from her own cinnamon curls and slipped it into Rosie's brown hair. "There now. It won't matter a whit that you haven't a bonnet. You look as fine as any lady in Dublin."

She gave Rosie a prod. Stunned at the young woman's act of kindness and equally dazed at the sight of Seth Hunter, Rosie found it was all she could do to move her feet in the direction of the wagon. Seth walked slowly toward her, a slight hitch in his gait.

"Afternoon, Miss Mills," he said. A grin tilted one corner of his mouth. "I hope Rustemeyer and I don't owe you a toll for crossing the bridge back there."

"No, of course not . . . no." She felt so silly inside. Like a jar of jelly left out in the sun. "Are you limping?"

"We had a little run-in with Jack Cornwall a couple of days ago. Low-down snake peppered us."

"Jack Cornwall!" Rosie glanced at Chipper. "Was anyone badly hurt?"

"Well, I winged Cornwall with Rustemeyer's pistol. I don't think it killed him. But maybe he'll think twice before coming after us again. And Rolf took a couple of pellets in his shoulder."

Rosie let out a breath. There was more to this story, and she intended to hear it—later. "I see you found seed," she said.

"Everything we went after. And then some."

"Hallo, Fräulein Mills," Rolf said, stepping up beside Seth. "How you are?"

"I'm fine, Mr. Rustemeyer." A sudden thought occurred to Rosie. A bright hope. A brilliant plan. "Sheena's sister has come from Ireland. Caitrin Murphy."

The German's gray eyes shifted their focus to the vision in emerald green. So did Seth's blue eyes. Both men instantly swept off their hats as Caitrin glided forward on her little kid boots.

"Pleased to meet you, I'm sure," she said tilting her pretty head of red curls at the two men. But her attention turned quickly away. "Jimmy O'Toole! How well you look! Sure you've put on weight since I saw you last—and all of it muscle."

Jimmy—as skinny as a fence rail—flushed bright red when his sister-in-law swirled over and gave him a warm embrace. "Caitrin Murphy, welcome to Kansas," he said. "We're happy to have you with us, so we are."

"Hi, Rosie!" It was Chipper. Rosie looked down to find Seth's son gazing at her. "How you been, Rosie?"

"I've been fine," she said, kneeling to wrap her arms around him. "But I've missed you, sweetie."

"We missed you, too. Look!" He opened his mouth and pointed to the gap where a lower front tooth had been. "Notice anything different about me?"

"You lost another tooth!"

"Yep. It was hangin' by a thread, and I couldn't eat nothin'. Papa pulled it out. I didn't even cry."

"Good for you. You're a brave boy." Rosie allowed herself a glance at the adults. Everyone had clustered around Caitrin Murphy—even Rolf and Seth. "What do you think of Sheena's sister?"

"Purty. She gots the same green eyes as Sheena an' all her kids, huh?"

"Yes, she does."

"You been plowin', Rosie? You gots dirt on your face."

"I do?" Rosie grabbed her apron and swiped the hem across her cheek. "Did I get it?"

"Naw. It's sorta all over."

"All over." Rosie shut her eyes. It was useless to feel envious of Caitrin Murphy. There was not a way on God's green earth that Rosie could compete with the Irish beauty. What little affection she had earned from Seth she was bound to lose now. After all, he had made it clear that true love sprang from passion. And what man in his right mind wouldn't feel passionate about Caitrin Murphy?

"Sure, I'm looking forward to meeting everyone in town," the young woman said in her singsong Irish accent. Rosie's heart nearly stopped.

"Town?" Seth looked around. "Nearest town is a fair distance from here."

"Nonsense! Sheena tells me I'm standing on the main street of a fine Kansas town." Caitrin gave Rosie a warm smile. "A town with a mercantile *and* a post office. And it has all been built by one very clever young lady by the name of Miss Rose Mills."

Everyone turned to stare at Rosie. She wished she could sink right into the hard prairie sod. She shrank into herself, her eyes pleading with Sheena for a rescue. But Sheena was suddenly preoccupied with her children.

"A mercantile?" Jimmy said.

"A post office?" Seth said.

"A *town?*" Rolf said.

"Right here!" Caitrin lifted her arms and turned around and around. "Surely Rosie, Sheena, and I are not the only ones who see it. It's Hope, of course. A town called Hope!"

Rosie had never known that things could go so very well—and so very badly—all at the same time. On the good side of things, August and September brought the planting and healthy growth of a whole new range of crops. Chipper and Stubby at his side, Seth worked the fields from sunrise to sunset, stopping only to wolf down the meal Rosie had packed for him in an oak splint basket.

Rosie had more to do than she could possibly accomplish. The post office and mercantile brought a stream of visitors day and night across the pontoon bridge. The stash of bright silver dollars rose to the top of the buried crock again—and Rosie was obliged to bury a second crock. And then a third.

Jimmy had flat-out forbidden Sheena to have anything to do with the enterprise. She was a mother, he reminded her, with five children who needed corralling. But every morning Caitrin Murphy strolled across the bridge bearing goods to sell to the travelers—baskets of hot bread Sheena had baked and bowls of fresh eggs the children had gathered.

Invariably, the young Irishwoman stayed most of the day at the barn. Not once did she mention a desire to set up a school or begin soliciting students. She loved the work of selling, bartering, and trading, and in the process, her greatest talent blossomed. Caitrin Murphy, as it turned out, was a genius in the art of transformation.

"We need windows," she announced one afternoon in early October. "Do you know what I mean, Rosie? Grand big windows right in the front of the mercantile. With glass panes to show off all our merchandise."

"Don't forget this building is really a barn, Caitie," Rosie said. She was folding bolts of fabric to stack on the row of shelves Caitrin had nailed up and down the barn walls. "I don't think Seth would like the idea of glass windows in the same place he'll be housing his livestock this winter."

"Livestock. Oh, the very thought of it! Sure we can't have the nasty beasts in here. They'll ruin all our work."

"It's a *barn*, Caitrin."

"Not anymore it isn't. Look at this place! We've put the chickens to roost in the new coop. The cows are out in the pasture. The mules work in the fields every day. We've carpets on the floor and even these glass-topped counters. It's not a barn anymore. Truly it's not."

"You're right," Rosie acknowledged. "You've changed it."

She still could hardly believe the way Caitrin Murphy had managed it. In the two months since arriving from Ireland, Cait had talked Rolf Rustemeyer into building a large wire chicken coop. She had talked Jimmy O'Toole into hauling three enormous counters across the trail from Holloway's station—after she had persuaded Rosie to buy them from the family who had taken over the Holloway homestead. She had talked Carlotta Pippeto into lettering a big wooden sign that read *Hope Mercantile and Post Office*, and she had talked Sheena into painting the sign in bold black strokes.

In fact, Rosie sensed the whole enterprise had gotten completely out of hand. And that was the bad part of the way things were going. Ever since Seth had returned from Topeka, he had retreated farther and farther from Rosie. He worked all day in the fields. In the evenings, he went out to the barn to cut shingles, sharpen tools, or build furniture.

When he did chance to cast a glance Rosie's way, his blue eyes were inscrutable. What was he thinking? What did he want? Why wouldn't he say it in words?

She could only assume he resented the mercantile and post office. She knew he didn't like people traipsing across his land any more than Jimmy did. And she had the feeling he was still concerned about Jack Cornwall. No rumors of the man's whereabouts had filtered out to the homestead, but Rosie couldn't imagine that any person so determined would give up.

Rosie sighed. "Mr. Hunter will be the one to decide about putting plate-glass windows in his barn," she told Caitrin.

"Mr. Hunter this. Mr. Hunter that!" Caitrin set her hands on her hips. "Why do you care so much what that man thinks?"

"I work for him."

"You love him!"

Rosie drew in a deep breath. "Caitrin, the harvest is starting to come in now. In a week or two, I'll probably be on my way back to Kansas City to work at the Christian Home for Orphans and Foundlings. My feelings for Mr. Hunter don't matter in the least. Winter is coming, and I won't be needed anymore."

"Not needed! That man needs you more than he needs his own life's blood."

"You sound just like Sheena."

"Of course I do. And I'll tell you the truth. If I were you and I had found a man as good as Seth Hunter, I'd marry him double-quick, so I would. But you go about your work, and he goes about his, and the two of you are just like a pair of courting chickens—dancing this way and that and never getting down to the business of it."

"Caitrin!"

"The business of *marriage* I mean. That's what this is all about, isn't it? Anyone with two eyes in her head can see that the two of you belong together. You should marry him, Rosie, and the sooner the better."

"I notice you didn't marry the man intended for you in Ireland, Caitie."

"That oaf? Not likely. Besides, I love a man I'll never marry." A wounded glaze came over Caitrin's green eyes. "Sean O'Casey is his name, and he's the finest man that ever lived. I love him. I'll love him always. My heart belongs to no other, nor shall it ever."

Rosie smoothed her hands across the flat folds of fabric. Caitrin's words mirrored her own feelings for Seth exactly. "Why didn't you marry Sean O'Casey?"

"Because he's already married, that's why. Don't look so shocked. Nothing wicked ever passed between us. Sean's father is a rich man. Four months ago, Mr. O'Casey forced his choice of a bride on his son.

It wasn't me. My own father had picked out my bridegroom, you see. But how could I live the rest of my life in that little village? Watching Sean and Fiona together day after day? Loving Sean as I do—and him loving me? No, I told my father I wouldn't do it. I would go to America to live with Sheena instead. And here I am. Bound to live alone the rest of my life and happy with my choice."

"Oh, Caitrin." Rosie didn't know when she'd ever heard such a woeful tale. It made her think of poor Rapunzel locked up in the tower by the wicked witch.

"But *you*," Caitrin said, "you have nothing to keep you from the man you love."

How little the Irishwoman understood, Rosie thought. "In many ways my problem is just like yours," she said. "You see . . . I believe that in his heart, Seth is still married to his late wife. Even though their marriage was difficult from the beginning, he must have adored her. When she died, I think something must have died inside Seth. He's afraid to let himself truly love again. He holds back. He throws himself into his work—night and day—anything to keep away from me and the feelings. . . ."

"That settles it," Caitrin announced. "The two of you belong together—never mind the man's long lost wife, God rest her soul. What we need is a grand occasion." She pondered a moment, then she snapped her fingers in delight. "I have it! We'll hold a harvest feast, so we will. We'll have it right here in the mercantile, and we'll invite all the farmers from miles around."

"Caitrin, if you want to have a party, why not hold it in Jimmy's barn? I'm afraid I've already pushed Seth too far with all these changes."

"But this is the perfect place for a feast. Two weeks should give us enough time."

"Enough time for what?"

"Enough time to get ready. Enough time to convince Seth Hunter he can't go on living without you."

"Oh, Caitrin, you don't know what you're saying! You don't know what you're doing. You're trying to change everything, but you can't! It isn't right. You can't just go around changing everything that doesn't fit with your dreams. You can't change barns into mercantiles. You can't turn a bit of prairie sod into a town. And you can't make Seth Hunter want to marry me. Besides, in two weeks, I'll be gone."

"Nonsense, Rosie. You'll be right here." Caitrin pressed a slender finger into the button at Rosie's collar. "I'm going to see that you wear the prettiest dress on the Kansas prairie. I'm going to arrange for music, dancing, and the perfect evening for a proposal of marriage. We'll have lanterns strung around the mercantile, hot cider, fried doughnuts, bobbing for apples, pies—lots of pies—and sticky buns with raisins on top, and . . ."

For a few moments, Rosie drifted in the scene that this genius of transformation painted with her words. It would be lovely indeed. The fragrance of cider and cinnamon drifting in the air, the aroma of freshly baked pies and cobblers, the scent of candles, the laughter of children. The feel of Seth's arms as they slipped around her and drew her onto the dance floor. So perfect.

Yes. She would wear one of Caitie's beautiful Irish gowns. Something in a pale silvery blue or deep russet . . . or plum, velvet plum. Caitie would pin up Rosie's hair and set jewels in the curls. Maybe she could even dust a little of Caitie's cologne across her skin. Seth would be entranced. He would fall under her spell. And then—

"Mail, Miss Mills!" Mr. Bridger from the Topeka post office marched into the mercantile and flopped a heavy sack of letters across the counter. "Got a letter for you this time. Seems like there might even be two."

Rosie sank out of her daydream like a hot cake in a drafty window. *Silly.* How silly to live in fairy tales. Seth hardly looked at her these days. Their conversations were short, matter-of-fact, and all about the business of daily life. If she had been right and working amicably side by side was all it took to make a marriage, it would be an empty lot in life. Now she understood how much more was needed to make a marriage truly fulfilling. Gentle touch. Quiet conversation. Longing looks. Passion.

No, Seth was not a man in love. And a harvest celebration was unlikely to change that. *Lord, help me to let him go. Please help me to do your will. . . .*

"Let's see now," Bridger said. "This letter here is for Rippeto. It come all the way from Italy. You ever seen such crazy writin' as this?"

Rosie studied the letter. She must concentrate on the here and now. And she must prepare herself for whatever God would lay in her future. "I can't read a word of it," she said. "Only the address."

"Hope," Bridger said. "Hope, Kansas."

Rosie rolled her eyes at the name and began to help him sort through the mail. "Here are two for Mr. LeBlanc," she said. "They look like business letters. Probably payment for milling. This one's for the young widow Hudson. Violet loves to hear from her sister in Ohio. This ought to cheer her up as the time for the baby draws near. And here's one for Jimmy, and two for Rolf Rustemeyer. Look at that writing. It's German, you know."

"Good thing that feller's been learnin' how to talk," Bridger said. "It ain't halfway hard to understand him now."

"Mr. Rustemeyer is a good man," Caitrin put in. She was sliding the letters into the cabinet of wooden mail slots she had talked Mr. Bridger into hauling all the way from Topeka for the mercantile. "He's a very hard worker."

Rosie chuckled. "I used to think that was enough in a man."

"Ain't a hardworkin' man good enough for you women?" Bridger asked. "Surely you don't figure to get good looks, a charmin' personality, manners, education, and all that out of a prairie farmer, do you? 'Cause if you do, you're gonna be in for a long wait. Here's your letter, Miss Mills. Looks like it come all the way from Kansas City."

Rosie held her breath as she took the letter. She recognized the handwriting at once. "Mrs. Jameson," she whispered. She tore open the envelope, and a scrap of paper that had been tucked inside fluttered to the floor. Scanning the letter, she absorbed the information.

"What is it?" Caitrin asked.

Rosie lifted her head. "I've been offered a position at the Christian Home for Orphans and Foundlings—where I grew up. The director writes that she has purchased a one-way coach ticket to Kansas City at great expense. I'm to be the head cook and earn three dollars a week plus room and board."

"Three dollars a week?" Caitrin exclaimed, sweeping the stagecoach ticket from the floor. "Why, that's highway robbery, so it is! You can make twice that in an hour with your bridge tolls. And the mercantile—"

"You don't understand, Caitie," Rosie said, taking the ticket. "They need me at the Home. They need what I have to give. Money is not, and never has been, the reason I work. I want to do God's will. I want to go where I can be most useful. And the children need me, Caitie, truly they do."

"*We* need you!" Caitie said. "We all do. Don't we, Mr. Bridger?"

"Hate to lose you, Miss Mills," Bridger said. "You sure have brightened up the prairie since you came along. Well, take a gander at this letter. Maybe it'll change your mind. Looks like it went all the way from here to Topeka and back again. That figures. It's from that German feller. Rustemeyer."

"From Rolf?" Rosie took the note and scanned it silently. English and German words were jumbled together, but the meaning was perfectly clear.

"Well, what does he write?" Caitie asked. Her green eyes flashed. "He doesn't want you to cook something for him, does he? The man eats like a horse, so he does."

Rosie looked again at the letter—so well-meaning and earnest, just like Rolf. These words would demand an answer. Confusion overwhelmed her, and in the end she could only chuckle and shake her head. "As a matter of fact, he does want me to cook for him—and wash his clothes, tend his garden, and have his babies. It's a formal proposal of marriage, Caitie."

"To that great *glunter*? Well, well, well. So you *are* needed out here after all."

"And in Kansas City, too. As a cook in both places." Dismay mingled with humor at the situation into which she had stumbled. "That skill seems to have emerged as my greatest offering to the world."

"What are you going to do, Rosie? Will you go and look after the fatherless children? Or will you marry that big hungry galoot? Or will you let me organize the harvest feast for you and Seth Hunter?"

Rosie slipped the letters into the pocket of her apron. "You can plan the feast, Caitrin," she said. "What I'm going to do is pray. In two weeks, I'm sure I'll have my answer."

CHAPTER 17

AFTER his return from Topeka, Seth had made up his mind to focus on his farming. His fields demanded his constant attention. And farming was a good way for him to spend time with Chipper. In the two months since their trip, the little boy had become his shadow. They plowed together, planted together, even hoed side by side down the crop rows. With three good rains and plenty of sunshine, it was beginning to look like Rosie had chosen a good name for the place. "Hope" was thriving.

But in his heart, Seth felt the coming of winter. Dormancy. The end of growing things. The long silences. The cold.

Would Rosie go away? Would she marry Rolf Rustemeyer? As Seth knelt to check his turnip crop, he turned the situation over in his mind. Rolf had insisted that Rosie was going to become his wife. Though Seth had doubted the German at first, he now felt sure it must be true. One day he had spotted a scrap of paper lying below the hook where Rosie hung her apron. As he picked it up, his eyes fell across the message. A marriage proposal from Rustemeyer. Had Rosie answered? Why not? She had nothing to turn to but a life in the orphanage where she'd grown up. She deserved more than that.

Seth longed to give Rosie a new life. A better life. Did he dare? He ran his fingers over the bright green leaves of his turnips. What kind of a future could he offer Rosie? Not much better than what she would have at the orphanage. Hard work. Children to mind. Clothes to wash. Meals to cook. Only real difference was that she'd have a house to call her own.

He looked up at the little soddy he had built. Not much to speak of there. A house made of dirt. No glass in the windows. Not even a real wood floor to sweep. When winter came, the place would be snug and warm enough. But there would be no idle pleasures—no trips to church or visits to a row of bright shops. Nothing but sitting by the woodstove and quilting or darning socks.

"Whatcha think of them turnips, Papa?" Chipper asked. "You been studyin' long an' hard over 'em."

Seth looked up at his son and realized the boy had been examining the crop as diligently as his father had been lost in thought. "I reckon we'll be pulling these turnips in a couple of weeks, Chipper. What do you think?"

"I think so, too. I bet Rosie'll put 'em into a big stew for us." He sobered for a moment. "A long time ago, Rosie told me she'd be goin' away in the fall. Is that true, Papa?"

"I don't know, son. There's not much to hold her here."

"There's me!"

"Yep, there's you. Rosie loves you an awful lot. But she's got to think about the rest of her life. She might not want to call a prairie soddy home, you know."

"I reckon she wants a family. And out here she gots me. She gots you, too, Papa."

Seth scratched the back of his neck. "I doubt I'm much of a catch, Chipper. I don't have a barrel of money to offer, or a big fancy house, or a carriage and team. Truth is, I'm about as poor as the dirt this turnip's growing in. So if Rosie had her druthers, I kind of doubt I'd be her first choice."

He stood and slapped his hands on his thighs to brush off the dust. As he and Chipper started toward the soddy, Seth glanced in the direction of the barn. Silhouetted by the setting sun, Rosie stood on tiptoe taking laundry off the line. Her slender hand reached for the pegs, plucking them one by one and dropping them into her apron. Across the field, Seth could hear her humming a hymn—something she did all day, every day. He tried to remember how it had been around his place before Rosie. Mighty silent, he recollected.

Lord, he breathed, lifting a prayer as he had seen Rosie do so many times when she thought he wasn't looking. *Lord, I've been awful angry with you. The grasshoppers and Cornwall and all. But I reckon Rosie was right when she said love took faith. Faith in you. Lord . . . I love that woman. I think . . . No, I know I love her enough to take the risk that I might lose her one day the way I lost Mary. But, Lord, dare I ask Rosie to take on this hardscrabble life? Show me. Somehow teach my heart the truth. Would Rosie want to mother a child who's not her own son? Could she love a man who is secondhand goods? And the house? Lord, could she ever come to feel that a dark, dusty, cramped soddy was a home? Her home?*

Seth sighed deeply and lifted his head. As he studied the little house he had built, he spotted something he had never noticed. Outlined by the pink sky of sunset, a large cluster of bright purple flowers nodded in the evening breeze—flowers growing on the soddy roof.

"What's that up there, Chipper?" he asked. "Up on the roof. Looks like some kind of weeds or something."

"It's purple coneflowers," Chipper said. "Don'tcha remember? You gave Rosie a seed head on our trip out to the prairie. She put it in her treasure bag that she wears around her neck. Back in the spring, she planted the seeds on the soddy roof."

"On the roof?" Seth gazed in amazement at the simple, natural beauty of the dancing purple wildflowers. "Why did she plant them on the roof?"

"So the soddy wouldn't be a house anymore." His voice took on a note of disgust. "Don'tcha know *anything* about Rosie, Papa?"

"Maybe not."

"She says you got to have flowers," Chipper said. "Rosie says flowers make a house into a home. That's why she planted them, Papa. 'Cause now we don't just live in a house anymore. We live in a home."

"Exquisite!" Caitrin Murphy crossed her arms and stepped back to admire her latest transformation. "Miss Rose Mills, you are a true beauty!"

"That you are, Rosie!" Little Erinn O'Toole fingered the ruffles on the deep claret-colored gown her Aunt Caitie had loaned away for the evening. "You look like a fairy princess."

"Snow White," four-year-old Colleen announced. "Rosie looks like Snow White."

"Where are the gloves?" Sheena asked. "Cait, you must let Rosie wear your gloves. The white kid ones with all the buttons. Where are they?"

Rosie stood in front of the stove in Sheena's house and stared down at the rippling, purple-red silk gown. Her waist, cinched tightly with a borrowed corset, curved inward and then out into the billow of a great hooped petticoat. She took a step forward. The skirt bobbed and swung. Beautiful! Oh, it was beautiful!

"Now the garnets," Caitie said, snapping her fingers. "Erinn, pass me the garnet necklace."

Rosie gasped as the chilled metal slipped around her throat. A narrow cascade of deep red garnets dripped down her bare skin to the delicate point of her bodice neckline. She had barely accepted the reality of wearing her first necklace ever, when Caitrin began screwing a pair of dangling earrings onto Rosie's lobes. Earrings! What would Mrs. Jameson say to such luxury? Such extravagance!

"Now my shawl," Caitie said. "The black one. Not that. The one with the fringe, Erinn dear."

Caitrin draped the soft wool shawl around Rosie's shoulders and gave a gentle squeeze. "There you are. Perfect. If only we had a looking glass, you would see you're a very queen tonight. Sure, your hair will be enough to send poor Mr. Hunter straight over the brink."

"You look like Snow White," Colleen said again.

"I think she looks like Cinderella," Erinn said.

"How do you feel?" Caitrin turned Rosie around and around on the packed dirt floor of the O'Toole soddy. "Do you feel like a queen?"

Rosie nodded—but not too hard. She was afraid her hair might fall down. Caitie had done it all up in loops and braids and curls. Then she had piled it so high and stuck it with so many combs and jewels and *shingerleens* that Rosie feared the slightest breeze would send the creation crashing like a great Christmas tree, scattering ornaments left and right. She wove her gloved fingers together. "I feel very . . . very wonderful."

"And you look it!" Caitrin clapped her hands together. "Now for the grandest surprise of all. A gift to you, Rosie. Can you guess who sent it? Seth! It's from Seth himself, so it is. He said, 'Give this to Rosie when she's getting ready for the dance. I think she'll like it.'"

"Seth said that?"

"Every word of it." Caitrin set a small flat box on the bed and gave Rosie a quick kiss. "We won't stay to see you open it. Sure, the rest of us must hurry over to the mercantile and join the guests. Rosie, you're to make your entrance at seven o'clock exactly. Not a second sooner. Erinn, the moment she walks through the door, you're to gasp loudly, so you are. Do you remember how we practiced?"

Erinn let out a loud gasp. "How's that?"

"Perfect. And Colleen, what are you to say?"

"I'm to say, 'Look at Rosie! She's magni . . . si . . fi . . shent. Magnishifent.'"

"*Magnificent*. Oh, just say she's lovely." Caitrin smoothed out the flounces on her own gown of deep blue. "Come along then, everyone. Rosie, we'll leave you here. Be sure to study the time. Don't be a moment late. Seven o'clock!"

Rosie stood, half afraid to move, as the O'Toole women traipsed out of the house toward the bridge. She gingerly took a single step toward the fireplace. The clock on the mantel read six-thirty. Half an hour to wait. She eyed the package on the bed. But she couldn't sit down to open it. If she did, how would she manage to keep from flipping the hoop straight up to the ceiling?

Rosie bent over carefully and picked up the flat box tied with a pink ribbon. For two weeks, she had watched the world turn upside down around her. Caitrin and Sheena—and even Seth himself—had slowly altered the character of the barn. While the two women were busy filling the front with lanterns and tables and paper decorations sent in the mail from Topeka, Seth was piling the back with radishes, lettuce, collards, cauliflower, carrots, and cabbages. His biggest cash crop would be the beets he was just beginning to harvest, and Rosie knew he had great hopes for them.

Three times Seth had stopped Rosie and asked if he could have a moment of her time. There was something he would like to say to her. But twice Caitrin had cut in—calling Rosie to help with customers or to rescue her from some little emergency. Once, just as Seth had been about to speak, Rolf Rustemeyer had dropped by. The moment had vanished—and Rosie had too. She was terrified that Rolf would ask for an answer to his letter. She wasn't ready to give it. She hadn't prayed hard enough yet. She didn't have an answer. She didn't know what to do.

With shaky fingers, she tugged apart the pink bow. Gingerly, half afraid to see what was inside, she lifted the box lid. Fabric lay flattened on a sheet of newsprint. She pulled it out into the light and let out a gasp of delight. It was a bright yellow calico bonnet!

Crisp and brand-new with long ribbons and a firm round peak, the bonnet had a gathered crown that would easily hold all her hair.

A bonnet! *Oh, Seth—what do you mean by giving me this? Is it a thank-you for my hard work? A farewell present? An apology for the loss of the old bonnet?* Or could it be . . . did he understand how much a new bonnet would mean to her? And did he want to please her with a gift that would draw her heart to his?

She needed to pray! *Dear Father, what do you want from me?* Rosie turned toward the door, and her dress spun like a carousel. How could she even concentrate enough to pray in this getup? This wasn't her. This wasn't Rosenbloom Cotton Mills. She should be cooking a big hot stew for Chipper and Seth. She should be tending a bowl of rising bread. She should be piecing her quilt. She should be seeing to the six-forty-five stagecoach from Manhattan. The stagecoach . . .

Father! Am I supposed to get on that stagecoach? Am I supposed to go back to Kansas City and help Mrs. Jameson?

Oh, she didn't know the answer. Why couldn't God hurry up and tell her what to do? She'd given him two weeks!

Maybe she was supposed to marry Rolf Rustemeyer. She could tell him her answer tonight at the harvest feast. *Yes, Rolf. I will marry you. We will be the Family Rustemeyer.* Washing clothes and growing potatoes and bearing him babies.

No! That wasn't right.

Rosie wrung her hands. What did Seth's gift mean? What had he been trying to tell her in those vain attempts to have a private word? Did he want to discuss her trip back to Kansas City? That must be it. What else could he have on his mind? The harvest was coming in. Winter was in the air. It was time to go back to the orphanage—and a new bonnet would send her off in style.

Oh, why was she wearing this silly outfit? She didn't belong in silk and garnets. She belonged in calico and gingham.

Father, what shall I do?

Knowing only what she *couldn't* do, Rosie stripped off the white kid gloves and threw them onto the bed. Then she began to pull the combs and ribbons from her hair. With every stage of her transformation from Cinderella-dressed-for-the-ball to Cinderella-of-the-ashes, Rosie felt better and better.

She unbuttoned the scores of tiny buttons down the back of Caitrin's dress, stepped out of it, and laid it across the bed. Then she took off the hooped petticoat. Then the corset. In seconds, she had slipped on her faded blue gingham dress and run her fingers up the mismatched buttons. She twirled her long hair through her hands and wound it into a familiar, comfortable bun. Slipping the new bonnet over her head, she tied the long ribbons into a bow under her chin.

Yes, the voice in her soul said. *Yes, Rosie. This is who you are, my child.*

In the distance, she could hear the six-forty-five stagecoach approaching, hoofbeats and wheels clattering down the trail. In moments it would pass the O'Toole house and cross the pontoon bridge. Then the driver would stop at Seth's barn to pay the toll.

If Rosie got on the coach, she would leave behind everything she had come to love—Seth, Chipper, the little soddy. But how could she ask more of Seth than he had to give? And how could she turn away from the orphans and foundlings who needed her?

The stagecoach. Yes, she should be on the stagecoach. She grabbed a piece of charcoal from the edge of the fireplace. *Dear Sheena*, she scratched out on the wood table. *I have gone back to Kansas City to help the orphans. It is the right thing to do. I love you all. Rosie.*

Yes, she loved them all. She did. But in the time she had spent on the prairie she had done little more than create havoc. Seth had never wanted a post office or a mercantile—or even her. She had forced her way into his life. It was time to go.

She shrugged her old white shawl over her shoulders and

stepped out into the darkness. Half blinded by unexpected tears, she reached into her pocket and pulled out the stagecoach ticket. As she started for the bridge, the coach passed her.

She waved and began to run behind it. The coach would stop at Seth's barn for only a moment. Rosie would speak to Mr. Dixon, the driver. She would get on with the other passengers. *Father, help me to leave! Help me to have the strength to leave this place!*

Rosie ran across the pontoon bridge. Up ahead she could see the barn strung with lanterns. Guests milled around the open front doors and gathered at the tables inside. The little band was tuning up. Children played hide-and-seek around the wagon wheels.

The stagecoach pulled to a stop. In the dim light, Rosie could see the driver talking with Caitrin. She took his toll money and chatted for a moment. Then he sauntered back toward the stagecoach. *Time to go, time to go.* Rosie brushed a hand across her wet cheek, lifted her skirt, and hurried up to him.

"Mr. Dixon," she said, thrusting out the ticket. "I want to book passage with you to Kansas City."

"Well, howdy there, Rosie. Kansas City, huh?" He looked her up and down. "You ain't stayin' for the festivities tonight?"

"No. I need . . . I need to go."

The driver raised an eyebrow. "If I was you, I'd stick around. Smells like some mighty good cooking's been done for this shindig."

"No, sir. I won't stay."

"Suit yourself then." He took the ticket. "Climb in round to the other side. I'll give the horses a quick check, and we'll be on our way."

Nodding, Rosie glanced inside the barn. She could see Seth talking with Violet Hudson. The widow was showing him her newborn baby. The look on the man's face was soft. Caring.

Let him go! Father, help me to let Seth go. Others need him more.

Rosie spotted Chipper in the doorway gnawing on a candied

apple. Will O'Toole had slung his arm around his friend, and the two boys were laughing at some shared joke.

Let him go! Let the child go. Others can care for him as well as I.

Where was Rolf? She really should say something to Rolf. There wasn't time. As he had written to her, so she would write to him from Kansas City—a kind letter, full of respect and admiration for him, yet firm in her refusal of his offer. She put her foot on the coach step and her hand on the door. As she leaned into the stagecoach, someone touched her elbow.

"Rolf?" She swung around.

"Miss Mills." Jack Cornwall took off his hat. "I'd really hate to accost you as I did once before, but I do need my nephew. So, if you'll just come with me now."

Seth's stolen rifle was slung across the man's back. He cradled his own shotgun in his arms, one hand resting loosely near the trigger. Her tears transforming instantly to icy fear, Rosie stepped back onto solid ground. Cornwall linked his arm through her elbow.

"Fine night for a party," he said. "You weren't thinking of leaving, were you?"

Unable to speak, Rosie walked beside him toward the barn. She could see Chipper and Will still munching on their apples, completely oblivious to the threat. In the half darkness, it would be easy to lure the boy away from the barn. Cornwall would use her to do it. She guessed he would take them both—using her as insurance—in his flight across the state. So she would return to Missouri after all . . . if Cornwall let her live that long.

"Call the boy," he said, prodding her forward a little. "Go on. Call him."

Rosie swallowed. "Chipper!"

"Hi, Rosie! Erinn said you were all gussied up. But 'cept for that bonnet, you look the same as ever to me." Chipper walked across the lighted open doorway of the barn and into the semidarkness. "Who's that with you?"

"It's your Uncle Jack," Cornwall said. "Hey, Chipper. How've you been?"

Chipper stopped and stared. "Hi, Uncle Jack. Did you come here for the harvest feast?"

"I just came to get you." His voice was soft, beckoning. "You want to go home to Gram and Gramps? They sure have missed you this summer."

Chipper took two more steps toward Cornwall. "I miss them, too. How are they?"

"I haven't seen them in a while. You know what happened? That ol' Yankee you've been staying with shot me. Right in the shoulder."

"Papa shot you?"

"You don't call that fellow papa, do you? Aw, he's just been tricking you. He's an ol' Yankee, don't you remember? He shot me, and I haven't been able to get home yet. But I'm ready to go now. Come on, and let's head out together, Chipper. You and me. I bet Gram will bake us one of her apple pies when we get home. You remember Gram's apple pies, don't you?"

"I love Gram's apple pies," Chipper said. "Can Rosie and Papa come with us?"

"We'll take Rosie part of the way at least. How about that?"

"OK. If Rosie's goin', I'll go, too. Lemme tell Papa good-bye first, Uncle Jack. He don't much like me to go off without tellin' him."

"Wait! Don't go. If you tell him you're leaving, he might try to stop you. Come on. Let's ride out. Just the three of us."

"Chipper—" Rosie began.

"Come on, Chipper," Cornwall cut in, squeezing her arm hard to silence her. "Let's go, buddy. I'll let you ride on my black horse. You'd like that, wouldn't you?"

Chipper stood for a moment. He studied Rosie. Then he eyed his uncle. Finally, he shook his head.

"Naw, Uncle Jack," he said with a shrug. "I reckon I'll just stay here with Papa. You can tell Gram and Gramps to come over for a visit. Know what? Papa says maybe we can all make peace one of these days. I sure would like that, 'cause me and Papa an' Rosie would really be happy if you lived near us. Wouldn't we, Rosie?"

Rosie did her best to nod. "Chipper, why don't you step back—"

"Come over here, Chip," Cornwall said. "Give your Uncle Jack a hug before I head off."

"Chipper, no!" Rosie said.

Cornwall jerked her with him as he lunged at the little boy. Chipper tumbled to the ground beneath his uncle. Behind him, Will O'Toole let out a howl. As Rosie fell, the shotgun barrel jabbed into her stomach. Shouts filled the air.

"Chipper!"

"Let go, Uncle Jack!"

"Stop, or I'll shoot!"

"Rosie, Rosie!"

"Seth, where are you!"

"Help them!"

Rosie struggled to move the gun barrel that was wedged beneath her ribs. She could hear Chipper shrieking in terror. *Father*, she prayed. *Father, help us!*

"Get off my boy, Cornwall!" Seth's big hand clamped onto the man's jacket. Cornwall sprang at his adversary. The shotgun jerked and went off. Rosie screamed as pellets peppered the dirt beside her.

"Chipper!" she shouted. "Chipper, where are you?"

"Rosie!"

In half a breath, the boy was in her arms. She scooped him up and struggled to her feet. Without a glance behind her, she ran with the child through the darkness, dodging around the stagecoach toward the bridge. *Get away. She must get Chipper away. Take him to safety.*

"Rosie! Rosie!" the boy cried.

"I've got you, Chipper. You'll be all right."

"Stop runnin', Rosie! We gots to go back. I don't want Papa to kill Uncle Jack!"

Rosie set the sobbing boy on the ground at the edge of the bridge. "Chipper, you can't save them both," she whispered, kneeling in front of him. "You have to let them see it through. Let God settle this thing."

"No, Rosie! Sometimes we gots to do what's right, even if we ain't had time to pray it over. Now come on with me!"

Taking her hand, the little boy pulled her down the trail, back toward the half-circle of light in front of the barn. She could see the two men there, slugging each other, fists flying left and right. Blood spattered into the air—a shower of droplets—and the gathered crowd drew back. Seth fell to the ground. Cornwall leapt at him, but Seth rolled over and came at his assailant from the side. They tumbled across the trampled earth.

Rosie and Chipper pushed through the crowd toward the two men. Chipper was sobbing, crying out, begging them to stop. Seth came to his feet again. Cornwall lunged. This time Seth was ready with a swift blow to the man's right jaw. Cornwall crumpled and sprawled backward.

"Uncle Jack?" Chipper rushed forward and fell to his knees beside the fallen man. "Are you all right, Uncle Jack? Papa, is he going to die?"

Seth limped over and looked down. He prodded his rival with the toe of his boot. "I reckon he's still with us, Chipper, though that shoulder doesn't look too good. Must be the place where I winged him a couple of months back."

Chipper ran a hand over his uncle's forehead. "You OK, Uncle Jack?" he asked. The man's eyes fluttered open. Chipper bent and kissed him on the cheek. "Uncle Jack, you didn't have to hit Papa just 'cause I said I wanted to stay here. Papa's been good to me. I love him, Uncle Jack. I love my Papa."

Rosie looked over at Seth. Though he was still breathing hard and a trickle of blood ran from the corner of his lip, he knelt beside Chipper. One big hand slipped protectively around the boy's shoulders.

"Jack," Seth said. "Can you hear me?"

The man's eyes slid open again. "I hear you."

"This boy is my son. I know you care about him. I know you loved . . . loved his mama. But I did, too." Seth wiped the blood from his mouth with the side of a finger. "Chipper's the child of my marriage to Mary. He's half of me. Maybe you don't like to hear that, but it's God's truth. I mean to keep Chipper with me, give him a home, raise him up right. He's my boy, and I love him. Three times now, you've tried to take him. I won't let you do that. Not ever."

Jack Cornwall struggled up to his elbows. The pain in his face told of an agony that went beyond his bruised jaw and wounded shoulder. "All right," he said, his words slurred. "I surrender. You win, Hunter. But it's not because of Mary. And it's sure not because of you. The only reason I'm giving my word I'll back off is because Chipper's made his choice." He turned to the boy. "You want to stay out here on the prairie with him, Chipper? You don't want to come live with Gram and Gramps?"

Chipper's lower lip trembled. He looked at his father; then he searched the crowd for Rosie. When he caught her eye, he let out a deep breath. "I want to stay here," he said. "I love my papa, Uncle Jack."

"All right, Chipper." Cornwall edged up onto his knees and then stood. Rosie was sure the man would collapse. Blood had soaked his shirt around his shoulder. He clamped a hand over the wound. "I'm going back to Missouri now."

"Uncle Jack, why don't you stay with us for a while?" Chipper said. "You look awful bad hurt."

"That's OK, little feller. I'd best be getting home to help your grandpa bring in the harvest."

The man staggered away from the barn and made his way through the gathered guests. As he vanished into the darkness, the crowd began to murmur and swarmed around Seth. "You done it, Hunter!"

"You whopped him good!"

"You sure gave him what-fer!"

"You got your boy back for good now, Hunter!"

Rosie slowly let out her breath. She could see Chipper clinging to his father's hand, his blue eyes shining up in adoration. It was going to be all right now. Cornwall wouldn't come back. He had given his word.

"Ready to head out, Rosie?" Mr. Dixon touched her elbow. "I held up the coach to see how this thing came out. But I'd best be pulling out. The next station's a good piece off."

"Yes," she whispered. "It's all right now. I can go."

CHAPTER 18

ROSIE squeezed between two men in the backward-facing seat inside the stagecoach. She tugged her shawl tightly around her shoulders and tucked her hands in her lap. As the coach began to move, she shut her eyes tight and swallowed the lump in her throat.

Yes, it was time to go. She had done everything God could possibly have wanted her to do. She had looked after Chipper during the difficult months of summer. She had helped Seth learn to be a good father to the child. She had kept his household running—food on the table, clothes washed and mended, floor swept clean. She had assisted in saving the homestead after the grasshopper plague. The toll money was safely stored away in the buried crocks, and Seth, Rolf, and Jimmy could use it as they saw fit. Her goal of leaving Seth and Chipper with something of value had been met. It was time to go.

"Quite a little to-do there," the gentleman next to her commented. He was clad in a fine gray coat and matching trousers. "Did you know the man who prevailed, madam?"

"Not very well." Rosie struggled to hold in her tears. Truly, she hadn't known Seth well. The pieces of his soul he had revealed to her, she had grown to love. But he kept back his heart. Always his heart. "I worked for him, that's all."

That was all. She had worked for Seth. Worked hard. Done her part. That was enough. It had to be.

The stagecoach clattered down the trail, and Rosie bid a silent good-bye. Good-bye to Sheena and Jimmy. Good-bye to all the children. And good-bye to Caitrin Murphy. Envy had not won a victory. Rosie truly liked Caitrin. They had become friends.

"Where are you off to, then?" the man asked. "Topeka?"

"Kansas City. I have a job there."

"A job? May I inquire as to your new position?"

"The Christian Home for Orphans and Foundlings. I'll be the cook."

"I should imagine they could find someone in Kansas City to do their cooking, couldn't they?"

"I am someone," Rosie said. "I'll do it. They need me."

"I'm sure you know best, but—"

His words were cut off by the sound of rifle fire. Rosie clapped her hands over her ears as the stagecoach began to sway. "It's Cornwall!" she cried out. "He's after us!"

"Cornwall? The man in the brawl?"

"That's him. He's come after us!" Rosie could hear men shouting outside as the horses whinnied and the coach began to slow. "Don't stop!" she hollered out the window. "Don't stop for him, Mr. Dixon!"

The stagecoach had barely halted when the door flew open. "Rosie?" Seth stuck his head inside. "Rosie, what are you doing in here?"

"Seth!"

"Where do you think you're going?"

"To Kansas City."

"Is this the man?" The dandy beside Rosie pulled a small pistol from his coat pocket. "Merely say the word, madam, and I shall put a ball through his heart."

"No!" Rosie cried out. "No, it's Seth. Seth Hunter."

"Get off the stagecoach, Rosie," Seth commanded.

"I can't." She shook her head. "I have to go to Kansas City. I can't marry Rolf because I don't love him, and it's autumn, and Mrs. Jameson needs me to cook."

"I need you to cook."

"She needs me more."

"*I* need you more. I need you, Rosie. I need you to sit with me by the stove in the middle of winter and read stories to Chipper. I need you to walk through the fields by my side. I need to talk with you . . . dance with you . . . wrap my arms around you. And I'll take care of you, Rosie. I gave you that bonnet as a promise that I'll always provide for you, always meet your needs. I want . . . I want you to be my wife. Will you do that?"

Rosie gulped as Chipper's head popped through the stagecoach door beside his father. "Hi, Rosie! Where ya goin'? We need you at home."

She looked up at Seth. His blue eyes were shining. "Chipper's right," he said. "We need you at home, Rosie."

"Well, my dear young lady." The man beside her slipped his pistol back into his coat. "I recommend that you give this gentleman the courtesy of an answer."

Rosie tried to breathe. All her life nervousness had made her talk a blue streak. But now . . . now she couldn't say anything.

"Mary," she managed. "You still love Mary."

"Mary's not with us anymore," he said in a low voice. "I know that, Rosie, and I've let her go."

"I need a new mama," Chipper said. "I pick you!"

"But how?" she whispered. "How can we be a family? I didn't give Chipper life. I don't know anything about . . . about being a wife . . . a mother. I never had a family, and I don't know how—"

"We're *already* a family," Chipper said. "It don't take flesh and blood to do it, Rosie. It just takes love."

"That's right," Seth said. "There's something you need to hear,

Rosie. I love you. I love you in a way I never understood before. It's deeper . . . stronger . . . crazier than I ever thought possible. Be my wife, Rosie. Let me love you for the rest of my life. No matter what the years bring us, let me love you. Will you do that?"

Rosie closed her eyes. *Father? What shall I say? Can you give me an answer? Is this what I'm supposed to do?*

"Come on, Rosie," Chipper said. "Sometimes you just gots to do the right thing."

"Yes," she said quickly. "Yes, I'll marry you, Seth Hunter."

His face broke into a grin, and the others in the stagecoach began to applaud. Seth reached in and slipped his arms around her. "Come here, my beautiful prairie rose," he murmured.

"I love you, Seth," she whispered as she drifted into his embrace, allowing him to carry her out into the brisk autumn air. As the stagecoach started up again behind them, his lips met hers in a tender kiss that sealed their vow. Joy flooded her heart, and she wrapped her arms tightly around his neck, savoring the promise of a lifetime with this man.

Seth turned his shoulders toward home and the bridge that linked his new family with a future he had placed in the hands of his heavenly Father. Then he lifted his heart toward a vision of Hope.

AFTERWORD

Prairie Rose mirrors the story of early settlers on the Kansas prairie. Seth's small soddy, barn, and pontoon bridge are similar to structures found on homesteads where struggling farmers battled to grow their crops. Six grasshopper plagues were recorded from 1854 to 1877, eight floods occurred from 1826 to 1892, six deadly blizzards hit between 1855 and 1886, fourteen prairie fires burned between 1890 and 1916, and countless tornadoes cut across homesteads, destroying homes and taking lives. Still the farmers toiled on, holding firm to faith in God and family.

Other settlers made a living running mills, mercantiles, and stagecoach stations. Bridge and ferry tolls earned a steady income, while post offices and churches provided a welcome means of communication for lonely farmers. Immigrants brought their traditions, their foods, and their languages with them from Europe. They also brought their enmities.

Prairie Fire tells the story of Caitrin Murphy and Jack Cornwall, whose blossoming love fans the flames of a fire that threatens everyone in a town called Hope. Look for it in the spring of 1998!

To learn more about life on the Kansas prairie, please read:

Dale, Edward Everett. *Frontier Ways: Sketches of Life in the Old West*. Austin: University of Texas Press, 1989.

Dary, David. *More True Tales of Old-Time Kansas*. Lawrence: University Press of Kansas, 1987.

Hertzler, Arthur E., M.D. *The Horse and Buggy Doctor.* Lincoln: The University of Nebraska Press, 1938.

Ise, John. *Sod and Stubble.* Lincoln: University of Nebraska Press, 1936.

Massey, Ellen Gray. *Bittersweet Country.* Norman: University of Oklahoma Press, 1986.

Schlissel, Lillian, Byrd Gibbens, and Elizabeth Hampsten. *Far From Home: Families of the Westward Journey.* New York: Schocken Books, 1989.

Stratton, Joanna L. *Pioneer Women: Voices from the Kansas Frontier.* New York: Simon and Schuster, 1981.

HEART
QUEST™

HeartQuest brings you romantic fiction
with a foundation of biblical truth.
Adventure, mystery, intrigue, and suspense
mingle in our heartwarming stories of
men and women of faith striving to build
a love that will last a lifetime.

May HeartQuest books sweep you
into the arms of God, who longs for you
and pursues you always.

Romance fiction from
Tyndale House Publishers, Inc.
WHEATON, ILLINOIS

Visit Tyndale's exciting Web site at www.tyndale.com

Edited by Kathryn S. Olson

Designed by Brian Eterno

Unless otherwise indicated, Scripture quotations are taken from the *Holy Bible,* King James Version.

Scripture quotations marked (NLT) are taken from the *Holy Bible,* New Living Translation, copyright © 1996. Used by permission of Tyndale House Publishers, Inc., Wheaton, Illinois 60189. All rights reserved.

Heart Quest is a trademark of Tyndale House Publishers, Inc.

3 IN 1   ISBN 0-7394-0311-7

Printed in the United States of America

For Sharon Buchanan-McClure,

My friend

I have come to bring fire to the earth. From now on families will be split apart, three in favor of me, and two against—or the other way around. There will be a division between father and son, mother and daughter, mother-in-law and daughter-in-law.
—Luke 12:49, 52-53, NLT

When you walk through the fire of oppression, you will not be burned up; the flames will not consume you. For I am the Lord, your God. . . . You are precious to me. You are honored, and I love you.
—Isaiah 43:2-4, NLT

CHAPTER 1

Hope, Kansas
October 1865

"THERE'S not a good heart among those folks," Jack Cornwall muttered as he led his horse across the bridge away from Hope. "Not a one."

With icy claws of pain gripping his wounded shoulder, Jack staggered down the road that would take him to Topeka. A chill wind whistled eastward across the Kansas prairie. He swung around and glared into the night, as if by sheer willpower he could intimidate the coming storm into retreat. Heedless, a frigid gust whipped beneath his lapels and ballooned his battered leather jacket.

Gritting his teeth, Jack stopped and bent over, fighting nausea. The stallion edged forward to nuzzle his master's neck with a velvet nose. A low snuffling conveyed the creature's unease at this midnight journey. Jack ran a hand down the coarse mane as he fought the reality that assailed him.

He had lost everything he'd ever fought for, everything he'd ever loved. His home. The Cornwall family farm. His sister Mary. Five of the men in his battalion—including his closest friend. The Confederacy and its goal of a new and vital nation. And now his little nephew, Chipper.

The darkness surrounding the man swirled through his thoughts. Hunger twisted his stomach. Thirst parched his tongue.

If he blacked out now—here—far from warmth, he might never make it back to his parents' home in Missouri. He tugged on Scratch's reins. The horse needed shelter from the autumn wind. They both craved decent food and a place to rest. But where?

The prairie dwellers who had dug their homes out of the Kansas sod despised Jack, and even now he tasted their hatred in the blood on his tongue. Earlier that evening the residents of Hope had gathered to cheer their neighbor Seth Hunter in the fistfight. The outcome ended any chance Jack had of taking Chipper back to Missouri. With his jaw nearly busted and his shoulder half torn apart, Jack had been forced to surrender. The crowd had parted, watched him pass, and then clamored around Seth with whoops of victory.

"Ah, forget the whole confounded bunch of 'em," Jack snarled. Then he gave a bitter laugh. "*Hope*. Yeah, sure."

A short distance down the road, a soddy formed a low hump in the endless, bleak stretch of tall prairie grass. Jack knew from hearsay that the homesteaders Jimmy O'Toole and his wife, Sheena, were his enemy Hunter's close friends, and this evening they were away at the dance. He doubted they would permit him to spend a night at their place. Not only were they loyal to their neighbor, but the O'Tooles lived with a passel of kids and relatives in the little soddy. The crowd itself would make a visitor unwelcome.

Jack snorted at the thought of the O'Toole family. Bunch of Irish street rats. Street rats turned prairie dogs. The image amused him, but his grin sent a stabbing pain through his jaw. Had Hunter broken the bone after all? Jack prodded the muscle and sinew beneath his roughly whiskered skin. Nah, it wasn't busted. Bruised, though. He'd be surprised if he didn't lose a tooth or two.

Checking his shoulder, Jack discovered that the bullet wound he'd suffered two months before had torn open during the fistfight. With all the travel he'd been doing, the blasted thing had never had a chance to heal right. Now blood seeped through his shirt and made his fingers sticky.

"Scratch," he said, eyeing the ramshackle barn near the soddy, "like it or not, the O'Tooles are fixing to have company. If you promise to keep quiet, I'll fetch you some fresh water and maybe even a few oats."

It didn't take Jack long to slip into Jimmy O'Toole's barn, tend to the horse, and locate a pile of hay in a back corner. He had half a mind to raid the nearby soddy for food, but he and his Confederate vigilante buddies had already run into trouble with the law. He didn't like the idea of landing himself in a Kansas jail. Bad enough to trespass into somebody's barn—he'd already been doing a good bit of that during the months of tracking his nephew. But busting into their house and taking their food was another matter. Yankee soldiers once had pillaged his home. Jack Cornwall would never sink so low.

He pried off his boots, stretched out on the hay, and shut his eyes. His shoulder burned like fire. If the injury didn't heal right, what would it mean to his dream of starting a blacksmithing business? How would he be able to work . . . take care of his parents . . . take care of Lucy . . . sweet, gray-eyed Lucy . . . ?

"I never saw such a *ballyhooly* in all my life," a woman's voice announced suddenly in the darkness—barely fifteen feet from where Jack lay. "Did you, Erinn? Now tell me the truth."

Jack stiffened and reached for his pistol.

"We all expected the fight." The second voice was much younger. A little girl. "All summer that wicked Jack Cornwall has been trying to make off with Chipper. Mama said Mr. Cornwall followed our Seth and Rosie the whole way from Missouri, so he did."

"Bad as Mr. Cornwall may be," the woman said, "we're to follow the good Lord's example of forgiveness. Jesus spent many hours in the company of the wicked, and his compassion helped them see the error of their ways. He never turned his back on a person, no matter how evil—and neither should we."

"If you turn your back on Jack Cornwall, he's likely to shoot you in it!"

"Aye, I can't deny 'tis a good thing he's gone."

So the O'Tooles had returned from the celebration. Jack had been expecting them, of course, but not in the barn. Not tonight. The family lived so close to the Hunter homestead they could have walked the short distance with ease. So what business did these two females have wandering around in the black night with not even a lantern between them?

"Shall I fetch a lamp from the soddy, Auntie Caitrin?" the younger girl asked. "It's so dark in here."

Jack shook his head. *No. Say no.*

"Yes, indeed," Caitrin said brightly. "I thought the moon would be enough to see by, but that wind has brought in too many clouds. You and I might be out in the barn all night fumbling with the latches on my trunk."

"Aye then, I'll be back in a flash."

"Take care now, Erinn! Don't run!"

Jack heard the child's footsteps on the beaten earth of the barn floor as she dashed toward the soddy. From his position on the hay, he studied the shadowed silhouette moving through the gloom. The woman was tall, straight, and as big around the middle as a freight wagon. It appeared she was expecting twins.

"Too ra loo ra," she sang, her voice meandering between words and humming. She bent over a large square trunk below the barn window, then she straightened again. "Too ra lay . . . Now where did I lay that pink bonnet?"

She waddled straight across the floor and stopped in front of the hay pile. Jack held his breath, willing himself to remain motionless. Leaning down, the woman began to grope around in the darkness. Her hand brushed against the toe of his boot, and she jerked backward.

"Oh, my goodness—"

"Don't scream." He caught the hem of her skirt. "I won't hurt you."

"Who-who-who—"

"Nobody. Just a traveler. I need a place to sleep."

"Take your hands off my—"

"Auntie Caitrin?" The child's voice sounded at the barn door. "I've brought the lamp."

"Don't let the girl see me," Jack hissed. "Send her away."

The woman wavered. "But I—"

"Let me rest in your barn tonight," he went on, "and I'll be on my way at dawn. I'm wounded."

He could hear her breath heavy in her throat. "Are you . . . are you that man? That Cornwall?"

"Auntie Caitrin?" the child called again. "Where are you? Even with the lamp, I can't find you."

"Protect me tonight," Jack whispered. "I'll never trouble you again."

Caitrin squared her shoulders. "I'm here, Erinn my love," she called. "Set the lamp on the shelf there by the barn door, and then you'd better go back to the house. 'Tis so late I've decided to repack the trunk myself. I'll be home in time to hear your papa read the Bible."

"But I wanted to help you."

As the light moved closer, Caitrin suddenly dropped the bulk of her immense girth on top of Jack—a pile of dresses and petticoats! He stared in surprise as a lithe woman danced across the barn and swept the lamp away from the child.

"There now, will you disobey your auntie, Erinn?" Caitrin said. "Scuttle back to the soddy, and tell your mama I'd adore a cup of hot tea before bed. Sure we'll work on my trunk tomorrow."

"Tomorrow I have chores!"

"We'll look through it right after lunch, so we will. I'll show you all my gowns and hats. I promise." Caitrin set her hands on her hips. "Now to bed with you, my sweet colleen."

"Oh, but you said—"

"Indeed I did, and my word is my vow. I wasn't thinking about the hour." She lowered her voice and cast a glance in the direction of the hay pile and the intruder shrouded in darkness. "What if there's a *pooka* in the barn?"

Erinn threw her arms around her aunt's waist. "Oh, Auntie Caitie! Could it be? I'm terrified of goblins!"

"Now then, I'm only teasing. Of course there's naught to fear. We've the good Lord with us always, and his strength is our shield. But 'tis never wise to wander about in the night. Go set the kettle on the stove to boil—there's a good girl. I'll be home before you can wink twice."

The child detached herself from her aunt and raced out of the barn, pigtails flying behind her. The woman strode to the back of the building and held the lamp aloft, bathing Jack in its soft yellow light.

"Now then, *pooka*," she said. "What do you mean by trespassing into Jimmy O'Toole's barn?"

Clutching his shoulder, Jack struggled to his feet. "Look, I said I wouldn't cause you any trouble."

"No trouble? You're Cornwall himself, are you not? Sure you're the very devil who caused such a ruction with our Seth tonight. You're the wicked fellow who's been chasing after poor little Chipper and trying to steal him away from his rightful papa."

She held the lamp higher. "Look at you standing there with your rifle and pistol and a knife stuck through your belt. Why then, Mr. Cornwall, you're trouble itself. You're the very man who—" Frowning, she peered at him. "Are you bleeding, sir?"

Jack glanced at his shoulder. "The fistfight tonight. An old wound tore open. A few weeks back your precious Seth Hunter pulled a gun on me. He shot me."

"Of course he did," she retorted. "As I recall the story, you were trying to shoot him first. Oh, this is an abominable situation. How can I go off to my tea and my warm bed if I must leave you out here bleeding? How can I sleep in God's peace tonight if I've abandoned one of his creations to a night of pain? Wicked though you are—and just one glance at your woeful condition confirms it—I can see I'm to play the Good Samaritan. Sit down, Mr. Cornwall."

With a firm shove on his chest, she pushed him down onto a milking stool. Then she hung the lamp on a nail that protruded from one of the barn's rough-hewn beams. Seizing his collar, she ordered, "Take off your jacket, sir. Quickly now, I don't have all evening. If you want Jimmy O'Toole traipsing out here with his shotgun, just dawdle."

Jack had barely begun to struggle out of his jacket when the woman grabbed a lapel and yanked off the garment. She took one look at his tattered shirt and seeping wound, and she clapped her hands against her cheeks. "But this is terrible, sir! Is the ball still in your shoulder?"

"No, it came out the other side."

He bent forward to show her the even greater wound on his back. At the sight, she gasped and sank to the floor, her purple-red silk skirts puffing around her. Covering her face with her hands, she let out a moan.

"Wouldn't you know?" she mumbled. "Papa was a fishmonger, and I nearly swooned every time he gutted one of those poor . . . miserable . . . And now this. Now *you*."

Jack studied the mass of auburn curls gathered at the woman's crown. Her hair was crusted with little trinkets—paste diamonds, silver butterflies, bits of ribbon. A delicate gold necklace hung with a heavy pearl draped around her long white neck. The scent of sweet flowers drifted up from her silk gown. Jack swallowed.

A beautiful woman. Jewels. A dark night. Common sense told him to take advantage of the turn of events. At the very least, he should snap the choker from her neck and ride away on his horse. If it was genuine, the pearl alone would feed him from here to Kansas City.

So why did he want to stroke a hand down the woman's back, whisper reassuring words, fetch her a drink of cool water?

"Ma'am?" he began, reaching out to her.

She pushed his hand away. "No, I can do this. Truly I can. And I will *not* swoon." Getting to her feet, she gathered up the clothing she had dropped earlier. "First I must pack the trunk as I promised Erinn. Then I'll fetch you something. Water. Medicine. Heaven help me," she moaned as she threw her garments into the open trunk, "I am not a nurse. What to do? Sheena would know, but of course I can't—"

"Ma'am," Jack cut into her agonized monologue as he rose to his feet again. "I'm not asking you to do anything for me. Just leave me alone here. Let me rest. I'll be gone at dawn."

She slammed down the lid of her trunk and faced him. "How can I leave you here with such grave injuries? I am Caitrin Murphy. I would never walk away from a person in need."

"Yeah, well I'm Jack Cornwall, and I don't need anything from anybody."

"Don't be ridiculous," she snapped. "Everyone needs *something*. You more than most, I should think. Even if you didn't have that . . . that awful bleeding shoulder . . . you're clearly in need of a good hot meal. Clean clothes. A haircut. A razor."

She took a step closer and looked him up and down. "Mr. Cornwall, if the condition of your flesh is any indication of the state of your soul, you are in need of a thorough cleansing both inside and out."

"What?" he said in disbelief. "Who gave you the say-so to judge me?"

"I always speak my mind. Now sit down." She pushed him back onto the stool. "Wait here."

Lifting her skirts, the woman stalked out of the barn. The scent of her fragrance lingered a moment in the air. Jack drank it in as he reflected on how long he'd been without female company. Too long. During the war, he'd spent months at a time on active duty or living in the woods with his vigilante friends and struggling to keep the Confederate cause alive. Then he had returned to find his home burned and the family farm sold to a Yankee out of failure to pay taxes. Mary was dead, Lucy suffering, and Chipper stolen away by a man who claimed to be his father. There had been no time for courting.

The auburn-haired beauty who had penetrated Jack's solitude stirred something inside him. Women had a certain softness about them, he recalled. A musical sound to their voices. A magic to their walk. He remembered now the whisper of silk skirts against petticoats. The fragility of a single curl at rest against a blushing cheek. The touch of a slender finger to the hollow of an ivory throat.

Miss Caitrin Murphy was certainly among the prettiest women Jack had ever seen. In fact, she might be perfect—except for that tongue of fire. Clearly she was no velvet-petaled flower just waiting to be plucked. The woman had thorns. Sharp, prickly spikes. She had labeled him wicked. Called him trouble. *Sit down,* Mr. *Cornwall. Wait here,* Mr. *Cornwall. Don't be ridiculous*. And what was that business about his soul needing a good cleansing?

High and mighty is what she was. Bossy, too. Just the sort of female to avoid.

"Now then, Mr. Cornwall," Caitrin Murphy said as she stepped into the barn, a wicker basket looped over one arm and a pail of water in the other hand. "I shall set you right, as a good Christian woman should. And then I'll rejoice at the sight of your backside heading out of Kansas."

"My pleasure," Jack returned. "I wouldn't live in a place like this for love nor money."

"And we wouldn't want you." She set down the pail and basket. "All the talk in the soddy is about you, so it is. 'That wicked Jack Cornwall attacked our Seth and tried to steal little Chipper,' says Sheena. 'Good riddance to bad rummage,' says Jimmy. You can thank the good Lord there's a flurry of tucking the wee *brablins* into bed or I'd never have made off with this food. Here, I brought you a loaf of bread, some apple cider, and a sausage."

She set the food in Jack's lap and busied herself with the water pail. He stared for a moment in disbelief. He had left home with twelve dollars in his pocket. When that ran out, he had resorted to eating what he could shoot or pick from kitchen gardens. But fresh bread? A whole sausage? And apple cider?

He picked up the loaf and tore off a hunk. The yeasty aroma beckoned, the crisp brown crust crackled, the center was spongy to his touch. He put the chunk in his mouth and closed his eyes. *Bread*.

"You like it?" Caitrin asked.

When he looked up, she was studying him, her head tilted and her eyes shining. Green eyes. Long dark lashes. He took another bite.

"It's good," he said.

"I baked it myself." Her lips curved into an impish smile. "Wouldn't my sister have a fine fit if she knew I was feeding our bread to Jack Cornwall? Sheena and I bake the loaves for sale, you see. There's a little mercantile across Bluestem Creek on the Hunter homestead. Rosie and I market goods to the travelers passing down the road."

"Rosie?"

"Rosie Mills. She's to be Seth's wife, so she is."

"Wife?" Jack frowned, thinking of his sister Mary and how deeply—and foolishly—she had loved Seth Hunter.

"Sure it happened tonight after the *ballyhooly* died down," Caitrin explained. "Rosie loved Seth all summer, and he loved her, too. But they were both too blind and stubborn to admit it. This evening she tried to leave on the stagecoach, but Seth fetched her back again and announced to everyone that she was to be his wife. So all is well, and in a few weeks' time, Seth will have a lovely wife, and Chipper will have a mama to call his very own."

Jack stiffened. "Chipper's mama—his *one and only* mama—was my sister Mary."

Caitrin wrung out a rag and took a step closer. "Take off your shirt, Mr. Cornwall. And while you do, I trust you will bring to mind the sad circumstance of your sister's death. Seth told us about the loss of his wife and your sister, and I'm sorry for it. But life does not always unfold as we wish."

"What do *you* know about life?"

Her eyes flashed as he shrugged off his shirt and tossed it onto the hay pile. "I know a great deal about life," she said. "Life is about losing, letting go, and moving on. I have lost more than a man like you could ever understand. I have lost love. Hope. Dreams. Everything I had lived for. But I did not go off in a rage of bitterness and revenge as you did, Mr. Cornwall. I am Caitrin Murphy. You destroy. I create."

She pursed her lips and began washing the bloody wound on Jack's shoulder. At the touch of the wet rag, flames of pain tore through his flesh, searing deeply into muscle and bone. He knotted his fists and stared down at the tips of Caitrin Murphy's shiny black slippers. Could this sharp-tongued snippet of a woman possibly be right? Had his life become a path of vengeance and destruction—a path so narrow he could find no room to turn around?

"You're a fiery little thing, you know that?" he said. "Aren't you the least bit afraid of me . . . big ol' blazing Jack Cornwall roaring into town and scaring the living daylights out of everybody?"

She gave a shrug as she began working on his back. "Fiery Caitrin Murphy and blazing Jack Cornwall. Sure we're a matched pair, the two of us. But where I've given myself to God to be used as his refining fire, you're naught but a swirling, raging, blustering prairie fire bent on destroying everything in sight."

"Fire's fire," Jack hurled back. "I'm a blacksmith by trade, and I know my business. Don't pride yourself, Sparky. One flicker of that refiner's fire can set a prairie aflame."

"Or draw precious gold from raw ore. 'Tis all in how a person chooses to make use of his fiery spirit, Mr. Cornwall. A contained blaze is a good thing, but you're a wildfire out of control. You need taming."

"Fight fire with fire, as they say." He touched the woman's arm. "Maybe you want to try taming me, Miss Murphy?"

"Wicked man. 'Tis no wonder they call you a devil." She pushed his hand away, rinsed the rag, and began to wash again. "This wound is frightful. Sure you must get yourself to a doctor, Mr. Cornwall. You might lose this arm, and then where will you be with your blacksmithing?"

"I don't need a doctor. Couldn't pay one even if I did."

"You have no money? But what have you been doing all the years before now?"

"Fighting."

"A soldier? Then a doctor will surely see you at no charge. You did battle for the honor and glory of your country."

"I'm a Confederate. I fought to save the South from the aggression of Yankees like Seth Hunter. No Kansas abolitionist doctor will treat the likes of me."

"Well, I've just come from Ireland, and I don't know much about your war and your silly politics." She dropped the stained rag back into the bucket. "But I do know you'll find better medicine at an apothecary than you will on Jimmy O'Toole's homestead. Here's a salve he uses on his sheep when they've got the fly. You must keep it near and use it often. And I brought clean bandages."

Jack studied the pile of lace-edged fabric strips she pulled out of her basket. "These are bandages? They look more like handkerchiefs."

"They were once a petticoat stitched by my own hand and edged in fine Irish lace. I could find nothing else to serve the purpose."

She handed Jack a swath of white linen and a crock of salve. "You tore up your petticoat?" he asked.

"'Twas an earthly treasure." With a shrug, she took his elbow and unhooked the lamp. "Come with me, Mr. Cornwall. You must sleep in safe hiding tonight. Perhaps Jimmy will take it into his head to check on his mules. Here's a little storage room the dear man built for me under the loft. We take more goods in trade than we can possibly display in the mercantile, so I use this room to stockpile the surplus. By the by, I shall thank you not to steal any of our inventory tomorrow when you leave. I keep careful records, and I shall know what's missing."

Using the key that hung from a ribbon around her neck, she unlocked the door to a tiny room stacked with bulky flour sacks and tinned goods. After spreading a pallet of quilts on the floor, she arranged a few things beside it. The bandages, salve, sausage, and bread she set into the basket. Then she rummaged around in her storage boxes and took down a comb, a razor, a small hand mirror, and a cake of soap. Finally, she lifted the lid of a square biscuit tin.

"Take this, Mr. Cornwall," she said, bringing out a handful of money and setting it into his palm. "It's my part of the earnings from the mercantile. I haven't much use for it out here on the prairie. Get yourself to a doctor, sir."

Caitrin turned toward the door, but Jack stepped in front of it, blocking her path. A look of dismay crossed her face as she realized he had trapped her inside the room. The light in her green eyes faded . . . to be replaced by a flicker of fear that Jack had seen all too often in his years on the battlefield. He didn't budge.

"Tell me something, Miss Caitrin Murphy," he said. He held up the wad of folded bills. "Why? Why'd you do this?"

"I told you, I . . . I have little use for money."

"I don't believe that." He took a step toward her. "Nobody does something for nothing. What's your motive?"

She swallowed hard. "Mr. Cornwall, I must go. Sheena will be looking for me. If Jimmy finds you—"

"Tell me!" He grabbed her wrist. "Nobody ever gave me anything for free. Now why'd you do it? Tell me."

"Because . . . because I found you here . . . and you'd been injured."

"Pity?"

"Only the weak are to be pitied." As she said the words, a strength seemed to fill her, and she lifted her chin. "I helped you because I am a child of God, and so are you. You were created for good, for a future and a hope. Though you may have burned out of control in your life, you are still precious to the Father. And because of him—with his love—I love you, Mr. Cornwall."

Before he could respond, she slipped around him and squeezed through the door. Jack stood for a moment, stunned, as if a bolt of lightning had shot through his head and come right out his boots. And then he shook off the daze, made a dash across the barn floor, and caught the woman by her arm.

Clapping her hand over her mouth, she stifled a cry. Her eyes widened in fear, and a curl of auburn hair tumbled to her shoulder. Jack didn't care if he scared her. Didn't care what she thought. Didn't care about anything but knowing. Knowing for sure.

"What did you say?" he demanded.

Breathing hard, she searched his face. "I said, you are precious to the Father."

"Not that part. What you said after. Say it."

"With the Father's love, I . . . I love you."

"*Again*."

"Why must I? Surely you've heard those words before!"

He stared at her, tongue-tied, trying to make sense of things. And then her face softened. The tension slipped off her shoulders.

"Oh, Mr. Cornwall," she murmured. Reaching out to him, she touched his injured shoulder with her fingers, and then she ran their tips down the length of his bare arm. Her green eyes softened and filled with a warm light that radiated to the smile on her lips.

"You are precious to the Father, Mr. Cornwall," she said, squeezing his hand. "Hear the words and believe them in your heart. You are precious, and with his love, I love you. *I love you.*"

She held the lamp before her as she turned again. Then she moved away from him, out of the barn, out of reach. The golden light faded, and he was left again in darkness.

CHAPTER 2

CAITRIN rolled over on the cornhusk mattress and gathered her niece in her arms. Young Erinn barely stirred. In the same bed, four-year-old Colleen snored softly against her auntie's shoulder, while tiny Jamie lay snuggled at their feet. At two, Jamie was already a bright, clever child, and Caitrin loved him dearly. Resting her cheek against Erinn's bright copper hair, Caitrin gazed out the window at the rising sun.

Jimmy had left the house well before dawn, and Sheena was already outside gathering eggs for breakfast. Will still slept in his parents' bed, but baby Mollie was stirring and beginning to coo. A wonderful family, the O'Tooles. Caitrin felt blessed that her sister had welcomed her into their crowded household after her long journey from Ireland. Busy with the mercantile and consumed by her chores, she had been happy enough . . . until last night.

Her thoughts turned again to the man who had trespassed into Jimmy's barn. Jack Cornwall had evoked the only welling of emotion inside Caitrin since she left Ireland. Moving through life with numb determination had kept her from facing the pain of losing the man she had planned to marry. But Cornwall's intrusion into her safe little world had sparked a conflagration of feelings . . . feelings she didn't want and couldn't seem to stuff away again.

Fear. Oh, he had frightened her. Lying there in the hay, shadowed by darkness, he had scared her half balmy. And then later, when he caught her arm, blocked her path, and chased after her through the barn, she had known the taste of terror. After all, the man was a criminal. He had shot at Seth Hunter more than once. Rumor had it, he'd even spent time in a Missouri jail.

Aversion. When had she last seen a man so greatly in want of a cake of soap and a tub of hot water? He must have been on the trail for months, with little food, no place to sleep, and the definite lack of a place to wash. Jack Cornwall carried on him the scent of horses, tobacco, and dust. His wound had horrified her, too. She could not imagine how such an injury could heal unless he saw a doctor and agreed to rest. The touch of his blood on her fingertips . . . the scent of his leather jacket . . . the warmth of his calloused hand . . .

Caitrin closed her eyes, remembering. What was that other emotion the man had aroused in her? She could hardly put a name to it. Confusion? Dismay? Fascination? Yes, that was it. He had fascinated her. Intrigued her. His voice was deep and resonant, almost husky coming to her out of the darkness. He spoke of himself with firmness, certainty, even pride. And those shoulders! But of course—he was a blacksmith. Even now, the image of Jack Cornwall's shoulders was planted firmly in her memory. Broad they had been, woven with thick sinew, and as hard as flint. Sure the man had been blessed with enough muscle for two.

Caitrin opened her eyes and studied the rosy light filtering into the soddy. Jack Cornwall would be long gone by now, far to the east, heading for Missouri and his family. She hoped he would find a doctor. And forgiveness. Hope. Love.

Father, please send Jack Cornwall someone who will love him, she prayed silently as she hugged Erinn's warm little form. *Let him hear the words again and again until his dark, empty heart is filled with the certainty of love. And Father, may he find you. May he know the taming of your . . .*

"Jack Cornwall's here!" Jimmy shouted, bursting through the

door into the soddy. His hair stood out on his head like a red flame, and his green eyes flicked around the soddy from bed to bed. "Where's Sheena? Gather the children! Caitrin, are you still abed? Get up! Get up, everyone!"

The baby burst into a wail like a banshee. Erinn jerked awake and grabbed Caitrin in a stranglehold about the neck. Colleen tumbled out of bed, hitting the floor with a thud. And then she began to howl.

"Caitrin!" Jimmy hollered over the hubbub. "You must bar the door. Hide the *brablins*. I'm after Sheena."

"Jimmy, wait!" Caitrin struggled out of bed, Erinn still hanging from her neck. "Jack Cornwall walked away from the Hunter homestead after the fistfight last night. Everyone saw the man leave. How can you say he's here?"

"His devil of a horse! 'Tis hobbled out behind the barn, so it is."

"Sure you must be mistaken." A wash of chills skidded down Caitrin's spine. She swallowed. "Have you searched the barn?"

"That I have, and he's nowhere to be found. Not a sign of the *sherral* but his horse. I fear he's stolen away my Sheena."

"Oh, Papa!" Erinn burst into tears.

"Now then, lass," Caitrin said, prying the child from her neck and looking straight into the pair of fearful green eyes. "If Mr. Cornwall's horse is hobbled behind the barn, he won't have gone away with your mama, will he? You must calm yourself, Erinn." She turned to her brother-in-law. "Jimmy, how can you frighten the children so?"

"Where is Sheena then?"

"She went to fetch eggs for breakfast. Have you looked in the coop?"

"The coop! Sure I'm a fair *googeen* this morning." Jimmy picked Colleen up off the floor and set her firmly on the bed. "Caitie, bar the door. Will, stand guard with the shotgun."

Jimmy thrust the double-barreled weapon into his son's arms.

Just as quickly, Caitrin grabbed it away. "What can you be thinking, Jimmy O'Toole? The boy is only six!"

"Look, there's Mama!" Erinn cried out, pointing to the soddy window.

Caitrin and Jimmy raced to the window to discover the plump little woman sauntering toward the house, a basket of eggs over her arm and a smile on her lips. The ribbons on her bonnet fluttered in the morning breeze as her skirt danced like a flag. On a whim, she set the basket of eggs on her head and broke into a little Irish jig, her feet deftly picking out a set of jaunty steps.

"Glory be to God, Sheena!" Jimmy roared through the open window. "Get your backside into the house, woman. There's trouble afoot!"

Sheena's head jerked up, and the basket toppled. Caitrin sucked in a breath as it fell . . . but Sheena reached out and caught it before it hit the ground. Clutching her prize to her stomach, she glared at her husband.

"The eggs, you old goat!" she shouted. "I nearly dropped them."

"Jack Cornwall is here. On our farm!"

"Awkk!" Sheena's hands flew up, the basket tumbled, eggs bounced to the ground and broke open. She grabbed her skirts, lifted them knee high, and raced to the soddy. "Cornwall! Lord save us, Cornwall!"

Jimmy threw open the door, pulled his wife inside, and slammed down the heavy oak bar. "His horse is hobbled behind the barn, so it is," he said, taking her by the shoulders. "I had just watered the mules when I rounded the corner, and there it was. Sure it's a great black devil of a horse, and Cornwall's saddle lay nearby. He can't be far."

"In the barn?"

"No, no. I looked there first. He's nowhere to be found."

"He'll steal the children!" Sheena grabbed the baby from the cradle and wrapped her arms around the infant. "Jimmy, you must go and fetch Seth. Tell Rustemeyer to come, too. The three of you must hunt Cornwall down. Kill him if you can."

"Now then!" Caitrin said, inserting herself between husband and wife. "Sheena, Mr. Cornwall won't be after our wee ones. What good would it do him to make off with a stranger's child? None at all. And Jimmy, if Cornwall's horse is here, why then it's a sign he spent the night in your barn, so he did. Perhaps he left the animal as a gift."

"A gift!" Jimmy snorted. "The man's a criminal. It wouldn't be in his nature to leave a gift."

"How can you be so certain of his nature? Perhaps Mr. Cornwall is not the fearsome man we all believe. Perhaps he has a . . . a certain longing in his heart, something none of us can truly understand. Perhaps he was lonely last night and was grateful for the shelter."

"There she goes again," Jimmy said, addressing his wife. "Ever takin' the worst and coatin' it in honey. Your sister would insist hell was nothin' more than a warm beach holiday, so she would."

"Jimmy! Watch your tongue in front of the *brablins*," Sheena scolded. "Maybe Caitie's right. If Cornwall stayed the night in our barn, he'd be long gone by now. He must have left his horse behind him."

"And set off for Topeka on foot? Sure the two of you are a pair of silly, beeheaded—"

"Then where is the man, Mr. Jimmy O'Toole?" Sheena demanded. "If Cornwall wouldn't go off without his horse, where is he?"

As Jimmy and Sheena fussed, Caitrin slipped over to the window again to study the barn. Was it possible? Could Jack Cornwall still be hiding out in her little storage room? He had promised to leave before dawn. Surely he wasn't foolish enough to risk staying in a place where everyone viewed him as the worst kind of villain.

Then another thought dawned, more awful than the first. Jack

Cornwall was dead. Perhaps his wound had filled his blood with contagion. Or the sausage she'd brought him had been too old. Or the salve for flyblown sheep had been poison to humans. Filled with remorse for his wickedness, perhaps he had ended his own life. The cider. The razor. A snake. Any number of things could have killed the man.

Caitrin gulped. First and foremost she must keep everyone away from the barn while she inspected the storage room. She would find a way to manage the consequences of her discovery later.

"Sheena's right, Jimmy," Caitrin said, turning from the window. "You must fetch Seth and Rustemeyer and search your land for Mr. Cornwall. If you don't find him, you will have no choice but to consider the horse a gift. An apology for the trouble he caused us all."

Before he could argue, she went on. "While you search, Sheena, the children, and I must carry on with our chores as usual. Sure we can't cower in the soddy day and night in fear of a lone, wounded, half-starved man. I am late to the mercantile as it is, and won't Rosie be scalded? Shall I go off without my breakfast, Sister?"

This appalling notion sent Sheena into a flurry of activity. Mourning the loss of the eggs, she barked orders left and right. Jimmy was to fetch a rasher of bacon from the smokehouse. Erinn must wash and dress the wee *brablins*. Will would stir the oatmeal and slice the bread. And Colleen must set the dishes on the table.

Her heart still in her throat, Caitrin quickly dressed and made up the beds, folding blankets and pushing the cornhusk mattresses back into shape. Then she helped Sheena cook the breakfast and serve it up. As the family ate, Jimmy announced that he would ride immediately to Seth's place. The two of them would travel upstream to speak with Rolf Rustemeyer, the big blond German farmer who homesteaded to the north. If they were lucky, other neighbors could be persuaded to assist in the search, and the O'Toole land would be scoured from top to bottom.

"We'll flush out that louse and pack him off to jail," Jimmy said. "If I have anythin' to do with it, the *sherral* will plague us no more."

"Aye," Sheena said, giving her husband a look of admiration. "That's the Jimmy O'Toole I know. Hunt down that blackguard Cornwall. Shoot him if you must. Sure you'll keep your family safe from evil, won't you, my sweet?"

Caitrin could hardly force a single bite down her dry throat. She took a gulp of water and pushed her chair back from the table. "If you'll excuse me, I must fetch a few tins of oysters from the storage," she said. "Sure Rosie will be wondering what's become of me."

"The storage room!" Sheena gasped. "Jimmy, did you check it for that Cornish vermin?"

Caitrin held her breath.

"Aye." Jimmy nodded. "The door was locked, of course. Our Caitie's a careful lass, so she is."

Caitrin managed a smile of gratitude. But she *hadn't* locked the storage room door the night before. If she had locked him in, Jack Cornwall couldn't have departed for Kansas at dawn. Then why was Jimmy unable to open it?

Sickeningly certain she knew the answer to that question, Caitrin threw her shawl around her shoulders and tied on her bonnet. After collecting the supply of fresh bread, butter, and cheese for the mercantile, she hurried outside and made for the barn.

Last night's wind had brought a nip to the air. Winter would not be long in coming. The prospect filled Caitrin with dismay. This autumn was to have brought her wedding to Sean O'Casey—a wedding she and the dashing young Irishman had planned in secret. But his father had made other plans, and in the end Sean had not been defiant enough to stand up for the right to marry the woman he truly loved. Though he had wedded the daughter of a wealthy mine owner instead, Sean had sworn he would always love his Caitie. She knew she could never love another.

Trying to push away the pain that gripped her every time she thought of her beloved, Caitrin stepped into the barn. Though her heart would always belong to Sean, he was lost to her now. Ireland was lost. Home was lost.

"*This* is the day which the Lord hath made," she whispered as she made for the storage room under the loft. "We will rejoice and be glad in it."

Caitrin repeated the verse of Scripture three times more for good measure. She knew she must seek out each day's joy rather than dwelling in its sorrow. God had given her this life and not another. Wishing would not change her lot. Anger would not change it. And certainly bathing herself in misery would never alter the fact that she lived on the Kansas prairie in a one-room dirt house with seven other people . . . and not in the O'Casey family's fine stone cottage on the green sod of Ireland.

This was the day the Lord had made. He was her strength. And no matter what came her way, she would rejoice and be glad.

Lifting her chin, Caitrin knocked on the storage room door. "Mr. Cornwall? Are you there?"

"Depends on who you are."

"I'm Caitrin Murphy."

"Then I'm here."

Relief that he was alive was replaced quickly by irritation. "And did you not promise me you'd be long gone from this place by morning?"

"Yep."

"Then why are you still here?"

The sound of heavy scraping was followed by the storage room door swinging ajar. Jack Cornwall's large frame filled the narrow gap. "Mornin', Sparky," he said.

Caitrin glanced at the barn door to make certain none of the O'Tooles had followed her, and then she slipped inside the storage room. "Don't wish me a good morning, Mr. Cornwall, when you've sent the entire household into a flap by leaving your black horse tied outside in broad daylight. Jimmy fears you'll steal his children away. Sheena dropped the morning's eggs. In short, the mere thought of your presence has thrown everyone helter-skelter."

"What does the thought of my presence mean to *you*, Miss Murphy?" he asked, his voice low. He leaned his good shoulder against a storage cabinet and studied her up and down. "Wish I'd gone?"

"Of course I do." Unwilling to let him see the consternation his appreciative appraisal caused her, Caitrin marched to a corner of the room and began sorting through the stacked tins. "Now you'll have to wait until tonight to make your escape. And what if Sheena decides to have a look in the storage room? Sure Jimmy O'Toole will string you up from the barn rafters if you're discovered. Even now, he and Seth and Mr. Rustemeyer are joining forces to scour the land for you. *Why* didn't you go?"

She turned to find Jack standing barely a heartbeat away. Catching her breath, she focused on the man's face, truly seeing him for the first time. He had gray eyes—terrible, steely gray eyes, as hard and cold and impenetrable as iron. A strong nose, its bridge slightly bent as though it had been broken once long ago. Cheekbones high and squared. A jaw that might have been carved from solid oak. And a mouth . . . oh, she hadn't expected such a mouth . . .

"Why didn't I go?" he repeated.

She jerked her attention to his eyes. "Yes, why? You've caused so much trouble."

"No one knows I'm here but you, Miss Murphy." That mouth tipped up at the right corner in a lazy grin. "Do I cause *you* trouble?"

Caitrin hugged her produce basket tightly, willing it to form a protective barrier between them. "You have not answered my question, Mr. Cornwall. Aren't you well enough to travel? Has your shoulder grown worse? Or did you simply fail to wake before dawn?"

"The shoulder's bad," he said. "I need the rest. But that's not why I stayed."

"Well, are you going to give me an explanation, or am I meant to guess and guess like a child at a riddle game?"

He smiled outright at that and seated himself on the lid of the pickle barrel that had prevented Jimmy from opening the door earlier that morning.

"I stayed because of the bandage," Cornwall said simply.

Caitrin glanced down at his bare chest and the white strips of linen wrapped around his shoulder. "The bandage? Are you quite well in the head, Mr. Cornwall? Or shall I write to an asylum and have you put away for a lunatic?"

His face sobered instantly. "An asylum is no place for a lunatic."

"No? Then what am I to make of a man who lingers in a place of danger because of a bandage?"

"Miss Murphy, are you going to listen to what I have to say, or do you intend to carp at me all morning?"

She swallowed down her annoyance. "By all means talk, Mr. Cornwall."

"I'm much obliged." He pointed to the collection of lamps Caitrin would sell later at the mercantile. "Last night after you left I lit one of your lamps and went to work on my shoulder. The salve is good, I think. Ought to help. Anyway, when I unrolled the bandage and started to wrap the wound, I noticed the lace. Fine Irish lace, I think you said?"

Caitrin nodded. "Aye, 'tis bobbin lace. In Ireland women work lace by the fire in the evenings; then we sell our creations to a laceman, who peddles them in the city. But that lace was a new pattern. I liked it, so I decided not to sell it. What does my lace have to do with your failure to leave this property as you promised?"

"I studied the stitches you'd used to sew the petticoat," he said, ignoring the question. "Tiny stitches. Even my mother would approve . . . and not much gets past her." He gave a low chuckle. "She's particular. My sister Mary always used to say . . ."

He paused and reflected a moment. When he spoke again, his voice was rough. "Been a long time since I saw fine lace on a lady's petticoat hem. Long time since I thought about a fireplace with a woman stitching beside it. Long time since anybody said to me the things you said last night. In fact, the more I turned your words over, the more I knew I hadn't ever heard such notions. I decided you were something different, Miss Murphy. So, that's why I made up my mind to stay awhile."

"Stay?" Caitrin snapped out of the daze his words had evoked. "Sure you can't stay here another night, Mr. Cornwall! Not in the storage room. I'm not a nursemaid, and I won't be fetching and running for you. I've my own work to be after, so I have. I'm busy sunup to sundown. And what if you're discovered? I'd bear the blame of it, so I would—harboring a criminal, sheltering the enemy. I'd be labeled a traitor to the whole town of Hope and everybody who loves Seth Hunter. Jimmy and Sheena would have every right to pack me off to Ireland, and I can't go back to Ireland. I *can't*."

"Nobody's going to find me. Lock the door when you leave. I'll read a few of those books on the shelf. Sleep a little. Rest my shoulder. Clean my guns. Get things back in shape. When I'm better, I'll leave."

"But you can't stay! I won't allow it."

"Are you planning to rat on me?" He crossed his arms over his chest and appraised her. "I didn't think you would. You're too blasted spunky to run crying for help. Fiery Caitrin Murphy and Blazin' Jack Cornwall, that's us."

"I'm *nothing* like you."

"No? All my life I've aimed to do something worthwhile, something that matters. I'll fight anybody to right a wrong and see that justice gets done. If I want something to happen, I do it myself. I'm bullheaded, contentious, and tough as nails. Are you any different?"

Caitrin clutched the handle of her basket, and the blood drained from her knuckles. "It terrifies me to see how the fire inside you matches that in my own soul, Jack Cornwall," she said in a low voice. "Sure we're a pair of candles burning brightly. Never have I known a man like you, a man whose flame will not flicker out at the slightest gust. But what can become of people like us out on this windswept prairie? Why will you linger here? What is it you want?"

"I want to watch you turn raw ore into gold."

"Only God can perform such a miracle." She met his eyes, determined to have the upper hand. "You cannot stay."

"I reckon I will."

"I'll lock you up and leave you to die."

"No, you won't."

"Sheena will find you."

"You'll keep her away."

"I'll tell Jimmy."

"Nope." He stood and held the door open for her. "I'm *precious*, remember? What was that you said about me last night? Oh yes. You *love* me."

"Turn my words against me, then. Make light of what I said to you in honest Christian charity." She squared her shoulders. "You *are* as wicked as they say, Mr. Cornwall. Though the good Lord commands me to love all men, I certainly don't like you. Not in the least. You are rude and stubborn and selfish. Sure I rue the moment I laid eyes on you."

Aware she must hurry to the mercantile or someone would come searching for her, Caitrin stepped past Cornwall. Relief at escaping him had just begun to seep into her when he caught her elbow. Her heartbeat skidded to a halt. Would she never be able to get away from the man without his barricading and accosting her?

She spoke through gritted teeth. "What is it *now?*"

"I wrote a letter to my parents last night." He pulled an envelope from the hip pocket of his blue denim trousers. "I understand you run a post office at that mercantile of yours. Suppose you could mail this for me?"

"Give me one good reason why I should do anything for a man like you."

"All right. A fellow I ran with at the end of the war has been searching for me. He thinks maybe I can pull our old bunch out of some hot water they got themselves into. My folks need to be on the lookout for this man."

Caitrin snatched the letter and stuffed it into her apron pocket. "Anything else I can assist you with, Mr. Cornwall?"

He smiled. "The key. You wanted to lock your storage room, remember?"

"Take it," she said, tugging the ribbon necklace over her head. "Lock the door yourself from the inside. And if my prayers are answered, you'll use that key to let yourself out tonight and leave us all in peace."

She whirled away from the man before he could capture her again. As she raced for the barn door, she heard his voice ring out behind her. "Good-bye, Sparky. Don't work your pretty little hands too hard." Mortified, Caitrin turned on her heel. "Whisht! Be quiet, you great rogue!"

Jack Cornwall was standing in plain view, his broad shoulders gleaming in a patch of morning sunlight and his brown hair ruffling in the breeze from an open window. If not for the blood-stained bandage on his shoulder, he would have passed for the finest specimen of a man Caitrin had ever seen. He wasn't handsome and elegant like Sean O'Casey. His face was rough-hewn. His form was lean—all flesh and muscle without the hint of softness.

His clothes were worn, dusty, faded. But he filled up the barn with a powerful presence that froze her breath in her throat and turned her feet into blocks of wood.

Clutching her shawl at her throat, Caitrin stared at the man. Outlined in sunshine, he stood calm and unafraid, studying her across the open space. And she understood.

Jack Cornwall was not staying in Jimmy O'Toole's barn in order to heal his shoulder. Nor to hide out from his enemies. Nor to filch himself a few free meals. In fact, he wouldn't care much if someone discovered him.

He was staying because of her. Because she fascinated him . . . just as he fascinated her. Fiery Caitrin Murphy and Blazin' Jack Cornwall, a matched pair.

"Auntie Caitie!" Erinn's high voice sang out just beyond the barn door. "Are you there, Auntie Caitie?"

Unnerved, Caitrin lifted her skirts and turned away. "I'm here, Erinn! Will you go with me to the mercantile this morning?"

The little girl danced into view, her pigtails bouncing at her shoulders. "Oh yes, I'll go with you! And after lunch may we open your trunk and look at your dresses?"

"Aye, that we shall." Caitrin glanced back over her shoulder as she left the barn. Jack Cornwall was gone.

CHAPTER 3

CAITRIN set her basket of tinned oysters on the glass display case and looked around in search of Rosie Mills. Evidence of the previous night's harvest celebration littered the large room that had begun as Seth Hunter's barn and had been transformed by Rosie and Caitrin into the Hope Mercantile and Post Office. Planks set on sawhorses still held stacks of plates and tin cups. A half-empty crock of apple cider sat beside a dish of stale popcorn. Lanterns, their wicks burned low, hung from nails around the room.

Caitrin frowned. It wasn't like Rosie to leave such a mess. It wasn't like her to be late to work, either. At that moment Caitrin spotted two figures framed by the door in the wall that divided the front of the mercantile from the barn at the back. Rose was caught up in Seth's arms as the man tenderly kissed her. Chagrined to have interrupted such a private moment, Caitrin quickly ushered Erinn back out of the mercantile, and then she called softly from the doorway. "Rosie? Rose Mills?"

A flushed face framed by a bright yellow bonnet emerged into the light. "Caitrin?" Rosie said. "Oh, it's you."

"Aye, and how are you this fine morning, lass?"

"I'm wonderful," Rosie murmured as Seth Hunter's tall frame emerged to stand behind his fiancée.

"Miss Murphy," he said, tipping his hat. "Good morning."

Caitrin noted the bright twinkle in Seth's blue eyes, and she smiled. "Finely and poorly, as we say in Ireland," she returned. "But I believe the pair of you have seen the day off to a better start than I. Now if you'll excuse me, I shall send Erinn to the creek to fetch water."

Grabbing her niece by the hand, Caitrin marched the protesting child through the mercantile door. "But Auntie Caitie, I wanted to fold the bolts of fabric this morning. You promised I could."

"Aye, that I did." Caitrin handed the girl a pail. "But we must scrub and mop first. The mail coach from Manhattan will be here soon. Shall we have our customers thinking we run a pigsty instead of a tidy shop?"

Scowling, Erinn headed for the creek, the tin bucket creaking as it swung on its handle. In a moment Seth's son, Chipper, burst from the nearby soddy and raced his dog toward the water to greet their visitor. Caitrin folded her arms and studied the children for a moment. Then she lifted an eyebrow at the mercantile.

Seth had emerged in the barnyard, whistling as he saddled one of his mules. "Jimmy was by here a few minutes ago," he called. "He has reason to believe Jack Cornwall spent the night in his barn. He's gone to round up Rustemeyer so we can search his land."

"The best of luck to you," Caitrin said. And she added under her breath, "You'll need it."

After allowing Rosie a moment to compose herself, she walked back toward the building. Caitrin was proud of the establishment and all it had come to mean to the growing community of Hope. Thanks largely to her initiative, the rough board siding wore a coat of bright red paint, a large lettered sign hung from chains over the door, and bright glass cases lined the walls. The mercantile itself was stocked to the rafters with everything a traveler could need on a journey west to the wild frontier or east toward the safety of cities and towns.

Caitrin peered around the door frame and gave Rosie a knowing grin. "Is it all right to come in now?"

"Don't be silly," the younger woman protested, her cheeks suffusing a bright pink all over again. "Why wouldn't it be all right?"

"Well . . . you and Seth . . . a pair soon to be married . . ." Caitrin gave a shrug.

"If you must know, Seth had just given me a good-morning kiss," Rosie said, stuffing a strand of wayward brown hair back into her bun. "I was upstairs in my little loft bedroom, and after I dressed, I came down the ladder to start cleaning the mercantile. Then Seth walked into the barn from the back, and when he saw me, he said, 'Good morning, my sweet prairie rose,' and I said, 'Good morning, Seth.' And then he kissed me—just like any man might kiss his future wife, which I didn't think was wrong in the least. Do you?"

Caitrin laughed. When she was flustered, Rosie Mills's tongue wagged faster than a dog's tail. "No, 'twasn't wrong," Caitrin said, laying a soothing hand on her friend's arm, "I think a good-morning kiss was exactly right."

"Yes, it was," Rosie whispered. "It was perfect." Then she flung her arms around Caitrin's shoulders. "Oh, Caitie, I'm so happy! So, so happy! I never believed I would see the day when Seth and I would marry. I was prepared to let him go. I was sure God meant for me to head back to the orphanage in Kansas City."

Caitrin smoothed a hand over Rosie's hair as her friend hugged her. "Sure I knew Seth would never let you get away from him," she said softly. "He loves you so much, Rosie. He loves you with all his heart."

"Yes, he does!" Rosie pulled away and spun around in circles again. "He loves me, Caitie. Seth Hunter loves me. All night long I repeated it to myself. Seth Hunter loves me. He wouldn't let me go. Not even one mile! He rode after me and claimed me as his very own. Oh, and Caitie, we're going to be married very soon!"

"Really? And when might the happy day be?" Caitrin began picking up dirty plates and stacking them one atop the other. Though her heart rejoiced for her friend, a hard knot had formed at the bottom of her stomach.

"The wedding is Sunday next, barely ten days from now," Rosie sang out, her voice musical. "Seth said he's going to round up a preacher if he has to ride all the way to Topeka. He doesn't think it's proper that I continue to live on his homestead. Seth says he wants to honor God and keep my reputation pure. He's going to ask Sheena if I can stay with your family the next ten days. I know it will be a terrible crush with all the children, and I told him I'd sleep in the barn."

"In the barn?" Caitrin looked up from the chin-high stack of plates, and her heart stumbled. "Oh, I don't think that's necessary. Jimmy's barn is nothing like Seth's."

"They're identical, Caitie. Except for the front of Seth's barn being a mercantile, they're exactly the same. If I could sleep in Seth's loft for an entire summer, why shouldn't I sleep just as well in Jimmy's?"

"It's dirty, that's why." Caitrin dumped the plates in the tub of water that had been used for apple bobbing. Instead of soiled dishes, all she could see was the image of Jack Cornwall standing in Jimmy O'Toole's barn. If he was discovered, everyone would know how he came to be staying in the storage room.

But Caitrin had to admit to herself that her concern for her own reputation was only half the problem. She didn't want anyone to find Cornwall because his life might be threatened. True, he was a dangerous man with those wicked gray eyes and that cocky grin. But she had unexpectedly formed a connection with him. Despite all his boldness, she sensed something vulnerable in the man. He was *human*, and he didn't deserve to die for it.

"We've cleaned Seth's barn," Caitrin said, praying she could keep Rosie away from Cornwall until she had convinced the man to leave. "It's tidy, and it smells decent. Jimmy's barn has those dreadful mules inside. The pig wanders in and out. And the goats! Have you ever smelled what a goat can do to a barn, Rosie?"

"I don't care how Jimmy's barn smells," Rosie said. "Anyway, it won't be for long."

"Well, I won't allow it." Caitrin feverishly scrubbed at the sticky debris of caramel apples and popcorn. "You can't stay in Jimmy's barn. A bride must have better."

"But there's no room for me in the O'Toole's soddy."

"Indeed there is. You'll sleep beside me, so you will. We can move Colleen into Sheena's bed for the time."

"I would never do that."

"You'll do as I say!" Caitrin announced, standing and waving a dripping fork at her friend. "You'll sleep in the soddy, Rosie Mills, and that's all there is to it."

A look of concern crossed Rosie's pretty face. "Caitrin? You're shouting at me." She paused a moment before crossing to the tub and draping an arm around the Irishwoman. "Oh, Caitie, I'm so sorry. I didn't stop to think how you must feel about all this. Here I am rambling on and on about my own wedding and all my dreams, completely forgetting that not so long ago you were planning to marry your beloved John."

"Sean."

"That's right, and the wedding would have taken place this autumn. But now you're all alone. I never once gave a thought to the terrible pain in your heart. Can you forgive me?"

Caitrin dropped the fork back into the tub and let out a breath. "Never mind about Sean O'Casey, Rosie. I hardly think of him more than four or five times a day anyhow, and then I realize there's nothing I can do to change what has happened. Sean is married, and I live in Kansas. My love for him will never die, yet I know I must not look back. If I do, I'll begin to wonder . . . to wonder . . ."

When she couldn't go on, Rosie spoke softly. "You'll wonder how it would have been to marry the man you love. You'll wonder about the children you might have borne. You'll wonder about the happy years you might have spent in his arms."

Caitrin shook her head. *No*, she wanted to say. *I'll wonder why Sean didn't come after me as Seth came after you. I'll wonder why he didn't stop me from leaving Ireland. Why he didn't put his love for me above all else. Why he let me go.*

"I'm so sorry, Caitie," Rosie whispered, holding her friend tight. "I'll try my best not to jabber about Seth."

Caitrin squared her shoulders and tugged on the bow of Rosie's yellow bonnet. "Never you mind, Miss Rose Mills and soon-to-be Mrs. Seth Hunter. You will talk about Seth as much as you like, and I shall enjoy hearing every word of it. If you'll permit me, I'll help you plan the finest and most elegant wedding Hope, Kansas, has ever seen."

Rosie beamed. "Hope has never seen a wedding. Ours will be the first."

"And the best." Caitrin watched as young Erinn entered the mercantile carrying a heavy bucket of water. "We must order ribbon from Topeka, Rosie. What color would you like? I love purple, so I do, but I believe you have a special place in your heart for yellow."

"Yellow ribbons!" Rosie whirled away, her gingham skirt billowing around her ankles. "Yellow ribbons and sunflowers! Oh, I wish Hope had a real church. We could put ribbons everywhere, Caitie. I'm going to sew Seth a new shirt, did I tell you? And Chipper will have brand-new shoes and a new hat from Topeka. But what should I wear for the ceremony? I love my blue gingham dress, but maybe I should think about spending a little of the money I've saved from the mercantile and the bridge tolls. I really love that bolt of pale blue cotton with sprays of roses everywhere. You know the one I mean? There it is, Erinn, can you see it? Climb onto the ladder and take it down from the shelf for me, will you please? And what about that pink there with the tiny dots all over it? Do you like that one, Erinn? . . ."

Caitrin sank back to the floor and the pile of dirty dishes. *Father, I love Rosie*, she prayed as she scrubbed. *I love her so much, and Seth, too. Help me to share in their joy and not for one moment dwell on my own sorrow. I don't want to grow into a bitter, angry woman eaten up by jealousy. And help me . . . please help me to put away all my memories of Sean.*

Oh, Sean. Caitrin's thoughts drifted away from her prayer. The young man's name evoked a blissful image of her handsome suitor marching up the hill to the Murphys' thatch-roofed cottage by the sea. Aye, but Caitrin had been proud to walk the streets alongside such a dashing man. With his dark curly hair and fine mustache, he had been the grandest looking gentleman in the county. And how Sean could dance! Never had a pair of feet moved so fast and with such perfection. When Sean O'Casey took Caitrin Murphy into his arms, a whole crowd gathered around to watch. How many years had he courted her? Four? Or was it five?

"It's the mail coach from Manhattan!" Rosie shouted, shattering Caitrin's reverie. "It's crossing the bridge, and look at this place. Erinn, grab the broom. Caitie, please help me put this fabric away. Oh, what if Mr. Dunham has brought passengers? They won't buy a thing!"

Caitrin leaped up and shoved the tub of water behind one of the makeshift tables. As she headed for Rosie and the swaths of calico piled on the counter, she spotted Jack Cornwall's letter lying on the floor in a puddle of water. Realizing it must have slipped out of her pocket, she swept it up and pressed it against her skirt. Blotting the paper did little good. The ink on the envelope had run, and the letter inside would be a sheet of soggy pulp.

"Hurry, hurry!" Rosie called. "Caitie, where did we hide the strongbox yesterday? And just look at this floor! Erinn, leave the sawdust alone and sweep up that popcorn over by the coffee mill."

Caitrin pushed the damp letter into her pocket and hurried to help. With only three of the fabric bolts folded and the floor still littered with remnants of the party, Mr. Dunham, the mail-coach driver, walked into the mercantile. Two fur trappers and a couple of soldiers followed him. They'd seen worse, Caitrin realized.

Rosie welcomed them and made excuses for the state of the floor. Mr. Dunham was more interested in hearing about the exciting events of the previous night. She was deep into the tale of Seth's chasing down her stagecoach when Chipper and his dog, Stubby, bounded into the mercantile. A moment later Seth, Jimmy, and Rolf Rustemeyer walked in. When they started telling the trappers and soldiers about the mysterious appearance of Jack Cornwall's black horse, Caitrin spied her opportunity.

She took out the letter, grabbed two sheets of blotting paper and a new envelope, and went to work at a back table. Cornwall's message must get to his parents—and as soon as possible. Certainly they should be warned about the troublemaker searching for their son, who was in enough hot water himself. They deserved to know about Chipper's decision to stay in Kansas with his father. They needed to understand that Seth Hunter had laid his memories of their daughter to rest and was planning to marry again. And they should be told of their son's injury. If Caitrin couldn't budge Cornwall from the storage room, perhaps a letter from his parents would.

Working quickly, she opened the envelope and took out the sodden page. She unfolded it and laid it between the sheets of blotting paper. Then she copied the address onto the dry envelope.

"Caitrin?" Rosie called from the front of the store. "Do we have any oysters?"

She barely glanced up. "In the basket on the counter. I brought some tins from storage this morning."

Caitrin peeled off the blotting paper and began to refold the letter. As she turned up the bottom of the page, she scanned the faded blue ink. She knew it was wrong to read Cornwall's words. Very wrong. But as surely as the blotting paper had soaked up the water, her eyes absorbed his words.

. . . *Keep a sharp lookout for Bill Hermann. He included my name when he testified, and he's hoping to implicate me in the Easton lynching. Don't tell him I'm holed up hurt. He'll come after me.*

Caitrin swallowed and folded up the bottom third of the letter. Mr. Cornwall's troubles were not her concern. All the same, she did wonder if he had mentioned anything about Jimmy's barn and the woman who had discovered him there in the darkness. She skimmed the letter for her name.

. . . *a* Miss Murphy *is looking after me here. She's about as Irish as they come—red hair, rosy cheeks, and a brogue so thick you could cut it with a knife. Don't have a fit of apoplexy about her being Irish, Ma. She's stubborn and mouthy. . . .*

Caitrin looked up and frowned. The very idea! How dare Cornwall call her mouthy? What else did he say about his rescuer? She glanced at the letter again.

. . . *How is Lucy? I know she misses me, and I don't like to think about her there alone. Please tell her I'm coming after her soon. Tell her she'll be with me the rest of her life, and I'll make sure she's the happiest woman on earth. Tell Lucy my heart is always with her. . . .*

Chagrined, Caitrin creased the last fold of the letter and slipped it into the envelope. So, there was a woman in Jack Cornwall's life. A woman he loved and intended to marry.

Good. A man so uncontrolled and ruthless ought to marry and be tamed by a loving wife. Best wishes to Jack Cornwall and his Lucy. May they live happily ever after.

Caitrin dropped the letter into the basket of outgoing mail. She didn't care in the least that Mr. Cornwall was engaged to be married. As for herself, she had too much work to do to ponder such matters. And besides, what gave him the right to label her *mouthy?* Certainly she spoke her mind, as any creature with a backbone ought. She held to her opinions, and she didn't mind sharing them if the situation called for it. She had a brain in her head, after all, and what good was a brain if a woman couldn't use it?

As she wiped the counters, she pondered the man's words. Why would Cornwall's mother have a fit to learn his caretaker was Irish? There was nothing wrong with Ireland and nothing wrong with Caitrin's manner of speech. *A brogue so thick you could cut it with a knife?* Of all the impudent, disrespectful—

"Caitie!" Rosie called. "Bring the mail over here, please. The stage is leaving."

Caitrin grabbed the basket and marched to the front of the mercantile. She dumped the letters into the driver's open canvas satchel, dusted off her hands, and stalked away. *There, Mr. Jack Cornwall,* she thought. *And may you be gone as swiftly as your letter.*

As the others walked out of the mercantile, she swept popcorn into a pile and pushed it toward the door. The chickens would like pecking at it, and she didn't suppose a little salt would kill them. In a moment she would finish the dusting. Then she could set to work measuring the front of the mercantile for its new windows. Rosie would certainly be surprised to hear how Caitrin had worked a miracle of persuasion at the harvest dance. The next time Mr. LeBlanc hauled a load of flour from his mill to sell in Topeka, he would return to Hope with a set of large glass windowpanes.

Floors. Shelves. Windows. Caitrin Murphy had more than enough work to fill her days. There simply wasn't time to mourn Sean O'Casey. As for Rosie and Seth, their wedding preparations would be her focus. If Rosie wanted to daydream and gush all day long, so be it. But Caitrin had more important things to do.

And Jack Cornwall? Well, he could rot away in the storage room for all she cared. She couldn't spare a second thought for a man with a cruel tongue, a troubled past, and a fiancée languishing after him. So much for the notion that he had lingered in Kansas out of fascination for Caitrin Murphy. That was a grand joke on her, but she was the better for learning the truth.

Whisking the popcorn out the front door, Caitrin straightened and leaned on the broom handle a moment. At the edge of the barnyard, Seth held Rosie in a farewell embrace. Oblivious to the two waiting men, he tenderly kissed her lips. Then he whispered against her ear, and she nodded eagerly in response. Reaching up, she touched the side of his face and straightened his hat. He kissed her on the cheek before mounting his mule. And then—as if he couldn't bear the thought of a single minute away from her—he leaned over, took her hand, and kissed her fingers.

Caitrin watched as Rosie stood on tiptoe to wave good-bye. Seth turned half around in the saddle, letting his mule follow the others across the pontoon bridge. As the men headed off, Rosie hugged herself, hardly able to contain her joy. Then she lifted her skirts, raced across the barnyard, grabbed up Chipper and swung him around and around.

Caitrin turned away. There was work to be done.

Jack Cornwall sat on the pickle barrel trying to read the text of *The Pilgrim's Progress* by lamplight and wondering if Caitrin Murphy would come. He had heard her in the barn just after noon that day. She and the little girl had opened a big wooden trunk and sorted through dresses, hats, and gloves until Jack thought he was going to climb the walls of the tiny storage room.

Their chatter about voile, tulle, satin, and silk hadn't bothered him. He didn't mind the endless discussion of fringe, ribbon, and lace. And he even held up under the lengthy debate about which kind of sleeves were the most flattering—flared, tiered, puffed, or capped. In fact, he could now declare himself a veritable encyclopedia of ladies' fashions. As if such knowledge were worth a plugged nickel.

No, it wasn't the female babble that had stretched his nerves. It was Caitrin Murphy's voice. Musical, it sang in his ears and sent his heartbeat stumbling like a dancer with two left feet. He craved the sound—the roll of the *R*s, the hint of laughter in every word, the lilt that made each sentence she spoke like the verse of a song.

Risking discovery, Jack had knocked out the center of a knothole and peered out at the two. Caitrin Murphy glowed in the dingy barn like a stained-glass window in a darkened church. Her hair flamed in shades of rust, cinnamon, and copper. Against the conflagration of auburn curls, her skin was as white and pure as snow. And her emerald green dress swished and swayed around her hips until Jack's head spun.

The image of the woman had burned in his thoughts all afternoon. Certain his decision to stay at the O'Toole place to recuperate had been wise, he spent the silent hours washing, shaving, and cleaning up. He focused his attention on medicating his shoulder and exercising the stiff joint. During the weeks of pursuing his nephew, Jack had tried to ignore the wound. But now he knew his recovery was crucial. If Bill Hermann found him, he'd need his wits and his strength. And a job in blacksmithing promised the only hope he had of caring for his parents and Lucy in the years to come.

Moving his arm in circles, he stared at the words on the book in his lap. *I would advise thee, then, that thou with all speed get thyself rid of thy burden; for thou wilt never be settled in thy mind till then . . .*

Jack slammed the book shut. Thee, then, that, thou? What kind of garbage writing was this supposed to be? The only *wilt* he knew anything about was a piece of soggy lettuce—and it never settled anybody's mind or stomach either.

He glowered at the book's green cover. Where was Caitrin? Was she going to leave him out here to starve? He glanced at the shelves stacked high with jars of apple jelly, beef and venison jerky, and dried apricots. OK, maybe he wouldn't starve. But didn't she want to see him? Wasn't she even curious about whether he'd left yet?

He was curious about Caitrin Murphy. So curious his brain fairly itched. What had brought a woman with so much life in her all the way from Ireland to the barren Kansas prairie? What spurred the ambition that drove her to tend a mercantile day after day? Where had she come up with the notion that God considered any man precious? The first battlefield skirmish he'd witnessed had taught Jack that human life was as fragile as a cobweb. If God thought people were precious, why did he let them die so easily? And what had possessed Caitrin to utter those amazing words—words that fluttered around in Jack's head like crazy butterflies? *I love you. I love you.*

"So, you're still here, *pooka,*" Caitrin's musical voice said in the semidarkness.

Jack jerked upright. The woman was standing a pace away just outside the storeroom door. "I didn't hear you come in."

"Sure you were too busy reading that book. What is it?" She leaned across him and studied the cover. "*The Pilgrim's Progress.* Good, perhaps it will scare some religion into you."

"What makes you so sure I don't have religion already?" Jack stood, hoping to catch another whiff of the sweet scent that had drifted up from her hair a moment before. "Maybe I'm a preacher in disguise."

"A devil more like." She shoved a basket into his stomach. "Here, *pooka.* It's all I could gather without the others taking notice. There's a chicken leg for you and some corn. I trust you won't mind eating it off the cob in the American fashion—you being such a fine citizen of this country, while I'm merely Irish."

She brushed past him and went to her money jar. Jack watched in amazement as she emptied her pockets and refilled her stash.

Obviously it would be a simple matter for him to steal everything she'd earned that day and add it to the cash she had given him earlier. Either she didn't care about money at all . . . or she trusted him. An odd thought.

"The Irish don't eat corn on the cob?"

She swung around. "We eat potatoes, don't you know? We dance little jigs and search behind every bush for leprechauns with their pots of gold. We're *Irish.*"

Bemused at the hostile tone in Caitrin's voice, Jack studied the woman in silence. She was arranging and dusting her shelves with enough steam to power a locomotive. He knew he should try to figure out what might have set her off, but his attention wandered to the more interesting fact that a single tendril of fiery hair had escaped her topknot and drifted down onto her long white neck. What was the scent in her hair? Some kind of flower, but he couldn't put a name to it. He took a step closer.

"I trust your shoulder's healing, Mr. Cornwall," Caitrin said, stacking and restacking small paper sacks filled with coffee beans. "Perhaps you're well enough to be off tonight. We've Rosie Mills living with us now, and it was all I could do to keep her from spending the night in that very loft above your head. She'll be staying here with the O'Tooles until her wedding, and if you think I can stop her from having a look in this room, you're wrong. If anyone is stubborn, it's her. In fact, I'd wager Rosie Mills is a great deal more mouthy—"

Caitrin caught her breath, and her hands paused on the coffee sacks. "A great deal more what?" Jack asked, wondering whether that auburn curl would feel silky or coarse to the touch.

"Talkative," Caitrin finished. "She talks a good bit more than I do."

"I don't mind your talk."

"Don't you?" She whirled around. "I suppose now you'll tell me you have all manner of fine opinions about me."

"I might." He took the tendril between his thumb and forefinger. "I've been thinking all manner of fine things about this particular curl."

Silky. He stroked down the length of the tress until his fingers touched the bare skin at her nape. "As a matter of fact, I'd have to say that this is the finest curl I've ever seen on a woman. And it smells nice. What is that scent, Miss Murphy?" He bent his head and traced the side of her neck with his breath. "Flowers. Roses?"

"Lily of the valley," she whispered, her voice barely audible.

He could feel the tension emanating from her as she stood motionless, barely breathing. But she didn't run. Didn't protest. So he took the tendril and feathered it against her earlobe. "This is a fine ear, Miss Murphy. A perfect ear. And as for your neck . . ." He trailed his fingertip down her velvet skin to the high collar of her dress. "It's a fine neck you have, Miss Murphy. What you said a minute ago was right. I believe I do have all manner of fine opinions about you."

"No," she managed. "No, you don't, and may the good Lord forgive you for your wicked lies."

Her green eyes assessed his, and her voice grew in strength as she faced him. "Though we both may be fiery of spirit," she continued, "you and I could not be more different in the way we have chosen to live our lives. You are a treacherous man, Mr. Cornwall, and I have great compassion for the poor woman who trusts you with her heart. You are not worthy of Jimmy O'Toole's sheltering barn. You do not deserve one kernel of the kindness I have shown you. From this moment, I shall pray that you will mount your black horse and ride as far from this place as possible. Your words disgust me. Your touch repels me. And though you may wither away in this room, you will never see me again."

Caitrin marched past Jack with her jaw set. He let her get as far as the storeroom door. "What was it you told me last night, Miss High-and-Mighty?" he said. "Those three little words?"

She stopped and faced him. "You'll be fortunate to ever know the honest love of a good woman. If you don't rid yourself of your burden of wickedness, you'll never receive the great blessings of our Father in heaven. And for those two losses, sir, I give you *these* three words: I pity you."

Caitrin was gone as quickly as she had come. Jack stared after her into the darkness. *Pity?* He clenched his fists, torn between desire for the woman whose scent still lingered in the room and fury at her bold rejection. She had labeled him a treacherous, wicked liar. What did she know about Jack Cornwall?

He yanked up his book and hunkered down on the pickle barrel again. Nobody was perfect, and Jack had his fair share of flaws. Sure, he possessed a lightning-quick temper, and he'd rather settle a score with a gunfight than a debate. He could hold a grudge better than any man he knew. He liked to do his work well, and he wouldn't tolerate imperfection in himself or anybody else. And he didn't have a lot of patience for nonsense.

Maybe he hadn't set foot in a church for years—but that didn't make him some kind of sinner condemned to the everlasting flames, did it? He'd sure prayed plenty of times on the battlefield. Caitrin had referred to his burden of wickedness. What did she know of the burdens he carried?

With a snort of disgust, he opened his book and took up where he'd left off. "Get thyself rid of thy burden," he read aloud. "For thou wilt never be settled in thy mind till then; nor canst thou enjoy the benefits of the blessing which God hath bestowed upon thee till then."

As the words sank in, Jack flung the book across the room. The movement tore through his injured shoulder like wildfire. Standing, he clamped a hand over his wound and stalked out of the room. Enough was enough. It was time to get on with life.

CHAPTER 4

"HAS JIMMY accepted the notion that Jack Cornwall has finally gone?" Rosie asked as she sat stitching beside the O'Tooles' warm stove with Sheena and Caitrin. "I noticed he went out after supper tonight to check on the black horse."

Sheena grunted. "Aye, after the men found no sign of the villain the other day, Jimmy vowed to keep combing the land. But he gave up on it today. The horse is ours, though we have no desire for it."

"No desire for a good horse, Sheena?" Caitrin asked, looking up from a wool sock she was darning. Any talk of Jack Cornwall made her uncomfortable. She had kept her word and stayed away from the storage room the past five days, but she couldn't seem to stop fretting about him. Though his horse remained, surely without fresh food or water the man himself had gone.

"Why wouldn't Jimmy want a fine horse like that?" she wondered aloud. "'Tis better than a mule, so it is, and there's no reason to hate the horse just because its owner was rotten. The trouble over little Chipper is ended. Cornwall must have surrendered the boy to Seth and Rosie and gone on his way. I can't think the horse is anything but a gift."

"A gift from a Cornishman?" Sheena spat out a snippet of thread. "I'd prefer a wheelbarrow full of rotten potatoes from a friend over a fine horse from a Cornishman."

Rosie looked up from stitching her wedding dress—a pale yellow gown with a row of pearly buttons down the bodice. "How do you know Chipper's uncle is a Cornishman, Sheena? Did Jimmy speak to him?"

"His name is Cornwall, isn't it? I should think that settles the matter."

"Cornwall is a county in England," Caitrin explained. "It lies along the western coast. A rough place, so it is."

"What's wrong with Cornishmen?" Rosie asked.

"The Cornish are the very pestilence of the earth," Sheena spoke up. "Tell her, Caitie."

Caitrin sighed. "Here we are in Kansas, Sister, and half a world away from the shores of Ireland. What use is it to hate the Cornish?"

"What use? For a start, Jack Cornwall's behavior toward us shows the very reason the Cornish are such a wicked people. They're a greedy, selfish lot. They'll lie and cheat an honest person into utter poverty if given half a chance. Tell Rosie about the Cornish, Caitie. Go on."

"The troubles go back hundreds of years," Caitrin said, unwilling to dispute the elder sister she always had loved so dearly. "The Cornish are a Celtic people, as are we Irish. They're clannish and warlike, and their tales of King Arthur are as ancient as our legends of Bran the Blessed. Sure the beloved green sod lies but a few miles from the coast of Cornwall, divided only by the Irish Sea."

"And there's half the trouble," Sheena cut in. "Fishing."

"The Irish claim certain fishing grounds, and the Cornish claim others. But it's never quite settled which is which and whose is whose. We've battled over fishing rights for centuries."

"Tell Rosie about the mining, Caitie."

"Tin mining," Caitrin explained wearily. She could hardly believe the scarlet hue that had risen to her sister's cheeks over this discussion of a trouble so far removed. "Ireland has few precious things to dig out of the ground beyond peat and tin. We burn the peat, but we can sell the tin for a profit." She thought for a moment about Sean O'Casey and his new wife, the daughter of a wealthy mine owner. "A man with an interest in a tin mine can earn himself a fair measure of riches."

"And those wicked Cornishmen are tinners, too," Sheena said, tucking pins into her unruly red hair. "Sure they try to undersell us, don't they, Caitie? They set their prices just a tad lower than ours, and all the market races after Cornish tin. Ooh, they're a scheming, nasty lot, those snakes. I knew Jack Cornwall was as wicked as the rest of them, so I did, the very moment I heard his name. 'Twould be just like a Cornishman to chase after a poor, wee child and try to steal him away from his rightful papa. Viper! I do believe if I ever clap eyes on Jack Cornwall or any of his breed, I'll wring their necks with my bare hands, so I will."

"Sheena!" Caitrin jabbed her needle into the toe of the sock. "Would you be so cruel yourself, now? And you here in Kansas without a mackerel or a tin mine in sight?"

"A Cornishman is a Cornishman is a Cornishman," Sheena said. "Take one of them out of Cornwall and put him in the middle of a desert—and he'll try to cheat you out of the very sand you're standing on."

At that moment Jimmy stepped into the soddy and tugged off his boots. Caitrin eyed him in silence. She had no desire to continue this ridiculous discussion. Good or bad, a man should have the chance to prove himself by his own actions . . . and not be judged by the entire history of his race.

Jack Cornwall, of course, *had* shown himself a liar.

In his letter he had called Caitrin mouthy and stubborn. But fancying himself at an advantage in the barn, he had tried to woo her with all manner of pretty words. And then he had touched her. Caitrin shut her eyes, willing away the memory of the man's fingers against her skin. Every time she thought of that moment, a shiver ran straight down to the tips of her toes. But Jack Cornwall had promised his life to another woman, a creature who even now sat waiting for him to come and make her a wife. How cruel of him to use two innocents for his own pleasure.

No, the man had proven himself unworthy—not because he was Cornish—but by his selfishness and troublemaking in both Missouri and Kansas. And *why* couldn't Caitrin remember those things, instead of the tingling caress of his fingertips sliding down her neck . . . and the way his broad shoulders gleamed in the lamplight . . . and the look in his gray eyes when he spoke to her . . . ?

"You left a lamp burning in the storage room, Caitrin," Jimmy said, crossing in front of the stove. "I spied it when I was seeing to that horse."

"A lamp?" Caitrin swallowed and glanced out the window.

"No fear. I went in and blew it out." He settled down on a stool with his pipe. "You'd left the door unlocked."

"Caitie, that's unlike you," Sheena said. "You always lock the storeroom."

"She's been working too hard on my wedding," Rosie put in. "You must be exhausted, Caitie. I'll go lock up for you. Where's the key?"

"No!" Caitrin stood quickly, almost knocking over her own stool. "I'll do it. I . . . I want the fresh air."

Jimmy gave a chuckle. "Fresh air? Sure it's cold enough to freeze your lungs out there. I'm expecting snowfall any moment. Leave the storage door unlocked tonight, Caitie. Nobody's going to steal your precious supplies."

"No, no. I'd better see to it." Before the others could try to dissuade her, Caitrin grabbed her shawl, pushed open the soddy door, and hurried outside.

As she raced across the open yard toward the barn, her heart beat out a frantic prayer. *Oh, Father, what shall I do if Jack is still here? How can I make him go away? And why does the merest thought of him leap into my soul on wings of hope and joy? He's not a good man. He's caused so much trouble for everyone. Father, I pray . . . oh, I beg of you . . . don't let my loneliness blind me! Show me the man as he truly is!*

The barn was pitch black inside, but Caitrin flew across the dirt floor without a thought for roosting chickens or clumps of hay that might trip her feet. Gasping for breath in the frigid air, she forced her steps to slow as she approached the storage room. She could see the faint outline of the open door, and she pushed it open with one hand.

"Mr. Cornwall?" she whispered. "Are you here?"

The little room was cloaked in silence. As she calmed, a chill crept up her bare arms. She stepped inside and peered around, but it was too black to see. "Mr. Cornwall?" she said a little louder. "'Tis Caitrin Murphy. Where are you?"

Again, nothing. Fumbling in the dark, she found the lamp on a shelf. She managed to light it and take it down. The faint yellow glow revealed an empty room. The pallet of quilts lay folded in one corner. The pickle barrel was shoved up against a wall. A stack of books sat beside it along with the crock of salve. The bandages lay in a heap on the ground.

So he had gone away tonight, just a little before Jimmy came in to blow out the lamp. Or perhaps Jimmy's near-discovery had caused him to flee. Perhaps even at this moment, he was riding his black horse toward Missouri and the man who wanted to hunt him down. Swallowing, Caitrin picked up the length of bloodstained fabric and studied the delicate lace edging. *Been a long time since I saw fine lace on a lady's petticoat hem.* Jack's deep voice drifted through her thoughts. *I decided you were something different, Miss Murphy. Something I've been needing a touch of.*

Why had he needed her? She reflected on their conversation, and the answer was obvious. Jack Cornwall had needed Caitrin Murphy because of the three words she spoke on their first meeting

. . . words he confessed he had never heard in his life. *I love you.* So simple, so easy to say. He had asked those words of her again and again. Yet she had not deigned to speak them to him a second time.

Despite his poor opinion of her in the letter to his parents, Jack had expressed a need. But she had been too proud . . . too high and mighty . . . to fill the empty place in him. Because he thought her stubborn and mouthy and because he had trifled and flirted with her while intending to marry another woman, she had railed out at him. Called him wicked, treacherous, a liar.

The Lord Jesus would never have done such a thing. Though Christ stood in righteous judgment of the unrepentant wicked, he also loved them so deeply he came to earth to give his very life for them. Aye, he dined with tax collectors, forgave thieves, and protected wanton women. *He that is without sin among you, let him first cast a stone at her,* the Master had said. *All things whatsoever ye would that men should do to you, do ye even so to them.*

Oh, but the haughty Caitrin Murphy had been wounded. Too miffed to see beyond herself to Jack Cornwall's need for true love—the love of God—she had spurned the man. And now he was gone.

Caitrin carried the lamp to the door. Who was the more wicked of the two? She knew very well the Light of Life, yet she had snuffed out that holy glow in the face of a man who had never heard a word of love spoken to him.

Shivering in misery, she pulled the door shut and glanced at the empty keyhole. Jack had gone off with the key. And that was all he had taken from this place—a little food, a few days rest, a head full of harsh words, and a key.

Remorse forming a lump in her throat, Caitrin set the lamp on a nail keg and fell to her knees beside the pile of hay on which she had first discovered Jack Cornwall. Clasping her hands together, she bent over and poured out her heart.

"Forgive my pride," she whispered, "forgive my cruel words, and forgive my selfishness . . . my jealousy. . . . Oh, Father, that was it. I was jealous of her, that woman in the letter. It was Sean and the miner's daughter all over again, and I was the one abandoned. Forgive me, please forgive me—"

A loud thump sent hay scattering across Caitrin's lap. "Who's Sean?"

Her eyes flew open to find Jack Cornwall himself crouched on the hay in front of her. Shirtless and smiling, he was the picture of vigor. For a moment, her mind reeled. Had God dropped the man from the sky? Was he an apparition to which she must beg forgiveness in person? She stared, unable to speak.

"Sean and the miner's daughter," Jack said. "Anybody I would know?"

Caitrin squinted up at the barn's rafters. Then she focused on him again. "Where did you come from?"

"The loft. I exercise my shoulder up there at night." In demonstration, he leapt up, grabbed a low wooden beam, and swung himself onto the loft ladder. From there, he seized a support beam with both hands and pulled up and down, his chin meeting the top of the bar as his muscles strained with the effort. Three, four, five, six. On the seventh, he let go and dropped down onto the hay again.

"I reckon I'm just about as good as new," he said, breathing hard. "Take a look at the shoulder."

Her tongue still tied in a knot, Caitrin studied the mound of hard sinew with its visible scar. Indeed, the wound had closed in front and back. Though the mark the bullet had left remained thick and tight, his shoulder obviously was flexible. Powerful. Massive.

"So, tell me about this Sean fellow," Jack said. He squatted on the hay across from her and draped his arms across his knees. "Somebody back in Ireland?"

Caitrin blinked and focused on his face. Shaggy brown hair, squared cheekbones, silver eyes. Her heartbeat faltered. "I thought—I thought you had gone away."

"Tomorrow. I wanted to get back in shape for the journey in case I run into trouble. Long way to Cape Girardeau. After I'm there, I'll need to find a job. The work I do takes a good arm." He looked her up and down. "Didn't expect to see *you* again."

"Jimmy said—"

"The lamp. I know. I watched until he'd gone into the soddy before I lit it, but he came back out to check on Scratch—my horse. He must have seen the light while I was up in the loft. I reckoned I was done for, but he just blew out the lamp and walked away."

"He assumed I'd left it lit."

Jack nodded. "So you came out to see if that wicked, lying scoundrel was still in your storeroom."

"The door . . ." She gestured vaguely in that direction. "I needed to lock it."

"Figured I'd finally gone, huh?"

"Oh, Mr. Cornwall, I must tell you how sorry I am for my harsh words," Caitrin burst out. "You have every right to think me mouthy and stubborn, for that is exactly what I am. And even though your dear mother believes ill of the Irish, she's no worse than my sister, Sheena, who holds a poor opinion of the Cornish—never mind how vigorously I dispute her. I should not have spoken so cruelly to you, for you are indeed precious to God and—"

"Hold on a minute. How do you know what my mother thinks of the Irish?"

Caitrin trembled in the cold, but she knew she must confess. "Your letter. It fell into a puddle at the mercantile, and while it dried, I read it. Not all, but some. More than I should. It was truly bad of me, and I implore your pardon. You see, when first we met and spoke here in the barn, our words together were heated and lively and full of spirit. I began to think of us as truly a pair of candles burning bright . . . as though we were alike in purpose and in heart. I believed we were something of a match, you and I, and a measure of my loneliness faded in the hope of a kindred soul. But then I read your letter. It was the knowledge of your beloved Lucy that provoked me so. When you spoke words of admiration for me the other evening, sure I could only think of poor Lucy waiting for your return and the day you would make her your wife."

"My wife?"

"Aye, and what you did was so like Sean O'Casey, you see. He declared his undying devotion to me, yet all the while he knew he would marry that miner's daughter. Instead of accepting you as a man like Sean—capable of wooing one woman while another waited in assurance of marriage—I expected better somehow. I always expect the best of people, and so often I'm disappointed. But I never learn, do I? Sure Sean spoke all manner of fine words and tender nothings until I was no better than butter in his hands. And when I heard your flattery—"

"Did you melt?"

She swallowed at the implication behind his question. "Your words put me in mind of Sean O'Casey and the miner's daughter. All the while you were speaking to me, I knew about your Lucy waiting at home. Aye, but I momentarily forgot what a wicked man you are, and that is where I made my error. Rather than hear you out and forgive you as a Christian ought, I grew angry at you for toying with me while Lucy sat in expectation of becoming your wife."

Jack shook his head as an odd grin tilted one corner of his mouth. "Miss Murphy, you're a wonder. A miracle. A flame-haired, green-eyed marvel."

Wariness stole over her. "What do you mean?"

"You've forgiven me for the sin of turning you into a puddle of melted butter. And all for the sake of Lucy. Lucy Cornwall—my pretty little sister."

Sudden heat raced into Caitrin's cheeks. "Your *sister?* But the letter said—"

"What was it I put in that letter meant only for my parents' eyes? Could you refresh my memory?"

"Please forgive me for reading it."

"Me forgive you? I thought I was the wicked one."

"Sure I'm wicked, too." She could hardly force out the words. Her face grew hotter as she studied her clasped hands. "You wrote that you would return to Lucy and never leave her. You intended to keep her with you all your life. I never thought—"

"I reckon you didn't." He stood and walked away.

Caitrin bent over and buried her face in her hands. Oh, this was too horrible. She had all but confessed to the man an attraction she couldn't admit even to herself. And she had mistaken his sister for a fiancée. She had to leave! The soddy would be warm and cheerful, and maybe she could put this wretched encounter out of her mind.

"Cold?" Jack's voice spoke behind Caitrin as he draped a thick quilt over her shoulders. "It's starting to snow. They'll come looking for you pretty soon."

"Aye." She sniffled and clutched the quilt at her throat. "I must go."

"Just a minute." He sat down beside her and slipped his arm around her. He had put on his jacket, but she could feel the bulk and strength of his arm through the fabric.

When he spoke again, his words were rough. "I'm going to tell you about Lucy. Maybe after I explain things, you'll see past my so-called wickedness to the man I really am. Maybe you'll understand why I went after Chipper the way I did. For years my parents have been embarrassed to speak Lucy's name beyond the walls of our house. I'm not sure Mary even told Seth Hunter about her. But I'm not ashamed of my sister, and I don't mind that you read the letter. You see, Chipper meant everything to my parents. My sister

Mary had died, and I was a grown man making my own way. In their minds, Chipper was all they had left of a real family."

"But what about Lucy?" Caitrin asked. "Why don't your parents claim her?"

"Never mind what they do or don't do—*I* claim her. Lucy is my sister, and she'll be my family long after the rest of them have passed on. Chipper already chose to stay here with Seth Hunter. My father isn't well, and he'll be gone soon. Ma won't be long after him. But Lucy is young. And she's . . ." He lowered his head for a moment. "Well, she's troubled. But I'm going to take care of her, I swear it. I plan to take a job in a livery and hammer horseshoes from dawn till dusk if that's what it takes."

"Your purpose in life is to care for your sister?"

"Protect her. I'll use my blacksmithing to provide for her. I learned my skills in the army. One day I'll have my own smithy. But now—Cape Girardeau—I'll work for somebody else to look after Lucy and my folks. I'll save what I can. Buy some land. Put up a house."

"Then you're a builder after all, Mr. Cornwall." Caitrin let out a shaky breath, finally beginning to relax in the warmth of his embrace. "I said you weren't, but you are."

"Maybe I am."

She ventured a glance at the man beside her. His face was so close she could see the texture of his skin. He smelled of shaving soap. Staring into a mist through which she couldn't see, his gray eyes were depthless.

"Your sister," Caitrin whispered. "What is the nature of her trouble?"

Jack looked at her, and she read the pain in his face. Clearly he was assessing her, weighing whether this mouthy, unforgiving, judgmental woman had the capacity to understand the sorrow that wracked him. Humiliated at the pride that had formed such a barrier between them, she reached out from between the edges of the quilt and laid her hand over his. Slipping her fingers through his, she became aware of firm sinew, callus, and a breadth that dwarfed her clasp.

"This is a hand that can protect a dear sister," she said softly. "You will bring healing to your Lucy."

"No." His jaw clenched tight, he shook his head. "No. Nobody can fix her troubles."

"What problem could hold a woman prisoner all her life . . . and offer no hope of solution?"

Jack was silent, but Caitrin could feel his heartbeat hammering against her shoulder. Finally he pulled away from her, the muscle in his jaw working hard. He looked up at the rafters of the loft. "Lunatic Lucy, they call her," he ground out angrily. "Touched in the head. Crazy as a coot—"

"Stop." Caitrin grabbed his arm. "Jack, you mustn't—"

"People throw rocks at her. Taunt her. And now, for her protection, we have no choice but to keep her confined. My parents can't manage her, but I can. And if anyone tries to interfere—if anyone hurts Lucy ever again . . ."

Beneath Caitrin's hand, the muscle in his arm bulged and hardened into solid granite. She laid her cheek against it, praying for the words to calm him. "You'll save your Lucy. I'm sure of it."

"Yeah, like I saved Chipper from the clutches of Seth Hunter."

"Chipper belongs with Seth. They love each other."

He grunted. "*Love*."

"Aye, and your love will save Lucy from her troubles."

"Nothing will save Lucy." His eyes hard, he scrutinized her. "What is it with you? You don't back away from me like I have smallpox. Don't you know I'm Loony Lucy's brother? You know what people say—maybe it's a family disease, and you'll catch it from me. Or maybe my wicked, lying ways brought Lucy's calamity on us. Maybe it's the punishment for my sins."

"Stop it, now." She covered his mouth with her hand. "Nothing you've done has brought this calamity on your sister. All of us have sinned in one way or another."

"I don't stand a chance of forgiveness for what I'm feeling right now, Caitrin Murphy, and I can't make myself repent." He pressed her hand hard against his lips. "The need you bring out in me burns like a fire inside. I think about you day and night, wanting a taste of those sweet lips . . ." He covered her mouth with his and pulled her roughly against him. His fingers slid into her hair, dislodging pins and combs. "Caitrin, hold me. Hold me tight. I've had the scent of your hair racing through my head like a cyclone whirling out of control."

For a moment Caitrin hung motionless as his mouth ignited a blaze across her lips. Shock captured her breath in her throat. Pleasure reeled through her, sending tingles dancing down her spine and shivers skipping into the base of her stomach as she arched into his kiss. And then truth tore through her heart.

"Jack," she said, clutching his shirt and pushing him away. "Sure you must not be so bold with me."

"Don't tell me that look in your green eyes isn't desire."

She shook her head. "I won't lie to you, Jack Cornwall. You're the first man since Sean to fill my thoughts for even a moment. Aye, I'm a woman, and inside me . . . there's also a need . . ." She bit her lip. "There's a longing in my heart that only the true love of a man can fill. But the Bible says—"

"Don't preach at me, Caitrin," he growled.

"No, but if you would possess my lips, then you must take my mind and spirit, too." She struggled to her feet and tugged him up to stand beside her. "I'm more than a creature with flaming hair, Jack. I've a brain, so I do, and you know precious little of what's inside it. I've a heart, too. The Spirit that dwells in my heart is not my own. Sure it's the very presence of God himself. You've a good face and strong arms, but I know nothing of your mind and heart. Indeed, you and I might find pleasure together. But pleasure lasts no longer than a season. And then what?"

Jack searched her eyes, and Caitrin refused to lower them in modesty. *Let him see that I meant what I said. Let him understand. And, dear God, please let my heart stop aching for another kiss from his lips.*

"It's time for me to go," he said. "Say the words, Caitrin. Say them to me before I leave. I want to hear them one last time."

Oh, Father, make them your words! she breathed upward in prayer. *Make them words of the Spirit. Let them come from you and not from me. Not from my heart.*

"Say the words," he repeated, gripping her shoulders.

She reached out again from her protective quilt and laid her fingertips against the side of his face. "You are precious to the Father, Jack Cornwall," she whispered. "You are precious. And with the Father's love, I love you."

"Caitrin Murphy." With a groan wrenched from deep inside him, he folded her into his embrace. "Please don't tremble. I won't hurt you."

"Aye, but you will."

"No, I swear it. I know I'm rough and bullheaded. I've done wrong in my life. And sometimes I don't think things through from start to finish before I act." His arms tightened around her. "But I'd never hurt you. You're something different, Caitrin. Every time you talk, little pieces of you get twisted around my heart. I don't understand the way you think. We're a matched pair, all right, but I don't understand that God who holds you so tight and keeps you apart from me. I need—" he paused and she could feel him searching—"I need . . . something from you. I don't know what it is."

"Maybe 'tis the three words. Not the ones you keep after me to say. Those others." She stood on tiptoe and whispered into his ear. "*You are precious*. Just think of it, Jack. You are precious to the Father—"

"Caitrin?" Rosie Mills's voice rose to a note just short of a shriek.

She was striding across the barn floor, a lantern hanging from her hand. "Caitie, what are you doing? Who's that with you?"

Caitrin jumped, but Jack pulled her close again. "It's all right, Miss Mills," he said. "Caitrin's been out here talking to me."

Rosie's eyes widened as they darted from one face to the other. Then her mouth fell open. "Caitie!" she gasped. "That's Jack Cornwall!"

CHAPTER 5

"I DON'T believe we've been introduced," Jack said, assessing the astonished young woman who stood before him. He could feel Caitrin quaking in his arms, and he tucked her hand inside his to reassure her. "Name's John Michael Cornwall, but most folks call me Jack. I'm Chipper's uncle. And you must be Miss Rose Mills."

"You-you-you—" Rosie stammered, pointing a finger—"you tried to kidnap Chipper! Y-you grabbed me at the party. You shot at Seth."

"All true. But not until after Seth had kidnapped my nephew from the only family he'd ever known."

"You're a Confederate!"

"Well now, that's a different matter entirely."

"Turn Caitrin loose!" she shouted. "You'll never get your grimy hands on Chipper this way. Let her go, you—you *Cornish snake!*"

"As I hear tell, Cornwall is not heavily populated with snakes, Miss Mills," Jack said, working to hold back a grin. "And I'm not inclined to turn loose of a good-looking woman who wants to be held." He bent to brush a kiss across her cheek.

"Caitrin Murphy!" Rosie gasped and clapped her hand over her mouth.

At that, Caitrin shrank into herself, mortified at his boldness. Jack was momentarily surprised at her response, but reality quickly became apparent. Fiery and stubborn Caitrin might be, but her loyalty to the O'Toole family proved she was no rebel. It wasn't likely she would fight them for the right to choose the man who would court her. And she would never defend a man with Jack Cornwall's reputation in the town of Hope.

The moment he'd been dreading had come. It was time to go, and he had made up his mind to leave with all the gallantry he could muster. If he could protect Caitrin from the hostility she would face over having cared for him in secret, he would do it. He loosened his embrace and stepped aside.

"Go ahead with your friend, Miss Murphy," he said. "I apologize for the inconvenience I've caused you."

"Inconvenience?" The flame in Caitrin's eyes roared to life as she turned on him. "You have caused me more misery—more *agony*—than you can ever imagine! Sure you've tilted me topsy-turvy, Mr. Cornwall. First you settle yourself in my storeroom and refuse to budge. And just when I think you've finally gone away, I begin to dread the thought of your leaving. You call me mouthy and stubborn—but the very next moment I'm your flame-haired Irish beauty. You try to kill my friend and steal his son, yet you treat me with a gentleness I've never known from a man. You command me not to preach at you, yet you beg to know what it is that makes me different."

She squeezed both her fists together and shook them at him. "A full half of my heart is praying for the moment you walk out of this barn and leave me in peace," she said. "And the other half can't—can't bear the thought of never seeing you again! After all the havoc you've caused, will you simply stand aside and wish me away with Rosie—as though I'm the merest of acquaintances?"

Jack stood rooted, absorbing her words and trying to make sense of the storm crashing around inside him. "Do you think I'm having an easy time here, Caitrin? I wandered into this barn broken and defeated. And then you came along with your lace petticoat and your red hair. You called me a villain, but you treated me like a man. You trusted me. You healed me. I don't know how, but you gave me hope. I should have left this godforsaken prairie days ago, but—"

"Now just a minute there, you smooth-talking scoundrel," Rosie cut in. Taking a step forward, she jabbed Jack in the chest with her finger. "This prairie is not godforsaken. I'll have you know a better class of people lives here than you'll ever be good enough to join! We take care of each other. We defend each other. And as for Caitrin—I don't know what kind of deceitful flattery you've tried to pull on her—but you can just take your black horse and ride straight out of here, because Seth and Jimmy won't abide your presence for a minute. Not a single, solitary minute!"

"Rosie, please," Caitrin said. "You don't understand."

"Oh, don't I? He's been toying with your heart. If he can't destroy us by stealing Chipper, he'll just ruin the prettiest, sweetest woman in our town. He's trying to sully you, Caitrin, but somehow you're blind to it. If he can't lure you into sin right here and now, he'll probably bamboozle you into running off with him."

"That's ridiculous," Jack spat out. "Caitrin has a mind of her own."

"Yes, she does," Rosie said. "And a home of her own, too. Caitrin, don't think for one second about leaving with this man. We love you, and you belong with us. Seth has planned a wonderful gift for you. I was supposed to keep it a secret until the wedding, but I'll just tell you the truth right now. This winter Seth is going to build us a brand-new house and barn—and he's giving *you* his soddy, Caitrin. Think of it. Your own house, a store to help manage, a town full of people who care about you. And if it's a husband you want, well, there's always Rolf Rustemeyer."

"Rolf?" Caitrin said.

"Who's Rolf Rustemeyer?" Jack demanded.

"He's a wonderful, upstanding, hardworking gentleman," Rosie said. "He would never steal children. He would never fight for slavery. And he would never seduce a poor, innocent woman in a dark barn. More than once Rolf has told me he would like to court you, Caitrin. So there! Your life is settled and perfect . . . and don't you listen to this man for one more minute. Now come with me before Jimmy walks out here and starts shooting."

Rosie reached for Caitrin's arm, but Jack blocked her. "Not so fast, Miss Mills. You seem to be forgetting that this poor, innocent woman you *love* so much has a right to her own opinions. As far as I'm concerned, Caitrin can choose where she wants to live, what she wants to do, and who she wants nearby. If she ever works her way through the tangle and chooses to have me at her side, you can bet your last dollar I'll treat her right. I'll protect her. And I'll fight any man who tries to come between us. Count on it."

Stamping her foot, Rosie glared at him. "I am not a betting woman!" she said. Then she swung around and faced her friend. "Fine, then, Caitrin. Choose."

"*Not yet*," Jack pronounced slowly and carefully in Rosie's face. "I have to go back to Missouri and take care of a little trouble that's been following me around. Besides that, I have people to look after. Responsibilities." Then he straightened and met Caitrin's green eyes. The look of bewilderment in them softened his fury. "I may not understand everything about you, Caitrin," he said. "But I respect you. You're something special. Something I've been needing. Maybe it's those three words, huh? What do you think?"

"Sure I don't know, Jack," she whispered.

"I don't know either, but I'll find out. You can depend on that. And now, if you ladies will excuse me, I'll get my stuff and head out before someone in this friendly little town starts shooting at me again."

He strode across to the storeroom, grabbed his shirt, his guns, and the bag of supplies he'd been accumulating, and headed for his horse. As Jack bridled Scratch, the stallion tossed his head, eager for some exercise. Jimmy had put the saddle on a sawhorse nearby. "OK, boy," Jack murmured as he fastened the cinch. "Easy, now."

Both women were standing just where he'd left them, stock-still and staring after him as he led Scratch out of the barn. It was all he could do to walk away from Caitrin Murphy, but he wouldn't cause her any more trouble than he already had.

Jack mounted and set off, peering through the swirling flakes of the now heavy snow in search of the trail that led to the road. The sky was black, as black as it had been the night he'd come to this place. But he felt none of the defeat that had burdened him then. The flame of Caitrin Murphy burned brightly inside him. So did the words she had spoken . . . those three little words. *You are precious*.

He threw back his head and stared up into the dizzying flurries, but the calm in his heart held firm. *You are precious to the Father,* her words echoed. *Precious to the Father.*

"Hey, God," he shouted upward. "Jack Cornwall here. I've been looking for you."

Watching the snow fly, he drank in a deep breath of chill air. *And I've been looking for you*, a voice answered softly.

Caitrin hurried across the barnyard toward the soddy, praying fervently to escape Rosie's questions. She had almost reached the door when her friend laid a hand on her arm.

"Caitrin?" Rosie asked. "What on earth have you done?"

Pausing, Caitrin took a breath and turned. "I know you want an explanation for what you saw tonight, Rosie, but I don't have one that will satisfy." She spoke quickly, hoping to put an end to the conversation. "Sure I found the man lying in Jimmy's barn the night of the harvest party. After his fistfight with Seth, the bullet wound in his shoulder was torn open and bleeding. I gave him a little salve and some food, as a Good Samaritan should. He was in no condition to defend himself, so I put him in the storeroom to keep Jimmy from finding him that night . . . then he refused to go away. But now he has, and that's that."

"Jack Cornwall kissed you," Rosie said, her eyes crackling beneath her yellow bonnet. "I saw it."

"He's not like we thought . . . not wicked through and through. Aye, he carries guns and rides a big black horse and shoots at people now and again. But only for a good reason. He *does* have his reasons, Rosie. You must believe that."

"I'll never believe anything that man says as long as I live. He's just like the serpent in the Garden of Eden, hiding in places where he doesn't belong and tricking innocent women with sly words."

"And what do you know of the words that passed between Jack and me?"

"Jack? You call him Jack?"

"He's a human being, Rosie, not a serpent. His name is Jack, and he has a heart far more tender than you could ever imagine. The wrong he did to Seth was done on behalf of his dear parents, so it was. Chipper is all they have of a family, except for—"

Caitrin caught herself. If she told Rosie about Lucy Cornwall, her friend's anger would surely soften. But that would betray the secret pain Jack had shared with her. If he wanted others to know of his sister and her burdens, he would tell them himself.

"Jack is loyal to his family," Caitrin continued. "He has said he would fight to protect those he loves, and that is exactly what he did in riding after Chipper. Does that make him evil?"

"Jack Cornwall also said he'd fight any man who tried to come between the two of you. Are *you* among those he loves, Caitie?"

Caitrin sucked in a breath. "Of course not. He hardly knows me. We spoke together but a few times, and never in the light of day. Jack has been away at war, and I'm likely the first woman he's met in a long time. I put a bandage on him and fed him some sausage. Sure he won't have found love in that."

"Do you love him?"

"Rosie!" Caitrin jerked the quilt up higher on her shoulders. "How can you ask such a silly question? As I've said a hundred times, I love Sean O'Casey as much today as I did the day I left Ireland, and even though he wed the mine owner's daughter, I shall never love another man as long as I live. But I won't brand Jack Cornwall a villain. I caught a glimpse of the true man that he is, and my eyes were opened."

"I think your heart was, too."

Caitrin looked away. "Think what you will, Rosie. He's gone away now. He'll be riding for his home in Missouri and the family who needs him. Work calls him, and responsibility, too. He won't trouble us again, you can be sure of that."

"After what I saw in the barn tonight, I'm not sure of anything," Rosie said. "For your sake, I pray he never comes back."

Caitrin's eyes filled with sudden, unexpected tears. "If you wish to pray about Jack, Rosie, pray for his soul," she choked out. "Pray that the Spirit of God will fill his heart. Pray for the troubled family who depends upon him. Pray for his safety from those who pursue him. Pray that he may find a good woman who has the courage to love him as he deserves. For my own part, I shall pray that if Jack Cornwall's name is ever spoken again in the town of Hope, you will remember that he is a man and not a snake. Perhaps then the Holy Spirit will direct your tongue to defend him with words of kindness, truth . . . and forgiveness."

Wiping a hand across her damp cheek, Caitrin pushed open the door and stepped into the soddy. Jimmy was snoring beside the fire. All the children were asleep. Sheena glanced up from her mending.

"Ah, Caitrin, there you are," she said. "Poor Rosie was in kinks of worry over you. You've been away such a long time. Are the stores all in place?"

"Aye, Sheena." Caitrin picked up her darning and sat down on the low stool. Behind her, she heard Rosie slip into the room. "All is as it should be."

"I'm glad to hear it," Sheena said. "With devils like Jack Cornwall roving about the place—"

"I'm sure Jack Cornwall is no more a devil than you or I, Sheena." Rosie spoke firmly as she took her place beside the fire and spread her wedding dress over her knees. "Caitrin, what do you think of this row of ruffles? Maybe I should take it off. I'm not really the ruffly kind of girl, am I?"

Caitrin blinked back the tears that threatened. "You're the good kind of girl, Rosie Mills," she said. "And ruffles or not, you will look beautiful on your wedding day."

"I do wish Hope had a real church," Sheena said as she and Caitrin slipped onto a bench near the front door of the mercantile. "A wedding should be held inside a proper sanctuary. Nothing else seems quite right."

"The real church is the body of Christ—everyone who believes in him," Caitrin said. "And with all of us collected here today, the Hope Mercantile is as fine a place as any for Rosie's wedding."

Caitrin surveyed the decorations inside the wood frame building and tried to take joy in her handiwork. Sprays of winter wheat tied in huge yellow bows hung on the mercantile's walls. Sunflowers with nodding brown faces and bright golden petals clustered in vases, bottles, and jars around the room. Every counter wore a length of sunny yellow calico or gingham topped with plates piled high with cupcakes and cookies. Seth had built a little pulpit, and it stood on the rough dirt floor facing the gathered crowd. Near it, hands clasped behind his back, waited a bald-headed little minister. The man had been imported all the way from Topeka just for the occasion.

As the community's motley band began to play on fiddles,

accordions, and mouth harps, Caitrin let out a deep breath. Well, she hoped Rosie and Seth would enjoy their wedding day. She had done all she could to make the surroundings beautiful. The good Lord himself had melted away every flake of the early snow that had fallen. He'd arranged for a sky the color of chicory blossoms and an afternoon sun in the exact buttery shade of Rosie's wedding dress. Caitrin had no doubt that the union established this day would be wreathed in happiness.

As for herself, all contentment had walked out of her life with Jack Cornwall. For the past few days she had been a tangle of nerves. Snappish, impatient words slipped from her tongue. She could find no pleasure in her neat rows of merchandise and the eager customers who stopped at the mercantile to buy. She could not even delight in Sheena's little brood. They vexed her, tried her patience, and made so much noise it was all she could do not to scream at them. Jack had stolen nothing from her—nothing but the very joy of living.

Against her own best intentions, Caitrin checked the barn storeroom at least three times a day. But of course, he was never there. When she tried to sleep at night, his words ran in dizzy circles around her brain. Worst of all, every time she thought about the years stretching ahead, she saw nothing but bleak isolation.

The prospect of owning Seth's soddy only served to remind her that she would spend the rest of her days alone. Always alone. *Was that such a terrible thing?* she asked herself time and again. It should not be. The apostle Paul himself had chosen the single life, better to dedicate himself to the Lord's work. Surely Caitrin could adopt such a holy attitude.

But no. The rapture in Rosie's eyes plunged a knife of agony into her heart. And she despised herself all the more for it.

Caitrin dug into her pocket for a handkerchief. Was every man who barely touched her soul bound to abandon her? First Sean

O'Casey. Then Jack Cornwall. Who would be next? *No one*, for she would never dare let another man near enough to hurt her. Caitrin sniffled. She could only pray that people would assume her tears were borne of happiness for dear Rosie . . . and never suspect that she wept out of vain, wretched pity for herself. Oh, could God ever forgive her for such a sin? And could she ever find a way out of this maze of misery?

A tap on her shoulder halted her recriminations for an instant. Jack? She looked over her shoulder to find a pair of warm gray eyes crinkling at the corners, a thatch of shaggy blond hair, and a smile as bright as heaven itself.

"*Ist* beautiful, the mercantile," Rolf Rustemeyer said, his words thick with German accent. The huge, solidly built farmer leaned closer and patted her arm with his heavy, work-worn hand. "You maken fery pretty, Fraulein Murphy. You maken happy day *für* Rosie *und* Seth."

Rolf's determined effort to communicate softened Caitrin's dismay. She gave him a warm smile. "Thank you, Mr. Rustemeyer. It is a lovely day."

"*Ja*." He nodded. "Goot day *für* vedding. Zoon Rolf Rustemeyer vill builden big *Kirche*. *Kirche*. *Für* veddings, peoples dying."

Caitrin frowned. What on earth was he talking about? "*Kirche?*" she repeated. "What is that?"

"*Ach*." He slapped his knee in frustration. "*Kirche*. Is *Gott's Haus*."

Caitrin used her knowledge of the Gaelic tongue to decipher the message. "A *Kirche* is like a *kirk*? A church. You're going to build a church for the town of Hope, are you?"

"*Ja, ja, ja!*" Rolf beamed.

The band began to play louder, and Caitrin glanced toward the mercantile door. Seth Hunter—straight, tall, and handsome—entered with little Chipper holding tightly to his hand. The proud father's new white shirt fairly gleamed, and his son all but danced in his shiny new shoes. Aye, but they were a fine pair, the boy a mirror image of his papa. Rosie had made herself a wonderful match indeed.

"Fery zoon, I vill *Kirche* builden," Rolf whispered, tapping Caitrin's shoulder again. "Here I builden. Near mercantile. You vill zee me on daytime. All days, *ja?*"

Caitrin's smile froze as the significance of his words sank in. Rosie had told her that Rolf would like to court her. Perhaps he would even want to marry her. To Rosie, that would be a wonderful solution to Caitrin's loneliness. And if Rolf spent day after day building a church near the mercantile, she would have no choice but to acknowledge him.

Caitrin studied the big man, all brawn and hardy good humor. Though his reputation in the community was spotless, Caitrin viewed Rolf more as a potential project than as a suitor. He needed a good haircut. A cake of strong lye soap would do wonders with the dirt embedded in his hands. And a few more English lessons would serve him well socially. Just as Caitrin had helped transform a barn into a mercantile, she might change a rough-hewn farmer into a gentleman. But to put her future into those large hands? To give her heart to Rolf Rustemeyer? Oh, heavens!

"'Tis the bride!" Sheena whispered, elbowing Caitrin.

Everyone stood as Rosie stepped into the mercantile. She was a vision . . . her yellow dress lit up the room, her brown hair gleamed, and her smile could have lit a thousand lamps. Seth looked as if he might burst with pride as she came to stand at his side. Love fairly poured out of the man's blue eyes. Rosie bent to kiss Chipper's cheek, and the little boy threw his arms around her neck.

"Hi, Rosie," he cried out. "We're gonna get married now!"

The nervous excitement in the room broke, and everyone chuckled as the happy threesome moved to stand before the preacher. When the familiar words of the wedding ceremony filtered through the room, Jimmy took Sheena's hand. It was a perfect moment, Caitrin thought. Two hearts joined as man and wife. One little soul given a brand-new mama.

The women in the congregation dabbed their eyes. Children sat transfixed. Men turned their hat brims in their laps and grinned with satisfaction. Chipper's gangly puppy, Stubby, wandered into the mercantile and lay down at Rosie's feet, his big tail thumping up puffs of dust.

"Seth, you may now kiss your wife," the minister said at last.

For a moment, silence hung in the room. Then Seth folded Rosie in his arms and gave her a kiss that was warm, tender . . . and much too long. The children giggled. One of the men called out, "Save it for later, Seth!" and everyone burst into laughter.

As the congregation rose, Caitrin stuffed her handkerchief into her pocket, determined to make a joyful occasion of the event. Rosie and Seth turned to walk out of the mercantile, and everyone rushed to engulf the couple. Caitrin worked her way through the throng until she was able to give the bride a warm hug.

"God's richest blessings upon you, Rosie," she whispered. "I wish you every happiness in the world."

"And you, too, Caitrin!" Rosie said. "I pray that you'll find as perfect a man for you as Seth is for me."

Seth leaned through the crowd and laid a warm hand on Caitrin's shoulder. "Thank you, Miss Murphy. The place looks great."

And then the couple were whirled away . . . out into the fresh air where tables and benches had been set up to feed everyone. Caitrin squared her shoulders against the tide of melancholy that threatened once again, and she headed for the serving line. Rolf Rustemeyer and Casimir Laski had been roasting a pig since dawn. Neighboring women had brought dishes filled with steaming corn, green beans, and black-eyed peas. There were bowls of mashed potatoes and crocks of brown gravy. And the fresh rolls piled in baskets almost could have fed the biblical five thousand without a miracle.

Caitrin rolled up her sleeves and took charge of the potatoes and gravy. By the time she had dished out a dollop for every visitor, her arms were aching. She filled her own plate and headed for a table near the barn.

"Caitrin, come over here!" Rosie called, beckoning from the heavily festooned central table. "Sit with us!"

Obedient, Caitrin turned and set her plate beside Chipper's. The little boy had fed half his pork to Stubby, who was licking his chops for more. "A grand day this is for you, Chipper," she said. "Sure I never saw a pair of shoes so fine."

"Yeah," Chipper managed around a mouthful of bread. "Papa bought 'em for me. I gots a mama *an'* a papa now, Caitrin. Rosie's gonna live with us in the soddy, did you know? An' Papa's gonna build us a new house this winter. A wood one."

"Truly? Not a sod house?"

"Nope. Wood." Chipper swallowed the bite. "Papa told me that Rosie might have a baby brother or sister for me one of these days. You need to get yourself a daddy, Caitrin. That way you can have babies."

"Now Chipper," Seth said sternly.

But Rosie was laughing. "You're exactly right about our babies, sweetheart. I'm going to pray that you'll have lots and lots of brothers and sisters. And then won't we all have fun?"

"I sure do wish Gram an' Gramps could be here now," Chipper said. "Uncle Jack, too. I miss 'em. Maybe they could all get married to us, an' live with us, an' then we'd be one family."

There was a moment of awkward silence, but Caitrin finally found her tongue. "What a big family that would be, Chipper," she said. "I think you and your new mama must want a family as big as the O'Tooles'. And where is poor Will O'Toole today? In all the excitement, have you forgotten your best friend?"

"Look down there at the end of the table," the child said, pointing. "There's Will with Erinn an' Colleen. They watched Rosie get married to Papa an' me today. Will says Rosie will be a good mama. Why don't *you* want to be a mama, Caitrin?"

"Oh, look, Chipper," Rosie cut in. "Jimmy's going to make a speech."

The gangly Irishman rose and lifted his mug of hot apple cider. "'Tis a fine day for our good friend Seth Hunter, and as fine a day for the rest of us here to have the pleasure of rejoicin' in his wedding. Sure there never was a man as good, honest, and hardworkin' as our Seth. Nor was there ever as pretty and lovin' a woman as dear Rosie—save my own sweet Sheena, of course. And if I didn't say that I'd be sleepin' in the barn tonight."

Jimmy paused amid the chuckles. "So, here's to the happy pair," he continued. "Seth and Rosie, may you live long, grow rich, and bear more wee *brablins* than you can count in a day!"

A chorus of hurrahs followed the toast. Caitrin glanced around, wondering who would stand up for Rosie. Sheena—though happy to speak her mind in private—would never have the courage to make a public pronouncement. And then Caitrin noticed that everyone's eyes were trained on *her*. Flushing, she realized that she was Rosie's close friend, and by all good grace she should offer a toast.

She stood, lifted her mug, and prayed hard for words to form on her tongue. "Rosie has brought the light of happiness to many here on the prairie," she began. "And I count myself blessed to be among those her life has touched. Not only is she good and kind, but she bears witness to the joy of Christian love that flows from her heart. In marrying Seth, our Rosie has found a partner . . . a friend . . . a true love . . ."

Caitrin squeezed her eyes shut and took a deep breath. "Rosie has found all the happiness she so richly deserves," she finished quickly. "Rosie and Seth, may your marriage be one of tenderness and everlasting love from this moment forward."

Sinking onto the bench, Caitrin buried her nose in her mug and took a deep drink. Oh, it had been a poor toast . . . unplanned and awkwardly spoken. Just when she meant to be strong, her own silly woes had swarmed out to engulf her. She *must* move past this self-pity. She *must* stop dwelling on a man who had been barely a flicker in her life. And she would. Truly, she would. God help her!

"Me now!" Chipper cried, climbing up onto the wobbly bench. "Who's gonna talk about me?"

The child looked around the crowd. Caitrin's heart went out to him. Perhaps Will would stand up for his little friend. She glanced down to the end of the table to find Sheena's son deep into a slice of cherry pie.

Chipper turned in a circle on his bench. "Does anybody have a speech about me? 'Cause I gots a new mama today, an'—" He paused and his face lit up. "Oh, look everybody! Here comes somebody to talk about me. It's Uncle Jack!"

CHAPTER 6

JACK rode his horse to within five paces of the nearest table, and the crowd broke into screams of terror. Women covered their children's heads. Men threw protective arms around their wives. A blond giant of a fellow leapt to his feet and came at the intruder. Heart hammering, Jack jumped to the ground and held up both hands.

"I'm unarmed!" he shouted over the roar. "I come in peace."

Head down, shoulder butted forward, the giant kept coming. Jack kept his hands up as long as he could. When he realized the fellow meant business, he went for the shotgun in his saddle scabbard.

"Stop, Rolf!" a woman's voice cried out. "Rolf, no!"

The giant skidded to a halt. Caitrin Murphy materialized at the man's side and grabbed his arm. "No, Rolf!" she said. "Look. Mr. Cornwall holds no weapon. You must let him speak."

Breathing hard, Jack waited in tense silence as the giant assessed the situation. "You not fight Seth?" the man growled, pointing a beefy finger. "Not little boy to take?"

Jack held out his empty hands. "I'm unarmed," he repeated. "I've come in peace."

"What do you want with us, Cornwall?" Seth called across the clearing. One arm clamped around Chipper, he rose from the wedding table. "You know you aren't welcome here."

Jack stepped forward, determined to keep his attention away from Caitrin. "I came to talk to you, Seth," he said. "You and everybody else."

In the wary hush, a child's voice rang out. "Hi, Uncle Jack! Guess what! Me an' Papa an' Rosie got married today."

"Hey there, Chipper." At the sight of the little blue-eyed boy, Jack's defenses faltered. This was his sister's son, the baby he had cuddled on his lap and rocked to sleep a hundred times. *Oh, Mary. If only you could see your child one more time. If only you could hold him . . . sing to him . . .* Jack swallowed at the knot in his throat.

"You know what, Uncle Jack? Nobody made me a speech." Chipper frowned. "Did you come to say a speech about me? Or . . . are you gonna fight Papa again?"

"I didn't come here to fight anybody, Chipper," Jack said, taking another step into the midst of the gathered tables. He searched the child's blue eyes and read the longing in them. "All right, little buddy, I'll make you a speech. How's that?"

"Yeah!" Chipper said, pumping a little fist. "Get a cup."

Aware of the tension racing through the crowd, Jack knew one wrong step could put him in danger. These people didn't trust him . . . and rightly so. He had tried to take the boy. He had disrupted previous gatherings. He had battled Seth Hunter with words, weapons, and fists. Any one of them might choose this moment to exact revenge.

If he had his way, Jack would speak his piece and get out. But Chipper was gazing at him with a plea for reconciliation. Jack glanced to a table in search of a cup.

"Take this, Mr. Cornwall." It was Caitrin's musical voice. Both hands outstretched, she offered a tin mug filled with cider.

Jack met the woman's eyes for an instant. It was all the satisfaction he could permit himself. Even so, the sight of shining green eyes, fiery hair, and lips soft with pleading nearly derailed him. Forcing his focus back to the boy, he lifted the cup.

"I've known Chipper since he was born," he addressed the gathering. "He used to weigh not much more than a sack of dried peas. Yep, he was a wrinkled little thing and about as bald-headed as an old fence post."

"Uncle Jack!" Chipper clamped his hands on his head and squealed in delight.

The crowd murmured, and a few low chuckles gave Jack the encouragement to continue. "Fact is, at the start I could hold Chipper in one hand. Right there in my palm, just like that. When he got bigger, he liked to ride around on my shoulders. Liked to eat mushed-up pawpaws. And he liked to holler, too. That boy could put up quite a squall to get what he wanted."

Chipper giggled, and the party guests began to relax. The blond hulk sat down on a bench next to Caitrin. "My nephew always knew what he wanted," Jack went on, "and not a one of us who loved the little rascal ever had the heart to tell him no. Now Chipper's made up his mind to have himself a papa and a mama."

Jack turned to Seth Hunter—the field hand Jack's father had driven from the Cornwall property, enraged at his Yankee sympathies and his secret courtship of beautiful, golden-haired Mary. Seth stood straight and tall, his hand on his bride's shoulder and his arm around his son. Behind Seth stretched his properties—a house, a barn, and fields that had brought in a good harvest. Around the man sat friends and neighbors who would defend him with their lives.

"The boy chose well," Jack said, lifting his cup to honor the man who had been his enemy for so long. Then he returned to his nephew. "Here's to Chipper. May his days be filled with fishing, swimming, kite flying, and all the joys of boyhood. And may he live a long, happy life in the sheltering arms of his parents . . . Seth and Rosie Hunter."

A stunned pause gripped the wedding guests for a moment. And then they lifted their cups and sang out, "To Chipper!"

Before he could choke on words that had been torn from his gut, Jack tipped up his tin cup and downed the cider. *That's right*, that voice inside him whispered. *Make peace. If you want to win, you have to lose. The last shall be first.*

His stomach churning in rebellion at words that reeked of weakness, Jack leaned over and slammed the tin cup on a table. *No! Fight. Stand up for yourself. Take the boy. Take Caitrin.* Bitterness rose in his throat, threatening to strangle him. From the moment he had ridden away from the woman, he had searched for a way to make her his own. But every scheme he cooked up involved violence and bloodshed. Every plan except this one.

That quiet voice had whispered a different approach. A new way. *Surrender. Let go. The last shall be first.* Jack never even got as far east as Topeka. In the stillness of a night as cold and alone as any he had ever known, he had hunkered down on his knees next to his horse and tried to listen to that voice.

Amid the blackness inside him, his own failings came to him one by one. He heard the clangor of his rebellion, his rage, his deceit. The echoes of his violent rejection of God drifted through the cavern of his empty soul. As he listened to the din of his stormy life, Jack recognized a future as hopeless as his past. Remembering the Jesus Christ to whom Caitrin's soul belonged—that refining fire who could bring gold from raw ore—he surrendered to the Master, begging to be filled with the harmonious melody of forgiveness.

At that moment the raucousness had stopped. Silence reigned. And then a sweet song began inside Jack. Peace filled the cavern. Hope stretched out before him like a bright pathway leading to eternity.

For the next few days after his night of repentance, he had walked on that shining path. He had listened to the music of that quiet voice. Drifting in a sort of daze, he had decided that a return to Hope was the answer he'd been searching for. He would make a public offer of reconciliation with his enemies. Then he would go one step further.

And that's when the buzz of rebellion stirred to life inside him. *Revenge, chaos, hatred,* it screeched, all but drowning the heavenly music in his soul. From that moment, Jack had been engaged in a different sort of battle, a fight that only prayer had seen him through. Gritting his teeth against the torment inside him, he lifted his head and faced his former foe.

"Seth," he said, "I've come to make peace."

Seth's dark eyebrows lifted a fraction. He looked down at Rosie. The woman's face had paled to an ashen white, but she gave her husband a nod of reassurance and gathered Chipper into her lap. Leaving her side, Seth walked around the table to stand in front of Jack.

"You want peace," he said. "Why?"

"For the boy. I don't want him to grow up with the notion that you and I hate each other."

"I'll see to that. I've never been a man of vengeance, Cornwall. The trouble between us doesn't change the fact that you're his uncle, and I'll make sure he always remembers his Gram and Gramps. Rosie and I plan to raise Chipper in a home where godly love is the rule."

Jack nodded. "It's good to know that."

"You didn't need to come back here and interrupt my wedding to get that promise out of me. What is it you want?"

"I reckon I came to put your notion of godly love to the test." Jack drank in a breath. *Say the words. Say them now.* He cleared his throat. "I'm here to ask a favor of you, Hunter."

A ripple of murmurs raced through the crowd. Seth's eyes narrowed. "There's only one thing I've got that you want," he said. "And you can't have him."

"This is not about the boy. I told you I gave him up, and I did.

Whether anyone here believes it or not, I'm a man of my word. I won't lay a finger on Chipper."

Seth's blue eyes still were hooded in wariness. "I'm a dirt farmer, Cornwall. What could you possibly want from me?"

"Permission."

"Permission for what?"

"Work." Jack listened to the hubbub that followed his request. He couldn't let the crowd's displeasure derail him. With God's help, he would win over his enemy and make a place for himself. He needed a place like Hope, a place where he could make time to silence the rebellion inside him and listen to the quiet voice. He needed time to learn and grow. He needed hope.

"Like you, Seth, I've been fighting a war," Jack said. "While I was gone, the family home was looted and burned. The farm was stripped. We had to move out. There are folks in Missouri I'd just as soon never lay eyes on again. I need to ply my trade, and I'm asking you for a place to do that."

"On *my* land?"

"That's right."

Some of the men began shouting at Seth, encouraging him to run off the intruder, kick him out on his backside, give him a taste of his own medicine. The blond giant stood to his feet again. Seth stared at Jack, his face expressionless.

"Let me get this straight," Seth said. "Your papa ran me off his farm. You spent the summer doing your dead-level best to steal my son away from me. You shot at me. You stole my rifle. You disrupted every iota of peace we had around here. And now you want me to give you a chunk of my land so you can work it?"

Jack rubbed the back of his neck as the jeers grew in intensity. This wasn't going well. Another minute or two and the whole crowd was liable to string him up. So much for making peace. So much for hope.

Jack settled his hat on his head. "I reckon your godly love

doesn't stretch that far," he said. "I don't blame you for it. Well, I guess I'd better head out."

Forcing himself not to look at Caitrin, Jack turned his back on Seth. Any man worth his salt would see this as a great opportunity to run his enemy into the ground. Kick him while he was down, and then spit in his face. Vulnerability made his spine prickle as he started for his horse.

"Hold on a minute, Cornwall," Seth called after him.

Yup, time for the payback. *Help me, Father, please help me here*, Jack prayed. When he turned, he saw that Rosie had raced to her husband's side. Well, this would just about finish things off, he thought. The last time he spoke with the woman, they'd wound up yelling at each other in the O'Tooles' barn. She was liable to spill the beans on him, hurt Caitrin in the process, and turn the hubbub into a hullabaloo.

"Mr. Cornwall," Rosie said, her shoulders squared. "What kind of work do you do?"

The question caught Jack off balance. "I'm a blacksmith, ma'am."

"A blacksmith," she repeated. She glanced over in Caitrin's direction and seemed to draw courage. "Well, I guess we don't have any blacksmiths in Hope."

"Nope." He saw a crack in the wall of opposition. "But you have a lot of wagons passing through here, ma'am. Broken axles, worn-out brake shoes, rusted undercarriages—I fix them all. I can patch a rusted kettle so good you'll think it's new. I can shoe eight horses a day. There's not a kitchen tool I can't produce. And even though my work has been mostly on weapons, I reckon I could learn to make and repair any farm tool you hand me."

"I see. Well, that's a useful trade." Rosie looked at Caitrin again. Then she elbowed her husband. "Isn't that a useful trade, Seth?"

The man's blue eyes focused on his wife. "Rosie, what are you up to?"

"I just think—" she twisted her hands—"I think Hope could certainly use a blacksmith. There *are* a lot of wagons. And that hinge on the door of our oven's firebox has been giving me no end of trouble."

"I fix hinges," Jack inserted.

"Your best shovel split clean in two the other day, Seth."

"I fix shovels," Jack said.

"And you can be sure we'd sell every ladle, knife, pothook, and trivet we could put in the mercantile." Rosie's eyes took on a light Jack had seen that evening in the barn. Only this time her ardor worked in his favor. "If we could repair the hoop on that big barrel by the barn, Seth, we could catch rainwater in it. Just yesterday I noticed that the bucket in the well has sprung a leak. And you were wishing for a new set of tools to build our house not three days ago. Seth, there *would* be value in a blacksmith. I think every one of us would profit, don't you?"

"Rosie." Seth shook his head and hooked his thumbs in his pockets. "Rosie, it's not any old blacksmith we're talking about here. It's *him*."

"I'll stand up with your wife, Seth," Caitrin said, walking to Rosie's side. "Mr. Cornwall has given his word he'll not trouble you again."

"He's troubling me right now," Seth said.

"Aye, but 'tis all in how you look at the matter. You cannot deny it took great courage for Mr. Cornwall to walk unarmed into our midst today and beg a boon of you. Something has driven him to it, Seth."

"I wouldn't doubt 'twas the devil himself!" Jimmy cried. "He's up to no good, Seth. Send the villain packing. And Caitrin Murphy, you'll sit yourself down before your sister flies into a fit of apoplexy."

"How can you be sure 'tis not God who has driven Mr. Cornwall to you, Seth?" Caitrin said. "Sure he's asked you for peace and forgiveness—"

"He's asked for your land!" Sheena shouted. "Don't give him a fleck of dust, Seth. He's Cornish, so he is, and they're all a pack of liars and cheaters—"

"Give him a chance, Seth," Caitrin cut in. "Clearly the man has shown a change of heart."

"Trickery! All trickery!" Sheena hollered.

"Seth, you could let the man work at the back of the mercantile after you've built the new barn," Rosie said. "He could have my bed in the loft."

"Run him off!" someone shouted.

"Can you fix a plow, Cornwall?" another called out.

"Send him packing!" Jimmy cried.

"I think now maybe this is goot man, Seth," the blond giant said. He held out his arms like a pair of tree limbs, and the crowd quieted. "Man is fighting you before. But now is vit no gun coming. Is ask vorking for you. Rolf Rustemeyer say yes. Is goot man now. Seth, you give vork this man."

"Hope does need a blacksmith," Casimir Laski added.

"A livery would bring in lots of customers," Rosie said.

"Don't do it, Seth." Jimmy shook his fist at Jack. "He'll ruin you. He'll destroy our town."

"He's asked for godly love," Caitrin reminded Seth softly. "How can we deny this man?"

Seth folded his arms across his chest and stared into Jack's eyes. "Can I trust you, Cornwall?"

"Yes."

"Prove it."

"That'll take time. Will you give me time, Hunter?"

"You're asking for more than time. You're asking for a place to live, a place to work, a chunk of my land, and a lot of my goodwill. Why don't you go on back to Missouri, Cornwall? Why work here?"

Jack's focus flicked to Caitrin for an instant. At the sight of her flushed cheeks and sparkling emerald eyes, he felt his resolve grow. "I need a fresh start," he told Seth. "Kansas is wide open and raw. Out here, a man can let go of the troubles in his past and make a new life for himself. You did that, Hunter. I'm asking for the same chance."

"For all I know, your troubles will follow you here." Seth studied his boots for a moment, then he shook his head ruefully. "Well, I reckon I'm a pretty big fool, but I'm going to give you permission to set up shop on my land. You can sleep in the barn loft. Rosie's made it a nice enough place. I'm not in the business of handing out loans, but if you can scrape together the cash, you can build yourself a smithy here by the main road and take in whatever work comes your way."

As the realization of victory coursed down his spine, Jack's spirits soared. "Thanks, Seth. You won't regret it."

"Yeah, well, we don't have any official peacekeepers around here, so we'll have to trust you to keep your nose clean. One slip, and we'll run you out of town so fast you won't know which way is up. Got that?"

"You won't have to worry about me for a while, anyway. I'm going back to Missouri to check on my family and take care of some unfinished business."

Seth nodded. "See you later, then."

"Later." Jack tipped his hat at Rosie and gave her the warmest smile he could muster. The young woman had risen to his defense . . . and her words had made all the difference. He felt sure he knew why she'd had a change of heart.

Caitrin Murphy was standing to one side as Jack mounted his horse. It was all he could do not to take her in his arms and thank her, tell her how deeply her words and actions had affected him, kiss her sweet lips in promise of the day he would return. But he could feel the hostility still emanating from the crowd, and he knew any sign he made toward Caitrin would cause her trouble in the town.

"I'll be back," he said. He gave her a last glance before he tugged Scratch's reins and headed for Topeka.

"I told you he wouldn't come back." Sheena leaned over a wooden chest in the mercantile and set the stack of paper valentines back into their box. "You stood up for him at the Hunter wedding. Rosie stood up for him. Rolf stood up for him. Even dear Seth stepped out and offered the scoundrel a place to work and a clean bed to sleep in. But he rode away without a backward look.

"Now what's it been? Three months? More? Not a soul has glimpsed a single sight of Cornwall's hairy hide. You thought he would return at Christmas, Caitrin. You mentioned he might appear for the New Year's Eve fancy dress ball. Then you speculated he'd show up for the Valentine dinner. Now you speak of Easter. As far as I'm concerned, Jack Cornwall is long gone and good riddance. I don't know why you even think of the rascal."

Caitrin wound lengths of red satin ribbon back onto their spools. She didn't know why she thought of him either. Jack Cornwall had stepped into her life for a few brief days. He had spoken sweet words and touched her heart with his bold request of Seth. And then he had vanished.

In the passing weeks Caitrin had invented all sorts of reasons why the man hadn't returned as he had promised. Something had gone wrong with his plans for his dear sister. Perhaps Jack hadn't been able to manage poor Lucy after all. Maybe she had fallen physically ill. On the other hand, the weather might have prevented Jack's return. It certainly had been a frigid winter, with so much snow that everyone had stayed cooped up for days at a time. Huge drifts had covered the roads, making travel difficult and communication all but impossible. Perhaps Jack had run into trouble with Bill Hermann, the man in Missouri who was trying to hunt him down and involve him in some sort of trouble. Or maybe his wound had taken a turn for the worse. Or he couldn't find the money to buy his equipment for the smithy. Or . . .

"He's no different from the rest of his kind," Sheena said as she packed a stack of lace-edged tablecloths into the chest. "Our father warned us never to trust a Cornishman, Caitie. Sure you and I saw the devils time and again in the fish markets. We knew firsthand the havoc they caused with their sneaking boats and their low prices. Our own papa denounced them, and if you can't trust Papa's word, who can you trust? The Cornish are liars, cheaters, and tricksters. Troublemakers. Jack Cornwall proved it with his wicked behavior toward Seth and Chipper. And the way he was casting sheep's eyes at you during the wedding feast! He's a scoundrel—can you deny it?"

Caitrin handed her sister the spools of ribbon. "He seemed sincere enough to me."

"Aye, and you'd believe a turnip was a gold nugget if someone looked into your green eyes and told you it was. That's the trouble with you, Caitie my love. You see things for what they could be . . . and not for what they are."

"Is that so wrong? Rosie believed this barn could become a profitable mercantile. She worked hard to bring the vision to life. And when she became a married woman and busy in her new house, she passed that dream along to me. Now look at the place."

Sheena lowered the lid of the chest, sat down on it, and studied the room. Caitrin couldn't deny the pleasure she felt as she stood on the brand-new plank floor and surveyed glass cases filled with merchandise, walls lined to the ceiling with shelves, and long plate windows gleaming in the afternoon sunlight. She had long nourished the idea of adding a small restaurant area to the mercantile, and she hoped she could talk one of the men into building a room or two at the back to rent out to passing travelers. Though her dreams of a husband and family had come to nothing, Caitrin felt sure God had given her a new goal, and she took satisfaction in her achievements.

"Rosie had a good idea," Sheena said. "And you helped her transform this smelly barn into an honest-to-goodness mercantile. But Caitie, you can't change everything you set your mind on. You certainly can't change people. Take Rosie herself for a perfect example. Each time the community gathers for a party, you dress Rosie up in your Irish finery, pin *shingerleens* into her hair, and push her feet into pointed-toe slippers. And halfway through every celebration, she races back to her house and changes into one of her ginghams so she can dance better with Seth. She pulls all the glitter out of her hair, puts on her worn boots, and turns back into our dear Rosie."

"I don't mind."

"Of course not, because that's who she is. She's *Rosie*. She'll never be a fine lady in silks and taffetas. She doesn't want to. And Rolf Rustemeyer will never be a gentleman speaking the King's English. He's a German farmer, so he is. He works all summer long in the dirt and heat. He's built half the church by himself this winter. He'd rather climb a ladder and nail shingles all day than try to learn the proper way of holding a fork and knife. Caitie, people are what they are. You can transform a barn into a mercantile, but you'll never turn a lying Cornishman into an upstanding citizen. You must permit Rosie to dress herself for the next party, and you must allow Rolf to eat everything on his plate with a spoon if he wants. And you must stop believing that Jack Cornwall will be true to his word and turn up in Hope again. He won't. He's not coming back."

Caitrin traced Sheena's flaming red hair and bright green eyes. How could two sisters brought up in the very same country, the same house, the same family arrive at such different beliefs? But they had, and they loved each other deeply in spite of it.

"Oh, Caitie," Sheena said, standing and taking her sister's hand.

"It's not that I want you to feel bad about all you've done. Sure I wish only for your happiness. I rarely see you truly happy these days, and I think it stems from all your wishing and dreaming. Look at Jimmy and me. He's as skinny as a fence post, so he is . . . and I'm so wide around the middle these days I can hardly tie on my apron."

"Are you going to have another baby, Sheena?" Caitrin asked with alarm.

"Oh, who can tell, and what of it? If I'm not nursing one child, I'm bearing another. That's what I'm trying to tell you. I'm me, that's all. And I'm happy. 'Tis because I accept my skinny Jimmy, and my vast brood, and my widening girth that I can find joy in each day that the Lord brings. I'm not always trying to change everything." She let out a deep breath. "Maybe if you'd stop looking on Rolf as a project in need of fixing, you might see he's a very good man in search of a wife."

Caitrin swallowed. "I don't want to marry Rolf."

"Why not? You expect him to be perfect like Sean O'Casey? Ooh, he was a fine one, prancing down the street with his black curls and his tailcoat. But he went off and married the mine owner's daughter, Caitie, and that makes him a poor match for someone as good-hearted as you. But Rolf—now Rolf would make a loyal husband, hardworking and true. If only you could accept him. If only you could change your attitude—"

"Now you're wanting *me* to change, Sheena!" Laughing, Caitrin flapped her apron at her sister. "Shoo with you! Back to your skinny husband and your brood of *brablins*. If I must stop having visions for what people can make of themselves, then I must stop being me. I must change, and I'm no more inclined to do that than any of these others."

"Aye, and you'll live a single, lonely life all your days." Sheena grabbed her basket of leftover heart-shaped cookies from the counter. "Stop waving that apron at me! I'm going, I'm going."

"Come and visit me tomorrow in the soddy," Caitrin called. "I think I've thought of a way to hang wallpaper."

"Wallpaper in a soddy!"

Her hearty laughter broke off as Rosie rushed into the mercantile. Face as pale as the snow that crusted the windowsills outside the store, she clutched her stomach and leaned against the wall, breathing hard. A long tendril of brown hair had come down from its pins. She brushed it aside and stared hollow-eyed at the two women.

"Something terrible has happened," she whispered.

"Rosie?" Caitrin hurried to the younger woman. "What's the matter? Is it Jack Cornwall?"

"Oh, Caitie!" Sheena squawked. "Must you bring up that scoundrel again?"

"This is worse than Cornwall," Rosie murmured. "Much worse."

"Sit down." Caitrin shoved a chair into the back of her friend's knees. Rosie collapsed and buried her face in her hands. "Is it Seth? Is it Chipper? Please, Rosie, you must tell us!"

Lifting her head, Rosie dabbed at the tears on her cheeks with the corner of her apron. "I have just realized the most awful thing," she said. She swallowed hard. "I'm dying."

"Dying!" Caitrin sank to her knees and took Rosie's hands. "Are you ill? Do you need a doctor?"

"It's been coming on very slowly," Rosie explained through trembling lips. "A slow, creeping sickness. It might be consumption . . . only without the cough."

"Consumption without the cough?" Sheena snorted. "I've never heard of such a thing."

Rosie shook her head. "I'm wasting away. I've watched my skirts' waists growing wider and my ribs starting to stick out."

"Are you eating?"

"Hardly. Everything I put into my stomach comes right back out. I can't tolerate the smell of Seth's coffee in the morning, and the fish poor Chipper caught the other day nearly knocked me flat. I've never been so sick. I've always worked like a twister—that's what Seth calls me, his little twister—but now I can hardly drag myself out of bed."

"Your cheeks are still rosy," Caitrin offered.

"Seth is going to be a widower again," Rosie wailed, "and Chipper will lose his second mother. Oh, I'm so upset, I can hardly think. How am I going to break the news to Seth? What will he say? We've just moved into our new house, and he's preparing for the spring planting. I don't want to die! It's not that I'm unhappy at the thought of heaven. Far from it. But you know I'd love to watch Chipper get bigger, and I want to have lots of babies and be a granny someday. I want to grow old with Seth!"

"Oh, Rosie!" Caitrin threw her arms around her friend. How could this terrible fate befall someone so precious? If anyone deserved a long life, it was dear Rosie. Now this!

"The truth hit me just a few minutes ago," Rosie said, dabbing under her eyes with the corner of her apron. "You see, I was in the kitchen counting the loaves of bread in storage. It seems like I'm having to make more and more loaves every baking day, just to keep up with the appetites of those two. Anyway, I got to figuring how many times I've baked bread this month. And then I counted up last month's baking days, and the month before . . . and . . . and . . . I suddenly realized that this is the third time that . . . that . . ."

"That what?" Caitrin implored, wondering what baking had to do with Rosie's impending demise. "This is the third time that *what?*"

"That she's missed her monthly!" Sheena exclaimed. "Of course Rosie can't eat, and she's losing her breakfast, and she's missed her monthly three times in a row. She's gone with child!"

"What?" Rosie and Caitrin said together.

"You're going to have a baby, Rosie, my sweet. Didn't anyone tell you the signs? Well, I suppose your caretakers at the orphanage forgot to pass along the important things mothers tell their daughters. Aye, I can see it as plain as the shoes on my feet. You're pregnant."

Rosie sat in stunned silence, her brown eyes fastened on Caitrin's face. Caitrin soaked in the news and squeezed her friend's hands. "A baby, Rosie," she whispered. "Sheena ought to know!"

Rising slowly, Rosie clutched the shawl at her throat. "Sheena, are you sure I'm not dying?"

"I'd lay my life on it. You should move past the morning sickness part of it any time now, and then you'll start eating so much Seth will go into shock. You'll have to let out all your skirts. You'll grow twice the hair you had before. And when you walk, you'll waddle like a duck."

"A baby!" Rosie shouted, twirling on the tips of her toes. "I'm not dying! I'm going to have a baby. Oh, miracle of miracles! Oh, joy and gladness!"

Caitrin laughed as Rosie danced around the chair onto which she had so recently collapsed. "Thank God!"

"Yes, thank you, Father!" Rosie whirled toward the mercantile door. "I've got to tell Seth! He'll be so surprised! He won't know how it happened!"

"I suspect he will," Sheena put in with a chuckle.

Rosie threw out her arms and spun out into the open, stumbling momentarily into the silhouetted shape of someone approaching the mercantile. Standing on tiptoe, she gave the man a kiss on the cheek.

"I'm going to have a baby! Glory hallelujah!" She popped her head around the door frame. "Oh, Caitie, isn't this the most amazing day? I'm going to have a baby. And Jack Cornwall has come back!"

CHAPTER 7

"OUT!" A plump redhead shrieked as she gave Jack a shove on the chest. "Out with you, devil!"

He took off his hat, looked over the shoulder of the woman attempting to eject him from the mercantile, and let his gaze settle on Caitrin Murphy. So, he hadn't dreamed her up. There she was, as real as life. Curly auburn hair piled high on her head. Bright green eyes and pink cheeks. Long, white neck. He was afraid he might keel over.

"Jack," she whispered, her lips barely moving.

"Get out of here, you wicked man!" The other woman bopped him on the arm with her basket. Heart-shaped cookies went flying. "We won't have the likes of you in our town. We don't want your kind. Wait a minute—where do you think you're going? You can't come inside here—"

"Miss Murphy," Jack said, stepping past the woman who seemed determined to beat her basket to shreds on his arm. "How have you been?"

"Finely and poorly," she said softly. "And you, Mr. Cornwall?"

"About the same." He thought his heart was going to jump straight out of his chest. "Mercantile looks good. You've been working hard."

"Aye."

As he came closer, she bit her lower lip and fumbled with a wisp of hair that had fallen onto her forehead. "I've come back," he said.

"No, you haven't!" The other woman whacked him again. "You shut your gob and listen to me, Mr. Cornishman. You'll not be casting sheep's eyes at my sister. You'll get onto your wicked black horse and ride back into the hole you crawled out of, so you will!"

Jack glanced at the stout woman and tried to make her resemble Caitrin in any way. Except for the hair and the eyes, they couldn't look more different. All the same, he realized this must be Jimmy O'Toole's wife, Sheena, in whose barn he had spent a good bit of time.

"Mrs. O'Toole," he said, nodding deferentially. "Pleased to make your acquaintance."

"Blarney!" she declared. "You'll not win me over with your sweet words. Sure I know the likes of you. You shot at our Seth, so you did. You tried to kidnap poor little Chipper. You fought with—"

"I know what I did, ma'am. I was there at the time." Jack turned his hat brim in his hands. "Point is, Seth Hunter gave me permission to build a smithy on his land. I'm aiming to do just that."

"Never! We won't have any Cornish people in our town. We won't allow Cornish—"

"And what's wrong with the Cornish, may I ask?" a high-pitched voice cut in.

Jack groaned as his mother strode into the Hope Mercantile. "Mama," he said, "maybe you ought to wait out in the wagon."

"Stuff and nonsense! I should like to make acquaintance with the inhabitants of my new hometown. And if I'm to do most of my shopping in this mercantile, I want to become familiar with the place." Her gray eyes sparked like flint as she studied Sheena O'Toole. "Jack, you didn't tell me the town was infested with Irish."

"Infested!" Sheena exploded.

"Mrs. O'Toole, Miss Murphy," Jack addressed the women over the hullabaloo. "I'd like you ladies to meet my mother, Mrs. Felicity Cornwall. Mama, this is Mrs. Sheena O'Toole and Miss Caitrin Murphy."

If calling on her sense of social decorum wouldn't calm his mother, nothing would. Nostrils white rimmed with distaste, Felicity gave the women a brief half curtsy. "Charmed, I'm sure," she said, patting her brown hair that lately had grown threaded with silver.

"Miss Murphy is one of the women who manages the mercantile here in Hope." Jack allowed himself a glance at Caitrin. Her cheeks were drained of color, and she had wadded up the end of a red ribbon she was holding. Though wishing he could speak to her alone for a moment, he knew he had no choice but to smooth out the trouble between the other women.

"Miss Murphy can show you around the store," he said to his mother. "Isn't that right, ma'am?"

"I should be happy to help you, Mrs. Cornwall."

"Is this the maid who hid you in the barn, Jack?" his mother asked. "Is she the one who took care of your wound after that brutal man shot you in the shoulder and then turned around and tried to beat you to death?"

Sheena gasped. Caitrin moaned. Jack rolled his eyes. This was not going well. He took his mother's elbow. "Weren't you asking about fresh eggs this morning, Mama? I believe I see a basket of brown eggs on the counter right over there. Maybe Miss Murphy—"

"You hid Jack Cornwall in *our* barn, Caitie?" Sheena demanded of her sister. "You hid from us the very devil himself?"

"My son is far from a devil, Mrs. O'Toole!" Felicity snapped. "I'll have you know he won a medal for bravery during the war, and I keep it right here in my bag. Show it to her, Jack!"

"Mama, please."

"Your son is a Confederate, so I'm told," Sheena said. "A soldier in the army that fought to keep the black man in chains. The army that burned cities. The army that looted the farms of good, honest people."

"It was Yankees who destroyed *our* farm! We had a beautiful place. My husband built our home with his own two hands the very first year we came to America."

"From Cornwall?"

"Yes, indeed." Felicity tilted her chin in the way Jack knew meant trouble. "We hail from the lovely seaside town of St. Ives. Perhaps you have heard of it."

"Me? Ooh, certainly not. And I have naught but pity for those who would choose to live on such barren, windswept cliffs. The Murphys, from whom my sister and I proudly descend, come from the parish of Eyeries in the township of Castletownbere in County Cork."

"Miners," Felicity said through pinched lips.

"And fishermen." Sheena's cheeks glowed.

"Amazing there's not a mackerel or a bit of tin ore in the whole state of Kansas," Caitrin said. "God has blessed us indeed to bring our families to such a bountiful new land. Mrs. Cornwall, you must be exhausted from your journey. Would you care for a cup of hot tea?"

"Just a half dozen of those eggs, Miss Murphy," Jack said before his mother could continue her argument with Sheena. "We've got to set up camp for the night."

"Camp?" Caitrin asked. "But Seth offered you the loft."

"We won't stay in an Irishman's store," Felicity said firmly.

"Seth Hunter isn't Irish. He's American—as are we all. Mrs. Cornwall, you're more than welcome to take lodging in the loft. There's a good bed, a chair, and even a table. I'll fetch a lamp."

"No!" She held up her hand. "We've caused a confloption just by our appearance here this afternoon. I had understood my son to say we'd be welcome. But I can see that the Irish community keeps to its accustomed clannish manners even in Kansas."

"And why should we welcome troublemakers—"

"Sheena!" Caitrin cried.

"Jack Cornwall tried to steal Chipper, so he did."

"My son was honor-bound to return my grandson to me!" Felicity huffed. "I raised Chipper from the day he was born."

"And kept the news of him from his rightful father," Sheena accused.

"Stuff and nonsense!"

"Stop your ballyragging!"

"Jack . . . oh, Jack." Caitrin's trembling voice silenced the argument. "Jack, someone's coming into the mercantile. Who is that?"

Expecting to see Seth Hunter armed to the teeth or Jimmy O'Toole with weapons drawn, Jack swung around to find a shrouded figure weighted with chains stumbling into the building.

He glanced at Caitrin and Sheena. "Ladies," he said, "this is . . . ah . . . this is my sister, Lucy Cornwall."

Caitrin stared in horror at the ragged creature whose hollow gray eyes gazed back at her in a lifeless trance. Heavy wrought-iron chains weighted down her thin wrists and clamped her bare feet together. Long brown hair hung in tangles that covered her cheeks and fell in uneven, limp wisps to her waist. Drooping shoulders barely supported the thin fabric of a dress with a torn neck. A ragged shawl trailed from the woman's elbow to the floor. A dark stain on her neck and a smudge across her forehead attested to the fact that she had not bathed in a long time.

"*This* is Lucy?" Caitrin asked.

"My daughter is not well," Mrs. Cornwall said tersely. "Jack, take her back to the wagon at once."

"No, Jack!" Lucy held out her manacled wrists. Her fingers, their nails bitten to the nubs, stretched toward her brother. "Jack, don't leave me out there."

"It's OK, Lucy." He shoved his hands down into his pockets and walked to her side. "We'll all go outside together. Come on, Mama."

"I'm scared, Jack," his sister whispered.

"Nobody's going to hurt you here, Lucy. This is a good place. Remember I told you about the mercantile and Miss Murphy who runs it? This is Miss Murphy, right here. She's a good woman."

The empty eyes focused on Caitrin. "Does she . . . does she know about . . . about the soldiers? . . ."

"Keep quiet, Lucy!" Felicity cut in. "You know you're not to talk of family matters in public."

"She doesn't know anything, Lucy," Jack said. "You don't have to be afraid."

"I'm happy to meet you, Miss Cornwall," Caitrin said. When she extended her hand, Lucy shrank back as if in fear she'd be struck. Caitrin lowered her hand and smoothed out her apron. "Sure you must be worn from all your travels, Miss Cornwall. Once I open my restaurant in Hope, I'll treat you all to a good meal. As it is, I can only offer a few chairs and that small table. But I'll be happy to lay out an afternoon tea for everyone. I've fresh rolls baked this morning, and perhaps I can even find a few sweets left from the Valentine party."

Sheena gaped at her sister, but Caitrin didn't care. If Jesus had treated all people with respect and honor, why should she be any different? Maybe Jack Cornwall was a wicked fellow, his sister troubled, and his mother ill tempered. Jesus had washed the dirty feet of his disciples, dined with prostitutes, and healed the slave of a rich man. Her Lord had been a servant, and she would do no less. Marching across the room, she began clearing the table of the receipts she'd been entering into her ledger.

"Sheena, will you please set the kettle on the stove?" she called. "Mrs. Cornwall, do you like sugar and milk with your tea?"

"Caitie, be reasonable!" Sheena hissed.

"Thank you for your offer of tea, Miss Murphy, but we must be going." Felicity Cornwall began moving her family toward the door. "We shall set up our camp near the Bluestem Creek, and Jack will begin building his smithy in the morning. Good day."

Caitrin set the ledger and receipts back onto the table as the visitors exited the mercantile. If the good citizens of Hope had thought of Jack Cornwall as a troublemaker before, she could hardly imagine what they were going to say now. What sort of man must he be to keep his sister in chains? Vile! And the mother—how could she allow her poor daughter to go unwashed and uncombed? It was disgraceful.

"Miss Murphy?" Jack Cornwall poked his head back into the mercantile. "Suppose I could talk to you a minute?"

"I should think not!" Sheena exclaimed.

"Oh, please, Sheena, do take your basket and go home to Jimmy. I must close the shop in a moment anyway."

"My husband will not be pleased when he hears the news that Jack Cornwall has returned," Sheena said, leaving the store with her nose in the air. "And neither will Seth."

Caitrin crossed her arms around her waist as Jack approached her in the empty building. Suddenly she wished she hadn't sent her sister away. The man was taller than she remembered, broader across the shoulders, and more deeply tanned. She had forgotten how he filled a room, as though the everyday things inside it had shrunk into themselves. But she hadn't forgotten his gray eyes.

"I owe you my thanks, Miss Murphy," he said, his hat in his hands. "That's three times you've come to my defense."

"I hadn't much choice in the barn when you lay injured. And at the wedding . . . well, I thought it bold of you to come unarmed and place your request before Seth. But I doubt my support will count for much in the days ahead, Mr. Cornwall."

"I know I'll have to earn the town's trust. I can do it, too . . . if they'll give me time."

Caitrin ran her hand along the edge of a counter. She tried to think of polite words to fill in the silence between them, but she and Jack had never spoken lightly. Their conversations of the past had always been urgent and often heated. Perhaps it was best that way.

"Why do you keep your sister in chains?" she spoke up. "You're a blacksmith. Surely you could remove them."

"I'm the one who made them."

"You made those dreadful manacles?" Caitrin stared at him. "But you're treating Lucy as badly as the most pitiful of slaves are treated! She must shuffle along instead of walking. She can barely even lift her hands."

"I know." He rolled his hat brim. "Look, Miss Murphy—Caitrin—you're the only human being I've run into lately with a lick of kindness. Don't judge my family until you know the truth."

"I'll not judge you even after I know the truth. But it's hard to stand by and watch a woman be treated in such an abhorrent manner."

Jack let out a deep breath and looked away. "We *have* to keep Lucy in chains."

"Why?"

"She tries to hurt herself," he said in a low voice. "There have been times when she . . . when she tried to take her life."

"Oh, Jack."

"The chains aren't to punish Lucy. They're for my own peace of mind. I have to protect her from herself. Not too long ago, she got loose from Mama, climbed up onto the roof of the house, and tried to jump off. I barely got up there in time to stop her. We don't have a choice in this, Caitrin. My sister may be chained, but at least she's alive."

Caitrin tried to absorb the terrible significance of what Jack had told her. "What kind of a life can she ever hope to lead?"

"Lucy has no hope . . . and she doesn't want to live."

"But God offers everyone hope for an abundant life. If only she knew her heavenly Father—"

"There's no easy answer to this, Caitrin," Jack cut in. "I told you before, nobody can fix Lucy."

Caitrin shook her head. "I cannot believe that. Perhaps if you bathed her, she would start to feel a little better. At the very least you could brush her hair and dress her in a pretty skirt."

"My sister won't let anyone touch her. If you get too close, she screams. When I walk near Lucy, I keep my hands in my pockets so she'll know I'm not going to lay a finger on her. She can't stand anybody washing her or combing her hair. We can't even get her out of that dress." He eyed Caitrin. "That's the way it is. But Lucy's my sister, and I'm going to stand by her no matter what."

"That's a good thing . . . but the chains are not. People here will think badly of you for keeping her in shackles."

"So, help them understand."

Caitrin swallowed. That was a grand wish. She couldn't even get her sister to be civil to the Cornish in their midst. Hope certainly had its share of different nationalities in the community—Rolf Rustemeyer, the German farmer; the Laskis from Poland; the LeBlancs from France; and the Rippetos from Italy. Thus far, the families had lived in harmony. She had a terrible feeling that was about to change.

"I shall try to make your family welcome," Caitrin said. "I'll do as the good Lord commands, but—"

"But how do *you* feel about it?" He touched her sleeve. "Caitrin, I told you I would come back, and I have. I'm not the man I was when I left Hope the first time. I've changed, and I want you to understand that."

"What has happened, Jack?"

"One night last fall, after I left the O'Tooles' barn . . . well, it was the lowest night of my life—and I've had some pretty bad times. Right out on the road, I got down on my knees, Caitrin, and I prayed so hard I thought I'd bust. It sure seemed like God was talking to me that night, forgiving me for my wrongs and welcoming me into a new life. I knew right then I had to come back here and get Seth to let me build the smithy. And I knew I needed to see you again. Every day I was gone, I thought about you. Thought about the words you said to me in the barn that first night. Did you think of me, Caitrin?"

Heat crept up the back of her neck. "I . . . I suppose I did, aye."

"Did you miss me, Caitrin?"

"I hardly knew you well enough."

"You knew me. Blazin' Jack and Fiery Caitrin, remember? You understood me better than anyone ever has." He searched her face. "And I understood you."

"Aye."

Though her heart had softened toward this man, she could not forget how the people in Hope would view him—as a hot-tempered avenger, a difficult and demanding presence, a man who would not be pushed around. Such a person would find it difficult to fit into a warm, loving community and become part of the team working to build the town of Hope. Though Jack professed a newfound commitment to the Lord, only time would allow him to live out his faith. And Caitrin could not be sure people would give him that time. She felt all too certain that the Cornwalls would not stay long, and her heart could not afford the pain of another loss.

"The people of this town will find it hard to accept you," she told him. "Sure you might as well realize that. Not only have you brought your own less-than-shining reputation, but you've brought other difficulties."

"Lucy."

"She's very troubled."

"My sister hasn't always been this bad off, Caitrin. Things got a lot worse when she found out Papa was about to die."

"Your father died? You didn't tell me! When did it happen?"

"Not long ago. That's why I couldn't get back here sooner. Papa took sick, and he lingered through the winter. We buried him one day and set out for Kansas the next. I reckon I don't need to tell you that Mama wanted to stay in Missouri. The only thing that calmed her was knowing she'd get to see Chipper again. Lucy loves the boy, too."

"Oh, Chipper! But that makes things even worse! I doubt if Seth will want the Cornwalls spending time with his son. He's very protective of the child. And now Rosie is . . . well . . . Seth will probably draw his family close around him. He loves them so much, and you caused such trouble before. Now things are going to be so . . . so difficult."

"Tell me a time when things aren't difficult." Jack gave a humorless laugh. "You're right in saying I brought more than my reputation along. I brought a group of decent people—the folks I care about most. Lucy has her problems, but I don't know a family that's perfect. Do you?"

Was he daring her to bring up the O'Tooles as the shining example of a family? Caitrin knew that must include her sharp-tongued sister. Aye, Sheena had her flaws. All of them did. No one in the close-knit Irish family could be called perfect, but at least they blended. Sheena had accused her sister of believing she could change everyone to fit an ideal image. But Caitrin obviously could do nothing to make Jack Cornwall blend into the peaceable community of Hope. Or the prickly Felicity. Or Lucy.

"No one is perfect," Caitrin said, untying her apron. "As the Good Book says, 'For all have sinned, and come short of the glory of God.'" With a sigh, she picked up her workbasket. "I won't lie to you, Mr. Cornwall. I was hoping you'd come back to Hope. You brought a bit of a spark into my life, so you did. And when you turned up at Rosie's wedding, you lit a little fire under the people here. You set them to thinking. You challenged them to move beyond their fears. You forced them to take a step toward forgiveness. But now that I see you again, I'm afraid."

"I never intended to scare you, Caitrin." His voice was low.

"Aye, but you have. Your Cornish mother and your troubled sister are naught but kindling to the fire you started last autumn. I'm afraid that fire will grow and spread until it changes into a roaring inferno that could destroy the town of Hope."

"No!" Jack hammered his fist on the counter and set the glass to shivering. "The only inferno I intend to light is the one inside my forge. I came here to work and take care of my family. I came for a fresh start."

"Only God gives fresh starts."

"I know that!" He took a step closer to her. "Caitrin, my past has been one rung after another on the ladder that proves a single man can't change the world. First, I thought I could bring Missouri a fresh start, so I fought in a bloody war that came to nothing. Next, I thought I could join up with a gang of vigilantes and keep the cause alive even when it was doomed. Not only did I fail to set Missouri free, but now one of my former friends is trying to track me down and haul me before the law. Then I got the notion to save Chipper. I lost that one, too. After that, I believed I could protect and help my sister. I stay right beside her every minute, but it's all I can do to keep her alive."

Jack lifted his hand to a tress that had tumbled from Caitrin's bun, and he sifted the strands of auburn hair between his thumb and forefinger. "When you told me you loved me—and God loved me—it was the first time in my life I realized there was hope outside myself. After I left you and Rosie that night in the barn, I got to thinking about all I'd tried to do and how it had come to nothing. I wondered if maybe I *didn't* have to change the world myself. That was when I realized there was only one way to get a fresh start. Only one Person who could turn things around for me."

"The Lord," Caitrin whispered, amazed at his repeated avowals of conversion to a living faith in Christ.

"I figured you were the person who could best help me to understand the nature of Jesus. And when I saw how everybody in Hope stuck together and helped each other out, I realized they were living the way God says folks should. So I thought I'd better come back here and join in. And then maybe things would get better."

"Oh, Jack, you mustn't look to *me* if you want to know who God is." Caitrin took both his hands in hers. "You mustn't set your eyes on the people of—"

"Cornwall?" Seth Hunter stood silhouetted in the open door of the mercantile. Behind him, Jimmy O'Toole stared, shifting a rifle he carried over his shoulder. Rolf Rustemeyer, an axe in one hand, made the third in the party.

"Yeah, I'm back." Jack moved away from Caitrin and took a step toward the men. "I reckon you remember agreeing I could build a smithy on your land."

"I haven't forgotten. I figured maybe you had."

"Mr. Cornwall was nursing his ill father," Caitrin said, joining Jack. "He recently passed away. The family has come to Hope for a new beginning. I'm sure we'll be happy to have them here."

The three men stared at Jack.

"My wife tells me you're a Confederate," Jimmy spoke up. "Kansas is an abolitionist state, so it is."

"And the war is over," Jack replied.

"You'd better not set your eyes on any of our women."

"Jimmy!" Caitrin cried. "What a thing to say. We shall include Mr. Cornwall as one of us, just as Christ welcomed all men into his presence."

"Sheena is say you haf crazy woman here bringen." Now Rolf

addressed Jack. "Vit chains. Maybe she is hurting children. Maybe killing."

"Lucy is my sister," Jack said. He squared his shoulders. "She will not hurt the children. She loves children. She . . . she trusts them."

Jimmy gave a snort. "Perhaps, but she's Cornish—as are her mother and brother. I lived my early life in Ireland, and I've run into your kind many a time. We're growin' into a good little village, so we are, with a church and even talk of a school. There'll be no Cornish tricks goin' on about the town of Hope, let me tell you that. Sure the first time you cheat somebody or tell a lie or make any trouble—"

"Do you expect the man to be perfect, then, Jimmy O'Toole?" Caitrin asked. "The last time I read the Holy Scriptures, I saw there was only one man perfect in all history. And the likes of us managed to kill him on a cross. Nay, Mr. Cornwall won't be perfect every minute, nor will you. All he's asked for is a chance. Will you not give him that much?"

"If his crazy sister comes anywhere near my *brablins*—"

"If you so much as lay a finger on Chipper, Cornwall—"

"If you haf plan to hurt anybody here—"

"Oh, it's the Welcoming Committee!" Rosie cried, dancing into the midst of the three men and slipping her arm around Seth's elbow. "We used to have a Welcoming Committee in Kansas City. When I lived at the Christian Home for Orphans and Foundlings, I'd see the committee sometimes after I'd climbed up into the big oak tree to pray. Come to think of it, that old tree is where I met Seth, isn't it, honey? And Mr. Cornwall, too, as a matter of fact. Anyway, sometimes when I was up in the tree, I'd see the Welcoming Committee marching down the street to visit the newest family in town. Five or six women in their Sunday best would take along baskets of fresh bread and candy treats for the children. All the businesses would donate gifts in order to introduce themselves to the newcomers. Well, now that's a grand idea! Mr. Cornwall, would you take your family a little something . . . a little . . ." She looked around the store.

"Eggs," Caitrin said, sweeping the basket off the counter. "Take these eggs to your mother as a welcoming gift."

"Thank you, Miss Murphy." Eyeing the men who stood gaping in the doorway, Jack accepted the basket.

"And you must present your sister with this brush and mirror," Caitrin added, laying the gifts on the eggs. "Tell the family they must come to tea tomorrow here at the mercantile. Isn't that right, Welcoming Committee?"

Seth cleared his throat. Jimmy shifted from one foot to the other. Rolf stuck his hand in his pocket.

"My mother enjoys a good afternoon tea," Jack said to Caitrin. "But I might ask Lucy to stay at the camp. Sometimes she's a little uncomfortable around strangers."

"That would be fine," Caitrin said. "Wouldn't it, Rosie?"

Rosie smiled. "Yes, that would be fine. Wouldn't it, Seth?"

When he didn't answer, she jabbed her elbow into his side. "Uh, yeah, I reckon," he said. "Welcome to Hope."

CHAPTER 8

CAITRIN sat beside the stove in the half-empty soddy and tried to think about wallpaper. Stripes. Flowers. Ivy. She would need a bucket, thick white paste, a brush. Scissors, too. She would start papering beside the front door and . . .

"Oh, this is hopeless!" She slapped her hands on her knees and stood. "I'll never make paper stick to these sod walls. Brown, ugly sod walls with grass roots growing right into my sitting room!"

Night had fallen, but the dim light cast by the oil lamp on the table revealed all but the darkest corners of Seth Hunter's old soddy—Caitrin Murphy's new home. Choking down tears, she stormed to the front door.

"Leather hinges," she said. "Dear God, why have you given me leather hinges? And no windowpanes! Couldn't I at least have glass windowpanes instead of this—this ridiculous half-rotted gauze?"

She hung her head. Was it wrong to shout at God? Was it wrong to moan and complain when she was blessed with her own warm home, loving relatives, and honest work to do each day? Shouldn't she be singing praises on this moonlit night?

"Spiders!" she cried, stomping the small black insect that scurried in front of her foot. "I hate spiders! Dear Father, why have you given me spiders and blacksnakes and prairie dogs? I wanted heather, bracken, sandy shores, and fishing boats. I wanted Ireland. I wanted Sean O'Casey! And now I must live out my life as a spinster shopkeeper on this freezing, blistering, grasshopper-infested plain with hardly a stick of furniture but this broken chair!"

She picked up the rickety chair and shoved it under a table Seth Hunter had built long ago. The end of one table leg had been chewed to splinters by Stubby, the Hunters' enormous mongrel dog. As the table wobbled back and forth, the lamplight flickered.

"Yes, I know they're only worldly goods," she said into the hollow room. "But God, you created me, and you know the kind of woman I am. I adore lovely things! I dream of castles and ivy-covered walls. I want silk pillows and Persian carpets. At the very least, I should like a set of dishes that match!"

Picking up a chipped white plate with a central rose bouquet that had been half scoured away, she searched for her reflection. She could make out nothing but the thousand scratches where knives had cut into meat or bread through the porcelain's glaze. She turned the plate over, hoping to find the insignia of a pottery in some exotic city. Perhaps it had been painted and kiln-fired in Staffordshire, Paris, or Japan.

"Ohio." She ran her finger over the raised, knobby letters on the back. Then she peered closer to discover that someone had misspelled the marking to read, *Mad in Ohio*.

"Oh, I just hate this!" Caitrin cried. "Shabby!"

She hurled the plate at the sod wall. The puff of dust, the burst of breaking porcelain, and the tinkle of falling shards were followed by a soft knock on the door. *Oh no!* Caitrin clapped her hands over her cheeks and realized they were damp.

"Caitrin?" It was Rosie's voice.

"One moment." Caitrin dabbed her eyes with the corner of her apron. She toed the bits of shattered plate into a pile and set a basket on top of them. Then she tucked a strand of hair back into her bun.

"Rose Hunter, what are you doing out and about after dark?"

Caitrin asked as she opened the door. "And in your condition! Do come inside at once. Does Seth know you're here?"

"He and some of the other men are meeting over at the mercantile." Hand in hand, Rosie and Chipper walked into the soddy. Stubby followed, his great tail thumping into Rosie's long, blue-gingham skirt.

"Looks different around here," Chipper said, surveying the soddy. "You don't gots very much furniture, do ya, Miss Murphy?"

"Not a great deal." Caitrin chewed on her lower lip as she followed the boy's gaze around her new home. Just as she feared, his eyes went straight to the basket perched atilt on the pile of plate shards. He and Stubby set off to investigate.

"It's broken glass," she warned.

"Oh no, it's that beautiful plate I left here for you!" Rosie hurried to Chipper's side and knelt beside the fragments. "This was my favorite of all the plates we had. Did you notice there were three roses in the center, Caitie? The one on the left was a bud, and the one on the right had just begun to unfold. But the rose in the middle—bright, glorious pink! Petals like velvet! Every time I washed this plate, I was sure I could smell that precious rose."

Caitrin sank onto her chair and rested an elbow on the rickety table. "I'm sorry," she mumbled.

"It's not your fault. Heaven knows I've let plates slip through my fingers before." Rosie pulled a stool to the table. "One time back at the home in Kansas City I was washing a teacup. It was the only cup I had . . . and almost the only possession I had, other than my bonnet that blew away last year in a storm. I had discovered the teacup lying in the neighbors' trash with just a little chip out of the rim. You know how people are so careless about what they throw away? There was no saucer, but oh, that cup was beautiful! It had been painted a pale, pale green with purple violets on the side. Anyway, wouldn't you know? I had covered the cup with soap, and it slid right out of my hand—*crash*—into the basin. The handle broke off. There were just two little nubs sticking out, so you couldn't hold it anymore without burning your fingers, but—"

"I threw the plate," Caitrin whispered.

"Threw it?" Rosie repeated loudly.

Chipper turned around, his blue eyes wide. "How come you threw Mama's good plate?"

"I was . . . I was angry." She wished she could crawl under the table. "I'm very sorry. It was the wrong thing to do. I'm afraid I got carried away shouting at God about my terrible lot in life. Such a dreadful thing to do after all the blessings he's given me."

"Nobody should shout at God," Chipper said.

"I'm not sure of that," Rosie said. "God is our Father. Every moment of every day, he knows exactly how we feel inside, what we're thinking, what we want, and what we need. It won't do any good pretending you're not mad if you're really seething. You'll never fool God. You might as well go ahead and tell him exactly what you think."

"But yellin' and throwin' plates?" Chipper asked. "That ain't good."

"The Bible tells us the Spirit prays for us in groanings that can't be expressed in words. *Groanings* . . . that's the very thing it says. And we know that Jesus prayed with such agony in the garden that he sweated great drops of blood. So if groaning and sweating blood are perfectly acceptable ways to talk to God, I don't see what's wrong with a little shouting and plate throwing."

Chipper laughed, and Caitrin couldn't hold back her grin. "Maybe all my ranting at the good Lord caused him to send you two along tonight," she said, laying her hand on her friend's arm. "I'm glad of your company."

Rosie's face broke into a smile. "I've been so excited about the baby, I just can't stop chattering. What do you think of Lavinia?"

Caitrin blinked. "Who's that?"

"It's the name of our new baby," Chipper said, crawling into his mother's lap. "Let's see, we gots lotsa names already. Lavinia and Priscilla and Vanilla—"

"Valerie!" Rosie said with a chuckle. She kissed Chipper on the cheek. "There's something so beautiful about the name Lavinia, don't you think, Caitie? It just rolls right off the tongue."

"I want a brother," the little boy announced, "an' I don't want him to be named Lavinia."

"Lavinia is a girl's name, silly. Oh, Caitrin, I'm just praying every moment for this baby. I so want her to be healthy. And why are you throwing plates?"

The change in subject caught Caitrin by surprise. "Because Jack Cornwall came back," she blurted, which wasn't at all why she believed she'd thrown the plate. "No, that's not it. It's really the wallpaper. And the table is wobbly, and the chair is rickety, and I don't know how Jack is ever going to fit in. Poor Lucy in chains. You should have heard Sheena! I could have stuffed a sock into her mouth. She was shouting *Cornish this* and *Cornish that*, hitting Jack on the arm with her basket. Then, in came Mrs. Cornwall talking about Irish infestations. Jack said that some former colleague is still trying to take him to court, and I gave poor Lucy a comb and brush, but it's not going to help at all!"

"Is she bald-headed?" Chipper asked.

"No!" Caitrin exploded, pushing back her chair and standing. "Of course she isn't bald-headed."

"Hide the plates!" Chipper shouted. "She's gonna start throwin' 'em again."

"Caitrin?" Rosie tugged on her friend's hand. "Do you remember what you told me to pray for last fall? You said, 'If you wish to pray about Jack, Rosie, pray for his soul.' You asked me to pray that the Spirit of God would fill Jack's heart. You wanted me to pray for his family and his safety. And last of all, you asked me to pray that Jack would find a good woman who has the courage to love him as he deserves. Do you remember that?"

Caitrin slumped into the chair again. "Aye. I've prayed for him myself. But what hope does a man like that have to make a fresh start of his life?"

"Hope is the very name of our town, Caitie! If Jack Cornwall can't find hope here, where can he find it?"

"But how can he have hope if he must keep his sister in chains, Rosie?"

"Paul and Silas were put in chains. That didn't stop God's love from touching them."

"Perhaps, but can Jack ever hope the people here will love him? You know the trouble he's caused."

"Folks will just have to forgive Jack's past and open their hearts to his family."

"But there's not a chance Jimmy and Sheena will accept the Cornwalls. Their Irish pride is so strong, and Jack's mother is thoroughly Cornish."

"And I'm a foundling from a livery stable." Rosie smiled, an inner triumph lighting her huge brown eyes. "I used to hate admitting that, but now I know it doesn't matter where we come from, Caitie. In time, people learn to look beyond such things. Folks around here have learned to love me, and they'll love the Cornwalls, too."

"Even if Jack can overcome all those things, a man is trying to find him and take him back to Missouri. He's being tracked."

"Uncle Jack tracked *me*," Chipper put in. "An' he found me. Now he's gonna live here with us. And Gram is, too. So maybe trackin' ain't all bad. I can't wait to see Gram tomorrow. Mama said she'd take me down to their camp first thing."

"It's going to be all right, Caitie." Rosie gave her friend's fingers a squeeze. "If God could create the miracle of life inside me, what can't he do?"

"You hear that, Laviliva?" Chipper said, his mouth against the soft apron around Rosie's waist. "Mama says you're a miracle."

"*Lavinia*. Oh, that name's never going to work." Rosie pursed her lips for a moment. "Why don't we throw a welcoming party for the Cornwalls? It could be a spring festival with fresh flowers and punch. We could hang a big banner over the mercantile's door: To the Cornwall Family—Welcome to Hope."

Caitrin smiled. "It's a lovely idea, but—"

Before she could finish, the soddy door swung open and Seth Hunter strolled in. "We made a decision," he began, stopping when he saw the women's surprised faces. "Uh, 'scuse me, Miss Murphy. I forgot I don't live here anymore."

"No, please. You're welcome any time." Caitrin stood as Jimmy O'Toole and Rolf Rustemeyer followed Seth into the small room. "Shall I put on a pot of tea?"

"*Ja*," Rolf said, grinning broadly. "Fery goot maken tea. I like."

"It's late, Rustemeyer." Seth clamped a hand on the big German farmer's shoulder. "We'd better leave Miss Murphy in peace tonight. We just wanted you ladies to know we've decided to let the Cornwalls stay in Hope—for one month."

"One month?" Caitrin cried. "But Mr. Cornwall will hardly have time to build his smithy. And you know the bridge travel won't get busy until late spring."

"A month's grace," Jimmy explained, "to see how they get along here. 'Round St. Patrick's Day, we three men will have another meetin' and judge if we'll allow the family to stay on. If Jack Cornwall causes one stime of trouble, he'll be out on his ear. His mother's to keep her Cornish gob shut tight, especially where my Sheena is concerned. They're to stay to themselves. And if we see the mad girl anywhere about, the whole family will be asked to leave."

"So you'll permit the Cornwalls to stay in Hope," Caitrin said, "as long as they keep themselves hidden, say nothing, do nothing, and contribute in no way except to bring business to the community. The rest of us, meanwhile, are to keep a sharp lookout so as to catch their slightest misstep. We're to turn our heads the other way when they walk past, and we're to pretend they're invisible at all times. Yet we'll be nosing about their business to find any flaws. Sure in a month, we'll have caught them at *something*, so we will, gentlemen. Then we can be rid of them like so much dust shaken from our boots."

Caitrin crossed her arms and leveled a stare at the three men. Never had she witnessed a more prideful act or heard a more unchristian decision than this one. Seth gave his wife an uncomfortable glance. Rolf rubbed the back of his neck and stared at the floor. Jimmy stuck his thumbs under his suspenders and regarded his sister-in-law.

"Shall we hold everyone in Hope to such exacting standards then?" Caitrin asked the men. "If so, we must run Rolf away immediately for his unforgivable misuse of the English language. And Seth, I'm afraid you'll have to go as well. Only yesterday you were helping Rolf frame up the church, and you must have hit your thumb with a hammer, for I heard a most unholy word escape your lips."

"Seth!" Rosie gasped.

"Well . . ." Seth shifted his weight from one foot to the other. "Well, it hurt. I'm sorry, Miss Murphy. It won't happen again."

"Too late for that, I'm afraid. Under the rules you gentlemen have laid out, one infraction is cause enough to be run out of town. We may be known as the town of Hope, but we certainly offer not a measure of grace. Jimmy will have to go as well, I'm sorry to say. Sure he's been known to walk outside of an early morning and put on a most unacceptable display of stretching, hawking, spitting, blowing his nose, scratching his—"

"That'll be quite enough from you, Caitrin Murphy!" Jimmy said. "You'll not be makin' light of our decision, young lady. Your own behavior toward Jack Cornwall has not gone unnoticed. Sheena told me you harbored that *sherral* in *my* barn last winter, so you did. You kept his presence a secret, fed him our grub, hid our own enemy from us. If you were not my wife's sister, I'd put you out on your grug for such wickedness. Sheena tells me she saw Cornwall throwin' sheep's eyes at you today, and you back at him. She said she left the two of you in the mercantile havin' a great cuggermugger, all cozy and sweetlike. What have you to say for yourself, lass?"

"I've nothing to say for myself. I'm not the person on trial here. It seems that Mr. Jack Cornwall has already been sentenced to a stoning by the likes of you Pharisees, so I'll speak for him—"

"You've spoken for that devil enough already," Jimmy snapped. "I never thought I'd see the day when one of my own family would turn against me. I gave you a home, food, and my good care, Caitrin. Is this the thanks I get? That you keep deadly secrets from us, that you speak out in defense of our enemy, that you accuse *us* of injustice?"

His green eyes were sharp as they stared into Caitrin's face. She felt her cheeks flush with heat. Half of her wanted to scream at the three pious men. But she couldn't deny that Jimmy had been correct in his accusations.

"I apologize to you," she told her brother-in-law. "I had no right to hide Mr. Cornwall from you last autumn. I put a stranger's well-being above loyalty to my own family."

"Aye, you did. I thank you for your repentance, and I'll welcome a change in your behavior. Never forget that you're Irish, lass. You're a Murphy from County Cork. Don't be swept away by that wicked stranger when you've better men here at home. And don't trade your allegiance to your Irish heritage for a few sweet words from a proven liar, a fighter, and a thief. Stay close to your own kind, Caitie. We love you, so we do. We'll see you're looked after."

"Thank you, Jimmy." Caitrin swallowed at the gritty lump in her throat.

"I am goot man here at home," Rolf said, thumping his massive chest. "Maybe you marry vit me, *ja*? Haf many childrens."

"Oh, dear Rolf," Rosie cut in, laying her hand on the German's brawny arm. "I think it's time for us to move past basic English and into learning good manners."

"Goot manners?" He grinned and shot a victory glance to the other men. "*Ja*, we are all goot manners, Seth, Jimmy, *und* me. I am goot man. Fery goot man. Tank you, *Frau* Hunter, for saying."

Rosie laughed. "You *are* a good man, and you will learn good manners in time. Maybe you can start by escorting Miss Murphy to the welcoming party for the Cornwalls."

"What?" Jimmy cried.

"We have to give the family a party, of course. Oh, don't worry yourselves, Welcoming Committee. Caitie and I will plan everything." Rosie gave Chipper a playful pat on the back. "Come on, sweetie. Grab that big ol' dog of yours, and let's head for home. I'm so tired! It's a good thing I'm having a baby, or I'd be sure this was another sign I was on the road to my own funeral."

Waving a cheery good-bye, Rosie hurried her family out the door. Jimmy settled his hat on his head and followed. Rolf gave Caitrin an awkward bow.

"You come to velcomen party vit me," he said. "I am fery goot manners."

"And *you* are Irish, Caitrin Murphy!" Jimmy called over his shoulder. "Don't forget it."

As the door slammed shut behind the men, Caitrin let out a breath. "I may have been born in County Cork," she said into the empty room. "But I live in Hope, Kansas. I'm not Irish; I'm American . . . and I won't be bound by petty prejudice."

All the same, she knew Jimmy had been within his rights to

chasten her. Her loyalty should lie with her sister and the O'Toole family. And no sweet words from a gray-eyed man could change that.

Jack set a block of sod on the slowly rising wall of his smithy, then stood back to survey his new domain. Though he had worked all day and his muscles ached, it would be another week before he could put a roof on the building. Cutting, hauling, and laying the heavy sod was tedious labor, but the natural material would keep his workplace cool in summer and warm in winter. More important, it wouldn't burn as easily as would the dry timber of a frame building. He sure didn't cotton to the idea of lighting his forge the first time and burning down the whole place.

Good thing Seth Hunter had allowed him to build near the mercantile, Jack thought as he trimmed the grass from another sod brick. Any wagon coming from east or west was bound to see the sign he would hang outside his door. In fact, he'd already had his first customers. Though he hadn't even built his forge, he'd managed to shoe five horses and patch a hole in a passing farmer's water bucket. The jingle of coins in his pocket sure felt good.

Whistling, Jack heaved the brick onto the wall and edged it into place. He'd seen Caitrin Murphy coming and going from the mercantile, but she had made herself scarce around his work site. He could hardly blame her.

After Jimmy O'Toole's unpleasant visit to his camp the night of the Cornwalls' arrival, Jack wasn't exactly on speaking terms with the family. Like some kind of self-appointed policeman, O'Toole had marched over and laid out a bunch of rules and regulations the Cornwalls were to follow. Then he'd announced they would have one month to demonstrate their good behavior, or they'd be expelled from the town. Jack's mother had responded with a flurry of loud verbal assaults about Irish slothfulness and stupidity . . . and that had ended the conversation.

"Hey, Uncle Jack," Chipper said behind him.

Jack swung around. At the sight of the little boy, he felt like the sun had just risen. An unexpected truth filtered into his heart. In spite of losing the child to Seth last autumn, Jack had been granted Chipper's presence—his snaggletoothed grin, his deep chuckle, his cheery conversation were a part of Jack's daily life again. God had given him the boy after all.

"Hey, Chipper," Jack greeted him, kneeling to give his nephew a hug. "I haven't seen you all day. What have you been up to? Trouble, I reckon."

"Naw!" Chipper giggled. "Me an' Will O'Toole was fishin' at the creek almost all day. Didn't catch nothin', though. I gotta go pick buffalo and cow chips for Mama now. But first, lookit what I brung you!"

He pulled half a cookie from the pocket of his overall bib. "Oops, I guess it busted when you gave me that squeeze. It's a sugar cookie. Mama made it."

Jack accepted the crumbly gift and took a bite. "Mm-mm. Now, that's one good cookie. You tell your mama I appreciate her thinking of me."

"Oh, Mama didn't send it to you. She baked a big batch of cookies to sell in the mercantile. Caitrin Murphy gave this one to me when I was in there fetchin' a coupla hooks for me an' Will this mornin'. It was warm, an' it smelled so good. I had all I could do not to eat it. But I saved it just for you!"

"Miss Murphy told you to give this to me?" Jack felt a ripple of satisfaction run up his spine. "What exactly did she say to you?"

"She said, 'Give this cookie to your Uncle Jack.'"

"And that's all?"

"She said in her funny way of talkin', 'It takes time an' hard work to build castles, so it does.' An' I reminded her that you was buildin' a smithy, not a castle. Then she told me the smithy is your castle, an' you're gonna build all your dreams right inside it. Is that true, Uncle Jack?"

"I reckon it is." Jack smiled and rumpled the boy's dark hair.

"But I thought you was gonna build stuff outta iron inside your smithy. Like wagon wheels and plows."

"I am. And with the money I earn, I'm planning to make my dreams come true."

Chipper tilted his head to one side. "Know what, Uncle Jack? I think Jimmy O'Toole was dead wrong the other night at Miss Murphy's house when he called you a liar an' a fighter an' a thief."

Fighting the fury that rose inside him at the child's repetition of O'Toole's slanderous words, Jack studied Chipper's bright eyes. "I have done some wrong things in my life, little fellow," he said. "Same as everybody. But you know what Miss Murphy told me once? She said God thinks I'm precious. He loves me. This winter I did a lot of praying and reading in the Good Book, and I found out she was right. The God who made this very sod we're standing on loved me enough to come down here and die for me. Now if he cares that much about an ol' scalawag like me, I figure he can help me leave behind whatever wrong I did and walk along a new road. And if Will's papa would look at who I am instead of who I was, maybe he could see that."

Chipper pulled the other half of the cookie from his pocket and handed it to his uncle. "I bet you're right, Uncle Jack. Well, I gotta go pick up cow chips for Mama. Guess what? We're havin' stew and corn bread tonight!"

"Yum! Come by and visit me tomorrow," Jack called as Chipper ran off to do his mother's bidding. "And tell Miss Murphy thanks for the cookie!"

The boy's laughter was ringing in the air as the mercantile door opened and Caitrin Murphy herself stepped outside. Jack caught his breath at the sight of the woman. In the past few days, he had reminded himself a hundred times to stand back and give her room. If he inserted himself between her and her family again, it would only cause trouble.

Besides, she wasn't all that special, he had told himself again and again. Just a red-haired gal, a little too skinny, and a lot too mouthy. Just a common working woman. A spinster at that. She was past the age when most women married—her midtwenties at least. And she had all those obnoxious relatives . . .

As she turned, Caitrin's green eyes flashed in Jack's direction. Behind her, the setting sun lit her hair like a roaring inferno. Her brown dress shimmered and glowed like molten bronze as it flowed down to her toes in cascades and swirls of fabric. She bent to insert a brass key in the mercantile door, and a lock of loose, curly hair slid over her shoulder. Jack had never seen a volcano, but that tress had to be like lava the way it burned and tumbled slowly forward.

He dropped the sod brick he was holding and started toward her. These past months he'd been praying so often that words seemed to form in his heart without his planning them. He knew God heard him, even though he couldn't always feel his Master's presence and couldn't always hear an answer to his constant request. *Father, I've tried to stay back,* his soul lifted up. *But there's something about her. Something I need. You brought me back here in spite of everything. Help me now. Help me to bridge gaps. . . .*

"Mr. Cornwall," she said, clutching her workbasket in front of her. "Good evening to you."

"And to you, ma'am." Belatedly, he remembered to take off his hat. "I . . . ah . . . I thank you for the cookie. Chipper gave it to me."

"Rose Hunter baked it."

"Tasted good."

She brushed the lava hair back over her shoulder and looked in the direction of her soddy. "Well, 'tis late. I must be getting home."

"I'll walk you."

"No!" The green eyes darted up at him. "Thank you, Mr. Cornwall, but I know my way."

He didn't care how much his presence unnerved Caitrin. He had seen the look she flashed him from the mercantile door, and he fully intended to spend a few minutes with her.

"I'll walk you anyhow," he said. "It's getting dark."

She let out a breath and picked up her skirt. "The sun is still on the horizon."

"Perfect time for the wild things to come out and feed."

Her focus darted his way as they started along the narrow path toward the soddy. "I'm not afraid of wild things."

"Really?" he said, matching her stride for stride. "Danger lurks in the most unlikely places."

"Does it now?"

"In empty barns on autumn nights."

"I'm not afraid of barns."

"On isolated paths across windswept prairies."

"I'm not afraid of paths."

He followed her to the door of her soddy. "In lonely hearts at sunset."

"I'm not afraid—" she paused and looked full in his face—"I'm not afraid of a lonely heart at sunset."

"You should be," he said.

CHAPTER 9

CAITRIN held her workbasket at waist level, hoping in vain that Jack might keep his distance. Instead, he rested one hand against the soddy, leaning on his arm and trapping her beside the open door. If she ducked inside, he might follow . . . and she could never allow that. Her back to the rough wall, she lifted her chin and met his eyes.

"Mr. Cornwall, you must not—"

"Jack," he cut in.

"As I was saying, Mr. Cornwall—"

"Jack."

She moistened her lips. "You must not come to my house, *Jack*. The men have allowed you only one month to prove yourself. If Jimmy sees you talking with me, he'll want to run you off."

"I don't care what Jimmy O'Toole sees. And I don't care what he thinks, either. The only opinion I care about is yours. What do *you* want, Caitrin? If you don't want to talk to me, tell me right now. I'll back off."

Caitrin could hardly believe how the man's very presence stirred her. This was nothing like the giddy, girlish sentiment she'd felt for Sean O'Casey . . . where pride in his position and his good looks had impelled her love. The force of Jack's determination cut into her, hewing down everything in its path. Jimmy had called him a liar. Yet she felt certain that this man, like none other she had ever known, was completely honest. He spoke his innermost thoughts aloud. He acted on his sincere convictions. And for the sake of peace, *she* must be the one to hide the truth.

"I think," she began, "I think you must not speak with me, Jack."

"I didn't ask what you thought. I asked what you wanted."

What did she want? Countless things! She wanted this man to take her in his arms and hold her day and night for the rest of her life. She wanted him to be her champion . . . to fight off every adversary that came between them. She wanted his deep voice ringing in her heart. She wanted his touch, his breath on her skin, his tender kisses. She wanted a world of passion and dreams come true!

"I want you to stay away from me, Jack," she choked out. "Because I don't want you to leave."

"What do you mean by that?"

She shook her head. "You cannot be seen with me, or the men will send your family away. I heard the words they spoke of you, so I did. Sure Jimmy looks upon you as the devil himself, Jack. Seth doesn't trust you. Rolf is confused by you and probably a little jealous. Do you want to leave this town?"

"Do you want me to go?"

"No, and that's why you must not come near me."

"What's the point of staying if I can't talk to you, Caitrin?"

"Sure you didn't come to Hope just for me! You wanted to make a fresh start. You wanted to build your smithy. You wanted to find a place of solitude and protection for Lucy. You wanted to earn a living for your family."

"I wanted to be with you." He took a step closer, all but engulfing her in his presence. "When I met you, I was sure God had abandoned me a long time before. One bad thing after another had happened in my life, and I blamed him. But then you walked into Jimmy's barn that night, and everything turned around. You're the only good I've known in many years, and I'm sure God put you in my life. I'm not about to back off unless you tell me to."

"Jack, God is not like a capricious fairy, showering us with bad luck or good according to his whims." Fearful of being seen, Caitrin tried to look over Jack's shoulder at the path to the mercantile. But the solid slab of muscle blocked her view. Praying for wisdom, she spoke quickly. "Life unfolds before us, good and bad. Often the bad is the consequence of our own personal sin. But sometimes . . . as with Lucy . . . dreadful things just happen. 'Tis the same with the good in life. Usually, we reap what we sow, and if we plant good seed, then good things happen in return. But sometimes the Lord permits good, even if his people don't deserve it."

"You're the good God brought into my life."

"But you mustn't look to *me* if you want to know God. I'm a human, and I make many mistakes. I'm willful and mouthy. I shout and weep, and I . . . I throw plates."

"Plates?"

"You must keep your focus on the Father, Jack. Talk to him and grow in him. Please . . . please don't view my presence in your life as a sign that God loves you. He has loved you always, through good times *and* bad. You must have a strong enough faith that when things take a turn for the worse, you won't believe God has deserted you. That's when you will need him the most. And if the men here chase you away—"

"No one's going to run me off, Caitrin. I'm a stubborn man." He fingered the tumble of curly hair that lay on her shoulder. "My convictions run deep, and I don't give up easily. You saw the way I went after Chipper. Last autumn I was sure God had robbed me of the boy, and I held the Almighty responsible for yet another loss in my life. But it hit me this evening when Chipper brought along that cookie . . . I didn't lose the boy after all. God gave him to me anyhow, just not in the way I'd planned. I'm beginning to think

God has good plans for me, and he can turn the worst problems into blessings."

Caitrin studied his gray eyes, reading the earnestness in them. How she loved to hear him speak! Though he was a common laborer, Jack might have been a scholar for the profound analysis he gave to his life and the world around him.

"When you look at it that way," he said, "you could say I've blamed God for a lot of losses that turned out to be gifts. I fought in the war for the cause of freedom from tyranny. The South lost the war, but God gave me freedom anyhow. Look at me out here, carving a life from this prairie. That's freedom, Caitrin. That's hope."

"I don't want them to take it from you," she whispered, her eyes misting. "Oh, Jack, please go away. Don't let the men see us together. They'll rob you of that freedom. They'll steal your hope . . . and mine."

"What hope do we have if we can't even speak to each other, Caitrin?" He drew her into his arms. "I want to hear your passionate words and see the flash of fire in your eyes. I want to get close enough to smell that scent you wear."

"Lily of the valley," she murmured, dropping her workbasket and slipping her hands up the broad expanse of his chest. "Jack, hold me tight. Sure my head is running in circles, and my heart . . . my heart . . ."

His lips pressed against hers in a tender kiss. She melted into him, reveling in the utter power of his embrace. For this moment she did not have to hold herself up. She could surrender . . . drift at peace in his strength . . . rest in the security of this man's presence. His hands slid into her hair as his lips found her cheek, her ear, her neck. Struggling for control, he drew her close and nestled her head in the curve of his shoulder.

"I don't care what they say, Caitrin," he mouthed, his breath warming her hair. "I don't care what they try to do to me. Unless you tell me to go, I won't abandon you. I'll never leave you. It's a promise."

With a last crushing embrace, he set her apart. Turning his back, he walked away into the dusk. Caitrin gripped the edge of the door behind her. In the distance she could just make out the glimmering light of oil lamps shining in the O'Tooles' soddy across the creek . . . and in the Cornwalls' small camp along the sandy bank.

"Lord, oh, Lord," she whispered in prayer. "Bring us light. May it be the light of your love and forgiveness, and not—" she stifled a sob—"not the spark of a fire that will destroy us all."

"*Three* pickles?" Caitrin eyed Mr. Bridger, the man who carried mail to and from Topeka. "Are you quite sure? You'll be thirsty enough to drink up the whole of Bluestem Creek before you're halfway home."

The man laughed. "They're not all for me. I've been raving about these pickles so long, my wife ordered me to bring her one. And then little Johnny piped up wanting a pickle of his own. If word gets out—and with my wife around, it will—you may have to shut down the mercantile just to make enough pickles to supply Topeka."

"That will be my sister's task, so it will. Sheena's the pickle maker of the town. I'll be sure to tell her of your abiding admiration."

"My admiration for her *pickles*," he clarified. "That Jimmy O'Toole may be skinny as a telegraph post, but I sure don't want to tangle with him over a misunderstanding about his wife."

Caitrin handed Mr. Bridger the wrapped dill pickles, their pungent green marinade already seeping through the brown paper. She needed to tend the customers who had ridden in on the mail coach, but she knew her first loyalty belonged to the mail carrier. It was he, after all, who brought the others.

"I'm sure Jimmy knows you're not the first to appreciate Sheena's skills," she said. "He's a good man, so he is."

"You're right about that, but I've heard stories about the hullabaloo he put up over the building of the Hope bridge. And I know he wouldn't allow the church to be raised on his land. O'Toole's a tough old buzzard, if you ask me. You make sure he knows it's the pickles that interest me, and not the wife."

"I'll do it," Caitrin said with a chuckle. "But you mustn't think too harshly of Jimmy—"

"Excuse me, ma'am." A short, bullnecked man leaned across the counter. "I don't mean to interrupt you, but when does the coach to Manhattan get in?"

Caitrin glanced up at the store clock. "It should be here already. It usually gets here the same time as the mail coach, and I can hardly catch my breath for the traffic. Are you bound for Manhattan, sir?"

"Yep." He squared his shoulders inside the ragged gray Confederate army coat he wore. "Headin' west. I'll cover the whole state of Kansas before I'm through, if need be. Fact is, I'm on the lookout for an old friend of mine. Name's Jack Cornwall. Ever hear of him?"

Caitrin's heart dropped to her knees. "Cornwall," she mumbled. "Is that a . . . a Cornish name?"

"Don't know and don't care." He rubbed the stubble of dark whiskers on his chin. "Near the end of the war, Jack Cornwall ran with my bunch over in Missouri."

"Your bunch?"

"Group of men, soldiers mostly. We kept the cause alive, protected the poor farmers gettin' eat up by Yankee aggressors, that sort of thing—not to mention a fair amount of drinkin', cuttin' up, and carryin' on with women." He gave a laugh. "Hoo, that Cornwall was a wild one, you know. Big tall feller, kind of a rough face, gray eyes. He worked as a blacksmith durin' the war—shoulders from here to here, arms like blocks of steel. Drove the ladies crazy. You'd remember him if you saw him."

Her back to the visitor, Caitrin busied herself tucking letters into the mail slots. "I'm sorry I can't help you," she said.

"If you run into my man, tell him Bill Hermann's lookin' for him."

"I'll do that." Through the window beside the mailboxes, Caitrin spotted Jack Cornwall dusting off his hands and starting for the mercantile.

"See, back around the end of the war, our bunch ran into a little unfortunate trouble," Hermann continued. "Messy business."

"What sort of trouble?" Caitrin asked, praying that Jack would change his mind and turn around.

"There was a lynchin'. Easton was the feller's name. After that, the bunch split up for a while. Cornwall went back to his family, and we ain't seen hide nor hair of him since."

"Does . . . does the bunch want him back?" Caitrin's heart slammed against her chest. Jack stopped to pat Stubby on the head as Chipper scampered up. *Go with Chipper,* she pleaded silently. *Go with your nephew.*

Jack knelt to talk to the boy. Chipper pulled something out of his pocket and the two bent to examine it.

"Yeah, the bunch wants his help," Hermann said. "See, most of 'em wound up in jail after the Easton troubles, but if Cornwall would testify that he was at the cabin that night and that none of the bunch was involved in the lynchin', the fellers might get off scot-free. 'Course Cornwall doesn't want to swear he was there for fear of gettin' his own hide strung up on the hangin' tree, and he's been runnin' ever since the trouble. Folks told me the Cornwall family had moved south, around Cape Girardeau. All I found out down there was that he'd gone to Kansas chasin' some kid. I rode across the state line lookin' for him, and folks said he'd come right here. To this town."

Caitrin could hardly breathe. "Is that right? I'm a newcomer myself. Not long of County Cork, in Ireland."

"You musta missed him. I hear he caused quite a ruckus—typical of Cornwall." He laughed again. "And then he headed back to Missouri. I spent most of the winter searchin' for him. But when I tracked him to the house where he kept his mama and his lunatic sister, the folks livin' around the place told me he'd up and took 'em off to Kansas."

Caitrin gulped as Jack stood and looked toward the mercantile door. "You're very dedicated to your purpose."

Bill Hermann stretched and twisted his bull neck, causing a series of crackling pops to echo through the mercantile. "I got motivation, ma'am," he said, giving his knuckles a similar bone-crunching flex. "Cornwall's testimony is the only thing that can get the bunch off the hook. The trial's scheduled for a couple of months from now, and I gotta get Cornwall back to Missouri in time."

He handed her a card. "This here's the place to write if you hear of Jack Cornwall. You'll let me know, won't you, ma'am?"

"Bill Hermann," she read from the card.

"That's me. Well, I hear the Manhattan coach pullin' up. Gotta go."

He started for the door just as Jack turned toward the smithy, putting his back to his former comrade. With the crazy notion that she could somehow protect Jack, Caitrin followed Bill Hermann out of the mercantile. *Dear God, don't let the men see each other!* she pleaded. *Please, don't let them see each other.*

When she stepped into the frigid February air, she realized she had broken a sweat. Mr. Bridger, the mail carrier, heaved a sack of letters onto his coach as his passengers climbed aboard. The driver of the stage bound for Manhattan was just stepping down from his seat.

"I'm sorry, Miss Murphy, I won't have time to stop today," he called out to her. "I know you always want customers, but I'm runnin' late."

"That's quite all right," she said. "Bring me twice as many the next time, will you?"

She squeezed her hands together as Bill Hermann followed a couple of other passengers into the coach. The driver latched the door behind them. When the horses began to pull away again, Caitrin waved and gave the driver her brightest smile. Inwardly groaning, she brushed a tendril of damp hair from her forehead. If Hermann had seen Jack . . . Remembering the man himself, she swung around toward the smithy. Chipper had just darted away with a wave of farewell. Jack Cornwall straightened, caught sight of her, and grinned.

"Well, well," he said. "This day just got a lot brighter."

Caitrin bit her lip to keep from bursting out with all the suppressed tension of the past few minutes. "Hello, Jack."

"Looks like Chipper found the first tadpole of the year."

"Bill Hermann was here," she blurted, rushing toward him. "Oh Jack, 'twas Bill Hermann himself, the man who's been tracking you! He just rode away on the Manhattan stage. He knows you were in Hope last autumn. He'll be back, I'm sure of it. And he says you were part of . . . part of a lynching."

Jack crossed his arms over his vast chest. "Bill Hermann is lying."

"Can you prove it?"

"Do I need to?"

"Hermann says you can testify on behalf of your bunch."

"I'm not going to testify. I don't have anything to tell a judge, because I wasn't around at the time of the Easton troubles. I don't know a thing about that lynching."

"Why does Mr. Hermann believe you were there if you weren't?"

"It was night. Dark."

Caitrin looked away. "And you *were* one of his bunch?"

"Yep." He took her shoulders and forced her to face him. "But I wasn't there that night, Caitrin. I swear it."

"Sure you don't need to swear such a thing to me. All I ask is that your words be true."

"I'm telling you the truth. I had gone to Sedalia that day. You can ask Lucy. We were together the whole time."

"Then Lucy can testify for you!"

"No." Jack shook his head. "She can't. She won't."

"But why not? Aye, the judge must listen to her words."

"I'd never ask Lucy to stand up for me." Jack raked a hand through his brown hair. "Look, let me handle this, would you, Caitrin? It's my problem. I can take care of Bill Hermann and the old bunch. I've put my past behind me, and I'm facing the future. I'm not afraid."

"You may have put your past behind you, but obviously your cronies haven't. Many of them are biding time in jail until their trial. They'll have plenty of good reasons to toss the past straight into your face . . . and Bill Hermann is their ringleader."

"Let it go, Caitrin. You'll never fix this one."

"What am I to do then?" She could hear the intensity in her voice, the edge of frustration knifing through her words. "Yesterday, you risked your position here in Hope by kissing me in full view . . . and it was all I could do to fall asleep last night for thinking of that kiss. Am I to be swept off by you, then, Mr. Cornwall? Is my heart to be placed in your hands? Is my very soul to be meshed with yours—only to have you ripped away by some demon from your past? And you ask me to stand by and do nothing! You promise you won't abandon me—yet I can almost see them coming now to drag you away. Am I to sit idly and watch?"

Jack enunciated each word slowly, "You *can't* fix this one, Caitrin. Leave it alone."

"Then you must fix it. You must help Lucy to write a letter to the authorities in Missouri."

"Never."

"Why not? She would do it for you."

The muscle in Jack's jaw flickered. "I won't ask her, Caitrin. Neither will you, and I'm counting on you to abide by my request. Do you understand?"

Caitrin lifted her chin. "Then do not expect me to allow you any further liberties with my affections, Mr. Cornwall. If you refuse to defend yourself and you will not permit me to help you, then I want nothing to do with you."

"Aw, Caitrin." Jack took her arm and pulled her close. "Get off your high horse, woman."

She trembled as his hand slid down her arm. "Jack, I cannot bear this. 'Tis bad enough that I must listen to the people here drag your family's reputation through the mud. I can't imagine you will ever win their hearts. But the thought that this man from your bunch—"

"It happened a long time ago, Caitrin. Almost a year. I've changed."

"Have you?" She rested her cheek against his chest. "I fear I'm a terrible weakling, Jack, unable to bear the pain of another loss. If you are genuinely innocent, prove it. Rid yourself of this millstone around your neck."

"When the time comes, Cait, I'll do that." He kissed her forehead. "But I have to walk this new life step by step. I can't alter the past. I can't fix up the whole world. And neither can you. I know I'm precious to God, remember? If I put this in his hands—"

"Caitrin Murphy!" Sheena squawked, racing toward the couple. "By all the goats in Kerry, sister, what are you doing? Get away from her, Cornish devil!"

"Oh no, it's the deadly basket again," Jack cried out, raising his arms in mock defense against Sheena's swinging workbasket.

"Get away from my sister!" The puffing woman clobbered him across the chest. "See to the children, Caitie!"

Caitrin gaped as Erinn and Colleen came to a stop just behind

Sheena. At the sight of their mother whapping the brawny man, Colleen popped her thumb into her mouth, and Erinn blinked in shock. Crouching beside the girls, Caitrin threw her arms around them.

"Is that Mr. Cornwall?" Erinn asked.

"Aye, and you mustn't be afraid of him. He's a very nice man, so he is. A good man."

"Then why is Mama hitting him?"

"Because he's . . . he's Cornish."

At that moment another stage rolled across the bridge and came to a stop in front of the mercantile. A fresh load of customers clambered out of their tight quarters. Caitrin sucked down a breath and turned to greet them. "Good afternoon, everyone," she called over the hubbub of her sister's drubbing. "Welcome to Hope. Won't you go inside and have a look around the mercantile?"

Dumbfounded at the sight before them, the visitors clustered together, wives clutching their husbands' arms. Caitrin turned to Sheena and attempted to grab the flailing basket. "Please, Sheena!" she hissed. "Please stop!"

"He's a villain, a very demon!" Sheena stood back, panting for breath. "A kidnapper!"

The crowd in front of the store broke into murmurs of surprise.

"This man is an attempted murderer!" Sheena cried in triumph, presenting her enemy to the gasping bystanders. "And now I have caught him in the very act of seducing my sister!"

"Listen here, feller!" The stagecoach driver pulled a pistol from the holster at his waist. "I don't know what you done to upset Miss Murphy's sister, but you better put your hands in the air and walk over here nice and slow."

"This is ridiculous," Caitrin said, stepping in front of the gun. "Mr. Cornwall is an upstanding citizen of Hope."

"I'll defend myself, Miss Murphy." Jack edged her to the side, his hands held well away from his body. "Ladies and gentlemen, I'm the town blacksmith. Mrs. O'Toole and her people have a little running feud with my kinfolk back in the old country, but you have no need to be alarmed. If you'll just step into the mercantile, I'll head over to the smithy and get back to my work."

The stagecoach driver glanced at Caitrin, then at Sheena. "Shall I let him go?"

"No," Sheena said.

"Aye," Caitrin overruled. "Of course, you must let him go. Good day, Mr. Cornwall."

"He was here to woo you, wasn't he, Caitie?" Sheena queried as Jack stood his ground. "Ooh, to think that my own sister . . . my beloved little Caitrin would—"

"I've done *nothing* wrong, Sheena." Caitrin didn't know whether to rush to her sister's comfort, try to ease her customers' trepidations, or run away with Jack Cornwall and never look back. "Sheena, please—ladies and gentlemen, do go inside and look around. We've plenty of freshly baked bread, and I received a parcel of bright new fabrics just yesterday."

"I hear Mrs. O'Toole's pickles are the pride and joy of Hope," Jack said, addressing the nearest woman. "Fact is, folks come from miles around just to taste them."

"Indeed," Caitrin said, encouraged by the flush of pink in her sister's cheeks. "Only moments ago, the Topeka mail-coach driver bought three whole pickles. Two for his family and one to eat on the way home. He's predicting a rush of orders from the city."

"Pickles?" A thin man took off his hat and stepped forward. "Dill pickles?" The stagecoach driver lowered his pistol. At that moment Felicity Cornwall raced up from the camp beside the Bluestem. Waving her arms over her head, she gave a wild shriek and headed for Jack. Women gasped. Men grabbed for their children. The driver accidentally discharged a shot into the ground.

"Jack, come quickly!" Felicity cried. "It's Lucy. She's drowning in the creek!"

CHAPTER 10

"LET'S GET out of this town," a customer called as Jack pushed through the crowd and sprinted toward the creek with Felicity following right behind. "These folks is crazy!"

"No, wait!" Caitrin held out her arms, but it was too late. Even the driver fled toward the stagecoach without a backward look. Swinging around, she grabbed Sheena's arm. "I must go with them to Lucy!"

"Caitie, this is not your business," Sheena insisted, clutching at her sister's hands. "Stay here and mind the mercantile. Let the Cornwalls tend to their own."

"How can you say such a thing?" Caitrin pulled back in disbelief. "Would you have the poor woman drown?"

"I would have you know your place, sister!" Sheena's green eyes crackled. "Sure you must choose between them and us, Caitie. You know we'll never permit that Cornish devil to become one of us. If you keep on championing him, letting yourself be duped by his charms, stumbling into his traps, we'll have no choice but to disown you. Please, Caitie, come into the mercantile with us now. Help Erinn and Colleen choose peppermint sticks and lemon drops to take to the boys."

Caitrin glanced at the little girls whose bright eyes stared in confusion. "Erinn, Colleen," she said softly, "Jesus commanded us to serve those less fortunate, did he not? Poor Miss Lucy, who cannot seem to find any joy in life, is certainly less fortunate than we. And that is why I must go to the creek and try to be of some service to her." She caught both her sister's hands. "You must understand, Sheena. Please, understand."

Without waiting for a response, Caitrin raced past the smithy toward Bluestem Creek. Lucy was nowhere in sight.

Felicity Cornwall darted back and forth along the sandy bank, shrieking in despair. Up to his chest in the creek, Jack was wading deeper as he called out the young woman's name.

"Jack!" Caitrin shouted, hurtling down the bank. "Where is Lucy? Where has she gone?"

"Drowned, drowned!" Mrs. Cornwall wailed.

Caitrin dashed into the frigid water just as Lucy's dark head bobbed up in midstream. The young woman drifted in the swiftest part of the current, her back to the shore. Gasping in shock at the icy chill that gripped her ankles, Caitrin waded to Jack's side.

"She's not done for yet," he panted. "She's got her feet on the bottom, but she keeps letting herself float off under the water."

"She's wearing those heavy chains. Sure they'll drag her down."

"Lucy!" Jack called out, reaching toward his sister. "Lucy, it's Jack. Can you hear me? Don't go under again, Sis."

"Lucy, Lucy!" Mrs. Cornwall shrieked. "Get out of that water at once! Do you hear me, young lady? Come here immediately!"

Lucy's head sank beneath the surface. Caitrin watched in horror as Jack lunged toward the spot, disappearing himself. Toes numb, she squeezed her hands together. Should she go ashore and calm Felicity? Her keening was only making things worse. No, there was no choice in this matter.

"Can you swim, Miss Murphy?" Felicity cried as Caitrin set out into the middle of the stream.

"Not much." She cast a backward glance. "If you're a praying woman, Mrs. Cornwall, now's the time."

Hardly able to catch her breath in the numbing water, Caitrin plunged ahead. When Lucy bobbed to the surface again, she was many yards downstream from the place Jack had been searching. Caitrin made for her at once. *Give me words, Father,* she pleaded. *And give her hope!*

"Hello, Lucy," Caitrin called in the most casual and unagitated voice she could manage. "It's a bit cold out here, don't you think?"

Lucy stiffened at the sound of the unexpected voice. Her hair streaming, she slowly turned to observe the woman approaching. Caitrin was horrified to see that Lucy's face had turned an ugly shade of gray, her lips a pale blue.

"Miss Murphy," Lucy whispered.

"Did you get the brush and mirror I sent with Jack?" Caitrin asked, working her way toward midstream. "They were meant as gifts for you."

Hollow-eyed, Lucy gazed in silence.

"It was a small tortoiseshell brush. I've a comb to match it in the mercantile." Teeth chattering, Caitrin kept walking closer until she was up to her chin in the bracing water. "I'd noticed that caring for your hair might be a bit difficult, and I thought perhaps you'd enjoy something pretty."

Lucy stared.

"I'm so glad you've come to Hope," Caitrin continued, chatting as though they were seated in a parlor somewhere. "Sure all the women who live close round here are married and busy with families. But I live alone, and the company of someone for tea now and again would be lovely. Perhaps you could come for tea this afternoon? I've Earl Grey, but please don't tell. It's wicked of me, but I don't want to share such a treasure with just anyone."

She stopped a pace from the young woman, hardly breathing in fear that Lucy would drift away again or that she herself might collapse from the cold. Ashore, Mrs. Cornwall had stopped shrieking, and Jack stood unmoving at the corner of her vision. Forcing her stiffened lips into a smile, she looked into Lucy's eyes.

"I'm a bit cold; are you?" Caitrin searched for recognition. "Can you feel the cold, Lucy?"

"I . . . I'm sorry . . . ," she mumbled.

"I think in the summer the water must be rather nice. The children enjoy paddling about in it, so they do. But it's awfully chilly right now."

"I don't . . . don't feel anything."

Caitrin cocked her head to one side. She could feel *everything*—the swift current tugging at her legs, the sucking mud beneath her feet, and the bone-aching cold creeping ever inward through her body. But Lucy's words had been filled with a kind of resigned peace.

"I suppose," Caitrin said softly, "I suppose you like it when you can't feel anything, Lucy. Sometimes . . . sometimes I can hardly bear the weight of my own thoughts. Do you know what I did the other day? I got so angry I threw a plate. Smashed it right against the wall."

Lucy gaped, blank-faced.

"And just now right outside the mercantile, I shouted at my sister," Caitrin went on. "Chipper says we shouldn't shout and throw things, but I think it's far more important that we be honest. God knows everything about us, and he's not going to punish us for sharing our true emotions with him. It's quite all right to feel what's inside your own heart, you know."

"No," Lucy mouthed. "I don't . . . I can't . . ."

"Grab her!" someone shouted from the shore.

"Get her now!"

Lucy's eyes darted away from Caitrin's face. A look of terror suffused her ashen skin. "No . . . no . . ."

"I'm not going to grab you, Lucy," Caitrin promised quickly. "Jack told me you don't like to be touched, and I certainly understand that. Sometimes I just want to hide, I feel so—" A movement caught her eye. "Oh, have a look at that blue jay on the other bank! Can you see it? Spring is almost here, Lucy. I can hardly wait. Did you know Rose Hunter and I are planning a welcoming party for your family? What's your favorite color?"

Lucy's focus shifted again from the shore to Caitrin's face. "I don't . . . I can't think . . ."

"Well, that's probably because it's so cruel cold out here." Aware that her legs had gone numb and the current was clutching at her with icy claws, Caitrin knew she had only moments before she would be forced to leave the water. "I've an idea, Lucy. Would you like to come to my house right now for a spot of tea? This very moment?"

"They'll . . . they'll . . ."

"No, they won't. I won't let them touch us. Jack will protect us, won't he? He loves you so much, Lucy. Sure I'll tell him to take off those ridiculous chains so you can lift your teacup. How's that? Will you come for tea? Do say yes."

Lucy turned toward the shore. Caitrin could see that a crowd had gathered—the Manhattan coach passengers who had let their curiosity get the better of them, Seth and Rosie, a horde of children. Even Sheena and the girls had traipsed down from the mercantile.

"Oh, good heavens," Caitrin said. "You'd think they'd never seen anyone taking a dip in the creek. Come along, we'll walk right past them, so we will."

Lucy shook her head and started for the center of the creek, the deepest part where the current surely would carry her off. Caitrin gulped down a cry and reached out to her. When she laid her hand on the young woman's shoulder, Lucy stiffened.

"'Tis the other way," Caitrin said, sudden tears clouding her eyes. "Please, Lucy, you must turn and go the other way."

There was a moment of utter silence, and then Lucy drifted toward Caitrin. Frail arms brushed against her. Huge liquid eyes blinked up at her. "I like Earl Grey," Lucy whispered.

"It's the bergamot flavoring." Caitrin let out a breath of relief and slipped her arm around the young woman's bony shoulders. "I think bergamot is a sort of herb, but then again it might be a fruit. The taste is rather citrusy, don't you think?"

"Yes," Lucy murmured.

"Because of that," Caitrin continued, beginning a slow walk toward the shore, "I should think one would want to drink it with a slice of lemon and a dollop of honey. But shall I tell you the truth? I love my Earl Grey with milk and sugar. Lots of sugar!"

Casting a pleading glance at Jack, Caitrin tried to think how to prolong the conversation. If only the people would go away and stop gawking like stupid cows. If only Caitrin's toes would come back to life so she could tell where the bottom of the creek was. If only she could touch . . . but she *was* touching Lucy, holding her close, speaking as one friend to another.

"I'll stoke up the fire in my oven," she said. "We'll be as warm as toast in a few minutes, and while we thaw, the tea water will have time to boil. You never did tell me your favorite color, Lucy. Mine is emerald green. I think I'm rather vain about green, but it really does go so well with my eyes."

"Blue," Lucy whispered as she and Caitrin straggled onto the shore. "I'm . . . I'm . . ."

"Teal blue?" Caitrin drew her closer, silently daring the gaping crowd to make a move as she led Lucy through them. "That's the color of a duck's back, you know. Sure I like that shade. But I'm rather partial to a soft cornflower hue."

"Baby blue." Lucy's chains clanked as she tried to keep up with Caitrin. "Baby."

"Jack, do come and take these off!" Caitrin called in frustration. At this rate, it would be an hour before they arrived at the soddy. Already she felt certain her skirt had frozen to her legs and her toes were going to chip off inside her wet boots.

Breathing hard, Jack knelt, dripping, at his sister's feet. As he inserted a key in the heavy padlock, his gray eyes searched Caitrin's face. She understood the terrible fear that consumed him.

"Lucy and I are going to take tea at my house," she told him, praying her words would reassure the man. "I'm sorry to say, but we can't invite you, Jack. This is a ladies' tea, and it's only for the unmarried women of Hope. That's Lucy and me, so there you have it. Now, please open the lock on her wrists."

Jack stared into Caitrin's eyes. "You take care of Lucy, hear?"

"I know you love your sister, Jack. Don't you?" She nodded. "Don't you love her?"

"I sure do. I . . ." His voice faltered as he bent to unlock the chain that bound his sister's wrists. "I love you, Lucy."

Jack knocked on the door of Caitrin's soddy, and then he gave his mother a solemn nod. Mrs. Cornwall stood to one side, as bug-eyed as a frog. They had waited more than an hour at their camp, talking over the terrible mistake they'd made in allowing Lucy to walk about unguarded. She'd headed straight for the creek, and Felicity had noticed her barely in time. If Caitrin hadn't come along . . .

"Well?" Felicity demanded. "Can't the woman be bothered to answer her own door?"

Jack gave his mother a warning look. "Miss Murphy won't like it that we're here in the first place. She wanted to be alone with Lucy."

"They've been alone long enough. That Irish maid doesn't have a single notion how to manage my daughter. She'll turn her back the first time, and Lucy will grab a pair of scissors—"

"Jack?" Caitrin opened the door to a narrow slit and peeped through. "What are you doing here? Mrs. Cornwall, I told you I would be taking tea with Lucy."

"Where is my daughter?" Felicity demanded. "She's sure to catch her death after all that swimming about in frigid water."

"Lucy is asleep," Caitrin said. "While she was warming up by the stove, she drifted off and hasn't awakened since."

"Typical!" Felicity said. "Lucy would sleep all day and all night, too, if we'd let her. She's the laziest maid you ever clapped eyes on. We must wake her at once and get her back to the camp."

"I should like your permission to keep her here tonight, Mrs. Cornwall." Caitrin turned her focus to Jack. "Please let Lucy stay with me."

"Never." Felicity's eyes hardened. "My daughter belongs in her own bed. And without the chains, one can't be sure—"

"You can't fix Lucy's troubles, Caitrin," Jack said over his mother's harangue. "Look, can I come inside and talk to you for a minute?"

Green eyes bright, Caitrin glanced from Jack to his mother and then back again. "Only you, please, Mr. Cornwall. I shouldn't want anyone to wake Lucy."

Jack let out a breath as he stepped into the soddy. That comment would set his mother off all over again—abandoned outside on a chilly February evening, as though she didn't have the sense to know what was best for her own daughter. Of course, Felicity probably *would* try to stir Lucy, and then Caitrin might fly off the handle. What a mess.

Standing just inside the door, Jack discerned his sister asleep on the rough-hewn wooden bed near the stove. Damp hair spread across the pillow in a dark tangle, she was covered with layers of thick quilts. Her long, angular frame lay perfectly still. His heart contracted at a sudden thought. How many nights had his sister been forced to sleep with her ankles and wrists bound by the chains he had forged? She looked so comfortable there on Caitrin's bed. So much at peace.

"Please speak to your mother about that constant carping, Jack,"

Caitrin whispered. "She must learn she will never shout poor Lucy into wholeness."

"And you'll never coddle her into it, either." Jack took her arms in his hands. "Caitrin, everyone in my family has done their level best for Lucy. We're all exhausted from constantly watching over her, trying to protect her, trying not to upset her. We've concocted every scheme imaginable to bring her out of these doldrums, but the doctors have told us Lucy's condition is incurable. Sometimes she'll seem a little better, but she goes right back into it. I don't want you to be fooled because you were able to bring her out of the creek today. Lucy does make forward strides. But in a few days or even a few hours, she always slides back into her black pit. Please listen to me, Caitrin—you *can't* change this."

"All I've asked is that Lucy be permitted to stay the night with me." She slipped her hands over his. "Jack, I'm not a fool. I know I haven't the training to manage Lucy. I certainly don't understand what caused this madness in her. But I do care about her. I want her to have one night of undisturbed rest. Please, Jack, allow her to stay."

His heart thudded as he looked into this woman's earnest face. Caitrin was so *good.* So perfect. And yet, one mistake with Lucy, and she'd be changed forever. If Lucy figured out a way to harm herself while she was in Caitrin's care . . .

"I'll stay here, too," Jack said.

"You can't do that!" Caitrin laughed in disbelief. "Sure I won't have a lone man in my home. What would people think?"

Jack fought the grin that tugged at his mouth. Caitrin Murphy didn't give a hoot what anyone thought about her relationship with Lucy or Mrs. Cornwall. But heaven forbid they should get any ideas about her and Jack Cornwall.

"I'll sleep just outside the door," he said. "That way you can holler if you need me."

"I won't need you, and I won't have you putting up a camp in my front yard." She set her hands on her hips. "Go along with you now. Your mother, too. You said yourself that everyone's exhausted from the constant care of Lucy. Relax then, and leave her to me this one night."

"Caitrin, if something happened—"

"Jack?" Lucy sat up in the bed, her eyes blinking in confusion. "Jack, I'm . . . I'm . . ."

"You're here at my house, Lucy," Caitrin said, going to her. "We were just about to have tea when you dropped off to sleep. Earl Grey, remember? Here's a dressing gown you can wear. Let me help you."

Jack shifted from one foot to the other, feeling awkward and useless in Caitrin's house. Though he was a little surprised at how sparsely furnished the place was, he could tell it was her private domain. She was completely capable of managing her life here, and she didn't need any interference.

"Good-bye, Jack," she called. "You can come over tomorrow morning and have breakfast with us if you like. Bring your mother with you. We'll have hot biscuits and gravy. It's an American dish, rather heavy if you ask me, but everyone seems to like it."

Jack watched as Caitrin helped his sister into a bright pink dressing gown, tied a big silky bow at her waist, and then began combing that tangle of brown hair. Combing! Caitrin was combing Lucy's hair! Jack stared at the two women in amazement.

Is it possible, Lord? he prayed. *Have you sent Caitrin to help Lucy? Oh, God, let Lucy get better. Please make her well again.*

"Ta ta, Jack," Caitrin called, giving him a wave of dismissal. "See you in the morning."

Jack stepped outside the soddy and pulled the door shut behind him. His mother stared at him in dismay, her face pinched. "You left Lucy in there?" she demanded. "You're going to let her stay the night with Miss Murphy?"

"That's right."

"Oh, Jack, you are besotted with that young Irishwoman!" she cried, frustration raising her voice to a falsetto. "How could you risk your sister's life? She'll be dead by morning."

"She'd be dead right now if Caitrin hadn't saved her," Jack said, brushing past her and starting for the camp. "Lucy's sitting in there wearing a pink gown and a bow. And Caitrin is brushing her hair."

"What?" his mother exclaimed behind him.

"Caitrin is brushing Lucy's hair."

"Really, Jack? Really?"

Jack paused and wrapped an arm around his mother's shoulders. "Really, Mama."

Caitrin woke in the night and felt the warmth of her new friend beside her in the bed. Odd how comfortable it was to share her little home with Lucy Cornwall. The place didn't seem quite so empty, so cold, so forlorn.

They'd had a good evening, sipping tea and munching sandwiches. If she hadn't seen Lucy drifting in the river hours before, Caitrin would hardly have believed anything was wrong with the young woman. They were almost the same age, and they kept up a comfortable conversation until the fire died down . . . planning the welcome party, discussing favorite foods and hairstyles. Lucy's speech was halting but lucid.

In fact, Caitrin realized as she lay in the darkness staring up at the ceiling, Lucy actually might have talked more freely if her hostess hadn't interrupted her every ten seconds. Chagrined, Caitrin mulled over the number of times Lucy had started to talk and then had fallen into her pattern of saying, "I'm . . . I can't . . . I don't know . . ." And Caitrin—with all good intent—had covered the awkwardness with cheerful chatter, changing the subject from one topic to another.

Rolling onto her side, Caitrin frowned into the blackness. Why hadn't she just listened to Lucy? Maybe her friend would have been able to share her deepest thoughts. Maybe she could have opened her heart to Caitrin if she hadn't been so rudely interrupted time and again.

Jesus, do you heal people like Lucy? Caitrin wondered. *The man you met in the cemetery had been as destructive to himself as Lucy—cutting his flesh with stones and screaming out in his anguish. But your touch brought him back to his right mind. Does Lucy have a demon inside her? Has she sinned in some terrible way to be tormented like this? Is it a dreadful sickness that one day will kill her? Oh, Father, I don't understand what's wrong with Lucy, but please touch my friend! Please make her well.*

"Caitrin?" Lucy had risen on one elbow and was gazing at the other woman. "You're tossing."

"Forgive me, Lucy. I didn't mean to wake you."

"No, I thought . . . I thought I might have . . ."

"You didn't disturb me at all. I've been thinking about . . ." Caitrin suddenly couldn't be honest. "I've been thinking about wallpaper lately. I want to paper the soddy, but I don't believe—"

Be still, a voice inside her spoke. *Be still.*

"I don't believe wallpaper will work," she finished.

"I'm not sure," Lucy said. "I can't . . . I can't think . . ."

"It's so late, and here I am chattering away—" Caitrin squeezed her fists. *Be still.* She let out a breath and finished, "Chattering about wallpaper."

Lucy was silent. Caitrin could hear her breathing softly. Her thin fingers picked at the tufts of yarn on the quilt that covered the two women.

"I don't think wallpaper will stick," Lucy said finally. "Your walls are dirt."

"I know."

"But I can't . . . I can't . . ."

"You—" Caitrin bit her lip to keep herself from blurting out some vapid nonsense.

"I can't think very clearly about wallpaper," Lucy said. "I don't . . . don't know . . ."

She lapsed into silence again. Caitrin thought perhaps she had fallen asleep, but then she sighed. "It's hard to think, you know," Lucy said softly. "My thoughts go around and around. I don't . . . I can't stop thinking about things that bother me."

"Like—" Caitrin cut off her own sentence.

"Like Mary. When she got sick. I adored Mary." Lucy's voice was high and fragile. "My big sister was golden haired and so beautiful. She loved to dance and flirt with all the men. But then . . . then . . . I can't . . ."

Caitrin managed to hold her tongue.

"Can't remember what happened to Mary," Lucy went on. "Oh yes, it was Seth Hunter. She fell in love with him, and Papa got out his . . . his shotgun . . . and how sad Mary was. She told me she had married Seth in secret. And then the baby . . ."

"Chipper?"

"Did I say there was a baby?"

"Yes."

"I'm not permitted to talk about that. We must keep our secrets well hidden. Others will stare at us if they hear the truth. No one has to know a thing."

"Who has told you to keep secrets, Lucy?"

"Mama." She lay quietly for a long time. "Some things can be mentioned. Mary died. The Yankee soldiers came. Oh, dear . . . I'm sorry, but I can't talk about that either. Jack was fighting in the war. And then Seth stole Chipper. Papa took sick. They put me in chains. I'm insane, you know."

"Are you sure?"

"Oh yes." Lucy nodded on her pillow. Her hand slipped across the quilt and covered Caitrin's. "Please don't be afraid of me. It's because of the thoughts going around and around. I can't make them stop. I try, but I can't . . . I can't . . ."

"You've had a great many sorrows," Caitrin whispered.

"Mary. The soldiers. The war. We lost the farm. Papa took sick." She trembled. "People die. There's such loss . . . and I can't . . ."

"I don't believe you're insane."

"No?"

"Anyone with as many griefs as you've known would find it difficult."

"Difficult to go on living."

"Aye, 'tis hard sometimes." Caitrin's thoughts wandered to Sean O'Casey and the terrible agony she had felt at his loss. But now—oddly—she no longer sensed that emptiness. There was something else . . . someone else . . .

"I have many sorrows," Lucy said. "And many, many secrets."

CHAPTER 11

IT WAS Rolf Rustemeyer's turn to lead the Sunday services. Jack heard that the big German farmer had been practicing his sermon on Rosie Hunter, but rumor had it there'd be slim pickings on the spiritual smorgasbord today. All the same, families from the homesteads around Hope began to gather in the mercantile around nine o'clock. By the time Jack walked in, the room was filled with the aroma of hot cinnamon buns, fresh coffee, and apple strudel.

In the short time he'd lived in Hope, Jack had tried to learn the names of the people who passed his smithy on their way to the mercantile for supplies. Few ever spoke to him, and when they did, it was only to ask how soon he'd be able to repair a plow or mend a wagon wheel. But Caitrin Murphy always followed her customers out the mercantile door to wave good-bye. "Come again, Mr. LeBlanc," she would call. "See you next week, Mrs. Rippeto!" And Jack would memorize the names.

They had all come together to worship on this bright, late-winter Sunday, and Jack had made up his mind to walk among them as one of the community. He'd been given a month to prove his peaceful intentions, and this gathering would be the perfect opportunity to do just that.

"Mornin', Mr. Laski," he said, extending a hand to the Polish fellow who owned a stagecoach station several miles down the road to Topeka. "I'm Jack Cornwall. Good to see you today."

The man's eyes narrowed. "Oh yes," he said. He gave a quick nod and turned away.

Jack shrugged. He wouldn't get angry. Couldn't afford to. Things were just now beginning to look up for the Cornwall family. Caitrin had convinced Felicity to let Lucy stay at the soddy a few days. His sister had lived with the young Irishwoman for almost a week now. And though no one had seen much of either one, Jack sensed that the community was beginning to relax about the notion of having a "madwoman" residing there. His mother—the only person from the creek episode to catch a cold—had stayed busy at the camp, either working or lamenting her drippy nose. Freed from his responsibility to help keep an eye on Lucy, Jack spent every free hour working to build the smithy. He would have the forge up and burning by Monday night.

"Mr. Rippeto," Jack said, giving the Italian homesteader his warmest smile. "Good to see you and Mrs. Rippeto here today."

"Keep your eyes off my wife," the man muttered, pointing a beefy forefinger. "Stay away from my family."

"Listen here, you—" Jack bit off his words. Swallowing his fury, he found a bench near the side of the mercantile, sat down, and opened his Bible. He'd be lucky to get through this morning without punching somebody in the nose.

"Hi, Jack," a voice whispered beside him.

He turned to find his sister slipping onto the bench. A cloud of Lily of the Valley perfume drifted around the startling array of braids and curls in Lucy's upswept brown hair. Clad in a silky dress of pale blue, she arranged her skirts to allow the tips of her kidskin shoes to peep out. Flushing a vivid pink, she patted the sagging bodice.

"It's too big," she whispered. "This is really Caitrin's dress."

Jack smiled. "Well, I reckon you look mighty pretty in it, Lucy."

His sister bit her lip and focused on her hands knotted in her lap. "I've been feeling better, Jack. You know . . . Caitrin lets me cook."

"Cook!" Jack instantly thought of the number of weapons Lucy could lay her hands on—knives, ice chisels, meat forks . . .

"I baked those cinnamon buns on the table over there," she said shyly. "Please don't tell, just in case they taste awful."

Jack took a deep breath. "Does Caitrin stay with you? Is she nearby all the time?"

Lucy nodded. "She or Mrs. Hunter. They take turns tending to me and the mercantile. Caitrin says . . . she says she's been dreaming of opening a restaurant one day, and she would like me to help with the cooking. We might build a little kitchen and have our own pots and pans. I could plan the menus."

"Is that so?" Jack hadn't seen his sister so animated in years.

"Caitrin's very good to me. I'm afraid I've worn her out, and Mrs. Hunter, too, but please don't make me come home, Jack. I really . . . I can't . . . can't . . ."

"It's OK, Luce," he said, calling her by her pet name. "I'll talk to Caitrin and see how she's doing."

The Irishwoman herself entered the mercantile in a vision of shimmering emerald green. Jack thought he might fall right off the bench. Red hair swept up in a mass of sparkling combs and doodads, she fairly radiated as she greeted one person after another. Little girls swarmed her, touching the emerald fabric and lifting the hem of her skirt to peep at the rows of petticoats underneath. Caitrin laughed and chatted, her focus roving the room until it came to rest on Jack.

His heart slammed against his chest as she gave him a brilliant smile and started across the room. At that moment, Felicity Cornwall marched into the mercantile, sneezed loudly, and made straight for Jack's bench. Cutting in front of Caitrin, the woman swept down beside her daughter and began to blow her nose on a violet-strewn handkerchief.

"I cannot believe this wretched cold," she announced. And then she noticed her daughter. "Lucy, how lovely you look! The dress is gorgeous—although two of you could fit inside it, of course. You didn't intend to wear that necklace, did you? Silver would look much better than gold with that blue."

Lucy dropped her focus to her lap and laid a hand over the offending necklace. Jack clenched his jaw. Two paces away, Rolf Rustemeyer tapped Caitrin on the shoulder, gave her a dramatic bow, and began to describe in detail his plan to escort her to the upcoming spring festival. Jack picked up his Bible, opened it right down the middle, and searched for an appropriate psalm to fit his dark mood.

"Let us begin with a familiar hymn," Casimir Laski announced, drawing everyone's attention. While people scurried to find places on the benches, he began to sing in Polish. As though directing a hundred-voice choir, he waved his hands to and fro, bellowing out the song at the top of his lungs.

The congregation listened in silence, bewildered by the unfamiliar tune and the foreign words. Jack fought a grin. So much for harmony in Christ. He'd located one of David's psalms pleading with God for justice upon his enemies. Jack found it particularly satisfying.

"Today morning, I talk about Gott," Rolf Rustemeyer said, taking his place at the front. Huge shoulders squeezed into an ill-fitting jacket, the German had attempted to comb his unruly blond hair into some semblance of grooming. As he held up a heavy Bible and stumbled through the Galatians chapter 5 passage about the fruit of the Spirit, his jacket sleeve worked its way up his arm almost to the elbow.

"Gott is maken beautiful day," Rolf said. "Fery goot the sunshine. Spring vill come soon, *ja?* But I haf question. Is spring inside you? In heart?"

Jack closed his Bible and tried to concentrate on Rolf's sermon.

His attention wandered over to Caitrin, seated with the O'Toole family two benches in front of him.

"*Ja,* I know I am goot man," Rolf said. "And many of you are goot manners. Excuse me, goot men. Goot vomens, too. And childrens. But in mine heart is sometimes bad things, *ja?* Maybe I am telling a story not true. How you say in English, Rosie?"

"Lying," she called out.

"Lying is bad thing. Or maybe I am want to have Jimmy O'Toole's fery nice mule, *ja?*"

"Coveting," Rosie spoke up.

"You are farmers, and in spring clear out all bad things from fields. Hoe, plow dirt, kill bugs, *ja?* Is because goot things cannot grow in bad dirt. So my question again. Is spring inside you? In your heart? Better you get all bad things out of your heart. Better you tell Gott, 'I am sorry. Forgif me.' No more hating, no more lying, no more covering—"

"Coveting," Rosie corrected.

"Let Gott bring spring into heart of *you,*" Rolf continued, his eyes blazing. "Then goot things vill grow. You can be happy, kind, forgif other people, *ja?*"

He looked around. Jack felt sure the sermon of the day was over, but Rolf crossed his arms over his chest and stared out at his congregation. It occurred to Jack that the German was probably a very intelligent man, no doubt frustrated at his inability to convey his thoughts as clearly as he'd like. But he had brought a good message. One they needed to hear.

"I say to you," Rolf boomed out, "no more talk bad about each other. Get rid of veeds! *Amen.*"

"Veeds?" Lucy whispered as Rolf returned to his bench and Casimir Laski stood to lead another song.

"Weeds," Jack translated.

Lucy nodded and smiled. The transformation on her face lifted Jack's heart. He could have kissed Caitrin Murphy right here in front of everyone. Lucy was better. *Thank you, God. Thank you.*

Another Polish hymn sung solo by Casimir Laski was accompanied by many dramatic gestures intended to encourage the congregation to sing along. As they hummed some semblance of the unfamiliar melody, it occurred to Jack that he ought to join Rolf Rustemeyer as often as possible in the final construction work on the new church. This town needed a pastor. And a song leader.

"How you like my talking?" Rolf asked, striding toward Jack as the congregation rose to make their way to the tables and sample the rolls and pies. "You understand what I say?"

"Perfectly," Jack said. He gave Rolf's huge hand a hearty shake. If anyone had determined to get rid of weeds in his heart, it was the German. He seemed to have decided Jack Cornwall was a friend, and his broad smile and strong white teeth displayed his acceptance of a former enemy.

"Who is pretty lady here with you, Jack?" Rolf asked, giving Lucy a little bow.

"Mr. Rustemeyer, meet my sister, Miss Lucy Cornwall." Jack reached for the young woman, but she shrank backward, a look of horror filling her gray eyes.

"Oh no," she mouthed. "No . . . please . . . I can't . . ."

"It's OK, Lucy," Caitrin said, joining the group and slipping her arm through her friend's. "Rolf, your sermon was an inspiration."

"Inspiration?" He squinted his eyes, clearly uncertain whether he'd just received a compliment.

"'Twas very good," Caitrin clarified. "Sure you might want to apply for the position of minister yourself. And Mr. Cornwall, how are you today?"

"Better now," Jack said, drinking in her bold green eyes and pink lips. "A lot better."

She laughed. "I'm certain you've heard about the spring festival that Rosie and I—"

"Lucy," Felicity Cornwall interrupted, "you'd better come back to the camp with me now, dear. I'm sure Miss Murphy has had quite her fill of mollycoddling you this week. And I know for a fact the mercantile has gone untended so often that rumors are spreading amongst the customers."

"Rumors?" Caitrin asked.

"I was in for eggs just two days ago," Felicity said. "No one behind the counter, of course, and the mail coach from Topeka pulled up. The driver told me you had ignored two sets of customers, you had left the mercantile doors wide open day and night, and you'd completely run out of pickles."

"Mr. Bridger," Caitrin gasped. "He wanted more pickles?"

"I realize you intended to do a good deed by watching over my daughter," Felicity continued, "but abandoning your commitments is quite irresponsible."

"My Caitie—irresponsible?" Sheena O'Toole said, approaching with a huge cinnamon bun in one hand. "I should think not! Caitrin Murphy took on *your* responsibilities when she welcomed this poor madwoman—"

"Well," Jack said loudly as his sister cowered behind him. "I reckon it's time to head out into the sunshine. Beautiful day! Great sermon, Rustemeyer. Mrs. O'Toole and Miss Murphy, good to see both of you this fine morning."

He shepherded Lucy toward the mercantile door, praying she wouldn't collapse before he could get her outside. Caitrin followed close at his heels, and he could hear Sheena and his mother exchanging volleys of insults. He hurried his sister out the front door.

"Mr. Cornwall!" Caitrin cried. "Won't you stay for a cup of coffee?"

The man stopped and faced her. "No, Miss Murphy. I won't be joining the citizens of this town for their Sunday fellowship."

"Why not?"

"Weeds," Jack snarled, scooping his wilting sister up in his arms. "Too many confounded weeds."

Caitrin hammered the last nail on the big sign outside the mercantile. "Welcome to the Spring Festival in Hope," she pronounced, reading the black letters she had painted on a white sheet. And then she muttered, "Hope, Kansas . . . home of the meanest, nosiest, grouchiest, and most intolerant people this side of the Mississippi River. Welcome one and all."

She gave the nail head a final whack and started down the ladder. The festival was doomed. People were already driving their wagons across the bridge, and she hadn't even bothered to dress for the occasion. What was the point? No doubt the event would erupt into another brouhaha just like the recent Sunday service. The guests of honor probably would be run out of town by the kindly folk of Hope. It would be a festival of welcome . . . and good riddance.

"I sound just like Lucy," Caitrin mumbled to herself as she stomped back into the mercantile. "One bad thing after another. Perhaps her disease is contagious after all, and I'm destined to spend my life in chains of my own making."

In frustration, she kicked at a marble one of the children had abandoned on the floor. The missile flew through the air, barely missing the glass counter that displayed men's white collars and ladies' lingerie, hit the wall on the other side, and bounced to the floor. Clapping a hand over her mouth in horror at the near catastrophe, Caitrin stood trembling. It was those horrid chains!

She couldn't stop thinking of poor Lucy . . . back in chains for jumping in front of the Topeka stagecoach and nearly succeeding in killing herself. The horses had panicked, the coach had careened across the bridge with screaming passengers hanging on for dear life, and Mr. Bridger, the driver, had tumbled from his seat and broken his wrist. Lucy was found huddled at the foot of the bridge, her pale blue dress covered in mud. Chains again.

Caitrin heard the mercantile door open behind her and a group of excited children pour into the room. "It's a party for Gram and Uncle Jack," Chipper told the others. "Aunt Lucy might even get to come."

"I thought she was crazy," Will O'Toole said.

"She is, but only if you look at her or touch her." Chipper tugged on Caitrin's skirt. "Are we gonna bob for apples at this festibal?"

"Not this one, Chipper," she said. "We'll have to wait until autumn for apples, so we will."

"Auntie Caitrin, where are all the fancy *shingerleens* you usually put into your hair?" Erinn inquired. "Sure I thought you were going to wear the purple dress again, but you've got on this old brown thing."

Caitrin tried to smile. "The color is bronze," she said. "Can't you see the fabric is all shot through with metallic threads? In the proper light, I shall fairly glow."

"Ooh!" Erinn closed her eyes, clearly imagining the moment. "Will I be as lovely as you one day, Auntie Caitrin?"

"Lovelier."

Caitrin bent to give her niece a kiss on the cheek as the Laski and LeBlanc families filtered into the mercantile. She was a little surprised they had come to the festival. After all, none of them had had a civil word for the Cornwalls. Of course, a quilt auction was planned for the late evening. Proceeds would be used to purchase the wood for pews in the new church. The women would want to see whose winter handiwork would bring in the most money. Certainly it wasn't the prospect of welcoming the Cornwall family that drew them.

In moments the mercantile began to fill. A self-designated band gathered near the canned goods and tuned their instruments. Lines of children and their parents formed in front of the little booths erected around the room.

As the festival officially got under way, Rolf Rustemeyer's harmonica provided a collection of tunes for a cakewalk. Carlotta Rippeto manned a make-believe fishing pond from which children could draw little candies, reed whistles, or cornhusk dolls. A group of young people gathered in a corner to play "graces," using crossed sticks to toss a hoop from one member of the party to another. Many of the unmarried farmers assembled near the food table and sampled the slices of pie and plates full of cookies.

"Hello, Caitrin!" Rosie fairly skipped across the room to her friend. "Guess what. I didn't spit up a single time today!"

"Wonderful," Caitrin said, mustering a smile. "Perhaps you're over the hump."

"Hump is right. You should take a look at my stomach! I ate all day long. Tonight I could barely button my bodice."

"Making up for lost time."

"I guess so. I started with tinned peaches, went on to half a loaf of fresh bread, then oysters, lemonade, and salt pork. Do you have any of those wonderful pickles Sheena makes?"

Caitrin chuckled. "As a matter of fact, I restocked the pickle barrel three days ago. It's right over there by Mrs. LeBlanc."

"I hope I don't make a pig of myself. Seth might stop calling me his little twister and start calling me his great big oinker!"

Rosie gave her friend a quick hug and started through the crowd. Caitrin searched the room for any sign of the Cornwalls. Not six months ago, Jack Cornwall had stirred up more than a little trouble in this very room—appearing at a party and accosting Rosie, and later fighting with Seth right outside the front door. Could the people of Hope ever put those events behind them? She had her doubts. Farmers had long memories, and Jack had branded himself a villain, as simple as that.

"Food is all gone from cakewalk," Rolf Rustemeyer said, coming up beside Caitrin. "I gif away already six pies, three cakes, and whole jar of peppermint sticks."

"Peppermint sticks?" Caitrin looked up into the German's smiling face. "But they weren't meant to be part of the cakewalk. We sell them in the store."

He shrugged. "I haf no more cakes and pies. Then I see peppermint sticks on counter, gif to children. Is OK?"

"Yes, it's OK," she said with a sigh. She hoped nobody else manning a booth would decide to give away merchandise as prizes.

"Is time for danzing now, *ja?*" Rolf slipped his heavy arm around Caitrin's shoulders. "You look fery beautiful tonight, Miss Murphy. Danz vit me?"

"Well, I—" Caitrin looked up to see Jack Cornwall and his mother stepping into the room. "Oh, the guests of honor are here! Excuse me, Rolf. I must ask Seth to introduce them. I wonder what they've done with Lucy."

Catching Jack's eye, she hurried away from Rolf. Poor Rolf! He was such a fine man, and so earnest. But Caitrin could hardly imagine an evening clomping around the dance floor with him, let alone a lifetime. He was desperate to marry, and Rosie had been his first choice. When she had elected to wed Seth Hunter instead, he turned his attentions to Caitrin. She was *not* desperate, however, and she certainly had no desire to marry in haste.

"Marriages are all happy," she muttered, quoting her mother's favorite Irish proverb. "It's having breakfast together that causes all the trouble."

She caught up with Seth beside the dessert table and asked him to announce the newcomers. Though everyone in the room already knew the Cornwalls by reputation, it would help their standing in the community if Seth would give them a public welcome. After avowing he wasn't much for speech giving, he motioned the band into silence and climbed up on a chair.

"I want to thank everybody for coming tonight," he said. "Are you folks having a good time?"

The question was answered with a cacophony of whoops and

hollers. Caitrin made her way across the room to Jack. Dressed in a clean white shirt and the gray trousers of his army uniform, he had clearly done his best to spiffy up for the occasion. Caitrin began to wish she'd taken time to arrange her hair and change into a fancy dress.

"Where's Lucy?" she whispered, as Seth welcomed by name the various families in the community.

Jack shook his head. "Mama didn't want to bring her along. The chains, you know."

"Did Lucy want to come?"

"Hard telling. She didn't say much—although she spent the whole day yesterday washing that blue dress. This morning she ironed it stiff as a sheet of tin."

"She *wants* to be with us, Jack. Please go and fetch her."

"Better not. We've got her locked up safe. She'll be all right, and I'll go check on her now and again."

Caitrin twisted her hands together. "Oh, please bring Lucy, Jack. How will she ever be accepted if she's locked away as though she has some shameful disease?"

"She does . . . in a manner of speaking."

"I'm not ashamed of her. Are you?"

"No." He rubbed the back of his neck. "All the same, if there's any trouble—"

"I'll take the blame, so I will," Caitrin said. "Gladly."

Jack let out a breath of resignation and started for the door. Seth's words stopped him. "We wanted to get together tonight," his former brother-in-law said, "to welcome the newest folks in Hope. I know a lot of you have been watching the smithy going up across the road. Well, that's Jack Cornwall's new place of business, and we're glad to have him here. If you need a new branding iron or a pair of tongs, Jack's the man to see. And I have it straight from the horse's mouth—or maybe I should say the mule's mouth—that he can nail on a shoe quicker than anybody around. Rumor has it, he's never been bit or kicked either. Now how many of you can say that?"

Amid the chuckles, Seth continued. "Jack is a good man, an honest worker, and my son's favorite uncle. I'm proud to call him a friend. Folks, would you give a nice welcome to Jack Cornwall?"

Caitrin held her breath as the smattering of claps gradually grew into a swell of applause. She noted that the crowd had looked uneasy at Seth's warm welcome of his former enemy. She really couldn't blame them for their misgivings after the things Jack had done in the past. Though Hope might appreciate having a smithy, Jack Cornwall himself was still on probation.

As Jack acknowledged the welcome and then slipped out to fetch Lucy, Seth began to introduce Felicity Cornwall. Caitrin belatedly remembered that years ago her husband had run off Seth with a shotgun, and that the Cornwalls had treated their daughter's husband as if he didn't exist. But Seth had managed to grow beyond his own memories of past hurts. He reminded everyone that Mrs. Cornwall was a recent widow, and he quoted Scripture admonishing Christians to take care of orphans and widows. Rosie must have put him up to that, Caitrin thought.

"Welcome to Hope, Mrs. Cornwall," Seth said. "We trust you'll be happy here."

Patting her silver-streaked hair, the woman nodded. "Thank you, Mr. Hunter. I always do my best to find a measure of joy in whatever circumstance God has placed me—no matter how bleak."

A rumble of mutterings at her comment crossed the room. Mrs. Cornwall simply stood there looking as though she'd just eaten one of Sheena's dill pickles. Caitrin studied the woman in disbelief. Did she *enjoy* causing dissent? Could she possibly think God wanted his holy name included in the context of an insult?

"Now we're going to dance awhile," Seth said, holding out his hands to quell the tide of dissent. "And then we'll have us a quilt auction!"

The roar of enthusiasm drowned out any bad feelings in the crowd, and the band struck up a lively square-dance tune that drew everyone from toddlers to grandparents to the middle of the floor. Rolf strode across the room and grabbed Caitrin before she could protest. As he charged around in circles, occasionally stomping her hem with one of his big work boots, she saw Jack and Lucy slip into the shadows in one corner of the room.

"Ouch, you great galoot!" Caitrin cried when Rolf's attempt at a two-step landed his foot directly on her big toe. "Oh, Mr. Rustemeyer, you really must take some lessons."

"I take many lessons. Talk English fery goot now, *ja?*"

"You need dancing lessons." She looked into his eyes and saw that he wasn't having much more fun at this than she. *Dear God, please send someone for Rolf*, she lifted up. *And don't let it be me!*

"Ven you marry vit me, is OK the mercantile," Rolf said. "I don't get angry. You can vork all days until baby comes."

"When I marry you?" Caitrin repeated numbly, her feet slowing. "Sure I never agreed to marry you, Mr. Rustemeyer."

"Ach!" He stopped dancing and gave his forehead a sound slap. "In German, *wenn* means *if*. I say this one wrong. I mean, *if* you marry me, is OK the mercantile."

"But I'm not going to marry you, Rolf," Caitrin whispered. "I . . . I love someone else."

"*Ja*, Sheena tells me about *der Irländer* you lof. But he is far away gone. Better you not to be alone. Better you to marry, *ja?*"

"Perhaps," Caitrin said, meeting Jack Cornwall's gray eyes. "Perhaps."

CHAPTER 12

AS SOON as she could disengage herself, Caitrin hurried over to the corner where Jack Cornwall stood beside his sister. Though Lucy looked haggard and pale, she had dressed in the silky blue gown Caitrin had given her, and she had made an attempt to put up her hair. A flicker of life leapt into her gray eyes as her friend approached.

"Lucy, you came!" Caitrin said, extending her hands.

"Oh . . ." Lucy drew back for a moment. Then she let out a breath and clasped the outstretched fingers. "Caitrin."

"That dress is positively stunning on you."

"Well, I . . ."

Lucy fell silent, and Caitrin waited.

"I got it dirty the other day," she whispered. "I'm sorry. I just . . . I can't . . ."

"It looks lovely tonight." Caitrin took a tentative step forward and folded the trembling young woman in her arms. "I'm so happy to see you, Lucy. I was sorry to hear you weren't feeling well. Sure you've no idea how I've missed your cinnamon buns for breakfast."

When Caitrin drew back, Lucy was smiling. "I just . . . I . . . I like to bake."

"And when we build our restaurant, the food will be famous thanks to you."

"Would you make some cinnamon buns for me, Luce?" Jack asked. "I've never tasted your cooking."

Lucy pursed her lips for a moment. "Usually I wear those . . . those chains."

She pointed to the iron handcuffs hanging from Jack's back trouser pocket, and Caitrin frowned. "I'm quite certain those aren't necessary tonight," she said. "Why did you bring them, Jack?"

"Just in case." He shifted from one foot to the other. "You know, Lucy's not real comfortable around crowds of people."

"Who is? I'd far rather be sitting in the soddy eating cinnamon buns and drinking tea with Lucy than allowing Rolf Rustemeyer to make minced meat of my toes. But here we are, and we'll make the best of it. Lucy, would you like something to drink?"

The wide gray eyes turned to her. "Punch," Lucy whispered. "And a slice of pie, please."

Caitrin gave Jack a victory smile. "I'll fetch us all something to eat."

When she returned, they still were seated side by side in the half-dark corner of the mercantile. Lucy was tapping her toe in time to the music, and Jack had managed to slip his hand around his sister's. Caitrin could have wept. *Father, please*, she pleaded in silent prayer. And when she couldn't think of words adequate to express her feelings, she turned the matter over to the Holy Spirit. *Groanings*, she thought. *Oh, God, my soul groans for Lucy.*

"This is one of my favorite tunes," Lucy shared as Caitrin joined her on the narrow bench. "Mary used to dance to this tune. But now . . . now Mary's . . ."

"Would you like to dance with me, Luce?" Jack asked his sister.

"No," she whispered. "You and Caitrin. Please, dance together."

Jack glanced at Caitrin, and she read the uncertainty in his eyes. Leave Lucy alone, and who knew what might happen? He would not likely abandon his sister.

"Where is your mother?" Caitrin asked. "She could sit with Lucy."

Jack grunted. "Mama's over there by the table. I don't want to bother her."

"Sure I can't see why not. She's only arranging the food—setting pies and cakes this way or that. Fetch her at once, Jack. She'll accompany Lucy while you and I dance."

Jack raked a hand through his thick brown hair. "Mama's had an ornery look on her face ever since I brought Lucy in here. She won't cotton to—"

"Mama doesn't like me to go out in public," Lucy said. "She's afraid I'll . . . I'll say something or do something shameful."

"Oh, Lucy, I'm sure that isn't so."

"I can stay here," she whispered to her brother. "I'll watch you dance. I would like it."

"Well, I don't know." Jack studied his sister. "You might get to thinking about things."

"I'll try not to. I promise."

Caitrin understood the man's concern, but she couldn't help feeling that this overprotectiveness was bad for Lucy. The young woman seemed fine at the moment, drumming her fingertips on her knees and chewing a bite of apple pie. *What is it that eats away inside Lucy, Father? What are these terrible secrets that gnaw at her soul and tangle her reason?*

"I don't think dancing is such a great idea," Jack said finally. "We'd better stay close."

Caitrin glanced at Lucy and absorbed the longing in her eyes. "Please escort me to the floor, Jack. After the dance, Lucy and I shall watch the quilt auction together. It's to start right after this song."

"Go on, Jack," Lucy said.

"Come along, Mr. Cornwall." Caitrin stood and looped her arm around his elbow. "If you don't take me out onto the floor at once, my feet will simply start dancing of their own accord."

"I'll be right back, Lucy," he said as he drew Caitrin into the midst of the crowd. The moment he stepped away from the darkened corner, a familiar teasing light filtered into his eyes. "Feet dancing on their own? Now that would be a sight. Allow me to ease your distress, madam."

"With pleasure, sir."

As Jack Cornwall whirled Caitrin through the crowd, she thought he was the most thrilling partner she had ever had. Though he wouldn't know the intricate steps of the Irish dances Sean O'Casey had performed, she began to understand that her young love's action had been just that—a performance. Sean had displayed his theatrical style with all the flair of a strutting rooster. Caitrin had been a flattering arm piece, a perfect foil to direct everyone's attention to the man himself.

But Jack Cornwall's focus was riveted to his partner. His whispered compliments sent her head spinning. His strong arms kept her close. He escorted her down a promenade, circled left and right, and fairly lifted her from the ground as they stayed in step with the music. By the time the music slowed, she was breathless.

"That was a delight!" she exclaimed. "I can't think when I've had such fun."

Jack gave her an extra twirl that lifted her skirts from her ankles. Laughing, she clapped her hands together as he caught her against his chest, dipped her low, and touched her lips in a warm kiss. "Caitrin Murphy," he said, "I could get lost in those green Irish eyes."

But when he lifted his head and looked across the room at his sister, his face sobered. Caitrin followed the direction of his gaze to find Lucy huddled into herself and staring blankly down at her lap.

"She's thinking about her troubles again," he said in a disheartened voice.

"I've missed your sister greatly," Caitrin whispered. "How is she, Jack? Please tell me the truth."

"Sometimes—like tonight—I start to think she's perking up. I tell myself I don't see any trouble, even when it starts to crop up again. I try to convince myself it's all right that Lucy sleeps day and night, and she won't get out of bed even to eat. Maybe she's just tired, I think. And when she sits staring at her lap for hours on end, I try to believe she's working out some kind of a tricky problem or something. But after a while, it's no use pretending."

"She told me her thoughts go around and around. She can't make them stop." Caitrin was aware that the crowd had moved toward the tables heaped with food. This rare moment with Jack must not be wasted. "What is Lucy dwelling on, Jack? What are these thoughts that plague her?"

"Memories, Caitrin." His face was solemn. "She's got a lot of worries and a lot of bad memories. Lucy always has been more sensitive than most folks to things that happen around her. Even as a little girl, she used to cry a lot. But she always laughed louder, hugged tighter, and loved deeper than everyone else, too."

"Maybe the trouble is something within the very essence of her spirit. Perhaps 'tis something she was born with."

"I reckon you might be right. And, too, she's had some pretty big hurts."

"Mary's death, your absence during the war, the loss of the family farm and your father." Caitrin recited the list. "Is there anything else, Jack? Did something else happen to Lucy?"

He looked away. "She just couldn't hold up under the pile of troubles."

"She said she has many secrets."

"I reckon so," he said. "In the Cornwall family, you keep certain things under wraps—no matter what. Lucy's always been the peacemaker of the bunch. She's so sweet, so trustworthy, that she's had a lot of confidences shared with her."

"Such as?"

He was silent a moment. "Seth Hunter, for one. Not until

everything had blown sky-high did I learn that Mary had been seeing him on the sly. Seth was just one of our farmhands, you know. He didn't have a hope in the world of earning Mary a good living, and he was a Yankee sympathizer to boot. Mary confided to Lucy about Seth, but Lucy kept the information to herself. Then Seth and Mary got married in a hush-hush ceremony, and before long there was a baby on the way—and not a soul knew about any of that except Lucy."

"Oh, my. What other troubles has Lucy borne?"

"When Papa took sick, he kept his illness a secret. The only way anybody found out was that Lucy used to empty his chamber pot every morning. She saw the blood, and that's how she knew. Papa made her swear she wouldn't tell Mama, but then when—"

"It sounds as if Lucy is the only Cornwall keeping secrets," Caitrin said. "'Tis as though she's been the hiding place for the entire family's sin and pain. What guilty knowledge have *you* laid on her fragile conscience?"

"Me? None." His eyes went hard. "Don't try to blame *me* for what's happened to Lucy. When she's feeling bad, she's like a sledder on top of a big snowy hill—going down fast and nothing can stop her. Once she's over the crest, you might as well give up. But I'll tell you one thing. It's never been me who gave her a push at the top. I've always stood by my sister and protected her."

"By clamping her in chains?"

"It's that or an asylum."

"For heaven's sake, Jack, why must you—"

A shrill shriek cut off her words. Caitrin swung around in time to see Lucy scramble from the bench, fall to her knees, and crawl into the corner. Rolf Rustemeyer leapt over the bench toward her, and Casimir Laski grabbed the German man by his suspenders.

"Stay away from that woman!" Laski shouted at Rolf. "She's crazy! A madwoman!"

"What I haf done?" Rolf said, turning toward the crowd in dismay. "I bringen her chocolate cake, no more."

"Get the Cornish strumpet out of here!" Jimmy O'Toole cried, pointing toward Lucy, who began to sob. "We won't have a lunatic—"

To Caitrin's horror, a string of foul language and denigrating epithets spewed from Jimmy's mouth. Lucy held her hands over her head as though she were being physically beaten as she screamed like a wounded coyote. Jack left Caitrin's side and shoved his way through the throng.

"Shut your mouth, O'Toole!" Jack shouted at the Irishman. "And you, Rustemeyer, get away from my sister. Leave her alone."

"*Aber* I only bringen *torte!*" Rolf returned, stumbling into his native language. He held up a plate bearing a slice of chocolate cake. "*Ich bin sehr* . . . I am fery goot man, *ja!* Not hurt nobodies."

"And you, O'Toole," Jack snarled, "if I ever catch you talking like that to my sister again—"

"You're as insane as she is!" Jimmy hurled back. "Your whole family is a pack of filthy Cornish—"

"Lemme tell you something, buster." Jack shoved his finger in the man's chest. "You stay away from my family or I'll—"

"Jack, Jack!" Felicity Cornwall grabbed her son's arm. "Get Lucy. You must get Lucy!"

Caitrin stood nailed to the floor, staring in disbelief while Felicity raced for the door as though ravenous wolves were after her. Jack scooped up his weeping sister and followed his mother out into the night. As the door banged shut, a hush fell over the room.

Finally Jimmy O'Toole cleared his throat. "'Tis a good thing they're gone. That family has no business in our mercantile. God created the different races to be separate and apart. The Cornish and the Irish. The black and the white. The Indian and the Spaniard. There is to be no mixin' of people."

An assenting murmur ran through the gathering. Caitrin glared at the self-righteous group—Poles, Italians, Germans, French—all a medley of racial backgrounds. Jimmy nodded importantly.

"Mr. O'Toole," Caitrin spoke up. "Could you please remind me where that particular verse is located in the Bible? Sure I'd like to read for myself the Scripture where God tells us he wants the different races to remain separate and apart."

The Irish immigrant folded his arms across his bony chest. "Tower of Babel," he said. "Genesis, I believe."

"At the Tower of Babel, God confounded the *language* of the people," Rosie Hunter spoke up. "Because of their conspiracy to reach God through human effort, the people were given many different languages. But the Scriptures in Genesis say nothing at all about the color of folks' skin or the place of their birth, Mr. O'Toole. Isn't that right, Seth?" She looked at her husband for confirmation.

"Well . . ."

She lifted her chin. "You said, 'Rosie, let's start at the beginning of the Bible and read all the way through.' And just last week we read that passage about the Tower of Babel. The story is not about the races; it's about languages. I remember the passage very well."

"Me, too," Chipper chimed in.

"My father told me that everythin' is in the Bible," Jimmy insisted. "Everythin' right and true. And he said 'tis true that the Cornish folk are wicked, and they cannot turn to good. For myself, I can hardly believe that a Cornishman has a soul. They're not completely human, but more like the devil himself, and so it cannot be right for us to have aught to do with the Cornish."

"No soul?" Salvatore Rippeto interrupted. "Then you are saying the Cornishman is like an animal, O'Toole? Maybe you think it's OK to *own* Cornishmen? Maybe you think slavery was a good thing, too. Is this what you say, O'Toole? You wanted Kansas to go to slavery?"

"Why do you think the girl is crazy, Rippeto?" Casimir Laski stepped into the argument. "God has given this illness to her because of some unconfessed sin! Sin drives the Cornwall woman mad. Sin from her past torments her day and night."

"I am an abolitionist!" Mr. LeBlanc roared. The miller leapt onto a bench. "I believe that all men have souls, Jimmy O'Toole! Cornishmen, black men, all men! I say it is wrong to own slaves."

"But if we'd had slaves," Laski shouted, "we could have gotten through that grasshopper plague a lot better last year! We could have replanted twice as fast!"

"Settle down, everybody," Seth Hunter hollered. "This is supposed to be a party, and we've just run off the guests of honor. Now everybody better get calm, while I go try to—"

"Down with slavery!" someone cried.

"And down with the Cornish!" Sheena O'Toole bellowed. "Down with soulless Cornishmen!"

"Defeat to the Confederacy!"

"All hail the Union!"

"Calm down everybody!"

"Secede! Secede!"

"Yankee!"

"Reb!"

Caitrin clapped her hands over her ears. As Salvatore Rippeto's fist smashed into Casimir Laski's nose, she ran toward the door. With the crack of a bench breaking and the wail of a child crying behind her, she let the blackness of night gather her into its arms.

Jack could hear the sounds of the quilt auction inside the mercantile as he strode toward it from the creek bank. The good citizens of Hope must have settled down after their hysterics, name-callings, fist swingings, and general conniptions. Cruel people. Sinners one and all. If he didn't have to go back inside and fetch

Lucy's handcuffs from where they'd fallen out of his pocket, he wouldn't come near the place.

Ever again.

It was time to leave. He should have known better than to return to Kansas—flat, dried-up old plain anyhow. Bunch of prairie dogs scratching out a living. He'd heard their cruel accusations against poor Lucy. Lucy had never done anybody a bad turn in her life.

"Sunshine and Shadows!" Seth Hunter called out from the mercantile. "This quilt was made by Mrs. Violet Hudson. Why don't you tell us about it, ma'am?"

Jack stepped into the crowded store as a woman stood holding a small baby. Five or six little children clung to her skirt. "It's the dark and light colors that make up this Log Cabin pattern we call Sunshine and Shadows," she said. "I used scraps from the dresses I made when my husband was alive. And then . . . well . . . I sewed myself some widow's weeds, so I had the dark scraps, too. So that's it, Sunshine and Shadows."

Thankful the crowd was facing away from him, Jack walked to the corner of the room where he had sat with Lucy. The whole mess was Caitrin Murphy's fault, he thought. She was so determined to do her good deeds and make her pious proclamations that she'd run everything straight into the ground. *Go and get Lucy, Jack. Please fetch your sister, Jack.* If he hadn't been swayed by her constant belief that all would be well . . .

As he picked up the chain, the clink of iron drew the attention of the crowd. Straightening, Jack stared at the onlookers, daring them to speak a word. Seth Hunter tossed the quilt onto a bench and took a step forward.

"Jack," he said. "I . . . ah . . . I was planning to come talk to you later. I hope everything's all right. Your sister, I mean."

"Same as ever." Jack squeezed his fist around the chain. Words of venom and bile filled his mouth and soured his tongue. He gritted his teeth.

"I am fery sorry for trouble I make you," Rolf said, standing. "I do not mean bad to your sister."

"That's right, Jack," Seth added. "I'd like to apologize to you and your family for the ruckus tonight. I guess things got heated up around here and . . . ah . . . well, some of us got a little carried away."

"Yep," Jack said. "I reckon you did."

The chain dangling from his hand, he walked toward the door. *Thanks for the welcome party*, he wanted to say. *Thanks for your show of neighborhood unity. Thanks for your godly example of Christian love and brotherhood.* But he swallowed the words and stepped outside.

So much for Hope.

Caitrin nearly cried aloud in fear when she saw the huge, shadowy figure moving toward her. But then she heard the clink of an iron chain and recognized the outline of the man's shoulders.

"Jack." She stood from the bench outside her soddy. "How is Lucy?"

"Needs her chains. And don't sass me about it, either. There's nobody to keep an eye on her while we pack up."

"Pack?" Caitrin took a step toward him, aching to touch and soothe but aware she had already caused so much trouble. "Are you leaving us, then?"

"It's for the best."

"Please don't go." The words slipped out before she had weighed them. "Oh, Jack, I know some of the men were unkind, but—"

"They spoke badly of Lucy. She's my sister, and I'll stand up to anyone who sullies her name. Fact is, before her troubles, Lucy was one of the sweetest little gals anybody ever knew—a good, upstanding Christian who showed her religion by her actions better than anybody around here. Jimmy O'Toole had no right to cuss her like that. I've been trying my best to pray, read the Bible, and walk the straight and narrow. But if I ever get my hands on that skinny little Irishman, I can't promise he'll live to see another day."

"Sure Jimmy is my own sister's husband," Caitrin said, recoiling at the harshness in his voice. "In spite of his ill behavior tonight, he's a fine hardworking man and a good father to his five children. You mustn't threaten his life, Jack. And the people of this town are not so wicked, either. Please try to remember they probably haven't met anyone like Lucy before, and they don't know what to make of her. Few of them have had such troubles in their own families. They haven't had time to get to know Lucy as a human being."

"Which they don't consider her to be. You heard what O'Toole said about us—Cornishmen have no souls. Aren't we worthy of God's love? Don't we deserve a measure of friendship from the townsfolk?"

"Of course you do."

"I reckon not. Ever since I started building the smithy, not a person in Hope has said more than two words to me beyond asking me to mend a shovel or patch a bucket. How's my family ever going to show our true nature if people judge us as demons?"

Caitrin lifted her eyes to the moon. She'd been sitting for almost an hour in prayer, begging God to show her answers to these very questions. Instead of a peace that passes understanding, she felt turmoil and anger. Fury raced through her veins at the cruel words that had been spoken and the wicked things that had been done. And now Jack Cornwall was forcing her to defend the very people who had disappointed her so deeply.

She let out a breath that misted white in the chilly night air. "I don't know how you can prove yourselves," she said softly. "But you certainly won't do it if you leave town."

Jack leaned his back against the wall of the soddy and dangled the chain against the toe of his boot. For a long time he said nothing. Then he hooked a thumb in his pocket. "All we wanted was a chance," he said.

"The question is not what *you* wanted, Jack. What does *God* want of you?" Caitrin rubbed her hands up and down her arms, trying to warm them. "Do you think I would have chosen a sod house on a barren prairie as my lot in life? Certainly not. But I felt the Lord leading me here to Sheena and Jimmy. I didn't understand why at the time, and perhaps I still don't. At first I felt I was to help my sister with her children, perhaps to start a small school and teach them their letters. Then I began working at the mercantile, and it seemed God brought my skills into use there. And then you came along. . . ."

She studied his face, the hard line written across his mouth, the rumple of his brown hair, the anger in his gray eyes. *Oh, Jack Cornwall. Why do you stir my heart and cause my very bones to ache? What is it in you that touches me so deeply?*

"'Tis not what we want," she whispered. "If we've given our hearts to the Lord, we must do his will no matter the cost."

"How's anybody supposed to know what God wants?" he asked. When Caitrin didn't answer, he mused for a moment. "If I were to put myself in God's shoes, I'd ask just one thing from folks—and it wouldn't have a thing to do with running smithies or mercantiles. I'd want love."

Caitrin tried to force down the lump in her throat. "Yes," she managed. *Thou shalt love the Lord thy God with all thy heart. . . .*

"I'd want people to love me so much that they had to tell everybody they met," Jack said. "And they'd show their love for me so clearly in everything they did that other folks would ask why . . . and then start begging to get to know me for themselves. If I were God, that's what I'd want."

Love, Caitrin thought. It was what Jack himself wanted and what she'd begged God to give him. How amazing that this often unloved and unlovable man understood so clearly the heart of his Lord.

He studied the moon. "I thought if I built a smithy here I could take care of my family," Jack went on. "I've got plans, you know. Dreams. And I sure thought God had led me back here to Kansas to make them come true. But after tonight . . . well, I'm not certain there's room for me in this town."

Caitrin gulped down a sob. How could she ever express the torment she felt over his words? She couldn't even make herself speak for fear she'd burst into tears. And what could she tell him? *Give these people time, Jack. Be patient, Jack. Let them learn to care for you . . . as I do.*

"If God didn't send me to Kansas to build that smithy," he said, still staring at the moon as though it were his companion on this night and not Caitrin Murphy, "if God didn't send me here to build that smithy, then why did I feel so sure I was supposed to come back? It was almost like I heard him talking to me that evening last winter after I left the O'Tooles' barn."

"You heard the voice of God?"

"In a way." He reflected a moment. "I told you about that night on the road when I got down on my knees and prayed for God's forgiveness. It was almost like God *told* me to come back to Hope. Why? Why did he want me here?"

Caitrin blotted her cheek with the corner of her handkerchief. *Why, Lord? Why anything? Why was Lucy so troubled? Why did Sheena scorn Felicity? Why didn't she have the answers for Jack? Why, why, why?*

"Because I'm supposed to love God here, and that's all," Jack said, his voice filled with an unexpected calm. "No big dreams. No big plans. Just love. *That's* why he wanted me to come back to Kansas. God wanted me to love him so much—right here in this podunk town with its mean-mouthed citizens—that people could look at me and see for themselves that God changes men's hearts."

Caitrin dabbed her eyelids and tried to dam the drippy faucet that her nose had become. Why did she have to cry *now?* Why this uncontrollable weeping when there was so much she needed to say? She wanted to affirm Jack, to encourage him, to beg him not to give up. She ached to reach out to him with words of acceptance and love. Instead, she gave a shuddering sob and buried her face in her hands.

"I doubt if the folks here will change, though," Jack said to the moon. "Their hate is dug in deep. Real deep."

Her handkerchief soaked, Caitrin blotted her cheeks with the cuff of her sleeve. Yes, it was true, she wanted to tell him. Hate and intolerance could spring out of the nicest people at the most unlikely times. And only God could change them. But her lip was quivering so much she couldn't form a single word.

"So I guess that's that," Jack said. He wound the chain around his hand. "If I leave, they won't have seen God in me. Not enough to touch their hearts anyhow. I reckon the Cornwalls will just have to be like that fellow Stephen in the Bible—keeping our mouths shut while folks throw their stones. It's not exactly in my nature to turn the other cheek, but I expect I better give it a try. What do you think?" He turned and looked at Caitrin.

"Oh, darlin'," he said. In a single stride he had caught her up in his arms and was kissing her hair, her damp cheeks, her wet eyelashes, her trembling lips. His warmth enfolded her.

"The first time we met, you told me you loved me," Jack said in a low voice. "I didn't know what that word meant. *Love.* Didn't really understand it. But I think I'm beginning to catch on. It's about opening your heart to what somebody else needs. And it's *you* I'm seeing that love in, Caitrin. I'm seeing God in you the way I want folks to see him in me."

He held her tightly, all but crushing the breath from her chest. "Thanks for talking to me about all this, Caitrin," he said, his lips moving against the skin of her forehead. "You're a wise woman."

With one last embrace, he stepped away from her, looked her up and down once, and then turned on his heel and walked away. She was quite sure *she* hadn't been the one talking to Jack Cornwall. And she hurried into the soddy for a dry handkerchief.

CHAPTER 13

"SOMETIMES I feel discouraged, and think my work's in vain," Jack sang as he pumped the bellows on his forge. "But then the Holy Spirit revives my soul again."

Jack thrust the red-hot nail header into his quenching bucket and heard the satisfying hiss of steam. "There is a balm in Gilead to make the wounded whole," he belted out the chorus. "There is a balm in Gilead to heal the sin-sick soul."

He gave the header a tap and a brand-new nail slid out into the pile on the table. With the church going up and folks repairing their barns and wagons, Jack could hardly keep up with the demand for nails. He was grateful for the work.

It had taken him two days to persuade his mother to stay on in Hope and less than two weeks to convince the townsfolk they'd be hard-pressed without him. Swallowing their pride, people had begun trickling into the smithy from the time he had his forge up and burning. Now a steady stream of customers dropped by wanting repairs or asking for the plows, shovels, wheels, and tools he crafted each day.

After talking with Caitrin the night of the welcome festival, Jack had made up his mind to keep a safe distance from her and the incredible lure of her sweet spirit and compelling beauty. If he was ever to have a chance of courting the woman in an open and proper fashion, he knew he'd have to win the respect of the

O'Tooles . . . and that wasn't going to be an easy job. All the same, he had found a way to stay in touch with Caitrin. She had agreed to let him sell his tools through the mercantile. The arrangement gave her a little profit, and it allowed him to talk with her every day, if only for a few minutes.

"If you can't preach like Peter," he sang, enjoying the rich round notes of his mellow baritone filling the smithy, "if you can't pray like Paul, just tell the love of Jesus, and say he died for all."

By the time he had sung the last word, Jack had made three more nails. Every fifteen seconds he could turn one out, he thought with some measure of pride. He had learned nail making at his father's side on the farm, and even as a child he had enjoyed the creativity and challenge that went with working iron. But it wasn't until the war that he'd come into his own. Assigned to a Confederate unit as the blacksmith, he had followed the troops and worked from sunup to sundown fixing broken weapons, repairing cannon, crafting tools. Hard work, but he'd loved it.

"Excuse me, sir, but where is Gilead?" a lilting voice asked.

Jack gave the bellows a push that blew fresh air onto the glowing pocket of coke in the forge and looked up. Caitrin Murphy stood in the doorway, a smile on her face and a bent poker in her hand.

"Caitrin," he said, his breath nearly robbed from his chest by the sight of her. "You look beautiful."

"No more beautiful than the sound of your voice drifting across the road to the mercantile." Then she gave him a little wink. "Tell me, sir, what is the exact meaning of the word *balm?*"

Jack laughed. "You know, I've been singing about the balm of Gilead ever since I learned that song at a church service last Christmas, and come to think of it, I don't know the answer to either question."

"Perhaps you'd better move on to 'Jacob's Ladder,'" she said, stepping into the room. "I recall the story behind that one, so I do.

Jacob dreamed about a ladder with angels going up and down it from earth to heaven."

"He was using a rock for his pillow," Jack said. "No telling what you'll dream if you do something knuckleheaded like that."

She chuckled. "That was when God gave Jacob all the land around the place where he was sleeping and promised him a long line of children, too. 'Tis a good verse for us here in Hope, Kansas. 'And, behold, I am with thee, and will keep thee in all places whither thou goest, and will bring thee again into this land; for I will not leave thee, until I have done that which I have spoken to thee of.'"

"Great ghosts, Miss Murphy," Jack said. "Where'd you learn all that?"

"Straight out of the Scriptures, sir." She laid the poker on a table. "And now down to business. I've a poor bent poker here that I took in trade for a bridge toll. Can you make it new again?"

"That's what I do best." Jack tapped another nail out of the header and onto the pile. Encouraged by his admirer's praise, he started in on "Jacob's Ladder" as he began the next nail. "Sinner, do you love my Jesus?" he sang, all but raising the rafters on the smithy roof. "Sinner, do you love my Jesus? Sinner, do you love my Jesus? Soldiers of the cross."

As he tapered the point of the nail, Caitrin joined in. "If you love him, why not serve him? If you love him, why not serve him—"

"Tush, Jack, you'll wake the dead with all that bellowing," Felicity Cornwall said, entering the forge with a lunch basket over her arm. "Oh. Miss Murphy. I didn't know you were here."

"I brought a bent poker for Jack to mend. Your son does fine work, Mrs. Cornwall."

Felicity sniffed. "I can hear you bellowing all the way down at the creek, Jack. You'd think it was a Sunday."

"Every day's the Lord's day, Mama." Jack glanced at the basket on her arm. "What did you bring me for lunch? I could eat two horses."

"Rabbit stew," his mother said, setting the basket on the table beside the new nails. "And if you don't get your hide out onto the prairie and hunt us a deer, we're going to be obliged to eat that horse of yours pretty soon. Of course, I suppose I could make a nice pot roast out of Scratch's flank, but—"

"All right, all right. It's just that I've got so much to do around here." He slung an arm around his mother's shoulders. "Guess what Salvatore Rippeto suggested this morning?"

"That Italian?" She wrinkled her nose as she set out a bowl and spoon. "No telling."

"He thinks I should set up a livery stable."

"You don't have the money, and I wouldn't like to see you fall into debt in a place like this. We could get ourselves mired here for good."

"As far as I'm concerned, we're already stuck, Mama," Jack said. Then he looked at Caitrin, eager to gauge her reaction to his news. "I'm going to ask Seth Hunter if I can put up a soddy."

"Oh, Jack!" Caitrin exclaimed, her face lighting up.

"Stuff and nonsense," Felicity barked, clanging the lid of the soup tureen. "Not in this town, you won't! I'll not live in Hope past the summer, Jack. I've told you once, and I'll tell you again. Earn the money to get us back home. That's all I ask."

"No disrespect intended, Mama," Jack said, "but where would we live in Missouri? Too many cities. Too many people. Folks here in Hope may not be comfortable around us, but they don't stick their noses into our business much. If we go back into one of those crowded Missouri towns, they'll have the law after us to put Lucy into an asylum."

"Exactly where she belongs," Felicity said, seating herself on a stool beside the door. "And don't argue with me, Jack. You should just see your sister today. She can hardly open her eyes. She's curled into a ball of misery on her bed with the quilt drawn over her head. The girl is completely useless to anyone."

"I should be happy to drop by and visit Lucy," Caitrin put in. "Perhaps she'd enjoy having a bit of company."

Felicity gave a snort. "Don't think you're some kind of a miracle healer, Miss Murphy. My daughter has her good spells and her bad. You just happened to catch her in one of her better humors last time. You won't talk her out of this with all your chatter about tea and cinnamon buns."

Jack tugged his leather apron over his head and hung it on a hook in the door. He wished his mother could find something to talk about besides Lucy and her woes. They'd had the same conversation over and over. He could almost say her part from memory.

"Lucy has such troubling thoughts," Caitrin said.

"She doesn't think about anyone but herself." Felicity picked up the poker Caitrin had brought in and examined it as she spoke. "Lucy's selfish, that's all. She pays no heed to the trouble she causes by demanding so much of our attention. She's wrapped up in herself and all her mournful little worries, and she never stops to consider how *we* feel. I must say, I am vastly weary of it all. It makes me angry."

Jack picked up his spoon and took a bite of stew meat. "Mama thinks Lucy just ought to come out of it," he said, stating what he knew would be his mother's next comment. Felicity always delivered her assessment of her daughter's condition in three parts. First, Lucy was selfish. Second, Lucy should just come out of it using sheer willpower. And third, if Lucy were a better Christian and prayed about her problems more diligently, God would deliver her from them.

"Yes, she could just come right out of it if she had the willpower," Felicity said. "And if she'd turn her worries over to the Lord, she would see everything in a new light."

"You think she could just pray herself right out of that bed and into her right mind?" Jack asked.

"I certainly do."

He gave the stew a stir. "What do you think about all this, Miss Murphy?"

"About Lucy?" Caitrin's eyes flashed in wariness. "Though I love her dearly, 'tis not my business to assess her troubles."

"You spent a lot of time looking after my sister. Why do you think she's the way she is?"

"Sure I don't know," Caitrin said. "But God does. I suppose the best we can do is ask him to help her."

"That's exactly what I said." Felicity nodded in self-assurance. "Lucy just needs to pray harder."

"Caitrin said *we* ought to pray, Mama," Jack corrected her. "I'm not sure Lucy can think clearly enough to pray. As a matter of fact, I don't believe she can think straight about anything. She sure isn't thinking about herself, how selfish she can be, and how much she can inconvenience the rest of us. The times she's tried to do herself in, she was just wanting everything to be over. She wanted to stop hurting."

"Hurting!" Felicity stood. "That child has everything a body could want. She's not in any pain. Stuff and nonsense, Jack. You're like putty in Lucy's hands. All she has to do is gaze at you with those big eyes, and you do anything she asks."

Jack looked up as a shadow fell across the door. Much to his surprise, Sheena O'Toole's bright red hair, green eyes, and rosy cheeks appeared in a patch of sunlight.

"Sheena?" Caitrin said. "What are you doing here?"

The woman moved one step into the smithy and stopped, as stiff as a statue. "Good afternoon," she said, her mouth tight and her focus on the rusty roasting spit in her hands. "Mr. Cornwall, I've come to seek your services, so I have."

"My services?" he asked. "You mean you want me to do some work for you?"

"Aye. That I do."

A flood of victory raced through Jack's veins. Now was his moment! He could skewer the little biddy on her own spit. He could send the Irishwoman and her sharp tongue right back outside with a message he wanted the whole town to hear: Nobody messes with Jack Cornwall. If you need me, you'd better treat me right.

He stood to his full height, towering over her. He could see the white skin around her knuckles as she clutched the rusty iron spit, and he recognized the incredible tension radiating from her. He recognized it. He had felt it himself when he went to Seth Hunter to ask permission to build the smithy.

A river of remorse washed right over the flood of victorious revenge in which he'd been about to drown Sheena O'Toole. At first he thought he couldn't even form the words that demanded to be spoken. But he'd prayed so hard that God's love would be revealed in his own life, the message just came flowing out.

"I'm glad to see you today, Mrs. O'Toole," he said, his voice more gentle than he'd ever heard it. "Looks like you've got a rusty spit bar there. That's a big problem with all those children of yours. I'll bet they want to eat day and night. If you were to put a big ol' roast on that bar, it would probably bust clean in two."

Sheena lifted her head just enough that the green of her eyes could be seen from under her dark lashes. "Aye," she said. "I was afraid of that myself."

"I can clean and mend your spit bar right here and now. But you'd do better with a new one. It would be stronger. Cleaner, too. I could have it ready for you by sunset."

"How much?"

Jack pondered a moment, and then it came to him. This was the perfect opportunity to begin building bridges between himself and Caitrin's family. The solution seemed heaven sent.

"Tell you what, Mrs. O'Toole," he said. "You invite me to your house for a sandwich of whatever's left from the first roast on your new spit—and one of your famous pickles—and we'll call it even. I won't charge you one red cent. How's that?"

Sheena sucked down a deep breath.

"She'll never do it!" Felicity crowed. "She'll never get her Irish mitts on that new spit unless she eats humble pie, and she's too proud for that. You've caught her now, Jack. Well done!"

"Wicked man!" Sheena spat at Jack. "I came here humbly offering you an honest bit of work, so I did, and you pulled one of your Cornish tricks on me! Wait until Jimmy hears about this—"

"Hold on a minute, there, Mrs. O'Toole." Jack caught her elbow as she made for the door. "I never meant a thing by what I said. I'll be happy to fix your spit. I'll make you a new one, if that's what you want. All I intended was to—"

"To worm your way inside my house!" she hissed. "You've already taken liberties with our Caitrin, drawn her heart away from her own family. Look at her here, chatting with you as bold as a strumpet! You've already used my Jimmy's barn for a camp. And now what would you have of us? Our very privacy? As if we'd let a man like you into our house! Demon!"

"Sheena!" Caitrin cried. "Please don't be so cruel."

"You were strutting about all cock-a-hoop before, Mrs. O'Toole," Felicity said, "flinging your Irish pride in our faces. But now you've found you can't do without my son, eh? Well, you'll never see his fine work in your miserable little soddy—"

"Now hold on a minute here, Mama," Jack cut in. "I just told Mrs. O'Toole that I'd make her the spit bar. I didn't mean to—"

"Oh no, you don't!" Sheena cried. "Don't try to turn your trickery around with one of your Cornish lies, Mr. Cornwall."

"Lies? Why, you witch!" Felicity raised the bent poker and shook it in Sheena's face. "Out of here, you little red-haired leprechaun!"

"Oooh!" Sheena leapt at the older woman, rusty spit thrust

forward like a sword. "Call me that, will you? Blast your soul, you're a cheeky thing! A strap is what you are! A bold, forward, Cornish strap!"

Felicity swung the heavy poker upward to parry the thrust, and the clash of metal knocked Sheena off balance. Recovering, the Irishwoman lunged at her opponent, and again spit clanged against poker.

"Stop this now!" Jack leapt at his mother, barely evading a jab from Sheena's spit. "Mama, put down that poker before you hurt Mrs. O'Toole."

"Sheena, don't do this!" Caitrin cried.

"Look at her, look at her!" Felicity shouted, dancing from side to side. "She's an imp of the devil himself!"

"Liar!" Sheena swung the spit, missed her target, and went spinning around in a wobbly circle. "Liar, liar!"

"Witch!" Felicity strained toward her adversary. "I'll get you now!"

In a burst of furious swordplay, the older woman fenced Sheena right out of the smithy. Jack grabbed Caitrin's hand and dashed after the two shrieking combatants. On the pale green springtime grass near the mercantile, the two women whirled and lunged at each other, their cries echoing like the wail of banshees across the open prairie.

"Stop this right now, Mama," Jack called as he sprinted toward the women. "Caitrin, help me out here."

"Sheena!" Caitrin headed for her sister, who was tottering off balance down the gentle slope toward the creek. "Jack, go after Sheena!"

"Witch, witch!" Felicity charged past Caitrin and chased after her foe, poker swinging.

"Shut your gob before I give you a sound larruping!" Sheena bellowed.

Caitrin grabbed Mrs. Cornwall around the waist, and at that

moment, the older woman hurled the poker at Sheena. The iron rod tumbled through the air. Jack reached for the teetering Irishwoman. Just as he put a hand on her arm, the poker slammed into her head. A bright splotch of crimson instantly appeared on her face as she slumped onto the grass. Arms covering her head, she wailed aloud in pain.

His blood racing, Jack dropped down beside the fallen woman. Caitrin turned Mrs. Cornwall loose, ran down the hill, and sank to her knees beside her sister. "Sheena!" she cried, throwing her arms around the bundle of moaning misery. "Oh, Sheena! Are you injured? Let me see your head!"

"What have I done? Oh, what have I done!" Felicity arrived at the creek bed as Sheena clutched her stomach in agony.

"My baby," the Irishwoman groaned. "I'm losing my baby! Caitie, where's Jimmy? Oh, heavens, the baby!"

"Sheena?" Caitrin exclaimed. "Sheena, you never said anything about a baby. Jack, sure you must run to the mercantile and fetch Rosie. Bring towels!"

God in heaven, help us all, Jack prayed as he raced up the slope toward the mercantile. "Mrs. Hunter!" he shouted. "Mrs. Hunter, come out here!"

The young woman appeared in the mercantile doorway, her cheeks flushed. "What's wrong, Jack?"

"It's Mrs. O'Toole. She's hurt bad. We need towels."

"Oh, Jack!" Rosie grabbed her skirts and dashed back into the mercantile. She reemerged in a moment, arms filled with white cotton tea towels. "What happened to Sheena, Jack?"

"Trouble. Go fetch Seth!"

He headed back down the slope. Sheena hadn't budged, her body doubled up and blood trickling down her temple. Felicity hovered over her, brushing back her tangle of red hair and trying to loosen the apron at her waist. Caitrin crouched in mute horror.

Jack dropped and slid the last two yards on his knees. "Mrs.

O'Toole, can you hear me?" He dipped a tea towel into the creek and pressed it onto the gash on her head. "Mrs. O'Toole, talk to me."

"The baby!" Sheena wept. "Don't let me lose my baby!"

"We'll do all we can. Caitrin, hold this cloth on your sister's head." He settled the young woman's trembling hand on the wadded tea towel. "Push down as hard as you can. And don't let her go to sleep. How far along are you, Mrs. O'Toole?"

"Four months, the same as Rosie. I didn't want to tell it round and cut in on her joy. I've had my other babies, and this is her first, and—oh, Mr. Cornwall, where's my Jimmy?" She clutched at his arms, her pretty face wreathed in pain. "I need my Jimmy!"

"I'll get him in a minute," Jack assured her. "Calm yourself, now, Mrs. O'Toole. Take a deep breath."

"I'm going for blankets," Felicity said. She leaped to her feet and ran toward the camp.

Jack took out his pocketknife and slit the ribbon that held on her apron. "Are you cramping up, Mrs. O'Toole?"

"Aye, I am." She was crying now, tears running down her rosy cheeks. "Oh, I'm a bad, wicked woman!"

"No, you're not. Things just got a little out of hand." He lifted her head into his lap and used one of the tea towels to blot her forehead.

"But I am, I am. I was miffed at my dear Jimmy—and at God, too—when I realized I was to have another baby. I've five *brablins* already, you know, and the soddy is terrible crowded, so it is. I said—" she grimaced in pain—"I told Jimmy I didn't want the baby. I prayed . . . prayed . . ."

"Now then, Mrs. O'Toole, try to calm yourself."

"I prayed I would lose the baby!"

"Oh, Sheena!" Caitrin whispered. "You didn't."

"A terrible thing to do," Sheena went on. "Wicked and sinful of me. I was so angry about it all. But now . . . oh, now . . . I want this child! I want my baby!"

"Of course you do." Jack could feel his heart slamming against his chest. Caitrin sat paralyzed with shock, her face as white as her apron. Jack had had plenty of experience tending wounds on a bloody battlefield, but he didn't have a clue how to take care of a woman in Sheena's condition. And he sure didn't know anything about hearing someone's confessions.

"Oh, it hurts!" she cried out, squeezing his hand. "Help me!"

"Turn her to the side," Felicity ordered, arriving back at the site of the catastrophe. "And for heaven's sake, take Mrs. O'Toole's head off your lap, Jack. She must have her feet up, not her head. Here, put this blanket under her legs."

Glad to obey orders, he wadded up the quilt and stuffed it under Sheena's feet.

"Drink this cup of cool water," the older woman commanded. "Sometimes the cramps can come on from a thirst. Now, I'm going to check the baby, all right?"

"Aye," Sheena sobbed. "Help me, Mrs. Cornwall, please help me! Save my baby."

"I'll do what I can. Try to rest now. Pray for the welfare of your unborn child."

While his mother worked, Jack traded the blood-soaked tea towel for a fresh one and examined the gash on Sheena's forehead. Her skin had been slashed, but a few strong stitches would probably hold it together until it had time to heal. As Jack dabbed the wound with water, Seth Hunter came barreling down the slope toward the creek. Rosie, skirts flying, was right behind him. She cried out in dismay as she absorbed the scene on the creek bank.

"Seth," she shouted, "run back to the house for my medicine bag, honey."

"Medicine bag," her panting husband repeated. Then he turned right around and started up the hill again.

"I'll go after Jimmy," Jack told Caitrin, touching her hand long enough to draw her attention. She nodded as she and Rosie took over the work on Sheena's forehead.

Jack ran across the bridge and covered the short distance to the O'Toole homestead. The children were playing in the yard, and the older ones directed Jack to where Jimmy was working in the field. Realizing something must have happened, they grabbed up the toddlers and started for the bridge.

"Jimmy!" Jack called, hailing the silhouetted figure whose mop of bright red hair easily identified him. "Come quick. It's Sheena!"

Jimmy dropped his plow and ran. "Where's my girl? What's happened to her?"

"On the bank. It's the baby."

"No!"

Paling, Jimmy took off like a shot. Winded from his run, Jack leaned against the O'Tooles' barn for a moment to catch his breath. At that moment, Caitrin came flying into the yard.

"Jack? Where are you?"

"Here, Cait!" He stepped out from the barn, caught her in his arms, and held her tightly. "I'm right here."

CHAPTER 14

WHAT'S happening with Sheena?" Jack asked.

"I don't know yet," Caitrin whispered. "Sure your mother's the only one with experience in these matters. I've come to fetch Sheena's sewing basket so I can stitch the wound." She clung to him, her cheek pressed against his shoulder. "Oh, Jack, how could this terrible thing have happened? Whatever shall we do?"

He swallowed, aware suddenly that this interlude with Caitrin might be the last. The trouble between his mother and Sheena O'Toole could seal the Cornwalls' fate in the community. There would be no courtship of Caitrin.

"We'd better pray," he said. "Pray for Sheena. Pray my mother can help her hang onto that baby." He took both her hands in his. "Father, please fix this mess. Look after Sheena, and show Mama how to take care of that baby. Amen."

"Amen," Caitrin murmured. "Oh, Jack, I'd no idea Sheena was expecting a baby. Which of them started the trouble? Sure 'tis all a blur to me now."

"They just went after each other."

"Aye, and they raced outside before I knew it. Then you and I tried to separate them. I took hold of your mother. You went for Sheena, and Mrs. Cornwall threw the poker—Oh, Jack!" She buried her head in the hollow of his neck.

"I've got you, Caitrin. I'm here." As he held her close, a warmth flooded through Jack's chest and filled him with determination. At all cost, he would protect this woman from pain. He would shelter her, shield her, from the fire that raged around them.

"'Tis the end of it then," Caitrin said softly. "You'll have to leave Kansas, Jack. They gave you a month of grace, and 'tis been less than that. Your mother struck Sheena with the poker. If she loses the baby—"

"The trouble wasn't my doing. It happened between the women."

"It doesn't matter. You'll bear the brunt of it, so you will. Sure Jimmy will latch onto any reason to drive out your family. He and Sheena have no use for Cornish."

Jack tightened his arms around Caitrin, looking into her green eyes, praying he could memorize her in case he never saw her again.

"Jimmy doesn't trust you," she said, echoing his own fears. "If he learns you were near Sheena when she fell, he'll cry for blood."

"Don't worry. I can stand up to Jimmy."

"Sure you can't save yourself and the whole world, Jack."

"No, but I'm putting my faith in someone who can. Caitrin, look at me." He took her shoulders in his hands and forced her to meet his eyes. "Tell me you want me to stay here. Tell me I mean that much to you—and not just as a child of God. Say you want me for the man I am, and I'll tear down anything that tries to come between us."

"I do want you to know how much I care about you, and I know you love God . . . but I'm . . . I'm sometimes frightened of the fierce spirit I see inside you, Jack. How can I be sure this boldness is all for good? The things you did before were so . . . I know you had your reasons, but you were a ruthless man. You were ironfisted and unyielding. You were merciless."

"Is that what you think of me *now*, Caitrin? Do you want me to carry my past around forever like an old sack of garbage?" Hands behind her neck, he stroked his thumbs across the velvet pink of her cheeks. "You once told me I was precious to God. Those were words I'd never heard. I believed you, Caitrin. I read in the Bible that if any man is in Christ, he's a new creature. Old things pass away, and all things are made new. That's why I came to Hope looking for a fresh start. I want to be different, inside and out. But I can't do that if people tie the bad stuff in my past around my neck and make me haul it around."

"Have you truly changed, Jack?" she asked softly. "Or will some spark set the flames to raging inside you again?"

Unable to resist, he kissed her lips, pressing her tightly to him. "I don't think the flames inside me have ever stopped raging or ever will. I'll always be ironfisted. I'll always be stubborn and rough. But I've come to believe that God can take the man he created and use me for his good purposes. He used Peter, didn't he? That fellow was no angel. He was always mouthing off and doing things before he thought them through. But Christ said he'd build his church on Peter."

"Aye, but—"

"So why can't he use me, Caitrin?" He crushed her against him. "Tell me the answer to that!"

"Christ *has* put his Spirit inside you, and he can use for his good the fire that burns in your heart. But Jack, I don't know that the people here in Hope have the wisdom and tolerance to see that far."

"I don't give a hot potato what the people here see in me," he said. "Who I am and what I do is up to God. You're the only person who matters to me, Caitrin. *You.*"

She clutched his shirtsleeves, knotting the fabric in her fingers. "Oh, Jack Cornwall, whatever is to become of us? More than ever now I see the matching zeal in our hearts. 'Tis true what I said so long ago—we *are* that pair of candles burning brightly. But I asked you before, and I'll ask it again: What future can a candle have on a windswept prairie? What do you want of me?"

"I want your fire. I want us to be a bonfire together. One big, blazing bonfire that God can use to turn raw ore into gold, a fire that everybody can see for miles around."

"Jesus taught that we're not to hide our light under a basket; we're to shine for all to witness. But Jack, I must think of Sheena and Jimmy. I love them! I want to honor and respect their wishes. They're the only family I have. And how can I be sure something won't go terribly awry? Sure your mother has a sharp tongue, and Lucy bears such troubles, and—"

"And people don't come in pretty little packages with bows on top, Caitrin. God loves all of us no matter what, and I reckon we should do our best to follow his example. But this is not about Mama and Lucy. This is about you and me, Caitrin. Say the word, and I'll leave town. Right now. But if you ask me to stay, I will. I won't budge an inch, no matter what anyone says or does."

As he held her, he could see the crowd hurrying across the bridge, Sheena hoisted on a blanket among them. Some of her children were crying. Jimmy was barking orders left and right. The mongrel dog yapped like there was no tomorrow as Chipper ran along beside him. Over all the clamor, Sheena's keening filled the air.

"They're coming," Caitrin whispered, turning to look.

Before she could push away, Jack bent and kissed her lips.

God, my heart cries out for her! The prayer was torn from his very soul. *Please don't take this woman from me. Make a place for us. Give us hope, Father God. I beg you, give us hope.*

"Stay," Caitrin whispered against his cheek. "I want you to stay, Jack."

"I will." His soul soared.

"But I cannot be with you in secret. If we're to be a bonfire, we can't go on hiding in the shadows."

"May I have your permission to come courting?"

She glanced up, surprise lighting her emerald eyes. "Aye," she said, a laugh bubbling from her throat as he caught her up in his arms and swung her around. "You may court me, Mr. Cornwall. I'll ask Rosie to chaperone. Now set me down before we turn the town on its head with our shenanigans!"

Before he could respond, she pulled out of his embrace and dashed for the O'Tooles' soddy. He followed, lifting up a prayer for Sheena. But his footsteps pounded out the song in his heart. *Stay! I want you to stay, Jack! Stay, stay, stay!*

"He'll have to go," Jimmy muttered. "The whole lot of them Cornish devils will have to go."

"Whisht, Jimmy," Caitrin said as she stood beside her brother-in-law in the silent soddy. "There may have been trouble between them, but Mrs. Cornwall is helping Sheena now. Don't spark up the strife again."

She clamped her hands together under her chin as she watched Felicity working. The younger woman lay unmoving on the bed, her head wrapped in a white bandage where Caitrin had stitched the gash made by the poker. The scent of burning lamp oil suffused the room, and the golden light gave it a churchlike atmosphere.

Felicity regarded Jimmy solemnly. "Your wife has kept her baby," she announced.

"Glory be to God," Jimmy said, letting out a deep breath. In two strides, he was at Sheena's side, kneeling by the bed and pressing his lips against her hand. Sheena stroked her husband's damp red hair. "Are you all right, my love?"

"Aye," she croaked. "The pains are going now. Oh, Jimmy . . ."

He muffled her sobs with tender kisses. "'Tis all right, my honey-sweet. Sure 'tis going to be fine now."

"I'm so . . . so sorry."

"Malarkey. You've no need to say that."

"But I . . . I . . ."

"If you'll leave us be now," Jimmy said, turning to the three women in the room. "My wife's a *donsie* thing. She'll be needin' her rest, so she will."

"Aye," Caitrin said softly. "Sheena, I must go and tend the wee *brablins*. Will you be wanting anything more from me?"

"Nay." Sheena sniffled.

Rosie picked up her medicine bag, wrapped her arms around it, and led the way out the door of the soddy. Felicity Cornwall followed, and Caitrin took up the rear. The O'Toole children stood barefoot on the hard-beaten earth yard and stared with great emerald eyes at the women.

"Your mama is fine now," Felicity told them. "And so is the baby. God willing, your healthy brother or sister will be born in the autumn."

Their faces broke into radiant grins as the woman turned and strode toward the bridge. Caitrin stared after her, wondering what thoughts had leapt into Felicity's mind during those terrible minutes when uncertainty gripped everyone. Would she admit her guilt in the conflict? Would she beg forgiveness of Sheena? Could Jimmy ever make peace with the Cornwalls?

"Caitrin." Rosie took her friend's hand and squeezed it tightly. "We saw you with Jack. As we were bringing Sheena across the creek, we saw the two of you by the barn. He was kissing you. Jimmy saw it, and the things he said against Jack were vile. Oh, Caitrin."

"Jack's a good man, Rosie. He's begging for a chance to show that he's changed."

"He won't get it. Not with that kind of behavior."

"He was comforting me."

"They'll drive him off, Caitie. I'm sure of it."

"No," Caitrin said, her voice low and determined. "Jack Cornwall is going to stay."

"He'll have to go," Seth said, wiping his face with a red kerchief. He looked at the two women on the front porch of his new house and shook his head. "I don't care how many horses Jack can shoe in a day, Caitrin. After Sheena nearly lost her baby the other day, Jimmy's bound and determined to run him off."

"But he's living and working on *your* land," Caitrin said. "Jimmy has no right to tell Jack anything."

Seth's blue eyes flickered. "You better figure out where your loyalties lie, ma'am. Don't get me wrong now; I understand the feelings that can grow between a man and a woman. But you deserve better than Jack Cornwall. A lot better."

"How well do you know him, Seth?" Caitrin asked, her blood heating. "Only the other day Jack asked me if he must live with his past tied around his neck. Is he to be forever labeled a wicked man, with no chance to prove himself changed?"

"It's just like those tomatoes I canned last summer, Seth," Rosie put in. "I pasted the labels onto the jars with good strong glue—TOMATOES. But then I found those awful grubs in them, and they weren't fit to eat. Just the thought of it makes me sick."

"Now, Rosie," Seth warned. "Don't tie your stomach in knots again. We've had months of that."

"Anyhow," she went on. "I threw out the tomatoes—flat got rid of those nasty things. And with the strawberries beginning to leaf out, I've been doing a lot of thinking about strawberry jam. I'd sure like to put strawberry jam in the jars—but I can't get those labels off no matter how hard I scrub!"

"Aw, Rosie, these days you're always thinking about food."

"I am talking about Jack Cornwall," she snapped, her brown eyes dancing. "Everybody in this town has pasted a great big label on him that says BAD MAN, when maybe he's trying to toss out the nasty stuff and put good things inside. He needs a chance to write himself a new label."

"Maybe so," Seth said, tucking his kerchief into his back pocket. "But it doesn't really matter what I think of the fellow, good or bad. Sheena's opinion ought to be what counts the most with Caitrin. Sheena and Jimmy are her kinfolk. Jimmy holds Felicity Cornwall accountable for the troubles the other day, and I can hardly disagree with him."

"But she helped Sheena after she'd fallen," Caitrin said. "'Twas Felicity who brought the water that calmed my sister's cramps. 'Twas Felicity who examined her for the health of the baby."

"It was Felicity who went after Sheena with a poker in the first place," Seth countered.

"Will you order them to leave then?"

"I don't know what I'll do." He settled his hat on his head. "I've got sixty acres to plow, a trip to town to buy seed, a wife who's about to eat me out of house and home, and a son who ought to learn to read and cipher if I don't want him to grow up wild and ignorant. Folks are talking about the need for a schoolmarm come fall, and they've asked if I'd consider putting a school near the church. The church is built all the way up to the steeple, and people are turning to me to find a preacher. After what happened to Sheena, everybody wants me to try to talk a doctor into moving to town. We've got more people passing through Hope than we can feed and house. And I'm supposed to help Rolf and Jimmy repair one of the pontoons on the bridge."

"All that, Seth?" Rosie asked. "Why didn't you tell me?"

"I don't want to worry you, honey. Not in your condition." He gave his wife a crooked smile. When he turned to Caitrin, the tenderness vanished. "All I ever wanted to do when I moved to Kansas was be a farmer. But I'm spending half my time as the sheriff, mayor, innkeeper, and general fix-it man. Now you're asking me to be the town judge, too, Caitrin? Frankly, I don't know whether Jack Cornwall ought to be kicked out on his backside or not. And I don't much care, either."

"Saint Patrick's Day is tomorrow," Rosie called after her husband as he stalked away. "You gave the Cornwalls until then. Are you going to run them off?"

"Don't know!" he repeated. "Don't care!"

"What a grump." Rosie shook her head. "Come on, Caitrin, let's hurry this bread over to the mercantile. Ever since Seth found out I was expecting a baby, he's been storming around like a big old rain cloud. He's worried the grasshoppers will come back. He's fretting about what to plant. He's crazy to buy another cow, but he wants to keep back some savings. You'd think the whole world dangled by a thread from Seth Hunter's fingers . . . instead of being cradled in the almighty hands of the Creator himself."

"Seth only wants to be sure his family will be cared for," Caitrin said as they walked down the path toward the mercantile. "He wasn't able to provide for Chipper and . . . and his first wife . . ."

"Mary. You can say her name; I don't mind." Rosie adjusted her skirt over the small bulge of her belly. "I know Seth was married before, and I feel sure his worries stem from that. While Mary was pregnant, he was away at the war. Then she died, and he had done nothing for her or for Chipper either. But, for Pete's sake, Seth is not the same man he was back then. And *I'm* sure not a thing like Mary Cornwall. Our family can live on wormy potatoes if we have to. I'm the best around at making do on nothing." She paused a moment. "Did that sound like bragging?"

Caitrin laughed. "Of course not, silly. But I think Seth's mood has more to do with his fears than with his worries about what you'll all eat."

"What fears?"

"Mary *died*. Seth lost his first wife, Rosie. He can't rest easy at the memory of that, and he doesn't want it to happen again. The birth of your baby will be a dangerous time for you, and after that, too. Seth's mood is a measure of his great love for you. Sure I think the loss of you would do him in. Truly I do."

Rosie stopped outside the mercantile. "Worrying won't keep me alive, Caitie. But you know something? This town *does* need a good doctor. And a preacher, too. I might just have to pester Seth about that . . . if I can get rid of that rain cloud he's under."

Caitrin studied the three wagons rolling slowly over the bridge and mentally tallied the tolls they would bring in. Jack Cornwall emerged from the smithy across the street and cocked a hand over his eyes to watch the travelers approach.

"More customers, and this itching is just about to drive me crazy!" Rosie exclaimed, scratching her belly. "We sure could use a doctor with some good medicines and lotions on hand. You know what might put Seth into a better mood? Another party."

Caitrin groaned inwardly. "He's not that much on parties, is he? And we're just past that disastrous welcoming festival."

"I'm thinking about spring. We could have a party in April when everything's budding out. The family who lived just beyond the limestone wall of the orphanage used to have an egg hunt every spring. I always wished I could join in. Wouldn't that be fun, Caitie? We could color eggs, and the children could search for them. Maybe if the Cornwalls are still around, Lucy would be feeling well enough to help out."

Caitrin frowned as the three wagons drew nearer. It would be wonderful to include Lucy in the preparations for a party. She could just imagine the poor girl's eyes lighting up and a smile softening her pretty lips. But after the incident between Felicity and Sheena, the Cornwall camp had become as closed off as a fort. Felicity was rarely about, and Lucy hadn't been seen at all.

"We could cut cookies into the shape of bunnies," Rosie said. "And we could sprinkle them with sugar."

"Bunnies and eggs?" Caitrin regarded her friend for a moment. "Spring is for celebrating Easter and the risen Christ."

"Well, sure it is. But I've always wanted to have an egg hunt."

Caitrin slipped her arm over her friend's shoulders. "I think a good Easter sermon and a round of hymn singing would lift your husband's gloomy spirits more than colored eggs and bunny rabbits."

Coming out of her springtime daydreams, Rosie stiffened suddenly. "Look, Caitrin, it's Jack Cornwall. He's coming this way."

"Go on inside the mercantile and open up for the day," Caitrin said. "Leave him to me."

"I don't think I should. What if people see the two of you talking alone? You never know what Jimmy might do."

"Aye, but I'll not alter my ways for a man with a closed mind," she said, giving Rosie her bread basket and walking toward Jack. "What can I do for you this fine morning, Mr. Cornwall?"

He jerked a thumb at the wagons. "Looks like you've got customers, Miss Murphy. Morning, Mrs. Hunter."

"Hello, Mr. Cornwall," Rosie said, her voice wary. "We've not yet actually opened for business today. Is there something I might bring you from the mercantile before you head back to the smithy?"

"Well now, that's a kind offer, Mrs. Hunter." Jack paused before the women and took off his hat. "As a matter of fact, I do have a request. I was wondering if you had planned to attend the prayer meeting Rolf Rustemeyer has called for Sunday night."

"Me?" Rosie gaped for a moment. "Yes, of course, I am. Why wouldn't I? Rolf thinks we all ought to take time out to ask God for some rain. It's been so dry, and Seth sure is worried about the spring planting. I wouldn't think of missing that service."

"Good." He cleared his throat. "I know I'm asking a lot here, Mrs. Hunter, but would you be willing to accompany me to the service? I'd be much obliged to you."

Two pink spots suddenly popped out on Rosie's cheeks. "Thank you for your kind offer, Mr. Cornwall, but I'll be attending with my husband. I'm a married woman, you know."

Now it was Jack's turn to flush. "I . . . ah . . . I didn't mean it that way, ma'am. The fact that you're married is the very reason I'm asking you. I was needing a chaperone for the evening."

"A chaperone?" Rosie looked at Caitrin and understanding dawned. "Oh, a *chaperone*."

"I'd like to take Miss Murphy to the service," Jack said, "but I'll need someone to accompany us for the evening."

"All evening?"

"As long as need be, Mrs. Hunter. If you wouldn't mind."

Rosie pursed her lips. "This is dangerous business, Jack Cornwall. And I don't like the notion that my dearest friend could get dragged into any more trouble than she's already in. From the night I first saw the two of you together in the O'Tooles' barn, I knew Caitrin was playing with fire."

"Blazin' Jack Cornwall, that's me. But in case you hadn't noticed, your best friend is mighty fiery herself. She stood up to everyone on my behalf, and that ought to tell you something."

"It tells me you've got her bamboozled."

"I hope she's as bamboozled as you are with Seth Hunter." His smile was warm. "You're right to be concerned, Mrs. Hunter. At one time, I was rough on you and threatening to the man you loved. I was hard and mean and bullheaded. But there's something you ought to know. The good Lord put Caitrin Murphy and me together in the barn that night, and out of that meeting I became a changed man. I turned my back on my old ways, and ever since, I've been living just to love Jesus Christ. That's all I know to do, Mrs. Hunter. Just love him."

Rosie glanced at her friend. "I didn't realize."

"I may be a new man, but I'm still stubborn," Jack continued, "too stubborn to let go of the light Caitrin has been in my life. I won't walk away from Hope just because other people can't see me for what I am. I won't run from trouble. And I won't hide my head in a hole out of shame over my family. I love my sister and my mother both. I want to make a home for them here."

"Yes, Mr. Cornwall," Rosie said softly. "I understand you. I know what it means to need a home."

"Then will you help me?"

"How can I possibly do anything that would help your reputation in this town?"

"Folks admire you. They respect your husband. If you'll stand up beside me, maybe I can walk Caitrin into that prayer meeting and not get myself shot."

"Caitie?" Rosie asked. "Do you want this man to court you in public?"

"Aye. That I do, and very much."

"Well, then." Rosie squared her shoulders. "I'll be pleased to serve as your chaperone for the prayer meeting Sunday night."

Jack broke into a grin that rivaled the sunrise. "Thank you, Mrs. Hunter," he said, grabbing her hand and pumping it up and down. "Thank you very much. I'll pick you up Sunday evening, then, Caitrin."

"Sunday," Caitrin said.

As the three wagons came to a stop before the mercantile, Jack turned and strode back toward his smithy. Rosie let out a little groan. "Seth Hunter is going to have a fit over this one."

CHAPTER 15

"A CHAPERONE?" Sheena lay in bed, her hands folded over her middle, and stared at her younger sister. "Did Rosie really agree to that?"

"Aye," Caitrin said. "Jack Cornwall asked her, and she said she would."

"What do you suppose he wanted a chaperone for?"

Caitrin swallowed. Now was the moment she'd been praying about, yet she didn't feel a bit of peace. If her sister exploded in rage at the news, there was no telling what might result.

"Jack wants a chaperone," she said, "because he intends to start courting. He's planning to go to the prayer meeting with a woman."

"And I suppose that woman would be my own dear sister." Sheena took another sip of the rich broth Caitrin had brought her. "I'm not wrong, am I?"

"No," Caitrin said. "Jack has asked to court me."

"I don't know why he bothered asking permission. The man seems to do whatever he wants without noticing how others might feel about it. He certainly hasn't kept his distance from you."

"And why should he? I care for Jack, Sheena. He's built a fine smithy, and his work is valued in the community. He's hoping to put up a soddy soon. Jack wants to see to the welfare of his sister."

Sheena grunted. "Lunatic. The children are frightened of her, so they are. Lucy Cornwall ought to be locked up."

Caitrin folded her hands in her lap and sat in silence. How could she possibly respond to this irrational hatred? Could God be pleased that his people—the creation of his own hands—despised each other because of race or language or outlook? There were so many things that made people different from each other. Skin color, size, interests, fears, dreams. What made a short person better than a tall one? a white-skinned person better than a brown one? an Irishman better than a Cornishman?

Nothing. Caitrin knew God looked on the heart of each man, and by that, his standing was determined. There were so many things in Hope to take people's time and attention, yet they continued to focus on their petty differences. The only problem large enough to band the community together was the drought.

Caitrin wished it didn't have to take something so serious to turn the focus of Seth, Rolf, Jimmy, and most of the other townsfolk away from the traumatic incident between Sheena and Felicity. While not forgotten, it had been relegated to a back burner as everyone worked to fill barrels with creek water in preparation to irrigate the dry fields. St. Patrick's Day had come and gone, and the Cornwalls remained in their own small camp beside the creek.

Caitrin spoke with Jack briefly at least once a day when he brought tools to the mercantile to sell, but he had kept their conversation to a minimum. This was all right with Caitrin, for until this day she hadn't managed to work up the nerve to tell Sheena and Jimmy that Jack had asked to court her. Or that Rosie had agreed to chaperone.

"What does Seth say about Rosie's part in this grand scheme?" Sheena asked.

Caitrin lifted the broth bowl from her sister's hands. "I don't know yet, but I'm sure he won't mind. Seth has done his best to put the past behind him and see Jack as he really is."

"A Cornishman." Sheena clamped her lips shut as if that settled the matter.

"But he's more than that. Sure he's a good man."

"A demon. How could he be else with that wicked mother of his?"

"That day in the smithy, Mrs. Cornwall let her anger get the better of her, Sheena. As did you."

"I was provoked."

"I can't understand why it happened at all."

"Cornish. Don't even let your thoughts dwell on those people, Caitie, my love. They're Cornish, and that's all you need to know." Sheena winced. "Oh, my head. At times it throbs so I can hardly bear it."

Caitrin tucked in the edge of the quilt that covered her sister. Poor Sheena. When she moved about much, her head ached or the cramping in her belly started again. She was hardly able to do her chores, and she still had months to wait before the baby's birth. If she were forced to stay in bed all that time, the O'Toole household likely would fall to ruin.

"Papa said the Cornish are all wicked," Sheena said with a sigh. "And wicked is as wicked does."

Caitrin considered this for a moment. "But Jack Cornwall is a Christian man, Sheena. He told me so himself. How can you call him wicked?"

"He's Cornish!"

"Do people always come to you in great batches like pickles, Sheena? These are the dill pickles, and they all taste sour. These are the bread-and-butter pickles, and they all taste sweet. These are the pickled green beans, these are the pickled watermelon rinds, these are the pickled pigs' feet—"

"What are you talking about?"

"People!"

"But you said pickles."

"'Tis the same thing with you, so it is. These are the Cornish people, and they're all wicked schemers and liars. These are the Italians. These are the Germans. These are the lunatics. You've put them into separate pickle jars, and you won't let each person stand on his own."

"Why should I?"

"Because I happen to know that Jack Cornwall is a man with a God-given talent. He can create beautiful tools from iron. He's a loyal son and brother. He's special and unique because he's *himself*."

"Jack Cornwall knocked me down, so he did."

Caitrin let out a hot breath. "He was trying to protect you, Sheena. Will you deny it?"

"Jimmy's furious with him."

"That's because Jimmy puts everybody into pickle jars, too. Jack Cornwall is a wonderful human being. And for all you know, Lucy may be a very nice young lady."

"Ha."

"Even though Lucy is deeply troubled, Christ taught us that he loves all people, not just the ones who behave as we'd like. In fact, the wickedest sinners and the most anguished souls need Christ the greatest. But if we shun them—"

"There you go again, Caitie. You'd change the whole world if you could."

"Aye, and why not?"

"Will you defend Jack Cornwall and his family even though they've treated us so ill?" Sheena elbowed herself up in the bed. "You believe I don't like the man purely because he's Cornish. Well, he's done nothing to prove himself any better than the worst scum of that lot. I cannot understand why you've allowed yourself to be swayed by his sweet words and bold kisses. Sure I thought my own darling sister wiser than that. Jack Cornwall has tricked you, Caitie. He's nothing but a lying, bullying—"

"I won't hear this, Sheena."

"You will hear it, because someone has to talk truth to you." She paused. "Get the door, will you? It's one of the children. Tell them to run and play with Chipper."

Feeling hotter than the late-March afternoon would warrant, Caitrin marched to the door. "I don't believe people are pickles," she told her sister. "I think each person stands on his own, and each person should have the right to prove himself. Rosie said if you glue a label onto a jar of grubby tomatoes, you'll never be able to put strawberry jam into it."

"Wait a minute, I thought we were talking about pickles."

"We *are*, but . . ." Caitrin pulled open the door to the sight of Jack and Lucy Cornwall.

"Who is it?" Sheena called.

"Pickles," Caitrin said, ushering them inside. "Mr. Cornwall is here, and his sister Lucy. It looks as though they've brought a gift."

"It's cinnamon buns," Lucy said. She was holding a basket with her unchained hands, and her hair had been brushed into a rough knot at the nape of her neck. "I made them for you, Mrs. O'Toole. Jack told me you weren't well, and he helped me last night with the dough. I . . . I hope you'll like them."

Caitrin met Jack's eyes as Lucy walked shyly toward the bed. He shrugged. "Lucy's had three good days in a row," he said. "Matter of fact, she's been looking after Mama a fair bit."

"I'm happy to hear it." Caitrin was delighted to see the young woman calmly set the basket on the bed and then take the stool beside Sheena. She wore the blue dress Caitrin had given her, its hem now dusty and its sleeves frayed. But she looked lovely all the same.

"Mama tells me if I'll just stop thinking about myself all the time," Lucy said softly to Sheena, "I'll get better. I'm not sure she's right, Mrs. O'Toole. It's others who fill my thoughts, memories and worries going around . . . and around. And . . . and . . . all Mama and Jack could talk about was you and . . . and your baby . . ."

Lucy shuddered and fell silent. Caitrin glanced at Jack. He started toward his sister. At that moment Lucy spoke again.

"I . . . I just thought if I could help you out, Mrs. O'Toole," she said. "I might feel better . . . and you might, too."

Sheena stared at the young woman beside her. "You baked cinnamon buns for me?"

Lucy nodded. "Jack helped."

"Not much," he put in.

"And then I got to thinking," Lucy said, "if you need some . . . some washing done, I can do that. And I'm good with a broom."

"Glory be," Sheena murmured. She sat in silence so long, Caitrin began to think she'd gone into shock. Finally a look of resignation crept over her face. "Well, there's the broom then, girl. See what you can do with it."

Lucy leapt to her feet and grabbed the broom propped against the wall. "Do eat one of those buns, Mrs. O'Toole. I used extra cinnamon."

While Lucy swept the rough dirt floor, Caitrin took her place on the stool and divided one of the sticky buns with her sister. One hand jammed in his pocket, Jack accepted another bun. All three watched, mesmerized, chewing slowly as Lucy worked her way around the soddy brushing up a pile that included bread crusts, potato peelings, ashes, and wood chips.

"Sure has been dry lately," Jack said. "This drought is about to get the best of everybody. Didn't have much snow, and we could use some rain."

Sheena looked startled, as if she hadn't expected the man to speak in normal human tones. "Aye," she commented. "Jimmy says this is the driest spring he can remember."

"Dry, dry, dry," Jack said. "And not a cloud in the sky."

"Have we had a rain yet this year?"

"Not a drop."

Caitrin sank her teeth into a cinnamon bun. It wasn't much of a conversation, but at least they were talking. She wouldn't have interrupted if she'd been paid.

"Bluestem Creek is running mighty low," Jack said.

"Jimmy heard someone saying the Kansas River itself is down," Sheena added.

"Sure is hard for the boats to get through when the water is low like that."

"Aye. I expect we'll have showers in April."

"Hope so. I sure do." Jack licked a dollop of cinnamon goo off his thumb. "I'm not a farmer, but I know the rain keeps folks around here going. I'd hate to see anyone go belly-up."

"Thank heaven for the bridge tolls. They saved us last year after the grasshoppers passed through, so they did."

"Well, I'm finished with that job," Lucy said, coming back into the soddy after tossing out the rubbish she'd swept. "Would you like me to wash those dishes for you, Mrs. O'Toole?"

Caitrin watched a smile form on her sister's lips—a warm smile, a smile reserved for people Sheena favored. She smoothed a hand across the quilt. "Not today, but thank you kindly, my dear," she said. "Perhaps . . . perhaps you'll pop round and visit me another time?"

Lucy beamed. "Yes."

"Would you be willing to bake some of your cinnamon buns for us to sell in the mercantile, Lucy?" Caitrin asked. "I haven't had time to start up the restaurant, but more and more people are stopping to take their meals at the mercantile. 'Tis the fresh-baked bread and Sheena's pickles that draw them. But I know they'd adore your cinnamon buns. You could have all the money you earned from them."

"Really?" Her gray eyes lit up. "Oh, Jack, I . . . I . . ."

"Sure, Lucy. You could do that." He squared his shoulders. "And about that spit, Mrs. O'Toole. I made you a new one. We hope you'll accept it as a gift."

He stepped outside and reentered carrying a heavy spit rod with a sharpened skewer bolted near one end. He laid it across the hooks over Sheena's cooking fire and gave the handle a turn. The shiny metal glistened as it spun, and Caitrin could all but hear the sizzle of meat.

"Thank you, Mr. Cornwall," Sheena said in a low voice. "'Twas good of you."

"You're welcome, ma'am." He straightened and took his sister's hand. "We'll be going now."

"Good-bye," Lucy called as he led her out of the soddy. "Good-bye, Mrs. O'Toole."

The door shut behind them, and Caitrin felt her shoulders sag with relief. Sheena picked up another cinnamon bun. "These are quite tasty," she said. "Lucy should do well with them at the mercantile."

"She's a sweet girl."

"I suppose so." Sheena licked her lips. "Of course, you and I both know they did all that just to soften my heart so that Jack Cornwall could court you."

"Lucy said she was worried about your baby."

"So she did. I don't suppose she has the wits about her to lie."

"I believe she does care about your welfare."

"And he hopes to court you."

"He does, Sheena. I've said I'll go with him to the prayer meeting."

Sheena stopped chewing. "Caitie, my love. You mustn't go out in public with the Cornish."

"Pickles, Sheena," Caitrin said.

"At least take Jimmy with you."

"Jimmy needs to look out for you. Rosie will act as chaperone, and that means Seth will join us."

"Honestly, Caitrin—"

"I might just wear my green dress for Jack Cornwall."

"Oh, Caitie!"

"Pickles, Sheena," Caitrin warned again.

"I don't care if he did make me a new spit," she cried. "That man is a dill if ever there was one!"

"We could color the eggs, Seth," Rosie was saying as Caitrin stepped out of her soddy into the evening. "Oh, hello, Caitie! We could paint them blue, pink, green, yellow—"

"Green eggs?" Seth asked. "Evening, Miss Murphy."

Caitrin walked toward Jack, who stood to the side, his hat in his hand. Glory be, but the man was a vision. Black coat, white shirt, a string tie at his neck, denim jeans, and a pair of boots . . . he wore clothing no more elegant than Seth's hand-sewn jacket, but a thrill ran up Caitrin's spine at the sight of him.

"Miss Murphy," he said. Thick and soft, his brown hair tumbled over his forehead as he gave her a little bow. "Good evening. You look lovely tonight."

Flushing with delight, Caitrin shook out the folds of her deep green skirt. "Papa bought this fabric for my sixteenth birthday, and Mama stitched it into a gown. This dress takes me all the way to the emerald sod of Ireland, so it does."

"What would it take to bring you back to the dry prairie of Kansas?" Jack asked, taking her hand and slipping it around the curve of his arm. As they followed Rosie and Seth down the narrow path toward the traveling camp, he whispered against her ear, "Would this do it?"

Bending over, he brushed a kiss on her cheek.

"Aye," Caitrin said, breathless. "I do believe I'm back."

"And cookies in the shape of rabbits," Rosie continued. "We could sprinkle sugar on top."

"I never have been crazy about rabbits," Seth mused. "If they get into your garden, that's the end of the lettuce, the beans, the carrots—you name it."

"I'm talking about rabbit *cookies*," Rosie protested. "It's for the spring celebration. Each child could eat a cookie after the hunt for the colored eggs."

"Green eggs," Seth repeated, his voice less than buoyant. "Somehow that doesn't sound too appetizing to me."

"Just the shells would be green, silly. Hard-boiled eggs with colored shells. Have you been listening to me at all, Seth Hunter?"

"Well—" he scratched the back of his neck—"I got sidetracked back when you started talking about those confounded rabbits."

Caitrin could hardly believe she was actually going to the prayer meeting with Jack Cornwall. Rosie had said she'd been all but tongue-tied when she started to speak to Seth about the notion of chaperoning. As it turned out, Seth already had made up his mind to see if he could get the Cornwalls over to the meeting. He thought a time of united prayer with the rest of the townsfolk might heal some of the trouble.

When Seth permitted Chipper to spend the evening with his Gram at the Cornwalls' camp down on Bluestem Creek, Caitrin all but smelled victory. God had somehow begun to heal some of the terrible rifts among the people in the little town. It was a miracle! Lucy was feeling well enough again to bake cinnamon buns. Sheena had not lost her baby after all, and she genuinely appreciated Lucy's offer of help. Chipper finally had been allowed to spend time with his beloved grandmother. And Seth had agreed to this outing with Jack. Caitrin's heart fairly sang.

"Tonight I'm going to ask Seth for permission to build a soddy," Jack told Caitrin in a low voice as they followed the Hunters. "I'll put it up next to the smithy. That way I'll be near Lucy in case she needs me."

"I think he'll agree to it."

"Mama's not keen on the idea. Ever since the trouble with Mrs. O'Toole, she won't even set foot outside our camp."

"I noticed she hadn't been up to the mercantile."

"She blames herself for the near loss of that baby, but she's turned her anger outward. Says everyone in Hope is dead set against us. Lucy bears the brunt of her temper, but I take my fair share, too. Mama's still talking to me about leaving."

"But you've just put up the forge."

"She doesn't feel welcome here. She reckons folks treat her worse than an old stray dog."

Caitrin could see the prayer meeting area clearly now. A wagon had been pulled over near the creek, and lanterns were hung on strings stretched from one tree to another. People were already gathering in the shadows. She knew her conversation with Jack would have to end in moments, and she could hardly bear it. This was the first time they'd been able to talk freely, man to woman, and with hardly a spark of tension between them.

"I don't like to think of you going away," she said. "I've been praying for the troubles here to end, but my thoughts keep turning to that dreadful Bill Hermann and his quest to take you back to the trial in Missouri."

Jack shook his head. "I won't go."

"How can you avoid it if he brings a subpoena?"

"There's nothing to pin on me." He slowed his steps. "Listen, Caitrin, don't tell folks about Bill Hermann and the Easton lynching, OK? That's my business."

"All right, Jack. Whatever you say."

They had stopped walking, and he was looking at her with those depthless gray eyes. She could hardly breathe as she gazed up at the man. The breeze toyed with the ends of his black string tie and feathered his thick hair. Lantern light gilded his high cheekbones. Moonlight silvered the bridge of his nose. Standing so close she could feel the heat of the forge still radiating from his skin, Caitrin prayed she would have the grace to behave like a lady this night.

The strongest urge poured through her veins to grab Jack's hand and race across the prairie grass until they came to a place that was completely free of strife. Completely silent. Completely alone. And there she would speak to him her every thought, listen to the music of his deep voice, and dance with him unattended by any but the cleansing wind and the presence of God himself.

"Do you want me to build a soddy here, Caitrin?" he asked, lifting a hand to her hair. "I'm asking you again. Do you want me to stay in Hope?"

She pressed her lips against his sleeve. "Aye," she said. "I do."

"I've always spoken what's on my mind, Caitrin. You've known that from the start."

"'Tis one reason I care for you as I do."

"Well, here's what I've been thinking. If I can get that soddy built, and if Lucy keeps on feeling good, and if the O'Tooles can come around to accepting us, and if Seth—"

"Are you two coming?" Rosie called. Turned sideways against the light, her silhouette clearly revealed the swell of the child within her. "Caitie, will you please explain to Seth about this spring party we're going to put on? He hasn't heard a word I've said past green eggs and rabbits. Oh, look at the crowd around the wagon! Is Rolf going to do all the preaching? I hope he's been practicing on some new subjects. I've about had my fill of *veeds*."

"Sure he was speaking the word of the Lord that Sunday, Rosie." Caitrin walked beside Jack toward the wagon. "'Twas a message we all needed to hear."

"The weeds have grown up mighty high in town," Jack said. "Let's hope they don't try to choke us tonight."

"We'll be all right." The tension in Seth's voice belied his words. "You said Sheena's aware of this arrangement, didn't you, Miss Murphy?"

Caitrin nodded. "I've told my sister, but I'm not sure Jimmy knows."

"The Lord wants us to place ourselves in his trustworthy hands and rely on him for whatever lies ahead," Jack said. "The purpose of this meeting is to pray for rain, and I suspect Jimmy will honor that."

"Look, the O'Tooles are coming across the bridge, Caitie," Rosie said. "Is Sheena fit enough to walk?"

"A bit." Caitrin slipped her hand through the crook of Jack's arm again. "Jimmy's helping her. I don't think he's seen us."

The two couples spread a quilt near the brightly lit wagon. The crowd began to quiet, individuals taking their places on blankets and wooden chairs as Rolf Rustemeyer climbed up onto a platform erected on the wagon's bed. For a moment the big blond German didn't speak, instead holding up a Bible before the congregation.

"This is Word of Gott!" he cried out suddenly.

The crowd gasped.

"Gott says where two or three manners comen togedder in his name," Rolf continued, "there he is among them! Now, how many comen togedder tonight? Fifteen? Twenty? *Ja*, Gott is here tonight vit us!"

Jack gave a grunt as he sat down. "I reckon we might ought to hire ol' Rustemeyer for the preacher's job."

Seth and Rosie joined them as they settled on the quilt. "Rolf is a farmer," Rosie said. "He'll never be a preacher, but he certainly loves the Lord."

"Now is springtime," Rolf went on. "Gott gif us goot dirt, goot seed, goot plow, goot mule."

"And lots of *veeds*," Rosie murmured.

Caitrin tried to suppress a giggle. Relaxing a little, she realized this might turn out all right after all. Though she could see the O'Toole family seating themselves not far from their own party, they had given no evidence of the hostility everyone feared.

"Now need only one thing from Gott," Rolf said. "Vater!"

"*Vater*," Rosie whispered and nudged Caitrin, who bit her lip to keep from laughing out loud. She felt like a schoolgirl, silly and lighthearted for the first time in many months. Here she was with a handsome beau, a precious friend, and a wonderful town in which to live. God was indeed here among them, and rather than giggling at dear Rolf, who was doing his best, she ought to start singing the Lord's praises.

Rolf held the Bible high. "Time to pray for rain. Gott listen to us pray. Everybody pray for vater to come."

"That reminds me," Rosie whispered, turning to Jack. "There was a fellow in the mercantile this morning asking if I could sell him a new water canteen. He said he'd been on the road for months and was headed back to Missouri without laying eyes on what he'd been after. When he told me he'd been looking all over Kansas for *you*, I could hardly believe it! I said, glory be, Jack Cornwall works right across the street in the town smithy. You should have seen his face."

The muscle in Jack's arm went as rigid as steel. "Did you get the man's name?"

"Herman somebody," Rosie said. Then she frowned. "No, that wasn't quite it."

"Bill Hermann," Jack said.

"That's it! But instead of stopping by the smithy, he took off right away on his horse, headed for Topeka. Bill Hermann is an old friend of yours, isn't he?"

Jack swallowed. "You might say that," he said. "Or you might not."

CHAPTER 16

JACK felt his blood boil up inside his chest. So Bill Hermann had found him. No doubt the snake was now on his way to Topeka to fetch the law. By now he probably held papers of some kind, a warrant or a subpoena ordering Jack Cornwall back to Missouri to testify in the trial of his former gang members accused in the Easton lynching. The only way he could testify was to swear he was at the cabin the night of the murder—and implicate himself in the crime.

"Are you all right, Jack?" Caitrin asked.

He studied the fiery tumble of her hair and the sincere concern in her green eyes. "I'm not leaving," he said. "I told you I'd stay here, and I'm a man of my word."

"Can Bill Hermann make you go?"

"*Nothing* can make me go."

Jack felt like a wild dog on a chain. The links in the chain that bridled him—his newfound walk in Christ, his desire to make a peaceful life, his growing bond with Caitrin, his responsibility to Lucy and his mother—were strained to the limit. Could such a chain hold against the forces that pulled at him?

Jack clenched a fist. He'd like nothing better than to knock Bill Hermann's teeth right out the back side of his head. And as for the other members of the bunch, well, they could rot in prison for all he cared. All their idealistic talk about keeping the peace, bringing vigilante justice, and restoring the glory of the South hadn't done any of them a lick of good. In fact, they had all walked on the wrong side of the law about as often as their Yankee enemies.

It had been the most futile, empty time in Jack's life, and he was thankful it had ended without too much bloodshed and loss of life. Now he had given all he had to Christ, turned his back on the past, and was doing his best to be pure and blameless. He was done with the men he'd once called friends. They'd better not try to drag him back into their midst. He knew it was right to turn the other cheek, but he found living peaceably the hardest thing about being a Christian. If his old pals tried to pull him into their troubles, he had a bad feeling he'd jump right into the middle of them and make them remember why they'd valued his fists and gun.

"Now manners and ladies," Rolf was saying, "who vill start the praying? Somebody comen up here onto vagon and pray, *ja?*"

The crowd murmured, and someone called out, "You pray, Rustemeyer. This meetin' was your idea."

"OK, I am starting, but I not practice this part so much," Rolf said. He bowed his shaggy blond head. "Dear Gott, for goot land and goot peoples here, I say tank you. I say alleluia. For Jesus Christ love us and gif his life on cross for us, I say tank you. My heart is full to top vit happy for all you gif us, dear Gott. But one thing needed only, and that is rain. Please send rain here to Kansas so crops can grow. In name of Jesus, I pray this. Amen."

When Jack lifted his head, he saw that Seth was already climbing onto the wagon. "Dear God," the gentle farmer prayed, "you've given us so much, it seems a little prideful of us to come begging for more. I want to praise your name for the gift of my family. Little Chipper and the new baby we're expecting are precious to me. And Rosie . . ." Seth was silent a moment. When he spoke again, his voice was strained with emotion. "Lord, I thank you for my wife. Thank you for Rosie."

Jack swallowed and took Caitrin's hand. In the past, he hadn't given marriage much consideration, but the beautiful Irishwoman sure managed to slip into his thoughts about two hundred times a day. Jack knew he didn't have the right to a happy home, as many times as he and the bunch had stepped in and messed up the peace of others. But if the good Lord ever saw fit to forgive him enough to let him marry, Jack would do everything in his power to honor and respect his wife.

"Lord," Seth went on once he'd composed himself, "I sure don't like to think about anything bad happening to Rosie and our young'uns. So right here and now, I'm stepping up to ask you for rain. We need it bad, and we're counting on you to send it. Amen."

Seth moved to the side of the stage as Jimmy O'Toole stepped up onto the wagon. Jack had never thought of Jimmy as a religious man. The Irishman had resisted any plan to build the new church on his land, and he often was absent from the worship services held each Sunday morning in the mercantile. His green eyes sparkled as he took his place at the front of the stage. When he began to speak, his voice was filled with passion.

"I've not come up here to pray for rain," he said, "because I think rain has more to do with clouds and wind than with the Almighty. If he wants rain to fall, sure there's naught we can do to stop it. And if there's goin' to be a drought, well then, all the prayin' in the world won't change that. But there is a matter we can change, and that's the presence of troublemakers among us."

"Jimmy," Seth called in a clearly audible whisper, "we're here to pray."

"I'll not stand about prayin' when my own wife and family are in danger from the Cornish ne'er-do-wells who've invaded our peace."

Jack took a deep breath and tried to calm himself as every eye in the gathering focused on him. Beside him, Caitrin went as still and cold as a stone. Rosie began fanning herself with a handkerchief.

"I say we run the vermin out of town!" Jimmy cried out. "The woman of the Cornwall family abused my wife and nearly robbed me of my own unborn child. She's a witch, so she is, a Cornish witch. She conked our Sheena in the head with a poker, and her son—right over there—threw the poor woman to the ground. Sure the Cornwalls would have killed Sheena if they could!"

"Jimmy." Seth took a step toward the Irishman and laid a hand on his arm. "I said, this is a time for prayer. We'll handle the matter of the Cornwalls later on."

"Nay, we'll handle it now! I won't stand for another day of livin' in the same town with them Cornish devils. You've seen the daughter yourself, Seth, and she's a madwoman sure as I live and breathe. She's tried to drown herself in the creek, and she threw herself in front of the stagecoach. She's a danger, a blazin' danger, I say!"

Caitrin squeezed Jack's hand. "I'm so sorry," she whispered. "I had no idea Jimmy would do something like this."

"He'd better stop talking about Lucy," he growled, the blood racing in his veins. "I don't like it."

"That Cornish madwoman is going to hurt one of us," Jimmy continued, heedless of Seth's attempts to move him from the stage. "She's got a demon in her, so she does."

"That's enough, O'Toole!" Jack shouted, coming to his feet. "Get off the wagon before I throw you off."

"No, Jack," Caitrin croaked, tears squeezing from her eyes. "Please calm yourself!"

"I'll not get off the wagon until I've had my say, Cornish!" Jimmy cried. "'Tis you I'm talkin' about. 'Tis your mother has tried to kill our Sheena. 'Twas you yourself who knocked her to the ground and near cast the child from her belly. Now look at you there with our Caitrin!"

Jack glared as the man's face grew red. The crowd's murmuring intensified, and their rumblings of discontent filled the night air.

All around him, people were staring and muttering snatches of affirmation for Jimmy O'Toole's tirade. Jack didn't care if this was a prayer meeting and God himself stood among them, he wouldn't tolerate anyone talking poorly of his family. Felicity Cornwall was his mother, and Lucy was his sister . . . and he'd fight to the death before he'd let harm come to either of them.

"You've bewitched our Caitrin," the Irishman growled, "and now you're tryin' to work your evil on Seth and Rosie Hunter." He faced the crowd. "Let me tell you people about the Cornish. They're liars and cheaters and thieves, all of 'em. You saw how Jack Cornwall tried to steal Chipper right away from his own papa, didn't you?"

"Hold on, there, O'Toole!" Jack shouted, unable to contain his growing fury. "Get off the wagon!"

"Nay, I'll speak my mind to these good folk. Jack Cornwall frightened the ladies and smashed our parties into smithereens! He stole Seth's rifle right off his wall. He trespassed on my land, fed my good oats to his devil of a black horse, slept in my barn, and wooed my own wife's sister for his evil purposes."

"You leave Caitrin out of this!" Jack said, pulling away from her and heading for the wagon. "I've never done a thing to hurt that woman."

"Harmin' women is his favorite pastime," Jimmy told the crowd. "You can see my poor *donsie* wife there with her head in a bandage and her feet barely able to walk from the injuries of that Cornishman, can't you? And there's no tellin' what wickedness the man has done to his own sister. You've seen the lunatic driftin' in the creek in the middle of winter, tryin' to end her own life. You've seen her shriekin' and carryin' on at the dance when Rustemeyer kindly offered her a piece o' cake, haven't you? Aye, you've seen the demon that lives with her, and his name is Jack Cornwall!"

"Stop slandering my sister!" Jack roared, leaping up onto the stage. So much for peace and purity. He grabbed Jimmy O'Toole by the collar, took hold of the backside of his britches, gave a big heave-ho, and tossed the Irishman off the wagon.

The crowd's shock turned quickly to fury. With a howl of rage, men stormed onto the platform. The first one landed Jack a glancing blow to the jaw. The second hit him square in the stomach.

Anger poured through Jack's veins. With the strength of every muscle that had ever forged iron, he threw himself into the fray. Though he could hear Seth shouting at him to run, he slammed a fellow straight in the nose and felt the crunch of snapping cartilage. He knocked another man clear across the stage. He caught one attacker on the cheekbone, and he drove a fist into another's gut.

Somebody smashed a heavy black Bible over Jack's head. The world swam for a moment as his legs buckled. Another fellow rammed his fist into Jack's eye. Yet another man's chop to the stomach knocked him to his knees.

Coughing and spitting out blood, Jack lunged upward again, throwing a forearm into an assailant's chest and knocking him flat. Maybe he was a goner, Jack thought, but he wouldn't go down easy. Screams and shouts rang in his ears as he fought his way across the platform. He elbowed somebody out of his way and dodged a fist directed at his nose. A man shoved him from behind. He stumbled forward as a gun went off.

Searing, blinding pain tore into the back of his leg. He tumbled to the ground. A blow landed on his jaw, another on his temple. Someone kicked him in the stomach. He gasped twice, unable to breathe. And this time, the stars went out.

"Let me go, Rosie!" Caitrin cried, trying to pull out of the woman's grasp. "Sure they'll tear Jack to bits!"

"You can't go over there, Caitrin!" Rosie said. "Look, here's Seth."

Her husband raced up to the women, took them by the arms, and hauled them away from the meeting ground. "Come on, you two, let's get out of here."

"But I heard a gun, Seth." Caitrin strained toward the wagon. "I'm sure I did! What if Jack needs help? He's in terrible trouble!"

"Jack Cornwall makes his own trouble."

"This wasn't his fault! Jimmy provoked him." Caitrin struggled as Seth dragged her and Rosie up the road toward the mercantile. *Oh, God, dear God! Please help Jack! Help me! Help us all.*

"Look, there's Mrs. Cornwall coming out of one of the Cornwall tents!" Rosie said. "Seth, you must tell her what's happened."

"She shouldn't get messed up in that craziness," Seth barked. "She's liable to get herself killed."

"Mrs. Cornwall!" Caitrin cried, heedless of Seth's admonition.

"Miss Murphy?" she responded. "That was a short prayer meeting. I was just fetching Chipper a blanket from the other tent."

"Oh, Mrs. Cornwall, you must go after Jack," Caitrin said. "There's been a terrible fight. Sure we've heard a gunshot."

"Gunshot!" Felicity glanced in the direction of the wagon and wrung her hands. "But I can't leave Chipper. And then there's Lucy! She's not doing well tonight. All day she's been dwelling on those Yankee soldiers and . . . and the things they did to her. She's troubled. Very troubled. I thought I might even need to fetch Jack back from the prayer meeting. Oh, heaven, what have those wicked O'Tooles done to my son? I told him I wouldn't have him marrying into that family, no matter how much he thinks he loves you. Now they've shot my boy, and I can't leave Lucy at a time like this!"

Breathing hard, Caitrin stared at Felicity Cornwall. What was the woman saying? Yankee soldiers had harmed Lucy . . . and Jack loved Caitrin . . .

"Papa! Mama!" Chipper dashed out of one of the Cornwalls' tents and threw his arms around Rosie's skirt. "Aunt Lucy's scrubbin' herself raw in there!"

"Goodness gracious," Rosie said, kneeling and tucking the child into a warm hug. "How about if we head home and find you an oatmeal cookie and some fresh milk? Then you can tell your mama all about it, sweetie."

"You'd better stay here with Lucy," Seth told Mrs. Cornwall. "I'm going to take Miss Murphy to her house, and then I'll make sure my wife and son get home safe. If I know Rolf Rustemeyer at all, he'll be trying to settle the crowd and help out your son. Maybe by the time I get back to the wagon things will have calmed down enough that we can pull Jack away without getting ourselves killed in the process."

"Yes, Mr. Hunter," Felicity said. "Please help us!"

"What about Lucy?" Caitrin called, as Seth tugged her down the road toward her soddy. "Can I do anything?"

"She's scrubbing herself, Miss Murphy," Felicity answered, staring ahead hopelessly. "She gets to scrubbing sometimes . . . uses sandpaper and a horsehair brush . . . and nearly takes her own skin off."

"Dear God!" Caitrin whispered. "Help us all!"

Caitrin was on her knees beside her bed when a knock fell on the door. Her heart contracted, and she squeezed her hands together. *Please, Father, let Jack be all right! Oh Lord, bring something good out of this terrible mess! Give us some reason to hope!*

"Caitrin Murphy? You in there?"

It was Jimmy O'Toole.

"I'm here," she said. "Just a moment."

She stood and hurried to the soddy door. After lifting the bar, she threw open the door on its leather hinges. Her brother-in-law stood outside as a huddled, blanket-shrouded figure cowered behind him.

"Is that Jack?" she whispered.

"Nay," Jimmy said. "Your not-so-secret beau is over at the mercantile getting the lead cut out of his leg by Seth Hunter. This here's your sister, who's so beside herself I daren't take her home to the *brablins*. Sheena's been weepin' like a blasted fountain, and I can't make her talk to me. Take her, if you will, Caitrin. She's mortal scared, so she is, and I know you'll have the words to comfort her."

"Sheena!" Caitrin clasped the woman in her arms and led her to a chair. "Are you all right? Is your baby well?"

The blanket fell back, and Sheena looked up, her great green eyes swimming with tears. Her red hair was topsy-turvy on her head, and her apron had fallen right off her dress. She sniffled and hugged herself around the middle.

"Sure I'm well enough," she whispered. "But I can't stay here. I need to look after the wee ones."

"Nay, you won't," Jimmy barked. "You'll stay here with your sister until I've settled them into bed and all of us have had a good night's sleep."

"Oh, Jimmy, let Sheena go home," Caitrin said.

"And frighten the *brablins* with her weepin'?" Jimmy shook his head. "If there ever was a man put upon, 'tis me, I'll tell you that much. Them Cornish is the root of all the trouble. My poor Sheena's laid up thanks to that devil woman, Felicity Cornwall. And now we've had a row the size of which would flatten Topeka. Men runnin' this way and that. Ladies shriekin'. Cornwall himself is shot, and several others has lost teeth, broke noses, and got their jaws knocked outta joint. Leave it to a Cornishman to start up a fray like that one."

"Jack didn't start the trouble—"

"I ain't finished yet," Jimmy said, taking a step toward Caitrin. "I was on my way over to your soddy with my poor wife there, when who should come runnin' out of the Cornwall camp but that lunatic lass. She was naked as a frog and all scratched up and bleedin'. And after her came her own mother, chasin' her across the prairie. Now, I don't know what to make of *that*, Caitrin, but what they're both of them mad as hatters."

"I can explain, Jimmy."

"You'll explain it to the fairies, so you will. I'll not listen to your bold tongue nor be swayed by your stubborn ways. I'm not like Sheena, ready to overlook the sins of a blood relative. Sure *you*, Caitrin Murphy, have caused every bit as much trouble as them Cornish!"

"I have not!"

"Aye, you have. All I wanted in comin' to this land was a bit o' peace and quiet. I built my soddy and plowed my fields. I planned to take care of my *brablins* and my wee wife and give us all a good life. But glory be, now we've a mercantile and a post office and a church and a smithy and a confounded prayer meetin'. We've lunatics and lechers and poker-wieldin' grannies about. We've more people crossin' that blasted bridge in one day than I ever wanted to see in a lifetime. And you, my dear lass, have been nearly the death of your own sister—consortin' with Cornishmen and takin' lunatics into your own home. Well, I'll tell you this. I've had enough of it, so I have. I'm tellin' you now, as I've already told Sheena—you're goin' back to Ireland, lassie. The first stagecoach east tomorrow, you're on it. And good riddance to bad rummage."

Caitrin clenched her jaw, willing herself not to erupt. *Please, God give me the strength, the patience, the courage . . .*

"Out!" she shouted, her faith utterly failing her. "Get out of my soddy, Jimmy O'Toole, and don't come back until you've had the good grace to apologize."

"When hell freezes over," he snarled. "Until then, I'll leave you to look after my wife as a good sister should. 'Tis high time you chose whose family you belong to—us or the Cornwalls. And if you decide to join the dregs, Caitrin Murphy, that's exactly what you'll be."

Hair flaming red in the lamplight, Jimmy turned and stomped out of the soddy. He slammed the door behind him. One of the leather hinges snapped loose from the frame. The door swayed, tipped, and crashed to the ground in a pile of loose boards.

"I want to go home," Sheena said in a wavering voice.

Caitrin swung around to find her sister pulling her blanket up around her shoulders and standing to leave. "Wait," Caitrin said, holding out a hand. "Please don't mind Jimmy. He's worried about you, and he's hot about the Cornish. I've been praying for God to soften his heart, and praying that I can rein my tongue. But so far, I fear we've both a bit more surrendering to do."

A tear trickled from one of Sheena's green eyes. "Jimmy frightened me tonight, Caitie. I've never seen him so angry. Sure he wasn't himself."

"Nay." Caitrin strode across the room and grasped her sister's hands. "Oh, Sheena, I never meant such trouble to come to Hope. My heart is bursting in two. How can I choose between my dear family and the man I love? You and Jimmy are all I have, so you are. I'll love you always. But Jack Cornwall . . . dear Sheena, he's a man like none other I've known."

"My poor Caitie." Sheena rubbed a hand under her damp eyes. "I . . . I don't know what to say."

"Say you'll stay with me this night. Sure you've had a rough time of it, and you can use the rest. We'll hang a blanket over the door."

"Jimmy's furious with me, Caitie! After the fighting settled, I told him he was wrong to speak out against the Cornish at the town prayer meeting. I shouldn't have gone against him. I should have . . . should have honored my husband." Sheena bent over sobbing. "I don't know what to do. I can't go on like this!"

"There now," Caitrin said softly, placing an arm around the woman's heaving shoulders. "A good cry is just the thing. I'm ready to join you myself, so I am. Never have I known such flames of hatred and fear and confusion in my life."

"Oh, Caitie, don't let's sit here and weep. Put the kettle on and make us a pot of tea."

Caitrin sniffled. "Aye, warm milk and a sugar will turn it that lovely caramel color and settle our nerves. As our dear mother used to say, there's nothing like a cup of hot tea for comfort."

Trembling, she headed for the fire. She had prepared the kettle earlier, hoping the two couples would take a moment after the prayer meeting to sit together and visit. How wonderful everything had seemed then. She had held great hopes that Seth and Jack would speak comfortably with each other, and then perhaps they could grow as true friends.

Was Jack all right? What if the bullet in his leg had done some terrible damage? Caitrin hung the kettle on the hook and stirred the fire. She couldn't leave Sheena alone to go and check on Jack. What if her sister's cramping started up again? But how could Caitrin bear to spend the night not knowing how Jack was? She ached to be near him, to hold and comfort him. And then there was Lucy . . .

The girl herself ran through the open doorway and into Caitrin's soddy. "I can't . . . I'm . . . I . . ."

"Lucy!" Felicity Cornwall was right behind her. "You'll be the death of me, girl!"

Caitrin gaped at the young woman. Lucy's flesh was raw and bleeding, and her hair hung in shaggy clumps. Coming to her senses, Caitrin grabbed a quilt from the bed and threw it over Lucy's shoulders. The girl shuddered and collapsed in a heap.

"Lucy!" Caitrin crouched beside her. "Lucy, 'tis Caitrin Murphy here. I'm going to hold you now. You'll be all right."

As she pulled the shivering woman into her arms, Felicity stood panting. "She was scrubbing herself with sandpaper, like I said," she told Caitrin between breaths, "and then she jumped up and ran off. I've been chasing her across the prairie for I don't know how long. She's right out of her head tonight. I never saw the poor child so bad!"

At that, Felicity sank down onto a stool and burst into tears.

"Now just calm down, Mrs. Cornwall." Caitrin tucked Lucy into the cradle of her lap, praying that God would settle the raving madness inside the young woman. "Lucy's going to be all right. She can stay here with me tonight. Sheena and I are just ready to have tea, and we'll welcome Lucy to join us."

Felicity glanced over at the chair where the Irishwoman sat. "Mrs. O'Toole," she said, and then she sobbed helplessly for a moment. "I'm so sorry! So . . . so sorry. I didn't mean to harm you that day, and . . . and your baby . . ."

"Nay, Mrs. Cornwall," Sheena whispered, blotting her own eyes. "'Twas I who came at you . . ."

"I struck you."

"I called you such vile things."

"Oh, whatever shall we do?"

"Mrs. Cornwall," Caitrin said, "I want you to go over to the mercantile and check on Jack. Please see that he's all right, and then come back and give me the news. If he needs me, I'll go to him at once. After that, you must make your way back to your camp and try to rest."

"Yes," Felicity said, dabbing a handkerchief on her cheeks. "I'll do that very thing."

As the older woman left, Caitrin held Lucy tightly and began to rock her. In a moment Sheena joined them on the floor. The three women slipped their arms around each other, and Caitrin thought of the despair and hopelessness that threatened. What hope of peace did any of them have?

And then she remembered. "The Lord is my rock and my salvation," she whispered. "Whom then shall I fear?"

Caitrin woke well past dawn the next morning. The blanket she had hung over the front door had fallen down in the night. Sunlight lit a golden rectangle on the bare earthen floor. Lucy lay nestled against Caitrin's left side, her sleep troubled and restless. Sheena slept soundly on the right. Caitrin stared up at the rough plank ceiling topped by blocks of heavy sod and thought of the time she had thrown a plate against the wall in frustration. As she recalled it, she'd been angry about grass roots burrowing into the house.

She hadn't known what trouble was.

Dear God, please protect Jack, she lifted up in silence. Felicity Cornwall had returned under cover of night to report that Seth had cut out the bullet, the wound looked clean, and her son was resting. Caitrin tried to feel relieved. *Father, what am I to do about that man? Why did you bring him into my life? I can't deny the stirrings of my heart for him. Jack is . . . he's so . . . what? He's interesting. He's dreadfully handsome. He's kind to children and to poor Lucy. He's intelligent. He's determined and hardworking. He loves you, Father, the best he can. But Lord, he isn't altogether tame.*

She looked at Lucy lying beside her. Lucy wasn't tame, but God loved her all the same. She was his child. And Sheena? Caitrin turned her head to study her dear sister. Certainly she wasn't perfect, yet it appeared she was willing to leave past troubles with the Cornwalls behind.

Caitrin's thoughts again turned to the shattered plate. She herself was far from docile. She had a fiery temper. She argued vehemently. She stood up against her brother-in-law. Jack once had referred to her as stubborn and mouthy. Imperfect. Yet, God loved her, accepted her, gave his life for her. And his Spirit willingly lived in her heart.

Sheena's always scolding me, Father, about wanting to change the world. I do expect the best of everyone, including myself. But you loved us in the midst of our failures, didn't you? You loved us in spite of our sin. Is it all right with you if I love Jack Cornwall? He's not everything he could be or everything he will be in time. But dear Father, may I have your permission to love the man?

Caitrin closed her eyes and hugged the two broken women beside her more tightly. *Beloved, let us love one another,* the apostle Paul had written, *for love is of God; and every one that loveth is born of God, and knoweth God. He that loveth not knoweth not God; for God is love.*

Though the sunshine crept across the soddy floor, Caitrin slept again, wrapped in an exhausted peace.

Dark clouds and an unexpected heat rolled across the prairie from the west. The promise of rain lifted Caitrin's heart as she hurried down the path worn in the creek bank. In spite of the town meeting's few prayers and violent battle, it appeared God had heard the people's plea and was sending water for their crops.

After feeding her two guests a late breakfast, changing the bandage on Sheena's forehead, and finding a complete set of clothing for Lucy, she convinced the younger woman to bathe. Never had Caitrin seen such a horrific sight as the self-inflicted scrapes and scratches that covered Lucy's pale skin. Sheena had gasped aloud, but she quickly took up a soft cloth and assisted Caitrin in the process.

When they finally had Lucy clean, dry, and dressed again, Sheena volunteered to brush out the tangled, matted hair. Though Caitrin's heart quaked at the trouble that might befall her two charges, she used the opportunity to leave them alone for a few minutes.

"Mrs. Cornwall?" she called outside one of the canvas tents. "Mrs. Cornwall, 'tis Caitrin Murphy, so it is."

Lightning flickered on the horizon. Within two hours, the rain should arrive. And it was about time. The long, dry prairie grass fairly stretched toward the heavens in a plea for water. Birds flocked around the wells hoping for a spare droplet spilled from a bucket. A child could ford Bluestem Creek without wetting his knees. The farmers would be thanking God at this very moment.

"Mrs. Cornwall?" she called again. "I've come to look in on Jack."

"Please go home, Miss Murphy." Felicity's voice grated like gravel. "I'll thank you to bring my daughter to me at once. After I've taken the horse and wagon to the smithy to load up Jack's tools, we'll be away by dusk."

Caitrin clasped her hands tightly. If Jack were too weak to resist, his mother could actually follow through on her plan. She might never lay eyes on him again.

"Please, Mrs. Cornwall, I've just come to see about your son. Is he all right?"

She listened to the silence from the tent. Finally she heard a groan. "Who's out there, Mama?"

"Jack!" Caitrin called. "'Tis I, Caitrin Murphy. Are you all right?"

"Come inside, Caitrin."

Fearing to incur Felicity's wrath after the previous night's fragile peace, Caitrin hesitated a moment. But her need to be with Jack overcame her concerns. Pushing aside the flap that blocked the entrance, she stepped into the shadowy tent. Felicity sat on a low stool near a pallet on the floor. She looked up from her knitting, her eyes swollen with crying.

Caitrin knelt beside the pallet and took Jack's hand. "Your mother told me the wound was clean. You'll be all right, won't you?"

"I reckon so." He reached up and touched a curly tendril of her hair. "You OK?"

"Aye. But worried."

"Listen, Caitrin." He winced as he elbowed himself upward. "About last night. I'm sorry for losing my head. I couldn't take Jimmy mean-mouthing my family, and I just—"

"Jack, you acted out of a right heart."

"A right heart maybe, but a reckless brain. Fact is, I didn't think. I just jumped up there and went after the fellow."

"And got a bullet for it," Felicity said. "That's the second time somebody in this wicked place has wounded my son."

"Now, listen here, Mama—"

"We're leaving, Jack, and don't argue with your mother. As soon as Miss Murphy brings Lucy to us, I'm going to load the wagons, and we'll be off. And none too soon."

Jack gazed at Caitrin. She could all but read the question in his eyes: *Do you want me to stay in Hope, Caitrin? Do you want me to stay?*

"Mrs. Cornwall," a man's voice called from outside the tent. "This is Seth Hunter. How's Jack?"

"Alive," she returned.

"I've come to give you a message. In light of what happened last night, the men around here feel it's important to discuss the future of the Cornwall family in Hope. We've called a meeting over at the mercantile one hour from now. Rustemeyer and I will keep order, and there'll be no guns and no fistfights. Jimmy O'Toole is coming to speak his piece in an orderly manner. We'd like you to come and stand up for yourselves."

"That won't be necessary," Felicity said. "We're leaving this wretched town."

Jack's gray eyes locked on Caitrin as if seeking strength and confirmation. "I'll be there," he told Seth. "I'll be at the mercantile in an hour."

CHAPTER 17

JACK hobbled into the mercantile at five that afternoon. His mother was busy packing up the tents and gathering the cooking gear and furniture they had used during their stay. Felicity had made up her mind to leave, and Lucy would go with her. The two women had no place to go in Missouri, and Jack knew he could not allow them to head off into the unknown. If he couldn't talk these stubborn townsfolk into letting them stay, he was going to have more trouble on his hands than he knew how to manage.

He eased himself down onto a bench and watched as the local homesteaders filed into the building. There was Casimir Laski, whose Polish hymns were a regular part of the Sunday services. Salvatore Rippeto entered the mercantile, glanced at Jack, and then turned away as if embarrassed. LeBlanc, the mill owner whose bevy of lovely daughters graced the community dances, followed Rippeto. Rolf Rustemeyer, Seth Hunter, and Jimmy O'Toole walked in, conferring in low tones. A handful of others, single young homesteaders—several of them sporting black eyes or swollen noses—took the benches around Jack.

"I reckon we ought to get started," Seth said, stepping up to the pulpit usually reserved for Sundays. "Some of you fellows have come a distance and need to get back before dark, so we'll try to make this quick. You all know Jack Cornwall here. Jack, would you mind coming up to the front here and taking this chair so we can all hear what you have to say?"

This was beginning to take on the aura of a courtroom trial, and Jack knew he didn't have much of a defense. All the same, he stood and hobbled painfully to the front of the room. As he turned to the chair, he saw Rose Hunter, Sheena O'Toole, and Caitrin Murphy enter the mercantile.

"Hold on a minute, ladies," Seth said. "This is men's business."

"Is that so?" Rosie returned, setting her hands on her hips and giving her husband a bold look. "It seems to me the Cornwall group is made up of one male and two females. That's more of us than you, by my calculation, and I think the women of this town deserve a say-so in the matter."

Some of the men chuckled as a flush crept up Seth's neck. "Now, Rosie, I don't need to tell you that women don't have any voice in the government of the state of Kansas. And since Hope is in Kansas—"

"We'll not vote then," Caitrin said. "But give us permission to listen to the proceedings. After all, we've done our part to make this a town."

"Suffragists," LeBlanc muttered. "I have a house full of them. You must be strong, Seth, or soon we will have women wearing trousers and putting their fingers into our politics."

"Aye," Jimmy agreed. "What are you doin' out of bed anyway, Sheena?"

"I'll be plucked for a goose if I won't watch this, Jimmy O'Toole! 'Tis my children who must grow up in this town, and I'll know what you men are about, so I will. Now will you kindly permit these ladies and me to sit down before we swoon in this unseasonable heat?"

Seth looked from Jimmy to Rolf, and then he surveyed the room for a reaction to the request. Jack noted that some of the farmers appeared more bemused than angry, but others looked downright irritated. "All right," Seth said. "You can stay and listen. But you're to keep quiet, and there'll be no female voting."

Jack watched a light of victory suffuse the women's faces. As glad as he was to see Caitrin, he wasn't too sure himself about letting ladies in on a matter like this. It was the men who would decide his fate.

"Back to business," Seth said. "There's two sides to the matter that has turned our town on its ear. On the one hand, we have a hardworking man in Jack Cornwall, a man who had the courage to put his past behind him and try to start a new life among us. He's built a fine smithy, and from what everyone tells me, he does good work. Matter of fact, I hear he's the best smithy from Topeka to Manhattan. Not only does the man do good work, but he stands up for his family. He has protected his widowed mother and his sister, and he has some loyal friends. I'd call myself Jack Cornwall's friend, despite some troubles we had in the past."

Jack shifted on the chair, trying to ease the pressure from his injured leg. He could see the thick black clouds moving closer across the horizon. Flickers of lightning licked the prairie. Puffs of dry dirt lifted into the air, spun around into dust devils, and danced away. That rain ought to be here before long, he thought, and a good thing. It would trap all the farmers inside the mercantile and give him time to argue his case. He had prayed for the chance to speak his mind. Maybe this rainstorm was God's answer.

"On the other hand," Seth said, "Jack Cornwall has brought with him quite a collection of troubles. Now as you all know, we gave him a month's grace here in Hope, and we've let him stay longer than that. But last night's ruckus over at the prayer meeting has brought us together to take a second look at the situation. Now let's consider that . . ."

Jack's attention wandered to Caitrin, and the hammering urge to defend himself with violence and revenge subsided. As long as he lived, Jack would never forget the night he met the red-haired

Irishwoman for the first time. *I love you*, she had told him. *You are precious to the Father, and I love you*. Because of those words, he had eventually surrendered his heart to Christ, given up his old reckless ways, and stepped onto a new path. He had left Missouri and the companions who had led him into trouble. He had done everything in his power to build a new life here on the prairie.

Love had always been a mystery to him, a word that had no real meaning, no definition. But through Caitrin, that word had become as bright, glowing, and real as the fire in his forge. By watching her example, he had come to understand that true love—for God and for people—couldn't just hide away in someone's heart like a cozy, personal secret. Love demanded an open demonstration in both words and actions.

Caitrin's love had led her to defend Jack, to believe the best of him, to trust him, and to honor him. In love, she stood by him with more than her words. She stepped out in active faith, taking his troubled sister into her home and helping Lucy find reason to hope. Caitrin respected his mother, in spite of Felicity's brusque ways and bitter tongue. Through love, Caitrin had stood tall against every flame of fire that threatened to consume her.

Faith, hope, and love, Jack thought, recalling the verse he'd read somewhere in the Bible. *The greatest of these is love*. He had learned how it felt to be loved. And Caitrin Murphy had taught him to love in return.

He loved her, he realized as he studied the woman across the room. He loved Caitrin Murphy with his whole heart. It was time she knew.

"I have something to say," he began, cutting into Seth Hunter's speech. He stood with difficulty and faced the congregated farmers. "I want to tell you why I came here to Hope and why I'm not leaving. It's Caitrin Murphy. I love her, and I'm—"

"Oh, Jack!" Caitrin cried, coming to her feet.

"You'd better shut your smush, Jack Cornwall," Jimmy O'Toole shouted, jumping up. "We're only halfway through the list of trials you've caused us, and you have no right to speak. And furthermore, Caitrin Murphy is my wife's sister, and she won't have you! We'll not allow it."

"You gentlemen better both sit down right now!" Seth ordered. "We've got a storm coming, and we need to get this over with so everybody can go home. Now, I already mentioned the problem with Miss Cornwall and her spells. Jack's sister has a passel of troubles, and those chains she wears don't help her a bit. But even though we all feel sorry for Miss Cornwall, a lot of you have confided to me that you don't like the notion of a grown woman throwing herself in front of stagecoaches, trying to drown herself in the Bluestem, and running around without her clothes on. She's scaring the children, and the women are complaining that they don't trust her not to hurt somebody."

Jack couldn't bring himself to sit. He didn't want to listen to a recitation of the trials that beset his family and in turn brought trouble on this community. Didn't *everyone* have troubles of one kind or another? And hadn't Jesus said something about bearing one another's burdens? Caitrin once told Jack that faith in Christ didn't take away the problems, but it gave a believer comfort and strength to bear them. Why couldn't these men just let him walk in that faith through the fires of his life? Why couldn't they support him with their concern and prayer. Was that too much to ask?

"And then there was that problem between Mrs. Cornwall and Mrs. O'Toole awhile back," Seth continued. "We all know Sheena has been suffering for some time as a result of her fall on the creek bank. Now I certainly don't believe Mrs. Cornwall has the same notions as her daughter, but she's caused a good bit of trouble in her own right. Which brings us to last night at the prayer meeting."

"First, I'd like to speak to the matter of the trouble between

Felicity Cornwall and myself," Sheena said, rising. "I'll have you know—"

"Sit down, wife!" Jimmy commanded. "You're not to talk, lass, and I'll thank you to mind the rules Seth set out."

Coloring a bright red, Sheena sank back onto the bench as Seth went on. "Now, things were going along all right, until—"

A crack of thunder shook the mercantile. Jack glanced out the window. A rusty glow had joined the boiling black clouds moving toward the town. Dust blew against the glass windows. A loose shingle slapped on the roof.

"Anyway," Seth said, speaking quickly, "you all know what happened. Jack jumped up on the wagon and threw Jimmy over the side, a fight broke out, Jack got himself shot in the leg, and about half the men in this room wound up injured. So, now you know both sides of the matter, and it's time to vote."

"Both sides?" Jack spoke up. "You told me to sit up here at the front. Now it's my turn to speak for myself and my family."

"Your actions speak louder than words," Jimmy shouted. "You came to us with a bullet wound in your shoulder, and you'll leave with one in your leg. That tells us all we need to know about you. Let's vote, men! I've chickens to pen up."

At that moment Jack's old comrade, Bill Hermann, walked into the mercantile with a badge-wearing lawman at his side. Jack let out a groan as the farmers turned to stare. Caitrin gave a muffled cry.

"I think I can make this whole mess easy for you, gentlemen," Hermann announced. He turned to Jack. "I've been searchin' for you a long time, buddy. Seems you stir up a ruckus no matter where you go."

"This is none of your concern, Bill," Jack said. "You stay out of it. I'm going to work things out with these men, and then I'll talk to you outside."

"I don't believe there's any workin' out to do." Hermann held up a sheet of paper and unrolled it before his curious audience. "This here's a subpoena, gentlemen. Your friend, Jack Cornwall, is headin' back to Missouri."

"Now just a cotton-picking minute, Bill," Jack exploded.

"You gonna come peaceful?" the lawman spoke over the hubbub.

"Am I under arrest?"

"No, sir, but if you resist me, I can have you arrested sure as shootin'. This subpoena says you're to appear at a trial in Jefferson City to testify for the defense in the matter of the Easton lynchin'."

"I wasn't at the Easton lynching, and Bill Hermann knows it." Jack turned on his former companion. "Don't try to drag me into that mess, Bill. You know I wasn't there that night, and I'll be jiggered if—"

"You were there, Cornwall," Hermann interrupted. "Admit it. You were there. You saw everything that happened. You know exactly who done what, and you can get the fellers off the hook. Come on, Jack, stand up for the old bunch."

"I'd gone to Sedalia earlier that day. I was with . . . with somebody." Jack raked a hand through his hair. He knew he couldn't prove himself—not without causing more trouble than ever. "I never saw one thing that happened out at the Easton cabin. You expect me to get up there on the stand and lie, Bill?"

"I expect you to do whatever it takes to defend the men you once called brothers. Deputy, looks to me like he's resisting."

"Now hold on a minute," Seth Hunter said, holding up both hands. He turned on Bill Hermann. "Listen, sir. We're in the middle of a proceeding here. Whatever trouble happened between you and Jack Cornwall can be worked out later. We've got to get on with our vote before the storm hits."

"Then make it snappy," the lawman said as he took off his hat and scratched his head. "That rain's gonna make me miss my supper."

"All right, men," Seth said. "I'm going to give Jack five minutes to state his case."

"He's had more than a month to prove himself," Jimmy countered. "'Tis time to vote. How many think Jack Cornwall and his family ought to stay here in Hope? Raise your hand."

"I have a right to speak!" Jack roared. "This is my life you're messing with, O'Toole."

"I vote to keep the blacksmith," LeBlanc said, standing and lifting his hand. "I have many repairs on my mill. Maybe the man makes trouble, but he does good work."

"I'm for letting him stay," Seth said. "Jack had the guts to come back here and carve out a business. He may have a hot head, but there's not a man among us who wouldn't have to own up to a fault or two. Jack, you have my vote."

Rolf Rustemeyer stood up. "I, too, think is goot this Jack Cornwall to stay here," he said. "I haf chance to come from Germany and make my farm. Here Cornwall can haf chance. Here Cornwall can stay."

"That's three," Jimmy said. "Any others? All right, how many of you vote that we ask the Cornwalls to leave Hope?"

Rippeto's hand shot up, followed by Laski's and those of the other farmers. Jimmy counted the men and included himself in the tally. "That's three for staying and seven for leaving. I say it's clear—"

"What kind of justice is this?" Caitrin cried. "'Tis only fair that you give Jack Cornwall the chance to speak for himself."

"Sit down!" a chorus of men's voices erupted.

"More trouble!" Jimmy cried. "Now Cornwall has the women rising up against us, so he does. You're voted out, Jack Cornwall. And as for you, Caitrin Murphy, I'll say it again—good riddance to bad rummage! You'd better pack your trunks—"

"Enough with your blather, Jimmy O'Toole!" Sheena said, leaping up. "Caitrin is my sister, so she is, and you'll not put her on any boat to Ireland!"

Jack took a step forward and squared his shoulders. He'd have his say, blast it, and not a man would drive him out before. He glanced out the window. The rusty cloud had transformed into a creeping tide of flames that lit the sky and sent up the black billows of smoke everyone had mistaken for rain clouds.

"Fire!" he hollered. "Fire headed this way!"

Men raced to the windows. "Fire! Fire!"

Sheena began to scream. Rosie ran to Seth. Heart slamming against his chest, Jack climbed up onto the chair. "Listen up, men," he shouted. "I'm a blacksmith. In the army, I learned how to handle a runaway fire. I'll tell you what we've got to do."

The farmers quickly left the window and gathered around him.

"Hitch up your plows," Jack told them, "and run a half dozen or so fresh furrows around your houses and barns. A few yards of bare dirt can hold back a raging fire. The minute you're finished, grab all the grain sacks and buckets you can lay your hands on, and ride down here to the Bluestem."

"What about the women?" Seth asked.

"Take the smallest children across the bridge to the O'Tooles' house. The fire won't jump the creek. Then all the women and the older children meet on this side of the Bluestem and start soaking grain sacks and filling buckets. My leg won't let me do much against the fire, so I'll hitch my horse to a wagon and haul the sacks and buckets out to the front line."

"But what are we to do against such a blaze?" Jimmy asked. "Sure I've never fought a fire in my life!"

"Some of you men take the wet sacks and beat out the flames. Others throw buckets of water. I'll start a backfire if I need to. The wind is driving the blaze this direction, and we don't want to lose the town. Let's go, everybody. And while you work—*pray!*"

Jack gritted his teeth against the pain as he stepped down from the chair. The farmers poured through the mercantile door. Jimmy huddled over Sheena, consoling her and begging her to stay abed in their soddy. Rosie gave Seth a quick embrace and started for the door, but he caught her hand and drew her close again. As they talked, Caitrin approached Jack.

"What about Bill Hermann?" she asked. "Jack, he says you know things about that murder."

"I wasn't at the Easton lynching," he said. "I told you that before. I may be hotheaded, but I'm no liar. Don't you believe me, Caitrin?"

He read the doubt in her green eyes and a fist knotted at the base of his stomach. He would fight the men of Hope to be allowed to stay here. He would battle Bill Hermann and the laws of Kansas and Missouri to be allowed to get his way. But if Caitrin lost faith in him . . .

"Oh, Jack," she said. "How has it come to this?"

He caught her by the waist and pulled her roughly against him. "What it's come to is that I love you, Caitrin Murphy. I love you, and I want you for my wife. I don't care what these rascals try to do to separate us, I won't leave you. I'll stand by you the rest of my life, and I'll make us a good home. A happy home. But I need to hear the words again, Caitrin. Those three words."

She stared up at him, her eyes filling with tears. "Jack—"

"Come on, Caitie!" Sheena cried out, grabbing her sister's hand. "Sure the whole place is going to burn down around us if we don't get busy. Save your gabbin' for later."

Caitrin swallowed. "Be careful, Jack," she said.

He held his breath as she pulled away from him and ran out of the mercantile.

"Lucy?" Caitrin sprinted into her soddy and looked around. "What are you doing here?"

The woman's head emerged from the hiding place she had made for herself. "I came back. I don't want to go away, Caitrin."

"Oh, Lucy, a prairie fire is coming. Sure you must go back to your mother."

"I'll look after Lucy," Sheena said, entering the soddy. Her cheeks were flushed. "I'll take her to our soddy, and she can bake cinnamon buns for the *brablins*. 'Twill take our thoughts away from the fire."

The young woman rose from behind the bed. "Mrs. O'Toole . . . I . . ."

"Come with me, Lucy. Help me."

The young woman held her hand toward Sheena. "Tell me what to do, Mrs. O'Toole."

Embracing Lucy warmly, Sheena led her out of the soddy. Caitrin gathered grain sacks and towels and hurried away to defend her town.

Black, pungent smoke clutched at Jack's throat as he drove Scratch down the line of men fighting the prairie fire. The horse tossed its head and neighed in terror of the flames, but Jack kept the creature moving parallel to the blaze. Dusk had settled as the fire crept ever forward, a bright, devouring glow that ate its way toward Hope.

Seth Hunter's new frame house stood directly in the fire's path. The shed would go first. Then the house would be consumed. Finally the new barn filled with the last winter hay would explode into flames. After that, it would be only a matter of time until the fire reached Caitrin's little home. The heavy prairie sod wouldn't burn, of course, but the smokehouse, the door, and the window frames would. The mercantile would be next—wood shingles, wood sign, new wood floor. All Caitrin's hard work would go up in flames. The new church would follow. Jack's smithy stood last in line before the Bluestem Creek would put a hissing stop to the crackle and flicker of this ravenous enemy.

"You'd better get the valuables out of your house," Jack called to

Seth as the homesteader unloaded a pile of dripping grain sacks. "Photographs, family treasures, that kind of thing."

Face blackened with soot, Seth stared up at Jack. "I spent all winter building that house. That's Rosie's . . ." The man looked away, fighting emotion. "That's Rosie's *home*."

"We'll do all we can to keep it safe, Seth. But I won't promise we can hold these flames at bay."

"Can you start a backfire?"

Jack studied the line of men, black silhouettes whipping at the tongues of orange flame and tossing bucket after bucket onto the conflagration. And still the wind pushed the fire ever forward. Behind the choking smoke, lightning flashed. The promise of rain. The hope of God's provision. But would it come in time? Would it be enough to stop the onslaught?

"Backfires are tricky," Jack said. "They can get away from you. If the wind takes this one the wrong direction—"

"It's worth a try. We're getting nowhere."

Jack tried to calm Scratch as he assessed the situation. "All right, but I'll need your help. We've got to keep fighting the big blaze until we can burn off a strip of grass a few yards away. Then we've got to get the men out of the way."

"We can do it," Seth said. "Help us, Jack."

They wouldn't have much time, and the wind was against them. But Jack pressed Scratch back toward the creek to alert the women and to pick up another load of sacks and buckets. Rosie had given out hours before and had joined Sheena and Lucy across the creek. With babies on the way, the women couldn't afford to push themselves too hard. But Jack was pleased to find Caitrin leading the others as they worked together at the creek.

Racing back to the fire, Jack prayed God would give him the wisdom to start the backfire in the right place. He prayed the wind would die down. He prayed the rain would fall. He prayed the homesteaders would have the stamina to keep fighting.

He could see the farmers now, gathering around Seth. Even Bill Hermann and the deputy had joined the effort. As the men divided into two groups, one to hold the big fire at bay and the other to manage the backfire, Jack climbed down from the wagon. He couldn't remember his shoulder ever hurting as much as his leg now burned. But there was no time to tend it.

"Stay near me," he told the group of men assigned to help him. "I'm going to light a line of fire. You fan it against the wind, keep it low, keep it safe. Once you've let the fire burn the grass for a couple of yards, beat it out and move to another place along the line. We can't let this thing get away from us."

As the men ranged out around him, Jack gathered a clump of dried prairie grass and lit it. Then he began moving slowly parallel to the encroaching fire and setting the grass aflame with his makeshift torch. The dry stems crackled like tinder, exploding as the sparks touched them. Alongside Jack, the men tended the backfire, carefully fanning into the wind.

Once he had lit the backfire and it was successfully burning a barrier of charred grass between the prairie fire and the town, Jack made his way around the flames to the other men. "Seth!" he called. "Come on out now! It's time to let it go."

Dark shadows against the scarlet light, the exhausted farmers left their posts and hurried to escape the encroaching flames of the backfire. As the men gathered in safety, they stood spellbound, watching the two lines of fire move ever closer toward each other.

"I think it'll work," Seth said. "I think we've got it licked."

"But fire can coming around?" Rolf asked, pointing to the vast stretch of prairie untouched by the backfire. "The big fire can coming this way around and still gif trouble?"

"Maybe," Jack said. "We'll keep an eye on it."

"*Ja*, goot." Rustemeyer clapped him on the back. "You helpen us. Now Jimmy O'Toole can see you are goot man. Where Jimmy is?"

Seth looked around, studying the soot-covered faces of the farmers. "Jimmy?" he called. "Jimmy?"

Jack scanned the flames. In a narrow patch of unburned grass between the prairie fire and the backfire, a lone silhouette whipped at the roaring blaze with a wet grain sack. Unhearing. Unseeing. Unaware of his peril.

It was Jimmy O'Toole.

CHAPTER 18

FOR AN INSTANT, Jack felt sure he was staring through the door of hell itself—and there stood Jimmy O'Toole, right in the middle of it. *Good riddance to bad rummage*, the Irishman had said to Caitrin. The words could just as easily be spoken to Jimmy himself. *Let him burn*, Jack thought. *He's a troublemaker—a spiteful, vengeful imp of a man without a redeeming bone in his skinny body*. With Jimmy out of the picture, Caitrin would have no reason to hold back. Would she?

But what kind of man was Jack to stand by and let another die? The words he himself had spoken came back to him. *Bear one another's burdens . . . Faith, hope, and love . . . the greatest of these is love*.

Love.

Grabbing a handful of wet sacks, Jack limped toward the fire. He could hear Seth shouting, ordering him not to go, but he picked up his pace. Rolf tried to catch his arm. The other farmers bellowed at him. "Too late," they cried. "It's too late!"

Jimmy turned now and saw the backfire creeping toward him. Eyes wide, face skeletal, he stared in helpless horror at the other men safe beyond the blaze. Jack edged forward across the blackened, smoking grass. Whipping at the flames that licked his trousers, he gritted his teeth and tried to ignore the pain that seared his injured leg. With agonizing slowness, he beat a path through the low-burning backfire.

"Cornwall!" Jimmy cried. Coughing, stripping away his shirt, the Irishman straggled back and forth on the narrow strip of unburned grass, looking for a way out. "Cornwall, help me!"

"I'm coming," Jack called. He lashed at the fire, smothering flames, pushing forward. Smoke swirled around his head and filled his lungs. Choking, he paused and bent over to gasp for air.

Jimmy's voice came to him through the pall. "Cornwall, Cornwall!"

"Where are you?" Jack cried. "Where are you, O'Toole?"

Silence overwhelmed him as he stumbled onto the unburned patch. He could see nothing. Heat stung his skin. The crackle and snap of burning brush swirled around his ears.

"Jimmy O'Toole!"

A low cough caught his attention, and Jack fell to his knees beside the crumpled man. Lungs crying out in agony, he lifted the Irishman onto his shoulders. His leg might give out, Jack knew, but his arms were strong. With Jimmy's limp body sprawled over his back, Jack struggled to stand. *God, help me. Help me!*

Inching upward, he straightened. Which way? Which way out? He coughed, sure he would choke on the acrid smoke that filled his chest.

I am the way. Follow me.

Jack thought he heard the words, but he could see nothing. He staggered forward.

Follow me. Follow me.

Stumbling, aware of flames that caught the hems of his trousers and wreathed his ankles, Jack followed. Night cloaked him like a heavy, black blanket. His shoulders ached. His legs cramped. His lungs clamped down, strangling him.

Follow me.

Seth's face suddenly appeared and blessed arms gathered Jack in.

The weight lifted from his shoulders. He drifted upward, sure he was floating. *Out of hell and into heaven*, he thought.

Follow me.

Caitrin heaved the dripping bucket out of the creek and turned toward the fire. Across the moonlit prairie she spotted a cluster of men moving toward her like wraiths. Flames flickered behind them, smoke billowed above them. Whips of white lightning cracked through the air.

"Jack!" Caitrin knew immediately he was one of the men they carried among them. "Oh no, 'tis Jack!"

She dropped the heavy bucket, grabbed her skirts, and started running.

"Here is two manners," Rolf said, leaving the group and trotting toward the women. "Is Cornwall and O'Toole both."

"What about the fire?"

"Is stop."

"To my soddy then!" Caitrin cried. "Follow me!"

Unable to hold back her tears, she led the men through the night toward the low mound that formed the roof of her small house. They stepped over the boards of the broken door and carried their two comrades inside. Caitrin lit lamps as the men laid Jimmy and Jack side by side on the bed.

"They're neither one breathing!" Seth said. "One time a fellow in the army fell out of a tree, and the captain of our troop breathed the breath of life right back into him. You reckon we oughta try it, Miss Murphy?"

"Show me," she said, swiping the back of her hand across her damp cheek.

Seth leaned over Jimmy, clamped two fingers on the man's nose, and breathed deeply into the Irishman's mouth. Caitrin placed her lips over Jack's mouth, held his nose tightly, and forced a breath down into his lungs. She saw his chest rise. As it fell, the cloying scent of smoke escaped his lungs.

"I love you, Jack Cornwall," she whispered through trembling lips. "Sure you're not a perfect man, but I love you all the same. No matter the consequences, I want to be your wife. Now breathe, Jack. Please, breathe!"

She bent over the man again and forced air down into his lungs.

Seth lifted away from Jimmy. "It worked on that soldier," he said. "I don't know what's wrong, Miss Murphy."

She drank in another deep breath. When she leaned toward Jack's mouth, his arms slipped around her, drawing her close. "Caitrin," he mumbled.

"Thank God!" Letting out the breath, she sank onto Jack's shoulder and sobbed. His hands moved up her back, his fingers slid into her hair, and he heaved a deep sigh. Beside him, Jimmy began coughing, shaking the whole bed, as Rolf and the other men gathered around with words of encouragement.

"Jimmy? Jimmy?" Sheena cried as she appeared in the doorway. Behind her were Rosie, Lucy, Felicity Cornwall, and the other women and children. At the sight of her husband sitting up and wiping the soot from his eyes, Sheena stopped. "Oh, Jimmy, are you alive?"

"Aye, but barely." Jimmy stretched out his arms. "Come here to me, Sheena, my love. I need a hug."

Bursting into tears, Sheena elbowed her way to the bed and threw her arms around her husband. Caitrin held Jack so tightly she was afraid she might suffocate him all over again. But she couldn't let go. Not now. Not ever.

"Caitrin?" Jack's voice was husky. "Say the words again."

"I love you," she said softly, knowing what he needed to hear. "'Tis those three words that will bond us forever. You are precious to the Father, and with his love I love you. But you are precious to me, too, Jack Cornwall, and with my whole heart I love you."

He let out a rattling breath and drew her closer.

"Pretty words and a happy scene," Bill Hermann said as he appeared at the door of the soddy and attempted to push through the crowd, "but I ain't got time for sweetness. Jack, let's go."

"You'll not take this man anywhere!" Caitrin cried, looking daggers at the rascal. "Sure he's a *donsie* thing, barely alive, and you want to cart him off to Missouri? You'll do no such thing!"

"I got a subpoena."

"I don't care if you've a letter from the president himself. Get out of my house!" She jumped to her feet and shook a finger in the man's face. "Out, villain! Out!"

"Listen, ma'am," the deputy said over Hermann's shoulder. "This ain't exactly somethin' I enjoy, but I've got my duty. This here subpoena means Jack Cornwall has to go back to Missouri to testify about that lynchin'."

"I wasn't there," Jack said.

"He's telling the truth," Lucy whispered. "My brother was in Sedalia with . . . with me the night of that lynchin'."

All eyes turned to the frail young woman. "Ma'am, you may be tellin' the truth, but a sister's word ain't gonna be worth nothin' in a court of law."

"It's OK, Lucy," Jack said, elbowing himself up. He coughed and then spoke in a raspy voice. "Listen, deputy, I've got a blacksmithing business to run here. Can't you just take a sworn testimony that I wasn't at the Easton cabin that night?"

"Nope. Says right here, you got to testify in person."

"He wasn't there," Lucy repeated softly. "Jack was . . . he was in town. He was with me. We were . . . we were—"

"That's enough, Lucy!" Felicity Cornwall said. "We don't tell our family business in public."

"Mama, please . . ."

"It's OK, Lucy." Jack studied his blackened hands. "Bill Hermann, you know if I lie for you, I'm going to land in jail myself. If

I tell a court of law that I was at the Easton cabin, I'm implicating myself in the crime. You expect me to do that for the bunch?"

"Don't you care about us no more, Jack?" Bill Hermann asked. "We was your family there toward the end of the war. We gave you a place to stay, food to eat, a cause to fight for. We loved you, Jack."

Jack lifted his head and eyed his former comrade. "You don't know the meaning of love, my friend," he said. He looked at Caitrin. "But I do. I understand love. It's more than just words. It's stepping out on a limb for someone, even if they don't deserve it—the way Christ laid down his life for me, bad as I've been." Turning back to Bill Hermann, Jack squared his shoulders. "So I'll go to Missouri with you."

"No!" Caitrin cried.

"Come on then," Bill said, reaching for Jack. "We'll get a wagon and—"

"He was with me!" Lucy elbowed her way around the bed toward the deputy. "Jack was with me. I can prove it."

"Don't do this, Lucy," Jack said. "Don't—"

"I know about love, too, Jack," Lucy said softly, her gray eyes huge and luminous. "I can . . . I can walk on limbs as good as the next person." She drew a locket from around her neck, pried it open, and pulled out a small piece of folded paper. "Here, deputy. I carry this with me everywhere."

"Oh, Lucy, how could you!" Felicity cried and fled the soddy.

The deputy took the paper and opened it. "This here paper is signed by Mr. Cornwall, Miss Cornwall, and by a Sedalia lawyer, too. It looks like a document turnin' over a baby for adoption."

Caitrin slipped her arm around Lucy's shoulders as she spoke in a voice barely audible. "The Yankee soldiers," she said. "They came to our farm and . . . robbed and . . . and burned . . . and . . ."

"Lucy," Jack said, reaching for his sister.

"After they . . . they hurt me . . . I was carrying a baby. Mama didn't want the shame. The shame . . ."

"Aw, Luce, you don't have to do this."

"I loved my baby," Lucy continued in the hush of the room. "But Mama said . . . said it was a good family . . . and Jack took me to Sedalia to sign the paper. It has the date and time stamped on it." With a trembling finger, she pointed to the document in the deputy's hand.

The man scratched his head. "Yup, that's the day of the Easton lynching, and the time is six in the evenin'. That Easton feller was swingin' by a rope at six o'clock that night."

One arm still around Lucy, Caitrin gripped Jack's hand. Confused, hopeful, and terrified all at once, she waited for the man's response.

The deputy looked down at the paper in his hands. "This lawyer a feller I can find in Sedalia?"

"Yes," Lucy whispered.

"You reckon he'd swear he signed this document?"

"Yes, sir."

The deputy folded the document and stuffed it into his own shirt pocket. "I'm hungry," he said. "I'm hungry, and I missed my supper fightin' that confounded prairie fire out here in the middle of nowhere. And now I find out this subpoena can't hold no more water than a leaky bucket. Bill Hermann, you better wangle up another witness, 'cause Jack Cornwall just got himself an alibi."

"You're not taking Jack back to Missouri?" Caitrin asked, scarcely able to form the words.

"I'm not haulin' any of you folks nowhere. I'm goin' home to my wife and my supper."

As the deputy exited and Bill Hermann stomped out of the soddy behind him, Caitrin clapped her hands over her mouth. A whoop of joy went up around the room. Rosie grabbed Lucy's hands and started dancing around in circles.

"Will wonders never cease?" Sheena said over the racket. Standing, she crossed her arms and surveyed the scene. As the group quieted, she lifted her chin. "An Irishman in bed with a Cornishman? And the pair of you as black as midnight and smelling like chimneys. Well, isn't this as cozy as two lumps of sugar in a teacup?"

"Aye," Jimmy said. With a grunt, he sat up. "And 'tis a cup of tea as sweet as any ever tasted. When I saw Jack Cornwall comin' through the flames, Sheena, he was no Cornishman to me. He was an angel of God himself. This man carried me out of that fire on his own two shoulders, and he saved my life. I'm an Irishman, tough as the sod and unforgiving as a winter wind, but my own sin is standing right before my eyes, and I'll not ignore it any longer."

Jimmy turned to the man beside him. "Forgive me, Jack Cornwall."

"And me," Sheena whispered. "Thank you for saving my Jimmy's life."

"Done," Jack said, shaking the Irishman's hand.

"Well," Felicity Cornwall said, stepping back into the soddy. "This is quite a sight. My son abed with an Irishman and in love with an Irishwoman. My daughter's shame spread into the open air for everyone to see. My husband dead . . . dead and buried, unable to . . . to defend his family . . ."

"Mrs. Cornwall," Sheena said, "there's naught to defend, for there's no longer an enemy."

Felicity set her hands on her hips and studied the faces around the room. "I don't understand this," she said. "I don't understand it."

"It's love, Mama," Jack said. "Accept it."

"Well," Felicity said. "Well, I never."

"I never either, Mama, but it's about time we did."

"You are precious to the Father, Mrs. Cornwall," Caitrin murmured, taking Felicity's hand. "And I love you."

"Well," Felicity said again. She swallowed hard. "Thank you,

Miss Murphy. And Mrs. O'Toole . . . thank you for . . . I'm sorry for . . ."

"La, Mrs. Cornwall," Sheena said, wrapping the older woman in a hug, "all's forgiven."

"Time for another vote!" Seth called out. "How many in favor of letting the Cornwall family stay in Hope?"

A roar of response filled the soddy as every hand in the room shot toward the ceiling. "Welcome to Hope, Mrs. Cornwall, Jack, Lucy," Seth said. "Now let's go check on that fire, men!"

His words were followed by a crack of lightning, a boom of thunder, and a wall of rain that raced over the soddy's roof like a bag of spilled marbles. Laughter filled the air at the knowledge that the town called Hope had been spared, that the creek would run high again, and that crops would flourish. Fathers lifted their sons onto their backs and headed into the downpour. Mothers took their daughters' hands and skipped outside to dance in the puddles.

Seth tugged a quilt around Rosie, grabbed Chipper, and headed for home, Stubby barking at their heels. Felicity took Lucy's hand and hurried her toward their camp to unroll canvases and cover the half-filled wagons. Jimmy hobbled out of bed, gave Jack a friendly squeeze on the shoulder, gathered his wife and his *brablins*, and made for the bridge.

Jack stood slowly, his arm around Caitrin's shoulders for support. Together they stepped out of the soddy into the night and let the cool water pour over them, washing away pain and fear along with the soot.

"The fire nearly got us," Jack said, holding Caitrin close.

"'Twas not a killing fire, as we feared," Caitrin answered softly. "'Twas the heavenly Refiner's fire, melting away the dross and impurities in our lives and welding us together with a golden bond that will never break."

"You know something, Caitrin Murphy?" Jack asked. "You're going to make some blacksmith a mighty fine wife."

"Aye," she said with a laugh. "And all because of three little words."

Their lips met, and a love beyond any she had ever imagined welled in Caitrin's heart as they melted into the Father's precious baptism of hope, grace, and peace.

AUTHOR'S NOTE

Dear friend,

From the ashes of the refiner's fire can emerge beauty both graceful and enduring. In *Prairie Rose* Rosie Mills and Seth Hunter overcome doubt and abandonment to build a new family bonded in Christ. In *Prairie Fire* the flames that threaten to consume the town called Hope are washed away in the flood of love and forgiveness that endures in the hearts of Caitrin Murphy and Jack Cornwall. *Prairie Storm*, in bookstores soon, will continue the story of A Town Called Hope.

My thanks to the many of you who take time to write and express your appreciation for the ministry my books have had in your lives. As I personally read and answer your precious letters, your words of love and faith become a ministry to me.

Blessings in Christ,

Catherine Palmer

Catherine Palmer
Tyndale House Publishers
P.O. Box 80
Wheaton, IL 60189-0080

ABOUT THE AUTHOR

CATHERINE PALMER lives in Missouri with her husband, Tim, and sons, Geoffrey and Andrei. She is a graduate of Southwest Baptist University and has a master's degree in English from Baylor University. Her first book was published in 1988. Since then she has published nearly twenty books and has won numerous awards for her writing, including Most Exotic Historical Romance Novel from *Romantic Times* magazine. Total sales of her novels number close to one million copies.

Her Tyndale House titles include *The Treasure of Timbuktu*, *The Treasure of Zanzibar*, and novellas in the anthologies *A Victorian Christmas Tea*, *With This Ring*, and *A Victorian Christmas Quilt*.

HEART
QUEST™

HeartQuest brings you romantic fiction
with a foundation of biblical truth.
Adventure, mystery, intrigue, and suspense
mingle in our heartwarming stories of
men and women of faith striving to build
a love that will last a lifetime.

May HeartQuest books sweep you
into the arms of God, who longs for you
and pursues you always.

Romance fiction from
Tyndale House Publishers, Inc.
WHEATON, ILLINOIS

Visit Tyndale's exciting Web site at www.tyndale.com

Edited by Kathryn S. Olson

Designed by Catherine Bergstrom and Julie Chen

3 IN 1 ISBN 0-7394-0311-7

Printed in the United States of America

For my earthly father,

Harold Thomas Cummins,

whose gentle love helped lead me

to my heavenly Father

My thanks to those whose vision and diligence helped bring the town called Hope to life: Tim Palmer, Ron Beers, Ken Petersen, Rebekah Nesbitt, and the whole HeartQuest team. My special thanks to Kathy Olson for her insightful editing and constructive suggestions as I wrote this series. Bless you all.

The Lord is slow to get angry, but his power is great, and he never lets the guilty go unpunished. He displays his power in the whirlwind and the storm. The billowing clouds are the dust beneath his feet. —Nahum 1:3, NLT

You have not come to a physical mountain, to a place of flaming fire, darkness, gloom, and whirlwind. . . . You have come to the assembly of God's firstborn children, whose names are written in heaven. You have come to God himself. —Hebrews 12:18, 23, NLT

CHAPTER 1

Hope, Kansas
June 1866

A SUDDEN, high-pitched cry caught Lily Nolan's attention. She sucked in a breath. A baby? Somewhere in the growing darkness, a baby was crying. Lily pushed aside the tent flap and stepped outside, listening. There it came again! Weak but insistent, the wail curled into the marrow of Lily's bones.

Abigail, she thought. *Oh, my darling Abby!*

No. That wasn't possible, was it? Abby was gone, buried in a little wooden box at the edge of Topeka. But whose baby was crying? Why didn't the mother rock the child?

Lily's body contracted and began to ache in response to the baby's cries. Could the voice be Abby's, calling to her mother from the spirit world? Beatrice had tried to assure Lily that the baby was an angel now, a soul drifting in the great unseen, a messenger who would come to her with hope and comfort from beyond. But this cry sounded so real. And so near.

Lily stepped out into the tall prairie grass. In the distance she could see the town of Hope, Kansas—little more than a mercantile, a smithy, a newly built church, and a few shabby soddies. Women wearing homespun dresses, men in tattered trousers, and barefoot children moved down dirt paths toward the main road. Seeking entertainment or hoping for a cure for some unnamed trouble, they came to the traveling show, just as such people did in every town across the country.

Clutching the velvet cape of her fortune-teller's costume closer about her, Lily concentrated on Beatrice's speech. "Are you sad and blue?" the woman called. "Does your heart ache, your blood race, your liver leap, and your stomach churn? Is your hair limp? Do your feet hurt? Are your fingers stiff? Whatever ails you, come and find the answers to your troubles!"

Lily knew it would be a while before "Madame Zahara" started peddling elixir, and even longer before she would send customers to the tent to have their fortunes told. With the cry of the baby haunting her, Lily gathered up her skirts and set off through the grass. If she could find the child's mother and gain permission to hold the infant for a few moments—maybe even kiss the soft cheek or sing a little lullaby—perhaps then she could stop aching so for Abby. Maybe she could find reason to go on.

Just a week ago, while the traveling show was camped on the outskirts of Topeka, an epidemic of diphtheria had swept through the city. With it came the nightmare of fever, listlessness, and the panicked struggle for breath. Though diphtheria was known as a childhood illness, the strain that tore through Topeka grew especially virulent and soon began to claim adults. Scores had died, young and old alike.

Lily pressed her knuckles against her lips to hold back a sob. After two days of unbearable suffering, her precious Abigail had slipped away forever. Before long Lily's husband had also succumbed—Ted Nolan, the dashing but lazy fellow she had married to escape her sanctimonious and abusive father. Hours after the women had buried Ted, diphtheria claimed the traveling show's manager, Jakov Kasmarzik. In a panic, Beatrice had loaded as much of the show's gear as she could into one of their two wagons and headed west, with Lily barely able to function in her grief. Now the two women were trying to fill all the roles of the traveling show, hoping to earn their way to California. Or at least that was Beatrice's plan. Lily had no intention of going to California, but she didn't think Beatrice needed to know that yet.

"Would you take a look at that gaudy wagon, Caitrin," commented a woman strolling with her three companions just ahead of Lily. She wore her rich brown hair piled on her head, and the bulge beneath her dress gave evidence that soon she would bear a child. "Dr. Kasmarzik's Traveling Show," she read from the sign painted on the wagon where Madame Zahara proclaimed her message. "Fine Theater, Singing, Juggling! Featuring Dr. Kasmarzik's Patented Elixir. Cures Guaranteed!"

"Aye, Rosie," the other woman in the group chimed in, "and my own father was a leprechaun."

With a giggle, the one called Rosie read from the sign Beatrice had put up, its black canvas painted with silver stars: "Madame Zahara—Fortunes Told! Palms, Tea Leaves, and Tarot Cards Read! Now that sounds interesting. I've always wanted to visit a traveling show. What do you think, Seth? Could we stop at the show before we go and listen to the preacher?"

Lily frowned at the woman's mention of the traveling preacher who was running a stiff competition for Dr. Kasmarzik's Traveling Show. Who did the fellow think he was, this Reverend Elijah Book, scaring off business and ruining her chances of a good evening's income? Lily could see him, outlined by the golds and pinks of the setting sun, as he raised his hands to beckon the gathering crowd. No wonder the women came, dragging their husbands behind them. The preacher was as good-looking a fellow as Lily had ever seen.

Straight and tall, with deeply tanned skin and piercing blue eyes, he towered over his congregation like a stately cottonwood tree. Rather than a fine silk top hat, the preacher wore a brown Stetson that perched just above his dark brows and straight slash of a nose. In a blue chambray shirt, worn denim trousers, and scuffed leather boots, he looked like he ought to be rounding up strays on a Texas cattle ranch. But there he stood, waving his big black Bible and barking out Scripture like John the Baptist himself.

Lily glared at him. Three or four months more with the traveling show and she would have enough money for a train ticket to Philadelphia. Though she had fled her pious father almost two years before and had vowed never to return, now Lily was determined to journey back to the big brownstone that once had been her home. The consequences would be severe, she knew, but her future with the show held no hope at all.

Lily heard the woman's husband, Seth, give a grunt of disgust. "This little town has had enough troubles without a bunch of ne'er-do-wells looking to skin the locals."

"Aye," the Irishwoman agreed. "These sorts of people wander through Ireland in bright caravans, selling useless potions and swindling innocents of their hard-earned coins. The doctors are bad, and the fortune-tellers are worse. But 'tis the actors who cause all the bawdy revelry."

Behind them Lily bristled. It was true that Dr. Kasmarzik's potion, which sold for ten cents a bottle, was nothing more than a mixture of corn syrup, vinegar, peppermint oil, and a dash of turpentine. But her acting had never caused one moment of bawdiness. She performed selections from Shakespeare and the poets of Europe. She played the melodeon and sang arias from the great operas. Educated at the finest school for young ladies in Philadelphia, she brought culture and dignity to Dr. Kasmarzik's show. If customers did sometimes get out of hand, it certainly wasn't due to her performances.

"I've seen whole villages run amok when the traveling caravans passed through," the flame-haired Caitrin continued. "Husbands neglect their chores, and their wives form long lines at the fortune-teller's wagon. Children roam about neglected and hungry. On top of all that, the members of the traveling shows usually manage to steal anything left unattended."

Of all the gall, Lily thought, clenching her teeth. How dare these provincial prairie hens accuse her of thievery! She considered passing around them, but they continued on in the direction of the baby's cries, so she followed.

The preacher had managed to draw a bigger crowd than Madame Zahara, Lily realized. At thirty-five, Beatrice Waldowski cast a commanding presence in her flowing robes, long raven hair, crimson lips, and sultry brown eyes outlined in black kohl. Lily was never sure whether it was Madame Zahara's mystic predictions or the intimidating woman herself who struck awe in the hearts of the most rough-hewn customers. Whatever it was brought them back night after night to spend their coins at her table.

But now she had stiff competition. The preacher had spread open his Bible in his big hand and was holding it out toward the people like a plate of tempting hors d'oeuvres. The evening breeze riffled the thin pages, lifting and turning them one at a time, but the preacher didn't seem to notice. He just kept right on talking, reciting the story of Nicodemus's visit to Jesus in the middle of the night.

Lily shook her head. How many times had she heard *that* sermon? She could probably preach it with as much accuracy as she could recite Jakov Kasmarzik's opening act for the traveling show. Before long the preacher would announce those familiar words, "For God so loved the world—"

Ha, Lily thought. If God loved the world so much, why had he allowed her father to beat her black and blue while her mother stood by wringing her hands and doing nothing? Why had God let Ted and Jakov die of diphtheria? Why had he snatched away helpless little Abigail? For that matter, why was God permitting that poor baby in the distance to go on crying unattended? Couldn't any of these pious Crawthumpers hear the child's sobs?

To her, the baby's wails sounded as loud and demanding as the clanging bells of a fire wagon.

"Do you suppose Madame Zahara really can tell a person what's going to happen, Caitie?" The woman named Rosie paused to look back at the tent where Lily's table was set up. "Do you think she might know whether I'm bearing a boy or a girl?"

When the two couples halted at the edge of the crowd, Lily tried to move around them, but they were blocking her path. The preacher had packed the people as close around him as oysters in a can. Rooted to the ground, the crowd gaped upward as the man expounded on his text.

"You'll not set foot near that wagon, Rosie," Caitrin said in a loud whisper. "Sure you recall the very words of Scripture about such deviltry."

"I do not. I've been to church all my life, and I don't recall anyone ever saying it was wrong to visit a fortune-teller."

"It's in the middle of Deuteronomy, Rosie," Seth drawled. "I remember reading it that time you made me search for the verse about foundlings."

"I declare," Rosie muttered. "One of these days Deuteronomy is going to do me in."

Lily searched for another way through the crowd as Caitrin pulled a small Bible from her pocket and scanned the pages. "Here 'tis. 'There shall not be found among you any one that maketh his son or his daughter to pass through the fire,'" she read in a low voice, "'or that useth divination, or an observer of times, or an enchanter, or a witch, or a charmer, or a consulter with familiar spirits, or a wizard, or a necromancer. For all that do these things are an abomination unto the Lord.'"

"Well, for Pete's sakey," Rosie whispered. "I had no idea."

Lily pinched her lips and tapped the woman on the shoulder. "Excuse me," she said. "Could you step aside, ma'am? I'm trying to find that crying baby."

Brown eyes focused on Lily, roving from her white blond hair down the purple velvet cape to the tips of her scuffed brown boots. "Oh, have you lost your baby?"

Lily swallowed as the question stabbed through her. "Oh," she breathed. "Yes, I've lost . . . lost my baby. My Abigail."

"I can hear her crying," Rosie whispered. "Where did you leave your child?"

"I don't . . . don't know where she is." Lily shook her head. That wasn't what she meant to say. She knew Abigail was buried in the little box. The wooden box. "I need my baby. I can't . . . I can't stop hearing the cries."

"We'll find your daughter," Rosie said, taking Lily's hand. "Come on, Caitrin. Let's help this poor woman look for her baby. In the crush of people, the dear child could get hurt. Seth, you and Jack stay right here. We'll be back in a minute."

"I hear the wee one now," Caitrin said, in a strong Irish lilt. "'Tis on the other side beyond the Reverend Book. Let's go around the crowd."

Lily tried to force down the tears that welled unexpectedly in her eyes as the two women began to move her toward the sound she had been following. She wanted to tell them it wasn't Abigail, that her baby was dead, that this was some other woman's child. But the preacher's voice rang too loudly, hammering every word into the silence like a nail into a coffin.

"'Except a man be born again, he cannot see the kingdom of God!'" he thundered. Lily huddled down between Rosie and Caitrin as they pressed her through the throng. "'How can a man be born when he is old? can he enter the second time into his mother's womb, and be born?'"

No, Lily thought. Abby was dead, and she could never be born a second time. Only once would that precious newborn be laid on her mother's exhausted body. Only once would Lily feel the gentle pressure of the baby's weight in her arms, the nuzzle of a pink cheek, the grip of tiny fingers. Abby was lost. Lost forever.

"I've found her!" Rosie cried, dragging Lily toward a leather saddlebag hanging on the side of a horse that had been hobbled near the road. Within the pouch, something pushed, wriggled, and flailed as a cacophony of desperate cries drifted into the evening air. "Here's your baby!"

"Abigail?" Lily whispered, approaching the bag. Her heart faltered as she laid her hand on the soft leather. At her touch, the wailing ceased. But this couldn't be Abby. There must be another mother nearby. Some woman had left her baby in this bag. But why?

"Goodness gracious," Rosie said, "why did you put your daughter into a saddlebag? That's no place for a baby."

"No, I—" The baby began to wail again, cutting off her words.

"Why don't you take the poor little thing out and feed her? I grew up in an orphanage, and I've taken care of many a baby. I can almost bet your sweet Abigail is wet and hungry."

Hardly able to make herself breathe, Lily drew open the leather pouch and slipped her hands around the warm, damp little body. Oh, Abigail! The baby felt just like Abby . . . only smaller . . . newer. She lifted the squirming bundle out of the bag and tucked it against her neck. The child's soft lips immediately began to root hungrily.

"Aw, she's precious!" Rosie cried. "But she looks like she's half starved. You'd better feed her."

"Aye, sit here on this blanket," Caitrin spoke up, guiding Lily to a square of brightly woven wool stripes spread beneath a spindly tree. "Is this your camp? Here, I'll put the pillow behind your back. There now, little Abigail is so hungry she can hardly bear it. Sure she's all wrinkled up like a newborn! How old is she?"

Lily couldn't make herself speak. The kicking baby clung to her, sobbing in anguish as she tucked it beneath the purple cape. Where was the child's mother? She was the one who should be feeding this baby.

"Do you need help with your buttons?" Rosie asked, kneeling on the blanket.

"No, I can . . . I can do this." Lily couldn't hold back her tears as she performed the familiar motions of slipping apart the row of buttons, untying her camisole ribbon, and nestling the baby close. The moment the child began to nurse, all crying ceased, and the tiny legs curled into a ball.

"Abigail was famished!" Rosie said with a laugh. "Goodness, I don't believe she'd been fed for hours."

"Whisht, Rosie," Caitrin murmured. "The lady's still weeping, can't you see? There now, madam, you've got your baby once again. The wee thing will forget all about her hunger in a moment, and the pair of you can have a good night's rest."

Lily tried to stop crying. Truly she did. But as the baby drank milk meant for little Abby, her pain and longing only intensified. All around her, the world drifted away—the two caring women, the rough blanket, even the preacher, whose voice droned like the hum of a lazy bee. The baby's fingers were splayed across the bodice of Lily's dress, and she knew they were not Abby's fingers. The tiny head wreathed in a cloud of dark curls bore no resemblance to Abby with her golden wisps. The face was smaller, the cheeks sunken, the skin wrinkled. Abigail had been plump and round, at four months the picture of health. This was not Abby.

"She's still crying," Rosie whispered to Caitrin. "I hate to leave her alone like this."

The Irishwoman glanced over her shoulder. "The preaching's nearly finished for the evening, so it is. Sure we'd best get back to our men." She laid a hand on Lily's arm. "Are you all right? I know you're not from one of the homesteads around Hope, so you must have come traveling our way. Perhaps Rosie and I could have a look in the crowd for your husband."

"My husband is dead," Lily whispered as she cupped the baby's tiny head. The child was still nursing as though every drop of milk must be drained into her tiny, shrunken stomach. Lily shifted the baby into her other arm, and the child began to suckle again. "Three days ago. He's buried near Topeka. My daughter lies beside him."

"Your daughter?"

Lily brushed her damp cheek. "I buried her in a wooden box."

"Oh, dear," Rosie said. "I'm so sorry. No wonder you're upset—a husband and a daughter both gone. I couldn't imagine how any woman could forget where she'd put her baby, but now I see you've been through a terrible trial. If I lost Seth and Chipper, I'd be just wild with grief. I couldn't bear it. Oh, honey, do you and little Abigail need a place to sleep tonight? I hate to think of you out here on the prairie with nothing but a blanket and that old horse. Seth and I have a great big house, lots of space, and we'd be glad to put you and your daughter up for the night."

Lily could feel that the baby had finally drifted off to sleep, warm and content at last. "No, no, you don't understand," she murmured, drawing the tiny form out from beneath the purple cape and gazing down at the child's blissful face. "This is . . . this is going to be all right. In a moment, I'll leave."

"Leave?" Caitrin exclaimed. "But 'tis almost fully dark now. You're a nursing mother and a *frainey* one at that. Sure you can't be tramping down the road in the middle of the night."

"Hey!" The preacher's voice pealed out like a clap of thunder. "What's going on here?"

Lily's head snapped up. Just beyond the blanket stood the two men who had accompanied Rosie and Caitrin. Between them, his boots planted a pace apart on the prairie grass, towered the preacher. He swept off his Stetson, took a step toward the women, and punched the air with his forefinger.

"Look here, lady," he snarled at Lily. "I don't know who you are or what you're up to, but you'd better hand over my baby. I've been given two jobs to do in this world. One of them is to preach the gospel. And the other is to take care of Samuel."

"Samuel?" Rosie and Caitrin said in unison. "*Samuel?*"

CHAPTER 2

"YES, Samuel. That's my baby." Elijah stuffed his hat back onto his head and took another step toward the pretty blond-haired woman in the purple cape. What was going on here? "Who're you?"

She looked up at him with big blue eyes and tearstained cheeks. "Lily Nolan," she said softly, holding Samuel out in her arms. "I'm sorry."

"Well, I reckon so." He knelt on one knee and took the baby. The instant his big hands closed around the damp little bundle, Samuel's eyes shot open and he let out a squall that could have shattered glass. Eli's heart sank. "Aw, don't start that again, fella. Come on, now, young'un, buck up."

He drew the baby close and awkwardly rocked him from side to side. Just like always, it didn't do a bit of good. The baby kept on hollering, his little fists pumping the air in a rage.

"Please," the woman said, reaching out. Before Eli could react, she took the baby, turned him sideways, and tucked him into the crook of Eli's elbow. "This is the way to hold your son," she said, "and put your hand under his bottom."

"He's wet!"

"He certainly is. Where's his mother? She ought to have changed and fed him hours ago. It's no wonder this baby's been crying his head off. He's miserable. He wants his mother."

"We thought *you* were his mother, Mrs. Nolan," the woman beside her said.

"What's going on here, Rosie?" Seth Hunter asked.

"This woman told Caitrin and me that she'd lost her husband and her daughter in Topeka three days ago. She said she could hear Abigail crying, and when we found this baby in the saddlebag, she started feeding him."

"You fed Samuel?" Eli demanded of the blond woman. He looked down at the baby, who had settled into a drowsy daze. As a matter of fact, this was the first time Sam had been quiet since Eli could remember. A miracle. "What did you feed him?"

"She nursed him," the other woman said. "She told us the baby was her daughter, Abigail."

"No . . . no, I didn't." Lily gathered her skirts and stood. "I said I had lost my baby. And I have. I've lost Abigail. Sometimes I think I hear her crying, but then I remember that she . . . that Abby is dead. My baby is gone . . . she's dead . . ."

Clapping her hand over her mouth, she fled. Eli frowned. A dead husband and a lost baby. A complete stranger nursing Sam.

But the baby was quiet. Quiet for the first time ever. Sleeping.

"Whoa, lady!" Eli bellowed. "Hold your horses there."

When she didn't stop, he took off after her. Samuel jerked awake and went to wailing again, but Eli had gotten so used to the ruckus he hardly noticed as he loped through the tall prairie grass. *God,* his heart cried out, *show me what to do here! You gave me this child, and I don't want him to die. Maybe you sent along this gal, too. Please make her stop running away.*

Her purple cape billowing behind, the woman jogged on as if she had no idea where she was going. Eli easily caught up to her, snagged her elbow, and swung her around. To his dismay, he saw that tears were streaming down her cheeks.

"Ma'am," he said over Sam's screams, "listen, I didn't aim to scare you. You don't need to be afraid of me. I'm just a preacher, and not much of one at that. Look, I don't know a thing about babies, feeding them or holding them or anything, and I'm real sorry to hear about your husband and your young'un passing on. Fact is, I appreciate you taking care of Samuel here."

"What?" She wiped her cheek with the heel of her hand. "Where's your wife?"

"I don't have a wife. I'm not married."

"You're not marr—oh, give me that child."

She took the screaming baby out of his arms, rearranged the wrinkled blanket, and tucked Samuel's head against the side of her neck. When she began to sway gently from side to side, the baby gave a big hiccup and fell silent.

"Where is this child's mother?" she demanded in a low voice.

Eli took off his hat and tapped it on his thigh a couple of times. "Dead." He spoke the word under his breath, as if the child could understand its significance. "A few days back when I was down south, inside the border of the Osage Indian reservation, I came upon a wagon on the trail. It had been shot full of arrows. I reckon you know the Osages don't like the way squatters have been moving onto their land and petitioning the government to move the tribe into Oklahoma. Anyhow, I saw right off that the man was already dead and the woman was a goner. She pushed the little fella into my arms and begged me to keep him safe. 'Teach Samuel to love the Lord,' she said, and then she breathed her last."

The swaying stopped. "How long ago?"

"Four days."

"But this baby can't be much more than a week old. What have you been feeding him?"

Eli scratched the back of his neck. "I tried mashed potatoes," he admitted. "He doesn't like them much. He did better on scrambled eggs. I don't have a bottle, and he's not real good with a cup. I manage to get a little water down him now and then. I know he needs milk, but I'm a traveling man—"

"The baby is starving. He'll die without proper nourishment." Her blue eyes flashed. "You'd better find this child some milk, Preacher-man, or you'll have his soul on your conscience."

"Brother Elijah?" Seth Hunter, Jack Cornwall, and the other two women were striding across the prairie toward him. Right after the preaching service that evening, Seth and Jack had approached Eli with an interesting proposition, and he wanted to hear more. But now all he could think of was this woman's prediction of doom.

"Brother Elijah," Seth called again. "I want you to meet my wife, Rose, and this is her friend Caitrin Murphy. Jack Cornwall here is engaged to marry Miss Murphy."

"Elijah Book," he said, giving the women a nod. "Pleased to meet you, ladies."

"Reverend Book," Rose Hunter addressed him. "It's our privilege to have you in Hope."

"I'm not much of a reverend, ma'am. I'm just a cowhand from Amarillo who heard the voice of God calling him to preach. I've been on the trail since March, riding from one place to another and speaking the word of the Lord."

"I've asked Brother Elijah if he would be willing to stay on in Hope for a couple of weeks," Seth told the women. "He could perform the wedding for Jack and Caitrin, and maybe he'd preach us a few sermons in our new church."

"A couple of weeks?" Rose Hunter cried. "Why not permanently? You could become our very own minister, Brother Elijah! You and your wife and son could live here in Hope while you minister to the homesteaders."

"I'm not married, ma'am," Eli said. "Samuel's parents were ambushed on the trail, and God put the boy into my hands to bring up."

"Then he's a foundling like I am!" Rose exclaimed, wonder lighting her pretty face.

"Brother Elijah, this is the answer to your prayers *and* ours," Rose's friend Caitrin said warmly. "Sure you can raise little Samuel in a town filled with loving people who will look after him as though he were our own. And instead of making poor Seth search all over Topeka for a preacher willing to move to Hope, God has sent you to us."

"Now hold on a minute there," Eli put in. "I appreciate the notion, and I know you folks mean well. But the truth is, I'm on my way to China."

"China?" Rose and Caitrin echoed each other again.

"That's right. I told the Lord I'd go wherever he sent me to preach his message of forgiveness and salvation, even across the seas to the farthest lands of the earth."

The woman holding Samuel gave a little grunt of laughter. "And what did God say to your grand offer?" she challenged him. "Look, Preacher-man, I've got to go. You'd better start feeding this baby on something better than mashed potatoes. And change his diaper now and then."

She held Samuel out to Eli. He shook his head and hooked his thumbs in his pockets. "If God sent anyone, I believe it was this lady to Samuel."

"Oh, no. I—"

"You just gave Samuel a taste of manna from heaven. Look at him lying there in your arms. That boy hasn't slept more than a wink since the day I found him. Now his belly's full and warm, and he's got the light of hope in his heart. Would you consider keeping it burning?"

"What are you talking about? I can't stay here. I have a job to do. I've got to earn enough money to get back home."

"Then I'll pay you to feed him."

"You're crazy." She glanced away for a moment, hesitating in spite of herself.

"Just a few days, ma'am. Just to get Sam on his feet."

Scorn flashed in her eyes. "He's a *baby*. He won't be on his feet for months—and it'll take a lot longer than a few days to make him healthy again."

"Please." Eli rolled his hat brim in his hand. "Please help me. Do it for the boy."

She gazed down at the baby in her arms, and Eli sensed her weakening. *God, she's a woman,* he prayed silently, *a tender, loving woman. Open her heart to Samuel. Touch her soul, please, Lord.*

"How much?" she asked, her voice flat. "I can make three dollars a day at my regular job, and that's for just a few hours of work. How many of those tithes and offerings are you willing to turn loose of, Preacher-man?"

Eli's eyes narrowed at the harshness of her words. Would it even be right to let such a bitter woman tend to the boy? The fact was, he couldn't come close to paying her three dollars a day. True, people often contributed to his ministry when he finished preaching a sermon. But he barely scraped enough money out of his hat to buy himself a little flour and a few mealy potatoes each week. Any extra money he could put aside, he kept in a pouch on his belt—the savings for his passage to China.

"All right," he said, untying the pouch. If God wanted to send him to China, he'd provide the means some other way. "You can take all I've got, ma'am. It's four dollars and fifty cents. That'll keep Samuel going for a day and a half."

He held out the pouch, pleading with God to make the woman take it. It didn't matter that she had a hard heart, or that he ought to get back on his horse and ride to another town to preach, or even that this would clean out his entire missions treasury. What mattered was Samuel. The baby had to live.

"Now hold on a minute there, Brother Elijah," Seth Hunter said. "Let's think the situation through. This woman needs pay. You need this woman. And we need you. Why not let us pay you to be our town preacher? Then you can pay her to feed the baby."

"The fact is, I'm on my way to China," Eli said.

"The fact is, I'm on my way back to Philadelphia," the woman spoke up. "And I don't intend to sit around all summer in a barren little town waiting hand and foot on some good-for-nothing preacher who thinks he can just pick a baby up off the road like an old discarded hat and . . . and feed it mashed potatoes and keep it in a saddlebag, when other people . . . other people's babies die of diphtheria . . . and fever . . . and they have to be buried in little wooden boxes . . . and what do you know about God anyway, Preacher-man?" She had started crying again, heavy tears dripping onto Samuel's blanket. "You don't deserve this baby. You didn't do anything to earn him. Nothing. You don't have any idea what it means to suffer . . . and . . . and marry someone you don't even love and live in a tent just so that . . . so that you can know the joy of one day holding your own baby . . . your own baby in your arms . . . and loving her . . ."

"There now," Rose Hunter said, slipping her arm around the sobbing woman. "Of course Brother Elijah doesn't know the terrible pain you've suffered. All he knows is that he cares for this little baby, and he needs your help."

"Won't you help?" Caitrin asked her. "Do it to honor the memory of your little Abigail. Do it for Samuel."

Stricken, Eli stared at the woman holding the child God had given him. Who was she? Why did anger bubble out of her like lava, searing everything it touched? She was beautiful, delicate-boned, as fragile as a porcelain teacup. Her golden hair gleamed in the lamplight, and her skin looked as soft as the petals of a white rose. Who had hurt her so deeply that raw pain tinged every word she spoke?

"All I wanted was to hold Abigail again," she was murmuring against Mrs. Hunter's shoulder. "I thought it might be my own baby crying, but then . . . then it was this little . . . this boy with dark hair and wrinkled skin . . . and he's not Abby. . . ."

"No, he's not," Rose Hunter said. "But he's alive, he's hungry for life, and he deserves the chance to grow and learn and become a man someday."

"Sure the best we could do for him here in Hope is feed him sugar water or cow's milk," Caitrin continued, "and you said yourself that he's already far gone. Samuel needs what only you can give him. Please do this."

"Please?" Rose whispered.

Elijah stared at the blond woman as though by sheer willpower he could force her to agree to help. *Care for the baby*, he mentally ordered her. *Care for him as much as I do*.

Growing up out in cattle country, Elijah had had only one person to look out for. Himself. He'd always lived a rootless life, as a child wandering with his father from job to job and then as a young man making his own way as a hired hand on one roundup or another. One night during the past winter, cold and hungry, he had broken into a settler's cabin and stolen everything he could lay his hands on. Including a Bible.

Three days and nights of nothing but reading the words in that book had broken him like a dried-up cottonwood limb. Down on his knees he had begged for God's forgiveness and surrendered his soul to Jesus Christ. He had returned the stolen goods, ridden into the nearest town, found a preacher to guide him, and started walking on the path of a new life.

And he'd realized that the world was not about Elijah Book. It was about other people—people who were hurting, empty, rebellious, and lost. People like this woman in the purple robe. Eli longed to reach out to her and touch her soul with the words of God. But he knew she held Samuel's future in her hands, and one wrong move from him . . . one misspoken word . . . *Please God, unlock her heart. . . .*

"All right," she said, nodding quickly. "All right, I'll do it for a few days. But I have to have money."

"Then I'll take the preaching job," Elijah told Seth Hunter. "Whatever the town can afford to pay for my work, give all the money to this woman."

Shock widened her eyes as she lifted her head to look at him. "Why would you do that? This baby isn't even yours. You don't love him. You don't know how to take care of him. You have no wife, no home, nothing to offer him. Why would you go to all this trouble for a baby you found on the trail like a—"

"Like an old discarded hat?" Eli settled his hat on his head. "The way I see it, ma'am, most folks are just like Sam here. We're lost, abandoned souls on the trail to nowhere. And we're all just about to starve to death. If we let him, God will come along and pick us up, feed us manna from heaven, and make us his own children. And that's the way Sam is my son, even though all I did was find him on the trail and pick him up out of his dying mama's arms."

"A very pretty sermon, Preacher-man," she said, her blue eyes unwavering. "Now where do you plan on holing up with this baby? Or are you going to keep camping on an old wool blanket under that skinny tree over there?"

Whoa, she was one tough little woman, Elijah thought. Hard as a rock and stubborn to boot. But he knew she had a softness somewhere inside her, and he was just going to have to trust God to touch it.

"Brother Elijah, you can live in the new church building," Seth Hunter said. "We built a little room in the back with the aim of starting up a Sunday school some day. You can stash your gear in there and stable your horse over at my place. And as for you, Mrs.—"

"Nolan," the woman said. "Lily Nolan. I won't be needing your charity. I have my own wagon, and I'll keep the baby with me until—"

"Lily?" A wild-looking female in a red Chinese silk robe, with long black hair and eyes smudged all around with black paint, came racing toward the group of people gathered around the baby. "Lily Nolan, where have you been? I sent the crowd to your tent half an hour ago, and they're already swarming around demanding their money back and threatening to tear me apart. What in the name of heaven have you been doing? Whose baby is that?"

"He's mine," Elijah said. "Who're you?"

"I am Madame Zahara." She straightened her shoulders and gave him a half-lidded gaze. "I know you. You're the preacher."

"I sure am."

"You've been luring away our customers the past two nights. Now I see you've put my assistant under your spell."

"Your assistant?" Elijah turned to Lily Nolan. "*You* work at that traveling show?"

"I perform operas and soliloquies," she confirmed.

"And she reads palms, crystal balls, and tarot cards," Madame Zahara added. "With the deaths of both her husband and our leader, Mrs. Nolan and I run the traveling show together. Now, Lily, you've got to get over to the fortune-telling tent and do your job. I've taken in almost two dollars from folks wanting to hear their fortunes, and they're mad as hops waiting for you to show up."

Elijah studied the golden-haired woman, waiting for her response. Would she buckle in to the witch in the red silk gown? Would she choose to return to that sinful, fleshly occupation of *actress*? Or would she take the higher path of sacrifice for her fellowman?

Eli's chest almost hurt with praying that she would give herself to Samuel. But now his gut twisted with doubt about her worthiness for such a high calling. A woman who had chosen a life as a performer with a traveling show—could this Lily Nolan do anybody any good?

"Well?" Madam Zahara snapped. "Give the fellow his baby, and come on!"

Lily bit her lower lip as her eyes traced over the small shape in her arms. "Not tonight, Beatrice," she said, lifting her head. "The preacher's offered me good wages to feed his baby. You'd better go read the fortunes yourself."

"What?" The woman's dark eyes hardened. "Are you running out on me, Lily? After all I've done for you?"

"I'm not deserting you, Bea," Lily said. "You know I would never do that. We'll stay here a few days and save up my earnings. While I look out for the preacher's baby, you can boil a new batch of potion. It'll be a chance for us to figure out how we're going to manage the show without Ted and Jakov."

"I know how to manage the show. All Jakov ever did was perform the opening act. I created the entertainment. I planned the programs and counted the money. Oh, Lily, I told you I'd take care of you, didn't I? We're partners, the two of us. We'll make it. We'll be fine."

Elijah had the awfulest feeling that Madame Zahara was about to cry, and he didn't think it would be a pretty sight. The woman herself was attractive in a mysterious, exotic sort of way. She had almond-shaped brown eyes, full red lips, and glowing olive skin. Her crimson silk gown was cut too low for any decent man to approve of, and her black hair draped around her shoulders like a luxurious cloak.

But every time she looked at Elijah, a prickle ran right up his spine. He felt pretty sure he recognized that prickle. It warned him of the presence of evil.

"Lily, let's head west like we planned," Madame Zahara said, her painted eyes persuasive. "We'll go on to Manhattan and set up camp. You can recite Ophelia's soliloquy there if you want. I know you've been under such a strain losing little Abby, and this preacher is preying on your kindness. Look at him, Lily. He's no different from the sort of man you've always despised. He's selfish and pious and unloving, and he's out to make all the money he can—and doing it in the name of God."

Lily's blue eyes focused on Elijah, and it was all he could do not to take off running. Truth to tell, he *was* selfish. Always had been. But God was working on him, breaking down the walls he'd built as a boy. And he sometimes was pious. Sure enough, not two minutes ago he had stood there mentally running Mrs. Lily Nolan into the ground for being an actress. What made *him* so perfect? Nothing but the forgiving grace of God the Father. And unloving . . . well, he never had been too warm around people. He wasn't much for hugging and kissing and all that. Made his back itch.

"I can read your spirit, Preacher," Madame Zahara said, turning her painted eyes on him. "I know what lies within your heart. If I looked into your palm, I could see the roads on which you've traveled. Paths of arrogance and self-importance. You believe you've found the one truth—the single answer to life. But you're wrong. All paths lead to God. Every person has the spark of divine truth within himself, and all we need to do is trust our own heart to touch the holiness inside us."

Elijah listened to her words. They had a ring of truth to them—but they weren't right. He knew there was only one path to God, and that was through Jesus Christ. On that path, he had found peace and comfort and hope. He had found forgiveness and a reason to live. Why was this woman trying to distort the truth?

"Let Lily go," she said, laying a hand on his arm. "Set her free to follow her own destiny. Don't try to control others with your words, Preacher. Let them seek truth and find that spirit in the place where it has always dwelled. In their hearts."

Elijah took off his hat and tapped it on his thigh a couple of times. "Well, ma'am, I appreciate your concern for Mrs. Nolan," he began. "Truly, I do. But the fact is, I've got a starving baby here, and she's got the means to feed him. Now, we've made a deal, this lady and I, and I aim to see that it's honored."

"That proves exactly what I was saying!" Madame Zahara exploded. "You are an arrogant, selfish—"

"I am a man with a hungry baby and nobody to—"

"Excuse me here," Lily Nolan cut in. "*I'm* the one who'll be making the decision. Beatrice, this baby needs a fresh diaper, another feeding, and a good night's sleep. I'm going to see that he gets it. And as for you, Preacher-man, you'd better start cooking up a humdinger of a sermon. It's almost Sunday, and I'll expect to find you over at the church reeling them in and emptying their pockets so you can pay my wages."

Eli swallowed hard as she turned and walked off toward the gaudy wagon of the traveling show. He didn't like Lily Nolan. Didn't like her at all. And sure as shootin', he didn't want her looking after little Samuel one more day than necessary.

"You're such a teensy little fellow," Lily murmured the next evening as baby Samuel regarded her solemnly. "But you've got big brown eyes and lots of hair. Where'd you get all that hair, huh? I think you're strong enough that we might try to wash it tomorrow. Yes, sir, Mr. Samuel, you need a bath and some warm oil on your skin." Lily had lovingly tended the tiny baby all through the night and today as well. After settling up with the irate customers, Beatrice had been pointedly ignoring Lily and her new little companion.

As Lily stroked the baby's cheek, he turned his head to the side and pressed his mouth against her hand. "I bet you're hungry again, you fuzzy little caterpillar. What has that big ol' preacher been feeding you? Mashed potatoes? And scrambled eggs, too? Glory be, no wonder you're so skinny. Next time he tries a trick like that, you just spit those potatoes right back in his face."

She reflected on the handsome preacher and his bold sermonizing. What a contrast to the frantic look in his blue eyes when he was pleading with her to feed the baby he'd found. Truth to tell, she would gladly care for little Samuel and never take a penny. But she had enjoyed watching the man squirm.

She sensed he was just like her father—held in high regard by the townsfolk, while they knew nothing of his true nature. She could picture her father marching into church with his head held high and his huge walrus mustache gleaming with wax. The grand gentleman, conductor of the Greater New England Symphony and minister of music at the First United Church of St. George, cut an imposing figure as he stood before the congregation and sang hymns in his melodic baritone.

No one knew, of course, that this same man could use his voice to subjugate his wife until she was sobbing in humiliation. The huge hands that held a baton with such finesse could slam a child to the floor or swing a leather belt across a little girl's bare flesh until it split open and began to bleed. The man who sang that "God is love; his mercy brightens all the path in which we rove" could turn on his family with hatred, rage, and unforgiving fury with a speed that rivaled the sudden flash of summer lightning.

Always fearful, yet somehow always unprepared for her father's wrath, Lily would crouch on the floor and cover her head until the storm of his anger had passed. And while he punished his daughter for the demons that lived in his own soul, she would journey to a secret place inside herself and listen to the sweet music in her heart.

"Forget me not, forget me never," she sang softly as she cradled the nursing Samuel. "Till yonder sun shall set forever."

Only after she had escaped her father, only in the sanctuary of the traveling show, had Lily ventured to sing aloud. Like a miracle, music had bubbled forth from her voice—arias, ballads, even meaningless jingles she had heard among her schoolmates. Beatrice had encouraged Lily to add singing and drama to the show, and as she performed, the young woman began to feel alive for the first time in her life.

"I gave my love a cherry that had no stone," she sang to the drowsy baby.

"I gave my love a chicken that had no bone.
I gave my love a ring that had no end.
I gave my love a baby with no cryin'."

Then with Abigail, Lily finally had known true love. Oh, Abby! Her baby's precious face formed in her memory. Deep blue eyes, downy golden hair, a sweet toothless smile. In the sea of misery, mistakes, and futility that Lily's life had become, Abby had been the only ray of hope. Gazing into that angelic face, a lonely woman could forget her father's rage-twisted features, her husband's wandering eyes, even her own desperate race down a darkened path with no end.

For the hundredth time, Lily's mind rebelled at the idea that the child was dead. Her heart refused to believe she would never again kiss that petal-soft cheek. Even her body had refused to acknowledge that the child no longer needed nourishment. Swollen, aching, tender, Lily hugged the orphaned Samuel close as she continued singing.

"A cherry when it's blooming, it has no stone,
A chicken when it's pipping, it has no bone.
A ring when it's rolling, it has no end.
A baby when it's sleeping, there's no cryin'."

"No cryin'," a rich voice echoed the final three notes. "Amen and amen."

A tiny female face with skin as dark and shriveled as a prune peered through an opening in the wagon's canvas covering. Gasping in shock, Lily clutched the baby tightly. When the old woman's bright brown eyes took in the sight of the nursing woman and contented child, a wide smile spread across her face.

"Mercy, mercy, mercy. Don't this beat all?" A gnarled hand with clawlike fingers reached out and gave the baby a pat. "Howdy-do."

"Hello," Lily said warily. "Do I know you?"

"Not yet, but you will. I'm Margaret Hanks. Folks round here call me Mother Margaret."

Lily stared in confusion. What business did this woman have snooping around in other people's wagons? Samuel had almost dropped off to sleep, and Lily herself was exhausted.

"Excuse me, ma'am," she began, "but I'm—"

"Oh, I know you, sure enough. You're the lady come to look after the baby. Folks is talkin' about it all over town, and I come out to see you for myself. When I heard you in here singin' like an angel, I knew God hisself done sent you. Mercy, mercy, mercy, child, and bless your heart."

Lily couldn't hide her smile, though she couldn't understand why her heart warmed so quickly to this odd little stranger. "I don't mind," she said softly. "I lost my own baby."

"I heard that, too. Child, I lost three of my fourteen, and my heart ain't never healed from the pain of it. Listen to Mother Margaret, now; why don't you and that baby come on over to our house and take supper with us? We got fried chicken and greens. Cherry cobbler, too. You eat with us, and then you stay the night in one of our beds. We'll make you a place with us, yes ma'am, and may the Lord be praised for his almighty wisdom. Amen and amen."

CHAPTER 3

LILY cradled the baby and willed herself to remain seated. Why did the old woman's words inspire such a sense of assurance and calm? How could a stranger know what a hot meal and a warm bed would mean to a grief-stricken traveler? And what had propelled this Mother Margaret across the prairie in the darkness?

"I know it don't seem usual," the woman said, "and maybe you wouldn't want to visit with folk who used to be slaves—"

"No," Lily said quickly. "It's not that. But you don't know me. You know nothing about me."

"Aw, sure I do. God sent you along here to help us out. Now you plannin' to come eat some of Mother Margaret's cherry cobbler or not?"

Lily's stomach tightened at the enticing thought. With her body depleted and this new baby so ravenous, Lily couldn't deny her own need. "All right. I'll come with you," she said. "And I thank you for welcoming me."

"Mercy, mercy, mercy," the old woman clucked as Lily made her way out of the wagon. "You're as welcome in Hope as anybody else. Look at the Hanks family! Two months back, my boy, his wife, and I followed the Cornwall family out here to Kansas. Hankses been in the Cornwall family for generations, don't you know. We was their slaves, of course, and now we're freed folks. Yes, ma'am, free as the wind. But the fact is, we respect the Cornwalls, and they always done us good. My Ben built us a fine house over yonder near the Cornwall smithy."

Lily tried to concentrate as she carried the baby through the tall grass. "I don't know the Cornwalls."

"You met Mister Jack earlier. He's a big tall fellow, lives with his mammy and his little sister, Lucy. The Cornwalls is as happy as fleas in a doghouse these days. It just took a little doin' for everybody in town to get used to them."

"Did the Cornwalls cause some kind of trouble here?"

"Hoo, you done said it, gal. But that's all in the past. Ben helps Mister Jack at the smithy, and Eva takes in laundry and mendin'. Me, I look after Miss Lucy when she's feeling bad. We're as much a part of things round here as quills on a goose." She paused. "Now, who's this a-comin'? She's got eyes that would chill a side of beef."

"Lily?" Beatrice Waldowski raced toward them. "Lily, where are you going?"

"Beatrice!" Lily stopped. "I didn't realize you were still about. It's very late."

"Have you gone mad?" Beatrice wore yet another version of her Madame Zahara outfit. "Of course I'm up. I've been reading palms and tarot cards in the tent. We have customers, you know. We have commitments. What are you doing?"

"I'm . . . I'm going with Mrs. Hanks." Lily swallowed, realizing how foolish she must appear to her friend. "She invited me for dinner, and I—"

"Dinner? Do you even know this woman? Oh, Lily!" Beatrice clasped the younger woman tightly and spoke against her ear. "I'm so frightened for you. You're not acting like yourself—taking in this baby and then wandering off with a stranger. Losing Abigail has distracted you and upset your spiritual balance. I'm frightened for you. Come with me, Lil. Come back to the wagon now. We'll pack up and leave in the morning, and I promise I'll take you far away from all this."

"Now just a cotton-pickin' minute," Mother Margaret spoke up, swelling to her full five-foot height. Her clawed finger shot upward and wagged in Beatrice's face. "Miss Lily is comin' to my house for supper, sure enough. You can come too, if you want, but don't you go turnin' this poor woman away from my door. Not now. Not when she needs me."

"Lily doesn't need you," Beatrice snapped. "She doesn't even know you."

"It's all right, Bea." Lily held up a hand. "Mother Margaret has offered me a meal. Why don't you join us?"

One eyebrow arched as Beatrice took in the small black woman. "I'd rather dine in hell."

She turned to leave, then swung back around. "And, Lily, don't think I'll let you go so easily. You're all I have. You're my dearest friend. I won't let your grief and these conniving people tear us apart."

Lily watched in dismay as Beatrice marched toward the wagon. It was true—they were close friends and had been comrades through many hardships. Beatrice Waldowski had believed in Lily when no one else would. Beatrice had helped Ted Nolan covertly marry and then spirit away the forlorn young woman who had appeared at their show night after night in Philadelphia. Elopement, escape, freedom. Beatrice had promised Lily a new life, and she had delivered.

True, they'd often gone hungry and unwashed. The show had been run out of many towns. No one but Beatrice had really appreciated Lily's soliloquies and arias. And then there had been Ted—a vain man, a drifter, a womanizer. But he hadn't beaten Lily, as her own father had, and he had given her Abigail. Beautiful Abigail.

"Hoo, I'm glad she's gone," Mother Margaret said. "That woman flat gave me the willies."

"Beatrice is my friend. She may appear harsh at times, but she has a kind heart."

"Uh-huh." The old woman sounded unconvinced. "Let me tell you about some kind folks. You see them lights a long way off, child? That's the home of Rosie and Seth Hunter. They've got a little boy named Chipper, and they're gonna have a new baby come autumn. Down the middle of town is the mercantile. Miss Caitrin Murphy lives in the soddy nearby, and she's fixin' to marry Mister Jack. The Cornwalls built them a place near the smithy, and my boy Ben put our house on the other side. Come on, now; I can smell that cobbler."

Reluctant to stray so far from her friend, Lily moved slowly up the road toward the smithy. Where would she be without Beatrice Waldowski? She'd be back in the brick house in Philadelphia, living under the thumb of her father and probably preparing for marriage. No doubt her parents would expect her to marry a man like Reverend Hardcastle's son, who was planning to take his father's place in the pulpit of St. George. Lily groaned. The last thing she wanted to do was marry a preacher.

"Mrs. Hanks?" Elijah Book stepped out of the small frame house and held up a lantern. "Did you find her?"

Lily stopped in her tracks. "What are *you* doing here? Is this some kind of a trick?"

"Brother Elijah is eatin' supper with us, same as you," Mother Margaret said as she headed for the front door. "Folks has got to feed the preacher, don't you know. It's mannerly."

Unbudging, Lily watched the tall man approach. He took off his hat, clearly as ill at ease as she. "Mrs. Nolan," he began, his blue eyes intense in the lantern light. "I was hoping you'd come to the Hankses' home."

"Why? Don't you trust me to take care of Samuel in my own wagon?"

He shifted from one foot to the other. "Well . . . as a matter of fact, it does make me a little uncomfortable."

"Because I'm an actress."

"But that doesn't mean I want you to stop feeding Samuel. Sam needs your help. I just thought maybe if you'd be willing to stay here with the Hanks family for a few days—"

"Do you mean to tell me you sent that poor old woman all the way across the prairie to rescue this baby?"

"No, it's not like that. Mrs. Hanks suggested it. I was over here visiting with the family, and I got to talking about the wagon and how maybe you'd like someplace quieter. I know you live in a traveling show, and that means—"

"What does it mean, buster?" Lily took a step toward him. "That wagon is my home, and Beatrice is one of the kindest people I've ever known. She took me in, and she gave me food and a bed and honest work—and don't you ever, *ever*—"

"I'm just thinking of Samuel."

"You're thinking of your own high-and-mighty reputation!" she snapped. "You want to make sure nothing around you looks too bad or too shameful because then it would reflect poorly on you. I'd wager you took in this baby just to prove to everybody how righteous and holy you are. 'Oh, the poor traveling preacher with his little orphan baby,' everybody will say. 'How sweet, how kind! Why, let's feed that preacher some dinner. Let's flock all around him like hungry little chickens. Let's give him our money.'"

"Now, listen here, ma'am," Elijah growled, his forefinger jabbing toward her. "I accepted that baby because God gave him to me. You think I'd be crazy enough to *want* to haul a squallin' kid around with me? I can't sleep, I can't think, I can't even pray with him hollering his head off every minute of the day and night. But I'm going to give that boy all I've got as long as I live because he's my responsibility, and I don't care what anybody thinks about it. Especially you."

As he spoke, Elijah advanced on her. Shoulders squared and head thrust forward, he was menacing, terrifying. "And as for the notion that I take folks' money," he barked, "I'll have you know I was supposed to go to China, but I gave all my money to you. That's where the money's gone—to you!"

Lily couldn't listen. She had to hide. Had to find that place inside herself where she could escape the anger.

"And if you think I'm so righteous and holy," he went on, "well, I'll tell you a thing or two about that. Not too long ago, I was just where you are. I was roaming around, doing whatever felt good to me, living my life just the way I liked it. I know how an actress in a traveling show lives. I know the kinds of things you do to earn money. . . ."

He was coming now. Closer and closer, he was coming. And soon, very soon, it would begin. Lily sank to her knees and covered the baby with her body. Both hands over her head, she squeezed her eyes shut and began to listen to the music inside herself. Golden melodies poured through her heart and filled her mind. The music lifted her up and away from his words, taking her far from the fear, the rage, the pain.

"Miz Nolan?" his voice asked.

She shrank from his touch, willing the music to keep her alive. Silver harmonies. Crystal notes.

"Are you all right, ma'am?" He was crouching in the grass beside her, his big hand gently laid on her arm. "I didn't aim to scare you. I'll admit I was a little frustrated, but . . . are you OK under there? You can come out. I won't do a thing, I swear."

Lily lowered her hands and lifted her head. It wasn't her father after all. It was Elijah Book. The preacher gazed at her with blue eyes full of concern. His Stetson had tumbled to the ground. A lock of hair had fallen over his forehead.

"You can keep Samuel in your wagon if you want," he said in a low voice. "I'm sorry. I'm sure sorry I scared you."

Unable to stop trembling, Lily straightened and held out the baby. "Take him. I can't do this."

"Please. I need you." He slid his hand down her arm and touched her fingers. "Don't be afraid of me. I would never hurt you."

"Mercy, mercy, mercy!" Mother Margaret's small feet appeared at the edge of Lily's vision. "What you two doin' down in the grass? I went in to check on the chicken, and next thing I know, you done disappeared. Everything all right?"

"Yes," Elijah Book said, his eyes locked on Lily's face. "It's going to be all right."

"Lemme see what you got there, Brother Elijah," Mother Margaret said as she and her family joined their guests outside on the front porch after the sumptuous meal. "You got the biggest, fattest Bible I ever did see. And what is that other book?"

Elijah showed the old woman the Holy Bible he had purchased right after his call to preach the gospel. He had traded his life's savings for the leather-bound volume, and he considered it a treasure. But the small hymnal he now placed in Mother Margaret's hand ran a close second. His mother had once owned the slender book of music, and she had sung the hymns to him as he sat on her lap. Elijah had found it in her trunk many years after her death. Even before he came to understand the message in the Bible, he had read those songs again and again. Their words had lit his path.

"That's my hymnbook," he said. "I can't carry a tune in a bucket, but I know every song by heart."

The old woman turned through the worn pages one by one. Her son, Ben, leaned over and examined the book with his mother. Elijah pushed back in his chair, hooked one boot over the other, and locked his hands behind his head. He could see Lily Nolan three chairs down on the porch, rocking the baby and humming some little tune. Maybe this was going to work out all right after all, though he never would have believed it.

That woman sure brought out the worst in him. She seemed to know exactly how to pull the anger right up out of his chest. Before he could stop himself he had been hollering at her, shouting in her face, and scaring the living daylights out of her. He'd never felt such shame in his life as when he saw her cowering in the grass, her arms over her head and her body sheltering the baby. As though he would hit her!

Sure, in his old saloon days, Elijah had been a rough and rowdy fellow, but he'd never touched a woman with a harsh hand. Now that he was walking in Christ's footsteps, he'd surrendered his old notion of "an eye for an eye, and a tooth for a tooth." He was working hard on turning the other cheek.

"This songbook ought to go to somebody who can use it right," Mother Margaret said. "Here, Miss Lily, you take it."

Elijah sat up straight. Lily stopped rocking the baby. Everyone in the gathering turned to the preacher as if awaiting his response. Ben Hanks, a strapping man with arms like tree limbs, gazed at him with soulful brown eyes. His wife, Eva, looked up from her darning. Mother Margaret just grinned as she held out the precious hymnbook.

"Miss Lily," she said, "you have the voice of an angel. Take this book, and keep it. You sing the baby every song in there, and he'll grow up right."

"Mother Margaret," Lily said, "the hymnbook belongs to the preacher."

"He don't need it. Can't carry a tune in a bucket; he said so himself. Take it, girl. And sing us somethin', would you? Sing the first song in the book. What's it called? You know, I can't read worth beans. Can't even sign my name."

Lily took the hymnbook and opened it. Elijah swallowed. That was his *mother's* book, his only memento of her. He didn't want some no-account actress—he caught himself and took a deep breath.

"Holy, holy, holy!" Lily began to sing.

> "Lord God Almighty!
> Early in the morning our song shall rise to Thee;
> Holy, holy, holy! merciful and mighty!
> God in three Persons, blessed Trinity!"

"Mmm," Mother Margaret said. "Ain't that the prettiest voice you ever heard, Ben?"

"Yes'm," her son agreed.

"Sounded like a funeral dirge to me," put in his wife.

"Eva!"

"Well, it did. Miss Lily, sing the verse about the darkness. Here we are out under the stars, and I can just feel the presence of the Lord. Sing it, Miss Lily. Sing it with joy."

Elijah studied the young woman as she gripped the hymnbook. Her fingers skeletal, Lily seemed mesmerized by the book. She swallowed twice, as though the words must be forced out of her throat.

> "Holy, holy, holy!"

Her voice began slowly, and then grew stronger as she sang. High, clear, perfect—each word formed on her tongue. Every note sounded like the ringing of a single crystal bell.

> "Though the darkness hide Thee,
> Though the eye of sinful man Thy glory may not see;
> Only Thou art holy—there is none beside Thee,
> Perfect in pow'r, in love and purity."

"Thank you, Jesus!" Mother Margaret exclaimed. "Love and purity. Yes, sir, that about says it all. The Lord of love is in my heart—holy, holy, holy. And he is pure! Amen!"

"Amen," chorused Ben and Eva.

Elijah eyed his mother's hymnbook, his chest tight and his heart dark. He didn't want Lily Nolan to have the book. It wasn't hers. A woman like her didn't deserve such a gift.

"Oh, Miss Lily, you have a voice that can rival the tongues of angels," Mother Margaret said. "You need that book. Take it with you, and sing to everybody far and wide. Sing to that baby God gave you. Sing to the preacher. Sing to God hisself!"

Lily lifted Samuel to her shoulder and began to pat his back. "I know plenty of songs by heart," she said. "I don't need Mr. Book's hymnal."

"It did belong to my mother," Elijah said, leaning forward.

"Belong?" the old woman said. "Nothing belongs to nobody but God. Everything we got is here on loan from the Almighty. This house, that songbook, even that young'un over there. You better start listenin' to the Spirit of the Lord, Brother Elijah. Don't act on your own will, now. You listen. Listen good."

Elijah stared at his mother's hymnbook and tried to listen to the Holy Spirit. But all he could think about was the afternoon he had discovered the book in a trunk and had realized that his own mother's hands had touched its pages. She had died when Eli was only four or five years old, and he mourned her to this day. She had sung to him out of the book, held him in her arms and sung hymn after hymn. . . .

He lifted his focus to the young woman cradling baby Samuel. *Nothing belongs to nobody but God,* Mother Margaret had said. She was right. The child had been given to him by God. Even this woman had been sent to him by God. He had to believe that. Hard and bitter as she was, Lily Nolan needed the words in that hymnbook more than Elijah needed a physical memento of his mother.

"You keep it," he said to Lily. "Sing to Samuel."

"That's right," Mother Margaret intoned.

"Well," he said, standing, "I reckon I'd better get going."

Eli settled his Stetson on his head and picked up his Bible. After thanking the Hanks family for their welcome, he walked toward the rocking chair. Lily Nolan was a vision out of a fine oil painting. Her golden hair glowed like a halo of holiness around her head. Her pale blue gown swept to her feet, and her slender arms enfolded the sleeping baby. With skin the color of fresh milk and eyes like a pair of bright bluebonnets, she could warm the heart of any man.

Lord, why does she have to be an actress in a traveling show? Elijah prayed silently as he approached her. *Why does she have a sharp tongue and a stiff spine? Why can't she be the kind of woman I asked you to send into my life?* Elijah longed for the gentle touch of a righteous woman whose eyes and heart were committed to the Lord. He envisioned someone sweet and pure. Why couldn't God have sent someone like that to tend Samuel?

"Mrs. Nolan," he said, "I'll be over at the church, in case the baby needs anything. You could send Ben Hanks to fetch me."

She gave the baby a pat. "You'll be preparing sermons, I guess. Make them good. I need the money."

He recoiled from the cynicism in her words. "Maybe you'd like to suggest a subject?"

"Hellfire and damnation, I should think. Isn't that what you preachers like to talk about the most? How about the thirty-second chapter of Deuteronomy as a text? 'For a fire is kindled in mine anger, and shall burn unto the lowest hell, and shall consume the earth with her increase, and set on fire the foundations of the mountains—'"

"Mrs. Nolan—"

"Or maybe something from Psalms? How about this, from Psalm 55?" She lifted her chin, narrowed her eyes, and recited in a venomous voice, "'Let death seize upon them, and let them go down quick into hell: for wickedness is in their dwellings, and among them.'"

Elijah shook his head in confusion. The woman knew the Scriptures better than he did. And yet her pain and anger were overwhelming. How could someone who had taken the Word of the Lord into her heart be so empty of his holy presence?

"I guess I could preach about hell," he said. "But I'd rather preach on the love and forgiveness of the God who sent his own Son to die for us."

"Hell is much more effective." She gave him a frigid smile. "If you haven't learned this lesson yet, Preacher-man, you soon will: fear is a great motivator. Humiliate, shame, and terrify a person if you really want to get something from him."

"Not if you want his love. Or hers." Eli bent down and ran his fingertips over the baby's velvety forehead. "Good night, Samuel. Good night, Mrs. Nolan."

He turned to leave, but her words stopped him cold.

"Love?" she said. "What would you know about love? You didn't even kiss your baby good night."

Eli squeezed his fists together in anger at her taunting words. Kiss a baby? What for? He was a man, and Sam was just a little pup—asleep, at that. Who would know the difference? Eli's own father had never kissed him. Not once.

Lily's voice was more gentle when she spoke again. "Please come and kiss your baby, Reverend Book."

Eli turned and walked back to her side. His father had never kissed him—and Eli had never felt his father's love. In fact, he hadn't understood what love was until Christ came into his life. If the woman Christ had sent was instructing him to kiss Samuel, then he'd do it.

Hunkering down on one knee, Eli set one hand on each arm of the rocking chair and bent over. He gave the baby a swift peck on the forehead and then drew back. "There," he said. "Done."

"Very good, Reverend Book. A truly loving gesture."

He frowned at her. "You kiss him then."

"All right," she said. As she gazed at the sleeping baby, her face transformed. Her blue eyes grew soft, her lips tilted into a smile, and her voice gentled. "Sweet Samuel," she whispered, "precious baby. Sleep softly, little one. Rest in comfort and hope. I love you, Samuel. I love you so much."

A tear slid from her eye as she pressed her lips to the baby's cheek. Then she kissed his little forehead. And then each of his eyes.

Elijah could hardly breathe. As though blinders had been stripped from his eyes, he saw Lily Nolan for the first time. This *was* the kind of woman he had begged God to send him. She was so soft, so tender, so perfect. He could hardly keep from taking her in his arms and holding her.

It wasn't the baby he longed to kiss. It was the woman.

Her spirit seemed to beckon him. She was fragile and vulnerable, so wounded she had built walls of bitterness around her gentle heart. He absorbed her trembling pink lips and tearstained cheeks. How could he break down those walls? How could he reach the soul inside? Had God sent her to him for this reason? *Lord, help me know what to do!*

"You'd better go on back to your church now, Preacher-man," Lily said, her walls rising stronger and higher as she faced him. "And take your baby with you. My place is in the traveling show, and I'll sleep in my own wagon tonight. I'll find Sam in the morning and feed him."

When Eli didn't move, she held out the tiny bundle. "Go on now," she said. "And here's your hymnbook."

Uncomfortable as ever at the notion of holding the fragile baby, Elijah tucked his Bible under one arm. Though Lily's voice had grown cold, he felt the warmth of her hands as he lifted Samuel from her. "You keep that hymnal," he murmured. "You sing better than any gal I ever heard."

Before she could cut him again, Eli pressed the baby against his chest and set off across the prairie. The moment the child felt the movement of the man's footsteps, he jerked awake and began to whimper.

"Aw, Sam, don't start that now," Eli mumbled as the baby let out a howl that could rival a coyote's. "We're not going to get a wink of sleep, and I have to come up with a sermon good enough to change the heart of Mrs. Lily Nolan."

"I've been consulting the cards," Beatrice said as she handed Lily a bowl of hot oatmeal made from the last crumbs in their storage bin. "I was up half the night, Lil, and I just couldn't get over how powerfully the cards spoke to me. It was a deeply spiritual experience, and I can't wait to tell you what I learned."

Lily stifled a yawn as she lifted a spoonful of oatmeal. She had been up half the night, too, and her wakefulness had nothing to do with consulting the spirits. Even from inside the church, Samuel's screaming, fussing, whimpering, and sobbing had been audible for hours. It had been all she could do to keep from crawling out of the wagon and racing to get him. When she dozed at all, she dreamed of Abigail crying out for her mother.

"The cards have told me there's a great future in store for us," Beatrice was saying. "Even though it seems impossible to believe, the deaths of Jakov and Ted are a part of the great plan. You see, you and I couldn't go forward on the path we're to take if we had continued in the shackles of those men. This is *our* time, Lily. Our destiny!"

Lily set the empty bowl aside and began folding the diapers she had just washed. Who could think about destiny? Who could see a path ahead? For Lily there was only this moment. She had to live through this day, surviving each hour, enduring each minute without Abigail.

"We're going to build an opera house," Beatrice announced.

Glancing at her, Lily placed a clean diaper on the stack. "A what?"

"An opera house! To make money!" The older woman seized Lily's shoulders. "It came to me in a vision. We'll go back to Topeka—"

"Topeka?" The image of Abby's makeshift grave inserted itself in Lily's mind. "I don't want to go to Topeka."

"But this is perfect. Do you remember those men who visited the show the first three nights before the diphtheria struck? Those two rich fellows who liked your singing so well? They're partners, and they own a saloon in Topeka. The Crescent Moon, it's called. You and I are going to go straight over to those men and ask them to back us in a venture to build an opera house right here in Hope, Kansas."

"Here?" Lily tried to picture a fancy theater with festoons and bright lights sitting out in the middle of the prairie.

"Hope is the crossroads of the East and the West. I saw it in the cards, Lil. Wagons travel over that pontoon bridge day and night. If we build our opera house beside the main road, we'll be bursting at the seams with customers. You'll sing and do your acts. I'll read fortunes, sell elixir, and manage the money. I'll bet those rich Topeka fellows know a fair number of talented men and women who would love to perform with us. We'll book touring shows, and we'll even let the townsfolk use the place for a meeting hall. They'll support our business, I just know they will. It'll draw all kinds of people here to spend their money. This'll be a regular boomtown in no time at all."

Lily drew a shawl around her shoulders and regarded her friend. "I need to go and feed the baby, Bea," she said softly. "We'll talk about the opera house later."

"There'll be no *later.*" Bea's lips hardened. "I can feel the forces pulling on you, Lily. Don't surrender to that preacher's whims. You know what he's like. You know that kind of man. He'll use you.

He'll wear you out and dry you up. He'll drain the very life out of you, if he can. Please, Lil, I'm trying to save you. Come with me to Topeka."

"Oh, Bea," Lily said with a sigh.

"When you see how those men are going to treat us, you'll forget all about that preacher and his scrawny little kid. We'll buy ourselves some new dresses. We'll go out to eat in fancy restaurants and sleep in a fine hotel. Elijah Book will be long gone by the time we get back to Hope." She clasped Lily's hand. "This is your chance to shine!"

Lily closed her eyes and thought for a moment. When she had first run away with the traveling show, the dream of one day performing in a real opera beckoned her with glory, fame, and riches. With each mile of the hard road and each day in her loveless marriage, her dream faded. Hope vanished. All she knew now was that she had escaped her father. Nothing more.

And then Abby had been born. A baby.

"You go to Topeka, Beatrice," Lily said. "I'm going to stay here and take care of Samuel."

Bea's nostrils flared. "I hope you're joking."

"I'm not. I'm needed here. You can talk to the men in Topeka without me. When you come back—"

"*If* I come back."

A stab of fear ran through Lily's heart. "You will come back, won't you?"

"Maybe." Bea shrugged. "The cards have shown me I'll build an opera house somewhere. But if you don't come with me, you might lose me forever."

Lily swallowed. To be left alone . . . abandoned . . . "I guess I could go to Topeka. You'd need me to sing in the opera house."

"You sing very well, Lily, but I can always find another singer. This is your chance to be part of the dream."

Silence filtered through Lily's heart as she pondered her choice.

Why did the future always look so black, so uncertain? Why did she have no direction in life? Where should she turn?

She studied the diapers. And then her eye fell on the hymnbook. "*God sent you along here to help us out,*" Mother Margaret had told her. "*Sing to everybody far and wide. Sing to that baby God gave you. Sing to the preacher. Sing to God hisself!*"

Lily didn't know who God was, but she did know Mother Margaret. Something about that tiny old woman filled Lily's heart with hope.

"I'm going to stay here," she told Beatrice. "I'm going to take care of Samuel."

"You're crazy!" Beatrice snapped as Lily scooped up the diapers and clambered out of the wagon. "That's not *your* baby. Your baby is dead, Lily. *Dead!* I'm going to Topeka. I'll leave without you! And I'm taking the melodeon!"

Lily halted. That was *her* organ. When she had left her house in Philadelphia, she had taken enough money from her father's vault to buy the small instrument. She had selected it herself, and it had accompanied her in every performance. Beatrice had no right to the melodeon.

On the other hand, Lily felt a certainty—a mixture of dread and anticipation—that Beatrice Waldowski would be back.

CHAPTER 4

ELI STOOD inside the empty church building, the baby wriggling fitfully on his blanket inside a small produce box on the floor. Through bleary eyes, the preacher squinted at the gaudy show wagon in the distance and prayed that Lily Nolan would hurry. He hadn't slept more than half an hour the whole night. Samuel had hollered and howled. He'd messed his britches three or four times—Eli had lost count. And he wouldn't eat a thing. It seemed that once the baby had tasted mother's milk again, he wouldn't settle for anything else.

Eli had been sorely tempted to go to the traveling-show wagon and rouse Mrs. Nolan to feed Samuel. But he knew that he'd frightened and insulted her at the Hankses' house the night before. And both he and Sam had paid for his carelessness.

And so Elijah had counted the hours until dawn, his sermon ideas lost somewhere in the haze of his sleep-deprived mind. As Eli stood waiting for the congregation to arrive, Sam began to wail. Then Eli noticed that the show wagon was starting to pull away from the campsite onto the main road.

What? Lily was leaving?

Eli groaned. Why had he expected more of her? Obviously the actress was a gypsy at heart, unable to commit to home and family, unwilling to labor at decent work, unfeeling and hard-hearted. Now what was he going to do?

"Hoo, that is one loud baby you got there, Brother Elijah." He turned to see Mother Margaret stepping into the church. Clad in a bright yellow dress tied with a crisp white apron, she was a ray of sunshine. Her dark eyes sparkled with joy. "You're liable to scare off more than the devil this mornin'."

Eli raked his fingers through his hair and mustered a smile. "Mornin', Mrs. Hanks. I reckon it is pretty loud in here, thanks to my buddy Sam. I don't imagine we're going to draw much of a crowd."

"Where's Miss Lily?"

"Heading out." He shrugged in the direction of the window. "The wagon is rolling toward Topeka right now."

"Mercy, mercy, mercy." Mother Margaret leaned over the sill and stared into the distance. "I do declare, I thought better of that pretty little gal. I was hopin' she'd caught a glimpse of heaven last night, but I guess the Lord's gonna have to knock her upside the head to get her attention. She's runnin' from him like a cat with its tail afire."

Eli nodded. "I reckon you're right, Mother Margaret. Something sure set her against God—and it was probably me."

"Don't blame yourself. The Lord has a good plan for each person's life. But the devil makes plans, too, don't you know? His schemes are low-down and wicked, and he'll try all kinds of sneaky tricks to keep people off the straight and narrow."

"Amen to that."

"Now, you better give that baby to me, Brother Elijah, and I'll see if I can get something into his belly while you preach your sermon. Mercy, he's a skinny thing. Puts up quite a fuss for bein' so weak and scrawny."

Eli studied the old woman as she hunched over the flailing bundle of damp blankets that had become his greatest burden. If he'd known what trouble a baby could bring, Eli wondered, would he have rescued Sam from his dying mother's arms?

Yes.

For some reason he couldn't explain, he had known God meant him to take the baby. He knew, even now, that he was supposed to care for Samuel. *But, Lord, have mercy on my weary bones*, he lifted up in prayer. *And please send help!*

"Yonder comes your flock, Brother Elijah," Mother Margaret said as she gave the baby a firm pat on his back. "What you plannin' to preach on today?"

Eli let out a deep breath. "I don't know," he said. "I have no idea."

With a sympathetic smile from the old lady to bolster him, Eli strode to the front of the church where he'd left his Bible. Before the baby entered his life, he had spent hours searching the Scripture for God's messages to the people. Eli loved to pray, silent and listening, in the early hours just after dawn. He pondered his own life and the lives of so many other sinners for subjects on which he could expound.

And when he finally delivered his sermons, God's Word seemed to pour through him. Women wept. Men fell to their knees in repentance. And the Holy Spirit went to work changing the hearts of sinners and renewing the vows of believers. Eli had never been so sure of anything as his call to preach the gospel of Jesus Christ.

And then he'd found that baby.

"Mornin', Preacher," someone greeted him as folks began filing into the new church building. Each family carried in a bench or two, and some hauled in chairs and stools. Eli recognized Ben and Eva Hanks from dinner the night before. And here came Jack Cornwall with the pretty red-haired Caitrin Murphy he intended to marry. Seth Hunter stepped inside, his round-bellied Rosie on one arm, their son on the other.

Next came a family of freckle-faced, green-eyed folks with more carrottopped children than a body could count. Following them, a big, tall man with shaggy blond hair gave the preacher an awkward bow before sitting on a chair that looked like it might splinter under his weight. There were others, too, so many Eli lost track as he thumbed through his Bible for an appropriate passage.

"Who vill lead singing today?" the shaggy blond man asked in a thick German accent. "Ve got new preacher, goot church, happy day. Who can sing?"

"Casimir Laski usually leads us," someone called. "But he's gone to Manhattan for supplies."

"All right, then, I'll do it." A skinny, bandy-legged fellow with bright red hair got to his feet. When he spoke again, his words danced with a light Irish lilt. "I'm Jimmy O'Toole, so I am, and I'll have you know I've not set foot inside a church for fifteen years. Sure I thought the whole lot of you were Crawthumpers who didn't have a grain of sense in your heads. I wouldn't allow the church to be built on my land, and I resisted the very notion of a preacher movin' into town."

"Aye, Jimmy," his plump wife said, "so you did."

"But as everyone knows, now I'm a changed man. Once I was walkin' so far from heaven that I nearly got myself burned up. Now I have the grace of forgiveness, and I'm a thankful man to set myself before you."

"And to Jack Cornwall we owe our gratitude," his wife added.

"We'll sing the first hymn to the tune of 'Llanfyllin'," Jimmy went on. "'Tis a Welsh air, but we'll forgive it that."

At that comment, his wife gave him a not-so-subtle elbow to the ribs. Unfazed, the skinny man lifted his voice in a hauntingly beautiful song, which the others joined him in singing.

"Sometimes a light surprises
The Christian while he sings;
It is the Lord who rises
With healing in his wings.
When comforts are declining

He grants the soul again
A season of clear shining,
To cheer it after rain."

Eli gulped as the song ended and the chorus of voices died down. *He* didn't have a season of clear shining. In fact, the waters of his future looked muddier than ever. He'd given away all his China mission money, Lily Nolan had run off, he didn't know what to do with his wailing baby, and now he was stuck for a sermon topic. *Lord, help me!*

Standing before the congregation, he turned to the middle of his Bible and prayed that a good psalm would jump right off the page. He read the first words his eye fell on—and realized to his chagrin that he'd landed in Hosea.

"'Hear the word of the Lord, ye children of Israel,'" he read. " 'For the Lord hath a controversy with the inhabitants of the land, because there is no truth, nor mercy, nor knowledge of God in the land. By swearing, and lying, and killing, and stealing, and committing adultery, they break out, and blood toucheth blood.'"

Oh, great. He'd preached plenty of sermons admonishing the wicked—in fact, the topic moved him deeply. But he didn't think a guilt-and-repentance message was a great way to introduce a preacher to his new congregation.

Eli looked out at the sea of expectant faces, tried to figure out what to say next, and went back to reading. "'Therefore shall the land mourn, and every one that dwelleth therein shall languish, with the beasts of the field, and with the fowls of heaven; yea, the fishes of the sea also shall be taken away.'"

He could feel the heat prickling up his back and onto his neck. This wasn't getting any better. Did he really want to do just what Lily had said and preach a sermon on the wrath of God? Eli fished in his pocket for his handkerchief to mop his brow, realized he'd tied it onto Samuel for a diaper in the middle of the night, and shut his Bible. *Oh, Lord, speak through me*, he prayed. *Say what you want to say, Father, because I'm up the creek without a paddle.*

He summoned his wits the best he could and began. "Do you want your land to mourn? Do you intend to languish here on the prairie? No? Then turn from your sin. Repent! Walk away from your evil—your lies, your swearing, your thieving, and your murder. Beg forgiveness of the Father!" He hammered his fist on the wooden podium. "Fall down on your knees and pray to be spared from the wrath of almighty God!"

At that, one of the little redheaded O'Toole children burst into tears. Dismayed, Eli watched the child's mother trying to comfort her daughter, and he prayed again for divine assistance. Not hearing any heavenly messages, he said the first thing that came to mind.

"Weep! Weep and wail for the sin that besets you. You enjoy your evil deeds. You argue, fight, and squabble among yourselves. You gossip and slander and lie. Repent now, I say! The hour of the Lord is at hand. He sees your wickedness. He knows even the smallest sin in your heart. You cannot escape!"

As Eli continued to expound on the wages of sin, a huge dog wandered into the church building. Tail thumping one bench after another, the mutt carried a meaty bone in his big chops as he meandered over to the Hunter family.

"Stubby!" the Hunter boy cried out. "What're you doin' in church?"

The crowd broke into muffled laughter as the dog flopped onto the floor and began gnawing his bone. But not even the loud crunching and slurping were enough to cheer the O'Toole girl, who continued to sob as though the world were coming to an end. At a loss for what to say next, Eli opened his Bible again. He glanced at the page and realized he was holding the book upside down.

When he lifted his focus to yet another disturbance at the back of the room, he recognized Lily Nolan silhouetted in the open doorway. Hands on her hips, she scanned the crowd in search of Samuel. Eli's spirits soared.

She didn't leave! She's here!

He swallowed a victory whoop. *Preach, Eli,* he heard the voice inside his heart. *Preach the Word of the Lord.*

But what had he been saying?

"You cannot escape," he repeated his last words. "You cannot escape God's wrath—"

He met Lily's bright blue eyes.

"And you cannot escape his love," he went on. "God hates sin—that much is true. But he loves you. He loves you more than you can ever imagine. All through the Bible, time after time, God showed his love for his people. But the greatest gift of love God gave us is his Son."

The dog dropped his bone, let out a loud groan of canine satisfaction, and stretched himself across the floor, tail thudding contentedly. Mrs. O'Toole stood up and carried her crying daughter out of the building. A rooster flapped up onto a windowsill and surveyed the crowd, his red feathers glossy in the sunshine. Lily's lips twitched in amusement.

"Most of you folks have heard about the baby God gave me," Eli continued, determined to ignore the interruptions. He didn't often mention his own life in sermons, but somehow he didn't feel much like he was preaching right now. He felt as though he were talking to Lily Nolan.

"Now little Samuel is my son," he said, "and I'm about as partial to him as any papa could be. Sure, he kept me up all last night with his hootin' and hollerin'. And I have no doubt he's messed more diapers than any baby on God's green earth."

At this, the crowd chuckled. Lily crossed her arms and leaned against the door frame, watching. Her dress was the color of new lilacs in the springtime, and she looked as wholesome as fresh milk. Eli's heart ached at the memory of the bitterness that rose so quickly to her tongue.

"The fact is," he said, "I'm not much fit to be a papa. I didn't ask for the job, and I don't have a wife to help me out. But God gave Samuel to me, and I love the boy. I love him more than I've ever loved anybody. Do you think I'd ever give him up? Do you think I'd turn him loose in a crowd that hated him? Do you think I'd ever let anybody hurt my son?"

He stepped away from the rough-hewn pulpit and faced his congregation. "Never," he said. "But I'm not God. 'For God so loved the world, that he gave his only begotten Son, that whosoever believeth in him should not perish, but have everlasting life.' God sent Jesus Christ among us—and we ridiculed him, tormented him, beat him, and finally killed him. God loves us so much he didn't want us to have to endure the punishment we deserve."

When he lifted his focus to the back of the room again, Eli realized that Lily had slipped away. His heart burning, he continued to speak as though she were still there. The rooster fluttered down from the windowsill and hopped over to inspect the dog bone. An elderly woman had a fit of coughing. Two children went to sleep. Eli didn't care. Maybe someone in this room needed to know about the amazing gift of God's love, and that was all that mattered.

The Word of the Lord was a flaming sword inside him—a sharp-edged, soul-cleansing, heart-piercing, all-protecting blade—and he had been commanded to wield it. Elijah Book was God's soldier, and for his Lord he would battle to the death all sin and wickedness.

"What a fine sermon, Reverend," Lily said when she spotted the long-legged preacher making his way down to the creek bank, where she sat nursing his baby. "And how many souls did you save from the fires of everlasting damnation?"

She saw him pause a moment, and she knew her words had wounded. Why did she feel such a need to strike out at the man? What brought on this compelling urge to hurt him? He'd done nothing against her. In fact, he had offered her good pay, searched out a place for her to stay, given her this chance to hold a baby once again. Though her heart ached with grief for her precious Abigail, she could not deny the pleasure she felt when little Samuel snuggled close against her, his eyes shut in peaceful slumber.

"I've never saved anybody, Mrs. Nolan," Elijah said, covering the last few feet toward her. "I just tell folks what God says in the Bible. He's the one who does the saving."

"Ah," she said, "how humble of you."

"You bring out the worst in me, Mrs. Nolan," he said finally. "Every time you talk, I get so angry I could just spit."

"The feeling is mutual, Mr. Book."

"Why is that?" He turned his blue eyes on her. "Are you upset because I found a baby and you lost yours?"

Lily swallowed. She hadn't expected him to be so direct. The men she had known in Philadelphia treated her with amused detachment. She had been a pretty prize to display at the symphony, a refined accessory at society's elite balls, an object for potential matrimony. But not a real woman. Not a package of emotions, dreams, hopes, sorrows, and joys worth opening and exploring. Yet this irritating preacher waded straight into her pain and demanded to understand it.

"It's none of your business how I feel or what I think," she said. She peered under the white shawl that covered the nursing baby and realized that Samuel had grown drowsy and was drifting to sleep. "I'm nothing to you. And you're nothing to me."

He flipped another stone into the creek. "Wrong. You mean a lot to me, Mrs. Nolan. Whether you like it or not."

Lily stared at the gurgling water to keep her eyes from Elijah Book. He was lying. She had never been important to anyone.

Only Beatrice Waldowski had found value in Lily. And then it was for the services the younger woman could perform. Lily's singing, her acting, her participation in the shows gave Lily worth. Of course, with the preacher it was no different. She was keeping his baby alive. That was all.

"You matter most because you're a special lady," Elijah said. His deep voice took on the same intensity she had heard during the most heartfelt words of his sermons. "God made you different from everybody else. You're pretty—prettier than most, though I'm not much of a judge of that kind of thing. You can sing. I'm not too good in that area, either, but Mother Margaret said you have a voice that can join with the angels. She's right, too. And you have a tender spirit inside. I see it when you look at Samuel. It's your heart that matters most to me."

"And to God. Isn't that what you're leading up to, Mr. Book?" She cast him a sidelong glance. "You're after my soul. If you can feed your baby and rope my soul into heaven, you can add a few more stars to your saintly crown. Well, I have news for you. I won't be one of your missionary projects. I've sat in church a hundred thousand times, read every Bible verse and memorized half of them, and there's nothing you can say or do to convince me that your precious religion has anything to offer. I like my life just the way it is."

"Then why didn't you head out with your friend?"

Lily stiffened. "Why should I? Beatrice is coming back here. I'm sure of it. The only reason I stayed is for the money. Last night Bea read a wonderful future for us, and she's on her way to Topeka to follow the plan in the cards."

"A stack of paper cards told her what your future would hold?"

"What's wrong with seeking truth in the tarot cards? You look for answers in the stack of papers between those leather Bible covers. There's not much difference between my cards and your book, except that the cards are a lot more accurate than a God nobody can see or hear."

"Maybe you never looked or listened."

Lily scowled. She didn't want to discuss religion with Elijah Book. As a matter of fact, she didn't want to discuss anything with the man. He made her uncomfortable. Look at him sitting there in his indigo trousers and homespun white shirt, his thick black Bible propped on his thigh, and his chin lifted as though he had the world by the tail.

How did he make his words sound so sincere? Why was he so confident in his faith? What made the man glow with assurance every time his resonant voice spoke?

"Anyhow," Elijah went on as though the conflict between them meant nothing. "I was telling you why you're important to me, Mrs. Nolan. It's not only because I could see right off what a special kind of woman you are, but it's also because of Samuel. I realize you're looking after my son because I'm paying you, but the fact is, you're keeping him alive. I meant what I said this morning. I do love him."

"Oh, please, Mr. Book. You picked him up off the trail, and you've hired me to feed him. Where's the love in that? He might as well be a puppy."

Elijah watched the gurgling water for a long moment. "Maybe I need someone to teach me how to love my son better. Will you do it?"

She looked up in surprise. "I can't *teach* you how to love. It's a natural thing."

"Not for me. I've never been real good with people."

"Then how can you think you're going to succeed as a pastor here in Hope? Oh, preaching is one thing. It's easy enough to wander around the countryside spouting Bible verses and warning people to repent of their sins. It's quite another thing to really know those same people—and to love them still. If you take on the responsibility of a church, Mr. Book, you can't just preach your clever sermons. And it'll be a lot more than deacons' meetings and committees and Sunday school picnics. You'll be called on to tend the sick and dying, and to comfort their despairing families. You'll be asked to heal troubled marriages and tame rebellious children and charm doddering old ladies who can't remember their own names. You'll be wakened in the middle of the night, called away from your dinner, interrupted in your bathtub—"

"Mrs. Nolan, is your father a preacher?"

Lily gave a harsh laugh. "My father is the devil."

"Whoa," Elijah murmured. "What makes you say that?"

"My life is my own business, Mr. Book," she said. "You stay out of it, or I'll set this baby at your feet and walk away."

Unwilling to let him read the emotion welling up inside her, Lily turned her back on the man. Elijah Book knew nothing about the path she had walked. And he never would.

"I can't seem to put two words together without making you angry," he said. "But you're right about one thing. I don't know beans about being a pastor. I was brought up on the cattle trail, and I never had much of a home. The only folks I spent time with were the trail hands—hardworking, hard-drinking, hard-talking fellows. In those days, my job was to keep an eye on the livestock. Flip over a cow and brand it, bob its ears, keep the wolves and coyotes from eating it, and drive it to market. There's not much room for love in that line of work."

"I guess not," Lily said, wishing the man would go away and leave her in peace. For some reason, ever since she'd had her baby, she couldn't control her tears. Abby's death had only made the situation worse. She didn't want this preacher to see her crying. Especially since nothing she said to wound him seemed to drive him away.

"When I saw you with Sam last night," he was saying, "I figured out right away that you knew some things I didn't. And I'm talking about more than how to put on a diaper. Mrs. Nolan, do you think you could teach me how to take care of Sam the way I ought? Not just when he's a baby, but as he grows. I want to raise him right. I want to love him."

"Then talk to him," she murmured. "And listen. Hold him close. Touch him. Comfort him when he cries. Kiss him. Take care of his needs. And bring a little fun to his life. That's all."

She brushed away a stray tear and blotted her finger on her skirt. What was it with men? Her father, a man she had struggled so hard to please, had been unable to love his only child. But Lily had loved Abigail so easily. So very easily.

"I'd offer you my handkerchief, but I had to use it for a diaper on Sam last night." Somehow Elijah had moved to within a foot of Lily and the baby. "Talk, listen, comfort, and have fun. Clean diapers and good food. That's all there is to it?"

"And touch," she said softly. "Don't forget to touch him."

He reached out to one of the baby's bare feet. Lily observed him as he set the little foot in his palm and ran his fingertip across the tiny toes. "They look like kernels of new corn," he said in a low voice. "You know how you shuck a cob sometimes, and you see those little white nubbins? That's what his toes look like. Nubbins."

He bent over, his head nearly touching hers, and examined the baby's foot. The preacher had good hands, Lily noticed. They had seen hard work and plenty of sun. But the nails were strong and clean, and the fingers conveyed a sense of power even as they gently explored the baby's tiny toes.

The man smelled nice, too. The fragrance of fresh soap mingled with the scent of his sunbaked leather hat and worn boots. He had rolled the cuffs of his sleeves halfway to his elbows, and she could see the mat of dark gold hair that covered his arms. If she dared to trust his words—and she didn't—she might believe that he was the simple man he claimed to be. She might accept that he truly cared about the baby, truly believed in God, and truly wanted to learn to love people. But it would take more than his pretty words to convince her. It was how a man lived that made the difference.

"You reckon I could hold him?" the preacher asked. "Of course, if he's still feeding—"

"He's not nursing." She slipped the baby from beneath the shawl. "Circle your arms, Mr. Book. Nestle his head in the crook of your elbow. Tuck your hand under him. There."

Elijah sat unmoving, as stiff as a statue, staring at the dozing child. "I'm scared I'm going to drop him or crush him or something."

"He's all right. You're doing fine."

"Hey, Nubbin," he cooed. "How ya doin' there, buddy? Look at his eyelashes. They're so long."

"He's pretty."

"Nah, he looks like one of those old potatoes you find at the bottom of the bin in the chuck wagon. Wrinkled and splotchy and all shriveled up."

"He's not well."

"I'm afraid that's my fault."

"You didn't kill his mother," she said. Then she looked up at him. "Did you?"

He looked up, his blue eyes flashing. "No," he whispered. "Why would you ask something like that?"

Lily met his gaze. "Why not? All I know about you is what you've chosen to tell. You say you're a preacher who found a baby in a wagon. Maybe that's true. Maybe not."

"Why would I lie?"

"Why not?"

"I don't have anything to hide. I told you who I am, where I've been, what I've done. You've hardly told me anything."

"And I don't intend to," she said, starting to rise.

"Look here, Lily Nolan." He caught her arm and pulled her back down beside him. "God put the two of us together, whether you want to believe that or not. I need you. Samuel needs you. And even though you'll argue yourself blue in the face about this—you need me."

"No, I—"

"I'll treat you right. I'll never lie to you. I won't hurt you or cheat you or play games with you. I'm just Elijah Book, that's all, and what you see is what I am. Now, you can fight me and try to drive me away. Or you can work alongside me. I'm asking you for peace. I'm asking you to be my partner. Will you do that?"

Lily drew back from Elijah, her heart hammering. "If I become your partner," she said, "I'll have to let you in. And I'll never let anyone in."

As she walked up the creek bank toward town, she could feel his eyes following her. A sparrow swooped down and perched on the end of a bowed blade of bluestem grass. Lily tugged her white shawl tightly around her shoulders and began to rebuild the sagging walls that fortified her heart. She could not afford to let Elijah Book come too close. Though he claimed to know nothing of love, he somehow reached out to her, touched her, held her, and caressed the wounded edges of her soul. She could not let him in. She would not.

CHAPTER 5

AS ELIJAH carried his son back up the creek bank toward the church, he recognized Seth Hunter standing outside the building. The man held a large woven basket topped by a bright, red-checkered cloth. "How about some lunch?" Seth called.

Eli grinned. "You read my mind, Brother."

"Rosie had a roast in the oven all morning, and we intended to invite you to eat at our house. But you got away."

"I went looking for Sam."

"How's he doing?"

"Half his breakfast is on my shoulder," Eli said. "I guess it's not a good idea to jiggle a baby right after he eats."

Seth laughed. "I'm fixing to learn all about that. My wife is due come autumn, and this will be the first baby I've helped with."

"I thought you had a son. The little fellow with the big dog?"

"Chipper was born to my first wife while I was away at war. Mary died before I could get back to her."

Eli tried to think what to say. He wasn't accustomed to hearing another man's personal matters. But he supposed that for a minister, it came with the territory.

"I've never been married," he mumbled. "Uh . . . and I'm sure sorry about your first wife."

"Well, God sent Rosie to me last spring. That was a miracle, if there ever was one."

"He does look after us." Feeling awkward, Eli patted Samuel. For once, the child was quiet.

"I sure would hate it if anything happened to Rosie," Seth said. "You know . . . while she's laboring over the baby."

Eli shook his head. "That can be bad. Boy howdy, it sure is trouble on a woman to give birth. My own mother died in childbirth when I was just five years old. She labored for three days. It was awful, all of it. The baby never did come, and finally my mama passed on. I don't believe my papa ever got over the grief of losing her."

Observing the farmer's stunned expression, Eli suddenly realized he hadn't said one word the man needed to hear. As a matter of fact, he'd only added to Hunter's fears. Eli's spirits sank. He didn't have any sense of how to comfort or reassure a person. Women did die in childbirth. They died often.

Lily Nolan had told him a pastor had to tend the sick and the dying. During the worst moments in their lives, the people of Hope would look to Eli for answers. He didn't even know how to begin.

"But—uh," he fumbled, "I'm sure Mrs. Hunter will be fine." *Lord,* he breathed, *help me out here*. "There's bound to be a good doctor around these parts."

"No," Seth said. "We don't have a doctor in Hope."

"No doctor."

"If you believe there's a God in heaven," Lily Nolan said, joining them, "then you'll remember he keeps his eye on everyone—even the sparrows. I couldn't help overhearing you, Mr. Hunter, and as I'd just noticed a sparrow near the creek, I thought I'd remind you of those verses in Matthew: 'Are not two sparrows sold for a farthing? and one of them shall not fall on the ground without your Father. . . . Fear ye not therefore, ye are of more value than many sparrows.'"

Eli gaped at the woman.

"Reverend Book," she went on, "why don't you reassure Mr.

Hunter that the God you trust with your eternal soul considers the lives of Mrs. Hunter and her baby important?"

Seth and Eli looked at each other. Eli swallowed. "Mrs. Nolan is right," he said. "God doesn't promise to protect us from every bad thing that comes along. But he loves us, and he's right here with us through thick and thin. He listens to our prayers, Mr. Hunter, so every day I'm going to talk to God about your wife. I believe he'll see her through the hard labor ahead. I'm going to have faith that come September you'll welcome a fine, healthy baby into your home."

Seth visibly relaxed. "You'll pray for Rosie?"

"Morning, noon, and night." Remembering Lily's instructions about how to show love, Eli reached out and laid his hand on the other man's shoulder. "You can depend on it, my friend."

"Thank you, Brother Elijah," Seth said. "I'll tell Rosie. She'll be mighty grateful, too."

"You folks pray, too, and we'll even do some looking for a doctor who might want to move to town."

"That would be great." Seth gave Lily a warm smile. "Mrs. Nolan, I've brought along some of Rosie's roast beef. Maybe you'd like to join Brother Elijah for lunch. We're happy to have both of you in Hope, and, Reverend, thanks again."

Eli took the heavy wicker basket in his free hand and gave Seth Hunter a farewell nod as the man started up the road to his own home. Then he turned to Lily. "You were hopping mad at me a few minutes ago. Why did you help me?"

She shrugged. "You were botching it."

"But you told me you don't believe in the Bible."

"I believe in comforting people." She lifted the lunch basket from Eli's arm. "Samuel has spit up all over your shoulder."

"I was jiggling him."

She rolled her eyes. "You're not much good at anything, are you, Mr. Book?"

"I can brand cattle."

With a laugh, she headed to a tree near the church and spread the checkered cloth on a patch of shaded grass. Eli let out a breath. *Lord,* he lifted up, *I don't understand this woman. I don't know what I'm doing in this town. And I can't see where you're leading me. Would you mind letting me in on the plan?*

"I am so hungry," Lily exclaimed, taking mismatched china plates and cutlery from the basket. "Nursing a baby just drains all the strength right out of a woman. Here's some roast for you. I'm surprised the Hunters would have beef. Surely they're trying to build up their flock of cows."

"Herd," Eli said, kneeling across from her. "Cattle run in herds. Sheep run in flocks."

Her blue eyes sparkled. "Maybe you're not as ignorant as I thought."

"Not about livestock, anyhow."

"Have you ever been to school, Mr. Book?"

"Once or twice. My father and I were on the move a lot. I like to read, though. I'll read anything I can lay my hands on. Did you get any schooling?"

"Certainly." She spooned peas onto his plate and set a warm roll beside them. "I am well educated and trained in all the proper social graces."

"Lonely, too."

"I am not." After giving him a withering glance, she set about buttering her roll. "Beatrice Waldowski is my good friend. She'll be back in a few days."

"I guess we'll see about that. She took the wagon, you know." Eli settled the baby on the blanket beside him. "Mind if I pray over this meal?"

"I'll try not to be offended by your beliefs as long as you're not offended by mine."

"Dear Lord," he began, wondering if there would ever come a

day when Lily Nolan didn't irritate the living daylights out of him. "We praise you for this beautiful afternoon and for the folks who came to the service this morning. Touch them with your message of hope and salvation. I want to ask for your special protection over Mrs. Hunter and her baby. Please keep them safe, Lord. And, if you would, help me figure out how to manage Sam. Most of all, I want to thank you for sending along Mrs. Nolan. Touch her heart. In the name of Jesus I pray. Amen."

"You forgot to thank God for the food."

Eli lifted his head. "You know this religion business pretty well, don't you?"

"I'm a walking university of religious folderol. Ask me anything. Go on."

"All right. Who parted the Red Sea?"

"Moses."

"Who walked on water?"

"Jesus. And don't forget Peter, the poor fellow. He managed a few steps before his faltering faith sent him under." She popped a bite of bread into her mouth. "Those are easy. Ask me something harder, like Who drove a tent peg through the head of Sisera the Canaanite?"

Eli worked a few peas onto his fork. "How can a person know the Bible front to back and not believe it's the Word of God?"

Lily paused. "It was Jael, the wife of Heber the Kenite, who drove the peg through Sisera's head."

"That's not the answer to my question."

"Well, it's all the answer you're going to get from me," she said. "Please pass the butter."

Eli set the small crock near her plate and watched her tear apart a second roll. "You're right that I'm not cut out to be a pastor," he said. "All I know is to preach the gospel and let the Lord do his work in people's souls. I can't comfort the sick and the dying, and I don't know how to reach a woman who's shut her heart up tight." He studied the hand-hewn shingles on the roof of the new church. "The folks here need a real minister—not some ol' Texas cowhand."

Lily tucked a strand of golden hair behind her ear. "Didn't King David start out as a shepherd?"

"Sure, but I'm not educated or tenderhearted or well mannered—none of those things you talked about. I know how to do a day's labor, earn my pay, eat a little chow, and sleep on the ground at night. I'm just a plain workingman."

"Jesus was a carpenter. Paul made tents. Peter fished for a living. You're not in bad company, Reverend Book."

"Right now, I'm in your company, and I can't figure you out."

"Why should you bother? I'm doing my job feeding your baby. Isn't that enough?"

"No." He reached across the checkered cloth and took her hand. "It's not enough for me. I thought about you all last night when I was up with Samuel. Today, when you walked into church and I saw you standing there at the back, I wanted to shout hallelujah. It didn't have a thing to do with the baby. You're not just Sam's nurse. You're a cyclone who's blown through my life and turned everything topsy-turvy. In the space of two days, you've made me boiling mad, lifted my spirits, bailed me out of trouble, challenged my faith in God, and filled my mind to overflowing. In spite of myself, Mrs. Nolan, I care about you."

Her hand was trembling as she slipped it out of his. "Please don't do that, Mr. Book," she said in a thin voice. "Care about these people—your church. Let them into your heart and learn to love them. Then you'll be a pastor."

"And you?"

"Don't care about me. I don't want anything from you except what you can afford to pay me. I have everything I need."

"A person who has everything she needs ought to be happy. You're not happy. You're angry and hurting. There's something inside you that's so sad—"

"No. I've chosen my path. I'm going to make my own way in this world. And I'll do it alone. I don't need the crutch of religion."

"My faith in God is no crutch. When I was trying to get through life without the Lord, I was limping along, stumbling and falling down every two or three steps. I tried to fill the emptiness with work, drink, cards, women—whatever. Nothing satisfied for long. Then I asked Christ to come into my heart, and he healed me better than new. A man doesn't need a crutch when he's whole and complete."

"Well, I'm a whole woman," she said, stacking their dishes. "My strength comes from within myself. I'm my own source of light and power."

Eli touched the sleeping baby's cheek. "I'm impressed. You must be a lot better person than I am, Mrs. Nolan. When I looked at my spirit without God, all I saw was confusion and nothingness. I didn't know which way to turn, and I sure didn't feel any power. Oh, I was strong all right—blustering around one saloon or another, fighting any man who looked at me crossways, running cattle from Abilene to Kansas City. But all my strength was on the outside. I pulled anger and hurt around me like a heavy suit of armor to keep everybody back. Inside, I was as empty as an old tin can."

Lily pursed her lips for a moment. Then she tucked a strand of hair into her bun. "It looks like rain," she said. "I'd better go and speak to Mrs. Hanks about her offer of a place to sleep. None of the other good Christian citizens of Hope have invited me in. I'm not surprised. When you're filled with the holiness of God, you don't want to sully yourself by spending time with a lowly actress from a traveling show."

Without looking at him, she set the dishes into the basket and stood. "You can fetch me when Samuel wakes up," she said. "I'll stay in town until Beatrice comes back from Topeka."

Eli sat on the checkered cloth watching Lily Nolan walk away from him for the second time that day. He thought about all his years on the trail. And he pondered his months on the preaching circuit. One thing seemed sure. God could use him like a cattle driver—spreading the gospel as he herded people into the kingdom of heaven. But Eli wasn't cut out to be a shepherd—guiding, nurturing, and tending a flock of lambs along the rocky paths of life day-by-day.

No sir. Right this minute he ought to go tell Seth Hunter he was quitting his job as pastor of Hope's church, and then he could head for China.

In the distance, Lily Nolan paused outside the door of the Hankses' house. She lifted the corner of her white apron and dabbed her cheek. She was crying, Eli realized. This woman who claimed to be whole, strong, and glowing with inner peace was weeping.

Lord, he prayed, *I want to run from this work you sent my way. But even more than that, I want to do your will. Teach me how to be a shepherd.*

"Mercy, mercy, mercy, girl. That storm is blowin' up fast. I hope we don't get us a cyclone."

Lily noted that Mother Margaret was taking her washing off the line even though the clothes weren't nearly dry. She chuckled at the older woman's now-familiar foibles. Four days in the Hankses' home had given Lily a sense of family she'd never known. Ben's siblings and his and Eva's children had long ago gone to work for other landowners, and the loss was palpable to this day. Often Mother Margaret mentioned a son or daughter, and at each meal Eva prayed for her absent children by name. Though lacking an extended family, the couple had created a warm and loving relationship with Ben's mother. Now they welcomed Lily as though she had always lived there.

"I'd better get that boy of mine to whittle some new clothes-pegs," the old woman said. "We toted these all the way from Missouri, and they're plumb wore out."

Sitting in a rocking chair on the front porch of the little frame house, Lily watched Mother Margaret drop gray wooden pegs into her apron pockets. For almost a week, clouds had been lingering on the horizon, promising rain but failing to deliver. The day before, in the mercantile, Rosie Hunter had told a terrifying story of a cloud of grasshoppers that had once plagued the town. Caitrin Murphy followed that with the tale of a raging prairie fire whose smoke everyone had mistaken at first for rain clouds.

Lily was beginning to wonder if life on this barren land might be a lot more intimidating than it appeared. These bucolic peasants were turning out to be warriors in disguise, battling the elements for their very lives. Though she was certain her reception at her father's house in Philadelphia would be unpleasant, she felt thankful she'd be returning there before the winter.

"Eva, you better run next door and tell Ben and Mr. Jack to carry their tools inside the smithy," Mother Margaret called. "It's fixin' to rain. I can feel it in my bones."

Eva peered out the screenless window of the house and gave Lily a wink. "I reckon those two men know enough to get their tools out of the rain before they get rusty, Mama."

"Mercy, I hope so."

Lily fingered the tight collar of her dress. The air hung dank and humid over the grassland, so heavy it was hard to breathe. She wondered what her parents were doing on this day in Philadelphia. No doubt they were attending a literary reading or a political speech. Her father would be preparing selections for the symphony to play during the Independence Day celebrations. Her mother would be agonizing over summer bonnets and gloves. The townhouse would be dark and cool, each table laden with a bouquet of fresh flowers, pungent smells wafting up from the kitchen, a coat of new wax gleaming on the hardwood floors.

How different from this toilsome prairie life. How empty.

Lily pushed up from the rocking chair and strolled across the beaten dirt yard to help Mother Margaret take down the rest of the laundry. Odd that she felt so comfortable in the home of former slaves. But here in Hope, Lily had discovered laughter that came from the belly, music that came from the heart, and food that nourished the soul.

"Sit yourself back down, child," the old woman said. "That preacher will be along here any minute with his squallin' baby. I don't know why he's takin' so long this afternoon anyhow. Seems like he comes a-runnin' to you the minute that little feller makes a sound."

Lily tugged a wooden peg from the line. She was a little concerned herself. Physically uncomfortable with her need to nurse the baby, she couldn't understand why she had seen Elijah only once this day. She had insisted that the baby spend most of the time with his father. After all, she would be leaving soon. But Lily found herself eagerly anticipating the moment when she would hear Samuel's wails drifting toward her from the church. Surely in a moment the preacher would march up to the house, his dark hair windblown and his blue eyes clouded with concern—as though Sam's every whimper spelled trouble with a capital *T*.

Though they hadn't spoken at length since the picnic beside the church, Lily had turned the man's words over in her mind. He might be uneducated and rough-hewn, but Elijah Book was sincere. At least . . . he seemed sincere. She hesitated to trust him too far. He was, after all, a man.

"What time did you nurse that baby?" Mother Margaret asked, dropping the last damp shirt into her basket. "I thought it was around midmornin'. Don't you reckon Sam's hungry by now?"

Lily set her hands on her hips and stared at the church. "Maybe Eva could go over there and check on things."

"Eva's cookin' supper. What's wrong with those two feet you got? Can't they make it across the street?"

"I don't want to bother Reverend Book. He might be resting."

"He's not restin'. That man's been working himself half to death over there. Hammerin' day and night. Plowin' up the ground. Splittin' fence posts. He hasn't done much visitin' of his flock, but he sure is sprucin' up the building."

"I guess I could walk over and check." Lily crossed her arms. "But he might be writing a sermon or something. With the wedding coming up this Saturday—"

"He never writes down a thing he says. Didn't you listen to him last night at prayer meetin'? Why, he just went to tearin' through the Scripture like a hound dog after a coon. One by one, he pulled those verses apart and put 'em back together—and he never looked at nothin' but the Good Book itself."

"I wasn't at the prayer meeting."

"Well, you missed a good'n. I don't know why you thought you needed to stay here at the house and wash your stockin's all secret-like. Everybody in town knows what a pair of lady's stockin's looks like. Mercy me."

Lily picked up the heavy load of laundry and carried it onto the front porch. The clouds looked no closer to town than they had the past three days, but at least Mother Margaret could stop fretting about her clothes getting rained on. The tiny old woman hobbled up the wooden steps and sank onto a chair.

"Go check on that baby, Miz Lily," she wheezed, "before I give myself a heart attack worryin' over him. Go on now. And don't you get caught in the rain."

Lily took a deep breath and started toward the unpainted clapboard church. She didn't want Elijah to think she ever missed Samuel. Or needed the baby. Or looked forward to seeing the two of them. He had to understand that the arrangement between them was just a job.

Taking care of Samuel would earn Lily the money to leave the nomadic life that had cost her a husband and a daughter. Going back to Philadelphia would return her to the shallowness and fear, but at least in the big brownstone townhouse she would have security. Life couldn't promise much more than that anyway.

A deep voice sang from the church's backyard.

"Hallelujah, Thine the glory!
Hallelujah, amen!
Hallelujah, Thine the glory!
Revive us again."

Hands dug into her apron pockets, Lily peered around the side of the building. For a moment, she failed to recognize the sweat-drenched, shirtless man who was digging postholes. Half built, the fence started from the back of the church in a razor-straight line, snapped into a perpendicular angle, stretched across the prairie to another sharp corner, and then set off back toward the church. In Philadelphia, Lily had never given much attention to such mundane things. But she could tell this was a beautiful fence.

The tall, well-formed man digging holes rammed his clamshell shovel into the ground, worked it around, and lifted out a clump of rich Kansas soil. As he lowered the shovel again, he returned to singing.

"We praise Thee, O God,
For the Son of Thy love,
For Jesus who died
And is now gone above."

Elijah Book was right, Lily thought. He couldn't carry a tune in a bucket. His heartfelt enthusiasm went a long way to make up for the off-key singing, but she cringed as the man plunged into a second verse. Attempting to keep a straight face, she stepped around the side of the church and approached him.

"Hallelujah, Thine the—whoa!" he said, taking a step backward. "I didn't expect you."

She was amazed to see the man flush a shade of deep rose under his tanned skin as he fumbled in his back pocket for a handkerchief. Mopping his forehead, he grabbed his shirt from the last post he had set and tugged it on.

"Good afternoon, Reverend Book," Lily said. He tried to fasten a button and finally gave it up. "I see you've been digging."

"Yeah." He pushed his fingers back through his damp hair. "I'm building a fence for the church."

"Ah," she said. "I thought churches were supposed to welcome people. Who is it you wish to keep out?"

At that he grinned. "Critters. I plan to put a little garden back here, so I don't have to rely on the generosity of the townsfolk for my food. And then—if need be—I can start a cemetery in that southeast corner. There's a little tree, and I thought I'd try turning over the sod and planting some flowers here and there."

"Flowers?"

"Well, sure. When they're grieving, folks like to come and spend some quiet time in a graveyard. Makes them feel better. I thought flowers would perk up the place."

Lily reflected on Abigail's barren grave. The baby had no headstone to mark her short life. No one would ever tend the spot where she lay. She had not even been given a little speech or a prayer—not that Lily thought prayers for the dead did any good. In fact, she hadn't found prayers of any sort to be worth much. God never listened.

"I could put up a stone marker for your baby," Eli said in a low voice. "I could ask Jack Cornwall to carve her name on it."

Surprised, Lily looked into the man's blue eyes. How had he known what she was thinking?

The preacher shoved his handkerchief back into his pocket and shifted from one foot to the other. "I just figured maybe—"

"Thank you," Lily murmured. "I would appreciate a marker in my daughter's memory."

"I'd be privileged to do that." After a pause, he asked, "Did I tell you Sam smiled at me this morning? Well, sort of. Anyhow . . ." He looked up at the church and frowned. "Sam's been awfully quiet."

Lily felt a twinge of dread. "Have you checked him lately?"

"He was sleeping, and I came out here to dig. But that's been a good while ago."

Tossing down the clamshell shovel, Eli started past Lily on his way to the church. She gathered up her skirts and ran after him. Side by side, they pushed through the narrow door at the back of the building and entered the dimly lit room where the pastor had been staying.

"Sam?" Eli dropped to his knees beside the wooden produce box on the floor. "Hey, Nubbin."

Lily sank down beside him and drew back the blanket. Heat radiated through the damp cotton gown as she lifted the tiny baby into her arms. Limp, listless, the child opened his eyes and gave a little whimper.

"Oh, Elijah!" she cried softly, covering the baby's forehead with her palm. "Samuel's so hot."

"Is he sick?" Eli took the baby and pressed his face against the child's cheek. "He has a fever. Oh, God, help us."

Lily uncurled the baby's tiny hand. "Elijah," she said, "we've got to have help. *Real* help. Let's take him to Mother Margaret."

CHAPTER 6

"MERCY, you got yourself one sick baby there, Brother Elijah." Mother Margaret watched the preacher carry a bucket of cool well water into her house and set it on the floor beside the washbowl.

"Isn't he any better?"

"He took a little milk," Lily said in low voice. "Just before dawn."

Eli knew that she and Mother Margaret had been awake all night, mopping Samuel's feverish body and trying everything they could think of to lower his temperature. He had hovered over the two women, trying to see what they were up to, asking questions, offering suggestions—until finally the older woman had shooed him outside to pray. Trudging back and forth along his fence, Eli had pleaded with God for the child's life. He was angry with himself for neglecting Sam all afternoon. He was dismayed at the absence of medical care in the little town. And he was truly frightened that his baby might die.

"He's going to be all right, isn't he?" Eli asked, kneeling beside the chair where Lily was rocking the baby. "This is probably just a head cold or something, don't you reckon?"

Her depthless blue eyes gave him all the answer he needed. On the frontier, babies often died for one reason or another. Lily had lost her daughter. Eli might lose his son.

"Here you go, Brother Elijah," Eva Hanks said, handing him a cup of steaming liquid. "It's sassafras tea. You need to eat something too. How about one of these biscuits?"

He shook his head. "My stomach feels like a knotted-up lasso. I don't think I can eat a thing."

"Ben has gone to the neighbors around Hope to let folks know about the baby," Eva told him. "Everybody will be praying."

Eli looked at Lily. Could prayer save Samuel? Obviously Lily didn't think so. Her face showed exhaustion and hopelessness. Her eyes were red-rimmed from weeping. She fingered the baby's thin blanket.

"I think he might have diphtheria," she said. "He's so limp and bedraggled."

"No." A chill of dread wrapped around Eli's heart. "Not diphtheria."

"He's still breathing comfortably enough. But I wish we could give him some kind of tonic to break the fever."

"What about that potion you sell in your show? Could you make up some of that?"

She shook her head. "It's useless. There's nothing in the elixir that would help Samuel. I can't think of anything—"

"Castoria." A cheerful redhead stepped into the house and held up a dark blue bottle. Eli recognized her as Caitrin Murphy, the woman whose wedding he was to perform on Sunday. "Sure I've brought Castoria for the wee one. Sheena—that's my sister, so 'tis—she says you must put a plaster on the baby's chest to draw out the infection, and wrap him tightly in blankets to sweat the fever from his body."

Eli grabbed the blue bottle. "How much should we give him?"

"Wait!" Lily said. "How can you be sure this medicine will help? He's so tiny. He can barely take milk."

"Sheena says he must have Castoria," the woman explained. "My sister has five children and one on the way. She knows about these things."

Eli laid his hand across the baby's heated body. "We've got to do something, Lily."

"Let me try to nurse him again first. If he can just get a little stronger, maybe he'll be able to fight the fever."

"I let him get too weak. I fed him mashed potatoes."

"It's all you knew to do. This is not your fault, Elijah. Abigail was in perfect health when the diphtheria struck Topeka. You mustn't blame yourself."

"But look at the little fellow. He's skinnier than one of those fence rails I've been splitting. What chance does he have?"

"You answer that question," Lily said. "You're the one who believes in a God of healing and protection. Where is your God when children are ill? Where is he when they're struggling to take in their last breaths? Where is he when they're hurting . . . and . . . and unable to defend themselves . . . and helpless . . ."

A tear started down Lily's cheek. Without thinking, Eli reached up and brushed it away with his fingertips. "Don't cry now, Lily," he murmured. "God's eye is on the sparrows, and he's watching Sam. He knows the number of hairs on our baby's head. He's holding Sam in his arms, and he's holding you and me, too. He's here with us, right now, this minute. I can't see the future, but he can, Lily. Why don't you sing for Sam? Sing one of the hymns."

Eli took his mother's hymnal from the table near Lily's chair and opened it. She shook her head as another tear trickled down her cheek. "I can't . . . can't sing," she said.

Eli began.

"Abide with me; fast falls the eventide;
The darkness deepens; Lord, with me abide!"

She joined in, her voice choked with emotion.

"When other helpers fail and comforts flee,
Help of the helpless, O abide with me."

"Keep on singing, Lily," Eli whispered. "Sing for Sam."

Standing, he followed Miss Murphy and Mother Margaret out onto the porch. Hands clasped, the two women waited with heads bowed. Eli stared across the vast plain and thought about Lily's questions—and more uncertainties crowded in. Where was God? Why did children have to suffer and die? What had Sam done to deserve the fever that raged through his tiny body? What had Abigail done? Did God really care about his people? And if he did, why wouldn't he heal Sam?

Mother Margaret began humming along with Lily's soft voice. "Yes, Lord," she murmured in prayer. "You are the Lord of life. You know the number of my days, short or long. Oh, God, I give them all to you. In health and in sickness, you are my comfort. In peace and in trouble, you are my strength. Lord, you fill my heart. Amen and amen."

Eli clutched the post that supported the porch roof. God would hold them all in his love—through life . . . and death. *But please, Lord*, his soul cried out, *don't let Samuel die!*

Lily's pure voice drifted out from within the frame house.

> "Hold Thou Thy cross before my closing eyes;
> Shine through the gloom and point me to the skies;
> Heaven's morning breaks, and earth's vain shadows flee;
> In life, in death, O Lord, abide with me."

Through the rest of that day and the next, tiny Sam battled the unexplained illness that raged through him. Though Lily was exhausted from lack of sleep and from her efforts to feed the listless child, she was touched by the warmth that poured from the townsfolk of Hope. Ben Hanks and Caitrin Murphy, it seemed, had rallied the forces in support of their weakest member.

Caitrin brought a sample of every medicine she stocked in the

Hope mercantile. Rosie Hunter, careful for the health of her own unborn child, sent Seth and Chipper to the Hankses' house with enough food to last a week. Sheena O'Toole bustled into the cabin with a batch of fresh bread and orders to *brauch* the baby. She and Mother Margaret tightly bound Sam's abdomen and then wrapped him so that no fresh air could reach his lungs. After a time, they removed the wrappings, rubbed his little body with vinegar and fat, moved his legs and arms in rhythmic motions, and prayed out loud. Then the wrappings were bound again, and the child lay in deathly silence.

Not only the neighbors close at hand, but everyone in the community reached out to the ailing baby. Violet Hudson, a young widow with many mouths of her own to feed, brought a new quilt to cover Samuel. The Laski family sent vegetables from their abundant garden. A Frenchman named LeBlanc arrived with oil to keep lamps burning all night as the caretakers watched over the baby. Even Rolf Rustemeyer, the big shaggy German, rode his mule into town and stopped by to see the Hankses and drop off a baby rattle he had carved from a piece of wood.

"Why?" Lily asked Elijah as Rolf stood on the porch that evening talking to Ben Hanks and Jack Cornwall. "Why have they brought all these things? They hardly know you, and most of them have never even seen the baby."

Haggard, the preacher studied the tiny child in his arms and shook his head. "Jesus," he said. "These people love Jesus. That's the only explanation I know."

"How futile." With a sigh of disgust, Lily pushed up from her chair and walked to the rough, hand-hewn table. "Look at all this food. What good can it do Sam? None. And neither can their precious Jesus. Some Savior he is. Why isn't Sam feeling any better? It's been two days. He's hardly eaten, and his fever keeps creeping higher. He's wrapped up so tightly he can hardly take in air. Has he even opened his eyes in the last hour?"

"I can feel him breathing. He's still alive."

"Oh, I can't bear this!" she cried out. "I wish Beatrice were here. She could read the tarot cards and tell us what to do. She has a crystal ball that foretells the future, and she knows how to study a person's skull. Phrenology, she calls it. She even has séances."

"You told me that elixir of hers is useless."

"But Beatrice has magical stones that can heal the sick. If she were here, she could put them on Samuel's body. Amethyst and garnet and quartz—they're very powerful, Elijah."

"Did Beatrice's crystals help your daughter?"

"Why must you bring Abigail into this?" She wrung her hands. "At least if Bea were here she could *do* something. That's better than sitting around praying to a God who doesn't listen. I'm tired of the silly prayers everyone is saying. I'm fed up with their trite little messages of hope: 'Oh, Samuel's so sweet that I'm sure God will let him live' or 'Maybe the Lord needs a new little angel in heaven.' That's horrible. It doesn't do any good. We need help here, Elijah. We need to *act*, not just sing and pray. I feel like I'm going mad!"

"You can't bring Abigail back, Lily," Eli said in a low voice. "Trying to force Sam to live won't bring your daughter back to life."

"I know that. Of course I know that. I'm not stupid." She pulled her handkerchief from the pocket of her apron. "But I can't lose two!"

"Mother Margaret lost three."

"She's obviously a much better woman than I am. I'm selfish and greedy. I want life. I want Abigail."

"Lily—"

"What do you know about anything?" she cried, turning on him. "You're so blindly trusting. You think God is protecting you and watching over you all the time. He's not, Elijah! If there is a God, he doesn't care about you. He doesn't care about Sam. You would understand that if you'd ever had to suffer!"

"I've suffered. I lost my mother when I was a boy. You think that didn't hurt me, Lily? You think I didn't hear my daddy crying in the night after he thought I was asleep? I was as helpless then as I am right now. I couldn't bring my mother back, and I can't make Sam well. But there's one thing I can do."

"Pray," she snapped. "Pray, pray, pray."

"I can trust that the God who created me and loved me enough to give the life of *his* Son for me cares about *my* son." He stood and walked toward her, the baby unmoving in his arms. "I can't see God's plans, but I believe they're good ones. My mama's death hurt, but God used it to pull me close to my father. It was the book of hymns you've been singing from that helped lead me to salvation. If Mama hadn't died, do you think I'd have counted her hymnal special? Do you think I'd have read it over and over? Do you think I'd ever have found the path to joy?"

"Joy? You can't tell me you feel joyful right now."

"At this moment, holding this dying baby, I have the greatest joy, the deepest peace, and the purest strength I've ever known." He slipped his arm around her and drew her against his chest. "Oh, Lily, I wish you knew it too. I wish you had hope."

"There is no hope." Desperate and frantic, she laid her hand on the baby's fevered little head. Abigail had been this ill in the hours before her death, and Lily had been unable to hold her daughter back from the precipice. All the love in the world had not kept Abby from slipping over the edge.

"Mercy, that's a sweet sight," Mother Margaret said, her bright yellow dress aglow in the light of the oil lamp she carried. "The three of you sure do make a pretty picture. Yes, sir. Once we get past this trouble, we're gonna have to fix you up. You belong."

Lily pressed her cheek against Elijah's shoulder, blotting her tears on the comforting homespun cotton fabric of his shirt. What was the old woman saying? Had everyone gone insane?

"But right now, we better head for a doctor," Mother Margaret continued. "We all been a-talkin' on the porch—Ben, Eva, Mr. Seth, Mr. Jack, Mr. Rolf, and me. We decided you need to take that baby to Topeka, Brother Elijah. Ben's hitchin' his mule to Mr. Seth's wagon, and Miz Rosie is sendin' some food down from her house. Miz Lily and I will take turns with the baby while you drive. You reckon you're up to goin' all the way to Topeka, Brother?"

As though a fresh wind had blown through the room, Eli lifted his head and gave the old woman a warm smile. "Sure thing, Mother Margaret. You're coming with us?"

"The Lord knows I'm not much use around here. I been hangin' up laundry and takin' it down wet for almost a week, waitin' for the rain to come. Maybe if I leave, Ben will finally have himself some dry shirts."

"I suspect it'll rain."

The old woman laughed. "You're probably right. Miz Lily, fetch the baby's box, would you? And let's take along some of them pickles Miz Sheena brought over yesterday. Mercy, I never tasted such fine pickles in all my life."

In a fog of sorrow and anxiety, Lily watched Mother Margaret bustle around the room gathering supplies for the sudden journey. Elijah tucked the jar of pickles under his free arm, and then he carried Samuel out the door to the wagon that Ben had pulled up to the porch.

As she gathered up her dresses and stuffed them into a bag, Lily reflected on her return to Topeka. Another long journey. Another sick baby. Could she bear to visit the unmarked grave where Abigail lay? She felt sure of only one thing. While in Topeka, she would search for and find Beatrice Waldowski.

The Lord allowed the rain to fall. Eli hunched under a sheet of canvas and, through a veil of pouring water, he watched the lights of Topeka grow closer. All night and all day, he had urged the reluctant mule eastward along the muddy road. They had sloshed through swollen creeks and rattled over rickety bridges. Barely stopping to rest and feed the mule, they had pushed onward.

Somehow, Samuel was still alive. Lily and Mother Margaret had taken turns tending the baby as they huddled beneath a makeshift tent on the wagon bed. Flashes of lightning and the crack of thunder had hardly disturbed Sam's fevered sleep. Now and again, the old woman would lean forward and call out some message: "He took a little milk," she would say, or "He's a-coughin' now."

As Eli guided the mule onto the main street of Topeka, he finally realized he could pray no more. He had begged, pleaded, wept, and cried out for mercy from his heavenly Father. He had searched his mind for Scripture of comfort and hope. He had offered the Lord well-reasoned arguments in favor of sparing Sam's life. He had ground his teeth in rage at the thought of the baby's death, and he had offered up every sacrifice he could think of—if only God would save Sam. "I'll go straight to China and preach your Word," he had told the Lord. "I'll stay in Hope and be a pastor all my days." "Africa? Do you want me to go to Africa? I'll do that, if you'll just let Sam live."

Finally he knew he had no choice but to surrender. He could not will the baby back to health. He could not bargain with the Lord. He could only relinquish Sam into the hands of the almighty God who could turn water into wine, make lame men walk, and calm stormy seas. "Thy will be done," Eli finally prayed as the storm of Sam's terrible illness raged around him. He was helpless against it. "Thy will be done on earth as it is in heaven."

Late evening finally brought an end to the downpour that had accompanied the wagon across the prairie. In the city of Topeka, oil lamps glowed in windows, and the aroma of suppers on the stove began to drift from chimneys. Children emerged to splash in puddles. Businessmen picked their way down wooden boardwalks. The humid chill carried the fragrance of fresh rain along with the reek of discarded, rotting food and open drains. Dogs shook themselves in a spray of droplets, while pigs ambled from the shelter of porches to wallow in the mud.

"You reckon we can find a doctor this late in the evenin'?" Mother Margaret said from under the tent. "I'm afraid they's all shut down, and besides that, it's Sunday."

Eli pushed aside the sopping canvas. He had been scheduled to perform a wedding ceremony this afternoon, but the thought of his obligation had barely crossed his mind. Jack Cornwall and Caitrin Murphy had been among those urging him off to Topeka. He supposed they would understand the delay.

"There's a doctor's place now," he said, spotting a dripping wooden sign that dangled over the boardwalk. "Doctor Schlissel" it read. "Cures." At least the message was straightforward.

As Lily emerged from the tent, Eli reined the mule to a halt and set the wagon's brake. He realized that the silent baby in her arms looked smaller and weaker than ever before. Was Samuel still alive? How could a human life possibly have endured the days of agony that this child had borne? Eli met Lily's somber gaze.

"I think he's still breathing," she whispered. "Elijah, this doctor had better be sent by your ever-loving God, or I don't know what I'll do."

Lifting the young woman down from the wagon, he noted how thin and fragile she was. Like a sparrow. *Oh, Lord, your eye is on the sparrow. Watch over Lily. Watch over us all.*

Eli knocked on the door of the doctor's office. Grumbling that she never had liked big cities, Mother Margaret chose to remain in the wagon. Lily stood shivering beside Eli, her kidskin boots soaked to the ankle. He slipped his arm around her shoulders and drew her close.

"What?" A bleary-eyed elderly man sporting a two-day growth of gray whiskers and the stub end of a cigar peered out the doorway. "Whatcha want?"

"We're looking for Dr. Schlissel," Eli said.

"He's off duty."

He started to shut the door, but Eli held it open. "Please, sir. We've got to have help for our baby. Would you ask the doctor if he'd just take a look at the boy?"

"Dr. Schlissel, would you like to take a look at the boy?" the man said. He thought for a moment. "No, I wouldn't. I'd like to prop my feet up and drink my tea, thank you very much."

As the door started to shut again, Eli stuck his foot out to block it. "You're the doctor? Please, sir, we've driven all the way from Hope. My son is dying. You've got to help us."

The old man took the cigar stub from his mouth and peered down at the tiny bundle in Lily's arms. "You've got him wrapped up like sausage meat in a pig's gut. Is he still alive?"

"Yes, sir," she said.

"You sure?"

"I think so, sir."

"All right, bring him in." Dr. Schlissel turned around and trundled back into the room. He wore a pair of house slippers that slapped the wooden floor when he walked. A set of bright red suspenders stretched over his ample belly, and a stethoscope dangled from his neck.

"I was having my dinner, if you must know," he said as he sorted through a collection of tools and instruments. "I don't like to be disturbed after a long day. Who would? We had a diphtheria epidemic here not too long ago, and I never worked so hard in my life. I'll tell you folks what. I need a vacation, that's what. I need to go set myself by a river someplace and catch some trout. If it isn't a boy with a broken arm or a mama with a burned hand, it's a baby with whooping cough or a grandpa with pneumonia. You name it, I've seen it all, and I think I've tended to one of every kind of disease there is today. Now, what's wrong with this baby? Great ghosts, do you think wrapping his stomach this tight is doing him any good? You've been *brauching* him, haven't you? *Brauching* is a bunch of hooey, if you ask me. Well, put him on the table, ma'am. Don't just stand there."

Eli took Samuel from Lily's arms and laid him on the long wooden table near the window. At one end stood a ceramic bowl filled with the doctor's tools; at the other end sat his dinner of a half-eaten lamb chop, a mound of potatoes, and a loaf of white bread. The man set his cigar down on his dinner plate, adjusted his suspenders, and peered at Samuel.

"Puny thing," he pronounced. "Looks like he's in bad shape. How many other children do you two have?"

"He's the only one." Elijah held Lily tightly, as though he could protect her from the pronouncement to come.

"Well, you're young yet." The doctor looked Lily up and down. "You'll have more."

Lily started to speak, then fell silent. Eli turned her away from the table and led her across the room to the doctor's horsehair settee. The room smelled of stale cigar smoke, the stench of infection, and the acrid scents of castor oil and ether. Together, the couple sank down onto the settee, and Lily buried her face in Eli's shoulder.

"Father," he murmured, his cheek pressed against her golden hair, "you gave life to Samuel. I know that each of us has a different length of time allotted, but has Sam lived all his days, Lord? Has he spent his whole life in these few short days? Oh, God, could you . . . could you see fit to lend him to us a little longer?"

Unable to continue, he wrapped his arms around Lily and gave himself to his grief. Her hands slipped up his back and clasped him tightly. She shook her head.

"No," she murmured. "This can't happen. God, if you're here, listen to me. If you can hear at all, hear me. If you care about us, reach out to us now. I'm not ready for Samuel to go. I can't bear to lose him."

She stopped and swallowed hard. "God," she went on, "don't do it for me. I know you didn't answer when I begged you for protection from my father. You didn't hear when I pleaded for Abby's life. Do this for Samuel. Please, let him live."

As Eli held the trembling woman, he could feel the agony wracking her. Without thinking, he stroked the side of her face and kissed her cheek. "God's been listening to you, Lily," he said, his hand cupping her head against his neck. "He was with you when your father hurt you so much. And he's holding your baby daughter in his arms right now. He'll bring good out of this sorrow. I know he will. If you'll give him your pain, he'll take it. And he'll give you joy in return. Not only joy, but peace, hope, and love."

"Just like a Mexican tamale," Dr. Schlissel announced. "All wrapped up in fifteen layers and hardly able to breathe. Hot as a tamale, too. You running a fever, little fellow, or are you just trying to stay alive under all those blankets?"

A weak cry from Samuel sent a chill down Eli's spine. He squeezed Lily's shoulders against his chest. The doctor was clanging his tools now, muttering to himself, asking where he'd left his cigar.

"How old is this baby?" he called across the room. "Couple of weeks?"

"I think so," Eli said, lifting his focus to the physician, who was gnawing his lamb chop as he prodded the tiny figure with his free hand. "I found him on the trail. His folks had been murdered."

The doctor gave a grunt and set down the chop. He wiped his fingers on his trousers. "Did you give him any kind of tonic?"

Eli looked at Lily. "We tried everything in the mercantile," she said. "We didn't know what else to do."

"So you gave him a little poison from every bottle. Figures. *Brauching*, tonics, sweating. What else have you tried?"

"Prayer," Eli said.

The doctor lifted Samuel's arm, and the baby let out a whimper of protest. "That's the only thing you did right so far. Did either of you happen to notice what kind of spider bit this baby?"

"Spider?" Lily leapt up from the settee and raced across the room. "A spider bit Samuel?"

"Don't tell me you never looked at the kid."

Eli hurried to Lily's side and stared down at the ugly red welt on Sam's tender skin just beneath his armpit. "We had him wrapped up to sweat out the fever," he explained. "The women in town told us—"

"Next time one of your young'uns gets sick, you look him over before you do anything else. It's real simple. Check his eyes. Open his mouth and look at his tongue. Listen to his heartbeat. See if there's a thorn in his foot or a bean up his nose or a plug of wax in his ear. You know what I mean? *Look* at your child. See what's wrong before you go pouring tonics down his throat and binding his stomach up tight. Now, let's see here. It couldn't have been too bad a bite, or you'd be long gone, little fellow. You're a fighter, though." He looked at Eli. "Your boy's a real fighter, isn't he?"

Eli nodded. "Yes, sir. He sure is."

"I'll have to clean this up and try to draw out the infection." He opened a cupboard that held a collection of dinner plates, wool stockings, raw eggs, and several tubs of ointment. He began to take out one medicine after another. "We'd better try some of this. And he could use a little of that. This ought to help. And this won't do any harm. I figured I wouldn't get through my dinner without interruption. A man sits down with his lamb chop and his tea. . . . Well, now, I forgot about this slice of apple pie I put in here the other day. Mrs. Truman gave it to me after I pulled her husband's teeth out. She swore it was the best apple pie this side of the Mississippi, and she's right. I believe I'll have this last slice for dessert. Yes, sir. We saved the teeth, but I don't think that man will wear the denture she's having me make. No, sir, he'll be gumming down his apple pie from now on. He's a stubborn old cuss. I guess that's why he's lived as long as he has. Well, that ought to do us. I don't suppose you folks are going to be able to pay for this. Dirt farmers never do. All the same, I want you to come back in three days and let me take a look at the boy. We ought to have most of the infection out by then, and the fever will be down."

Eli blinked as the old man slid the plate of apple pie down the table to join his lamb chop, and then he set three small packets of ointment and a bottle of tonic beside the baby. "You mean," Eli said, "you mean, Sam's not going to die?"

"If you'd kept him wrapped up like a sausage any longer than you did, he would have died. And it's no wonder he couldn't eat with his belly all caved in under that bandage."

"He's going to live?" Lily asked.

"That's what I said, wasn't it?" The doctor adjusted his suspenders and started toward his dinner. "Go on now. You folks did your best to kill him, but he's a fighter. Your prayers helped too. I've been in this business more than fifty years, and I don't understand it to this day—but folks who pray have an edge. So keep it up."

Eli looked at Lily. Then he turned back to the doctor. "Samuel's going to be all right?"

"Are you folks deaf? Take him and go," the old man barked. "I want to eat my apple pie. I'll see you in three days. All of you."

CHAPTER 7

"I WANT to find Beatrice," Lily said softly. She cuddled the tiny baby beneath her white shawl and shivered with relief that Sam was nursing again. Though she and Elijah had only stepped outside the doctor's office and climbed back into the wagon, somehow a wind of hope had lifted her spirits. The child would live. A future stretched ahead, filled with possibility and promise.

Beside Lily on the wagon bench, the broad-shouldered preacher fiddled with the mule's reins. He hadn't spoken since they told Mother Margaret, who was seated in the rear of the wagon, the good news.

It was clear to Lily that Eli was all but overcome with emotion, knowing the baby would be all right. A *man who truly loves a child. A man who can express something more than rage. A man who can weep. How rare and beautiful*, she thought.

"Beatrice will be able to find us a place to stay," Lily said, laying her hand on Elijah's arm. "She knows Topeka better than I do, and she has acquaintances here."

Though she had no intention of letting Elijah in on her plans, Lily had made up her mind to retrieve her melodeon from Beatrice Waldowski. With the money she had secreted out of her father's vault in Philadelphia exhausted long ago, the small instrument was Lily's only asset. Here in Topeka, she would sell the melodeon.

With that money and the wages she was earning from Elijah Book, she could plan what to do next. For the time being, she would return to Hope to see Samuel back to health. After that, she couldn't be sure.

All she knew was that something had touched her during those dark, agonizing minutes in the doctor's office. Desperate, vulnerable, she had allowed the possibility of God to enter her heart. For the first time in her memory, she had let down the walls that barricaded her soul—and she had caught a glimpse of genuine hope, faith . . . and love. Though Lily had no idea which direction her life should take, she now knew she would never continue west with Beatrice and the traveling show.

"There's a hotel here in Topeka," Lily said to Elijah. "It's called the Crescent Moon, and Beatrice knows the owners. If we go there, they'll be able to tell us where she's staying."

Eli swallowed and clenched his hands around the reins. "God spared Sam's life," he said, his voice rough. "And you want to carry my son into a den of iniquity?"

Lily felt a familiar curl of defiance slide into her chest. "The Crescent Moon is not a den of iniquity. It's a hotel."

"Hotels have saloons."

"I wasn't planning to lead Samuel down the path to strong drink and loose women."

"What were you planning? To find Madame Zahara and tell her to put one of her spells on my son's body? To ask your friend to read the bumps on his skull? *Jesus Christ* saved Sam's life, Lily, and that's all there is to it. I won't bring dishonor to the miracles of almighty God by letting the handiwork of the devil taint my child."

"Beatrice is not a devil!"

"She's no saint."

"Neither are you, Preacher-man." Lily felt the baby squirm with discomfort at the stormy voices around his cocoon of comfort. "I suppose you'd rather camp out on this rain-drenched night, risking pneumonia and who-knows-what diseases on this poor baby, than let anyone catch a glimpse of your holy hide in a saloon."

"My hide's not holy, but it is sanctified by the blood of—"

"Sanctified and saved. Washed in the blood. Whiter than snow. Glory hallelujah." Lily tried to catch her breath. She suddenly felt ill from the whirlwind that raged inside her. "I seem to recall that Jesus invited himself to the house of Zacchaeus the tax gatherer when he needed lodging and food. And when the disciples questioned Jesus about eating with publicans and sinners, he told them, 'They that be whole need not a physician, but they that are sick—'"

"How do you know that verse?" He turned on her, taking her shoulders in his strong hands. "You know the Bible better than I do, Lily, but you throw the Scriptures at me as though they were stones."

"You deserve it." At his rough touch, she shrank into herself, fearful of the outcome yet determined to have her say. If the man became violent, she would survive as she always had. She would retreat to the protection of the quiet place inside herself, to the golden solace of her music.

"You believe the Bible's words without testing them," she went on. "You put your trust in your own righteousness. You think you know everything, but you know nothing. You don't even know who Jesus Christ was."

"Who was he?" In the sky overhead, the storm clouds had rolled away, and Eli's blue eyes shone in the moonlight. His hands tightened on her shoulders. "Lily, who *is* Jesus Christ?"

She sucked in a breath. "If you don't know—"

"I know. I don't always follow him the way I ought. I make a lot of mistakes. You're right that I judge folks when I shouldn't, and I say things without thinking. But I know Jesus Christ. I know what he's done inside me. I know how he changed my life. If you see a bunch of mistakes being made by a big ol' fool, you can figure it's probably me. If you see love and healing and hope and freedom and peace, that's Jesus."

"I'm sorry," she whispered, lowering her head. "Sorry I lashed out at you. Sometimes you just make me furious."

"You make me so mad I could spit nails."

A smile tickled the corner of Lily's mouth. "At least you're honest about that, Preacher-man."

"I'm honest about everything, even though sometimes it means I put my foot right into my mouth. And the honest truth is, I don't want to look for your friend Beatrice."

"Why not? She knows this town. She can help us."

"What if she lures you back into her—"

"Den of iniquity? You make her sound like a spider."

Elijah studied the reins in his hand, and Lily realized that her description fit the man's opinion of her friend perfectly. To the preacher, Beatrice Waldowski was a spider. A poisonous insect. A venomous instrument of the devil, determined to inflict her evil on the lives of everyone she touched.

"It's because of you, Lily," he said finally. "I don't want to lose you. I know Samuel needs you. But I . . . well, I like having you around, too. We're kind of a team, you know, with the baby. Hearing you sing always lifts my spirits. And I enjoy watching you take care of Sam."

"And she's purtier than a shiny new tin whistle," Mother Margaret finally spoke up from the back of the wagon. "Brother Elijah, I'd sit here all night under this wet tent and listen to you work up to tellin' Miz Lily how you really feel about her. But I figure you might go on for hours before you get it right, and in the meantime, you'll probably make her mad two or three more times. A body can only take so much fussin' and makin' up. Now, I want to get me some supper and some sleep. We gonna head over to the den of iniquity or not?"

Lily chuckled at the old woman's blunt question. Leave it to Mother Margaret to get to the point. Elijah was staring into the back of the wagon as though he'd forgotten they had another rider.

"I'd prefer to camp by the river," he said.

"And sleep under this drippin' ol' tent? On these wet blankets? With nothin' to eat but Eva's soggy biscuits? Please, Brother Elijah, have a heart. Don't you know how old I am? I'm *real* old. Now, I got me a son lives here in Topeka, I recall, but I won't be able to locate him without a good bit of askin' around. We was slaves, don't you know, and all my children but Ben was sold out from under me. When my little Moses was ten years old, he was bought by a man from Topeka, and no tellin' what become of him since. So I reckon I better wait until tomorrow to start lookin'. Meanwhile, I expect the Crescent Moon Hotel has got itself some dry beds and a pot of soup a-boilin' on the stove. Kansas is a free state, so let's see what we can find there."

Elijah tugged on his Stetson brim and gave the reins a flick. "All right, Mother Margaret," he said. "Publicans and sinners, here we come."

Although Topeka, Kansas, had a reputation as a sleepy little cattle town, for Lily the place was steeped in sorrow. It was in Topeka that her daughter had been captured in the deadly grip of diphtheria. It was here that her precious baby had been ripped from her heart and buried in an unmarked grave. It was here that her husband and his employer had died. In Topeka, Lily felt, her own life had ended as well.

Now as she huddled beside Elijah Book, she had the impression that she was traveling in a landscape of hell. One muddy road turned into another. One rickety clapboard house followed another. Hollow-eyed children stared at the wagon through waxed-paper windowpanes. Even though the moon shone overhead, darkness crept around each corner and lurked under every porch. Dogs slinked across the streets, the hair on their spines lifted in wariness. Turn after turn led the wagon down narrow alleys and across vacant, treeless lots.

Now and then, Elijah called out to someone to ask directions to the Crescent Moon Hotel. "Turn left," came one response. "Two streets down," came another. "Turn right and then right again. I think that hotel's near the Boar's Breath Tavern. You'd better check with the night watchman on the corner up ahead."

Lily tried not to shiver, but exhaustion and fear crept into her bones. She wanted to pray again, as she had in the doctor's house. Her heart longed to cry out for help, guidance, and safety. But she was too wary to venture a prayer. She didn't want to trust a God who had let her down so many times before.

Leaning her head on Elijah's shoulder, she gave herself to the swaying, creaking wagon. Why hadn't God helped her when she'd cried out to him all those times when her father's uncontrolled rage poured over her? Why hadn't God saved her? She'd been such a little girl, so thin, so frightened, so helpless.

God will protect you, the preacher had announced in his sermons at church. *God will protect you*, the Sunday school teachers had assured their pupils. Lily had clung to that promise. But God hadn't protected her. Without warning, her father had struck out at his only child, and his fury had blackened her eyes, striped the backs of her legs, jarred her skull, cracked her ribs. Philadelphia's finest doctors puzzled over Lily's series of baffling injuries. Her teachers labeled their precocious student "clumsy." Her friends wondered why so often she could not come out to play—and after a while, they stopped asking.

Until she was sixteen, Lily had thought it was all her fault. She was a bad girl. So naughty. Then one day her father was whipping her after the rehearsal for his orchestra's rendition of Handel's *Messiah* had gone badly. A giant wave of realization washed over her. *No*, she thought, *I do not deserve this beating. My mother will not save me, and God will not protect me. So I'll find a way to take care of myself*. And she had.

"You know," Elijah said suddenly, "I may never find that hotel, but I've had a good chance to do some thinking out here on the streets of Topeka. And here's what I think. You're right, Lily. You're right that I ought to put my trust in the words that come right out of the Bible. Not what some preacher tells me, or what I heard some religious person say, or what I might think sounds right and good. I ought to believe the Bible, nothing else. And that means I need to know the Scriptures as well as I know my own name. I need to learn them—the way you have."

Lily focused on a lamplit building just down the street. "Crescent Moon Hotel and Saloon" a sign read. Almost there, and yet she must know one thing.

"Does the Bible promise that God will protect us?" she asked Elijah. "Because I don't—"

"There it is," he cried out, giving her a brisk hug. "Hey, Mother Margaret, it's the Crescent Moon. We found it." He turned to Lily. "Of course God protects us. Look right there at that sign. He brought us here, didn't he?"

"Did he?" she mouthed, but Elijah was busy reining the tired mule and setting the wagon brake. *Had* God promised to protect her? Did the Bible she had read again and again offer even a single promise of God's abiding shelter at *all* times through *all* things?

Lily sat on the wagon, numb with confusion. Preachers had said it. Teachers had said it. Elijah Book had said it. But had God said it?

And if God didn't promise protection, what good was he? What use was trust in an all-powerful Creator who wouldn't defend his creation?

"Let me have that little fellow," Elijah said, raising his arms toward Lily. "If we're going to walk straight into the valley of the shadow of death, I'd better protect my boy."

Elijah tucked Samuel into his arms as Lily had taught him. *Yea, though I walk through the valley of the shadow of death, I will fear no evil; for thou art with me.* The familiar psalm slipped into Lily's mind. A loving father protects his children, she thought, watching

Elijah make a fuss over the little bundle he carried. A loving father keeps his children safe.

But bad things happened to God's children all the time. Did that mean he didn't love them? Or was God like her own father—outwardly perfect as he put on displays of his own brilliance and talent, yet privately inflicting merciless punishment upon the helpless?

Lily realized that Elijah was holding out his free arm to her. She took his hand and slid down into his embrace. The preacher held her for just a moment too long before he moved away. "Mother Margaret," he called. "You planning to come out of that tent?"

"Go check if they let black folks come into the hotel," she returned. "'Cause if I'm not welcome, I'll take my business somewhere else."

"Serve 'em right, too," Elijah said. "Come on, Lily. Let's go look for your friend."

"I trust you'll restrain your tongue from referring to Beatrice as evil incarnate and this hotel as a den of iniquity."

Eli stopped at the steps to the front porch and took Lily's hand. "Even though I wish you wouldn't walk back into Miss Waldowski's life, I won't try to stop you. You make your own choices. But if you need me, Lily, I'll be right beside you."

As he turned to climb the steps onto the porch, Lily gathered her shawl around her shoulders. The chill of realization filtered down her spine. The preachers and teachers were wrong. Elijah Book was wrong. God had never promised to protect her. He didn't promise to protect anyone.

"Yea, though I walk through the valley . . ."

That's right, Lily, you will walk in paths of danger and places of harm.

"I will fear no evil . . ."

But you don't have to be afraid.

"For thou art with me . . ."

I'll be right beside you. All the way.

Elijah sat on a bench in the lobby of the Crescent Moon the following afternoon and waited for Lily and Mother Margaret to emerge from their room. After hours of searching and questioning strangers, Lily believed she had tracked her friend to a small boardinghouse at the edge of Topeka. When she finished nursing Samuel, she and the others would go in search of Beatrice Waldowski.

With growing discomfort, the preacher watched businessmen and cowboys file into the saloon situated just down the hall from the lobby. His Stetson held loosely in his hands, he turned the brim around and around. Though he tried to calm himself, he could almost hear the thunder of his heartbeat in his chest.

Preach to them, the steady voice inside his soul commanded. *Preach, Elijah Book. Lead the lost to the light of salvation. Guide the wicked onto the path of righteousness*.

How could he just sit idly by and allow these unrepentant and ignorant souls to continue in the darkness of their wicked ways? The men had no idea that Jesus could make a difference in their lives—and they would never hear the message of Christ's sacrifice and love unless somebody told them.

Eli had to do it. He had to preach.

After a quick search for his black leather Bible in the saddlebag beside him, he realized the valued book was missing. Distressed but unwilling to let the moment pass, he climbed onto the bench where he'd been sitting. "'The Lord is my light and my salvation,' " he cried out in a loud voice, "'whom shall I fear? The Lord is the strength of my life; of whom shall I be afraid?'"

A passerby stopped and stared. A little boy in a sailor suit ran out of the dining room to see what the commotion was about. His mother quickly followed. The hotel clerk popped up from behind his desk.

"Last night," Eli addressed them, "I wandered the streets of this town without light, without direction, without security. I confess to you that I stumbled in the darkness. I lost my way many times. I shivered in dread of the unknown."

He spotted three men ambling through the lobby toward the saloon. "Do you gentlemen wander in darkness on this sunny Kansas afternoon?" he called to them. "Do you believe the fleeting pleasure of strong drink will bring you lasting happiness? Do you mistake the passing fancies of a loose woman for the security of true love?"

"Shut yer trap, cowboy!" one of the men called back. "Take yer preachin' to church."

"I used to ride the cattle trails just like you boys," Eli went on, extending his open hand in their direction, "and I worked hard night and day. Long hours, sore muscles, and nothing but a bedroll to call home. I thought I deserved the light refreshments and the sweet-smelling fancies in the towns I went through. But they were empty pleasures. All empty!"

"Sir," the clerk said, approaching from behind his desk. "We have a policy against solicitation in the—"

"Jesus Christ gave my life meaning," Eli continued, searching his mind for a verse he had tried to memorize a few weeks back. " 'Woe unto them that call evil good, and good evil; that put darkness for light, and light for darkness. . . . Woe unto them that are mighty to drink wine, and men of strength to mingle strong drink—' "

"Ain't nothin' wrong with a stiff belt of whisky, Preacher," one of the men chimed in.

"Let him be," his companion said. "He's a-preachin' the Word of God."

"Sir, would you please step down from the bench?" the hotel clerk pleaded.

"I'm no different from any of you," Eli went on, ignoring the man. Out of the corner of his eye, he saw Lily and Mother

Margaret edging warily down the staircase. Their faces registered surprise. "I thought I could be the trail boss of my own life, but I knew I was getting nowhere fast. Then I read the words of truth I'd been looking for: 'Seek ye the Lord while he may be found, call ye upon him while he is near: Let the wicked forsake his way, and the unrighteous man his thoughts: and let him return unto the Lord, and he will have mercy upon him.'"

Eli focused on the gathering crowd, but his thoughts were on Lily. "God loves you," he said, "and he wants to live inside you. He wants to wash away the sins that have stained your soul. He wants to make you as white as snow. If you'll let him, the Lord will lead you onto his path. He'll direct your steps. He'll fill your life with joy and peace. Will you ask him in? Sinners, will you give your heart to Jesus Christ?"

Closing his eyes, Eli began to pray aloud the prayer that filled his heart. Pleading with God, he begged for the souls of the lost men and women in the saloon down the hall. He prayed for the lost in the lobby. He prayed for the lost on the street outside the hotel. "Open their hearts. Give them strength to stand up. Fill them with love. Amen and amen," he said, lifting his head. The floor around the bench where he stood was filled with kneeling men and women. Some wept. Others clasped their hands in prayer.

For a moment, Eli was stunned. What had happened? He'd only been speaking aloud the words inside his heart—words that demanded an outlet. But God had used his simple, disjointed message to touch these people. He stared in confusion. Again and again, this happened when he preached. People heard the Word of the Lord. People responded. People repented.

Oh, Father, what am I supposed to do now? I'm no good at this part. I don't know how to touch them one by one. I can't . . .

Lily was teaching him how to love. He could do it. Climbing down from the bench, Eli knelt on the floor among the people. Slipping an arm around the man beside him, he instructed all of them to pray with him if they wanted to invite Jesus Christ to become Lord of their lives.

"Yes, Lord," the man beside him said softly.

"I believe Jesus Christ is God," Eli went on. "I believe Jesus came to earth and died in my place to take away my sin. I believe he came to life again after his death, and I know he sent the Holy Spirit to live inside me. Take me now, Father. Take my heart, my soul, my whole life. I give myself to you. Teach me to walk in your path. Amen."

"Mercy, mercy, mercy," Mother Margaret said in a low voice as the crowd rose and gathered around Elijah. "Hallelujah and amen."

Some people shook the preacher's hand; others tried to press money on him. Elijah refused the gifts, giving each person a hug instead. This wasn't half as bad as he'd thought. In fact, he kind of liked touching folks, speaking an encouraging word and seeing their eyes light up.

"Go find yourselves a church tomorrow," he called after the dispersing crowd. "And get a new set of friends, you hear?"

"What have you been up to, Brother Elijah?" the old woman said, folding her arms over her chest. "We can't hardly leave you alone for a minute without the gospel a-comin' right up out of you and a-spillin' over onto everybody."

Eli gave Mother Margaret a sheepish grin. "I hope I didn't keep you ladies waiting too long. I just got to feeling real unhappy about that saloon down the hall."

"They're not feeling too happy about you, either," Lily said, nodding in the direction of a pair of angry men storming down the hall toward them.

"You, sir!" one of them called, pointing at Elijah. "What do you mean by drivin' away our afternoon's trade? We lost half our customers when you went to speechifyin'."

"You have no right to do business in the lobby of this hotel!" the other cried. "I'm George Gibbons, owner of this establishment, and you'd better get your bags and get out of here before we call the law on you."

"Yes, sir," Elijah said, nodding with as much politeness as he could muster. He felt like punching them both in the nose. Clearly, these two men ran the saloon—and probably managed the soiled doves who plied their trade in the back bedrooms, too. But they were right. He hadn't gotten permission to preach.

"I apologize for upsetting you, gentlemen," he said, adjusting his Stetson on his head. "The ladies and I were just leaving."

"For good," one of the men added, sticking a stubby finger in Elijah's chest. "Take these women and your bags, too. We don't need the likes of you folks at the Crescent Moon."

"I'm afraid he's right, sir," the clerk said with an apologetic smile. "The manager just told me that we can't let you stay the next two nights, like you'd planned."

Eli glanced at Lily. With a roll of her eyes, she transferred Samuel into Mother Margaret's arms and headed back up the stairs to fetch the women's baggage. In a moment she returned carrying their few possessions, and the group left the hotel.

As Elijah steered the wagon in the direction of the waning sun, he mused on the disturbance he'd created in the lobby. Truly, he hadn't intended to upset anybody. Something inside him demanded that he speak. He thought of the apostle Paul and his determination to preach in spite of shipwrecks and stonings and prison sentences. That was just how Eli felt. He *had* to tell folks about Jesus—no matter what.

Glancing at Lily seated beside him on the bench, he tried to read the expression on her face. Was she angry? Disgusted? Did she think him a fool?

Becoming aware of his steady gaze, she met his eyes and lifted her determined chin. "You were wrong, Reverend Book," she said.

"I probably should have asked permission," he agreed. "A fellow ought to respect those in authority."

"You were wrong about something you said."

"I was?" He scratched his forehead, trying to remember his own sermon. It wouldn't surprise him a bit if he'd put his foot in his mouth. Maybe he'd even gotten his Scriptures mixed up. Without his Bible, he couldn't be sure. Where had he put that book anyhow?

"Was it the part about being the trail boss of my own life?" he asked her. "I know that didn't make much sense. See, when all us cowhands were driving cattle north to market, we followed a trail boss who—"

"You said God protects us always."

"I did?" He didn't remember that. "I said he loves us. He wants to forgive us and live inside our hearts."

"Last night, right here in this wagon, you told me the Bible said God always protects us. You were wrong."

Eli tugged on the reins and turned the mule south. He did recall talking with Lily about that. But he couldn't remember exactly what he'd told her.

"I couldn't sleep last night," she said, "so I slipped into your room and borrowed your Bible." She pulled the book from beneath her white shawl and set it on his lap. "Hope you don't mind. Anyhow, I searched all night and I never did find a single verse that promises God's constant protection. You were wrong."

Lifting his focus to the pink-tinged sky, Eli tried to make sense of her statement. Why was she telling him this? What did it mean?

"I guess I *was* wrong," he said finally. "I was thinking about the apostle Paul a couple of minutes ago, and I recollected all those shipwrecks he suffered. Also, folks threw stones at him and tossed him into prison. He wrote down that he figured he'd gone through just about every terrible problem a fellow could face—and you're right, God didn't spare him from any of that."

"Ha!" she said. "Everybody lied to me. God doesn't protect us. He's useless."

"If all you want to do is skip through life on a rainbow, I guess so. But Paul said he was filled with joy in all his sufferings. If you want to grow into someone beautiful and useful to God, Lily, I suspect he's got to do a little molding. I don't know exactly what you've been through, but I do know one thing. You can let your trials turn you bitter and angry, or you can give your heartaches to the Lord. Then he'll use you to reach out to other folks hurting just as bad, and through you, he'll draw them to himself."

Lily sat in silence after that, and Eli didn't know what else to say. He figured he'd probably done enough preaching for one day. Besides that, he was scared he might run Lily off, and Samuel was just beginning to perk up. The baby's cheeks were pink again, and he'd done a fair amount of fussing during the night. Eli had never thought he'd actually look forward to the sound of Sam's squalling.

"There she is," Lily said suddenly, shrinking toward him. "There's Beatrice. Oh, Eli, you've got to help me."

CHAPTER 8

LILY?" Beatrice Waldowski leaned forward, hands on her hips, and squinted at the approaching wagon. "Lily Nolan, is that you?"

Taking a deep breath and shifting away from Elijah, Lily lifted her hand in greeting. "Hello, Beatrice! We came from Hope yesterday. How are you?"

"I knew you'd come to your senses!" Grabbing her green silk skirts, Bea hurried down the steps of the rickety boardinghouse. "Oh, Lil, just wait till you hear what I've been up to! I've got everything organized. You won't believe the things we can do with—"

She stopped and stared at Elijah. "Who's he?" she said. "Is that the preacher, Lily?"

"Elijah Book," he answered for the woman at his side. Taking off his hat, Eli gave Beatrice a polite nod. "Been awhile."

"Not long enough," she said. "Lily, I hope this man doesn't plan to stay around. You and I have a lot of work to do. We've got plans—plans that *don't* include him."

Lily swallowed. "Mr. Book, Mrs. Hanks, and I came to Topeka to see a doctor about the preacher's baby. A spider bit Samuel." She motioned to Mother Margaret cradling the child in the back of the wagon. "He's better now."

"That's nice," Bea said, her voice flat. "I hope you don't expect me to put them all up here, Lil. This isn't a hotel, you know."

"I was hoping we might be able to stay for a couple of nights. Maybe we could sleep in the show wagon. Bea, you and I need to talk about some things."

The woman pushed her mass of dyed black hair behind her shoulder and gave Lily a sneer. "If you're still choosing to work for that preacher instead of me, Lily Nolan, I don't see that we have much to say to each other. You've made yourself clear."

Hurt that her friend would reject her once again, Lily started to climb down from the wagon. Elijah's hand on her arm stopped her. Turning toward him, she read the plea in his blue eyes. *Don't go. We can find another place to stay. You don't need this woman.*

But Lily did need Beatrice. She needed the melodeon. And she needed . . . perhaps . . . the reassurance that she hadn't completely lost the one true friend she'd ever known. Pulling away from Elijah, Lily stepped down from the wagon and walked toward Beatrice.

"Don't turn me away, Bea," she said softly. "You saved me from my father once. For so long, you and Ted and Jakov were all the family I had. I trusted you."

"I trusted you, too. You let me down."

"I'm sorry." Lily stopped a pace away. "I chose to take on a job that would put food in our mouths, Bea. I wanted to help you the way you helped me. What's wrong with that?"

Bea's painted eyes flicked to Elijah. Slipping her arm quickly through Lily's, she turned the younger woman away from the wagon. "You scared me so bad, Lil," she whispered when they were far enough away that Elijah couldn't hear. "Can't you see how that preacher is just like your father? I knew he'd fill your head with his pretty lies. What's he been telling you? Does he cast doubt on your certainty that holiness lies inside your very own spirit—that you are the essence of the divine?"

"Well, he does preach from the Bible, but—"

"Does he try to woo you into his confidence and make you

believe he's telling you the truth? You know what religious men are like, Lil. Look at your father—how different is that cowboy preacher from the man who told you about God's love and then blackened your eye?"

"But Mr. Book is not—"

"Has he put his arms around you? Has he tried to kiss you? You know what he's after, Lily. He'll tell you he's trying to win your soul, when it's your body he wants. Tell me he hasn't kissed you."

Lily flushed. "Well, he did kiss my cheek—"

"I knew it! He'll use you up, just the way your saintly father did. He'll tell you one thing and treat you the opposite. Oh, Lily, honey, take your things out of that wagon and come with me right this minute. I'll get you into the house where he can't reach you. I'll keep you safe."

Lily took her friend's hands and held them tight. "Elijah Book is not hurting me, Bea. He has no power over me, and I'm sure he doesn't want to use me in the way you think. The truth is, the preacher and I fight all the time, just like a pair of twisters stirring up twice the trouble every time we get near each other. The baby brought us together, that's all. Samuel needed my help—and he still does. Yesterday that poor child was nearly dead, Bea. He's only just beginning to perk up. I can't abandon him now."

"Are you telling me you tracked me all the way through Topeka only to turn away from me all over again?" Bea pursed her trembling lips. "I swear, when I saw you on that wagon, Lily, I thought this was going to be the best day of my life. You don't know how my spirit rose inside me. It was like all the angels were singing. But now . . . now . . ."

"Beatrice, don't cry." Lily drew her friend close and wrapped both arms around the older woman. The familiar scents of heavy perfume and incense drifted up from Bea's green silk dress. "I'm here now."

"It's just that . . . that the cards told me that today was going to bring a surprise . . . and I was hoping . . . hoping you'd come. Oh, Lil, I've been working so hard to set things up for us. I wanted to tell you everything. It's going to be so wonderful, and I wanted you to share in my joy."

"Why don't you let us stay here with you a short while, Beatrice?" Lily asked gently. "You can tell me all your plans. We'll take Samuel back to the doctor in a couple of days, and once he's completely well, we'll know which way to go."

"Will you let me read your fortune?"

Lily's heart sank. It wasn't that she didn't trust the tarot cards. It was just that . . . well, she didn't want to cloud her thinking with Bea's psychic premonitions and forebodings. For so many years she had put her faith in the words of her ministers and Bible teachers. After rejecting them, she had come to trust Beatrice's mystic powers.

But now . . . for the first time . . . Lily didn't want to count on anyone. She wanted to search for truth. She wanted to find answers. And she wanted to do it alone.

"Has that preacher turned you against the cards, Lil?" Bea asked, her eyes moist. "Because if he has—"

"The tarot cards let me down, Bea. The cards didn't predict Abigail's sickness. They failed to warn me." Lily looked down at her knotted fingers, fighting the tears that arose every time she thought of her beloved daughter. "But even worse than that, the cards didn't offer any comfort after my baby died. I had nothing but emptiness. No hope, no future, no peace."

"And you think the Bible can do any better?"

"I think I want to sit down and nurse Samuel Book. I want to rest my tired bones. And I want to figure this out for myself."

Beatrice sniffed. "If that's how you feel."

"Do you have room for us?"

"The old woman will have to sleep in the wagon. The preacher can bunk down in the men's quarters. You can stay with me."

"I'll sleep with Mother Margaret," Lily said as she gave her friend a quick hug. "I don't want to leave her alone."

Her sense of relief mingling with uncertainty, Lily returned to the wagon and told the others the news. As Elijah climbed down from the wagon, he assessed her, clearly trying to ascertain the truth in the situation. After he removed his saddlebag, he caught Lily's sleeve and drew her to one side.

"You all right?"

She nodded. "But please don't start preaching in the boarding-house and get us tossed out. We can't see Dr. Schlissel again for two days, and I won't risk Sam's health over another one of your outbursts."

"Outbursts? Was that what it was?"

"Oh, Elijah, you know you rolled right over those people like a great big thunderstorm. You didn't care a whit about the consequences. You just went right ahead and—"

"The consequences were that ten people came to know Jesus Christ this afternoon. I cared about *that*."

Lily bit her lip and stared into his sparkling blue eyes. Yes, he did care about that. No one could deny the fervor in the man's heart. Beatrice Waldowski embraced her faith in the spirit world, held it tightly, claimed it for herself. But Elijah shared his beliefs with everyone he met, as though he was so full of Jesus Christ that he could do nothing to dam the flood of his joy.

In a way, the two were as opposite as two people could be. Bea trusted her inner spirit to be her guide; Elijah trusted the Spirit of God to lead him. Bea pursued self-fulfillment; Elijah emptied himself to everyone around. Bea made plans that would bring glory to herself; Elijah took on a dying baby and gave away his life's savings to rescue the child.

"Elijah," Lily said, "I wanted to find Beatrice for one reason. She took something valuable of mine. I need to get it back."

The preacher slung his saddlebag over his shoulder. When he

spoke, his voice was filled with tenderness. "Oh, Lily, I hope what you're looking to get back from that woman is something more valuable than diamonds or gold. I hope it's your precious soul."

Elijah was getting so good at tracking folks that he thought he might ought to hire on with the Pinkerton Detective Agency. That wouldn't leave much time for preaching, though, and it had been all he could do to keep his mouth shut during the past two days at the boardinghouse. Now, pulling up to a wood-frame shanty on the outskirts of town, Eli reflected on the men he'd come to know in Topeka. Not a single one of them knew the Lord—not as a friend and Savior, anyhow. That burdened him.

"What if Mother Margaret's son doesn't live here?" Lily whispered as the wagon rolled to a stop beside the yard of the little house. "She's going to be so disappointed."

"We'll just keep looking for the man," Eli said. As Samuel had grown steadily better, Elijah and Lily had joined the old woman in her search for her long-lost son. Not many hours before they were to return to Dr. Schlissel's office, a tenant at the boardinghouse had told them of a Moses Hanks who lived on the south side of town. Mother Margaret's face spoke of her anxiety and hope.

"I'm afraid he won't remember me," she said, leaning forward on the wagon bench between Eli and Lily. "He was only ten years old when they sold him off. Did I tell you that?"

"Yes, Mother Margaret," Lily said. "You told us."

"He was such a little boy. So skinny and scared. It like to broke my heart."

"I'm sure it did."

"Jack Cornwall's father done it. He was a good master most of the time, but he didn't understand how it felt for a mother to lose her children one by one. Oh, look at that little boy peerin' through the window. You don't suppose that's Moses, do you?"

"Moses will be a grown man, now, Mother Margaret. He's older than Ben, remember?"

"How come I keep forgettin' that? Mercy, somebody's comin' out of the house." She took Lily's hand. "Miz Lily, I'm plumb addled over this. Do I look all right? Is my bonnet tied on straight?"

Lily arranged Mother Margaret's bonnet bow while Elijah jumped down from the wagon and walked toward the approaching man. He was a big fellow, ebony skinned, broad-shouldered, and rawboned. He cradled a rifle under one arm.

"Afternoon, sir," Eli said, taking off his hat. "We're looking for a man by the name of Moses Hanks."

"What for?"

"We'd like to talk with him."

"I'm Mo Hanks. Speak your piece."

"Moses?" Mother Margaret stood up on the wagon. "Moses, child, is that you?"

The big man turned and spotted the little woman. Instantly the hard lines left his face. His caramel eyes lit up with joy. "Mama? Mama, you found me!"

Suddenly a ten-year-old boy again, he dropped his rifle to the ground and sprinted toward the wagon. In one scoop, he lifted the little woman into his arms and engulfed her. Swinging her out of the wagon, he turned her around and around until they were both laughing and crying at the same time.

"Moses, Moses, honey, you're liable to squeeze the stuffin' right outta me!" Mother Margaret squealed.

"I can't believe it's you, Mama. You came for me!"

As he lowered her to the ground, she pressed her face against his chest. "Oh, my precious baby. My sweet child. My darlin' boy. Let Mama hold you now."

"Mama, you found me. You found me."

"I'm here now, baby. I got you."

Elijah stepped back as others began to trickle out of the house.

He glanced at the wagon to find Lily dabbing her cheeks. With Samuel propped on her shoulder, she was rocking back and forth and patting the baby's back. His tiny pink fingers curled into her golden hair as she nestled her nose against his neck.

Father, Eli began, and then he didn't know what to say next. At the sight of Lily and Samuel, something welled up like a fountain inside him. He couldn't identify it. Couldn't control it.

Father, I . . . Lily's hand tucked the thin cotton blanket around the baby's legs. Eli swallowed hard.

Father, I care . . . I need . . . I think I love Lily. I love something about her. Help me, Lord. Show me what to do.

"Brother Elijah, this is my son!" Mother Margaret cried, taking the preacher's arm and pulling him close. "This is my sweet Moses. I found my baby!"

The big man pumped Eli's hand. "Thank you for bringin' my mama to me, sir."

"Glad to do it."

"You precious man!" The old woman threw her arms around Eli. "Moses, I want you to know Brother Elijah. He's my preacher from back home. Mercy, can he give a sermon! And that's his little baby over there in the wagon. That's Samuel. There's Miz Lily a-holdin' him, and I do declare, this must be the happiest day of my life. Thank you, Lord! Amen and hallelujah!"

"You haven't changed a bit, Mama," Moses said with a laugh. "Come over here now and meet my wife and all your gran'kids."

"Gran'kids!" Mother Margaret threw up her hands. "Wait till Ben and Eva hear about this! Mercy, I think I'm about to faint."

Grinning, Eli watched the happy pair hurry across the yard to introduce Moses' family to their long-lost matriarch. The preacher strolled back to the wagon and climbed up beside Lily and the baby.

"I think that's the first thing I ever got all the way right in my life," he said. "Have you ever seen so much laughing and crying all at one time?"

Lily blotted her handkerchief across her cheek. "It's wonderful."

"You look about as happy as a tick-fevered calf."

At that, she actually chuckled. "Now you've got *me* laughing and crying at the same time."

Aching to take her in his arms, Eli did the next best thing. He leaned toward Lily and gave Samuel's soft head a light kiss. "What are you sad about?"

"I was thinking of all the other children Mother Margaret lost," she said softly. "She once told me she'd given birth to fourteen. Three of them died, and all but Ben were sold. Now we've found Moses, but nine are still missing."

"You think Mother Margaret's worrying about the nine she's missing—or rejoicing over the one she found?"

He studied the chaotic scene on the front porch of the little frame house. Never in all his days had he heard so much carrying-on. Little children jumped up and down. Dogs barked. Somebody began to sing. A couple of folks were even dancing.

"I think," Lily said, "that she's mourning the nine, even though she's rejoicing over the one."

"You're missing Abigail, aren't you?" Unable to stop himself, he slipped his arm around her. "I guess you can't ever replace someone you've lost. No matter how hard you try."

Lily leaned against his shoulder, the drowsy baby nestled between them. "No one can take Abby's place."

Eli observed the joyous family on the porch, and his own imminent loss grew sharper. "Nobody can take *your* place, Lily," he said finally, voicing the fear that had troubled him for days. "Am I going to lose you?"

She looked up. "You can't lose something you don't have. Do you have me, Elijah?"

"A little bit, I hope." He tightened his arm around her. "At least you choose to keep feeding my son. You talk to me without shouting. You don't pull away when I touch you."

She shivered. "Elijah, I . . ."

"What is it, Lily?"

"I need to talk to you about something." She drew in a deep breath and began. "Beatrice told me she has the money to build an opera house. Those two men who ran us out of the Crescent Moon Hotel are the ones she had met the last time we were in Topeka. She asked them if they'd finance a new show house, and they agreed to put up the cash. She's already paid for a shipment of liquor and lined up a bartender. She's planning to hire a cook, a juggler, a magician, and a ventriloquist."

"How about a singer?"

"She wants me to sing," Lily said. "She's offered me good wages."

"Better than I can pay?"

"Yes," she said in a hushed voice. "Much better."

Elijah was pretty sure his heart had sunk to the bottom of his stomach, but he knew he had to keep talking. If Lily got wind of how much he cared about her, she'd hightail it right off.

"Where's Beatrice going to put up her opera house?" he asked.

"Lawrence. A lot of the town was burned during the war, you know. They're eager for people to move in and build."

"Lawrence, Kansas."

He repeated the name, even though he already knew where the city was located. *Oh, Lord, help me. I can't figure out what to say to Lily. I know I'm not supposed to think this way about her. She's not a believer. You don't want the two of us to feel tenderness for each other. But, Father, she's special to me. It's more than the baby, Lord. There's something about Lily.*

"Beatrice took my melodeon with her when she left Hope," she was saying. "It's stored in the show wagon."

"Melodeon?" Eli tried to make sense of her words. "Is that something like an organ?"

Lily nodded. "It's mine. Will you help me get it?"

"Get the melodeon?"

"That's what I said. Are you listening to me?"

"Sure, I'm listening. You said Beatrice is building an opera house in Lawrence, Kansas. She wants you to sing, and you need me to take your melodeon out of the show wagon."

Lily drew back from him and looked into his eyes. "I'm not going with her."

Elijah stiffened up like he'd been shot. "You're not going to Lawrence? You're not going to sing?"

"No." She shifted Samuel to her other shoulder. "I'm going to Philadelphia."

"Philadelphia!" He was sure he'd been shot a second time. "That's in Pennsylvania."

A smile crossed her lips. "You know your states very well."

"I borrowed an atlas one time when my pa and I were living near Albuquerque."

"I see." She squared her shoulders. "Well, when I sell my melodeon, I'll have some money for my train ticket. So, I'll be going back to my father's house in Philadelphia . . . after I've spent another month or two in Hope."

Hope! Eli didn't need an atlas to know where that was. He felt so light he could have soared right over the wagon. But surely he'd heard her wrong. If Lily had the money for a train ticket to Philadelphia, she wouldn't go back to the prairie. Would she?

"You're going to Hope again?" he asked. "With me and Sam?"

She gave a little laugh. "Are you losing your hearing, Preacherman? I'll need to earn the rest of the money for my ticket, and I want to make sure this baby is strong and healthy."

"But what about your singing? What about Beatrice?"

Lily lowered her head. "Bea has a good future ahead of her. With an opera house to run, she'll stay busy and make good money. She can find another singer."

"Hallelujah!" Elijah said. "Praise the Lord. Amen and amen."

Lily laughed. "You've been listening to Mother Margaret

too long. Oh, Elijah, I need a fresh start. I tried once when I ran away from Philadelphia. I thought I'd found the answers I was looking for. But even before Abigail died, my life became so . . . so . . ."

"Mercy, you two, listen to this!" Mother Margaret called as she fairly flew across the yard. "I got me six gran'kids and three great-gran'babies! Three—can you beat that? Brother Elijah, you and Miz Lily better come meet all these folk. There's more kin here than I can shake a stick at. Miz Lily, I want you to know God done blessed me with good measure, pressed down, shaken together, and runnin' over! The Lord is wonderful; praise his holy name!"

"Amen!" Eli said.

"Hallelujah!" Lily added. "Amen and amen."

"This is the fighting-est baby I ever saw," Dr. Schlissel said. "I suspect it's going to take more than a spider and his careless parents to do him in."

The doctor lifted Samuel and turned the baby around in his big hands. Lily had been pleased to discover that during regular office hours, Dr. Schlissel's dinner and smoldering cigar were not in evidence on the long table. Although the physician seemed determined to chide her and Elijah for failing to notice the spider bite, Lily took a measure of pride in the baby's present state of health. After all, she had nursed him faithfully night and day, and his scrawny frame was starting to fill out.

"You say you found this baby in a wagon that was shot full of arrows?" the doctor asked, turning to Elijah.

"Yes, sir."

"Did you happen to notice anything unusual about the folks in the wagon?"

Elijah shook his head. "I mostly prayed over them while I buried them. I couldn't think too clearly just then."

"Did you see which of them was a redskin?"

Lily stared at the dark-haired baby in the doctor's hands. A redskin? An *Indian?*

Elijah rubbed the back of his neck and shifted from one foot to the other. "It was the mother," he said finally. "I couldn't tell what race she was. Maybe Indian or Mexican. She had real black hair."

"Then you got yourself a half-breed here." The doctor laid Samuel back on the table. "You sure you want him? There's a home for orphans and foundlings over in Kansas City. I could put the baby on a mail coach headed that way."

Lily clasped her hands together in disbelief. Put Samuel on a mail coach? Send him to an orphanage? Surely Elijah wouldn't do such a heartless thing.

She didn't care what color the baby's skin was or whether his hair would stay black as he grew older. His heritage didn't matter in the least. Samuel was a beautiful child, a precious little boy. Everyone who saw him would recognize that, wouldn't they? Surely people wouldn't reject Samuel because of the circumstances of his birth or the color of his skin.

"I didn't really give the whole notion much thought before now," the preacher said. "I guess Sam's going to have a hard row to hoe in life."

"He sure is."

"Good thing he's a fighter." Scooping up the baby, Elijah planted a big kiss on the boy's soft forehead. "Come on, little fellow. Let's go home."

Relief flooding through her, Lily grabbed the baby's bag and gave the doctor a final glance. *A hard row to hoe.* Whose life wasn't? Elijah's was. Hers certainly had been.

Perhaps Samuel would face many difficult times ahead—maybe he would even walk through the valley of the shadow of death. No telling what kind of evil and heartbreak might lie in his path. But with Elijah Book as his father, the child would be watched over, tenderly loved, and diligently nurtured. Samuel Book, Lily decided, would grow up to be a strong and courageous man.

"Thank you, Doctor," she said. "For the medicine."

Out in the street, Mother Margaret was lifting Samuel into the wagon. Her face was suffused with the light of the waning sun as she hugged the tiny baby. "Mercy sakes, you're gettin' heavy," she cooed. "Your mama's gonna have to sew you some regular people-clothes. You'll be crawlin' before long."

Your mama, Lily thought as Elijah helped her into the wagon. No, she wasn't Samuel's mother. But if anyone had tried to put that baby into an orphanage, she would have fought tooth and nail to prevent it. Already the thought of abandoning the child in a couple of months seemed unbearable. She had told Elijah that no one could take the place of Abigail—and she had meant it. But Samuel had carved out his own niche in Lily's heart.

Taking Samuel from Mother Margaret and gathering him close, Lily brushed a light kiss across the baby's cheek. "I guess we're ready to go back to Hope now," she said. "After a stop at the boardinghouse to pick up my melodeon."

"There's one more thing," Mother Margaret said from her place in the wagon. "Once we fetch our bags, Brother Elijah, I'd like you to drive by Moses' house one more time. I been considerin' on this matter for a few hours, and I've made up my mind. Moses and his wife asked me to stay with their family as long as I want, and I believe I'll do that. Would you tell Ben and Eva where I am? Would you give them my love?"

Elijah gave the old woman a hug. "I don't know how we'll make it without you, Mother Margaret."

"Well," she said, softly. "You've got the Lord, ain't you?"

CHAPTER 9

LILY handed the baby to Mother Margaret and stepped down into Elijah Book's arms. Though she dreaded the moments to come, she had made up her mind to confront Beatrice Waldowski. Elijah had reminded Lily that it would be a lot simpler just to take the melodeon from the show wagon and then head for Hope. But Bea deserved better.

The flamboyant woman had befriended Lily at a desperate time, and she had continued to support her through the ups and downs that came their way. Most important, Bea had recognized and encouraged Lily's singing ability. For that alone, she must be treated with respect.

"Do you want me to come with you?" Elijah asked as he walked Lily a few paces toward the boardinghouse. "I told you I'd stand by your side. I meant that."

She shook her head. "Bea doesn't trust you. She thinks you're trying to convert me to your religious ways."

"I am."

"You are?"

At her startled look, he gave a chuckle. "I'd be lying if I told you I didn't want you to know Jesus Christ the way I know him. But that's not why I'm choosing to stand by you, Lily."

"It's Samuel, isn't it?"

"God brought the two of us together for Sam's sake, but it's gone way beyond that. In spite of your hard ways, Lily Nolan, I care about you. I've come to know the woman inside you. I'd give my life to protect you."

Lily fingered the fringe on her shawl. She thought about telling Elijah how much he had come to mean to her in the past few days—how she enjoyed the deep sound of his voice, how she looked forward to his laughter, how she treasured watching him hold Samuel. She even liked fighting with the man.

But she didn't want to say too much. Philadelphia would be her destination before long. She couldn't afford to let a man's blue eyes and gentle heart sway her from her own path in life.

"I'll be back soon," she said, touching his arm. "Elijah . . . pray for me."

Without waiting for a response, she hurried up onto the porch of the boardinghouse and knocked on Beatrice's door. In a moment, she heard the sound of chairs scraping and voices murmuring. Lily had rarely known Beatrice to entertain gentlemen callers, but—

"Lily?" The door swung open. Behind Beatrice stood a tall, beefy man with a thin black mustache. His face hardened at the sight of the young woman on the porch.

"Beatrice," Lily said, focusing on her friend, "I've come to tell you that the preacher's baby is well."

"You interrupted me for that?" Bea pushed up the shoulder of her red silk gown. "Can't you see I'm doing business, Lil? This is George Gibbons from the Crescent Moon. He's one of the *owners*, if you catch my drift."

"I'm pleased to meet you, Mr. Gibbons," Lily said. The man looked familiar, and she remembered seeing him at the hotel. "I've decided to go back to Hope, Bea," she went on. "I wanted you to know that. And I'm going to take my melodeon with me."

For a moment, Beatrice stared in silence. Then her black-rimmed eyes narrowed. "You're going with *him?*"

"The baby needs me."

"You've let that preacher bamboozle you." Her lips tightened to a white line. "You're a coward and a weakling. You disgust me, Lily Nolan."

Stung, Lily stood her ground. "I'm sorry you feel that way. I was hoping we could part as friends."

"Who is this gal, Bea?" the man from the Crescent Moon asked. "I've seen her over at the hotel."

"She's a traitor, that's who she is," Bea said. "I saved her from her pious father, and now she's taken up with a preacher."

"I remember her," George Gibbons said. "She was with the fellow we threw out of the hotel the other day. That preacher just about ruined our saloon business for the whole night."

For some odd reason, Lily felt a surge of pride in Elijah. "Mr. Book speaks from the heart."

"I'd like to punch him in the gut."

Just give it a try, Lily thought. Considering Elijah's years on the cattle trail, she had no doubt the preacher could lay this loser out cold. Of course, Elijah had told her he was trying to turn the other cheek.

"Good-bye, Bea," Lily said, choosing to ignore the man. "Thank you for all you've done for me. I'll never forget you."

She had turned to go when Beatrice burst through the doorway to embrace her. "Don't leave me, Lily!" the woman cried. "I need you. I've counted on you. You've got to help me with the opera house."

"Beatrice, please—"

"You can't go with that man. You're all I have. Oh, Lily, you have to sing for me. How can I have an opera house without a singer? You're not really leaving, are you?" Bea pleaded, clasping Lily tightly. "Everything depends on you! You can't take the melodeon. You can't go."

"Bea, I've made up my mind," Lily said. "I'm going back to Hope."

"You're mad! I've offered you twice what that preacher can pay. Why would you turn me down?"

"I need to help the baby."

"It's not the baby!" Bea's eyes were streaming now, black paint staining her cheeks as her desperation turned to rage. "It's that preacher. He's trapped you with his words. He's snared you in his web of lies."

"This is my choice, Bea. I want to go back to Hope."

"No, Lily! You can't. Tell me you won't do this to me."

"I'm leaving, Bea."

"I'll tell your father where you are!" Bea burst out. "I'll write to him and tell him you've gone insane. He'll come to Hope and find you. He'll beat you black and blue."

Lily grasped the porch post beside her. "Beatrice!"

"I will! I'll tell him you ran off with a show man, and I'll tell him everything you've done. We'll see what happens then! You'll pay for this, Lily Nolan."

"Bea, please don't tell my father where I am." Lily's lips trembled. "When the time is right, I'm going back to Philadelphia. I'll make peace with him."

"Not after he knows where you've been, how you've lived, the things you've done! You won't live to see the next day after he catches up with you! I'll tell him everything unless you stay with me. This opera house is all the future I've got, Lily. I won't let you ruin me. I'll make you stay."

Lily took a step backward. Her plans to return home hinged on her father's ignorance of her past. She could never tell him about the traveling show, about Ted Nolan and Abigail, about the reckless, desperate choices she had made in her life . . .

"Everything all right here?" Elijah Book stepped onto the porch. "You OK, Mrs. Nolan?"

Lily swung around. "Elijah, I—"

"Don't touch that woman, Preacher," George Gibbons said,

stepping into the doorway. "I've had my fill of trouble from you."

"I'm not here for trouble. I just want to make sure Mrs. Nolan is treated right."

"Treated right?" Beatrice exploded. "How are you treating her, Preacher? Have you managed to get her into your bed yet?"

"Beatrice!" Lily clasped the woman's shoulders. "Bea, please don't say such things. Can't we part as friends? Can't you let me go?"

"I'll never let you go, Lily," Bea snarled. "I made you. I brought you here. I own you."

"Bea—"

"You watch and see, Lily Nolan. I'll tell your father everything you've done. And I'll build my opera house in Hope."

"Hope?"

"I'll put my place of business so close to that church, we'll drown out the preacher and shut down his whole operation. Before summer's out, I'll have you singing for me, Lily. You can count on it."

Lily took a step closer to Elijah. "Bea, what are you saying?"

"I won't let you go, Lily. I have plans, and you're part of them. If you won't help me out of love, you'll do it out of fear."

"But I do love you—"

"You don't know the first thing about love, Lily. You only know fear. Fear drove you out of your father's house. Fear brought you to the traveling show. Fear made you Ted Nolan's wife. And fear's binding you to that preacher and his baby."

"I care about Samuel."

"You're scared he's going to die just like Abigail. That's all you can think about, isn't it? Fear eats you up inside just like a worm in an apple." Bea set her hands on her hips and stared at Lily. "I can't believe you're so ignorant. Can't you see the preacher's onto you just the way your father was? He's playing your fear, Lily. Well, I can play you, too. I'll make you so frightened, you'll do anything I ask. And I'll start by telling your father where you are."

"Don't you dare!" Lily cried.

"Listen here, Madam Whoever-you-are," Elijah said, pointing a finger at Beatrice. "I don't know what kind of hex you're trying to put on Lily, but it isn't going to work. She's a strong woman and a good woman—and what's more, she has a heart. You're not going to scare her into anything, you hear?"

"You shut your trap, Preacher," George Gibbons said, drawing back his coat to reveal a holstered six-shooter. "Now get back in your wagon and head out."

"I'll leave when I'm good and ready. And you'd better cool down that itchy finger. I'm a minister of the Lord, and I'm unarmed."

"As if I care!" Gibbons drew the gun. "Back away nice and slow, Preacher. Bea, grab the singer."

"No!" Lily cried as Bea reached for her. "I won't stay here. Run, Elijah!"

Gathering up her skirts, she leapt off the porch and landed in a bed of peony bushes. As she tumbled forward, Elijah scooped her up in his arms. As Gibbons fired warning shots into the air, the preacher dashed for the wagon. Lily flung her arms around his neck and buried her head against his chest, tensed for the moment when a lead ball would tear into his back.

"Hunker down, Mother Margaret," Eli called as he tossed Lily into the wagon bed and clambered onto the seat. "Come on, ol' mule. Let's go, sweetheart."

As the wheels began to roll, Lily pushed herself up and peered over the side rail. Gibbons was reloading his six-shooter, while Beatrice glared after the retreating wagon. Her heart sick, Lily read the utter hatred on the woman's face.

How many hours had the two women sat together—chatting, laughing, darning socks, or making show costumes? How many times had they dried each other's tears? Oh, Beatrice! What had driven her to such desperation? Why was her voice so filled with hatred? They had shared dreams of a happy future . . . plans for wealth and luxury . . . an opera house . . . music . . .

"Wait!" Lily cried suddenly, clapping her hand on Elijah's shoulder. "Pull the wagon around to the barn. I have to get my melodeon."

Eli's head turned, his hair whipping his cheeks. "Forget the melodeon. We've got to get out of here before that loco-brain blasts us to kingdom come."

"But I need it, Elijah. I can't get home without it."

"Mercy, child," Mother Margaret said, patting Lily's arm as the wagon rolled out onto the main road. "You don't need no melodeon to get home. You're goin' home right now. Home to Hope."

Elijah studied the vast prairie that stretched out on either side of the road and wondered how it compared to China. He didn't know much about that foreign land, only that it was about as far from Kansas as a man could get.

A part of him really wanted to be there.

As the wagon rattled down the rutted trail between seas of bluestem, broom sedge, and switchgrass, Eli searched the horizon for the shingled roof of the little Hope church. He was headed back there to be a pastor again. Not a missionary. Not a traveling evangelist. Just the pastor of a little flock. Lily had warned him that meant weddings, funerals, planned-out sermons, and deacons' meetings.

Oh, Lord, are you sure you wouldn't rather send me to China? he prayed. *Surely they don't have committees in China. Or deacons. Or cemetery funds.*

Eli reached down and picked a stem of purple coneflower from the side of the road and twirled it between his thumb and forefinger. The pale petals fanned out from the dark brown, prickly eye. In a few weeks, the petals would fall and the central black pod would cast its seeds across the fertile prairie sod.

Cast seeds, Elijah, the voice in his soul whispered. *Spread my*

Word across the prairie. The harvest truly is great, but the laborers are few.

"Yes, Lord," he murmured in response.

"What?" Lily Nolan straightened on the seat beside him. "Did you say something, Elijah?"

Embarrassed, he shook his head. "Just praying."

"I guess I was dozing. It's such a hot afternoon."

With Mother Margaret at her son's house in Topeka and the baby sleeping in the back of the wagon, Lily and Elijah had been sitting for hours in total silence. He felt uncomfortable alone with her. She was too pretty. She smelled too sweet. His thoughts kept meandering off the main trail and wandering around the notion of what it would feel like to take Lily Nolan in his arms and kiss her pink lips. He wanted to touch her hair too, all that long gold silk. And he wouldn't mind the feel of her soft cheek against his neck or her—

"What were you praying about?" Lily asked.

Eli blanched. Had he been praying?

"Being the pastor in Hope," he said, forcing his thoughts back onto the main trail. "I reckon it's going to be hard work."

"You'll be tending lambs among wolves," she said with quiet assurance. "That's a terrifying responsibility."

Eli shifted the reins from one hand to the other. No, he wanted to tell her. He'd been a pastor in Hope just long enough to realize it would be the tedium of the job that oppressed him. The same people with the same petty arguments and the same complaints day after day. They'd be pulling on him, tracking him down, sucking him dry. The grind of it all would do him in.

Nothing like being a missionary in China—or even a roving evangelist. In Hope there would be no unknown trails to explore, no hordes of unrepentant souls to gather in, no rugged wildernesses and savage tribes to tame. Nothing but Hope, Kansas. Dirt farmers. Broiling sun. Relentless wind. Cows. Chickens. Wheat.

"When I think about the task of a minister," Lily said, "and I mean a *real* minister, someone who's honest and loves his flock and truly has faith in God, I think it must be the highest calling in the world."

"You do?" Eli took his Stetson off, fanned the flies a moment, and put the hat back on. "The highest calling?"

"Mother Margaret could explain what I'm trying to say." She let out a breath. "Oh, I miss her so much. I feel lost without her."

"I'd like to hear your thoughts, Lily. How do you figure a preaching job in an outpost like Hope is a high calling?"

"Because the pastor is the only shepherd the people have. That means he sees to the welfare of the flock—their physical health, their daily needs, their harshest trials, and their sweetest joys. A true minister—if there is such a thing—lays down his life for his flock."

"In Hope?"

"The wolves are all around, Elijah. The hungry lion is on the prowl."

Seeing the call to preach in a different light, Eli squared his shoulders and lifted his chin. "Maybe you're right. I never lived anywhere long enough to have a real pastor, but I sure heard a lot of traveling preachers. That seemed like the best way to get the message across."

"An evangelist came to our church once," Lily said. "He was a mighty man with a hypnotic voice. He left everyone in tears. But the main thing was, *he left*. It was our minister, Reverend Hardcastle, who reached out to all the broken spirits and contrite hearts. He was the one who really made the difference."

"You liked your minister, Lily?"

She shrugged. "Reverend Hardcastle is a loving man—kind to everyone. And that makes him blind."

"Blind to your father."

"I don't want to talk about my father."

"But I do." He took her hand and wove her slender fingers between his. "Tell me about him, Lily."

She looked away, across the prairie, seeing places and events Elijah could only imagine. The thought that anyone could hurt Lily was almost more than he could bear. For one thing, she was so delicate, almost fragile. How could anyone—let alone a father—treat her roughly? Thinking about it made Eli so angry he could taste it.

The man had damaged Lily's tender, childlike trust in God. That sin seemed unforgivable. Had her faith been destroyed completely? Or did Lily still nurture a tiny seed?

"Consider the lilies how they grow." The voice inside Elijah whispered words from Jesus' teaching.

Could Lily still grow? Was there hope for her? Did God have a plan for her life . . . even though her heart was hard and her spirit had been shut away?

"Seek ye the kingdom of God; and all these things shall be added unto you." Eli raised a prayer of thanksgiving as the words of Scripture flooded through him. It was never too late. Never. Not even for Lily.

"My father is a great musician," she said softly, her fingers gripping his. "He conducts the Greater New England Symphony Orchestra, and he directs the choir at the First United Church of St. George, the largest church in Philadelphia."

"People respect him," Elijah said.

"Yes." She nodded, but her focus had left the vast freedom of the prairie and was directed on her lap. "He's a great man. He's always very busy attending meetings and speaking out on behalf of his orchestra. They travel often to perform across the East Coast."

"Has he heard you sing?"

"No," she said, her voice hushed. "No, never."

It was as though the very mention of the man lapped at Lily's spirit. She began to shrink and wither, her voice growing small and her shoulders drawing together. Elijah rubbed his thumb gently over hers, stroking away the tension.

"I went to the finest schools," she continued. "I always wore expensive clothes. My father liked to show me off to his associates."

"I guess you had a lot of friends."

"Father didn't like children to come to our house. He didn't want me to spend time with anyone but our family, so he kept me inside. He had to protect me from bad influences."

"You must have been pretty lonely."

"Yes, but my father wanted only the best for me. He needed to keep control of things, he said. Everything had to be in order so I would grow up well. He didn't like for me to speak out my own ideas or go places without him. He always kept my mother close, too. She did everything he told her to do, but I . . . I was naughty sometimes. I liked to climb trees, and twice I tore my pinafores. One afternoon I ate half a cherry pie all by myself. Another time I hid under my father's desk because I wanted to make a house there for my dolls. But he found me and—"

She squeezed her eyes shut and shook her head, unable to continue.

Not far ahead, Elijah could see the little town of Hope, its collection of soddies and timber-framed buildings glazed orange by the setting sun. The glass panes gleamed in the mercantile windows. A drift of pale gray smoke rose from the smithy's chimney. White sheets fluttered on a line. So small and simple the town seemed. A place where children could climb trees and eat cherry pies without fear.

"Your father had no right to hurt you," he said. "You were just a little girl. You were playing."

"Rights? What rights do children have? My father was preparing for an important concert that weekend. I disrupted his . . . his thoughts."

"Did he beat you?"

She bit her lip as she nodded. "His baton made a good whip. Convenient. But Elijah, *most* children are punished when they do wrong. I know that. I realize I was—"

"Most children don't wind up black and blue. A papa or mama might give their child one quick pop on the backside to set him straight. But not a beating. Not pouring out anger on a young'un. That's not right, Lily. Is that what your father did to you?"

"I'm sure he didn't intend to hurt me—"

"Did he bruise you?"

"Yes," she whispered. "He . . . he broke my ribs once. I remember how hard it was to breathe. My mother told the doctor I had fallen down the stairs."

"She lied."

"She didn't want anyone to think less of my father. He has such a fine standing in the community. He's very—"

"Cruel. Vicious. Mean."

"Talented. He's brilliant and high-strung. They say he's a genius. Sometimes he just can't control everything."

"He can't control himself."

"He couldn't control me. Not completely. I frustrated him."

"You were a little girl. A child, Lily. No one ought to hurt a young'un—no matter what."

She let out a breath, as though the weight of the past had slipped from her shoulders for a moment. "I know," she said finally. "For so many years I took it all inside myself. I defended my father. I blamed myself. I accepted my mother's lies to the doctors. I managed both sides of my world—the glittering parties, fine gowns, soaring music . . . and the shouts of rage, the cruel baton, the bruises and broken bones. And then one day . . . when I was older . . . I stepped outside myself, and I saw it."

"That's when you ran off with the traveling show."

"Beatrice has not had an easy life either, you know. She took me in when she and the others were barely able to feed themselves. At first, Jakov didn't want me, but Bea argued on my behalf. She said she would rescue me, and she did. Ted Nolan became my husband after that. I didn't know him well when we got married, and over time I liked him less and less. But I needed shelter, and he offered it. In return, I worked for the show."

"So now you've run off a second time," Eli said, "and you're feeling just as guilty as when you left your father. You're making up reasons why those people deserve your love and your respect—even though they never loved or respected you."

"Bea loved me," she returned. "I know she did."

"True love doesn't try to control folks." Eli guided the mule off the road, past a grove of shady cottonwood trees, and down the main street of Hope. "I don't know much more on the subject than what you've taught me, Lily, but I know what I've read in the Good Book. If people love you, they're not going to threaten you or make you feel low. And they're sure not going to make a habit of hurting you."

"I think Bea lashed out at me because she's terribly frightened. All her life, she's struggled just to survive. She never had anything to call her own until she joined up with Jakov and the traveling show. She truly needs my help."

"You'd sing in an opera house?"

"You make it sound like another den of iniquity."

"Ever been inside one? There's drinking and gambling and all kinds of carrying on. That's not a place for someone like you."

"Someone like me? Who do you think I am?" she asked, turning her blue eyes on him. "Don't be fooled by my appearance, Elijah. I'm not a porcelain doll. I've made a lot of wrong choices, and I've done things a good woman shouldn't. I've been hard and angry and bitter. I've gone my own way in life, and I've carved out a rough path. An opera house would welcome the likes of me. I'd fit right in."

Eli pulled the mule up to the front of the Hankses' house. "I would have, too, in the old days. I did a lot of things a man couldn't brag about, Lily, and I expect I'll make my share of mistakes in the years to come. But there's one big difference inside me now."

"Please don't start preaching, Elijah."

"I'm not preaching—I'm telling you about *me*. Who I am. Do you care at all?"

"Yes," she said softly.

"I'm walking God's path, not my own, Lily. I'm following his light, not stumbling around in the dark. I won't choose wrong when he shows me what's right."

"But I'm scared."

"Be scared of your father. Be scared of Beatrice. Be scared of me, if you want. I'm a long way from perfect. But don't be scared of God. All he wants to do is love you, Lily. He wants to love you with the kind of love that never fades."

She clenched his hand. "I can't let go. I've worked too hard to take hold of my own life."

"Are you holding it? Or is Beatrice?" He reached up and touched her cheek. "Lily, don't give your life away anymore. Not to people. We're selfish and greedy and pretty rotten most of the time. And don't try to hold it yourself. You told me you've made a lot of wrong choices, and you're bound to make more mistakes. But God isn't. He won't. You can count on that."

Eli reached down and pulled up the brake lever on the wagon as Ben and Eva Hanks stepped out of their house to greet them. This had been a long road. A wearying path. But it was the right path. He was sure of that.

CHAPTER 10

"MY HUSBAND built that pew and brung it to church, and that big ol' German feller has took to settin' on it ever' Sunday." Mrs. Hudson's small dark eyes sparked. "That's *our* pew, Preacher, and you better tell him to find another!"

Elijah took the elderly lady's hand in his and regarded her seriously. "I'm sure Rolf Rustemeyer doesn't mean a thing against you folks by sitting on your pew," he said. "This will be my fourth Sunday in Hope, and I've never heard a selfish or harsh word out of the man. In fact, I think he regards your family with the highest esteem."

Mrs. Hudson patted her silver hair. "I reckon he should. We're good people."

"Yes, you are."

"If my son hadn't died, we'da never come to Hope. But we aim to keep helpin' his poor widder with all them young'uns as long as we's needed. Violet and them kids is all we got in the world, Brother Elijah."

"They're good young'uns. And the Widow Hudson is a mighty fine mama to them."

"She sure is, and I don't want that shaggy ol' German to get no designs on her! You hear me?" She shook her finger at Eli. "Him a-settin' on our pew ever' Sunday and makin' big puppy-dog eyes at Violet. It's a downright disgrace."

Bull's-eye! Elijah struggled to hold back a victory grin. He hadn't been at this business of shepherding a flock for long, but he was getting better at it all the time. Maybe he wasn't tracking down the wayward and lost in the wilds of China, but he was working just as hard at rounding up the truth in little old Hope. And he liked the challenge.

"I don't believe Rolf Rustemeyer sitting on your pew is what's really troubling you, Mrs. Hudson," he said in a gentle tone. "I suspect it's the prospect of a man courting your daughter-in-law. You don't want anybody taking your son's place in her heart, do you?"

"I certainly do not." Her righteous indignation began to dissolve into sorrow. "Jim was our only son, don't you know. We didn't have no other kids, Preacher. When we heard about him a-passin' on, well, I just like to have died myself. But now, thanks to the good Lord, we got more young'uns than we know what to do with. Don't you see how it is? We lost our son, but we been given that passel of kids in his place. If that long-haired German feller thinks he can take Violet and them babies away from us—"

"Rolf Rustemeyer would never want to deprive you or your husband," Eli said, patting her hand. "I'm sure he sees you two as part of the family."

"You reckon?"

"I know for a fact that he's a lonely man, and I have a feeling he'd make Violet a fine, hardworking husband. I'm sure he'd welcome all her kin into his home—young and old alike."

She considered this new thought for a moment. "Well, that might not be so bad. He's got hisself a nice place, I hear."

"He's one of the most successful farmers around. Plus he was partners with Seth Hunter and Jimmy O'Toole in building the bridge and founding the town of Hope. That means he's taking in some of the profits from the bridge tolls. Why, he's one of our most prosperous citizens. You never know, Mrs. Hudson. God may have sent Rolf Rustemeyer your way. That hardworking German might be the best thing to come along for your family in a mighty long time."

Her dark eyes lighting up, Mrs. Hudson gave Elijah a smile. "I do declare, Preacher, you might be right."

"Even if nothing comes of his friendship with Violet, it wouldn't hurt to have such a fine man sharing your pew on Sunday, would it?"

"We'll see that Mr. Rustemeyer has the best seat in the house of the Lord." Standing, she shook out the folds of her patched calico skirt and slipped on her faded bonnet. "Brother Elijah, I do declare, I believe you was the one sent here by God. I heard what you done 'bout fixin' up a town graveyard behind the church. That's gonna be mighty welcome, don't you know. And folks is talkin' over the way you sat with the Rippeto family when their littlest was took sick. You're doin' a good job. Such a good job that I don't even hardly mind givin' my tithe of a Sunday."

Elijah stood and tucked his Bible under his arm. "I appreciate your kind words, Mrs. Hudson."

"I'm a-goin' now, and I thank you for your time."

"Much obliged."

With a smile tickling his mouth, Eli watched the diminutive lady make her way down the aisle between the rows of rickety benches. A little sheep heading back into the safety of the fold. With the Lord's help, he had rescued another lamb from the wolves of jealousy, fear, greed, and covetousness that threatened Christ's body in Hope.

"And one more thing, Brother Elijah," Mrs. Hudson said, turning in the doorway. "We-all think you'd best get yourself a wife. A preacher ought to have a wife. It just ain't right any other way. Especially if he's already got hisself a baby."

"Well, I appreciate your thoughts, Mrs. Hudson."

"We-all like that Lily Nolan pretty good. She's got a nice face and a gentle hand, and she seems to take to your boy."

Eli's humor faded. *We-all.* Who were *we-all* to stick their noses into his personal business anyway? If he wanted their opinion, he'd ask for it.

"She seems to like you real good," Mrs. Hudson went on. "We-all took note of how she laughs at your stories and turns bright pink when you look at her. We-all think you ought to court her formal-like. Make it official, Preacher, and you'll do the town good."

Eli drank in a deep breath to calm himself. "I do care about this town, Mrs. Hudson, but I've got to think about other things, too. I'm sure you'll be the first to know when I make up my mind to go courting."

With a laugh of delight, the old woman stepped out of the church into the afternoon sunshine. Eli gave the bench nearest him a shove with his boot. *Baa, baa, you little sheep*, he thought. *Head back to the fold and gossip with your friends*. If she and her cronies knew what he felt like inside—torn to shreds every time he so much as caught a glimpse of Lily Nolan—they'd think twice about prying.

Truth to tell, he'd been doing all he could to keep away from Lily Nolan. After a week back in Hope, he was hoping that Beatrice Waldowski would fail to make good on her threat of returning to the little town. He could tell that Lily was starting to feel free of her past—freer and lighter and happier than he'd ever seen her. She fairly lit up the whole sky when she walked by. In his effort to avoid the woman whose presence stirred him so deeply, he'd finished the fence around the church, dug and planted a garden, visited everybody in town at least once, and almost read the whole New Testament straight through.

She's not a Christian, he wanted to tell the snoopy Mrs. Hudson. *Lily isn't a believer, and because of that, she wouldn't make me a good wife. A pretty face and gentle hands aren't enough to build the foundation of a good marriage. It takes a shared faith, a joint trust in Jesus Christ, a united front against the destructive forces of the world.*

Not only had his Lord discouraged marriage between a Christian and an unbeliever, but Elijah knew it would never work from a practical standpoint. Whether he was going to be a pastor in Hope or a missionary in China, he needed a full-fledged partner. And Lily Nolan could not be his—not in any way.

Grabbing his hat, Eli stalked toward the room at the back of the church where he made his home. He couldn't understand why Lily had started attending his preaching services. And he wished he'd never asked her to talk so honestly about her father. Now, every time he recollected their conversation in the wagon, he wanted to smash in the man's nose. How dare anyone hurt Lily? She was so sweet, so kind, so tender—

"Hello, Elijah," Lily said as he walked into his living room. She was sitting on the floor playing with Samuel. "Hope you don't mind that I came inside. Eva and I baked some cookies this morning. It's Mother Margaret's recipe. I brought you some."

Eli stopped dead still and stared at her. Her pale blue skirt swirled around her on the floor like a rippled pond. Sunlight danced in the fine strands of her golden hair. As she looked up at him, her eyes sparkled with a blue flame.

"Lily," he managed.

"I trust I'm not interrupting."

"No." He cleared his throat. "I was just . . . just talking things over with Mrs. Hudson."

Had Lily heard their conversation? Did she know what the townsfolk were saying about the two of them? If Lily thought for a minute that he would ever betray his vow to the Lord by courting a nonbeliever . . . but what if she thought he didn't care for her? What if his words to Mrs. Hudson made her think he didn't appreciate her as a woman? He did. *Lord, help me. I do wish I could take Lily into my heart.*

"I'll bet Mrs. Hudson was complaining about Rolf Rustemeyer sitting on the pew her husband built," Lily said as she wiggled Sam's bare toes. "She wants it reserved for Violet and her children."

"Aren't there any secrets in this town?" he asked, a little more gruffly than he intended. He walked across the room and set his Bible on the table. "I don't know when I've ever met such talkity people."

"The truth is, Mrs. Hudson's afraid Mr. Rustemeyer will marry Violet and move her and all the children away to his farm," Lily said, giving Sam's tummy a soft poke. "Why don't you have a cookie, Elijah? I want to know if you like them."

Eli turned. "What did you just say?"

"Have a cookie. They're oatmeal."

"I mean about Rolf and Violet. How did you know that's what was really troubling Mrs. Hudson?"

"It's just a feeling," she said. "I've watched them all in church, and that's what I suspect."

"You mean you just *know?*"

"Beatrice would say I'm psychic. She'd say the spirits told me. But I think I'm just a woman with two good eyes."

Eli sat down at the table and thumped his fingers on the Bible. "It took me a good bit of tracking to piece together Mrs. Hudson's real trouble with Rolf Rustemeyer. But you figured it out right away. How did you do that?"

"I'm a *woman*, Elijah," she said, giving a shy laugh. "We notice these things."

"Maybe I ought to just take you on rounds with me. Then I wouldn't have to spend half the time beating the bushes to figure out what's really troubling folks. I've learned the problem is never what they tell me to start off with."

"I'll go visiting with you," she said. "I'd like that."

"No." He stood quickly. "That wouldn't be a good idea. Folks might get a wrong notion about us."

"Oh?" She smoothed down the soft cotton gown Sam wore. "What's a right notion about us, Elijah?"

He gave her a wary glance and began to pace. Being cornered

like a hunted grizzly was not a good feeling. If he told her he couldn't socialize too much with her because of her lack of faith, she'd be hurt. She'd believe he thought he was too good for her. It might even turn her more against the Lord.

But if he told her how he really felt about her—how much he enjoyed talking to her, listening to her, laughing and even crying with her—well, she'd think he was starting to care about her. He *did* care about her. But he couldn't. Shouldn't.

"You're taking care of Sam," he said finally. "We're like business partners, I reckon. Aren't we?"

"Are we?"

Confound it. He paced across the room and then back again.

"I'm paying you," he said.

"You kissed me."

"Not on purpose."

"On accident?"

"Well, I'm not trying to seduce you the way Beatrice said, if that's what you think."

"No. I never thought that."

"I'm a man of honor."

"I know."

"I'm doing the best I can here."

"You're doing a wonderful job. I heard how you sat up with the Rippeto family when their youngest was sick. Everyone in town speaks well of you."

"There you go! See? I can't do a thing without everybody watching. And I'm trying my best to stay on the right track. But I'm just a man, and you're a woman, and—"

"It's Ted, isn't it?" She looked up at him, her face pale. "You're put off by the fact that I was married before. That I took a husband out of necessity. That I'm not pure."

He frowned for a moment, trying to understand. "What?"

"On the wagon from Topeka, you and I spoke so honestly

together. You held my hand. After all we endured with Samuel, I just thought we were . . . we were friends. But since we've been back in Hope, you've hardly looked at me. You won't speak to me more than a moment or two. Do I repulse you?"

"Repulse me?" In disbelief, he knelt on the floor beside her. "Lily, it's all I can do to hold back from you. You're the most beautiful, precious, gentle—" He leaned away. "No, I can't do this."

"Do what? You're not doing anything."

"It's not you, Lily. It's me. I have to focus on being a pastor. There's the Cornwall wedding tomorrow and two sermons the next day. And Seth Hunter asked me to give a little talk at the Independence Day fish fry next week."

"Do I get in the way of your work?"

"All the time." He shook his head. "That's not what I meant to say. It's just that I keep thinking about you. Thinking about . . ." He tried to make himself breathe. "Thinking about what's going to happen to you. You'll be going back to Philadelphia."

"Not until I've earned the money for my ticket. Without my melodeon to sell, I won't be able to leave until fall." She moistened her lips. "Elijah, I wanted you to know that Rolf Rustemeyer has asked me to go with him to the fish fry."

"Rolf Rustemeyer?" Eli slapped his hand on his thigh. "I thought he was after Violet Hudson!"

"I think he's after a wife. Anyone will do."

"You're not anyone. You're *you*. You're . . . you're Sam's . . . Sam's aunt."

"Aunt?" She stared at him. "Is that how you see me? As a sister?"

He raked a hand back through his hair. Confound it, he wasn't about to let Rolf Rustemeyer marry Lily Nolan. If he thought he was in torment now, he could hardly imagine how bad *that* would feel.

But Elijah couldn't court Lily himself. He could never take her as his own wife. And he couldn't tell her why. Or could he? Should he just blurt out the whole thing? *Lord, help me here!*

"I thought Beatrice was wrong about you," Lily said as she tucked the baby's blanket around him. "She insisted you were like my father—concerned only about how the world viewed you. On the way back from Topeka, I was sure she was mistaken. I saw you as a real man, caring and honest. It didn't matter what I'd done wrong. You accepted me and made me think that God would too."

She stood, her blue skirt swirling down to the tips of her black boots. "Now I understand that Beatrice was right about you, Elijah," she went on, her voice taking on that harsh quality he knew too well. "In the watchful eyes of Hope, you're the high-and-mighty preacher. You can't be friendly with a woman from a traveling show. You can't be seen talking to me too often or caring about me too much. I'm not a real person anymore, am I? I'm your business partner. Samuel's aunt. Your sister."

"No, you're wrong—"

"It's all right, Elijah. You warned me you were only human. You told me I couldn't count on you."

"I said I'd stand by you, and I will." Rising, he took her shoulders. "Lily, listen to me."

For a moment he stared down into her blue eyes, trying to make himself speak. What did he want to say? That she was everything he'd ever wanted in a woman? Spunk and determination mingled with gentleness. Intelligence and talent softened by a tender heart. Fragile beauty, a loving spirit—

"Oh, Lily." Without meaning to, he pulled her into his arms and held her tight. He didn't have the words he needed to say. So he pressed his lips against her forehead . . . and then her cheek . . . and finally her mouth. Her hands slid tentatively around his back. He could feel her trembling as he struggled against the war inside his heart.

"Lily, I—"

"Brother Elijah?" Seth Hunter stepped through the church door into the little back room. "Oh, 'scuse me. I didn't mean to interrupt."

Lily jumped like she'd been shot. Elijah wheeled around to face the visitor. He could feel the heat creeping up the back of his neck.

"Seth," he said, jamming his hands into his pockets. "Come on in. How's the farm? Rosie feeling OK today?"

The tall farmer eyed the two as Lily scooped the baby up from the floor. "I was just coming to tell you the news," he said. "Looks like that traveling show is back. And they've brought wagons loaded with lumber. Jack Cornwall and Ben Hanks went down to see what was up. Turns out those folks have plans to build an opera house."

Lily fled out behind the church with Samuel wriggling unhappily in her arms. She could hardly hold back the tears of dismay as she raced across the rutted main street toward the Hanks house, where she'd been living since her return from Topeka. She needed to talk to someone, to pour out the confusion and agony in her heart. But Mother Margaret was gone. Eva Hanks wouldn't understand. No one would understand.

She hurried into the shadowy depths of the small frame house and laid Samuel in the little crib Elijah had built for his son. Instantly the baby let out a wail that would deafen heaven. Lily set her hands on her hips and stared down at the screaming, frustrated bundle of tiny arms and legs.

"Well, I'd like to cry, too," she told him. "Go ahead and yell for both of us, Sammy. Are you hungry? I just fed you an hour ago, didn't I? Are you wet? Is that it?"

She felt the baby's diaper. "You're dry. You're full. And there's not a pin pinching you or a bug biting you. So what's the matter?"

By now Sam's face was bright red. His little fists pumped the air, and his legs churned as though they were working milk into butter. At her wit's end, Lily stared at the baby's wide mouth, twisting head, and frantic squirms.

"What's wrong?" she asked. "*What . . . is . . . wrong?*"

By now tears were streaming down her own cheeks. What was wrong with *her?* Everything. Beatrice had come back to Hope. Samuel was screaming. Rolf wanted to take her to the fish fry. And Elijah . . . oh, Elijah!

"You just want somebody to hold you close," she said, lifting the baby back into her arms and snuggling him against her neck. "That's all you want, isn't it, Sammy? Calm down, now. I'm here. I won't leave you alone, sweet boy. I love you."

As the baby's wails began to subside, Lily rocked him from side to side. "I love you, Samuel," she whispered, feeling the tension slide from her own body. "I can't protect you from every hurt. I can't choose the path you'll take. But I'm here, Sammy. I'm here, and I love you."

Closing her eyes, she swayed alone in the stillness of the little house. Even now, she could feel Elijah's arms around her and his lips against hers. Oh, it had felt so good to kiss him. So right to be held in his warm embrace.

But Elijah had made plain his feelings about her. She shouldn't count on him. No matter what he might feel—what either of them might want—Elijah would not be more to Lily than her employer, her brother . . . her pastor.

As a woman, she sensed the power his male attraction gave her. If she chose, she might be able to tempt him away from his calling. She could lure him into her arms and away from the very purpose of his life, from the work that made him the man he was.

But she would hate herself for it. He would hate her, too, in the end. It would come to nothing but pain. More pain.

No, she thought, brushing her cheek against the baby's downy dark hair, she would not be alone with Elijah again. She would not tempt him. She would not even speak to him. By September she would have enough money to buy her ticket back to Philadelphia. And then she would leave Hope behind.

If only she had someone to talk to. Someone with whom she could share the terrible ache in her heart. Someone she could trust.

"I wish to goodness Mother Margaret was here!" Eva said, racing into the house and throwing her apron onto the table. "Oh, Miz Lily, there you are! It's a terrible thing. Just awful! They've picked out a place right next to the road. The opera-house people, I mean. The lot is not on Mr. Seth's land, so he doesn't have the right to run them off. And they've got a deed for that land! It's all legal, too. You should just see Ben. He's about to have a conniption."

She threw open the oven door and took out two steaming pies. "Some folks are saying that one of 'em's the same wagon you came in on," Eva continued as she set the tins inside the screened pie safe and then began rearranging every plate on her shelves. "They want you to go down there and talk to them, Lily. Ben says you'll convince those folks to leave. But Mr. Jack thinks maybe you're the one who encouraged them to come back here. And Mr. Seth says he doesn't care why they're here, he's not going to allow that kind of folk in his town. He's thinking of holding an election come the Fourth of July fish fry, and setting up a town government, and a mayor, and all that. And Mr. Rolf says we need a sheriff before we need a mayor. Those folks are unloading their lumber already!"

She restacked her plates and turned all her tins and canning jars label-side out. "Why, you know what an opera house is like," she went on. "It'll be painted some bright color and hung with red curtains. There'll be a saloon in there; I just know it. Anyhow, Ben says they're planning to serve liquor. Just think what kind of undesirables that will attract."

Lily walked across the room to the rocking chair and sat down to nurse the baby again. Maybe if Samuel took a little milk, he'd drift off to sleep. As she rocked, she watched Eva begin to scrub her rough-hewn wooden table.

"Dancing girls," Eva said. "They'll have dancing girls. The men will flock down there—you can count on it. And they'll be too tired to come to church of a Sunday after they've stayed up half the night watching the dancing girls. Oh, mercy, I miss Mother Margaret. Ben's mama could put us all to peace about this."

She wrung out her rag and began to scrub again. "I hear they put on plays in those opera houses. You know what I mean? They act things out. How can that be right?"

"Now, Eva," Lily finally interjected, "some very great and moving dramas have been written. They touch people's hearts."

Eva paused in her scrubbing. "I don't know. I never saw a play. But I can't imagine folks dressing up in costumes and pretending they're something they're not. That's just plain strange, if you ask me. And singing! Ben says they sing the rowdiest songs you ever heard at those opera houses."

"Not all the songs are rowdy. Some of them are beautiful. They often present selections from the great operas of Europe."

"Well, they won't let a black man into an opera house anyhow, so I don't have to worry about my Ben. Thank the Lord for that." Eva hung her rag over the side of the washtub. After straightening her colorful scarf, she sank down onto a stool and pressed her hands together. "You're not going back to them folks, are you, Miz Lily? You wouldn't join up with those actors and dancing girls, would you? Not after all this time with us. And knowing how much Samuel needs you. And seeing how the preacher feels about you."

Lily looked up from the dozing baby. "How does the preacher feel about me, Eva?"

"Why, he loves you," Eva said with surprise. "Can't you see that? He loves you, Miz Lily. Sure enough."

CHAPTER 11

"BY THE power vested in me by God and the state of Kansas," Elijah said, "I now pronounce you man and wife."

He took Caitrin Murphy's slender hand and placed it on the large callused palm of Jack Cornwall. The young couple, beset by delays ranging from Samuel's illness to a huge order for nails from the nearby military fort, had postponed their wedding date two weeks. Finally, on this sun-warmed Saturday afternoon, they were pulling it off.

The bride wore a white gown trimmed in tiny beads, her flame red hair caught up in a small hat adorned with plumes and a wispy veil. The groom stood tall and handsome in his new black suit and fine store-bought top hat. Roses and prairie wildflowers festooned the church. Ribbons decorated every pew. In all, the Murphy-Cornwall wedding was the most lavish event Eli had ever witnessed.

"May I kiss the bride, Brother Elijah?" Jack Cornwall asked, drawing the preacher from his reverie. "Or are we supposed to stand here all day?"

"Kiss her?" Elijah said. "Sure, go ahead."

No one had told him about *kissing* being part of a wedding ceremony. He'd memorized his part from start to finish, but there wasn't a word in the instruction manual about smooching. As the bridegroom drew his wife into his arms, a collective sigh of delight rose throughout the church.

Eli glanced to the back pews near the door. Lily hadn't come. Everyone in town had been invited to the wedding, but she had chosen not to make an appearance. Disappointment darkened his spirits. The reception would be starting in a few minutes, and he had looked forward to sitting near Lily. Maybe he would ask her to dance. Seth Hunter had evidently kept quiet about seeing their stolen kiss. Speaking of kisses . . .

"Whoa, you two," Eli said, tapping Jack Cornwall on the shoulder. "The guests are all eager to have a slice of wedding cake. Or are we supposed to stand here all day?"

As the crowd chuckled, Jack and Caitrin parted. Her cheeks rosy, the bride gave a musical laugh. Linking her arm through her husband's, she set off beside him down the aisle. The other celebrants clapped as the pair led the way out of the church.

When the building was finally empty, Eli let out a deep breath and slumped onto the chair near the pulpit. He bent over, covering his face with his hands, and prayed for the storm inside his heart to calm.

That opera house was going up faster than a dandelion after a spring rain. In just twenty-four hours, the framework for a large, two-story building had already been erected. Had Lily visited the site or spoken with Beatrice? Was she planning to take a job there? He gritted his teeth.

Why had he kissed her yesterday afternoon? He'd tried so hard to keep himself away from the woman. And now that he had finally run her off, he could hardly bear the distance that stretched between them.

Every morning, Lily sent Eva to fetch Samuel, and Ben returned the baby each night. During the day, Lily stayed busy helping Eva weed the garden, wash and iron laundry, bake bread, and mend shirts and socks. The two women worked side by side, as though they were sisters. And never once did Lily glance in the direction of the church.

Eli was sure he looked her way at least five hundred times a day. Not only was he curious about her relationship with Beatrice and concerned about the welfare of little Sam, but he couldn't make himself stop thinking about Lily herself. Why had she come into his life? Would it really be so wrong for him to court a nonbeliever? Maybe they could just see each other on Sunday afternoons. Eli could borrow a wagon and take Lily for a drive down the main road. Would there be any harm in that?

Eli rubbed his eyes. He hadn't slept much lately. Confusion and turmoil rolled around inside him like thunder.

Of course he couldn't court Lily. If he took her for a drive, he'd want to kiss her again. And if he kissed her, he'd want to tell her how he really felt about her. And if he told her how he felt, he'd want . . .

Well, he'd want to spend the rest of his life with her. That's what he'd want.

He slammed his palms against his thighs and stood. *God, I need your help!* He picked up his Bible. *I need it right now. I don't know what I'm going to do about Lily. I can't change her. I can't unlock her heart. But I care about her. I care about her too much. Lord, you allowed her to come into my life. Please help me now.*

As he cried out his earnest prayer, Eli strode down the aisle to the double-hung front doors. The turmoil inside him felt as though it were raging—a huge twister building up speed, gathering power, and threatening to destroy everything in its path. If he hadn't given his life to Christ, there was no telling what he would do with all this pent-up frustration inside his heart.

Elijah, do you love me? a familiar voice inside him whispered. The preacher stopped, listening.

Feed my lambs.

Eli took a deep breath. The sheep. That was it. He would head over to the reception taking place inside the mercantile, and he'd visit with every member of the church. He'd ask about the health of the Rippetos' youngest, Mrs. Hudson's grandchildren, Mr. LeBlanc's new millstone, and Mrs. Laski's ill sister in Poland. He would inquire after Mrs. Hunter and Mrs. O'Toole and their expected babies, Mr. Rustemeyer's ailing cow, and Miss Lucy Cornwall's latest batch of cinnamon buns.

Elijah, do you love me?

Tend my sheep.

He wouldn't look at the Hanks house. He wouldn't think about Lily. He wouldn't even—

At the sight of a slender figure just down the street, Eli stopped walking. There she was. Her blue skirt fluttered as she hurried along, clutching her white shawl close around her shoulders. Though she wore a cotton bonnet with wide ruching that hid her face, he knew it was Lily. And she was headed for the opera house.

Elijah, do you love me?

Eli clenched his fists and squeezed his eyes shut. "Lord," he murmured, "you know I love you. I've given my heart to you. I've turned over my whole life. Of course I love you."

Then feed my sheep.

"What do you mean by that, Lord?" he breathed, bowing his head. "Your sheep are over in the mercantile."

The words of Luke's Gospel came over him like a drenching rain: "*What man of you, having an hundred sheep, if he lose one of them, doth not leave the ninety and nine in the wilderness, and go after that which is lost, until he find it?*"

Eli shook his head. He couldn't go after Lily. He couldn't be her shepherd. He could probably preach to the lost in China. He might even be able to pastor the Lord's flock in Hope. But not Lily. He didn't know how to reach her. Worse than that, he didn't know how to hold back his feelings for her. He didn't know how to be her pastor when he really wanted to be her—

He wanted to be her husband. That was it. That was all there was to it.

Lord, I love Lily Nolan, he prayed. *I love her like a woman, not just another one of the flock. I can't think of her any other way. I know you don't want that. I know you would never want me yoked with an unbeliever, and I'd do anything to keep from disobeying you, Father.*

Eli swallowed hard.

Tend my lamb, Elijah.

The voice was unmistakable. When God spoke to him, the words reflected those of Holy Scripture. Elijah started walking. He trudged past the mercantile, deaf to the laughter and the sounds of fiddles and dancing feet inside. He forced his boots down the rutted main street of Hope, Kansas. And he looked across the prairie toward the frame of a new two-story building.

The opera house.

Lily paused in the shade of a large cottonwood tree near the Hope bridge. She had waited for this moment when the whole town was busy celebrating Caitrin Murphy's wedding to Jack Cornwall. No one would notice a lone woman headed down to the construction site of the new opera house. Lily could slip over to the building, perhaps speak with Beatrice for a few minutes, and then return to the Hankses' home before Sam awoke from his afternoon nap.

There wasn't a thing wrong with her plan. So why did she feel sick inside? Why was her heart as heavy as a piece of Ben Hanks's unforged iron?

Lily laid her hand on the gnarled trunk of the old tree and studied the framework of the large building. How had it gone up so fast? Determination, that's how. Men swarmed over the frame of the opera house, raising walls and laying floorboards. Within a week or two, the structure would be finished and painted, the roof shingled, and the furniture moved in.

Beatrice's dream would come true. And Lily could join her. All it would take was a step out of the sleepy security of Hope and into the raucous, lively, on-the-edge life of an entertainer. Lily would have the chance to get rich. She would meet travelers with interesting tales to tell. Maybe she would find a husband. And, of course, she could sing.

Lowering her head, Lily considered the lure of the opera house. She had been rich once in her life, but her fine dresses and expensive education had brought her no happiness. She had adventured with the exciting characters the road brought her way, but she had found no joy. She had been married, but it had given her no lasting pleasure.

Singing. How she loved to sing. With Beatrice at her side, Lily could again sing the great arias. She could stir people's hearts and bring a thrill to their weary lives. If she returned to Philadelphia, she would never sing again.

Stepping out, Lily walked across the cleared ground and up to the site of the opera house. This could be her new home. This could be her realm.

"Out of my way, lady," a man called as he shouldered a load of planks past her. "I've got to get this wall up before the sun goes down. Don't want to miss the party, you know. The whisky flows!"

Lily pursed her lips and scanned the construction site. Not far away, George Gibbons from the Crescent Moon Hotel stood deep in conversation with a group of workers. His thin black mustache took on a life of its own as he spoke. At the sight, a light bubble of laughter rose up inside Lily. This could be fun. Parties in the evenings. Lots of men to dance with. She didn't have to feel lonely. She wouldn't even think about Elijah Book across the way in his white clapboard church. She would be the belle of the ball.

"Excuse me," she said as another man hurried by with a load of bricks. "Do you know where I could find Beatrice Waldowski?"

"Who?"

"Madame Zahara?"

"The only madam around here is Mrs. B. You one of her girls?"

He gave Lily the once-over and grinned. "I might have to be first in line."

A chill ran down Lily's spine. "Excuse me, please," she said, brushing past him.

It couldn't be true. Surely this building was not going to become a brothel. Beatrice had said it was to be an opera house. There would be plays and ventriloquists, juggling and dog acts, raucous music and lighthearted operas.

Breathless, she strode around the building site until she found Beatrice. The older woman was looking up at the half-constructed second floor, her bright red dress sparkling in the late-afternoon sunlight. She had piled her long black hair high on her head and topped her bun with a crimson silk rose.

"Beatrice," Lily called across the empty space. "I heard you had returned to Hope."

The woman turned, her painted eyebrows arching in momentary surprise. "Lily?" Then she held out her arms in welcome. "You've finally come."

Stepping into the embrace of her friend, Lily was enveloped in the scent of Bea's exotic, spicy perfume. Lily had expected to feel as though she were coming home to the comfortable and familiar, but something about the moment of intimacy repulsed her. Moving back, she slipped her hands into her pockets.

"Your dress is luxurious," Lily said.

"George bought it for me." Bea gave her hips a toss and then laughed. "He's the most wonderful man. Oh, Lily, I've never been so happy in all my life."

"Are you in love with him?"

"Of course I am! He's the best thing that ever happened to me. So much for Jakov and his traveling show." Her hand made an arc to take in the building. "I'm on my way now!"

"Bea, I'm so happy for you. Has Mr. Gibbons asked for your hand?"

"Why should he want my hand when he's got the rest of me?" With a giggle, Bea slipped her arm around Lily's shoulders. "Oh, Lil, I'm sorry you and I parted with angry words back in Topeka. I was just sick about it for days. All those harsh things we said to one another. It was horrible."

"Let's move forward now, Bea. This is a nice place. You and George must have big plans for it."

"It's going to be a gold mine, honey. We'll have the theater down below, the saloon to one side, and all those rooms upstairs."

"So, it's going to be a hotel?"

Beatrice laughed again, and this time Lily realized her friend's breath smelled strongly of liquor. "In a manner of speaking," she said. "George is going to bring in some girls. Soiled doves, they call them. I hear they're everywhere out West, California especially, and most of them are eager to move to someplace nice."

Lily stiffened at the confirmation of her fears. "A brothel, Bea?"

"Why not? The money is good. Every lonely farmer, merchant, and traveler from the Mississippi to the Rockies can belly up to our bar, have himself a few good laughs at our show, and then buy an evening's pleasure with one of our gals. With that bridge nearby, we'll get them coming and going. Why, we might even lure that pious preacher friend of yours over here for a night of fun. What do you think?"

Hardly able to breathe, Lily reflected on the simple, good-hearted townsfolk celebrating a marriage within sight of this place. Jack Cornwall and his bride. Ben and Eva Hanks. Seth and Rosie Hunter and their growing family. The O'Tooles and their gaggle of red-haired children.

A brothel? A saloon? She felt like she was going to be sick.

"We can make a place for you here, Lily," Beatrice was saying. "There's lots of room."

"Oh, I wouldn't want to—"

"Not with the other gals, silly!" Beatrice laughed and took a small flask from the pocket of her red dress. "You could sing in the theater. We've got a troupe of actors coming from Topeka early next month. They have a bear—can you believe that? A live bear! I know they'd be happy to make room for you in their plays. You could sing, too, Lily. I've told George how wonderful you are. He'd love to hear what you can do. We could make you some costumes. Remember the old days when you and I would sit together in the show wagon and sew ostrich plumes onto our skirts?"

Chuckling, she took a swig from her little bottle and then held it out to Lily. For a moment, Lily hesitated. She had walked this path with Beatrice. They had reveled and laughed and behaved in reckless ways—the best of friends, enjoying the good things in life. Or that's what they had told themselves.

"Don't you want a drink?" Bea asked.

Lily shook her head. "No thanks, Bea. I've got to get back to the baby. He's taking his nap right now, and I—"

"The baby?"

"Samuel."

"Don't tell me you're still tight with that preacher and his brat. I thought you'd come over here to join me, Lily. I thought you wanted to work for me."

Lily swallowed. "I promised to keep feeding Sam for a few more weeks. He's grown a lot, Bea. He's starting to smile at us, and he sleeps all through the night now. Elijah says—"

"Elijah?" Beatrice frowned. "Lily, there's fifteen men right here who can beat the charms of that sour-faced preacher. Why don't you stay with us this evening? Every night we have a party like you wouldn't believe. It's been so much fun, I can hardly believe this is happening to me. It's like a dream. A flat-out dream. George is going to put me in charge here at the opera house; did I tell you? I'll manage the women and schedule the shows and keep the bar stocked in whisky. I'm going to run the whole operation."

"Mr. Gibbons is going back to Topeka?"

"Well, sure. He's got a wife and five kids to feed."

"But, Beatrice, I thought—"

"You thought wrong. Much as I care for the man, he's not free for the taking. We'll see each other now and again, and I don't really mind. I never wanted to marry anyhow. This way I'm still available in case a more interesting offer comes along." She gave Lily a squeeze. "Come on and stay with me tonight, Lil. We'll talk till all hours like we used to. I'll paint your toenails red, and we can have our pick of dancing partners. What do you say?"

Through the window, Lily studied the little town that stretched down the narrow main street of Hope. The celebrants were filtering out of the mercantile now, their laughter carrying to her. She thought of Elijah Book and his warm blue eyes. He had kissed her, but he didn't want her. Eva had been wrong. Elijah didn't love Lily. He couldn't. No matter how her heart ached for the man, no matter how she tempted him, he would keep himself from her. She wasn't good enough. She wasn't pure enough. And he had his reputation to protect.

Just like her father.

"We've got a big pot of stew on the fire," Bea said, turning Lily toward the wagons. "And you should taste the bread that cook of ours can bake. I'll tell you what—if the show, the liquor, and the girls won't draw customers, the food will! Come on, I'll introduce you to Milton. He's the sweetest little fellow you ever met."

Lily walked beside Beatrice toward the show wagon. A place to live, friends to call her own, good wages, the chance to sing—what more could she ask for? In a few weeks, Samuel could start to eat solid food. He could survive without her. Ben and Eva were already making plans to go to Topeka to visit Mother Margaret, Moses, and the rest of their newfound family. Rose Hunter would give birth to her baby. Caitrin Murphy would be busy in her home. After the harvest, everyone in Hope would prepare to settle in for the winter.

Why shouldn't Lily have a place of her own too? Why not here at the opera house?

Beatrice would probably fail her in the long run. Lily knew that. Elijah had warned her not to place her trust in the woman. That was wise advice. But he'd also cautioned Lily not to put her life into his hands . . . or even to rely on herself.

God was the only one to count on. God.

Oh, God! Lily's soul cried out. *Oh, God! God!*

"I can smell that stew from here," Beatrice said. "Bill, where's George? Round up that man of mine, would you? And call Milton over here. I want those fellows to see who's come to join us."

Lily clenched her jaw and pulled away from Beatrice. "I can't stay, Bea," she said quickly. "I won't. I won't do this."

Before Beatrice could stop her, Lily dashed across the cleared ground toward the main street of Hope. The moment she passed the old cottonwood tree, someone moved out of the shadows into the road.

"Lily?"

She swung around. "Mercy, you scared the living daylights out of me, Elijah."

"I'm sorry." He took off his hat as he walked toward her. "I didn't aim to scare you."

"What are you doing out here? I thought you were at the mercantile with the wedding party."

"I told you I'd stand by you." He held his hat in both hands. "I wanted to be nearby in case you needed me."

"You followed me out here?" She didn't know whether to feel flattered or angry.

"I spotted you down on the street right after the wedding. I remembered how things went between you and your friend back in Topeka, and I thought I'd better stay close."

"I'm all right."

"Is there anything I can do for you?"

She glanced across at the opera house and the workers gathering in front of it. A tinny song filtered up, a guitar and a hollow-sounding piano. And then over it all she heard the round, rich notes of Mozart. The song was poorly executed, but she recognized the tune.

"Beatrice is playing my melodeon," she said in a low voice. "She's beckoning me."

"Will you join her?"

"It's going to be a brothel, Elijah."

His nostrils flared as he drank down a deep breath. "Are you sure?"

"I won't be a part of any of it. I've taken enough wrong roads, and I don't want to make more mistakes."

"Lily, I've been needing to—" He reached out to her and then caught himself. Pulling back, he tucked away whatever it was he had almost confessed. Instead, he pulled a small book from the pocket of his black coat.

"I've been needing to ask if you'd sing a special song for us at the fish fry." He handed her the hymnal that had belonged to his mother. "Eva told me you hadn't been looking at this book much, but I thought you might be able to find something in here you'd enjoy singing. Casimir Laski has offered to perform a solo, but I hear he only knows Polish songs. Since this is an Independence Day celebration, I was hoping maybe you could sing something in English."

Lily took the hymnal and held it against her chest. "I have to get back to the house. Samuel will be waking from his nap."

"Lily, about the other day—"

"It doesn't matter."

"It does matter. I was forward with you again, and I shouldn't have been. I'm doing my best to keep back and let you make your own choices. You've had a rough time. I don't have any right to elbow in and try to influence you. No one can decide about your life but you."

He was standing so close now, she could smell the scent of starch in the freshly pressed shirt he'd worn for the wedding. It was all she could do to keep from rushing into his strong arms and burying her head against his shoulder. He would hold her close and shelter her. He would protect her from brothels and saloons and all her poor choices.

He would save her from Beatrice.

But Elijah, too, would fail. He had warned her of that already. He was human, and he would make mistakes. He would let her down. She couldn't trust him. She couldn't trust anyone.

Only God. God!

"Are you all right, Lily?" Elijah was asking. "You look . . . a little off-kilter."

"I'm so confused. I'm being pulled one way and then another. I can't decide on my own. I can't do this by myself."

"Lily." Again he reached out to her—and again he drew back. "Lily, I can't do it for you. Make the choice. Decide now."

She clapped her hands on her head, feeling as though she might explode in the raging storm of torment. Winds of indecision buffeted her from every side. *Go back to Beatrice*, the thunder growled. *Cling to Elijah*, a chill breeze whistled. *Stand on your own*, the lightning flashed.

God! Turn to God! It was a small whisper in the tumult. Small but beautiful. As beautiful and golden as music.

"Lily," Elijah said, touching her arm. "Will you let me lead you to him?"

"No." She shook her head. "Stay away from me, Elijah. You tear me apart inside. When I'm near you I can't think."

"I don't mean to trouble you, Lily. I only want to—"

"I know what you want. You want to be my brother. You want to be my employer. You want to be my pastor."

"I want to be your friend."

"Well, you can't!" she said, grabbing his coat sleeves and gripping them in her fists. "Friends don't kiss each other the way you kissed me. Friends don't hold each other and pray together and look into each other's eyes like you look into mine. Don't try to tell me you just want to be my friend, Elijah. It's a lie."

He studied the ground for a moment, obviously stung. She steeled herself for his wrath. But when he raised his head, she could see that his eyes were rimmed in red.

"You're right, Lily," he said in a rough voice. "I can't just be your friend."

"You can't be anything to me. No one can be anything to me. I don't trust you. I *won't* trust you."

"I'm a man, and as hard as I try, I can't keep from seeing you as a woman. You're right not to trust me. I don't trust myself." He stuffed his hat onto his head. "But confound it, Lily, you can trust God. You can put your life into his hands and count on him to stand by you every minute of every day."

"Elijah—"

"What in tarnation do you think I am, anyhow? I'm not perfect. I nearly killed Sam feeding him mashed potatoes. And then I let a spider bite him. I got us all run out of the Crescent Moon. I've talked when I should have kept my mouth shut, and I've kept quiet when I should have spoken up. I've preached some of the measliest excuses for sermons you ever heard. And I'll tell you something else. When I was sitting up with the Rippetos and their sick young'un, I was wishing I was home in my own bed. You're right not to trust me. I'm just a man, that's all. I'm weak and foolish and so crazy about you I can't see straight. You'd better not count on me for anything. But you can count on God. That's the only thing I know for sure. You can count on him. There, I've said my piece."

Without another word, he turned on his heel and stalked away down the road, leaving Lily alone in the darkening shadows of evening.

CHAPTER 12

BETWEEN the town and the opera house, the old cottonwood tree offered the only hiding place Lily could find. Sinking to her knees in a patch of tall bluestem grass, she pressed her face in her hands. Samuel would be awake and hungry by now. Eva and Ben would wonder where their houseguest had gotten to at this late hour. Even Beatrice might be standing on the porch expecting her to come back. Lily sensed their faint beckoning, but she could not move.

If she returned to the opera house, she would face Beatrice and the lure of her old life—a life she now knew for certain she did not want. If she walked into Hope, she would face Elijah and the call of a man she could never have. Though he cared for her, though his desire was obvious, he would not give in to his passion. His commitment to God controlled his entire life, and Lily knew that no matter what happened, he would never permit himself more than friendship with her.

If she turned inward, relying on herself, she would face the emptiness of her heart. Dependence on her own wits had led her to the traveling show. Led her to Ted Nolan. Led her to Beatrice. Mistakes and more mistakes. She had acted unwisely and made choices out of desperation. Eventually, she had lost her precious Abigail. As strong as she had become in the months since she had left Philadelphia, Lily knew she would never be able to rely on herself.

Fighting tears, she lay down in the grass and pulled her knees up to her chest. She felt so lonely. So hopeless. Everyone had betrayed or abandoned her. And why not? They were all humans, too, fallible and shortsighted.

Why did she feel such a need to turn to someone to fill the emptiness inside her? Why couldn't she do it herself? She was resourceful, intelligent, talented. Surely she didn't need anyone but herself.

Rolling over, Lily swallowed at the gritty lump in her throat. Of course she needed someone else. Like Samuel, she could not exist in this world alone. She would wither, grow frail, and die. No one—not even the most powerful human on earth—could live without sustenance and nourishment.

"*Whosoever drinketh of the water that I shall give him shall never thirst.*"

Lily clenched her teeth as the silent words filtered into her heart. She had memorized them long ago in Sunday school. Meaningless words. How could Christ quench this burning thirst inside her? How could he become the nourishment that would fill her?

"*I am the living bread which came down from heaven: if any man eat of this bread, he shall live for ever.*"

But her emptiness went too far! It was all-consuming. Her very soul was devoid of hope and life and love.

"*Behold, I stand at the door, and knock: if any man hear my voice, and open the door, I will come in to him, and will sup with him, and he with me.*"

Lily turned until she was lying flat on her stomach, her arms stretched out and her tears wetting the crushed grass. Would Christ really come and dwell inside her as he promised? Could his Spirit really fill the emptiness?

Oh, Lily knew she needed more than filling, though. She needed guidance so she could keep from making such foolish mistakes. She needed direction. She needed a clear path.

"I am the light of the world: he that followeth me shall not walk in darkness, but shall have the light of life."

Unable to move, Lily sobbed out. "God, be my water and my bread. Be my light. Be my friend."

"Ye are my friends, if ye do whatsoever I command you."

But what did God command her to do? She had spent so much time in his presence, yet she had never truly understood him. For many years, she had been able to do nothing but cling to the hope of God's protection from her father. Now she understood that difficulties would come her way. Elijah had explained that God never promised to protect her from all evil—instead, God had vowed to stand beside her and hold her in his loving arms. She could confidently place her trust in his constant presence, light, nourishment, and guidance. But what did he want of her in return?

"Believe on the Lord Jesus Christ, and thou shalt be saved."

Lily let out a deep breath. Believe. Surrender. Give up the anger, the bitterness, the confusion, the doubt. Stop being a child, and become a woman with the courage to place her life in the hands of a living Savior.

"Yes, Lord," she murmured. "I confess my failure. I believe. I surrender. I give you my soul."

For a long time she lay in silence, reveling in the sweet calm that slowly crept through her. Katydids buzzed in the trees overhead. The scent of fresh earth and sun-warmed grass bathed the air. Not far away, the Bluestem Creek gurgled its way toward the Kansas River. When she finally felt fully at peace, she curled up onto her knees. Around her, the darkness of the Kansas night wrapped her in a warm cocoon. It hadn't been hard at all. Just a few words and a release of what she had been trying to carry on her own.

Now she would never walk alone again. Feeling the weight of the little hymnal in her pocket, Lily reached for the book. It was too dark to see, but still she opened it, fingering pages filled with words she knew so well. How odd that she had been brought up to know Christ, and yet she had never given herself to him—until now. She began to sing softly.

"My faith looks up to Thee,
Thou Lamb of Calvary,
Savior divine!
Now hear me while I pray,
Take all my guilt away,
O let me from this day
Be wholly thine!

"While life's dark maze I tread,
And griefs around me spread,
Be Thou my guide;
Bid darkness turn to day,
Wipe sorrow's tears away,
Nor let me ever stray
From Thee aside."

"I don't think I'm cut out for the pastor's job." Elijah sat beside Ben Hanks on a bench near the Bluestem. Despite heavy storm clouds hanging on the horizon, the Independence Day fish fry had gone off without a hitch. Many in the community had come down to the water's edge to eat and have fellowship. Though Eli had been asked to join a game of horseshoes, he didn't have the heart for it.

"I wouldn't agree with that," Ben said. "Folks are still talkin' about the way you sat up with the Rippetos and their sick baby. I think everybody's glad you came to Hope."

"I should have gone to China."

"I bet you don't even know where China is, Brother Elijah."

"I sure do. It's over there on the other side of the world."

Ben took a bite of batter-fried bass and chewed in silence. Finally he shook his head. "What do you want to go all the way over there for anyhow, Preacher?"

"The Chinese people need to know about Christ."

Ben considered this. "I reckon they do. Somebody ought to go tell 'em the Good News. But what makes you think that 'somebody' is you? There's plenty of folks right here in Hope who don't know the gospel either. And we need you to help us guide our town in the right direction. There's a rumor afoot about that opera house they're puttin' up down the way. Somebody heard those folks are plannin' to bring in whisky."

Elijah plucked a stem of grass and stuck it in his mouth. *That's not all they're bringing in*, he thought. Every time he considered the prospect of a brothel at the edge of town, his gut churned. Half the time he caught himself cooking up ways to demolish the infernal den of iniquity. The other half of the time, he was preaching imaginary sermons that would drop Beatrice and the rest of those wild-living sinners to their knees in repentance before almighty God.

And he knew he couldn't do either. If he preached against the opera house too strongly, he might incite the townsfolk to do something ill advised—like burning it down. That would be just as great a sin as the wickedness taking place inside the building.

In fact, this very afternoon he had led the short worship service with a message on the glory of the Lord—and he was disgusted with himself over it. He had spoken not a single brimstone-laden word about brothels or saloons. He hadn't even extended an invitation to confess sin and be saved. It was just a simple talk about the beauty of the nation—words so lukewarm they would never convict anyone.

"Mr. Jack is thinkin' about starting up a Sunday school," Ben said. "He figures the town ought to get the children off to a good beginnin' in life. They can learn the Bible stories and maybe a little readin' and cipherin', too. And Mr. Seth wants to have a fund-raisin' so's we can put a steeple on the church roof. How about that? A real steeple—and maybe a bell. Wouldn't that be dandy?"

Eli nodded. "It'd be nice, all right."

"Miz Rosie said if we can find us a teacher willing to move to town, we could start a regular school inside the church buildin'. And there's folks talkin' of formin' a cemetery committee. Now that you built us such a nice graveyard, Brother Elijah, why, we want to keep it mowed and maybe even plant some flowers."

"There's not anybody buried in it yet, Ben."

"That don't matter."

"What matters is that I'm no good at leading folks to Christ. Not after they get to know me. It's one thing to preach a sermon to a bunch of strangers and then move on. But here in Hope, people can see I'm just a regular fellow. I don't have much book learning, and I'm not trained to preach. I'm just an old cowhand, Ben."

"Nobody expects you to be God."

Eli considered that for a moment. It was true that he himself could not save a single soul. That was God's business—and in Bible times, God had used some of the most low-down, ornery fellows to do his mighty work. But look at what a mess Eli had made of his talk with Lily Nolan the other night. He cared about that woman so much, but he had only blurted a bunch of outright nonsense and then stormed away. If he couldn't lead Lily to the Lord, who could he lead?

"Take Miz Lily," Ben said. "Now there's one fine lady. I reckon she knows you about as well as anybody does, Brother Elijah, and she don't seem to mind you a bit. She's been comin' to the church services real regular, and of late, she's always singin' hymns out of that little book of yours. You made a difference in her life. Look at her over there right now showin' off that baby to all the womenfolk. Anybody would think Sam was her own young'un. Why don't you make things right with the woman and marry her?"

Eli studied Lily as she stood at the water's edge. Her laughter, musical and light, drifted up the bank. She had pulled her hair into a loose bun at her crown, and it gleamed like a golden halo. Since that night on the road, he had managed to avoid her, but just the sight of her now made his insides hurt.

"I'm not going to marry Lily Nolan," he told Ben. "And I wish you and everybody else would stay out of my business."

Ben fingered a transparent fish bone out of his mouth and tossed it to the ground. A flicker of lightning in the distance led quickly to a low growl of thunder. "Gonna rain," Ben said. "Sure am glad my mama's in Topeka with my big brother. She'd have hung the washin' on the line and took it down again fifty times today already. Mercy, I miss that God-fearin' old woman."

"I'm sorry I was sharp with you," Eli said. "You're not the first who has told me what to do with my life."

"It's all right. I know you're in a pickle. You think God's tellin' you to go to China, when it's clear as daylight to everybody else that he brung you to Hope to do his work right here. And I know you're fit to be tied over Miz Lily. I don't understand what's keepin' the two of you apart when we can all see you belong together."

"She's not a Christian, Ben," Eli said. "I can't marry a woman who doesn't serve my God. I won't do it."

Ben set his tin plate on the ground and nodded in understanding. "I reckon that explains it then. Miz Lily come home late the other night after Mr. Jack's weddin', and she told Eva she'd been out talkin' to you on the road. Did you say somethin' to her?"

"I made it clear we couldn't be anything but friends, that's all."

"She must have took it pretty good, because you ought to see her the past couple of days. She's a new woman, Brother Elijah. It's like a load come right off her back. She's been chipper as a jaybird—singin' and talkin' and scurryin' around till Eva can hardly keep up with her. Maybe you tellin' her where things stood eased her mind so she could get to feelin' better. Look at her right now, climbin' up onto the table to sing. Don't she look a sight?"

Eli groaned. He had asked Lily to perform from the hymnal, but he hadn't really had much hope she would do it. Now how was he going to sit through this? He couldn't, that was all. He just couldn't do it. Grabbing his Bible, he jumped to his feet and headed for the church. With the storm blowing up, he needed to make sure the shutters were latched and that he'd put away the tools for painting the cemetery fence.

As he stepped inside the stuffy building, he could hear Lily's voice lifted in song. She had chosen one of his favorite hymns, "My Faith Looks Up to Thee." Elijah's own mama had sung it to him while he sat on her lap, and he could almost feel her warm arms around him. Almost, but not quite.

Eli quickly fastened the shutters and tried not to think about how lonely he felt all of a sudden. He'd never been lonely on the range. All he'd had out there was a bunch of cowboys and some cattle, but they'd been company enough. Here in the middle of a busy town with people coming and going all around him, he felt a sharp sense of longing.

He'd go find Samuel. That's what he'd do. With Lily spending most of the time with the baby each day, Eli had been free to work on the church and tend to the needs of his flock. But he'd hardly seen the boy except at night, and now the notion of cuddling the little fellow seemed like the best plan he'd thought up in days.

He set the paint bucket and brush inside his back door, and then he walked down to the creek again. Lily was still singing, but Eli walked around the edge of the gathering and found the woven basket in which his son lay. The moment the child laid eyes on him, Sam's small round face lit up with a toothless grin.

"Hey, Sammy," Eli said, kneeling by the basket. "How are you doing there, little Nubbin?"

Slipping his hands under the baby, he savored the warm, living weight. Sam had grown. He was thriving. If God saw fit, this little boy would one day become a man. Eli settled Sam on his shoulder, patted his small, curved back, and stroked his fingers along the baby's dark hair. It was going to be up to the father to see that the son turned out well.

"You want to take a walk, Sammy?" Eli asked, rising. "Let's go down to the edge of the creek and see if we can find any crawdads. We might even catch us a frog or two. You ever seen a tadpole?"

Suddenly the baby gave a huge leap in Eli's arms. Surprised, the preacher nearly lost his grip. As he struggled to settle Sam, he realized who had caused the child's reaction.

"Tadpoles?" Lily said, stepping up to join them. "Surely you're not going to introduce this sweet, innocent child to tadpoles and crawdads."

Eli breathed up a quick prayer for help. If God had sent down fire from heaven and parted the Red Sea, surely he could perform another miracle now. Eli needed one. Badly.

"I expected you to talk about the opera house in your sermon," Lily said as they made their way to the creek. "I was surprised you didn't mention it."

"This didn't seem like the time or place," he managed.

"Are you resigned to it then?"

He felt the steam rise up his spine and his heart rate increase at the mere mention of the opera house. "You might as well know, I *will* preach out against that place—and soon. I realize the folks running it are your friends, Lily, but drunkenness and adultery are sins. The Bible makes that real clear."

"I know it does," she said softly.

"I won't stand by and watch this little town catch sin like a killing case of influenza. I've been in Hope long enough to see these people struggling against enough kinds of sin—greed, jealousy, covetousness, lies, and faithlessness. Why should I stand around and watch that opera house import a whole new form of evil?"

"You shouldn't."

"I'm the minister of the church," he continued, "and it's up to me to set an example. Either that or I'd better ride off to China and let the whole town burn down like Sodom and Gomorrah."

"I'd hate to see that."

Elijah knew he was walking faster now, but he couldn't make himself slow down. With Lily Nolan, he had always been able to speak his mind. Somehow the woman drew his thoughts right out of his head. If he was planning to denounce her friends and their place of business, well, she had the right to know. Besides, it felt good to talk.

"Seems to me there were two kinds of fellows in the Bible," he said. "Pastors and prophets. Prophets didn't tend flocks; they hollered out for God to send down justice. They called folks to repentance. They showed people their sins. I reckon I'm supposed to be a prophet. In my sermon today, I stayed away from what was really on my heart, and I feel sick about it. So even though you're going over to that opera house to find work, Lily, I'll be preaching out against you every Sunday."

"No, I'm not," she murmured.

"See, I never have been much good at pastoring," he went on. "I get too het up. I have to preach the Word of God, and that means calling folks to look at their lives and make a change." By now they were halfway to the grove of trees where he'd spoken with Lily the other night. Just the memory of his failure there made him sick inside. "I think I'm supposed to be a prophet, not a pastor, and that means—"

"You're supposed to be like Christ, Preacher-man," Lily said.

Eli stopped and looked at her. For the first time, her voice remained gentle when she accosted him. Standing in the road, she gave him a warm smile and lifted her eyebrows.

"Isn't that right?" she said. "Prophets and priests were God's messengers *before* Christ came. After that, our job has been to emulate him."

"Emulate?"

"Copy. And Christ is both prophet and priest, isn't he? What's wrong with shepherding a flock—and pouring God's Word out to the sheep at the same time? Can't you do both?"

"Are you mocking me?" He shifted the baby to his other shoulder, uncomfortable and more than a little confused at her words. "Go ahead and throw Bible verses and religious talk at me like you usually do. I don't mind, Lily. I realize you know the Scriptures better than I do, and you've been to church a lot more years than I ever have. But it doesn't matter. Ever since our talk the other night, I've been doing nothing but thinking and praying. And I've come to see that the only thing I can do is to walk in Christ's footsteps. That's all. Just follow him. So even if you make fun of me or I mess up a sermon or I give someone lousy advice, nothing matters but that I keep on following Christ the best I can."

By this time, they had come to the shelter of the trees beside the creek. Elijah realized he was patting the baby with such vigor that poor Sam had gotten himself a bad case of hiccups. Every time he "hicked," his whole body wriggled, and every time he "upped," out came a gurgle of white milk onto the shoulder of Eli's black jacket.

"Aw, confound it, Sam," he said, balancing the baby in one arm while he searched his pockets for his handkerchief. "Don't you know I borrowed this coat from Jack Cornwall? It's his wedding jacket, and now it's a mess, sure as shootin'. He's liable to hog-tie and skin me, young'un. Where in tarnation is that handkerchief? Lily, would you . . ." He looked up to find the woman convulsed in giggles, her laughter poorly hidden behind her hand. "What's so funny?"

"Here, give me that baby, would you?" She held out her arms, and Sam eagerly went to her. "It's you, silly. You're so hopeless with babies."

"I am not." He began wiping the wet spot on his shoulder. "What have you been feeding that boy anyhow? The smell is enough to gag a polecat. What am I supposed to tell Jack Cornwall? And would you quit that infernal cackling?"

Lily leaned against a tree and laughed as though she'd never seen anything so funny. He took off the coat and hung it on a tree branch. There. Maybe it would rain soon.

Looking out across the prairie, Eli felt his heart contract at the sight of the sickening green color of the sky. Though rain hadn't begun to fall, the air felt as heavy as a damp dishrag. Lightning licked the horizon like a snake's tongue. Purple and blue mingled with the pea-soup green, a livid bruising of the heavens.

This was going to be worse than a heavy rain, Eli realized. There could be hail. Hail would mean crop damage right in the middle of summer. If the crops were ruined, there'd be no time for replanting before the onset of autumn. The farmers had barely made it through the past winter after last year's grasshopper plague. He ought to get back to the people. Back to his flock . . .

"We've got to go, Lily," he said. "The sky's looking bad."

Sobering, she turned to look in the direction of the oncoming storm. "Oh, Elijah." She took a step toward him. "The sky is green. I've never seen anything like that."

"We'd better find shelter before the hail hits." He let out a breath. "You know, even though you were challenging me again, Lily, you were right. I've got to follow Christ's example—and that means I'll be both a prophet and a priest."

"Elijah," she said, her hand on his arm to stop him. "Before we go, I need to talk to you. I want you to know I wasn't mocking you earlier. I was trying to help you see how important you are to the town. The people need you. Truly they do—and they need you for the man you *are*, not some imaginary ideal of the perfect pastor."

A sudden gust of wind ripped Eli's hat from his head and sent it rolling down the road. He started after it, but Lily tightened her grip on his arm. "Elijah," she went on, "I want you to know what happened to me the other night. I've been waiting for the right time to speak. I want to tell you about my decision."

Eli watched his Stetson tumbling farther across the prairie, and he wanted to go after it. Not because he needed his hat, but because he didn't want to hear Lily's words. She would tell him about her plans to join her friend at the opera house, and that would tear her away from him completely.

The way things were going right now, at least he could be near her sometimes. He could talk to her. He could listen to her beautiful voice. He could pretend he would be able to hold onto her forever, even though he knew she never would be truly his.

"I'd better get my hat," he said. "We'll talk after the storm passes, Lily. I'll walk over to Ben's, and you and I can sit on the porch."

Disappointment clouded her eyes. "But I'd rather—"

A shrill screaming wind cut off her words. On the horizon a huge black funnel dropped suddenly out of the boiling green clouds. Tearing through trees and fences like a giant plow, the twister churned up dust and kicked sheds out of its path. Haystacks exploded. Brush ripped free from its roots. Birds flew screeching, their wings beating the air in a futile effort to escape.

"Cyclone!" Eli hollered. "Come here, Lily."

Grabbing her arm, he tucked her and the baby against his side and began to run down the road toward the picnic site. He'd seen twisters tear across Texas and New Mexico, and he knew the destruction they could cause. Quicker than a man had time to think, the whirling wind could blast his house to kingdom come, strip the skin off his livestock, and suck his children into the air—never to be seen again. The townsfolk needed to take cover, and Elijah knew the creek bed wasn't deep enough to protect everyone.

"Where are we going?" Lily cried as she struggled to keep up with him. "What will we do?"

"We've got to get everyone into the empty soddy. It's half underground."

As he and Lily reached the site of the fish fry, the crowd had just noticed the black funnel bearing down. Over screams and barking dogs, Elijah bellowed for everyone to run up the slope and take cover in the soddy. Rushing Lily and the baby toward the little house that had once belonged to Seth Hunter, he could hardly believe the chaos. Some people were actually trying to pack up their belongings. Others had elected to race toward the grove of trees. Mr. Rippeto was even hitching his mule to his wagon in hopes of outrunning the cyclone.

"Salvatore!" Eli called to the man. "Run for the soddy!"

By now, stinging hailstones peppered the bare skin of Eli's face. Sam was crying and Lily could barely move against the howling wind. Her long dress tangled around her legs, and her hair streamed back from her face. The cyclone was headed straight for Hope, Eli calculated, and there was not much hope it would avoid the town. His heart sick, fear an acrid taste on his tongue, he swept Lily into his arms and ran the last few paces toward the soddy.

The old door had blown off its hinges, but townspeople were crushed together in a huddled mass on the floor. Children sobbed as husbands called out to their wives, making certain of their presence in the room. Eli worked his way through the throng to the back of the soddy, and he shoved Lily onto the dirt floor beside Caitrin Cornwall and Rosie Hunter. Chipper gripped his dog around the neck. Rolf Rustemeyer hollered at everyone in German. Sheena O'Toole shouted her children's names. Jack's sister, Lucy, began to shriek.

Just as Salvatore Rippeto burst into the soddy and was yanked to the floor by groping hands, the cyclone churned across the sod roof of the little dugout. The sound of ten train locomotives deafened Eli's ears. Praying for protection, he surrounded Lily and Sam with his arms.

Oh, God, dear God, he pleaded as the wire screens ripped off the soddy's windows and the black of night descended. He could feel hands gripping him from every side, as though the whole town was clinging together in one lump of trembling humanity. *Save us, Father! Please save us!*

But God hadn't protected Lily from her own father, Eli remembered as he held the woman close. His Lord didn't promise shelter from all evil. The buildings would be flattened. The crops ruined. The town devastated. *God, please don't destroy Hope. Please save your people!*

A chair flew out through the open door and vanished into the darkness. A mother clung to her child as the wind lifted the toddler up, pulling, sucking, greedy for ruin. At that moment, a heavy iron plow drove straight through the soddy's front wall, splintering wood, grinding up sod bricks, slamming into the gathered people. Screams mingled with cries for help.

It was no good, Elijah thought as he left Lily's side and crawled toward the injured. The twister had them in its grip. In moments it would devour the whole town. The soddy couldn't hold up under the pressure. It was bound to explode or collapse, and then—

"My faith looks up to thee—"

A beautiful voice lifted over the screams of babies, above the sobs of the wounded, even beyond the growl of the tornado.

"Thou Lamb of Calvary,
Savior divine!"

Amid the storm, other voices one by one joined with Lily's.

"Now hear me while I pray,
Take all my guilt away,
O let me from this day
Be wholly thine!"

CHAPTER 13

LILY sang, rocking the baby in her arms as howling winds wrapped around the soddy.

"Bid darkness turn to day,
Wipe sorrow's tears away,
Nor let me ever stray
From Thee aside."

The others in the room had joined in, and as Lily began the fourth verse of the hymn, the roaring, growling tornado suddenly faded into nothing more than shutter-banging gusts. And finally, the tumult transformed into utter silence, eerie in its intensity. The sheer terror gradually ebbed from Lily's body, leaving her trembling and chilled. Next to her, Rosie wept in her husband's arms.

"The cyclone got our house," she cried in an anguished whisper, "I just know it did. All your hard work . . . the new front porch . . . Chipper's toys . . . the baby's room . . ."

"Hey there, sweetheart," her husband said. "We're all alive, aren't we? Even ol' Stubby."

Nearby, the big mutt thumped his tail and gave a whimper. The little boy lying against him patted the dog's massive head. "It's OK, Stubby. God brought us through, an' now we're all gonna be fine."

"Sure we'll rebuild the mercantile, won't we, Jack?" Caitrin Cornwall asked her new husband, her usually hearty voice carrying a note of uncertainty. "We'll be back in business before the month is out, so we shall. At least, I hope so."

"Caitrin, I'm worried about Lucy," Jack said. Lily knew the man was referring to his sister's fragile mental condition. "She's holding onto Mama for dear life."

"She'll be all right. We'll put Lucy to work cooking for everyone, shall we then?"

"Oh, Caitie, must you always be so cheerful?" her older sister, Sheena, groused. "Next thing we know, you'll be callin' the cyclone naught more than a stiff breeze."

At that, the crowd hunched together in the little soddy began to chuckle and relax. Outlined in the open doorway, Elijah got to his feet and addressed the people.

"Folks, I'd better tell you there's a couple of us injured up here." At the reaction of concern, he motioned for calm. "Salvatore Rippeto was clobbered by the plow that came through the wall. I think his leg is broken, and we may need to get him to Topeka. And one of Violet Hudson's little boys fell and skinned his knee pretty bad running up here. Other than that, the main thing we need to find out is how many of us made it into the soddy. Before we head outside, we ought to know who we're looking for."

Lily could see dull, gray rain streaming down in a torrent, veiling the destruction left in the wake of the black funnel. Never in her life had she imagined anything so powerful, so all-consuming, so relentless. Never had she felt as small and helpless as she had racing up the hill toward the soddy. Even when her father had been bearing down on her, she had sensed that she would survive the pain. But the cyclone had been a thousand times more frightening than her father, for in its fury, the storm held the potential for death.

Lily had felt terrified, unprotected, panic-stricken. Yet she had not felt alone. Through the growling wind and the grinding dirt, she had sensed a calm fullness within. Not once had she thought to crawl into the secret place inside herself—the place where golden music had blocked the pain of her father's abuses. Instead, in the very midst of the cyclone, a song had erupted from her heart, music both strong and serene. She had known the overwhelming presence of God's Spirit within, for as he promised, Christ had not left her comfortless.

Hugging Sam, she hummed to the baby as Elijah, Seth, and Jack checked on and counted the families crowded into the soddy. Some of the groups elected to brave the rain the moment they were all accounted for—eager to race home and inspect the damage. Others chose to huddle in the security of the thick sod walls until the storm had subsided.

"Are you and Sam all right, Lily?" Elijah asked her as he finally worked his way in the darkness to the back of the room. "I didn't intend to leave you alone, but when that plow—"

"I'm not alone," Lily said.

"I guess not. I never knew so many folks could cram into one house. I reckon we must have looked like a can of oysters all bunched up together. I'm glad nobody got hurt worse."

"Is anyone missing?"

"A couple of the young single farmers took off for the trees near the creek. I sure hope they found some low ground. I'll tell you what; I've seen whirlwinds racing across the desert, tossing around tumbleweeds and darkening the sky, but I've never known anything like that twister."

Lily gathered the baby closer as Elijah sat down beside her. "Thank you for seeing me to safety," she said. "I was frightened."

"Who wasn't? I'll bet that cyclone tore up the whole town." He slipped his arm around her shoulders. "God just barely gave us enough time to get to safety. You sure you're OK?"

"I'm fine." Enjoying the warm comfort of the man's embrace,

she leaned her head against his shoulder. "I'm worried about the church."

"It'll be standing. I have no doubt God saw to that. He wants his folks to have a place to worship—especially after something as terrible as that twister. I sure hope the Hunter place is still up. Seth just put on a new front porch, you know, and they've got the baby coming this fall. They need to have things all ready by that time, but this could set them back. Jack Cornwall's smithy is made of sod, so it ought to be all right. But his house and the Hanks place might have gone. I wonder about the opera house."

He fell silent momentarily. Lily stroked Sam's cheek, praying the child would relax enough to sleep. If most of the houses in town had been destroyed, she and the others would be forced to take shelter in the soddy until morning. There wasn't even enough room for everyone to lie down. How had Beatrice, George Gibbons, and their workmen fared in the storm? What if they lay injured even now?

"I'll bet that place is flatter than a hotcake," Elijah said. "A pile of toothpicks."

"Oh, Elijah, that would be terrible."

"Would it? Don't you know the Lord works out his will in this world? If he wanted to get rid of that opera house as badly as I did, he probably smashed it to smithereens."

"But what about the people? What about Bea and the others? You sound as though you'd be glad to find them dead."

Elijah stiffened at her accusation. "I don't want anybody to die, Lily. But I wouldn't object to seeing those folks pull up stakes and head back to Topeka."

Lily busied herself tucking Sam's blanket around him. She had turned from her past and asked Christ to be Lord of her life, but that didn't mean she had stopped caring about Beatrice and the others. Though she had no desire to join them in their business, she would never wish evil upon them either.

"I'm sorry, Lily," Elijah murmured. "What I said just then wasn't really about your friends. It wasn't even about the opera house."

"Well, what was it about then?"

"It was about . . . about not wanting to let you go. I don't want you to leave town, Lily. I don't want you to leave Sam." He was silent for a moment. "I don't want you to leave me."

Lily closed her eyes, soaking up the sound of words she had longed to hear. Could it be possible that now, after all her mistakes and all her pain, she had found a man with whom she could build a future? Would God really allow Elijah to care for her? Did hope for true love really exist for someone like her?

"I know you're angry with me," Elijah said, "and I don't blame you. First I tell you I'm going to do one thing, and then I do the exact opposite. One time I'm walking away from you, and the next time I'm holding and kissing you. Lily, I wish I could explain to you how mixed-up I've been feeling."

"Why don't you try?" Though the darkness around them was alive with people, the pouring rain drowned out all but the sound of his low voice. "Because if you could only tell me how you really feel—"

"I feel two ways." His fingers on her shoulder tightened as he struggled to express himself. "On the one hand, I think you're . . . well, you're a good woman."

"Good?"

"Kind and sweet, you know."

"You're talking about the way I take care of Sam."

"And how you are with Ben and Eva Hanks. They love having you at their house. Everybody in town really likes you a lot."

"Do you like me, Elijah?"

"Sure I do."

As Eli fell silent, Lily could almost feel the man breaking into a sweat. Why was this so hard for him? What held him away from her? She felt sure it must be her past—her marriage to Ted, her life with the traveling show, her friendship with Beatrice, even the fact that she'd given birth already. How many times had her father told her to stay pure? "Men don't want used goods," he had shouted across the parlor during her first and only courtship.

But she wasn't pure. Not unless Elijah was willing to accept the cleansing she had received from the Lord. "*Though your sins be as scarlet, they shall be as white as snow.*" Lily felt sure God viewed her now as whole and pure again. But would Elijah?

"I care about you, Lily," he said finally. "And not just the way a shepherd cares for the sheep."

A smile tilted one corner of her mouth. "I'm glad you're beginning to see yourself as a pastor."

"But not with you. With you, I'm . . . well, I'm flat-out confused." He leaned his head back against the sod wall. "See, I'm a preacher. And that means God has some special work for me to do."

"God has special work for each of us."

"Sure, but I've got to be an example, you know. I can't be a stumbling block to folks. I'm supposed to lead them on the right path."

"And I'm a stumbling block to you?"

"Phew." He shook his head. "You just say whatever you're thinking, don't you?"

"More or less. You said you felt two ways about me. On the one hand, you like me. At least, you like the way I take care of Sam, and you appreciate the fact that I've helped Ben and Eva. Let me guess the other. You see my past life as though it still exists. I'm still that woman who came in with the traveling show, that fortune-teller, that drifter. Am I right?"

"The thing is, Lily, that God might want to send me to China. And if I let myself care about you . . . more than as Sam's helper . . . I'd pretty soon be wanting to cart you off to China."

Lily stroked the sleeping baby's head. Though she was sure she knew why Elijah refused to accept his growing feelings for her, she intended to make him speak plainly. He was hedging. Evading the truth. He didn't want to tell her she was "used goods" and not pure enough for him. If she was to be rejected, she would have the reasons clearly stated.

"You're not worried about whether I'd want to go to China, Elijah," she said. "You know good and well that if God wanted to send me to China, I'd be able and ready to go. And I *would* go to China, because I'd know I was supposed to be there. You're the one who told me we're never alone. Christ's Spirit is always with us—in China or in Kansas. Whether you want to hear it or not, I have the strength to go anywhere and do anything so long as I'm walking the right path and following the light of my salvation. It's true I've made mistakes. I married for the wrong reasons. I ran from my fears. I fell in with tricksters. But you said a life can be changed, made brand-new, made pure again. Because of my faith, I am healed, Elijah."

"What?" His voice was low and filled with disbelief. "What are you telling me, Lily?"

"I'm saying that it's *you* who's veering off the straight and narrow." She set Samuel in his arms, fighting the urge to run out of the stuffy little soddy and breathe freely. "Take your son, Preacher-man. You were so sure God gave him to you. Without doubting the Lord's plan for a moment, you just picked that baby right up out of his dead mother's arms and went on your way. But you've been too blind to see what else God gave you. You don't even know what's right in front of your nose. It's *Hope*, Elijah. The Lord sent you here."

"Well, I—"

"God puts people in places because he has work to do there," she went on, determined to force the man to face the truth. "These townsfolk were hungry for the Word of Christ. They had even gone so far as to build a church. God was already at work in Hope, don't you see? He led you here to be his instrument. It's not just Sam who needs you, Elijah. It's the Hunters, the O'Tooles, the Cornwalls, the Rippetos. It's me. I need you. God brought us together—and it wasn't just so I could feed Sam. It's because he has a plan. Can't you understand that? He has a plan! Now are you just going to veer off the path and live with one foot on the road to China, or are you going to start looking forward into the light of your own salvation and following God's plan for you in Hope?"

Finished, depleted, even angry, Lily pushed to her feet. "I'm going to see what's left of the town," she said. "I'm too tired to talk anymore."

She started off through the huddled figures, most of them now dozing. As she stepped over Stubby, Elijah jerked on the hem of her skirt.

"Hold on there, woman," he said, coming to his feet behind her. "Just one cotton-picking minute."

Wobbling backward, she braced her hand against the soddy wall.

"I'm going to look for Ben and Eva."

"It's the middle of the night. There'll be critters out. You won't be able to see a thing."

"Would you two be quiet?" someone whispered loudly. "We're trying to get some shut-eye here."

Lily folded her arms and stood as rigid as a fence post in the inky blackness. It was true that she couldn't see. She didn't know which way to turn, which path to take. But she wasn't alone.

Lord, be near me, she prayed silently. Letting out a breath, she sat down on the floor again. *This infuriating, stubborn man is your servant. He knows you and he loves you, but for some reason he won't listen to you. He won't see what you're trying to show him. Speak to Elijah, Father. Please speak to him.*

"Lily," Elijah whispered in the darkness. "Are you there?"

"I'm here," she said. "I'm going to sleep now. Don't bother me."

"Did you say the *Lord* sent me here to Hope?"

"Yes. Be quiet."

He obeyed, but only for a moment. "Did you say *God* brought us together?"

"Shh."

"Did you say you're healed?"

Lily tucked up her knees and rested her head on them. *OK, Lord, he heard that much at least. Thank you.*

"It happened that night under the cottonwood tree by the road," she said softly. "After you left, I realized what I'd been running from, and I . . . I stopped running."

"Hallelujah!" he shouted suddenly into the silent soddy. "Hallelujah! Thank you, God!"

"Hush, Brother Elijah," someone muttered. "Folks is tryin' to rest."

"Hallelujah!" he said again. He was back on his feet. Lily could just make out his shape as he swung the baby around in a circle. "You hear that, Sam? She did it! She really did it! Hallelujah!"

"What?" the voice grumbled. "What'd she do?"

"Yes!" Elijah cried. "Yes, yes, yes!"

"Preacher, much as we love you," another voice called, "we's gonna have to shove you out on your backside if you won't be quiet."

"Come here, woman!" Elijah said, reaching down into the darkness and grabbing Lily's arm. "I'm free now! Don't you see? You're free! He set us free! I didn't have to do it myself. God did it! We're free."

His arm came around her and pulled her close. Lily felt half sure the poor man had suddenly gone mad. At the same time, his jubilation thrilled her as he hugged her tight. This was how she had been feeling ever since that night under the cottonwood tree. She was free! Free and filled with peace and hope and love. Laughing in spite of herself, she allowed Elijah to move her through the room.

"Sorry!" she called softly as she tripped over someone's foot. "Oh, excuse me! Elijah, not so fast! Slow down."

"Glory to God!" he shouted as they finally burst out of the soddy into the damp night. The rain had stopped falling, but the ground was soaked and littered with debris from the tornado. "Yes, Lily, yes!"

The baby in one arm, he pulled her against his chest. Reeling from the sudden outburst, she slipped her arms around the man and held him close.

"Elijah," she said as Sam caught a clump of her hair in his tiny fingers. "Elijah, what does this mean?"

"Oh, Lily, it means everything." He was breathing hard, his voice ragged with emotion. "You're right; I haven't been looking at the path right in front of my feet. I haven't been trusting God with my life. I've been trying to figure it all out myself, trying to get what I thought I wanted instead of letting God take care of me. But I can see it now—I know why I'm here, what I'm supposed to do. I can see everything. It's all going to work out fine."

"Brother Elijah, that is you there?" Rolf Rustemeyer, lantern in hand, came running through the darkness toward the soddy. "You must hurry. Come quickly!"

"What's wrong?"

"Is the church!" The big German came to a stop, his boots caked in mud. "Is the church!"

"What about the church?"

"Cyclone caused much troubles. Barn of Seth Hunter is blown away. All windows in mercantile broken. Part of Cornwalls' roof is torn off. O'Toole house is missing front porch. But only building completely gone is church."

"The church?"

"No church left. No fence. No cemetery. No benches. All is gone."

Lily covered her mouth with her hand as Elijah let out a cry of disbelief. Taking the baby from him, she stood in a chilly puddle as Rolf handed the preacher his lantern and the two men raced down the street toward the scene of the disaster.

No church!

Lily lifted her head toward heaven as a scrap of doubt fluttered into her heart. "There's no church," she whispered. "I thought you had a plan for him here. He said you wouldn't take it. But you did. You took the church."

As Sam began to whimper, Lily made her way back to the soddy.

Elijah stared at the gaping hole in the ground where Hope Church had stood. Dawn bathed the prairie in a gentle pink glow that softened the edges of the tornado's destruction. Around him, lumber lay scattered on the ground like windblown hay. Shingles hung from tree branches and floated at the edge of Bluestem Creek.

A wagon rested upside down on the roof of the O'Tooles' house, while a length of wet canvas now covered the place where their porch had stood. The Hunters' barn had been lifted, carried to the plot of land behind the mercantile, and dropped with such force that it had flattened like a stomped-on tin can. Caitrin Cornwall's shining plate-glass windows lay on the ground in a thousand knife-sharp shards.

Rolf Rustemeyer's cow had been discovered an hour ago chewing her cud in Ben Hanks's backyard. Three of Rosie Hunter's chickens had landed in Sheena O'Toole's oak tree, barely alive and with only a handful of feathers among them. Jack Cornwall's hog had slid into the creek and drowned. A pair of mongrel dogs no one had ever seen before were found eating sausage in Jimmy's smokehouse.

But not a single person had perished in the storm. Salvatore Rippeto was the only man seriously injured. A couple of young farmers sported bumps and bruises. Will O'Toole had stepped into a hole and twisted his ankle.

And the church was gone.

Elijah swallowed hard as he counted the postholes he had dug with such vigor. Not one of them contained a fence post. Of the hundred rails he had split, not a one lay in sight. His vegetable garden had been stripped bare. Half of a ceramic chamber pot lay where the corner of the cemetery had once stood.

As if in mockery of his fervor to beautify and strengthen the place, the only portion of the church still intact was the door frame to his little room—the cans of white paint and the wide brushes still neatly stored in readiness for the next project he would undertake. He walked over and kicked them skyward. There.

"Elijah?" Lily's voice showered warm rain through him.

He swung around, emotion hanging in his throat like a lump of dry bread. "It's gone, Lily," he said. "The whole thing is gone."

She looked at the ragged, water-filled cavern in the ground, the scattered boards, the empty postholes. Without speaking another word, she walked to him and wrapped her arms around him, holding him close. Elijah rested his head against hers and let the loss wrack through his chest.

"I don't understand it," he said. "We didn't do anything to deserve this. We were trying our hardest to please the Lord. Why did he take the church, Lily?"

She stroked her hand down his back. "You're the man who taught me that bad things can happen to people who don't deserve them. God doesn't protect us from all evil, Elijah."

"But this was his church."

"It was a building."

"It was my work."

"His church is the people of Hope. Your work is the people of Hope. And Christ is right here with us now. He's with us always, remember? Have you lost your faith?"

He gripped her tightly. "Oh, Lily."

"Come on," she said softly. "Eva's watching the baby for me. Let's start cleaning up."

He couldn't let go of her, agony washing over him as the tormented confusion in his mind tumbled forward. Maybe this destruction was a sign for him to leave. Maybe God didn't want him to stay in Hope after all. Lily insisted that the Lord had led him to this town, but hadn't that same Lord just swept away the church building?

Should Elijah gather up the baby and head east? Or should he stay here and rebuild? Did God really have a plan as Lily claimed?

"I don't know," he said. "I've been wandering around here for hours, and I just can't make myself think straight. After the storm, after you told me about your new life, I was so sure I understood what God wanted me to do, Lily. Now I wonder if I was wrong."

"Christ calmed storms and walked on water. Do you think he would allow a single cyclone to change his almighty plan for your life?"

He studied the gentle woman, painfully aware of the trust and hope shining in her blue eyes. She had pulled back her hair into a lump of gold, rolled up her sleeves, and washed her face. Her cheeks glowed pink, her chin tilted upward in confidence, her lips curved into a soft smile.

"We're never alone," she told him. "Not in the midst of the cyclone. And not now. Don't you trust that, Preacher-man?"

He let out a breath. Had the storm blown his faith in God away along with the church building? Was he really that shallow rooted?

No, he lifted up. *Father, I believe you're here with me. And I'm going to look into the light of my salvation and step forward on the path you've stretched out in front of me. Amen and amen.*

"Well?" she asked, hands on her hips.

"I believe those boards over there belong to Seth Hunter's barn," he said. "Mrs. Hunter told me that's her favorite shade of red."

Lily turned and observed the tangle of painted lumber, long square-headed nails protruding like porcupine quills. "You might be right. If they're his, Seth will be wanting them back. But I'm sure I saw part of your split-rail fence hanging on Eva's clothesline."

"We'd better go fetch it. Jack Cornwall already lost one hog. I don't want him to get the idea he can pen in the rest of those critters with the church's fence." He took Lily's hand and headed for the road. "A church cemetery needs a fence."

"And thank the good Lord no one needs the cemetery."

Elijah laughed as he walked beside her across the street to gather up the fence rails. Eva Hanks spotted them coming and stepped out into the yard, the baby in her arms. "Hey, you two!" she called, giving them a wave. "You look happy as foxes in the chicken house—and that's a mighty good sight after all the troubles we been through."

"God is good," Elijah said, feeling his heart swell with courage even as the words left his mouth.

"All the time," Eva replied. "I'm going to see if Miz Caitrin will write Mother Margaret a letter for us. If we tell her about the cyclone, maybe she'll come home to check on us."

"That's mighty low-down and conniving, Mrs. Hanks," Elijah said as he tugged the fence rails from the clothesline. "But I sure could use a good dose of her common sense and godly faith."

"So could I," Lily agreed. "Mercy and hallelujah."

Eva laughed. "We're going to be all right. I don't believe this baby of yours even knew what hit him. You should have seen him a minute ago when Ben came home to eat a bite of breakfast. I do believe Sam winked at that big ol' man of mine."

"Winked!" Lily chuckled and began picking up the painted white rails from the yard. "You're seeing things now, Eva."

"Maybe so." The other woman gave the baby on her hip a pat. "Ben said he thought he was seein' a ghost last night when he come upon that opera house a-standin' there by the road."

Elijah stopped and straightened. "The opera house?"

"Perfect as a new penny," Eva said, giving Lily a glance. "That storm didn't touch it. Not even a lick."

Lily picked up a shingle and dropped it among the others in the hammock she had made of her apron. "The Lord works in mysterious ways," she said, setting off for the church site, "his wonders to perform."

CHAPTER 14

IN THE late afternoon of the third day, when the sun beat down on the scorched earth and cicadas screeched in the denuded trees beside Bluestem Creek, Elijah finally understood why God had let the cyclone take the church.

From every part of the countryside around the devastated town of Hope, people had come, driving wagons filled with lumber, nails, quilts, benches, window glass, cans of paint, and food. Without being asked, they set about repairing barns, nailing shingles to roofs, and putting up new split-rail fences. Although most of the folks who showed up had never set foot in the Hope Church, they began rebuilding the temple of the Lord with the zeal of King Solomon himself.

Elijah had eaten more apple pie in the last three days than a body could rightly hold. He had hammered so many nails that the smithy could barely turn them out fast enough. He had greeted more newcomers than he'd known lived in the area. And he had never seen people work as hard or as long or with such determination.

"Brother Elijah," an old man called out, hurrying toward the preacher on bandy legs. The fellow lived three miles west of Hope, and he'd been laboring on the church building as though it belonged to him alone. "We got a problem here, Preacher. I say we ought to put a baptistry right up at the front where everybody can see what's a-goin' on. You know, we could haul in water and baptize every new believer the way it should be done. But Simeon over there says we don't need nothing more than a bowl of water to do the baptizin'. He thinks we ought to use the space up front to put in a choir. But everybody with half a brain knows the choir sings at the back of the church, not the front."

Elijah regarded Simeon-the-adversary standing beside the rapidly rising walls of the church. The fellow had his jaw set and his eyes narrowed like a feisty old ram ready to butt the stuffing out of whoever stepped in his way. Aware that the pastor was observing him, he stepped forward.

"At the church where I growed up in Ohio," he said, "we sprinkle babies."

"Sprinkle babies?" the other man bellowed. "In Kentucky, where I come from, we dunk full-grown believers."

"And the choir sets in the front."

"In the back!"

"Now just a minute here, fellows," Elijah said, stepping between them. "We'll work this out—"

"Next thing you'll be wanting to drink grape juice at the Communion!" one of them cut in.

"What else?" the other barked. "You don't reckon we'll be servin' wine, do you?"

"All right, gentlemen," Elijah said, holding up his hands. It was time for the shepherd to come between these two old rams. "We'll use the water God has already provided us for baptizing—and that's Bluestem Creek. If a river was good enough for John the Baptist, it'll be good enough for us."

"What about the choir?" Simeon snapped. "Where's it gonna set?"

"We don't have a choir," Elijah returned. "We don't have a song leader. We don't have a piano. And we won't even have a building if we stand around arguing all day. Now let's get back to work, shall we? Brother Simeon, would you mind helping those fellows frame up that wall back there? And you, sir—"

"Hubert."

"Brother Hubert, I couldn't help but notice what a fine job you do planing down shingles. Would you be willing to supervise the roofing of the new church?"

The old man's chest swelled. "Indeedy-do."

As the fellow hobbled away on his bowed legs, Elijah let out a breath. Shepherding a little flock was turning out to be challenging work. If the sheep weren't butting heads over one doctrinal detail or another, they were bleating that someone was sitting in their pew or not giving a fair share of tithe. Then there were the struggling lambs that needed his tender care—the sick, the lonely, the widowed, the fearful. Just as important, all these new sheep had come to town to help with the rebuilding—and Elijah was bound and determined to round up every last one of them and bring them into the Father's fold.

"Elijah?"

"Hello, Lily," he said without even having to look. The woman's touch on his arm and her sweet voice had become so familiar in the last three days. As he turned to her, Lily's blue eyes lit up. How amazing to see the changes God's love had wrought. When she sang hymns, the words flowed from her heart. When she recited Scripture, the verses poured out like honey. She no longer hurled religion at Elijah like accusing stones. Instead, she used her greater store of biblical knowledge to gently help him find the right pathway.

"Lily, just look at all these good folks," he said, wishing he could tuck her under his arm and hug her warmly. "Instead of sending me out to round up the flock, God used the cyclone to drive the sheep right here to us."

"But the wolves have followed, too," she said. "Some of the builders from the opera house are coming down the road. They've been drinking, Elijah. I think they mean trouble."

This was not the first time the Topeka men had wandered through town calling insults to the laborers and casting lewd suggestions at their wives. Seth Hunter had confronted them once, and they had retreated. This morning Jimmy O'Toole had brought his rifle to town.

"Maybe I should go talk to Beatrice," Lily said. "I'm sure this is partly her doing. She's angry that I haven't returned to the opera house, so she encourages these fellows to come to town and bother people."

"I wish you'd stay clear of that woman," Elijah said. "If you go back to her—"

"What's the worst that could happen? I've made my choice."

He studied the way the rays of late sunlight sent sparks of gold into her eyes and gilded her pale skin. Lily knew the Bible back to front. She'd heard a thousand sermons. But she was a baby in Christ. The woman had no idea of the power of sin to grip a struggling believer, tangle his feet, and try to drag him down. It was true—Lily had made her choice. But Elijah knew from his own experience that the chosen were subject to the devil's sneakiest attacks.

"I'll go talk to that fellow from the Crescent Moon myself," he said. "He's a businessman. He'll understand the town's need to stick to the job of rebuilding. Maybe he'll call off his wolves."

"You can't go over there, Elijah. Beatrice views you as her personal enemy, and Mr. Gibbons doesn't think highly of you either. You ran off his saloon customers, he figures, so why shouldn't he run off your congregation? There's nothing the two of them would like better than to keep the church from going up again."

"We haven't done anything to them."

"They're afraid your preaching will turn the town against the opera house." She shook her head. "I learned a few things in my time with the traveling show, Elijah. Places like the opera house depend on a town's support. They'll rely on the mercantile for mail and supplies. They'll use the local farmers to supply their restaurant with fresh vegetables and butter. They'll hire women from town to clean and cook. In order to function, they need Hope."

"Well, Hope doesn't need them." He tossed down his hammer. "And they're not going to drive me out of town. I'm here to stay."

The lines of worry between Lily's eyes softened. "Is this the same Elijah Book who was on his way to China?"

"I'll go to China if that's where God sends me. But right now he's sent me to Hope. A shepherd protects his flock, Lily. I'm going to talk to George Gibbons."

"Well, if it ain't the preacher!" The group of five Topeka men swaggered up to the church. Their leader, a fellow in a filthy homespun shirt and a pair of ragged denim trousers, stepped forward. "And there's Miss Lily herself. The flower of the frontier. I do believe you read my palm back in Topeka, Miss Lily. You told me the two of us was gonna have a fine time one of these nights."

"Listen here, buster." Elijah nudged Lily behind him and moved toward the intruder. "I won't have you talk that way to Mrs. Nolan."

"What claim you got on the lady, Preacher?"

"She's a citizen of this town and a member of my congregation. You stand back from her, you hear me?"

"Aw, don't you wanna shake your skirts at me, Miss Lily?" the man said, leering over Elijah's shoulder. "Come on, gal. Let's have us a little dance the way we did back in Topeka."

"Leave the lass be!" Jimmy O'Toole shouted, lifting his rifle as he walked toward the five men. "We don't want your kind of rabble comin' around our town. And you shan't be actin' disrespectful to our ladies."

"Nothin' wrong with a little dancin', is there, Irish?" The man began to sway his hips and wave a half-empty whisky bottle around. His companions laughed and elbowed each other. "Me and Miss Lily's gonna have us a fine time tonight, ain't we, gal? We'll sashay around the town a time or two, maybe stop by the saloon for a sip, and then I'm gonna give you a great big smooch!"

"You better take that back," Elijah growled, grabbing the man by his collar. "Take it back. *Now!*"

As Elijah jerked the man half off his feet, the man's Topeka cohorts drew their six-shooters. The gathering crowd sucked in a collective gasp. Around the circle, Elijah discerned the men who had become his closest friends. Seth Hunter, Jack Cornwall, Rolf Rustemeyer, Jimmy O'Toole, and Ben Hanks—all of them but Jimmy unarmed. He could not let this confrontation turn into a bloodbath, and yet he wouldn't allow anyone to sully Lily's name.

"Set him down, Preacher," another of the Topeka men said, ramming the barrel of his gun into Elijah's side. "Take your hands off'n my cousin, you hear?"

"I'll turn him loose when you fellows put your guns away and head out of town."

"You turn him loose before I blow your guts to glory."

"Elijah, please," Lily said, laying a hand on his arm. "Let me speak to them."

"Stay back, Lily. Rolf, take her out of here."

"No!" she cried as the big German farmer reached for her. "Elijah, please let go of that man. What do you boys want, anyhow? I've already told Beatrice I'm staying here in town to earn my pay. I'm not going to sing for her."

Elijah slowly released the fellow's collar as Lily pushed her way to the center of the crowd. Giving his neck a vigorous rub, the man spat a gob of tobacco juice at Elijah's feet. Then he straightened his shirt and faced Lily.

"Mrs. B says you don't belong with these folks," he told Lily. "She says they've bamboozled you into joinin' them and givin' up your true friends and your callin' as a opera singer. That preacher done suckered you in by gettin' you attached to his baby. Now you're as stuck as you were back in Philadelphia. Mrs. B told us to come down here and remind you of all the fun you're missin'—and all the money."

He took a leather pouch from his back pocket and shook it in her face. The jingle of coins told the crowd he meant what he was saying. Giving his pals a smirk of victory, he pulled a silver dollar from the pouch.

"There's good wages to be had over to the opera house," he told the crowd. "Don't you folks want to get out of the sun? Don't you want to put your plows away for good? We got all kinds of work to be done and steady pay for anybody who'll do his job. Ain't that right, boys?"

The other men let out a roar of agreement, lifting their liquor bottles and stomping their feet. "We're gonna open up for business tomorrow night," their leader shouted. "How many of you want to join us? Come on, Miss Lily, you be the first to step forward. Show these folks you know how to live!"

Elijah clenched his fists in anger as Lily lifted her hands for silence in the midst of the gathering. *Lord, don't let them take her. Protect her, Father! Protect her now!*

"I'm sure you boys have big plans," she said, her voice taking on the worldly bravado Elijah had heard so many times before. "Sounds good, doesn't it, everybody? Big, fat purses filled with coins. Easy work. Cheap liquor. Lots of fun."

"That's right, Miss Lily!" the Topeka man said. "You tell 'em."

"I've been there before. I've done that kind of work, and I'll tell you gentlemen exactly what it's like." She looked into the eyes of each farmer standing around her. "It's sleeping all day and staying awake all night—long, cold, lonely nights. It's a full stomach but an empty heart. It's footloose and fancy-free—but no home to call your own. No family. No true friends. If you want to give up your dreams, your hopes, your very future, join these fellows over at the opera house. But if you want peace, comfort, and an eternal home, you'd better stay with Brother Elijah, this church you're building, and the town of Hope. As for me, boys, I've already made my choice."

Without meeting the preacher's eyes again, she turned and walked back through the crowd toward the Hankses' little house. Eva joined her, and then Caitrin, Rosie, Sheena, and Lucy followed. Elijah's heart swelled as he watched the women of Hope stand united against the opera house.

Spotting the stump of a tree the cyclone had blown down, Elijah jumped up onto it. "Hear the Word of the Lord," he called. "'Thou shalt love the Lord thy God with all thine heart, and with all thy soul, and with all thy might.' If you love God, you'll keep his commandments, gentlemen! I tell you today, that opera house down the road stands as an enemy of the Lord. I've kept silent until now, but if I keep silent any longer, the stones will cry out."

Allowing the Word of truth to pour out of him, Elijah watched the Topeka men laugh among themselves as they walked off down the road. But the others in the group gathered closer, and he could feel the strong rod of the Shepherd moving through him to draw the flock into the fold.

"A saloon," he said, "is a place with a wicked purpose. I know, because I've spent a lot of time in saloons from Missouri to California and back again. A saloon has three aims. To get you drunk, to help you gamble away your money, and to make you lust after women. Not only does that opera house have a saloon, gentlemen, but they're bringing in women!"

"Lord, have mercy!" old Hubert cried out, his eyes shooting wide open in shock. "Did you hear that, Simeon?"

"That opera house is really a brothel," Elijah told the crowd. "It'll lure the men traveling down our honest roads, and it'll try to lure you fellows, too. The Lord makes plain his commandments about fallen women. 'Let not thine heart decline to her way,' he says, 'go not astray in her paths. For she hath cast down many wounded: yea, many strong men have been slain by her. Her house is the way to hell, going down to the chambers of death.'"

"Amen, Brother Elijah!" Simeon cried.

"Preach the Word of God," Jimmy O'Toole hollered, firing his rifle into the air. "Let's tear down that house of wickedness! Let's drive the sinners out of our midst!"

"'Vengeance is mine, saith the Lord,'" Elijah countered, recognizing the mood of the restless crowd. These men had labored in the baking sun for three days to rebuild the town of Hope. With the opera house looming as a threat to their hard work, there was no telling what they might do to destroy it.

"The best thing you men can do to stop that place from taking root here in Hope," he told them, "is to steer clear of it. Don't set one foot inside those doors. Don't sell those folks your crops. Don't let your women clean and cook for them. Keep yourselves pure and holy before the Lord, fellows, and he'll drive that place out of our—"

A cry from the Hanks house drew the instant focus of the men. Caitrin Cornwall raced out the front door, followed by Sheena O'Toole and Eva Hanks. "Brother Elijah!" Sheena cried. "Sure you must come at once!"

"Where's Lily?" He leapt down from the stump and began to push his way through the crowd.

"She's inside," Caitrin called. "'Tis not her; 'tis the baby! Your baby is gone, Brother Elijah! Sure he's been taken clean away."

Lily lay crumpled at the foot of the cradle, fighting the nausea that had swept over her.

"Lily, what in tarnation is going on?" Elijah dropped to his knees beside her. "Where's Sam?"

"I don't know!" She took his sleeves in her fists. "He was alone for only a few minutes—"

"It's my fault!" Eva wailed. "I left the baby to go watch the opera house men feudin' with the farmers over by the church. I wanted to make sure my Ben didn't get himself into a fix. When all us women came back to the house, we were so busy talkin', we didn't notice for a minute. And then Lily saw the cradle. Mercy, Lord, someone took that child!"

As Eva wept, the other women tried to console her. Lily lifted the blankets and pressed her hand on the soft warm spot where the child had lain. Abigail's little bed had been warm in the minutes after her death. Another child. Another loss. The image of her baby's face drifted into focus, blended with her memory of Samuel's precious smile, and dissolved into tears of disbelief.

It was Lily's fault. She had insisted on helping with the cleanup in town. She had left Eva in charge of Sam, when the baby was truly her own responsibility.

"Oh, Elijah," she said, "I'm so sorry."

"Did an animal drag him off?" He ripped the blankets out of the cradle. "I don't see blood."

"Perhaps 'twas was one of the wild dogs that were in Jimmy's smokehouse after the cyclone," Caitrin cried. "Sure those wicked creatures have been wandering about for three days looking mean and hungry."

Letting out a strangled cry, Lily jumped to her feet and ran to the open back door of the house. "Elijah, you've got to go looking for those dogs!" She grabbed the door frame. "Take Jimmy's rifle. You have to find Samuel."

"I don't think it was a dog," Rose Hunter said. "Stubby's been right here in town all day, and he'd have barked if he caught wind of any strays. I think a person took the baby."

"Who would take him?" Elijah demanded. "Sam's *my* baby. He belongs to me."

"There've been so many strangers in town," Rosie said. "Maybe there's a husband and wife who've been trying to have a child of their own—"

"What about that peddler who came through selling pots and pans this morning?" someone asked.

"I think it was those opera-house ruffians. I'll bet they took the baby for spite."

"Somebody ought to go look for them stray dogs."

"Maybe it was a coyote."

As the crowd around the Hanks house grew louder and more restless, Lily searched the room for Elijah. They had nearly lost Sam once before. With God's grace the baby had pulled through his illness.

God help us!

Head and shoulders over most of the men in the room, the preacher caught her eye. They communicated in silence for a moment, and Lily felt sure she knew the direction of his thoughts. Who would take Samuel away? Who would be so wicked, so heartless, so cruel?

Without speaking, she walked through the back door as he headed out the front. They met in the yard, and he took her hand. As one, they began to run—out into the yard, down the rutted street, past the half-built church and the mercantile with its new glass windows, and alongside the grove of cottonwood trees.

"Why?" Lily gasped as the opera house came into view. "Elijah, why would she take him?"

"I don't know," he said. "But I aim to find out. That boy is my son. If she's hurt him—"

"She wouldn't do that. Bea's confused, but she's not wicked." Even as she spoke the words, Lily doubted them herself. Beatrice had chosen a path that took her in direct opposition to Christ and his commands. Not so many weeks ago, she had been willing to peddle a useless potion as a healing elixir. She had admitted to making up fortunes and inventing readings from her crystal ball.

Now she had cast herself, body and soul, into the arms of a married man—a conniver willing to lure the unwary with liquor and fallen women. One step down the wrong road had led to another and then another. Lily wondered if Beatrice would stop at anything.

"Let me speak to the woman," Lily said, grabbing Elijah's arm. "I can reason with her."

"I don't trust her. There's no telling what she'll do." His blue eyes bored into her face. "I'm going in alone."

"We'll go together."

"It might be a trap, Lily. She might have taken Sam to lure you over here."

"Or you."

Lily clutched his hands and knew, no matter what the consequences, she was going in after Samuel. He was Elijah's child in name, but he was hers in heart. She had fed and nurtured him, and she treasured the baby as her own.

"I'm not his mother," she said in a low, firm voice, "but I won't let anything happen to Samuel, Elijah. I love him."

"Stay close to me, Lily," he said as he started toward the steps of the opera house.

Climbing onto the shady porch, Lily realized that Elijah couldn't protect her. He was unarmed and outnumbered. But he would do all he could to keep her safe. She could trust him. She could rely on him.

"Well, if it ain't the preacher!" The front door flew open, and the leader of the men who had come to town earlier stepped outside. "You finished up that fancy sermon you was dishin' out, I see. And you brung Miss Lily. Did you come to take me up on my offer of a dance, darlin'?"

"I think you have my son here, buster." Elijah jammed a finger into the man's chest. "I want him back."

"Your son?" A grin crept across the fellow's face, revealing rotted teeth. "I don't believe so."

"Somebody from your camp took my baby while you and your

cronies were causing trouble at the church. Now hand him over before I fetch the law."

"The law?" The man laughed. "Well, ain't that a how-de-do? Come on in here, Preacher, and let me introduce you to the law."

"Don't go," Lily whispered. "It's a trick."

"Bring the baby out here, and we'll settle things up," Elijah said.

"What baby are you talkin' about?"

At that moment, Samuel's distinctive cry drifted through the open window of the opera house. Lily caught her breath and dashed past the man into a cavernous foyer trimmed in flocked red wallpaper and hung with gilt chandeliers. "Sam!" she called.

"Lily!" Elijah was at her side in an instant. "Where is he?"

"Sam?"

Again the baby's hungry wail sounded faintly. Lily pointed to a heavy pocket door. Elijah stepped toward it and forced the two sliding panels apart. As they burst into the room, the group gathered there on tufted settees rose as one.

Lily stopped, her heartbeat hammering in her ears.

Beatrice Waldowski and George Gibbons stood beside a massive fireplace. On one side of the room, a crude wooden box held the sobbing baby. Across the thick Oriental carpet stood a short fellow wearing a sweat-stained Stetson and the silver badge of a deputy. Beside him, a giant of a man straightened to his full height, his diamond tie pin and dark frock coat bearing testimony to wealth and importance.

"Lily," the giant said.

Though her every instinct ordered her to rush to the baby, Lily could not make her limbs move. Her blood sank to her knees, and her mouth went dry. Sucking in a breath, she managed one word.

"Father."

CHAPTER 15

"REVEREND Book, I assume?" The imposing gentleman stepped forward and extended his hand to Elijah. "You must be the minister of the church in Hope."

"That's right," Elijah said, giving the man's hand a single, quick shake. "And that's my son over there. I don't know how Samuel came to be in this place, but I'm taking him home now."

"Not so fast, Preacher." The sheriff's deputy placed himself between Elijah and the box in which Samuel lay crying. "We had a report in the Topeka office that you found the baby in Indian territory."

"Who sent in that report?" Eli demanded.

The deputy glanced across the room. "Mrs. Waldowski told us about the incident."

"I figured. Listen, mister, I've never kept anything about Samuel a secret. I found the baby when I was passing through Osage land down south. His parents' wagon had been shot full of arrows, and his pa was dead. Right before she died, his mama handed her son over to me and asked me to take care of him. I promised her I would, and that's what I've been doing ever since."

"Do you have any legal papers to show you've adopted the boy, Reverend?"

"Of course I don't. His parents weren't in any shape to sign him over to me."

"All the same, we've got ways of doing things around here. An abandoned baby doesn't just belong to the first fellow that picks him up."

"Well, who does he belong to?"

"The state of Kansas."

"But his mother gave him to me."

"Do you have any witnesses to that?"

Elijah felt like he was about to explode. "My horse."

With a scowl, the deputy scratched the back of his neck. "I guess you noticed that baby's not all white, Reverend Book. He's got some black or Indian blood in him. Maybe Mexican."

"His blood is red, same as yours and mine, Deputy. Now, if you'd please step aside, I'll see to it that he's given some food and put back into his own cradle where he belongs."

"Is this your wife?" The deputy gestured at Lily.

"No, she's not."

"That's a relief." The tall gentleman gave a benign smile as he addressed the deputy. "This young woman, good sir, is my daughter. Lily, what a surprise to find you here. Your mother and I are very grateful to Mrs. Waldowski for alerting us to your whereabouts."

Lily cast a withering glance at Beatrice before facing her father. "If you gentlemen will excuse me," she said with the barest trace of a tremble in her voice, "I need to tend to the baby."

"I'm sorry, ma'am, but I can't allow you to take the child out of my sight," the deputy said. "He's a ward of the state, and I'm going to have to take him with me back to the state-run orphanage in Topeka."

"Now just a cotton-picking minute—," Elijah began.

"Shall I nurse the child in full view of the public then, sir?" Lily cut in.

"Nurse him?" the deputy and Lily's father said at the same time.

"You don't think he's old enough for meat and potatoes, do

you?" She swallowed hard as she walked between the two men. When she lifted the baby, his sobbing began to quiet. "Come on, Samuel, sweetheart," she murmured. "Are you a hungry boy? Wet, too! Oh, poor little fellow."

Turning, she gave the deputy a hard stare. "This baby is in good hands, sir. Better hands than he would be in at an orphanage in Topeka. I'll go and feed the pastor's son now, and when I come back, I trust you'll have seen reason."

As the deputy and her father stood silent, Lily carried the baby out the parlor door. When Elijah turned to follow her, the lawman spoke up.

"You'd better stay here, Reverend. We've got some talking to do."

Elijah took a hard-backed chair as near the door as he could. He felt outnumbered, and that made him uncomfortable. But more than that, he sensed that, although God's presence was inside him, the Spirit was not in this room. An oppressive heaviness hung in the air, sitting on his chest and weighing down his heart. He leaned forward and rested his elbows on his knees.

"Look, what is it you want from me, Deputy?" he asked. "You know I'm a man of God. There are plenty of folks in town who'll testify to my calling as a preacher. I took the baby out of kindness to his dead mother, and I've grown to care about the boy. I'll do whatever I need to do to make him legally mine."

"A warm and godly expression," Lily's father cut in, flipping back his coattails as he sat down on the settee. "You, sir, are a man of righteous intent and pious purpose. I therefore appeal to your reason in the matters at hand. First and foremost, the child's welfare must be addressed. Second, my daughter's future is of great interest to me."

Elijah studied the man's blue eyes, reminiscent of Lily's, yet somehow devoid of the life and spirit that sparkled in hers. So this was the father who had beaten his child black and blue. This was the man who had broken his little girl's ribs and arm. This was the great, respected conductor of the Greater New England Symphony Orchestra—a man in control of everything but his own temper.

"Dr. Richardson has come all the way from back East to fetch his daughter," the deputy said. "And I'm here to take the baby to Topeka. The way I see it, that settles both problems."

"I don't think so," Elijah countered. "Lily has been nursing and tending to Samuel for a long time now. The baby had a rough start in life, and he's still not as strong as he ought to be. If you take him off to Topeka, Deputy, he might die. Does the state of Kansas want to be responsible for the death of an innocent baby?"

"How can we be sure the kid doesn't have relatives on the Osage reservation?" the deputy asked. "It's clear he's part colored. Maybe he's got an Indian grandma or something."

"His folks were dirt farmers," Elijah explained. "They were passing through the reservation."

"How do you know?"

"They were in a wagon filled with belongings—plows and seed and rocking chairs. Look, Deputy, can't you go through your records and search for an account of somebody finding the wagon? I can tell you exactly where it was. That ought to prove me out. I buried the bodies right there by the side of the road."

"Well, I reckon—"

"They were a couple of folks heading west to start a new life—just like thousands of others—when they ran into trouble with some renegade Osage. The wife was Indian, maybe, or Mexican, or even Italian. I don't know, and I don't care. All I do know is, she begged me to take Samuel and raise him up in the Lord. And that's what I intend to do." He turned to Richardson. "As for your daughter, sir, it looks to me like Lily's made up her own mind about her future. She lives with a good family in town, she's got work to do, and she's happy."

"Happy?" Richardson straightened his tie. "Reverend Book, you tell us you care for that baby you found by the roadside. Do you have any *idea* the depth of love a mother and a father have for their natural-born daughter? When Lily vanished from our home, her mother became hysterical. She was inconsolable."

"I'm sorry to hear that, sir. I'm sure Lily didn't mean to upset her mother."

"For more than a year now, we've been forced to accept the conclusion that our only child might be dead," the man went on. "And suddenly, a miracle is sent from heaven! Mrs. Waldowski writes us a letter, informing us that our Lily lives! Though you tell me she is happy, Reverend Book, I cannot accept your judgment. Clearly my daughter is not well. That she would willingly leave our home, the tender care of her mother, a future of comfort and security, illustrates the fragile condition of her mind."

"There's nothing wrong with your daughter's mind," Elijah said.

"But I've been given to understand from Mrs. Waldowski that our Lily has been living with a traveling show, roaming about aimlessly, surviving in the direst of circumstances. I want you to know, this young lady received the finest education money can buy! She is trained in the fine arts of womanly decorum. She has been prepared for a life in the highest echelon of society. And you tell me she chooses to live in abject poverty? Of course she's gone mad!"

Elijah felt like his drawers were crawling right up his back. Lily Nolan wasn't crazy. She'd chosen to run from this very man who claimed to have given her a happy life but in reality had tormented her with his abuses. Everything in Elijah told him to spill the beans on the pompous Dr. Richardson. But why would the deputy trust the word of a down-home preacher with a foundling baby over that of the conductor of the Greater New England Symphony Orchestra—a man with a diamond stuck through his tie?

"Your daughter, sir," Elijah addressed Richardson, "is not only sound of mind, but she's shown herself to be a respectable citizen of Hope. Any number of folks will tell you how she's helped out the Hanks family, taken good care of my son, and even pitched in to rebuild the town after a cyclone hit us. But you ought to let Lily speak for herself. She can tell you what she wants to do with her life."

"My dear man," Richardson said, his mouth pulling into an expression of disbelief, "you of all people should understand a woman's place of submission in Christian society. Surely you've read the scriptural admonition that woman may not be allowed to 'usurp authority over the man, but to be in silence.' I trust you've been trained in a detailed explication of the Bible, and you are aware that the apostle Paul taught the Corinthian church that 'the head of the woman is the man' and that 'it is not permitted unto them to speak; but they are commanded to be under obedience, as also saith the law.'"

Elijah twiddled his thumbs. Well, he'd read the Bible through a few times, but he didn't exactly recall those particular verses. Truth to tell, he'd gotten the impression that Christ loved women as much as men, and that a godly woman could fulfill an important role in the church. Wasn't there somebody named Priscilla who helped her husband hold worship services in their home? And then there was a lady named Lydia—

"You *have* studied at a seminary, have you not?" Richardson asked.

The preacher shifted uncomfortably. "No, sir."

"Then what makes you think you're qualified to preach the gospel?"

"I heard the voice of the Lord calling me to tell other folks about him, so I got on my horse, and I went out and did it."

A triumphant look crossed the conductor's face. "Upon my word, young man, you are completely ignorant! You have no formal training, no religious education, and no experience in matters of family instruction or spiritual guidance—and yet you proclaim yourself a minister of God's Holy Word! You have had the effrontery to place yourself in a position of leadership over the church of Jesus Christ in Hope, Kansas! I am astonished."

Elijah felt about as low as a snake and twice as dumb. The man was right, of course. Elijah had no business pastoring a church or giving anybody advice.

"Young man, you must get yourself to a seminary before the week is out." Richardson adjusted his diamond tie tack. "I cannot, in good conscience, endorse your presence among the people of this warm and earnest little town. Do you not recall the words of St. Paul to young Timothy? 'Give attendance to reading, to exhortation, to doctrine. . . . Take heed unto thyself, and unto the doctrine; continue in them: for in doing this thou shalt both save thyself, and them that hear thee.'"

"I have been reading the Bible, sir, every day. And I'm studying it as well as I can."

"Your sincerity impresses me. In fact, I am quite willing to write a letter of recommendation on your behalf to the dean of the institution of higher learning to which you aspire. I shall personally address myself to this matter in order that your future education is assured. I am well acquainted with the presidents of various venues of religious instruction, and I shall provide you with a list of recommended schools. You strike me as a man of untrained but sincere caliber. An education will transform you into the model of a minister."

With a nod, he indicated that the subject was closed. Feeling about like he had the night the twister hit Hope, Elijah studied a pair of sparrows building a nest under an eave of the new opera house. Dr. Richardson was right that he didn't know much about pastoring. He was uneducated, too. But he wasn't ignorant. Elijah knew his Savior. And he knew that God had promised to keep his eye on Lily and Sam—just like he was keeping watch over those sparrows.

"As for the foundling child," Richardson went on, "it is

abundantly clear that his future lies in the competent hands of the state of Kansas. Do you not recall the admonition of the Lord to Jeremiah the prophet? 'Leave thy fatherless children,' he warns, 'I will preserve them alive.' It is God's work—not yours, Reverend Book—to provide for the orphan. An unmarried, uneducated man in need of schooling cannot hope to rear a helpless baby. The child must be placed in the good hands of the orphanage."

"I reckon you're right," the deputy chimed in. "Although I've got to tell you—"

"My daughter, of course, will return to Philadelphia with me on the next train from Topeka." Dr. Richardson rose and straightened the tails of his coat. "Obviously her mother and I must attend to the immediate repair of her mental condition and the reconstruction of her reputation. Following that, we shall see that Lily is secured in the good marriage and societal position for which we prepared her."

Elijah stood. Though he knew his boots were on solid ground, he felt a little off-kilter. Richardson was obviously a man who knew God, knew the Bible, and knew the right way of doing things. Educated and wealthy, he cited Scripture as though there could be no arguing. And why would Elijah argue with the Word of the Lord, anyway? But for some reason, the whole thing didn't sit straight.

Could a man like Richardson possibly be wrong in what he said? Even lying? Could someone in a position of leadership in a church and in a city really be speaking in error—especially when he backed up everything he said with verses from the Bible?

As the esteemed gentleman made casual conversation with Beatrice Waldowski, George Gibbons, and the deputy, Elijah thought about Lily. Maybe the woman had deceived him about her father. Maybe Dr. Richardson hadn't hurt her at all, but instead she had chosen a willful and rebellious path away from family and Christ. Maybe Elijah didn't have any business pastoring the Hope church. And maybe Samuel would be better off in an orphanage in Topeka.

"I'm assuming you know the place to which my daughter has taken the child," Richardson said as he walked to the parlor door. "Perhaps you would be so good as to lead us there, Mister Book."

Elijah pictured Lily sitting under the big cottonwood tree beside Bluestem Creek. She would be holding Samuel, singing some little lullaby the way she always did, and stroking his soft dark curls. It was under the cottonwood that Lily claimed to have opened her heart to Christ. Elijah had to believe that much was true. With his own two eyes, he had seen the changes in her.

And he knew a few other facts, too. Lily and Samuel belonged together. Lily and Elijah belonged together. Sam was Eli's son. And Christ had joined the three of them. This image in Elijah's mind of the group of people united for a higher purpose seemed true and quite real. Yet Dr. Richardson's words rang powerfully to dismiss it. Elijah must go to a seminary, the baby to an orphanage, Lily to Philadelphia. God had ordained their futures.

Unable to see clearly, unable to sort through the whirlwind in his mind, Elijah headed into the foyer of the opera house. "I'll fetch your daughter, Dr. Richardson," he said.

"I don't think it would be wise for you to go alone. 'Be sober, be vigilant,' young man, 'because your adversary the devil, as a roaring lion, walketh about, seeking whom he may devour.'"

Eli stopped, frustration rising to the point of anger inside him. "Now what's that supposed to mean?"

"Ah, ignorance! Ah, bliss!" The conductor clapped him on the back. "How easily you fall prey to the limitations of your own fallible mind. I am telling you that you must stay away from my daughter at this vulnerable time in your life. The powers of the seductress are great, and you—like most men—are hard-pressed to resist them. Come, we'll all seek out my Lily as one party. Deputy, will you join us?"

The lawman was chewing on a wad of tobacco as he studied the inside of the opera house. When Richardson addressed him, he focused again on the matter at hand and nodded his acquiescence. The three men stepped outside, followed by Beatrice and her cohorts, and they all set out for the grove.

With every step Elijah took down the road toward the cottonwood tree, the noose tightened around his neck. If he let Lily go with Dr. Richardson, would she find the happiness God had planned for her, as her father insisted? Or would she fall victim to a man who had no control over himself? At this moment, Dr. Richardson was in control not only of himself but of the whole situation.

And what if Elijah let the deputy take Samuel away? Would the baby really live a better life in an orphanage than in the home of a man who loved him as a son? Of course, love didn't make up for ignorance and inexperience. Eli knew he possessed both of those in abundance.

And what if Eli left the town of Hope and headed east to get himself an education? Would he be turning his back on the call to shepherd that little flock? Or would he be freeing the people of Hope to find themselves a minister who really could meet all their needs?

"There she is," Beatrice Waldowski said. "There's Lil, hiding behind that old tree."

Her voice jerked Eli right out of the cyclone and set him on his feet. The noose around his neck loosened. A peace that passed all understanding filled his heart.

"I'll talk to Lily," he said.

"*I'll* fetch her," Bea insisted.

Eli grabbed the woman's arm. "She left you, Madame Zahara. She chose a new life."

"I suppose you think that means she chose *you*."

"She chose Jesus Christ."

"Oh, please. Lily's as naive and stupid as that baby she's so attached to. She couldn't make a decision on her own if her life depended on it. You tricked her into leaving me. You seduced her away from a good future—"

"In your brothel? I don't think so, Beatrice. Lily doesn't need you, me, or her father. Truth be told, she's given her future to someone she can really count on."

"What's this about a brothel?" the deputy asked.

"Lily!" Beatrice called. "You can come out of hiding now, little girl. Daddy's come for you."

Before anyone else could move, Eli took off through the grove of trees to the place where Lily sat nursing Samuel. As he approached, she tugged her white shawl over the baby's head and looked up at the man, her blue eyes clouded with uncertainty.

Eli hunkered down beside the two of them and let out a breath. This was where he belonged. Right here with Lily and Sam.

"How's my little Nubbin?" he asked, touching one of the baby's bare pink toes.

Lily managed a smile. "He's asleep."

"And how's my Lily?"

"Oh, Elijah!" She leaned her head on his shoulder, and he drew her into his embrace. "I can't believe my father came all this way."

"I can. He's determined."

"Determined to take me back to Philadelphia." She shook her head. "There was a time when I believed I should go home. I knew my life with the traveling show was taking me nowhere. At least in Philadelphia I would have food to eat and a roof over my head. I'd lived so many years under my father's thumb, and I figured I could do it again."

"He wants to take you back today."

"I know."

"He's going to recommend me to a seminary so I can learn how to be a pastor."

"I see."

"He says Sam would be better off in an orphanage."

"Since you'll be in school, and I'll be in Philadelphia."

"That's right." Eli cupped the baby's tiny foot in his palm and stroked his thumb across the puff of soft skin. "He says it's all God's will."

"I'm sure he backed up his position with Scripture."

"Yep." He met Lily's blue eyes. "Your father sure does know the Bible."

"So did I," she said. "Before."

"I remember."

"But I didn't know *him*. I didn't know Christ."

Eli thought for a moment. "You reckon somebody could twist Scripture around? I mean, could a man take verses right out of the Bible and use God's Holy Word for wrong reasons?"

"I was very good at it."

"But a fellow who claims to be a Christian . . . claims to believe in Jesus . . . claims to serve him. Could he be lying?"

Lily lifted the baby away and tucked the shawl around him like a blanket. Elijah leaned over her and kissed Sam's pink cheek. Without speaking, Lily laid the baby in his arms. As Eli gazed down at the pair of long-lashed eyelids, the soft nub of a nose, the tiny rosebud lips, a certainty filled his soul.

"'Ye shall know them by their fruits,'" he said in a low voice. He had read the verses that morning, and he'd been working all day to memorize them. "'Every good tree bringeth forth good fruit; but a corrupt tree bringeth forth evil fruit.' Evil fruit. A corrupt tree. 'Beware of false prophets, which come to you in sheep's clothing, but inwardly they are ravening wolves.'"

The verses had slipped unbidden into his mind, but Eli knew who had put them there. Though the Pharisees had appeared holy, Jesus had called them serpents, a generation of vipers.

Yes, it was possible for a man to clothe himself in the sheep's wool of Christ's flock. But in reality, he could be a wolf, a serpent, a predator, distorting truth and preying on the tender lambs. Possible. But was Dr. Richardson a sheep or a wolf? A lamb or a viper?

By their fruits, a small voice whispered to Eli. *By their fruits . . .*

"You've got to go face your father," he told Lily. "You have to talk to him."

She nodded. "I know, but . . . Elijah, would you pray with me first? I need you as my pastor. I need your help."

"I'm right here beside you." He took her hand and bowed his head. "Father, we've got trouble. Lily and I . . . we love Sam, and we believe you gave him to us. We ask you to watch over the little fellow and put him where he needs to be so he can grow up right. As for Lily, Lord, she's your daughter. She belongs to you more than she ever belonged to Dr. Richardson. Please protect her."

"Amen," Lily whispered.

"Listen to me, darlin'," Eli said as they stood. "I won't make your choices for you, and I won't go against God's plan for your life. But I'll stand beside you. I love you, Lily, and that's the truth."

As he spoke the words, her eyes filled with light and a smile lifted her lips. "I love you, too, Elijah Book," she said softly.

Eli nodded as he tucked Sam's small round head into the curve of his neck and gave his little bottom a pat. Yep. That was the truth.

CHAPTER 16

As LILY walked through the trees to the road, she felt herself shrinking inside. She knew Elijah, cradling Samuel in his arms, walked beside her. But each step forward took her back, further and further into her childhood. She was a little girl again, a willful child who had disobeyed her father. What would he do to her? Where could she run to hide? Who could protect her from the coming storm?

"Lily." His voice assumed that tone of disappointment with which he always began. "Lily, Lily, Lily."

She looked up into his face, into ice blue eyes above the stern mouth. "I'm sorry to have troubled you, Father."

"Indeed." Hands behind his back, thank heaven. "Lily, your mother is awaiting your return. I have engaged the services of a coach and driver, and we shall depart for Topeka at once. I assume there is nothing of value here that you wish to retrieve before you go."

Lily studied the tips of her toes. From the corner of her eye, she could see Elijah's scuffed leather boots. Nothing of value? Only the man she loved. Only the child she had come to treasure as her own.

Oh, Father God, is it wrong to disobey my parents? I love Elijah, but I'm so . . . so afraid of this man. Please be with me, Lord.

She lifted her head and spoke. "I'll not be returning to Philadelphia with you, Father. I'm going to stay right here in Hope."

There. She had done it. She steeled herself, drew in her breath, and forced her eyes to meet his. The man's chest swelled. A sneer twisted his mouth.

"I beg your pardon?" he said.

Lily tried to make herself breathe. "I'm staying here," she managed. "I won't go with you."

"You *won't* go with me?"

"No, sir."

"You'd better do as he says, Lil," Beatrice interjected. "He's your father, remember?"

Lily cast a glance at the woman she had once called a friend. "I trusted you, Bea."

"I warned you not to cross me."

"You betrayed me."

She shrugged. "You let me down. I figured if you wouldn't work for me, you might as well go on home to daddy. 'Honour thy father and thy mother,' you know." Smiling smugly, Beatrice swung around. "Come on, boys, let's head back to the opera house. She's going to get exactly what she deserves."

As they walked off down the road, Lily shook her head and turned to the man who had caused her terror, humiliation, torment. *Honour thy father?* she thought. *No, not him. He surrendered his right to wear the name* father.

"I won't go with you," she said. "I'll write a letter to Mother and explain myself. You'll have to go back without me."

"You impudent little fool!" Richardson swung around and addressed the deputy and the preacher. "She presumes to tell me what she'll do. My own daughter refuses to obey me."

It would come now, the black storm. She could feel the pressure building inside her father. First a few raindrops. A slight wind. Then the sky would transform to a sickening green. Hail would begin to fall. And then trees would be ripped from their roots. Barns would topple. Homes would be torn up and dashed to the ground.

"Lily, you will do as I say or suffer the consequences," the thunder rolled. "Are you mad, child? Or are you simply stupid? Can you not see that your life is already settled? I've given you everything. Everything. And you treat me like this? Like I'm nothing? Like I'm dirt under your fingernails?"

"No, sir," she whispered.

"Indeed, you do!" the lightning flashed. "You have the impudence, the absolute gall to dishonor your own father! Ingrate!"

"Now, hold on a minute," Elijah cut in, shifting the baby in his arms.

"You stay out of this, bumpkin." The wind turned, its gale blowing now in a huge circle that encompassed everyone and everything in sight. "You've defiled and dishonored my daughter. You're a disgrace to the calling of the church. What are you? A rube. A rustic. A cowboy."

"No, sir, not any longer. I'm a shepherd, and your daughter is one of my flock."

"Your flock," he snarled, grabbing Lily's arm and jerking her toward him. "This pathetic creature is mine, not yours. She belongs to me, and I'm here to take her back where she belongs. Now, move your feet, Lily. I've had enough of your nonsense."

He pushed her in the direction of the opera house, but she struggled loose. "No," she cried. "I won't do it!"

"You'll obey me, or you'll wish you had."

"I can't obey you."

"Can't?" He drew back his hand, and she ducked, crouching into the fabric of her skirts. "Can't or won't?"

"Stop!" Elijah shouted.

"Can't or won't?" her father bellowed.

Lily covered her head with her arms, and at that very moment, the eye of the storm passed over her. Calm filled her. Security wrapped her in holy arms. She looked up into the red, swollen face hovering over her.

"'The Lord is my light and my salvation,'" she murmured into the storm, "'whom shall I fear? the Lord is the strength of my life; of whom shall I be afraid?'"

"What?" her father roared.

Now the final winds would come, Lily knew. She closed her eyes in readiness. "'Behold, I see the heavens opened, and the Son of man standing on the right hand of God.'"

"Blasphemer!"

"'Lord, lay not this sin to his charge.'"

"Demon! Witch!"

Lily drank down a breath in preparation for the coming blow, but a loud cry startled her. As her eyes flew open, she saw Elijah Book, baby in one arm and the wrath of God on his face, slam a balled fist into her father's face. The huge man toppled backward onto the road and lay in stunned silence. For the space of a breath, Lily thought it was over. The storm was finished. But then the man scrambled to his feet with a bellow of rage.

"I'll kill you!"

"Stay clear of Lily!" Elijah shouted.

"That's enough, men!" The deputy drew his pistol and stepped between the two. As Lily's father came at Elijah, the lawman pivoted and aimed the six-shooter at his heart. "Stop right there, mister, or I'm gonna make wolf meat outta you."

Crouched on the road, Lily could see her father hesitate. "Father, please stop this," she called to him. "It won't work anymore. All these years it's been wrong. You can't win this time. Please, Father. Set me free."

The towering man stood heaving for breath, his shirt stained with sweat and his collar sprung from its buttons. His sledgehammer hands clenched and released, clenched and released. A trickle of blood worked its way down the corner of his mouth.

"By your fruit," Elijah said in a low voice, "by your fruit, Dr. Richardson. The fruit of God's Spirit is love. Look at *your* fruit huddled there on the road. What you see is fear. Anger. Sorrow. Confusion. Torment. The Good Book says that folks who sow fruit like that can't inherit the kingdom of God."

Lily watched her father's face as the storm began to die. The red in his cheeks faded. His lips drooped. His blue eyes lost all expression.

"I can't quote the Bible back to front like you do," Elijah went on, giving the baby on his shoulder a pat, "but I've read all about the fruit of the Spirit. That's *love*. *Joy*. *Peace*. *Gentleness*. Are you gentle, Dr. Richardson?"

When the man didn't speak, Elijah continued. "*Longsuffering*. Near as I can figure, that means patient. Are you a patient man, Dr. Richardson?"

Lily watched her father begin to sag as Elijah went on. "*Meekness*. Christ asks us to be servants, not slave masters. *Temperance*. That means we're supposed to control ourselves."

The preacher paused, and his voice was low when he continued. "Maybe some grown-up whipped you when you were a boy. Or maybe somebody told you it was a father's business to beat on his little daughter. It's not. I'll admit, my daddy popped my tail feathers a few times, but he never really hurt me. He never ground me into the dirt or backed me so far into a corner that I didn't have any choice but to run away, fearing for my life."

Lily's father had covered his face with his hands, and she tried to imagine what he was thinking. Was the storm building inside him again? Would he emerge with his fists raised against Elijah? Would he turn on her? In his uncontrollable wrath, would he force the deputy to shoot him?

"I reckon you owe your daughter an apology, Dr. Richardson," Elijah said. "You think you could settle up your unfinished business before you go on your way?"

Lily held her breath as her father took a step toward her. But when he lowered his hands, she realized that his eyes were rimmed with tears. His lip quivered as he dropped to his knees in the dirt in front of her.

"Lily," he said. "My daughter."

Folding in upon himself, he pressed his face into the road as sobs tore from his chest. With a trembling hand, Lily reached out and laid her hand on the man's head. *This* was her father. Not the great conductor, the imperious musician, the overlord of the Richardson household. His hair damp beneath her fingertips, she traced the curve of his head with her palm.

"Father," she whispered.

"Lily, I hurt you. I know what I did."

"Father." She lifted his shoulders and drew him into her arms. "Papa, my papa."

"Oh, Lily," he wept, "I'm so sorry."

As she clung to him, she looked up into Elijah's face. The pastor held his own child close, his large hands stroking the baby's soft curly hair. "I love you, Father," she said. "I forgive you."

"God, have mercy on me," he groaned. "Have mercy on my soul."

"He does," Elijah said.

"I don't deserve—"

"No, but you'll get it anyhow. That's called grace. Amazing grace." The preacher reached down and took the man's arm. "Dr. Richardson, welcome to Hope."

On the front porch of the Hankses' house, Lily sat in a rocking chair and laid Samuel lengthwise on her lap. As his big brown eyes focused on her face, his mouth broke into a wide grin. With a laugh, she chucked him under the chin. Folds of soft skin testified to his bouncing good health and made Lily think of one of Lucy Cornwall's fresh, doughy cinnamon buns.

"Hello, precious boy," she whispered to him. "How's my little

Samuel this afternoon? Did you have a nice nap? You did! Guess what I've been doing? I've been ironing sheets with Auntie Eva, and I'm so hot."

The baby gurgled in response and gave his tiny feet a kick. Lily clasped his pudgy legs and pumped them up and down as the baby cooed with pleasure. Three days had passed since her father's repentance on the road between the opera house and Hope, and he had chosen to stay on for a few days to help rebuild the town. Though father and daughter didn't speak often, he sometimes came to sit with her on the porch while she nursed the baby.

"Look, here comes that big ol' fellow right now," Lily murmured, spotting Clement Richardson making his way up the street. "Do you want him to hold you today? Shall I ask him if he'd like that?"

She pictured her father's great hands cradling the child. Did she dare allow the man who had hurt her to touch the baby she loved so deeply? Could she trust that he'd changed? Really, truly changed?

"Good afternoon, Lily," her father said, stepping up onto the porch. "Rather hot, don't you think?"

Lily began to rock a little, swaying the baby back and forth. She wished she could get past feeling uneasy around the man, but she'd spent too many years in fear. "Yes, it's quite warm today," she said. "I've been ironing sheets with Eva on the back porch."

Her father took the chair beside her, removed his hat, and mopped his brow with a monogrammed white handkerchief. "It must be difficult for you," he said. "You once led such a pampered life. Now you're reduced to pressing sheets as though you were a slave woman yourself."

Lily swallowed. "Eva's not a slave, Father. She's my good friend. I'm happy to work at her side."

"Of course, of course. I meant no ill will in my comment." He leaned back in the chair. "Lily, I've been trying to decide how to speak with you. Nothing is simple anymore. I don't know what to tell you of my deepest thoughts. I'm not sure which tone to take with you. But I do know that matters must be addressed. We must talk about the past and the future."

"I prefer the present, Father. I'm happy here."

"Are you?" His face showed the hint of a scowl. "You were brought up with art and music, with gardens and servants, with beautiful gowns and parties every weekend. Now you wash and iron, you cook three meals a day, and you tend that . . . that baby."

"I told you why I care for Samuel, Father."

"Yes, yes." He shook his head. "I'm sorry to be brusque. This is difficult. All of it. I find it so . . . impossible . . . to imagine my daughter, my own flesh and blood, wandering about with that woman, that Beatrice Waldowski. To think that you actually married a stranger in order to escape your home. . . . Well, I find myself both humiliated and enraged by the entire episode. That you bore a child, my grandchild—"

"Abigail."

"Please don't speak the name. I blame myself."

"No, Father—"

"Yes, I do. I am responsible. And yet I am also determined to make amends. To God, to your mother. To you, Lily. I must try to repair my errors in your upbringing. I must atone for my wrongs."

"Wrongs can be forgiven, Father. I've chosen to put my own past behind me and look ahead to a new day. I'm certain that the Lord has a good plan for my life—and for yours. He is a God of great mercy. When I look at all he's done for me in these past months, I am almost dumbfounded. All this time he's been leading me toward him, waiting for me to open the door and let him into my heart. In spite of everything I did, all the wrong choices, all the willful and irresponsible actions I took, God brought Samuel into my life, and he gave me this home, this town, and Elijah."

"The preacher is a good man, Lily." Her father paused for a moment, as if turning over in his mind the novelty of the man who had led him to the brink of repentance. "I'm thankful that Reverend Book wants to further his education," Richardson went on. "Though he is a bit rough around the edges now, I can envision him in a large church one day. He's good with people. He has intelligence. And he has a way with words."

"Yes," she said softly. The fact that her father admired Elijah pleased Lily. For three days she had pondered her last conversation with the preacher under the cottonwood tree. *"I love you,"* he had said. But what did those words mean to him? Was his affection that of a pastor for one of his flock, or had Lily come to mean something more to Elijah?

"He cares for the townspeople here," her father was saying. "And perhaps he should stay on in Hope for a time. Practical experience is never a bad thing."

"Hope would be poorer for losing him."

"Indeed." He rocked for a moment. "As for you, Lily, I know your mother will be heartbroken should I return to Philadelphia without you. I cannot describe the depths of her agony at your disappearance."

"I'm sorry. Truly I am."

"Then you'll come with me? I've kept the coachman waiting as long as I can. I'm afraid I must leave tomorrow."

Lily lifted her focus to the church. She could see Elijah hammering board-and-batten siding with some of the other men. The deputy, who had stayed on to help with the rebuilding, was handing him nails.

"I can't leave Samuel," Lily said. "Elijah and I . . . we almost lost him once before, Father. He was bitten by a spider. And you know he was terribly weak when Elijah brought him to—"

"The baby will be going to an orphanage tomorrow, Lily." Her father laid his hand on hers. "The deputy has confided in me that he intends to take the child. Without legal grounds for adoption, with no information on the baby's parentage, with no wife or home, the preacher cannot hope to obtain permission to keep an orphan. Everyone knows that you and Reverend Book have become attached to the child, but Lily, you must think in a reasonable manner. This baby needs a stable situation."

"But I—"

"The longer you remain in the picture, Lily, the easier you make it for the preacher to keep the boy around. But for how long? And to what end? This child in your lap is a human being, Lily. Samuel shouldn't be shuffled from one adult to another—neither of whom is truly his guardian. And look at these living conditions! You live with the Hanks family, while Reverend Book resides on a cot in the back of the church. Neither place is suitable for the rearing of a child."

"Father, I'm sure Elijah plans to—"

"Even should there be a proper home one day, Lily, you know that this town has no school, no physician, none of the amenities of polite society. . . . My dear, please set your emotions aside and allow the child to have a chance at security. Come with me to Philadelphia, to your mother. Allow the deputy to take the baby to Topeka. And permit God to have full use of his instrument in this town. Elijah Book must be set free to grow into the man God intends. Only you can see that such a thing happens."

Lily ran her fingertip over the baby's tiny knuckles. Soft, velvety bumps. But this baby didn't belong to her. Sam was not Abby's replacement. He was a child of God, rescued by Elijah, and deserving of a good future. Maybe her father was right. But, oh, how could she part with this child she loved so much?

And how could she leave Hope?

No, it wasn't the town so much as it was the preacher. Elijah Book. She loved him. She couldn't walk away from him. Her heart would break in two.

But what if she and Samuel truly were hindrances to God's plan for Elijah? What if they kept him from doing the work he was intended to do? What if Elijah would be better off without them?

"Lily," her father said, patting her hand gently. "Will you come home with me? Will you restore joy to your mother's face? Most important, will you allow me to become to you the father I never was? It would be a gift greater than anything I have ever received."

Lily gathered Sam into her arms and held him close, fighting the cry that rose up inside her. *No, no!* she wanted to shout. *I want to stay here. I want Elijah. I want this baby. I want my way—my way!*

"Oh, Lily," her father murmured. "Say you'll come home."

"Nevertheless not my will, but thine . . ."

Blinking back the tears that misted her vision, Lily nodded. "Yes, Father. I will."

"This area back here is the cemetery," Elijah explained, nodding toward the expanse of untouched prairie he had just refenced. For three days, Dr. Richardson had been good enough to stay on in town, spending his nights at the Hunters' house and his days helping shingle the church's new roof. A few minutes ago, he had wandered across the street to visit with the preacher.

"I don't see no headstones," the deputy observed. He, too, had elected to remain. He'd been meeting with town leaders to discuss legal problems the citizens of Hope were up against. He had promised to look into helping the town hire a lawman, but so far, he hadn't mentioned carting Sam off to the orphanage in Topeka. Elijah was praying the subject was closed. "How can you call this a cemetery if there's nobody buried in it?"

"I reckon we'll lose one of our people one of these days," Eli said. "In the past couple of years we've had a plague of grasshoppers, a prairie fire, and now a cyclone. There's another winter coming up, and who can tell what that might bring?"

"You're right about that."

"I'm learning that prairie life is hard, real hard. Without a doctor in town, folks don't have any place to turn for healing. I know from experience that sometimes homemade doctoring doesn't work too well. Fact is, I believe a pastor's job is to take care of his flock—and that includes providing a resting place when they go on to be with the Lord. A cemetery kind of helps comfort the family, too, you know, and that's what a church ought to do."

"I'd say you're cut out for the job, Brother Elijah," the deputy commented. "Nobody in town has a bad word to say about you."

"Well, I don't have much training."

"Reverend Book," Richardson said, "would you like to study theology here in Hope?"

The man hadn't said too much to Elijah since that day on the road. In fact, he really didn't talk to anyone. In the evenings, Eli had observed Lily and her father sitting on the front porch of the Hankses' house, but they didn't seem to be speaking to each other. They just sat and rocked. Eli thought that was OK.

"Hope doesn't even have a grade school, Dr. Richardson," he said. "And I don't know where I'd find the nearest seminary."

"You have a post office, I assume. If you wish, I shall correspond with one of my acquaintances in the East. He's a professor of biblical studies. I believe he would be willing to post a series of his lessons to you."

Eli's heart swelled. "I'd like that very much, sir. Thank you. Thanks a lot."

"You'll be staying in town, then?" the deputy asked him.

"Yes, sir, I will. I promised the Lord I'd go wherever he sent me. And he sent me here."

The deputy grinned. "You preachers are quite a bunch. I wish the Lord would talk to me the way he talks to you."

"He might be. Are you listening?" Eli asked, giving the man a slap on the back. "Listen, has anyone invited you two gentlemen to the all-day singing and fellowship we're going to have? You're both welcome to join us while we dedicate the new church building. Let me tell you, the ladies in this town can bake pies like you wouldn't believe."

The deputy took off his hat. "Thank you kindly, Brother Elijah, but I'd better head on back to Topeka. Which brings me to the matter I came here for in the first place. We need to talk about that baby you found."

"That baby is my son," Eli replied.

"No he ain't. Not legal, anyhow."

Eli could hear Lily singing to Samuel across the way, and his innards knotted up just thinking about losing either one. "What do I have to do, Deputy?" he asked. "I'll do anything you say. Just don't take my boy away."

The lawman plucked a stem of grass and stuck it in his mouth. "What's a man like you aiming to do with a baby, Preacher? You don't have a wife or a house or even a good-paying job. I'm the father of six, and I've got news for you. Before long here, that little fellow is going to be up on his feet, running everywhere and climbing on everything. I've watched you work this town—visiting with folks day and night, sitting up with the sick, tending to quarrels, building fences and graveyards, reading that Bible of yours at dawn. You don't have time to chase around some snot-nosed kid. Why don't you let me take him to the orphanage in Topeka? I'll admit it's not the best life a child could ask for, but the war brought in a lot of homeless young'uns. He'd have company, food in his belly, maybe even a little schooling. You did your part, Preacher. Now let the state of Kansas do the rest."

Elijah stuck his hands into his pockets and drifted for a minute with Lily's singing. He knew the tune well; it was one of her favorites. Maybe this evening he could carve out a few minutes alone with her.

"I'm going to tell you something else," the deputy added. "That boy's going to have a tough row to hoe, being a half-breed and all. Don't take that on, Preacher. Let him go."

"I know it's going to be rough," Eli began, "but Lily and I—"

"My daughter is going home to Philadelphia with me," Richardson said. "She won't be able to look after the child."

Eli felt the bottom drop out of his stomach. "Lily's leaving Hope?"

"Our reconciliation has opened new doors. My daughter would like to see her mother. We all hope to make a new beginning, thanks to your intervention, Reverend Book."

"Well, I—"

"There's a fine young gentleman, a doctor, whom I have in mind as a husband for my daughter. He's a stable and very honorable man, and he lives and practices medicine not three houses from ours in the city. He comes from a prominent family, his reputation is excellent, and he earns a more than satisfactory income from his profession. Despite my daughter's brief period of indiscretion, I am certain this young man will welcome her into his heart."

Elijah tried to scrape his stomach up off the ground. "So Lily is really leaving town?"

"Indeed. We depart tomorrow morning."

"All the more reason to send that baby on with me, Brother Elijah," the deputy said. "Ain't gonna be nobody to look after him when she goes. You'd better let the orphanage take over."

"I need to do some thinking." Eli paused. "I need to pray."

"I hope it won't take too long, Preacher. The longer I dawdle here, the less my wife is going to like it. Like I said, we've got six young'uns. . . ."

As the man rambled on, Elijah felt his heart stand still in his chest. He had to see Lily. Had to talk to her. Under the cottonwood tree, she had told him she loved him. But loved him how? Like a preacher? Like a brother?

He wanted more from Lily than that. "Excuse me, gentlemen," he said. Then he nodded to the two men and sprinted out of the cemetery toward the Hanks house.

CHAPTER 17

AS LILY carried Samuel down the road toward the opera house, she watched a peregrine falcon soar high above in the bright blue sky. Drifting on a current of warm summer air that swirled upward from the prairie, the majestic bird surveyed its territory with an eye that missed nothing. Alone, regal, ever vigilant, the falcon hovered, almost unmoving.

"*They that wait upon the Lord shall renew their strength.*" The words of Isaiah whispered through Lily like a soft breeze. "*They shall mount up with wings as eagles; they shall run, and not be weary; and they shall walk, and not faint.*"

Wait upon the Lord. In her awkward, stumbling life, God had revealed himself as the master of time. He had led her, matured her, nurtured her, and finally knocked at a moment when she was willing to open the door of her heart. She had to trust that even now, in the midst of her utter sorrow, God would work his will. In his time.

If she could only be patient, Lily thought as she stepped onto the porch of the gaudy building, he would give her strength. Though right now she felt as worn and ragged as an old dishcloth, she believed that one day God would help her to mount up with wings just like that peregine falcon. She would be able to run and not grow weary, to walk and not faint. Some distant future moment, even without Elijah and Samuel, she would learn to soar.

Oh, Father, guard me now. Please permit me to give Elijah this one gift, something to help him in his work, something from my heart.

She had barely lifted her hand to knock when the door swung open. Beatrice emerged, her purple velvet dress blending with the shadows in the room behind her. A smirk lifted one corner of her red-painted mouth.

"I saw you walking down the road, Lil." She stepped aside and gestured toward the dusky foyer. "Won't you come in?"

Lily tightened her grip on Samuel. "Thanks, Bea. I was hoping you and I could speak for a moment."

"Sure. Old friends, after all."

Entering the room with its red wallpaper and gilt chandeliers, Lily nestled the baby's head against her neck. The sound of laughter and poorly played music drifted through the room from the saloon down the hall. She had hoped to leave Sam with Eva. But the woman's "short trip" to the mercantile had lasted more than an hour when Lily decided to go ahead and finish the matter. Evening approached, and she didn't want to be out after dark.

"How do you like the place?" Bea asked, giving a twirl that sent her velvet gown billowing above her ankles. "The saloon's that way. The girls' rooms are up the stairs. The opera stage is through those doors. Can you believe this is all mine? It's just like the cards foretold, Lil. Grand things are happening to me. And this is the grandest of them all. What more could a woman want?"

True love, Lily thought. *A family. A home. An abiding faith in a saving God.*

"Our girls came in yesterday," Beatrice confided. "We've got five of them, and every one is just gorgeous. We have a singer, too. She's not as good as you, but she'll do. The saloon is fully stocked, and business is good already. George has been counting the wagons and stagecoaches passing this place ever since we started building. He thinks we've got ourselves a regular gold mine."

"Are you happy, Bea?" Lily asked softly.

"Of course I'm happy. I'm ecstatic. Who wouldn't be? This is everything I've ever wanted." With a frown that belied her words, she crossed her arms. "So, what brings you out here? I see the deputy wasn't able to pry you loose from that baby yet. You know, your daddy was fit to be tied when he found out what his little girl had been up to. I guess you two have worked things out. At least, I don't *see* any bruises."

As she laughed, Lily lifted her chin. "I'm going back to Philadelphia with my father tomorrow morning, Beatrice," she said. "I've come for my melodeon."

The woman's face froze. "You've come for what?"

"I want my melodeon."

"What for?"

"Because it's mine. I bought it. Please give it to me."

Bea's face, harsh in the light of the chandelier's oil lamps, twisted into a sneer. "The blasted thing is *here*, isn't it?" she said. "That means it belongs to me."

Lily shook her head. "You know it's mine, Bea."

"I know who's got it, and that's me." She gave a sniff. "You robbed me once already of my biggest asset. You refused to stay with me, even though I'd taken care of you and given you everything I had to give. You left me penniless and hopeless, with nothing to my name but that old show wagon, while you went prancing off after that preacher and his baby. Now you think I'm going to give you the melodeon? Think again, Lily Nolan."

Lily had expected this. She knew Beatrice still wanted to punish her, and she sensed that honor and fairness would never rule in the heart of her false friend. To move Beatrice Waldowski to action, it took money.

"You know the melodeon is mine by rights," Lily said. "If you won't give it to me, I'll buy it from you. Here's everything I've earned working for Elijah Book. You can have all the money in my purse, if you'll let me take my melodeon."

Shifting Sam to her other arm, Lily tugged a cloth pouch from her pocket. The weight of the coins pulled on her arm. Elijah had earned this money by tending to his flock, faithfully ministering to their needs, and laboring day and night on the church. But he had given it willingly to Lily to pay for Samuel's care.

In the beginning, she had felt she deserved every penny. Up most of the night, worn out from washing diapers and helping Eva keep the house, her body depleted by the baby's constant need for nourishment, Lily had taken Elijah's money gladly. Now it meant nothing to her. Nothing but a way to get the melodeon.

"How much is it?" Beatrice asked, giving the pouch a look of disdain. "Five or six dollars?"

"More than that. You're welcome to count it." Lily handed her the pouch. "It's enough to help pay for a piano. That would suit your needs better anyway."

"What are you planning to do with the melodeon, start your own opera house in Philadelphia?"

"I want the church of Hope to have it."

"A church? You want to put that organ in a church?" She smiled. "Well, too bad, Lil. I'm keeping the melodeon. I like the way it sounds."

She tossed the pouch at Lily before whirling away. Lily strode after her. "You have to give it to me, Bea. It's mine. You have no right to keep it. I need it."

"You can't have it!" Beatrice stormed into the saloon. "Go on back to Philadelphia, little girl. Let your daddy beat on you. You don't need a melodeon for that."

"Where's Mr. Gibbons?" Lily demanded, following on her heels. "I'll speak to him about it. He'll take the money."

"George won't care about your paltry pennies, Lil. He's a rich man." She sashayed across the room toward a table where a group of men were playing cards. "Get rid of this woman for me, would you, George? She's pestering me."

The big man stood up from the table, dropping his cards face-down beside his glass of whisky. "You again?" he said, facing Lily. "What are you doing on my premises? Get out."

"That's my melodeon in the corner," Lily said. "I bought it when I joined the traveling show. I paid for it myself."

"With money she stole from her daddy's vault," Beatrice shouted.

"I've offered to pay for the melodeon," Lily countered, laying the cloth pouch on the table. "There are thirty-two dollars here. Count them if you like, Mr. Gibbons. It's a fair price."

"Get outta here, lady. We don't need your money, do we, Bea?"

"We don't need anything from her."

"Get out, before I send one of my boys to throw you out. You ain't caused me nothing but trouble since the first time I laid eyes on you. You and that infernal preacher. First he drives off my saloon business, and now you try to take my music."

"It's *my* melodeon," Lily repeated firmly. "I have nothing else to leave these people. Nothing to give Elijah. I want the town of Hope to have the melodeon. Please, sir, listen to reason. Take this money and give me my instrument."

"Out!" he roared, grabbing her arm. "Out, out, out!"

As he pushed Lily across the saloon, the customers broke into jeers. The women in their bold silk dresses called out to her. Samuel began to cry. Lily covered his head with her arm and hurried out into the foyer, barely able to stay on her feet as George Gibbons shoved her toward the front door.

As she reached for the brass knob, the door flew open. Elijah, the deputy, and Dr. Richardson—followed by half the town of Hope—poured into the building. George Gibbons and his men drew their pistols.

"Turn the woman loose," Elijah demanded, taking a step toward Gibbons. A half-dozen six-shooters pointed at Elijah's chest clicked to full cock. He held up his hands. "I'm unarmed. I'm the preacher in Hope, and I'm asking you to let Mrs. Nolan go."

"She's trespassing," Gibbons spat. "And so are you, Preacher."

"Well, I'm not," the deputy said, moving into the open circle. "Put your guns away, men. Won't be no bloodshed. We'll settle this peaceable, or I'll haul every one of you off to Topeka."

"We've done nothing wrong," Beatrice said. "We have a deed to this property, and we're just minding our business. It's Mrs. Nolan you ought to haul off. She came over here to stir up trouble, Deputy—and she brought that poor little baby right into the saloon. If that doesn't show what kind of person she is, I don't know what would. Arrest her, sir, and we'll all be better off."

Lily let out a cry of disbelief. "Beatrice, how can you say such things? I came for the—"

"She came here looking for work," Bea said. "She tells me you're planning to take her back to Philadelphia tomorrow, Dr. Richardson. She was hoping to hide out here at the opera house until you left without her, and then she thought she could get a job singing in our shows. I reminded her of all the trouble she's caused you and everybody else, but she said she didn't care a bit. Look at her standing there with that baby, all sweet and innocent. She knows good and well what she's up to, don't you, Lily?"

"Why would I come here for work, Bea?" Lily said. "You've already got a singer. Don't you, Mr. Gibbons?"

"Well, yes, but—"

"Did you want to join our *other* girls, Lily?" Beatrice asked. "Maybe that was your real reason for coming."

Cornered, Lily spotted one ray of light.

"Maybe so, Bea," she said. "Maybe you'd like to hire me on with the other girls. Why don't you tell the deputy what my duties would be? And while you're at it, you can show him your license to operate a brothel."

Amid the cries and shouts that followed her remark, the deputy hollered for order. "Now what's going on here?" he demanded.

"What's this about girls, Mr. Gibbons? I've been hearing rumors ever since I stepped into this town. You operating a brothel here?"

"Absolutely not, sir." Gibbons's face flamed bright red. "We run a legitimate opera show and a saloon."

"What's all this about hired girls?"

"Maids. Cooks."

"And those rooms upstairs? What do you use them for?"

"We rent them out to travelers passing through. Kind of like a hotel."

"I guess you wouldn't mind if I took a look." Without waiting for an answer, the deputy headed for the stairs.

In the ensuing confusion, Lily spotted her opportunity to escape. Hugging Samuel tightly to her chest, she darted through the front door and slipped out onto the porch. Oh, this had been a disaster! How could she have misread the warning signs? How could she have been so naive as to think Bea would agree to her request? She could hardly wait to get back to the quiet security of Eva's house.

"Lily!" Elijah's voice stopped her short. "Lily, can I talk with you a minute?"

She stopped at the edge of the porch and squeezed her eyes shut. She could only pray for strength. At this very moment, she must hand Samuel over to Elijah. She must let them both go, and she had not even the melodeon to give the man she loved. Her father would be coming to get her, and she must leave with him. That was her decision—to do God's will and put her own desires behind her. *God, give me strength!*

"Lily?" Elijah's warm hand covered hers. "I was worried about you. I went looking for you at the Hankses' house. And then Caitrin Cornwall said she saw you walking this direction. Your father and the deputy heard the news, and after that, it seemed like the whole town joined in the parade down to the opera house. Are you all right?"

She drank down a breath, unable to meet his eyes. "I'm sorry to have caused trouble again."

"Lily?" He placed the crook of his finger under her chin and tilted her head. "Lily, I know you're supposed to go to Philadelphia tomorrow morning. I also have a feeling that in some ways you're still scared of your father. Did you come here to get work from Beatrice?"

She couldn't keep the tears from rolling down her cheeks. "No, I came to get my melodeon," she wept. "I wanted you to have it for the church. I wanted to leave the town something. Bea wouldn't give it to me, not even when I offered all the money I've earned working for you. She's keeping the melodeon, and I left the pouch on the table in the saloon, and now the money's all gone, and I don't have anything to give you. . . ."

His arms slipped around her, encompassing both the woman and the baby. "Lily, you already gave me the greatest gift you could give. You gave my son his life. You gave me your music, the sound of your voice, your smile, your words of wisdom, your laughter. You gave yourself to me and to this whole town, Lily. We don't need . . . *I* don't need anything but you."

"No. I've interfered with your work for the Lord. Samuel and I keep you from doing—"

"Keep me from it? You give my ministry meaning, Lily. When I think of you and Sam, I realize why I've got to help folks. I understand how I'd feel if anything ever happened to either of you. I think about what I'd need in a pastor, and that gives me the strength to keep on working for God. It's the thought of seeing you and Sam on the porch every evening that fills my heart with joy and keeps my feet on the servant path. It's you who comes into my mind when I'm praying and planning sermons. What do I want to say to Lily to help her grow? How can I encourage Lily? What words can I offer to make Lily stronger in her walk with God? It's you . . . you and Sam . . . who make this pastor work worth all the hours I spend at it."

He stopped, his breath shallow. "I know you want to go home with your father," he went on. "I know you need to see your mother. And I would never want to put a barrier in the path God has laid out for you. But I meant what I said under the cottonwood tree the other day, Lily Nolan. I love you. I love you the way a man loves a woman. I love you so much, I'm willing to ask you to leave your mother and your father and cleave to me. Which, if I understand Scripture right, means I want you to marry me, Lily. I want you to marry me and live with me every day of my life from here on out. No matter what."

Lily covered her mouth with her hand, unable to believe the words that had tumbled from this man's overflowing heart. "Oh, Elijah, I love you so much!" she cried out. "But I don't want to be a stumbling block—"

"You're my wings, darlin'."

"Wings!" Lily lifted her gaze from the prairie and focused on the falcon still tracing lazy circles in the twilight. "I want you to soar, Elijah. I want God to use you. I'll do all I can to lift you up."

"Then you're saying yes?" He set her away from him, his hands on her shoulders. "Because your father told me—"

"My father can go home to his wife," she said firmly, "and I'll stay here with . . . with my husband. I'll visit my parents soon enough. But then I'll come back here, where I belong."

"Mercy!" Elijah laughed. "Mercy, mercy, mercy."

"Amen," she murmured, slipping into his arms again.

"Brother Elijah!" Seth Hunter dashed out onto the porch. "Brother Elijah, you've got to—oh, I didn't mean to—"

"That's all right," Elijah said. "At least it's you cutting in on us again."

The tall man gave a chuckle. "You two need to make this thing official."

"We are. Just give us a week or two."

"A week!" Lily said, giving Sam a squeeze. "You hear that, Sammy? Your daddy and I—"

Elijah was staring at her. "Lily, do you think Sam would be better off in an orphanage?" he asked in a low voice. "I don't have a house yet. I don't get paid much. And there's no school here in Hope."

"I think you're his God-given father," she said. "He couldn't be better off than that."

"I don't know about that baby of yours," Seth Hunter cut in, "but there's a ruckus going on inside the opera house, Brother Elijah. We could do with a man of God to help sort things out."

"A ruckus?"

"Those ladies came out of their rooms wearing next to nothing, and the deputy was rounding them all up when Jack Cornwall's mother fainted. Then Beatrice Waldowski went to screaming, and all of a sudden she bit the deputy on the arm, and Jack knocked out two of the saloon customers, and George Gibbons fired a bullet into the ceiling, and . . . and, well, I'm just rambling on to beat the band," he said. "I've been living with Rosie too long. You'd better come in and help us, Preacher. It's a mess."

Elijah reluctantly stepped away from Lily. "Go on back to the Hankses' house," he told her, "and start planning our wedding. I want to marry you before anybody gets it in mind to come between us again. You hear?"

"Yes, sir," she said, giving him a mock salute. "And you get in there and round up your sheep, Reverend Book. Don't you know a pastor's work is never done?"

With a laugh, he caught her and gave her a warm kiss right on the lips. As he turned to go back into the opera house, Lily fairly skipped down the porch steps. *"They shall run, and not be weary,"* she thought as she scampered onto the road, her spirits soaring on eagles' wings.

CHAPTER 18

"THAT ought to do it for you, Mrs. Nolan," Jack Cornwall said, stepping back from the small stone cross he had set into the ground. "Is it all right?"

Lily held Samuel close as she knelt beside the marker lit with golden sunlight on this bright Sunday morning. "Abigail Nolan" it read. "1866. Rest in peace." She reached out and ran her fingertips over the coarse stone that Elijah had asked the town blacksmith to carve as a memorial to her lost baby.

"Thank you, Mr. Cornwall," Lily said softly. "Elijah was right about the cemetery. It does help."

"Sure the man himself will be back soon enough," Caitrin Cornwall said. She laid her hand on Lily's shoulder. "Perhaps he'll arrive this afternoon before the all-day singing is finished. I know he planned to be here to dedicate the church, but Topeka is a long way."

Lily nodded. "I know."

"If you're sure you'll be all right, then, we'll just pop round the front to help set up tables."

"That would be fine, Caitrin." Lily smiled at the Irishwoman, whose concern was plainly written in her green eyes. "I'll join you soon."

As the young couple left her alone, Lily sank farther into the lush green grass at the foot of the stone cross. Elijah Book had left town along with the deputy and Dr. Richardson a full ten days before, and no one had heard a word from them since. The three men had planned to escort the entire troupe of opera-house employees to Topeka, where they would have to speak to the authorities about their activities. At the same time, Elijah was hoping to begin the paperwork that would give him the right to call Samuel his son. The deputy had predicted success, but Lily couldn't make herself relax.

What if Beatrice had pulled some kind of trick? What if George Gibbons had gone off half-cocked? What if Elijah had run into legal problems over the adoption? What if . . . what if . . . what if . . . ?

"It's hard to put your whole faith in the Lord, Samuel," she told the baby in her arms. Spreading a small quilt, she laid the child in the grass beside her. "I've always tried to manage things on my own, even though I never did a very good job of it. Sometimes, I'm afraid to trust."

She studied the small stone cross and thought of the wrenching grief she had suffered. "This marker is in memory of Abigail," she told Samuel as the baby took one of his own bare toes in his tiny fist. "Abigail was my daughter. Your sister, in a way. I loved her very much."

Watching the baby through misted eyes, Lily pondered her loss. What if Elijah couldn't get permission to adopt Samuel? What if the baby were taken from them? What if something terrible had happened to Elijah while he was in Topeka? What if . . . what if . . . what if . . . ?

"Here I am worrying again," Lily whispered, giving Sam's nose a gentle pat. "You'll have to learn from your papa rather than me on this matter of letting God take control. I do miss Abby, Samuel. She was my precious daughter. But I'm so grateful to God for putting you into my arms. I want to be your mama, sweet boy. Is that all right?"

"It's all right with me."

Elijah's voice took Lily's breath away.

She swung around to find the man himself standing beside the church's back door. "Elijah!" she cried, getting to her feet. "You came home! You're safe!"

With a laugh, he caught her in his arms. "Where's your faith, darlin'? We tried to make it back last night, but we were just too tired. Spent the night down the river a way, and then got up at dawn to make it here in time for the singing."

"Oh, Elijah, what happened in Topeka? You have to tell me everything."

"The judge shut down the opera house and threw George Gibbons in jail for operating an illegal business. Beatrice hightailed it off someplace before she could even get to court, and nobody could find her. She's long gone. Seems the deed she and Gibbons were so proud of was nothing but a fake. So the judge gave the building to the town of Hope to start up a county school. How about that?"

"But what about Samuel? Can you adopt him? Is it going to be legal?"

"*We* can adopt him," he said. "I found out that Reverend and Mrs. Elijah Book will have an easy time of it—easier than Brother Elijah all by himself, anyhow. So what would you say to taking care of first things first?"

"What do you mean?" Lily asked. She watched in confusion as Elijah took two strides across the grass, scooped up the baby, and headed back to the church. "Where are you going?"

"To get married. Care to join me?"

With a laugh of disbelief, Lily followed the preacher into the church. As they stepped into the crowded room, the round rich notes of Lily's melodeon suddenly filled the air. Everyone rose from the newly built benches and began to clap. Lily covered her mouth with her hand and stared in shock.

"Welcome home, Brother Elijah!" Rolf Rustemeyer called from

his accustomed position beside Violet on the Hudson family's pew. "We are waiting for you long time!"

"I had to round up another preacher," Elijah said as everyone laughed and clapped again. "And I needed to find just the right person to play the music for our wedding."

Lily glanced in the direction he pointed. There sat her melodeon. And playing the wedding march was . . . her mother! But how?

"Your father wanted her to come," Elijah explained, "so he sent a wire to Philadelphia. She came on the first train."

With a cry of joy, Lily dashed across the room and threw her arms around her mother. Tears streaming, the older woman lifted her hands from the organ and gathered her daughter close.

"Oh, Lily," she whispered. "Your father told me everything . . . I'm so sorry. So very sorry."

"Mama, you came. You're here. That's all that matters."

The older woman's moist blue eyes crinkled at the corners. "Well, you'd better not interrupt the music any longer, my dear. You know how your father feels about that sort of thing."

Lily lifted her head to see the grand gentleman himself step into the small building along with Dr. Hardcastle, the pastor from the huge stone church in Philadelphia. As the music swelled, the two men marched to the front and took their places near the podium. Lily sat dumbfounded as her father began to sing "Ode to Joy." His magnificent baritone filled the church, rattled the windows, and silenced the birds in the trees.

With a smile as broad as all outdoors, Elijah walked across the room and took Lily's hand. "Will you marry me," he asked, "this morning?"

Unable to speak, Lily nodded. Cradling Samuel in one arm, Elijah encircled Lily with the other as they walked to the altar. Dr. Hardcastle smiled and held out both his hands to her.

"Welcome, Lily," he said gently. "Welcome to the family of Christ."

Lily tried her best to listen to the service, truly she did. But all she really managed was to soar through the heavens on eagles' wings. Her mother had come all the way from Philadelphia. Her father was singing for her wedding. And beside her stood a man more handsome, more kind, more loving than any she could have dreamed possible. In spite of her rebelliousness, her weak faith, her many failings, God had blessed her beyond all imagining.

As she listened to Elijah express his deep love for her, Lily heard herself speak words of the vow she meant with all her heart. For richer, for poorer, in sickness and in health, till death do us part.

"I do," she said as the minister set her hands inside the warm grasp of her new husband. "Oh yes, I do."

"Mercy, mercy, mercy!" The joyous voice at the door to the church drew everyone's attention. Mother Margaret, hands lifted in praise, stepped into the building. As the melodeon began to play, the old woman trundled down the aisle.

"She told me she was ready to come home to Hope," Elijah whispered, leaning close to Lily. "And she didn't want to miss this moment."

As the organ music swelled through the room, Mother Margaret took her place at the front of the church and raised her voice in blessing.

"My faith looks up to Thee,
Thou Lamb of Calvary,
Savior divine!
Now hear me while I pray,
Take all my guilt away,
O let me from this day
Be wholly Thine!"

A NOTE FROM THE AUTHOR

Dear Friend,

In *Prairie Storm* I wanted to capture the pain that I and many others have felt by the betrayal and hypocrisy of some who claim to follow Christ. When storms of hurt, anger, or bitterness threaten to overwhelm us, let's remember that Christ promises to calm the waves if we will keep our eyes on him. We must never place our ultimate faith in other Christians or even in our church leaders. They often are all too human. Jesus alone should be our guide and our hope. His faithfulness is forever!

I pray you've enjoyed *Prairie Storm*. In case you missed the others in this series, be sure to look for both of them: In *Prairie Rose*, Rosie Mills and Seth Hunter overcome doubt and abandonment to build a new family bonded in Christ. In *Prairie Fire*, the flames that threaten to consume the town of Hope are washed away in the flood of love and forgiveness that endures in the hearts of Caitrin Murphy and Jack Cornwall.

My thanks to the many of you who take time to write and express your appreciation for the ministry my books have in your lives. As I personally read and answer your precious letters, your words of love and faith become a ministry to me.

Blessings in Christ,

Catherine Palmer

Catherine Palmer

ABOUT THE AUTHOR

Catherine Palmer lives in Missouri with her husband, Tim, and sons, Geoffrey and Andrei. She is a graduate of Southwest Baptist University and has a master's degree in English from Baylor University. Her first book was published in 1988. Since then she has published more than twenty books and has won numerous awards for her writing, including Most Exotic Historical Romance Novel from *Romantic Times* magazine. Total sales of her novels number close to one million copies.

Her Tyndale House titles include *Prairie Rose*, *Prairie Fire*, *Prairie Storm*, *The Treasure of Timbuktu*, *The Treasure of Zanzibar*, and novellas in the anthologies *A Victorian Christmas Tea*, *With This Ring*, and *A Victorian Christmas Quilt*. Look for *Finders Keepers* and *A Victorian Christmas Cottage* coming soon.

Catherine welcomes letters written to her in care of Tyndale House Author Relations, P.O. Box 80, Wheaton, IL 60189-0080.

Current HeartQuest releases

- *A Bouquet of Love,* Ginny Aiken, Ranee McCollum, Jeri Odell, and Debra White Smith
- *Faith,* Lori Copeland
- *June,* Lori Copeland
- *Prairie Rose,* Catherine Palmer
- *Prairie Fire,* Catherine Palmer
- *Prairie Storm,* Catherine Palmer
- *Reunited,* Judy Baer, Jeri Odell, Jan Duffy, and Peggy Stoks
- *The Treasure of Timbuktu,* Catherine Palmer
- *The Treasure of Zanzibar,* Catherine Palmer
- *A Victorian Christmas Quilt,* Catherine Palmer, Debra White Smith, Ginny Aiken, and Peggy Stoks
- *A Victorian Christmas Tea,* Catherine Palmer, Dianna Crawford, Peggy Stoks, and Katherine Chute
- *With This Ring,* Lori Copeland, Dianna Crawford, Ginny Aiken, and Catherine Palmer
- *Finders Keepers,* Catherine Palmer—coming soon (Fall 1999)
- *Hope,* Lori Copeland—coming soon (Fall 1999)

Other great Tyndale House fiction

- *The Captive Voice,* B. J. Hoff
- *Dark River Legacy,* B. J. Hoff
- *Embers of Hope,* Sally Laity and Dianna Crawford
- *The Fires of Freedom,* Sally Laity and Dianna Crawford
- *The Gathering Dawn,* Sally Laity and Dianna Crawford
- *Jewels for a Crown,* Lawana Blackwell
- *The Kindled Flame,* Sally Laity and Dianna Crawford
- *Like a River Glorious,* Lawana Blackwell
- *Measures of Grace,* Lawana Blackwell
- *Song of a Soul,* Lawana Blackwell
- *Storm at Daybreak,* B. J. Hoff
- *The Tangled Web,* B. J. Hoff
- *The Tempering Blaze,* Sally Laity and Dianna Crawford
- *The Torch of Triumph,* Sally Laity and Dianna Crawford
- *Vow of Silence,* B. J. Hoff

HeartQuest Books by Catherine Palmer

Prairie Rose—Kansas held their future, but only faith could mend their past. Hope and love blossom on the untamed prairie as a young woman, searching for a place to call home, happens upon a Kansas homestead during the 1860s.

Prairie Fire—Will a burning secret extinguish the spark of love between Jack and Caitrin? The town of Hope discovers the importance of forgiveness, overcoming prejudice, and the dangers of keeping unhealthy family secrets.

The Treasure of Timbuktu—Abducted by a treasure hunter, Tillie becomes a pawn in a dangerous game. Desperate and on the run from a fierce nomadic tribe looking to kidnap her, Tillie Thorton finds herself in an uneasy partnership with a daring adventurer.

The Treasure of Zanzibar—An ancient house filled with secrets . . . a sunken treasure . . . an unknown enemy . . . a lost love. They all await Jessica Thorton on Zanzibar. Jessica returns to Africa with her son to claim her inheritance on the island of Zanzibar. Upon her arrival, she is reunited with her estranged husband.

A Victorian Christmas Tea—Four novellas about life and love at Christmastime. Stories by Catherine Palmer, Dianna Crawford, Peggy Stoks, and Katherine Chute.

A Victorian Christmas Quilt—A patchwork of four novellas about love and joy at Christmastime. Stories by Catherine Palmer, Ginny Aiken, Peggy Stoks, and Debra White Smith.

Coming soon from Catherine Palmer

Finders Keepers—Blue-eyed, fiery-tempered Elizabeth Hayes hopes to move her growing antiques business into Chalmers House, the Victorian mansion next to her small shop. But Zack Chalmers, heir to the mansion, has very different plans for the site. And Elizabeth's seven-year-old son, adopted from Romania two years earlier, has plans of his own: He thinks it's time for his mother to marry—and the tall, handsome man talking to her at the estate sale is the perfect candidate. In this first book of a new contemporary romance series, each must learn that God's plans are not our plans and his ways are not our ways. *Fall 1999.*

A Victorian Christmas Cottage—Continuing the popular Victorian Christmas anthology series, this collection of four original Christmas stories once again leads off with a heartwarming novella by Catherine Palmer. In "Under His Wings," a young widow leaves her home in Wales to settle with her beloved mother-in-law in a small cottage in England's Lake District. Finding work in the kitchen of the dashing Lord William Levine, earl of Beaumontfort, Gwyneth soon attracts the earl's attention. He is charmed by her wit, her love for her mother-in-law, and her devotion to Christ. But unexpected developments at the lavish annual Christmas gathering threaten their growing love. *Christmas 1999.*

English Ivy—Ivy Winton, a beautiful but destitute young widow, finds herself at the mercy of her young brother-in-law. When he insists that she marry his closest friend—a known rake and wastrel—Ivy is horrified. But in the interest of providing a stable home for her three young daughters, she consents to marriage, in name only. When the man turns out to be a delightful father, a brilliant manager of his property, and a kind and gentle husband, Ivy is torn between her commitment to honor Christ and her growing feelings toward her new husband, a man with whom she is unequally yoked.

The Treasure of Kilimanjaro—Alexandra Prescott, looking for inspiration for the line of exotic fabrics she is designing, fully expects her trip to Kenya to be an adventure. But an attempt on her life wasn't quite what she had in mind! Anthropologist Grant Thorton wonders what he has gotten himself into when this beautiful stranger suddenly invades his world. Although they seem to have nothing in common, he is drawn to her—and to her unnerving faith in God. And when the hired killer strikes again, Grant finds that there is far more to Alexandra than meets the eye. The third book in Catherine Palmer's contemporary romance adventure series set in Africa.